GENTLEMAN CLIFFORD,

AND HIS

WHITE MARE BRILLIANT;

OR,

THE LADIES' HIGHWAYMAN.

𝔄 𝔯𝔬𝔪𝔞𝔫𝔠𝔢 𝔬𝔣 𝔱𝔥𝔢 𝔯𝔬𝔞𝔡.

LONDON :

PUBLISHED BY E. HARRISON, MERTON HOUSE, 135, SALISBURY COURT,
FLEET STREET.

[THE AUTHOR RESERVES TO HIMSELF THE RIGHT OF DRAMATIC ADAPTATION.]

PREFACE.

————◆————

THIS work professes to be no more than a compilation of dramatic incidents, linked together by a series of biographical sketches of characters who have played conspicuous parts in the criminal history of this country. The portraits of Wild, Colonel Jack, the German Princess, &c. &c., are purely historical. That of Clifford is, on the other hand, entirely fictitious. To various standard works, particularly those of Ainsworth, and the "Lives of Highwaymen," the writer is indebted for many of the facts he has worked into his novel. The author asks that his book may be judged by the standard he has set for it. Its claims to originality are but few. Its merits as a work of fiction may fairly be judged by contemporary works of its class.

LONDON, *June* 4, 1864.

CONTENTS.

CONTENTS.

ILLUSTRATIONS.

R.PROWSE.   A.DORRINGTON.Sc

GENTLEMAN CLIFFORD AND HIS WHITE MARE BRILLIANT.

GENTLEMAN CLIFFORD

CHAPTER I.

THE HAND OF DEATH — A MALEDICTION — THE WILL
AND ITS MYSTERIOUS DISAPPEARANCE.

AN old, old English hall! Remnant of feudal times!
Crumbling memento of a sturdy, honoured, and
honourable race of Englishmen!

Night—a cold, clammy November night—had thrown
its sombre mantle over Winterleigh Hall.

Winterleigh, in 1748, was a little retired village
nestled snugly in the very bosom of Buckingham.

It was a delicious retreat in the summer time, when
full choruses of birds made glad the day and the night,
and green foliage and verdant meadows sparkled in
sunshine. It was beautiful when the little rivulets
rippled and rippled, and sparkled and danced through
Holwell meads; but in winter there were no such attractions.

Winterleigh was then dull, monotonous, and sombre,
and in the midst of its gloom stared forth the old Hall,
the residence of Sir Lascelles Winterleigh, the eighth
baronet of that name.

There was at the date of our story, and there still

CLIFFORD AT LENGTH FINDS HIS FRIEND WILFRED.

remains to some extent, many superstitions extant among the rustic population of England, and the people of Winterleigh did not hesitate to give the Hall the reputation of being *haunted*!

"Give a dog an ill name, and hang him!"

Give a house the reputation of being haunted, and it not only becomes objectionable in itself, but spreads its gloomy influences over a very large extent of ground, and, consequently, the village of Winterleigh did not stand high in the estimation of the sturdy men of Bucks.

To add to the bad reputation of the place there lived, in a little lone cottage in Winterleigh Woods, an old woman of the name of Clifford, who was supposed to be a witch and sorceress of great power, and animated in her actions by bad passions and malignant feelings against all who crossed her path.

How far she deserved this reputation we shall hereafter see.

Let us now return to our opening scene.

It was, as we have said, a cold and altogether objectionable November night, and the year was that of 1748.

It was fast approaching the hour of midnight, and the gloom deepened, and the darkness became more dense, and the solitude more fearful, as the hour approached; and the winds wept more fitfully over the meadow land, and rustled the old trees in the park and adjoining woods.

There were lights in the upper apartments of Winterleigh Hall.

Not the brilliant, cheering, dancing lights which illumine a house of festivity, but dull, sad, steady glares, which spoke of sorrow, sickness, and death.

Lights which only partially illuminated the dingy old chambers in which they appeared, and cast dark shadows about them, out of which started the many phantoms solitude and sorrow will create.

Many lights were moving, but all was silent.

Sir Lascells Winterleigh, eighth baronet of Winterleigh, was dying.

A career of seventy-five years was fast, very fast drawing to a close.

Altogether, Winterleigh and the neighbourhood looked more gloomy than ever on that particular November evening, and those late travellers who passed through its boundaries hurried on their horses, and shivered involuntarily at the awful silence, the deepening gloom, and the sickly, sickening lights.

On, on! no matter about punishing the jaded steeds. On! on! anywhere out of Winterleigh!

From among the towering trees which overhung the terrace of the Hall the outline of a human figure might have been seen advancing to a spot from whence an uninterrupted view of the windows might be obtained.

It was the bent and decrepid form of a very old woman.

Hideous in aspect, crawling with the stealth of a fox, and chuckling with the malignity of a jabbering raven, she advanced to within fifty yards of the terrace, and then, uplifting her long, bare, and shrivelled arm, she spoke:

"Lascelles Winterleigh, of Winterleigh," she said, "thine hour is come! The lamp is almost burnt out; it flickers, and it will soon expire! Years I have waited for this night — years I have prayed for it, for I have been more wicked, more terrible, as thy lease of life ran out! Hateful as I am to others, I have been more hateful to myself, for I have known no rest since they told me thou wert sick and dying. I would have thee dead, for I hate thee and thine! I would have thee in thy tomb, that me and mine may enjoy the wealth in which thou hast so long revelled. I would have thee quit the earth, that my vengeance shall be complete. The curse, the bitter curse, of a wronged woman follow thee to the other world! Take with thee the malediction of the injured, and may it bring thee and thine to the eternal fire of Hell, that thou mayest there know in death the pains I have felt in living! But I will see thee before thou diest!"

Uttering these fearful words, and still jabbering as she hobbled along, the old hag made for the Hall, which she entered through a small door at the east end of the terrace.

*   *   *   *   *   *

A chamber of death!

Sad scene! Terrible reminder of what we are and what we shall be! How do we dread and pray against an acquaintance with this harrowing detail!

How do we avoid thy terrors! How do we fight against thy mysterious realities!

But all humanity must make thy acquaintance sooner or later, and in his turn came Sir Lascelles Winterleigh.

Power and wealth could put off the day no longer. The time was come, and nothing could delay the fatal moment.

Nature is a hard creditor, and, when it makes its demands, they must be settled in full. There can be no compromise. Great and small must bow to the claim, and all that can be done is to submit.

Lewis Norman, nephew to the baronet, was seated in the apartment adjoining the chamber of death.

"Well," he said, to a medical attendant who had just quitted Sir Lascelles, "What is the news?"

"Still sinking."

"Any faster?"

"Yes, I fear much faster."

"Umph!" The young man swallowed a large tumbler of wine.

"Do not drink any more wine," said the doctor; "your uncle may send for you directly."

"The more need of wine."

"I must beg of you to put the bottle on one side. You would not enter that chamber in a state of intoxication?"

"I would enter it in any state. Better that of drunkenness than any other. What does it matter?"

"Much *to Christians*; nothing *to beasts*. Do as you will."

The doctor quitted the room.

"I'll kick him out directly the old fellow croaks," said the hopeful nephew. "I shan't stand any fellow's humbug when I'm master of Winterleigh."

In this speech the reader has a strong clue to the youth's character.

He was an illiterate, brutal, drunken, fox-hunting badger-baiting fellow, who lived but for what he pleased to term sport, and the delights of the bottle.

But we will allow his character to develop itself, and not weary the reader with long and useless descriptions.

Suffice it now that his principal idiosyncracies are hinted at. Of his personal appearance nothing more flattering can be said. He was a square built, ungainly lout, and the lines of his face denoted cunning, animal passions strongly developed, and a love of cruelty. His eyes were small and deep set, and his mouth hard and brutal. Such was the heir prospective of Sir Lascelles Winterleigh.

"Why don't the old ass die at once, and save all this bother?" said the dutiful nephew. "Such old birds ought to drop off suddenly, and save trouble. But people now-a-day have no idea of saving bother. I hate bother, and I hate foolery; and I believe, if it wasn't for these d——d doctors, the old 'un would have kicked it long ago."

With this kind of speech the young gentleman again applied himself to his bottle.

Let us leave him for a while, and seek the presence of the dying man.

He was surrounded by a group of attendants and doctors, in the midst of which was conspicuous a young girl of rare beauty and exquisite contour.

This was Evelina Courtenay, a supposed orphan, adopted by the old baronet in her infancy, and who now stood weeping bitterly by the side of his couch.

"Have I long to live?" asked Sir Lascelles, very feebly.

"Not an hour, Sir Lascelles," said a physician. "Therefore, if there be anything you could do, let me entreat you that it be done at once, or it will be too late."

"Too late!" repeated the baronet; "Too late!"

He relapsed into silence for a few moments.

At length he turned his eyes upon the group, and fixed his gaze upon the young girl.

"Evelina," he said, in an almost inaudible voice, "tell them all to go—all—all."

She did as she was desired, and they were alone.

"Evelina," he said again; "be seated, and I will tell you the story of my life."

"My dear sir, let me entreat——"

"You think I am too weak, and that the exertion will be more than I can undertake. But you mistake. Is Mr. Warrington here?"

"Yes; he has been here some three hours, expecting you would send for him."

"I did not think I should have any commands for him; but within the last few minutes I have changed my mind. I shall want Mr. Warrington."

"Then I will call him."

"Not till you have heard my story. Listen: My father, the sixth baronet, died, leaving two sons—my brother Adolphus, who was the elder, and myself. My brother was delicate from his birth, and at the age of twenty exhibited marked signs of decline. Shall I confess that I marked the ravages of his disorder with feelings much akin to satisfaction? Well, it was so. You shudder; and so do I—now. I was ambitious and covetous. My brother stood between me and the title and estates. I now lived for but one short hour. I would not, however, take any means to hasten his death—for, in spite of my worst passion, there lingered down in the depths of my heart some tenderness for the companion of my infancy and boyhood. I could have endured his presence, though I might not have been pleased at it: but at last he fell in love, and married. In this act I beheld the wreck of my hopes and ambition, and I was maddened to desperation. The wife of my brother was not of noble birth; in fact, her father was only a well-to-do yeoman; but she was beautiful, and accomplished beyond her position —beyond, very far beyond, the majority of her sex. I loved her, too; but she only had a heart for the elder brother. This, together with my craving after the property, was sufficient incentive for setting the whole of my energies at work in accomplishing the downfall of their happiness and the consummation of my aspirations. Fortune favoured me, and in two months from the day of their wedding I succeeded in making my brother believe his wife false to him; and the result was, that she was thrust from the house, and the marriage annulled by Act of Parliament."

"Was she, then, false?"

"She was as pure as the light of heaven; but I was false, and, heaven pardon me! I succeeded in my black designs. I have not strength to relate how I succeeded. The tale is too long and intricate, and I grow weaker each moment. To conclude: The poor girl was thrust from her home, and had to wander the country over for shelter and food. Forced from village to town and from town to hamlet, she at last died, leaving, as I am told, a child. If this should be so, I can at least make some tardy amends; and it is for that purpose I shall require Mr. Warrington."

"Is this all you have to say? Shall I call Mr. Warrington?"

"Not yet—not yet. I have not yet told all. My brother died broken-hearted a few short months after the disappearance of his idolised wife, and I became possessed of the title and the revenues of these vast estates. It was then that the elder sister of my brother's persecuted wife crossed my path. She, too, was beautiful; but unlike her sister, inasmuch as she was dark and fierce-tempered, loved not restraint, and had bad passions. I

cannot say I loved her; but she gratified me, and I made proposals to her which ultimately led to her fall."

"This is a terrible tale," said the young girl, clasping her hands over her forehead, as if to shut out the vision of the past conjured up by the old Baronet's words.

"It is indeed; but bear with me for a while, for I have almost finished. At the end of twelve months this woman bore me a child, and it was then I cast her from me."

"Oh, shame, shame!"

"It was a terrible act; but I stood at nothing then, and the very night of her confinement I had her thrust from the Hall, and she had to seek the shelter of her mother's cottage. It was a bitter night, and the journey to her mother's cottage in Winterleigh Woods, short as it was, killed her. But the child lived."

"But where is the child? Surely you have not abandoned it?"

"Yes."

"Oh, this is too terrible!"

"It may appear so; but listen: The child turned out a poor God-forgotten thing, more resembling a brute than anything human. You have heard of the Dwarf of the Willow Marsh?"

"I have indeed, and report says, never was there so hideous a creature."

"True, true; that is my son."

The young girl shuddered.

"Heaven is just!" cried the baronet, "and you see my reward."

"It was an awful punishment for your crimes."

"It was; but I now acknowledge its entire justice. I am deservedly punished. There are only a few words more. On the night of the birth of my hideous offspring my sister, the wife of Sir Alfred Norman, gave birth to a son, and he—"

"Is Lewis, your heir."

"He is my next male relative, but he shall not be my heir."

"Indeed!"

"I have determined. Justice shall be done to the offspring of my poor brother if it yet lives, and therefore I shall immediately execute a will, leaving all I possess to the poor defrauded child of the union I made so unhappy."

"It is just."

"I feel it is so. I will, however, leave Lewis a sufficient annuity to keep him in comfort. Fortunately, not an acre of the estates is entailed, and I can therefore dispose of the wealth as my fancy dictates. I thank God that that fancy at last dictates something in the shape of justice."

"And now?"

"And now call Mr. Warrington."

Evelina flew to do as she was ordered.

In a few moments the lawyer was at the bed-side, and the sinking man briefly explained what manner of instrument he desired to execute.

It was a very straightforward task, and was soon accomplished.

Provided the child of his brother still existed, all the estates of which he was possessed in Lascelles Winterleigh he bequeathed to the said child. After deducting certain annuities then enumerated, viz., one of a thousand a year to Lewis Norman, during the term of his natural life, one of two thousand a year to Evelina Harcourt, so-called, the adopted daughter of Sir Lascelles, and several others to servants and retainers of the baronet.

After this deed was executed the old man continued to sink, until he became insensible.

Seeing that his last moment was drawing near, the physician called in the servants and Sir Lascelles' nephew.

The latter rolled into the room in a state of semi-drunkenness, and came to the side of the fast-expiring old man.

Sir Lascelles turned his eyes upon him, and warned him away with expressions of disgust.

'Go, go," he said, "I cannot bear the sight of thee."

"Leave the room," said the physician to the drunkard. "Your presence pains him."

A servant, one of the men in his interest, followed Lewis from the room.

"Well," said the master, "that looks very much like a cut direct."

"Yes," said the man, "but that is nothing to what ollows."

"What do you *mean?*"

"I mean that the old man has made a will."

The young heir staggered back aghast.

"Well," he said at length, "what next?"

"All is given to the child of your uncle, provided one can be found."

"Well?"

"You are left in trust."

"I breathe again. It's not likely the brat, if there should be one, will ever turn up again."

"Don't be too sure. Strange things happen now-a-day."

"Bah! fetch some more drink for me. I'll not go to bed."

"Very good."

And as the man went away to execute the commission of the young bully, he turned into his chamber to reflect on what he had heard, and still deeper sodden himself with wine.

*   *   *   *   *

"I am dying," said the old man, shortly after his nephew had disappeared, "I am dying; leave me alone—alone with my thoughts for a few moments. Go, all."

It was a strange request, but the physicians humoured it.

"It is his last wish," said one, "it will be well to obey it. He has not many minutes to live, and it is not likely he will require any further assistance from us. He will go off in sleep."

The room was immediately cleared, and the old man turned on his side, and for a moment gazed at the lamp flickering on the table.

On the bed was a jewelled casket, in which reposed the newly-made will.

The old man placed his hand on it, and drew forth the document. He unfolded it, and placed it near his eyes."

"I cannot see," he said, "I cannot see. It is useless."

"Yes," said a voice near him, "it is useless. All is over with thee at last. Ha! ha! at last. The vengeance is at last complete."

"Who are you?" said the baronet, opening his eyes, "Who are you, and what do you here?"

"Look on me. Do you not know me?"

"My eyes grow dim. I cannot see, and yet your voice is familiar to me."

"It should be."

"Your name?"

"Madge Clifford."

"Ah, I know you now. How dare you come hither?"

"I dare do anything in my hour of triumph. I would not miss this opportunity for my life."

"Begone. I am dying. I have repented and made amends, so leave me alone with Heaven."

"I will, when I have commended thee to Hell."

"Do not curse me. See what I have done. Even now I have made a will in favour of the child of my brother's wife. It is here."

"Indeed."

"Yes, it is thus I have made reparation to the persecuted Agnes."

"Bah! You are cunning as the fox. Where is the child of Agnes? Who knows whether the babe lived? Such justice is a deceit and a snare."

"Something tells me the child lives."

"Dotard! Can you believe it?"

"I cannot doubt it."

"Then your justice shall be set aside. It shall not be as you wish. No, you shall not even die with the satisfaction of having done one righteous act if I can prevent it."

"What would you do?"

"This. I will have the will!"

The woman darted forward and seized the casket and the will.

"Now," cried the hag, "I will leave thee. Accursed be thy soul for ever."

"The will," screamed the old man, starting up in the bed. "The will—give it me.'

He started up in the bed, but the hag was upon him; her long fingers closed upon his throat, and she dashed him back on the bed.

The noise attracted the attention of the watchers in the next chamber, and they rushed into the room.

All was silent and still. No trace of the intruder could be found.

"I swear I heard voices," said one of the physicians, "but there is no one here."

Mother Clifford had disappeared, as she came, through a secret panel, bearing the will with her.

"He is dead," said one of the medical men, taking the hand of the baronet in his, and placing his fingers over the pulse, "he is dead. All is over."

"But the casket," said Warrington, glancing over the room; "the casket and the will. Where can it be?"

"Gone," said another, "There is no trace of it."

"Ah, ah," cried Lewis Norman, "gone, then *I am master of all.*"

With this he rushed from the room.

"I fear some treachery here," said the lawyer, "but I cannot comprehend it, for I was watching the chamber door during the whole of the time we were absent."

Evilina gazed on the body of her departed frien Bad as he had been, she at least regretted him. The sight was too much for her, and she fell senseless across the bed.

"Poor girl," said the lawyer, "unless the will be found, she will be without a friend in the world. What will become of her, I know not."

CHAPTER II.

THE MEETING NEAR THE TERRACE.

THE room in which Sir Lascelles died was an old panneled apartment, hung in some places with faded, but once magnificent tapestry.

It was from behind this Mother Clifford came, and behind it she disappeared from sight on gaining possession of the will.

She threaded a secret passage, known only to herself and the late baronet, and thus wended her way to that part of the building which she entered. In doing this she had to pass through the wall of the great Hall, for it was this way the passage ran, and on a line with the great pictures of previous generations of the family.

Behind that of the baronet who had just expired was a sliding panel. This the hag opened, and by a vigorous blow dashed the picture to the ground; closing the panel with the rapidity of lightning, but yet not before her wild scream echoed through the Hall.

There were a number of servants collected in the large apartment, and these stood petrified at the strange sight they beheld.

"It is a warning," said the servant, "the baronet is dead."

At the same moment a nurse came from the chamber of death to announce that Sir Lascelles Winterleigh was no longer among the living.

Mother Clifford passed on rejoicing in having fooled the people of the hall.

"It is thus," she said, "we impose upon the credulous and simple."

She passed on, and in a few minutes stood on the terrace.

Reaching this she paused, and glanced up at the shadows on the blinds.

"Ah, fly about! All your care, all your hurry, will not undo the work of death. He is gone, and I triumph!"

In another moment she was joined by Lewis.

"Who are you?" demanded the young man. "Ah! I recognise you. You are the witch of Winterleigh Woods. Ah! I am master now, and I will soon rout you and all the wild, dissolute crew who cling about the place. I will—I swear it. And now clear off from this, evil one — clear off. How dare you come hither?"

"How dare I? Dog!—hound!—poor drunken, half-witted fool! To whom do you talk? But, ah! it is right you should know, and I will tell you who and what you are and what I am. We must understand one another sooner or later. Perhaps this is the very best time it could occur."

"What can you have to tell me, or to what am I to listen? What can there be between us?"

"You shall know. Now, listen to me, boy, and mark me well. You are not Lewis Norman!"

"What do I hear?"

"Truth, as I live!"

"Who, then, do you say I am?"

"The bastard son of the man just dead and my daughter."

"I am confounded. And yet what proof have you of this? Why should I believe it?"

"I have ample proof, should it be needed, but you will not trouble me to furnish it; your own feelings will convince you of my truth. On the night of your birth—the very night your unhappy mother died from being turned from under this roof—Lady Norman was delivered of a son. A scheme of vengeance crossed my brain, and wrapping you in the folds of my cloak I sped with you to the very chamber wherein lay the heir of Winterleigh. 'Now,' I said 'for revenge!' I snatched up the sleeping boy and substituted you in his place. 'He will be heir of Winterleigh,' I muttered, and the young Norman be reared as the son of my unhappy child would have been but for this scheme.' And I have lived to see its consummation—I have lived to see its consummation. Does not your heart confirm my words?"

"Yes, for you can have no motive in deceiving me; but the young Norman, where is he?"

"Ah, you have naught to fear from him. Have you ever heard of Cackalo, the hideous dwarf of the Willow Marsh?"

"Frequently, and once I have seen him."

"Well, then, in him you saw the young Norman."

"Can I believe my ears?"

"I still speak truth, strange though it may appear."

"It is indeed strange. But I fear neither Norman nor myself will receive any benefit from these vast estates. The old man executed a will to-night, leaving all to the child of his younger brother."

"I know it; but still you have naught to fear."

"And wherefore?"

"Because the will will never be found."

"You know, then, of its loss?"

"Yes, for I stole it."

"Indeed. Then it is in your possession. Give it to me."

He advanced to take it.

"Stand back, fool!" cried the old hag; "do you think I will spare it? Never—never! It is mine—mine, and I alone will hold it."

"Do not play with me. Give me the will."

"I would rather part with my heart's blood."

"Be it so. The will or your life!"

"Idiot, I defy you! Make but one step to lay a finger on me, and I will cast you to the earth and trample upon you. Beware, for I am dangerous."

"Pshaw! Stand back from a decrepid woman like yourself! Ridiculous! Listen to me. You know too much for my safety and peace, and therefore we will square accounts here. I thank you for your confidences, but having uttered them you have no more to do with this world."

He sprang towards the old woman with the wild bound of a tiger, but she stepped back a pace, and, avoiding his spring, turned suddenly upon him, and seized him by the throat.

Lewis was in a vice of iron. In vain he writhed and struggled and exerted his enormous strength. The old hag had the power of a giant, and, after partly strangling him, she cast him to the earth with a violence which crushed out all his remaining sense, and he lay like a mangled corpse.

"Fool!" muttered the hag, "I could kill thee, though thou hadst ten times thy strength! But the time is not yet come. Live on, and living be my tool!"

With this she glided from the spot, and disappeared among the trees.

CHAPTER III.

GENTLEMAN CLIFFORD.

"HURRAH for Captain Clifford!"

"Hip! hip! hip! hurrah! hurrah!"

"Thanks, friends, thanks! I am glad to see you have not forgotten me, though I have been absent a full month."

"Forget the captain! - Forget Gentleman Clifford! that's not very likely."

The foregoing words were uttered in the principal drinking room of a low public-house in one of the least reputable neighbourhoods of London.

The place was completely full of persons whose appearance said but little for their character.

They were a rough, ill-favoured set, and the scene in which they took part was one of wild confusion and debauchery.

Vessels of all descriptions and all sizes covered the tables, and around them were seated some fifty persons of both sexes, presenting a scene to which only the pencil of Hogarth could do justice.

The men were drunk with wine and spirits, and the women with excitement, and riot was at its height.

The occasion of the burst of enthusiasm from this crew, with which we commenced this chapter, was the advent among them of a young and remarkably handsome man, dressed to perfection in an elaborately but chastely trimmed scarlet coat, and riding boots of glazed leather.

He also wore a splendid handkerchief of the finest lace about his throat, and his hat was embroidered in gold with extreme neatness and elegance.

Everything about him denoted polish and good breeding, and there was a smile in his face which spoke of a kind and generous nature. This personage was no other than Paul, otherwise "Gentleman" Clifford, well known on the road as The Ladies' Highwayman—a distinctive title he had earned by his wonderful grace and deportment, and the effect it had on the fair sex.

It was commonly said in Paul Clifford's day, that half the women of London crossed Hounslow Heath at midnight, solely for the pleasure of being robbed by so daring, and withal so splendid a man.

Report was rife as to who he was, and what was his birth and parentage. Some set him down as the natural son of the king. Others, in turn, fastened him to half the nobility of England, and the remainder set him down as an aristocrat in disguise; but not one knew his real parents, or the story of his life.

The fact was, Paul himself was entirely unacquainted with it.

He remembered something of his mother—a poor pale, half-crazed, wholly dejected woman, He had a dim recollection of a wild but beautiful face gazing down into his own, and devouring it with her eyes. He had also a recollection of a plaintive voice soothing his sorrows, and uttering words of love to him.

Beyond this he knew nothing.

The reader will at once divine that Gentleman Clifford was no other than the son of the elder brother of Sir Lascelles Winterleigh.

A brief sketch of his career may now be given.

His mother dying while he was yet in infancy, he was left nurseless and friendless on the mercy of the world.

On the day of her death the poor outcast had wandered into the haunt of the worst characters of the metropolis.

She had begged for many days in the streets of London, but at last, failing to excite sympathy and obtain the relief of which she stood so much in need, and feeling that her earthly race was almost run, she staggered into the haunts of sin and crime, "for," she said, "they at least will let me die in one of those obscure hovels."

Chance threw her at the door of a woman named Granville, the keeper of a poor lodging-house for thieves, of the lowest order.

It was a wretched place; but fainting, dying, the poor woman could not choose but enter it.

"Well," said the woman who kept the place, seeing the poor wretch stagger in at the door; "well, what d'ye want here? This is no place for drunken people. Get out of it."

It was too late. The divorced bride of Winterleigh fell with a crash to the floor, her poor babe under her.

"Filthy drunk," said the woman; "filthy drunk, as I'm a living sinner."

"Get away, you fool," cried a man, rushing from one of the rooms at the sound of the fall. "Get away! Don't yer know death from drunkenness? Can't yer see that she's a gone case?"

"Then why the devil did she come into my house to die?"

"Because she didn't choose to die like a dog in the street, I suppose, and very sensible too. Look to the child, while I carry the poor thing into a room."

"She'll be carried into no room of mine, Bill Waters."

"She'll be carried just wherever I like to take her. Turn her out, and you'll see what is likely to come of it. There's been some ugly work done here before, and you might get into trouble if you raised people's suspicions over this poor devil. People don't believe in sudden deaths like this without good reasons can be shown for 'em, and that's why I say you'll do well to let the body be here until arter the inquiry. Besides, won't yer get paid for it?"

The prospect of receiving money seemed to pacify Mother Granville, for she made no opposition to the man placing the body in one of the upper rooms.

After the inquiry into the cause of death the authorities offered to take the child under their protection, placing it in the usual institution for the reception of such poor, unfortunate wretches—the parish poor-house. But, strange to relate, Mother Granville positively refused to part with the child.

"No," she said, "I will rear him myself. I've no children, and there'll be something for him when I die, so he shall stay with me."

The linen of his mother was marked "Agnes Clifford," and so the child was called Paul Clifford—the Christian name being that of the woman Granville's late husband.

Years passed, and little Paul grew in stature and improved in appearance, until he presented a promise of a glorious manhood.

He was quick at learning, and loved books, and his protectress determined to educate him to the full extent of her means.

Brutally ignorant and sinful as she was, it was the pleasure of her life to educate Paul, and keep him from the path she had followed.

"Paul shall be a gentleman," she said, and to do her justice she strived to keep her word.

Paul learnt rapidly, and there was a hope that he would realise all the expectations of Mrs. Granville; but, unhappily, the boy took a wonderful fancy to the society of Bill Waters, a notorious highwayman and burglar, and the constant *habitue* of Mrs. Granville's lodging house.

In the society of this man, as may be expected, Paul learnt but little good.

"Bill Waters delighted in nothing so much as recounting his adventures, and setting forth in glowing colours the delights of a lawless life.

The boy's fancy was caught by the false dazzle, and at twelve years of age he determined on his future course.

"Mother Granville," he said, "wants me to be a gentleman; so I will, but it shall be a gentleman highwayman. Yes, I'm for a life on the road."

"That's your sort," said his friend Bill, "that's the style of thing to stick to. Only you keep on growing up good-looking, and give yer mind to gentility at the same time, and you'll be the King of the Road; that's what you'll be, or my name ain't Bill Waters."

Paul did continue to grow good-looking, and he did give his mind to gentility, and at last realised the prophecy of Bill. At the age of twenty-two he was the veritable King of the Road, and the wonder and admiration of all England.

Paul's fame was increased by the possession of a magnificent mare, which he named "Brilliant," and which was the envy of all who ever looked upon her.

She was a miracle of form and courage, and, singular enough, had not a spot of black about her.

"Milk-white," Bill Waters said she was, "and as beautiful as an angel, as sleek as a greyhound."

Thy sympathy and affection between master and horse were almost miraculous. They seemed to live for and in each other, and to be inseparable.

With Mrs. Granville Paul could go to live, and it was difficult to say whether the old woman was most proud of his gentility or his daring deeds.

"I always said he should be a gentleman," she would say," and he is. There ain't one like him throughout the length and breadth of the land."

We must now return to the house in which we introduced Paul to the reader.

The warm greeting over, Paul seated himself at the head of the table, and was immediately supported, one on each side, by two women. Both young, and both beautiful; but beyond a kind nod of recognition, Paul took but slight notice of them.

"Your health, captain," said Bill; your health and happiness."

"Thanks," said Clifford. "Gentlemen, I drink to you."

"There," said Bill, looking with admiration on the young highwayman; "there, ain't he a real picture? See him toss off that glass. It's beautiful to see; that's what it is; nothink less than beautiful."

"My old friend Bill is a consummate flatterer," said Clifford, with a smile. "He is ever singing my praises in the most enthusiastic manner."

"Who could resist doing so?" inquired one of the females; "who could withstand the blandishments of Paul?"

"I hope you will, ladies," said Clifford; "for the fact is I can make you no return for expressions of affection. I am wedded to the road and to my mare, and, like the Knight of Malta, the Knight of the Road is, if he is ambitious to succeed in his profession, condemned to celibacy. So waste not your sweets on me."

"There's a beauty," said Bill, once more in ecstacies. "What's pleasure to him, what's all the world to him, that don't concern his lovely profession? Not a bit.

Not the value of a fig. He don't care; not he. There's Mistress Louisa and Mistress Fanny, two of the magnificentest creatures in the world; but they might as well be Dutch dolls, for all the captain cares. It's my opinion he's above all human weaknesses, and is a sort o' spirit. If he isn't that, I don't know what he is. *That's* what he is."

Bill, doubtless, thought he had been extremely logical, and nodded his head with evident self-approval; but what he really made out the object of his admiration to be must for ever remain an impenetrable mystery.

" Clifford is a dolt," said Mistress Louisa. " He's the only highwayman who does not love a woman."

" And yet they call him the ladies' highwayman," said the fair Mistress Fanny, with a sneer. " What a mis-application of terms."

" No matter—no matter," said Louisa, pouting her pretty lips, if he will not love us, there are doubtless others who will."

" That's as may be." interposed Bill; " but there's only one Gentleman Clifford. Mark that."

" That's the truth," shouted the men. " There's only one Gentleman Clifford, and he's the best fellow in the universe."

" So he is, gentlemen," said a tall and commanding man, who now entered the room. " So he is; and sorry am I to be forced to drag one so much appreciated by you from your company; but necessity has no law, and so, by your leave, the idol must disappear from the gaze of the worshippers."

" Hillo," cried Bill, " here's Wilfred Barnard, the Bird of Night. What's the game now?"

" Nothing in which you can assist," said the new comer; " so sit down and drink. I require only Clifford."

" It is already too late for business," said Clifford, rising and walking towards the door;" but I attend you if you have aught of importance to communicate."

" Importance!" said Wilfred Barnard. " My dear fellow, it's of the utmost importance, or I would not have disturbed you. Come along."

They passed from the room, and entered an adjoining apartment.

" Now," said Clifford, " what is in the wind?"

" Much, I have raised some game: will you join in the chase?"

" In other words, you know of a house to rob, and wish me to join in the business."

" That's a literal translation of my words. Are you inclined for the sport?"

" I do not know. Where does the game lie, and what is it?"

" Well, the game lies in a splendid old hall down in Bucks, and it consists of good bright gold. What do you say to that?"

" I say that Buckinghamshire gold is quite as good as any other, provided there is no more risk in obtaining it than there would be in any other place."

" Not a jot; not a jot."

" Well, then, just make yourself intelligible."

" Which can be done in a very few moments. A few days ago I met up at the west-end of town a young fellow from this same nest in Bucks. He was far gone in drink, and was naturally communicative. He informed me that his uncle was Sir Lascelles Winterleigh, of Winterleigh Hall, Bucks, and that he was his heir. The old man, he said, was on his death-bed, and there was no hope of his living over the week. He assured me that he should be master; that there was lots of money there, and that he would desire nothing better than my company, particularly if I brought a jolly friend or two with me. Now, I don't see why we should not enjoy his hospitality and—"

" Thieve his money and valuables. A very generous proceeding, on my life."

" Just so, but you'll consent?"

" Yes," said Clifford, " I'll consent: but when do you propose to set off?"

" Before daylight. We must get clear of London to-night."

" Very well. I have not long been off the heath, but Brilliant will be fresh enough by this time. A roll in the straw and feed of corn sets her straight enough for anything."

" Very well, then. In two hours we will start. Where shall we meet?"

" On the road. It will look bad for two horsemen to dash through London at this hour, and interruption is to be avoided."

" You are right. At the third milestone then in three hours."

" 'Till then adieu."

" Adieu. Ah! hang those French words. If you can pronounce 'em 'tisn't everybody else that can."

CHAPTER IV.

AN UNPLEASANT INTERVIEW.

THE incident detailed in the last chapter took place on the night preceding the death of Sir Lascelles Winterleigh; and on the night of the old man's decease Clifford and Wilfred Barnard were at the village. At nightfall they missed their road, and only regained it after many hours' hard riding, consequently it was full an hour after the decease of the baronet and the interview between Lewis and Mother Clifford that the travellers reached the hall.

As may be expected, their appearance occurred at a most inopportune moment, and their reception was not what it would have been under different circumstances.

The old man was dead, and the nephew, half strangled and wholly frightened, sought his own chamber to regain his equanimity, and rid himself of the fumes of the wine he had consumed so largely during the night.

Therefore, on inquiring the host, that worthy, who had some difficulty in recollecting that he had ever given any persons in London an invite, sent a message excusing himself from receiving his unexpected guests, and placed the position of his establishment before them with a request that they would establish themselves at the Winterleigh Arms in the village until the following day, when an arrangement could be made for them if they still chose to remain in the neighbourhood.

" Stalled off," said Wilfred. " A nice thing this to come such a distance for. But if they won't open the doors to us there remains an alternative, and that is —"

" To get in at the windows."

" Precisely my idea. It wants many hours to daylight, thanks to the November gloom, and we can do all we want to and get well off by daylight. Hang the country lout! Does he think to bring gentlemen from London to make fools of them? If he does he will be much mistaken in our case."

" He will," said Clifford, as they moved from the Hall, " I was never fooled yet, and I have not come into Bucks to experience the sensation."

They walked their horses towards the village, but suddenly Paul stopped, and, pointing to Winterleigh Wood, said—

" That's our spot. No village inn for our cattle, my boy."

" Yes," said Wilfred, " that looks a nice likely spot, and it's close to the house, so we safely go there. For my part, I hate pothouses. A fellow gets too much quizzed by the louts hanging about the tap-rooms to suit my book."

" Then the wood be it."

" They were in the road, and the wood extended away beyond some meadows to their left.

" Now, Brilliant, old girl," shouted Paul to his mare, " over that hedge !"

He gathered up the reins in his grasp, and with a slight cheer set the mare at the hedge.

A light bound, and she was over.

"Like a dove," said Paul, tapping the beautiful creature on the neck, and looking back for Wilfred.

"Yes, like a dove, indeed," cried Wilfred, in admiration. "I wonder how this brute will get over it. Hey !"

He dashed his spurs into the flanks of his horse, and the poor beast raised its head, and gathered itself up for the leap.

A bound, and down he came, crashing through the hedge like an elephant rather than a horse.

"The deuce take it !" shouted Wilfred. "I'm scratched to pieces. Ah, if I were on the road regularly my first thought would be to find an animal equal to Brilliant, and if I failed I think I'd stick to my own line, and give up all thoughts of your more graceful business."

"Then you would fail to the greatest certainty in life, for throughout the length and breadth of the land there is but one Brilliant."

"And lucky are you to be her owner."

"Lucky indeed, and yet I fear she would never have found so fond a master. I am as careful of her as if she were a Christian and a companion rather than a poor beast of burthen, but, then, no one could be otherwise than kind to so faithful a beast." A scamper across half a mile of meadow land brought the adventurers to Winterleigh Wood, and there, covering them with their cloaks, and securing their bridles to the trees, they left their steeds.

"Now for the Hall," said Paul to his friend. "They have been up during the greater part of the night, and will now be sleeping soundly."

"The more sound the better," said Wilfred. "I hate disturbances of any kind."

Meanwhile, Lewis Norman had, to some extent, shaken off the effects of this night's carouse, and its almost fatal termination.

"Hang the old witch," he said ; "she has the strength of a giant, and the nerve of a devil. I shan't forget her grip for some time. Now, what's to be done with her? She must be got rid of ; but how ?   No means suggests itself to me ; for she is a dark and terrible being, and if report speaks correctly, endowed with supernatural powers, which would render her unassailable. And, besides, her vengeance of an attempt here made and failed would be too terrible to contemplate."

"That her tale is true I have no reason to doubt. She could have no reason for deceiving me. No ; it is evident that I have been the vehicle through which she has wrought her vengeance on the old baronet. Well, then, she is not likely to interfere with, to betray me. Why should I dispose of her? *She holds the will !* That is the secret. The will ! the will ! if I could but grasp that I should fear nothing. But I'll think no more. Thought distracts me, and I'm in no humour to reflect on unpleasant things. For the time, at all events, I am master of Winterleigh ; so a fig for care ! I'll be gay. There's Evelina ; I'll turn my attention to her. She, at all events, will prove a salve to my perturbed feelings. But then, again, she loves me not. I have long noted it ; and had it not been for her respect for Sir Lascelles, would have long since exhibited her repugnance. But I forget that I am master now, and that will make all the difference. Yes ; now that I am able to gratify her ambition and her wants, she will not despise me, and I shall enjoy her society as long as — well, as long as she pleases me."

At this moment Evilina entered the room.

"Well, Evelina," said the young baronet ; "what has brought you here ?"

"I heard you were ill, and I came to see if I could render you any assistance."

"No, I thank you ; I am better now."

"Then I will retire."

The girl moved towards the door.

"And yet, stay a few moments," said Lewis ! "you can render me a service. Sit down on this lounge."

He pushed a luxurious pile of cushions towards her.

"There, sit down, and I'll take my seat by your side, and tell you all I want to say."

There was something in his eye that alarmed the poor girl, and she would have fain retired : but the brutal fellow caught her hands in his, and looking into her eyes, said :

"You are as beautiful as an angel to-night."

"If this is all you would say to me." said the girl, attempting to disengage her hands, "I will retire."

"No you will not," continued the ruffian ; "no girl feels offended at being told she is beautiful, and I'm sure you cannot ; so I'll say it again. You are beautiful ; and I'll tell you something more—I love you."

"You, sir !" cried the orphan ; "is this a time, is this a place for such language ? Remember the scene we have so recently witnessed."

"Oh, curse the scene ! what do I care about it ? The scene has nothing to do with me, and I can only think of it as the snapping asunder of the chain that bound me down to a hateful routine, and kept me from my pleasures. I can only think of the old man's death as the obstacle removed from between you and I. I can only think of it with joy ; for it throws you into my arms, and makes me the most envied of men."

"Dullard !" cried the girl, tearing herself from the impious wretch by her side, " dullard and villain, know that I hate and despise you, and that rather than become yours I would spring into the river yonder, and cut short my existence. Your very shadow is hateful to me, and I would shun the spots on which you walk as if they bore the trail of the creeping serpent. I despise you, and so I will leave your presence."

"Oh ! you will, will you ? come, you've had your say, and now hear me. No will has been found, if one was ever made, which I beg to doubt, and you are thrown upon my mercy. Without me you are homeless, and a beggar. There is not a penny for you, and when I cast you forth you can only starve. I offered you a pleasant alternative, and you have thrown it back in my teeth with scorn. We will now see who has most occasion to be haughty, the penniless orphan, or the master of Winterleigh."

"Were you a thousand times more powerful I would still address you in the same tones. I hate and despise you, and I would not receive a favour at your hands, though my life depended upon its acceptance."

"Indeed ! Then begone this moment ! This very moment quit this roof, and for ever. Beggary and misery be your doom."

"Beggary may be my doom, but not misery. I leave all that to thee."

"Begone !"

"You could not pronounce a more welcome word. I will hasten from the house with all despatch."

"The sooner the better."

Evelina flew rather than walked from the apartment, and sought her own chamber in order to make the few preparations that were necessary for her instantaneous flight.

"I have been a fool," cried Lewis, as soon as Evelina had quitted his sight. "Was this the way to win her ? Idiot that I was, I might have known her better. But what can be done ? She must not quit the house ; and yet it is too late to persuade her to remain. Well, then, force must be used. Yes, I will take means to make her stay."

With this he followed her from the room, and rushed after her to her chamber.

"He burst open the door, and entered.

"Evelina," he cried, "in spite of all I cannot lose you. I am come to bid you stay."

"Begone, monster, and pollute not the air I breathe with your presence."

"Evelina, hear me. I love you, but I can hate as well

No. 2.

as love. I am desperate—maddened—and I have determined that you shall not quit the house."

"You had best not attempt to detain me."

"By hell, I will do so. I swear you shall not go."

"I will call for help."

"It is useless. We are away from the remainder of the household, and all are steeped in slumber too deep to be disturbed, even if your cries could reach their apartments."

"What would you? You would not kill me?"

"No; but you shall be mine, and if not by fair means, as I would have it, it shall be by foul—as you choose. Any way, you must and shall be mine. I will possess you, and so you know what you have to put up with. Now choose."

"Lewis, Lewis, spare me! By the memory of him who now lies stark and cold under the same roof with us —by the memory of our childhood—by all that is good and generous—I conjure you, spare me!"

"Evelina, I love you! Let that answer suffice."

"Lewis, have mercy upon me! I am a weak, unprotected, helpless girl. If there is one spark of generosity in your nature, let me go forth and persecute me no longer."

"I am immovable, Evelina. Destiny itself is not more so."

He glared at her from out his wild, inflamed eyes, and the poor girl shrank back in affright. She could only cry—

"Spare me, spare me!"

The voice was touching enough to melt a heart of adamant, but it affected not Lewis Norman. He was maddened with passion and burning with unholy thoughts, and he sprang towards his victim with the bound of a tiger.

In another moment she was locked in his powerful arms, and his lips sought hers.

Maddened with terror, the poor girl struggled with immense power, but it was in vain; she wasted her strength on an immovable, unfeeling monster, and in a few minutes she sank into a fainting fit, but still murmuring—

"Spare me, spare me!"

At length she was dead to all outward feelings, and lay in his arms like a statue of pure marble.

"At length," he cried, feasting his eyes upon her face, and embracing her still more warmly, "at length she is mine, and the moment I have waited years for has arrived."

"Has it, you abominable scoundrel?" said a voice at his elbow. "Not if I know it." This was accompanied by a crashing blow on the face, which at once forced him to relinquish his hold of the fair girl. "Take that —and that; and now what have you to say?"

The young libertine fell back with a fearful howl of pain. As he fell his eye rested upon the young and splendidly dressed man, who took Evelina carefully in his arms, and supported her head upon his shoulder.

It was Gentleman Clifford.

"Somehow," said Paul, "I am constantly coming to the rescue of some distressed damsel or another, but I do think this is the most beautiful I ever had the pleasure of doing a service. What a glorious face—what hair— what a complexion—what a form! Heaven save us! and a fellow with the form of a human being, and wearing the semblance of a well-bred man, could descend to ill-using such a miracle of beauty. I'm confounded."

Clifford gazed on the prostrate form of the libertine, and then into the face of his inanimate victim.

He had never before been so deeply impressed with a face.

"She is indeed lovely," he said, as his heart beat with a rapture quite new to him. "Oh! if my lot were but cast with hers—if I could but dare to press those lips— but, soft—she wakes."

Slowly the poor girl regained consciousness.

At length she was sensible that her waist was encircled, and that a hand clasped hers.

With a deep shudder, and an expression of repugnance, she darted from where she stood, and almost stumbled over the prostrate form of her persecutor.

"Fear nothing, fair lady," said Clifford, raising his hat, and bowing low to Evelina, "you are safe now," and he pointed to the prostrate form at his feet.

"Oh, yes, yes," cried the terrified girl, "I remember all now. The scene in the other room—the preparations for flight—his following me, and my awful position."

"From which you are happily rescued."

"Yes, and by you."

"I have had that extreme pleasure, lady, although I deeply regret the pain you must have experienced in a situation requiring so rough a rescue."

"Ah! you remind me that this is no place for me. I must fly. Should he recover and find me here."

"While I am here, at least, you have no cause for fear."

"True; but I dare not remain. If you but knew him."

"Lady, I do know him. Although I never saw him until this moment, I can read him most thoroughly. He is a mean, brutal coward; and from my heart I despise him."

"He is all you say of him, or he would not have persecuted me as he has done, and with his uncle but two hours dead."

"Such men can do anything, lady. But can I render you any assistance?"

"No, no, many thanks, but I cannot trouble you."

"I am never troubled in assisting a lady."

"But I know not how you can assist me."

"You said you were quitting this place?"

"Yes."

"Then permit me to see you to your destination."

"My destination! God help me! Where shall I find it?"

"What, lady! quit this house at such an hour, and not know whither you are going: you cannot be in earnest."

"Alas! I am only too deeply in earnest. Would that it were a jest."

"But your friends. Where are they?"

"The only one I ever had lies dead in another part of this house."

"An orphan?"

"Yes; unhappily an orphan. A poor friendless, homeless wanderer."

"Like myself. I sincerely pity you. But what can be done?"

"Nothing, nothing. I thank you for the kindness you have shown me. Now leave me to my fate."

"Never! I should be less than a man were I to contemplate such an act. Lady, you must not, shall not, wander from this house under these painful circumstances. You say you are an orphan. Were you the ward of the baronet who died to-night?"

"I was his adopted child."

"He has surely not left you without a provision?"

"Alas, alas! He made an ample provision for me in a will executed to-night, but it was no sooner accomplished than Sir Lascelles died, and no trace of the will could be found."

"Then you are totally unprovided for?"

"Yes. The man from whom you have saved me inherits all."

"Then I have determined on the course I ought and will pursue. You must go with me to London."

"With you?"

"Yes, with me, lady. Fear not to trust yourself to me; for I will treat you with all the consideration a brother could have for a dearly loved sister. I will place you in safety, and will see to your wants until the mystery attending the disappearance of the will of which you spoke is cleared up; or, at all events, until something can be done to place you beyond that want, suffering, and danger which stares you in the face, if you leave this house as you intended. Do you not see that I am right?"

"Oh, yes—yes, I do, indeed. But such a kindness from an entire stranger, I cannot, dare not, accept it."

"Lady, pardon me if I say you must. It is no kindness. It is an act of duty to a fellow-creature. I should be a despicable wretch, indeed, were I to abandon you in such an hour of peril."

"God will bless you."

"I trust he will," said Clifford, devoutly. "But see, the villain moves. If you desire no further scene with him, fly at once."

Evelina hesitated a second only, and then, placing her hand in Clifford's, she said—

"I will go with you."

CHAPTER V.

WHAT BEFEL WILFRED BARNARD — THE BODY ON THE WILLOW TREE.

WE must retrace our steps for a short period, having gone in the last chapter somewhat in advance of our theme.

Having seen the bold Clifford rescue the fair Evelina it is only right that we should explain how he came so opportunely to the rescue.

The lights were out, and the old Hall wrapped in gloom, when the two friends returned to it from the wood of Winterleigh.

The gloom had still deepened, and the wind still continued howling and moaning through the leafless trees.

"All still now, Wilfred," said Paul to his companion. "How miserably quiet and awe-inspiring the place is, to be sure. Ugh! it is enough to give a fellow the cold shivers."

"Now," said Wilfred, "what are your plans?"

"Rather let me ask what are yours, for your experience in this sort of thing by far excels mine."

"You compliment; but I am at a loss to know what to do, for I have not got a clue to the repository of the valuables. We must trust to chance."

"Yes," said Wilfred, "that will be best. When we have effected an entrance we will separate, and each take different paths. You range the upper apartments while I confine my attentions to the lower regions, and mind that neither awaits the other. Bungles are often made by that means. As soon as each has secured his booty he will make for the wood, and, if not pursued or in trouble, await the coming of the other."

"Good! You are the best of generals, and I admire your skill."

"Ah! Paul," said Wilfred; "I know not how it is, but I have a presentiment that this night will be the last occasion I shall have for the exercise of that skill."

"Psha! Wilfred; you are a fatalist. I thought better of you."

"I thought better of myself; but I cannot control the feelings which now overpower me. I dread lest this night should be my last."

"Why, how long has this feeling possessed you?"

"Since I first looked upon this gloomy old pile. But, no matter, I am not a croaker, and am not afraid to look danger straight in the face."

"Shake off your qualms, then, and prepare for work. We will enter by the windows which open on the terrace yonder. See, there are shutters, and an entrance may very easily be effected."

"You are right; you know our plan. Now let us shake hands, and prepare for danger."

They clasped hands.

"This hand will be stiff in death when next you touch it," said the burglar."

"Nonsense, Wilfred; you unnerve me."

"I am sorry; but you will find that I am right. If such should be the case, go to my lodgings, and in my iron box you will find a small case containing papers. Open them, and follow out the instructions therein given; and above all preserve the certificates of a birth and marriage you will find secured there, together with a wedding-ring, and other articles which, although trivial in themselves, may one day prove of the greatest value."

"To whom?"

"To you."

"To me?"

"Yes; to you. *I knew your mother.* I loved her, and she confided in me; but suddenly I lost sight of her, and when I heard of her again she was in her grave, and you were under the protection of Mistress Granville. Finding you were so well cared for, I left you with the woman, but determined to keep a watch over you. I have done so to the best of my power. It is to serve you that I am here now."

"Indeed!"

"Yes, indeed. The young fellow of whom I spoke to you as having tendered the invite to myself and friends to assist this place was sought out by me; and the invite was drawn from him in order that I might enter the Hall, and learn what progressed here uninterruptedly."

"But what has all this to do with me?"

"Much, as you will find hereafter. But now we must separate. You go on your mission, and I will go on mine."

They were at the window, which, by a little skill, was easily opened.

"Now," said Clifford, who began to look upon his companion as either mad or dreaming; "now, Wilfred, my boy look alive!"

"I am ready," said Wilfred, stepping into the room; "and here we separate. But before you go, I wish you to make me a promise."

"What is it?"

"It is that if we meet again you will not recur to this topic unless I first broach it."

"Why should I not do so?"

"Do not ask me, but promise."

"Well, I promise."

"It is well, and now adieu, or, if we meet no more, farewell."

Clifford would have spoken, but Wilfred waved him off, and the highwayman passed from the room into the darkness beyond, without uttering another syllable.

He groped his way up the great staircase, and it was whilst traversing the great gallery that the cries of Evelina fell upon his ear.

"He is gone," said Wilfred, "and I shall see him no more. Oh! this terrible gloom upon my mind. Would that I could shake it off. Too late—too late. This robbery, too. Why should the risk be run, and there is nothing to gain, and all to lose. By Heaven! I fear I am mad. But it is all for the best. Cursed fate! Little did I think that this night would have so strange an ending, but I am not a free agent. Some governing power sways my actions, and I am but the puppet of fate. I have done wrong in speaking as I have done to Clifford. Should I not die, he will demand explanations which my oath to his mother forbids my giving; but why speculate thus: I *shall* die, so it is useless to hide the fact."

He commenced his search for valuables, and in a short time had found a great quantity of plate and jewellery which he secured in a bag and slung across his shoulder. He waited a few moments for some sound of Clifford, but none came, and giving a final glance in the direction his companion had taken, then made from the house with all speed.

His footsteps were bent in the direction of the wood.

The horses were tied securely in a spot where the trees were less numerous than in any part of the wood, the spot forming a little glen or hollow, carpeted with soft green sward.

When Wilfred reached this spot, he observed that the horses trembled as if from fright, and that something unusual was irritating them."

"Whoo, whoo!" said the man to the horses, steady, steady, what ails you. Poor fellows, then.''

"Whoo, whoo!" echoed a most unearthly voice, "steady, steady ! what ails you, poor fellows, then ?"

This was followed by a yell which froze the very blood in the veins of him who listened to it.

And the horses trembled more violently, and snorted and chafed fearfully.

Next moment the eyes of Wilfred fell upon a form whose hideousness he had never seen equalled.

Before him stood a frightful dwarf, of singularly in-human proportions.

An enormous head covered with a matting of long shaggy red hair, was set upon shoulders of preternatural breadth, terrific brawny arms which almost touched the ground as they hung by the side, were bare to the shoulder, and exhibited a knotting of muscles which told of a lion's strength. The legs were bowed, and in pro-portion with the arms ; but the body was extraordinarily small, but every muscle stood out on it like a knotted rope.

This was the descendant of the house of Norman !

Wilfred was speechless. He had never dreamt of meeting such a being, and the shock to his system was one he could not recover for many moments. At length he spoke :

"Who and what art thou ?" he asked.

"Who and what art thou ?" echoed the dwarf, with a diabolical grin.

" No human being ever wore a form like that."

" A form like that !"

"Good God," said the terrified man, " he can only echo me."

" Echo me !"

"The only faculty with which he is endowed, is that of imitation.''

"Imitation, imitation !"

The dwarf repeated this word a dozen times, at length raising his voice into a wild chant he screamed out the word, varying the accent on the different syllables and thus realising a kind of monotonous song which was positively frightful to hear, but which appeared to give him the greatest possible pleasure.

"Imitation, imitation," screamed the dwarf.

Away, away !" cried Wilfred, waving him off. " For the love of Heaven leave me."

" Leave me, leave me."

" I cannot bear it," cried Wilfred ; " I must fly."

" Fly, fly !"

Uttering this, the dwarf sprang forward, and, snatching the bag of treasure of Wilfred, poured its contents out on the ground.

With a terrible yell of delight, he fell upon the gold and silver, and commenced biting it furiously.

He literally tore the heavy pieces of metal into shreds, his passion increasing as he found that it was tasteless, and defied his efforts to masticate it.

He continued his task until he was mad with fury, but while he was thus engaged, Wilfred stole quietly to the tree to which his horse was secured, slipped the bridle, and sprang lightly on his back.

Quick as the motion was, it was not quick enough, for the dwarf who, observing it, sprang to the side of the horse, and clung to it.

Wilfred drew his knife, and attempted to strike the dwarf, who avoided the blow, and, grasping the knife, tore it from Wilfred's hand.

" Knife, knife," cried the dwarf ; "Sharp, sharp."

Gash, gash, and blood came.

Terrified to death, Wilfred dashed spurs into his steed, and the beast sprang forward with him, but the dwarf, leaping at the horse, plunged the knife into its side.

The poor beast leaped forward, and galloped of at an enormous pace, leaving a fearful trail of blood in its rear, along which the dwarf followed with tremendous speed.

Along dashed the horse, and after it went the dwarf.

Through the road and over the meadows ; along by the river, and out into the open country, spreading away in a tract of desolate marsh land.

On, on, stopping at nothing.

On, on, went the maddened suffering steed.

The race was a fearful one, but it was soon to end.

The blood flowed from the awful wound inflicted by the dwarf, and the life-blood of the beast oozed out, and its strength waned, until it reeled out, and at last fell.

Wilfred cleverly extricated himself from the stirrups and sped onward, drawing his pistols, and relying upon them as last resource ; the man flew onward, but the dwarf gained upon him at every step, and it became palpable to the fugitive that he must soon stand at bay. His object was to reach an old willow tree which overhung the sheet of stagnant water which was in the middle of the marsh.

On he sped, and in a short time reached the spot he sought by straining every nerve.

As he clutched it, and turned himself suddenly from its trunk, the dwarf was upon him, and the knife dashed forth.

The blade, however, entered the trunk of the tree, and Wilfred had time to raise a pistol.

Presenting it at the head of the dwarf he fired.

The dwarf was hit, and staggered slightly, but with a scream of pain he prepared once more to pounce upon his victim.

" *My last chance*," said Wilfred, drawing a second pistol, and pulling the trigger.

It *missed fire*.

"God help me !" cried the wretched man, "for all is over now."

It was over.

The dwarf foaming at the mouth with rage, and smarting from the pain of the bullet wound, raised the knife of which he had become possessed, and darting at his victim, caught him by the arm, and dragged him from behind the tree.

" Blood, blood !" screamed the dwarf, "gash, gash, and blood, knife cut and gash. I know what to do."

" A horrible, malignant glare shot from his eye, and he dashed his victim to the earth, and raised the knife.

" Blood !" he screamed again, "blood : see it, see it. Down came the knife, with a dull sound on the prostrate man's throat, and as it was drawn forth, out spur ted the crimson stream, saturating the hand which inflicted the wound.

The body quivered under the fatal stroke, the eyes half started from their sockets, one half-uttered exclama-tion escaped from the lips, and there was a gurgle in the throat, and all was over.

As the terrible dwarf gazed upon his hand, he uttered an exclamation of disgust, and turned ghastly pale.

" Ugh !" he cried ; "ugh ! Blood, blood ! ugh ! the smell. Clammy blood. It sticks to me, sticks to me, sticks to me !"

He threw himself on his face, and bathed his hand in the water, striving, but for some time striving in vain, to free himself from the awful stains.

" Off, off !" screamed the awful heap of deformity. "Off, off !" and he plunged his great hand deeper into the water, and paddled it about for some minutes.

After this he drew it forth and looked upon it.

With a scream of delight he marked the disappearance of the stains.

He then turned his attention once more to the pros-trate man, and all his malignity returned.

Catching the body in his brawny arms he tossed it up, and let it fall to the earth. Then he untwisted the long neck-cloth, and, avoiding the blood-stained portion, made a knot at one end about the throat of his victim.

Taking the other end in his hand he sprang with it into the willow tree, and dragged the corpse after him.

Crawling with his victim out to the extreme end of a bough overhanging the water, he fastened the neck-cloth thereto, and left the body suspended.

Jumping to the ground, the terrible being uttered a shriek of delight, and picking up his knife, which he secreted in his scant clothing, he danced about the gibbet he had made, and then started off; but, after running a distance of about a hundred yards, he turned to gaze once more upon his bloody handiwork.

The sight appeared to fascinate him beyond measure, and he once more sped back to get a near view of it.

This manœuvre he repeated again and again; but at last his fancy was satiated, and he sped away and returned not again.

CHAPTER VI.

CLIFFORD AND EVELINA—THE MYSTERIOUS FIGURE IN THE CORRIDOR—THE CHAMBER OF DEATH AND THE SECRET PASSAGE—A CLUE TO THE MISSING WILL.

"I WILL close the door, and he will be safe," said Clifford to the fair fugitive, as he sped from the chamber wherein Wilfred lay.

He turned, and secured the bolt as he spoke.

"Now we will fly."

"Oh!" cried Evelina, "my courage fails me. I fear I know not what, but presentiments of a thousand evils flock upon me, and weigh me down."

"It is a night of ill omen," said Clifford. "There is a something in the air we breathe that crushes us, and drives us to despair."

"Yes," said the girl, shuddering and clinging to her new-found protector; "it is the presence of death."

"Speak not thus, or, bold as I am, you will unnerve me. I have already undergone much to-night, in listening to the incoherent raving of a friend; let me not be tried further, lady, or my brain will reel under the oppressive load."

"How dark it is."

"Yes," said Clifford, "and the nearest window is nearly at the other end of the corridor. Do you know your way?"

"Yes," said Evelina, "to the private staircase. Softly, or we may be overheard."

"Who watches in the dead man's chamber?"

"It is tenantless. No one could be induced to stay there after the mysterious disappearance of the will."

"I do not wonder at it. Superstition is rife on such a night, and the circumstance of which you speak was sufficient to frighten all the poor ignorant people of the house from such a region of mystery, if not of enchantment."

"Do you fear?"

"I fear nothing. Are you prepared?"

"Yes, yes; but my feet cling to this spot, and a weight of lead appears to hold me fast."

"Shall I carry you?"

"No, no; I can walk."

"Come, then."

The girl made an effort to quit the spot on which she stood, but could not move. Her body fell forward, and she would have fallen but for Clifford, who caught her in his arms, and supported her.

"Heaven help me!" cried the girl; "I am paralysed!"

"Yes," said Clifford, "but only with fear. Lean on me, and I will assist you."

He was about to move forward, when the girl grasped his arm with a violence which made him start.

"What is it?" he whispered.

"Look! look!"

The girl's eyes were fixed upon the gloom beyond the window of which Clifford had spoken.

"I see nothing."

"Look! look!"

"Heaven save us! There is nothing there. Come on."

"Not for worlds. Look again."

"I repeat, lady, I see nothing."

"It nears the window—strain your eyes."

"Ah!"

"Now, now do you see it?"

"Yes, distinctly."

As he spoke, a dark shadow flitted across the window of the corridor, and advanced towards them.

Neither of them moved or breathed.

In another minute the figure of a woman stole by them.

"The vengeance is complete," said a voice—an old, croaking, ill-omened voice. "The vengeance is complete, and I conquer. I conquer, now my children are avenged."

The blood of the watchers froze in their veins as they listened.

Another second, and the figure was out of sight.

"What was it?" muttered Evelina, clinging still more tightly to the arm of her protector; "what, in the name of Heaven, was it?"

It was the figure of an old and withered woman," said Clifford, "but the voice was that of the raven. Oh! I shudder as I think of it."

"It was terrible."

"I never heard the like."

"Now I believe all I have heard of the place. The old superstitious tales of the villagers must have a foundation. The house is haunted."

"It is," said Clifford; "but I strongly suspect it is by evil-disposed mortals. A will was lost to-night?"

"Yes."

"And you suspect no one?"

"Who could one suspect? There was no one in the chamber."

"And yet the will disappeared from the chamber?"

"Yes."

"Then it was taken by mortal hands."

"I can scarce believe it."

"I feel convinced of it, and so shall you."

"Which way did that mysterious figure take?"

"I thought it passed to the corridor to the left."

"Where is the chamber of the baronet?"

"In that corridor."

"So I suspected. This mystery must be rooted out. Be assured you shall have justice done you if I can compass it. Come."

"I dare not."

"There is no danger. I swear it. Come."

"Oh, if I could but think as you do."

"Try. Come, fair lady, reassure yourself. There is no cause for alarm. Let us hasten to the chamber of death, or we may be too late."

"Too late! For what?"

"To find there the purloiner of the baronet's will."

Clifford took Evelina by the arm, and dragged rather than assisted her towards the much-desired chamber.

"Where is it?" asked Clifford.

"There," said Evelina, pointing to a doorway about half way down the corridor, but without turning in the direction.

"Come," said Clifford, "have courage. Let not your heart fail you now."

"Oh! if you but knew the terror that possesses me."

"I can guess it, but let it pass. I am with you."

They approached to the door of the chamber of death.

"Listen," whispered Clifford, "I hear a voice."

Evelina clung to him as if her life depended on the prowess of her hold.

"What do you hear?" she asked as plainly as her parched lips would allow her; "what is it?"

"A female voice.   Hark !"

"Cold and stiff in death," came the sounds of a voice from within the chamber: "Cold and inanimate, dead to sound as thou art to feeling : I still spurn thee, still feel the same bitter hatred for thee.   Murderer of two innocent girls, accursed of thy race !   I revile thee in death, and hurl imprecations on thy memory !   Powers of heaven and hell, hear me curse him again and again !   He dried up the fount of humanity within me.   He made my life a barren waste.   He tore from me those I held most dear, and robbed me of all that made life endurable.   He it was who unsexed me, and made me the thing I am ; and therefore I call for retribution, and ask that he may meet that punishment in the bourne to which he has gone that he escaped here !   I pray for the torture of his soul, even as he has tortured mine !"

"Horrible ! horrible !" said Clifford.   "I will see who dare utter such words in the presence of the dead."

He released himself from the hold of Evelina, and dashed into the chamber.

He was too late.

As he entered the tapestry on the wall was shaken and disturbed, and the intruder heard the click of the closing of a secret door.

He rushed to the entrance of the chamber, and drew in Evelina.

"Here," he said, as he closed the door, "here is the secret of the lost will.   There is a passage in the wall through which the old hag who swept by us in the corridor has fled."

"Indeed !"

"Yes ; I am convinced that what I say is the fact. Here, then, the mystery of the will is revealed.   Do you know who the woman is ?"

"I think I recognise the voice ; and I know there is but one who has ever had occasion to hurl such bitter curses at the dead man."

"And who is that ?"

"An old woman who lives in the wood hard by."

"Her name ?"

"Clifford."

Paul started in amazement.

"Why do you start ?   Do you recognise the name ?"

"It is one with which I am familiar," said Clifford, somewhat confused as the words of Wilfred Barnard occurred to him.

"Strange," he muttered ; "strange and terrible."

"To what do you allude ?"

"Pshaw !" he said, recovering himself by a violent effort ; "what folly !   I believe I am infected with your fears, for I am grown dull and almost imbecile.   We must to business."

"What will you now do ?" asked the maiden, casting a timid glance at the corpse."

"I will seek for this secreted passage," replied Clifford, drawing on one side the tapestry, and seizing one of the wax candles which burned beside the corpse.

He hurried behind the tapestry, and Evelina followed him—for she could not bear to remain alone in the presence of the dead.

She stood trembling and half fainting as Clifford went from panel to panel, tapping them with his hand, in order to find the one sounding the most hollow, and likely to conceal the passage.

At length he detected the one he sought.

"This is it, " he said ; "and now for the spring—for there must be one concealed here somewhere."

Narrowly he scanned each inch of the wood, and with eager eyes glanced at every spot likely to prove the one he desired to find.

At length a peculiar knot in the framework of the panel attracted his attention, and to this he applied his thumb with some force.

There was a movement of the panel, and then it slid away, revealing a concealed staircase, which apparently wound round all the walls of the house, and terminated in the vaults.

"Strange," said Evelina, regarding the opening in the wall with eyes extended in amazement, "strange that I should have lived here from infancy, and never heard of this passage before."

"Not at all strange," said Clifford ; "I'll wager this passage was known to but one person, and that person is the one I saw escape by it but a few moments since."

"You will not enter there," said Evelina ?

"And wherefore should I not, lady ?"

"Because you know not what danger it may lead to."

"I will answer for it there is naught to fear.   The woman was alone, and it would be cowardice to shrink from following the footsteps of one so helpless and infirm.   Come, lady, and fear nothing.   I will conduct you in safety."

"I will still trust you," said Evelina, placing her hand in that of Clifford.

"I will repay your confidence."

He drew her gently through the opening, and, closing the panel after him, commenced his descent into the vaults, steadily supporting the rescued girl, and carefully guiding her footsteps.

In about five minutes they came to the end of the passage, and their way was blocked by another secret entrance.

Clifford groped about for the spring, and at length found it.

A large stone slid away, and presented a narrow entrance, through which the two adventurers crawled.

They found themselves in the vaults of the old Hall.

They were in total darkness, and quite at a loss how to proceed.

Clifford endeavoured to find some passage by which they could continue their flight, but it was useless.   He felt they were spacious vaults, but he could see nothing, and knew not how to proceed.

In this emergency he determined on returning as he came.

"Let us re-enter the passage," he said, "for without light it is impossible to find our way out of this place."

"Yes," said Evelina, much alarmed at the awful stillness and darkness, "let us return."

Clifford stepped back to the place from which he had descended, and, after passing his hand over the wall for some moments, uttered a slight exclamation of terror.

"What is it ?" demanded Evelina, in an agony of fear.

"Horror !" cried Clifford, "the entrance to the passage is closed, and we cannot return."

Evelina staggered toward the spot from whence Clifford's voice came, and, overcome by the excitement of the past hour, sank helpless and motionless into his arms.

Clifford was distracted.   He knew not where to move, or what to do.

"It may be," he said, "that we are entombed alive, and that we may lie here and rot before we are discovered.   Heaven save us !   What is to be done ?"

It was useless to ask that question, for there came no answer.

Listening to the beating of his own heart, Clifford held the poor girl in his arms, and gave vent to his pent-up feelings in a torrent of invectives.   He cursed himself, fate, and all the world.   He felt as if madness was stealing over him, for his brain reeled, and a sickening sensation came over his heart.

He was in the embrace of the demon of despair.

"What shall I do ?—what shall I do ?" he cried.

This time there was an answer.

It came in the shape of the faint glimmer of a light, far away in the distance.

Faint as it was, it caught the eye of Clifford.

"Ah !" he said to himself, "it is the old woman of the corridor ; I must follow the light."

Lifting his senseless burthen in his arms, he sped with it quickly, but noiselessly, in the direction of the light.

It was Madge Clifford, and the highwayman followed her as closely as he could without risking a meeting.

She sped towards some steps, which Clifford readily divined led from the vault to the upper apartments.

"All right," he thought, "now the crone can get out of the way as fast as she likes."

In a few moments Madge Clifford had mounted the flight of steps, and opening a door on the top, disappeared from view.

Clifford drew a long sigh of relief, and catching Evelina in his arms, once more sped lightly up the steps.

Opening the door, he found himself in the great hall of Winterleigh.

As he entered the spacious apartment he beheld the old crone depart by a distant door, opening on the park.

"Fortune favours me," cried the highwayman gaily. "Safe above ground once more; now for the wood. Egad, though, Wilfred will be surprised to find what my expedition has resulted in."

Faint streaks of dawn were visible as Clifford stepped out into the air once more.

The sharp morning breeze at once revived the drooping girl, and, opening her eyes, she demanded where she was.

"Safe," said Clifford; "safe at last, lady, and once more with the clear sky above you."

"Saved," she murmured; "saved from worse than death. How shall I express my thanks?"

"By endeavouring to fly as quickly from this fatal spot as you possibly can."

"Yes, I will exert myself," said the girl. "I feel that it is best to be far away from the place. Danger lurks at every turn, and there is no peace within the precincts of the place. I will fly. But still," she continued, "it is not right that I should thus hamper you without again giving you time to reflect on what you do. I am a poor, helpless, indigent girl, and shall be a great burthen to you. Pause and think ere you incur further trouble on my account."

"I will die in your service, lady," cried Clifford, with enthusiasm in his voice: "All I can do to serve you will be a pleasure, therefore there is no occasion to pause another moment. Let us hasten to the spot where my horse awaits my coming."

They hurried towards the wood.

"You have not yet told me your name," said Clifford, as they sped on their way.

"It is Evelina," replied the maiden.

"But your surname?"

"Alas, sir, I have none. Sir Lascelles gave me that of—"

"I see my question has pained you, but I sincerely regret it. I meant not to wound you in any way."

"I am well convinced of it," said Evelina, "and now let me, in return, inquire the name of my deliverer?"

"Paul Everton," said Clifford, blushing at the false-hood he uttered, but he dared not give his real name.

"I shall treasure the name in my heart for ever," said Evelina. "I can never be sufficiently grateful to him who owns it."

"He is amply repaid to hear you say so."

"Ah," said Evelina, "you undervalue the services you have done me, but I never can. My gratitude is stronger than words can express."

After this they were silent again until they entered the wood.

"You will doubtless see a friend of mine who awaits my coming. I must ask you to pass over in silence anything you may see that strikes you as being singular and inexplicable. Strange things occur every day, and do not admit of explanation to those unconnected with them, therefore let me entreat you to close your eyes as well as ears should anything of the kind I have hinted at occur to you."

"There is a mystery in your words, and I cannot find a clue to it, but I will, as you desire, follow you blindly, for I can suspect no ill to me or others where you are concerned."

Clifford passed his hand over his brow as if in pain; but, shaking off the emotion the words of Evelina had occasioned, and which he endeavoured in vain to hide, he said,

"You think well of me: better than I deserve, but your confidence will never be betrayed."

Once more they moved on, and at length Clifford saw his mare standing patiently where he had left her, but his companion was gone.

"How is this?" said Evelina, in amazement; "what disturbs you?"

"My friend is not here, and his horse is gone."

"Did you, then, rely upon finding him here?"

"I did, indeed."

"He will, perhaps, return anon."

"What is this?" cried Clifford, stooping over the glittering heap of plate which had been subjected to the passionate usage of the dwarf.

"What further mischief is in store for us?" cried Evelina, in great terror.

"For you none; for me, perhaps some; but I fear my poor friend has fallen a victim to some treachery here."

"Indeed."

"Aye, indeed! What do I see?"

His eyes fell upon the blood of the horse.

"Blood!" he cried; "blood! His blood, perhaps."

"You alarm me."

"Calm yourself, lady; calm yourself. There is nought to fear."

"But you speak of blood."

"Yes, yes; look on the sward; there is the trace of it, and it runs to that path leading to the marshes beyond. I must seek my friend."

"Do so; let me not interfere with his safety. If you can assist him, fly, in the name of Heaven."

"I must do so," said Clifford, hastily pulling his cloak from the back of the mare, and throwing it over the shoulders of Evelina to screen her from the chill blast of morning; "remain you here until I return. There can be no danger to you, and I will not ride beyond the limits of the marsh."

"Think not of me, but fly."

"Good, generous girl. I will return immediately. Do not move from the spot, or I may miss you."

"I will not. God speed you."

The next moment the white mare was dashing through Winterleigh Wood by the path Wilfred had taken on his wounded horse.

Clifford rode hard, and his magnificent mare bounded with him over the ground with the speed of the fawn.

On he dashed until he reached the spot where the horse of his friend had fallen dead.

Without pausing, he continued to ride until he reached the willow tree, and there, with the pale moon struggling to maintain her brilliancy against the dawn, shining full upon it, he beheld, dangling from the bough of the fatal tree, the lifeless body of his friend and companion.

At first Clifford sat regarding the spectacle in silent horror, and then he gave way to a passionate burst of grief.

"Poor Wilfred," he cried, "friend of many long years, noble and generous companion, who can have done this? My curses light upon him, whoe'er he be, and my vengeance pursue him. Poor, poor Wilfred."

Tears streamed down the cheek of the strong man, and a storm of grief raged within him.

In all probability he would have sat there until broad daylight, with his eyes bent upon his friend, and thoughts fleeting back to days gone by; but suddenly the memory of Evelina, and the position in which he had left her, came upon him, and with a start he gathered up his reins.

"I cannot assist you," he cried; "and it is useless for me to remain here; but I will know no rest until I have sought out your murderer, and wreaked my vengeance on him."

With a last long look at the pitiful sight before him, he turned his horse's head, and galloped from the spot.

*   *   *   *   *

Evelina had not been left alone many minutes in the wood when she was startled by a peculiar cry.

It rang in her ears with startling shrillness, and made her very blood curdle as she listened to it.

Nearer and nearer it came.

Still nearer and nearer, and at last it appeared to proceed from a part close by where she stood.

Darting behind a large tree, she partly concealed herself just as the dwarf stepped into the little glade.

Evelina had often heard of this singular freak of nature, but had never before looked upon him, and it may readily be imagined how the sight electrified her.

The dwarf, without discovering her place of concealment, sat down close by the spot, and re-commenced crushing up the plate that strewed the ground.

The poor girl was terribly frightened, and shrank within herself.

She scarcely breathed for fear of attracting the attention of the monster who pursued his task of crushing the heap of gold and silver with untiring pertinacity.

At length a wood pigeon started from the tree behind which Evelina stood, and, with a cry, started off on the wing to another spot.

The dwarf started to his feet, and gazed about.

He then looked up into the tree.

"More, more," he cried. "I'll find more."

He advanced to the tree, and was about to climb it when his eyes fell upon Evelina.

The girl started back, and sought to fly, but her terror rooted her to the spot.

The dwarf uttered another of his frightful cries.

"I know you, I know you," he screamed, flapping his great arms against his sides—"Evelina, Evelina of the Hall—Evelina of the Hall—the Hall."

Still repeating these cries, he performed a kind of wild dance around the spot on which the girl stood.

Next, he approached her nearer, and extended his great hand toward her.

As it touched her, she fell shuddering with fear to the ground.

The dwarf stooped and bent his face over hers. Fortunately, the girl had fainted, or the gaze which the brute fixed upon her would have driven her mad.

"Mine now, mine now ! Alone in the wood : alone in the wood ; mine now."

He seized her in his arms, and was about to fly with her, when Clifford galloped to the spot, and at a glance saw the position of the lady.

Without hesitation, he drew a pistol and fired.

The shot partially took effect, for the dwarf dropped his prey.

Terrified as he was at the sight of the being in whose presence he stood, Clifford never for a moment forgot his presence of mind, and bounding towards Evelina, he caught her in his arms.

The dwarf had now recovered the shock of the bullet, and drawing the knife he had obtained from the unhappy Wilfred, he prepared to spring upon his assailant.

"Terrible being," cried Clifford, presenting his second pistol at the head of the dwarf ; "avaunt, or this moment will be your last."

"Evelina, Evelina," screamed the dwarf, lifting his knife, and glaring savagely at Clifford.

It now flashed across Clifford's brain that before him stood the murderer of his friend, and steadying his aim, he discharged his second pistol full at the dwarf's head just as the deformed wretch was about to spring upon him.

This shot took effect, and the recipient of the ball fell to the earth with a yell of pain.

Scarce pausing to glance at what he had done, Clifford sprang on his mare, and setting Evelina before him, urged his pet forward.

Notwithstanding the double burthen the gallant animal

dashed away at great speed, and in a few moments was clear of the wood.

And now Clifford set off in the direction of London at the top of his mare's speed.

He dared not spare the poor animal, and so urged her on and on until Winterleigh lay far behind him.

CHAPTER VII.

WITHIN TEN MILES OF LONDON—THE WAYSIDE INN—ARRIVAL OF THE OFFICERS—CLIFFORD IN DANGER—THE ESCAPE FROM THE STABLE, AND TERRIFIC LEAP OF THE WHITE MARE, BRILLIANT.

THE Harvest Home was a little inn situated in a village lying about ten miles from the boundaries of the city of London.

Job Winchurst, the jolly host, was well known as the man who never refused a snug room and a good drink to a knight of the road, nor a stall in his stable and a feed of the best oats to the knight's steed.

"As far as I can see," Job would say, "they're decent fellows enough, and don't harm any but can afford it ; and many's the pound they put in my way of a dark night, by keeping those within my house who, if the roads were clear, would ride on to London. So, if they come to me, I'll wink at their calling, and treat 'em like lords "

Now, it was well known to every London thieftaker that these were Job's sentiments, and if any particular gallant horseman happened to be particularly required by the authorities, it was pretty certain that the limbs of the law would seek him in the neighbourhood of the Harvest Home, failing to find him in any of his metropolitan haunts.

It so happened that on the very day Clifford rode from Winterleigh, and made for this village, which we will name Hanford Wells, two officers from London took it into their heads that they would seek him at the "Harvest Home.'

"If he isn't there," said one, "it's just possible that he will come there sooner or later, and so there we will wait for him."

The plan being determined upon, the men disguised themselves into very fair parodies on opulent City travellers, and immediately set out on their expedition.

By a strange misfortune, Paul arrived at the inn, and placed his horse in the stable, just a few minutes before the officers came in sight.

"Show this lady to the best room in the house," said Clifford, and let her be attended as becomes her."

"Your orders shall be obeyed, sir."

"Give the mare a feed, and let her lay down. She must want it by this time."

"Yes sir. Had a hard ride ?"

"A very hard ride. Put half-a-gallon of your best ale in her water, and throw a rug over her. She must not get chilled."

"Ah! sir, you deserve to have a good horse, you know how to take care of one."

"Serve those well who serve you well, Job," said Clifford, "and you can't do wrong. That is the motto I act upon."

"And a very good motty, it is ; and I'm sorry more people as perfess honesty don't act up to it."

"The profession of honesty is oftener heard than the practice seen ; but that is neither here nor there. Give me some good wine, and take care of Brilliant."

"That I'm sure to do."

Paul seated himself at the window of the room into which he had been shown, and after the landlord had placed a bottle of good wine before him, he gazed out upon the road, and reflected on the strange adventures in which he had taken part during the night.

He had not been thus occupied long when the two men to whom we have alluded drew rein before the inn door.

They were so well disguised for the characters they personated that Paul had not the faintest suspicion of their real errand to that place.

"A nice, likely pair of old gentlemen," he said, as the men drew up. "Now they would be worth stopping between this and London on a dark night. But it's no use to let my thoughts run in that direction this journey, for I have other and more weighty business on hand; so my opulent old friends may stand over to the uses of some of my disengaged friends. I wish them health and success."

We leave Paul to discuss his wine, and descend into the court and see how matters progressed there.

The officers on pulling up were at once waited upon by Job Winchurst and the ostler, Bob Brassley—a gentleman whose further acquaintance we shall make in the progress of this tale.

"What house is this?" demanded one of the officers.

"This is the Harvest Home, at Hanford Wells."

"The Harvest Home; I've heard of this spot, and I'm sorry to say that what I've heard does not redound to the credit of the place. They say it's a regular house of call for highwaymen and thieves."

"Then they tell infernal lies, whoever they are," said blunt old Job. "It's a house of call for all travellers, and one's as welcome as another. Great and small, gentle and simple may come, for all I care. Those as pays best is most welcome, and one man's money is as good as another's; but the one as spends most is most welcome. That's the real principle of trade."

"Well, my good man, I didn't say it wasn't," returned the officer; "so don't fly into a passion without a cause. For my part, I've no particular objection to highwaymen, as long as they let me alone; and, to speak the truth, I've nothing much to complain of in their attention to me, for they have hitherto managed to steer clear of me, and let me travel the roads in peace."

"And I may say the same," said the other. "They rather shun me. I suppose there's something about me they don't like."

He accompanied this speech with a loud laugh, and winked at his companion, who laughed, and returned it.

"Somethink about yer they don't like," said Bob Brassley, walking away with the horses, after the men had stripped them of their saddle-bags; "so I should think. I'm cussed if there ain't somethink about yer I don't like, and I'll keep my eye upon yer."

"And now," said the most talkative of the two officers to Job, "if you don't see any objection we'll see our horses fed. It's a rule of ours."

"Oh, all right," said Job. "We ain't in the habit o' cheating dumb critters; but you can have yer way. Come along."

He walked towards the stable, and the officers followed him.

"Now, then, Bob," cried Job Winchurst; "these here gents wants to see their hosses fed. Look alive, and give 'em some corn."

With these words Job turned away with an air of disgust, and walked across the courtyard to the house.

He had not been gone an instant when the eyes of the two thieftakers fell upon the mare Brilliant.

"Hillo!" ejaculated one.

"Whew!" whistled the other.

"I've my eye upon yer," said Bob quietly, as he entered a stall with a feed of corn. "You knows that mare, if I ain't mistaken."

"Baker," said one of the officers to the other, "Baker, that's a good-looking mare."

"She's a clipper, Harris, and no mistake about her."

"Oh, you're very much interested in her, no doubt," said Bob to himself.

"I say, ostler," said the man addressed as Baker, "whose mare is that?"

"A gentleman's."

"So I suppose; but what gentleman's?"

"I don't know."

"I suppose that means you won't know."

"It may be so, and it mayn't. It's just as people takes it."

"Oh, you're a nice sort of fellow, you are."

"Yes," said Bob, with extreme gravity, "its generally supposed so by them as is judges of people's characters."

"Yes, a promising candidate for Newgate," added Harris

"A place," said Bob, "with which, I've no doubt, you're both tolerably well acquainted."

"Ah," said Baker to his companion, "there's not much to be made out of this fellow; let's get into the house."

"All right," returned the other; "but we're about right this turn. That mare belongs to Gentleman Clifford, or I'm a Dutchman."

They walked into the house.

"Officers," said Bob, as they disappeared, "officers, as safe as eggs! Clifford's caught in a nice trap; but he shan't walk into it with his eyes shut, if I knows it."

With this he gave vent to his indignation by giving the horse belonging to Baker a sound punch in the ribs, narrowly escaping a sharp kick in return.

"Take that, you varmint," said the ostler, "and I'm precious sorry to think it wasn't your master's ribs I was a punching."

He went into the yard, and seeing his master standing at the door of the house, he beckoned him into the stable.

"Yer see them hosses, don't yer?"

"Well, o' course I do," said Job; "and very likely beasts they are."

"Yes, they are—too likely, it strikes me."

"Now, what are you driving arter?"

"Just this: them hosses don't belong to no travellers, they don't."

"Oh, don't they," said Job; "then you'd better call me a fool, and tell me I don't know nothink about it."

"No more yer don't."

"Hey?" said Job, opening his eyes; "hey? But I see yer game; you're drunk."

"Oh, o' course I is. That's werry likely, considerin' I've had nothink to drink. Drunk! You'd take care o' that, you would."

"Well, then, if yer ain't drunk you're mad."

"I s'pose so," said Bob: it's werry possible. I've come into a large fortin, I s'pose, and that's done it; or you're going to give up the house, and give it to me, and the news has turned my brain! That's likely to be it, ain't it?" The ironical tone in which this was conveyed meant, as plainly as possible, that *that* was not likely to be, under any circumstances.

"Well," said Job, "if yer ain't drunk or mad, what's up?"

"I've discovered somethink."

"Yer have?"

"Yes."

"What?"

"Them travellers ain't travellers."

"Ain't they? Then who are they?"

"Officers."

"No."

"Yes."

"Whew!"

Mr. Job Winchurst whistled in astonishment, and raised his eyes until the whites only were perceptible.

"What s to be done?" inquired the jolly host. "They mustn't have the Gentleman this journey."

"They mustn't have him any journey out of the Harvest Home," said Bob; "it ain't to be thought of, no how."

"No more it ain't," said Job; "they shan't say the little house was ever a trap for the catching of anybody, while Job Winchurst's name is on the signboard."

"That's the right sort o' sentiments, guv'nor," said Bob, in extreme enthusiasm; "that's the kind o' thing I like to hear, and no mistake."

"Now for action," said Job; "Clifford must at once know what's up; meanwhile, saddle and bridle the mare, and make all straight for instant flight. D'ye understand?"

"Yer shall see."

"I know I can leave it to you. So, now for the bold knight."

Job crossed the courtyard, and entered the house.

Assuring himself that the men were not watching him, the host hastened up the stairs, and entered the front room occupied by Clifford.

He opened and shut the door with the greatest haste, and turned to Paul.

The highwayman at once saw, by the manner of his friend, that there was something wrong.

"Hist!" cried Job; "hist! there's danger!"

"How?"

"The hawks are on the wing, and have spotted their prey."

"Where?"

"Here; they've covered you."

"Ha!"

"Yes; a pair of them—and sharp 'uns, too."

"How did they spot me?"

"Knew the mare directly they saw her. Tried to pump Bob; but it was no go in that direction."

"How long have they been here?"

"A very few moments."

"Indeed!"

"Yes, indeed. Have you been looking out of window?"

"Yes."

"And did you see no one come?"

"Yes; two travellers from the London-road."

"That's the werry identicals."

"You surely jest. I was only just thinking what a nice pair of fellows they would be to me this evening."

"They would—if you wanted to go with them to Newgate."

"Well, it appears I'm caught. Devil take it! How unfortunate at such a moment!"

"You're not nabbed yet, my boy; and shan't be, if old Job can help it."

"Thanks. You're a good fellow; but I'm afraid there's no way out of this scrape. To attempt to get the mare from the stable would be to startle them and bring them down upon me, and without the mare I should be useless. Then, again, the lady—how can I leave her?"

"You can trust her to me until you can return for her, can't you?"

"Yes. But how can I explain this peculiar act?"

"What explanation does it require?"

"Much. She knows not who I am, and will not understand my flight."

"Oh! some excuse must be made, some bait offered that she can easily swallow. There's no time to hesitate."

"You are right: but I know not how to excuse myself to her, and I would not have her know the real secret of my affairs for worlds."

"I see, a clear case of love. Well, you're to be pitied, for love's an awful thing, and shouldn't be indulged in by men in your line. You see what a mess it has put you in now. If it wasn't for this good-looking young woman you'd not hesitate to jump on the back of the mare and fly on the instant, but you see how you're now sitiwated. It's an awful position to be put in. Howsomever, there's no time to lose, and you best see about doing somethink at once. Now see the young woman, and tell her some-think or other, and then follow me."

"See her! No! I could not tell her a lie to her face. I'll write!"

"You will best be quick."

"Why should I be quick? It strikes me I am much better here with her than on the road at this hour. It is just possible I may be running from one danger into another. It's too near London to go parading the roads in broad daylight."

"Well, it is light, but it won't be so much longer; for at this time o' year there ain't much light after four, and it's now past three."

"Just so. Perhaps I am safer in the saddle, and if I can only give these fellows a pelter across the country,

I could leave them behind in an hour, though they were mounted on winged horses, for there's nothing on four legs that can match Brilliant."

"I believe yer. But there's pen, ink, and paper. Are yer going to write?"

"Yes."

"Very well, then. I'll just take a turn into the b k room that overlooks the yard, and see what's up. I'll tap once when I come back."

"I understand."

The heart of Clifford sank within him as he was left alone in the inn chamber.

A dismal foreboding of evil—an unaccountable and unconquerable dread of something being about to happen—possessed him, and he trembled as he took up the pen to write.

The shadows of the November afternoon now began to creep into the grim old chamber, and make it still more dismal.

The fire in the large grate threw out its lurid glare, and cracked anything but pleasantly. Without, the aspect of things was no more enticing.

The sky was tinted with that dull, misty red, peculiar to the evenings of November.

Far away over the hills stole a heavy mist, and with it came the wind.

A dull, monotonous soughing and sighing through the branches of the leafless trees ensued, and the night promised to be dark and stormy.

"Psha!" cried Clifford, throwing down the pen, and walking towards the window, "what a cur I am. What a craven heart, that I should be thus disconcerted at the presence of two men, perhaps not so well armed, certainly not so well mounted, as myself. But yesterday I should have looked upon this as a pleasant adventure; now, alas! now I am as disconcerted as if the fetters were about my body, and the gates of Newgate yawned to receive me. I know not how to account for it, unless it be that I am weak from want of rest, or that I am growing sick. But no! My eyes are not heavy, and my pulse is even, and beats healthily. What, then, is it? Ah! it is the memory of the night I have passed. The visit to Winterleigh—the fate of Wilfred, and the supernatural events attending the death of the old Baronet. But what have these to do with me? I am grieved for Wilfred, grieved as one man can be for the untimely end of another whom he has loved, but beyond this there is nothing to disconcert me. What has the Red Hall, its mysteries, its nocturnal visitants, its dead owner, its distressed damsel, or its idiotic dwarf to do with me? Echo should answer, 'Nothing!' but it does not. Strange! There is a voice within me that tells me all these things have to do with me. I am warned that a special Providence brought me to Winterleigh last night, and that my fate is by some mysterious link bound to theirs whose acquaintance I have made within the last few hours. Strange, very strange! All these things appear as familiar to me as if I had experienced them before. I must have pictured similar scenes in my dreams. But it grows dark, and the wind whistles more shrilly through the trees. I must shake off this weakness, and do the bidding of my friend."

He returned to the table, and again resumed the pen.

"What shall I write?"

"THE TRUTH!"

Paul started to his feet.

"God of Heaven! What was that?" he cried.

There was no one present. There came no reply to this question. But the room grew more gloomy, and the fire threw out a still deeper glare; and the shadows deepened and deepened. Paul shuddered and pushed the table.

The blood ran coldly through his heart, and every limb of his body quivered as if ague-stricken.

"What was it?" he murmured, hoarsely; "what could it have been? It was the voice of the old hag I saw stealing through the corridors and vaults of Winterleigh.

But, no ! It could not have been so. The distance, the place ! Psha ! Idiot that I am ! I am as nervous as a child. It was but an echo from my own heart. THE TRUTH ! Yes, I should write the truth, but I dare not— I dare not !"

He seated himself once more, and attempted to recommence his note to Evelina.

For at least five minutes he failed to make a mark on the paper, and then he dipped his pen in the ink with the mechanical motion of one in a dream, and arranging his paper, wrote the following lines :—

"I am forced to leave you here, lady, until I can return or send for you. I am at this moment in a serious difficulty, and have to fly to London. But fear not that I will return with the speed of lightning to convey you to a place of safety until something can be done for you. This may appear a strange line of conduct, but heed it not. All is for the best.

"Believe me, yours devotedly,
"PAUL CLIFFORD."

Unconsciously he had signed his real name, forgetful that he had called himself Everton when asked his name by the lady to whom he had written.

He hastily folded this scrawl, and, lighting a piece of paper at the fire, he sealed it and threw it on the table.

"There," he said aloud, "I have at least told no lie."

"*But you have not told the truth.*"

"The voice again," cried Clifford. "Heaven preserve me, the place is haunted."

"Yes, haunted : haunted as every place will be in which you for the future set your foot. As every spot must be until you give up your pursuit of Lascelles Winterleigh's will, and banish Winterleigh from your thoughts."

"That will never be."

A shadow seemed to flit between Clifford and the fire.

He started forward to grasp it, but his arm enfolded air.

At this moment Job returned.

"Didn't you think I'd been a great time?"

"I did not note the time."

"Indeed ! why I've been just an 'alf-hour."

"No matter."

"Oh ! isn't it, though. I beg your pardon, but I think it is."

"What do you mean ?"

"Why, I mean that those officer fellows have taken up their places in the yard, from which the devil himself won't move them."

"Well ?"

"Well, there's no getting at the stable, that's all."

"No matter."

"Oh ! isn't it ? I'm glad you think so."

"Pardon me," said Clifford, "I knew not what I said ; I am almost distracted."

"All right—no offence, only I don't see what's to be done."

"Let me look out at the yard. I may be enabled to see a way out of the scrape. I'm more used to difficulties of this sort than you can possibly be."

Clifford walked into the adjoining room with the landlord.

The window of this chamber faced the yard ; and, hiding behind the curtains, Clifford looked down into the yard

The officers stood at the door of the house, smoking their pipes, and Bob, with a pipe in his mouth, stationed himself at the stable door, and fixed his eye upon the unwelcome guests.

Job quietly threw up the window and popped his head out.

The three men smoked away silently for a few minutes, and then one of the officers looked up, and fixing his eye upon Bob, grunted out—

"Well !"

"Well !" reiterated Bob, puffing away in great complacency.

"You don't seem to mind the cold," said the officer.

"No," said Bob, "I don't usually mind it ; but you look as if you rather enjoyed it."

"I don't know what I look like," said the officer, "but I don't enjoy it at all."

"Then what d'ye stick there for ?"

"Because we can't move."

"Got the cramp ?"

"Got the devil ! No."

"Then why *can't* yer move ?"

"We may as well tell him," said the officer who had spoken : "it must come out sooner or later."

"All right."

"Look here, What's-yer-name, I suppose you take us for City travellers, don't you ?"

"No, I don't."

"Well, it's all the same if you did, because we ain't anything of the sort."

"I know that."

"Oh, you know that, do you ; then *how* do you know that ?"

"Because I can see."

"What can yer see ?"

"Newgate written in yer faces, that's all."

"Oh, that's all. Well, you've hit it."

"Of course I have."

"Well, since you know who we are, I 'spose you also know why we came here ?"

"I can guess."

"I suppose so."

"Yes, you come here because t's the best house you can stop at between this and London."

"Oh ! Well, then, that's *not* why we came here."

"Well, then, I don't know, and I don't care."

"Well, then, I'll tell you, whether you know or care. We want the fellow who rides that white mare."

"Do yer ?"

"Yes."

"Well, then, I wishes as how you may get 'un, that's all."

"Oh ! we'll have him fast enough. If he isn't here now he'll come, and as sure as we lay hands on him—"

"You'll get something for your trouble," said Bob.

"Perhaps."

"Yes, perhaps ; only there don't seem to me to be much doubt about it."

"Well, your opinion ain't up to much."

"It's worth something."

"In your opinion !"

"Yes, and in other people's ; so don't make a mistake about it."

"We are not going to make any mistakes at all, my friend, and to convince you of that we'll commence business at once."

"What's yer game ?"

"Well, in the first place, our game is to show you who we are."

The officers rose and advanced to the stable door.

"Now," said the spokesman, "look at that."

He drew a short brass mace from his pocket and held it up to Bob.

"Do you see that ?" he asked.

"Oh, yes."

"Well, now you know who we are, and knowing who we are, you'll just aid and assist us in effecting the capture of Paul, *alias* Gentleman ' Clifford, an offender against the laws, a disturber of the king's peace, and a desperate highway robber upon whose head a price is set."

"How much ?" demanded Bob, with imperturbable gravity.

"One hundred poun's."

"He'd be cheap at the price !"

"Now, without further gab," said the officer, "we'll trouble you for the key of that stable."

"What's the use of it ?"

"The use of it is simply this—it will lock the door and save us the trouble and danger of dividing our strength while we search the house for the man we want."

Bob looked np and caught the expression of Job's eye as he peered down from the window above. It said as plainly as eye could speak, " Give him the key."

" So you want the key," said Bob.

" Yes we do, and we mean to have it."

" Werry good. Here it is."

He drew the great key from his pocket and handed it to the officers.

One of them took it, and instantly closed and locked the stable door.

" Now, that's done," said Bob, "what's the next move ?"

" The next move is to see who's in the house, so now amuse yourself till we come back."

" That's easily done."

" We're glad of it."

" Ha ! ha !" said the second officer, " I fancy we've got the bird this time."

" I wish you may keep him," said Bob.

" Oh ; that job's not so difficult."

" Yet your betters have failed at it."

" That may be. It proves nothing."

The men went into the house.

In a moment Bob closed the door.

" Now," he said, looking up at the window, " What's to be done?"

" The ladder," cried Job.

" All right," said Bob, running to the further corner of the yard, and picking up a ladder with which he returned immediately.

" Now then," said Job, " up with it."

" No sooner said than done."

Bob lifted the ladder to the window, and Clifford instantly stepped through the casement and descended.

" They boned your key," said Job, " but they didn't think there may be a twin brother knocking about. Look out, Bob—catch."

" Job Winchurst flung down a key, which Bob caught in his hat, and with which he started off to the stable.

In an instant the door was flung open, and Clifford and the other entered.

" Come, mare, come, softly, softly," said Clifford.

Hearing his voice, the faithful animal turned in her stall, and picked her way daintily towards the door.

" Steady, steady, and softly," said Clifford.

Almost without a sound the mare came into the courtyard, and Bob re-locked the stable door : catching up a handful of mud and flinging it into the hole.

" If they open that in a hurry I'll eat 'em," he said, eyeing his work with great satisfaction.

" Thanks," cried Clifford, about to spring into his saddle ; " thanks, I shan't forget you."

" Look out !" screamed Bob in reply.

Clifford looked towards the house and saw the two officers sliding down the ladder.

He was not in the saddle when the first of them touched the ground.

At the end of the yard were two folding gates of considerable height, opening unto the road.

The tops were covered with long iron spikes and altogether the gates proved a most formidable barrier.

With extreme foresight the officers sprang to this point and before Clifford had well recovered from the surprise their sudden appearance had occasioned him the gates were closed and he was bound in.

" Devil take 'em," cried Bob, they've done for you."

" Not yet," cried Clifford ; " hey, mare, hoy, hoy ; at it ; over my beauty."

He drew the mare back and showed her the task she had to perform.

It almost appeared suicidal to set a horse at such a barrier, but Brilliant was no ordinary animal, and pricking up her ears and uttering a neigh which appeared to be for the purpose of assuring her master of her capability of bringing him safely through the danger, she flew towards the gates.

Taking the leap at a miraculously well-judged distance, Clifford raised his mare and, with a wild shout of defiance, he was the next instant flying over the barrier, over the heads of the officers. They looked up and fired their pistols wildly after the fugitive, but he was on the other side and springing lightly over the road to London.

" Gone," cried both the officers in a breath ; gone clean off."

" You see, my friends," said Bob, taking up his cap and dancing with great glee, " you see I was quite right. The little job's more difficult than you took it to be."

" Go to the devil," was the polite reply.

The officer who had taken the key of the stable from Bob now drew it forth and tried to insert it in the lock, but Bob's mud had almost filled up the wards, and the door obstinately refused to open.

" You'd better give it up," said Bob ; "the gentleman is about a mile in advance and your horses won't catch him in a week."

" No, thanks to you," said one of the fellows.

" What d'ye mean by thanks to me?"

" I mean that you've aided in the escape of a highway robber after having been called upon to assist in his capture."

" How have I aided ?"

" Why you've filled up the wards of the lock, and we can't get our horses out."

" Well," said Bob, " it's the first time in my life that ever I knew a feller had not the right to do what he liked with his own locks and keys, and what's more, it's the first time that I knew gentlemen want to get at their horses until they've paid their bills."

" Open that door," shouted the enraged officer."

" Yes, when you've paid your bills. Officers or no officers you don't leave the Harvest Home without paying."

" We'll pay you over the head with the butt of our pistols if you don't open the door."

" Oh, that's your game is it," cried Bob. " You refuse to pay your bills and threaten to maim the ostler if he don't give up your nags ; now my fine fellows," cried Bob, seizing a stable-prong and brandishing it, " there ain't no law as admits of ostlers being served like that, so if you don't walk into the house and pay yer bills at once, I'll smash yer into little bits."

Thoroughly beaten and crest fallen the thief takers did as they were ordered by Bob, who enjoyed their discomforture to the utmost.

As soon as the men entered the house Bob set himself about opening the door, a task of some difficulty, but one which he ultimately accomplished.

He then walked the horses of the two officers to the front door of the house, and held them until their owners came out.

Silently and sullenly the men got into their saddles and prepared to move away.

" Remember the ostler, gentlemen," said Bob, touching his hat.

" Remember you," said the men, " d—n you ; yes—we'll never forget you."

" Haw, haw, haw," roared Bob, " that's a good 'un."

" Good 'un or not, you'll repent it. Mind you've not yet heard the last of this."

" Oh, yes I have."

" What do you mean ?"

" Why I mean that you'll be ashamed ever to say a word about the matter. People in your line don't care about boasting of such a beating."

" The fellow's right," said one to the other ; "yes, he's right."

" Then you will remember the ostler."

" Hark ye, Mister Bob," cried one of the officers ; " if

a penny would save your life, I'd see you eternally choked before you'd have it of me."

"And hark ye, Mister Officer," returned Bob, "if a penny of your accursed blood money would save me from choking, I'd see myself eternally cursed before I'd touch it. Now what dy'e think of that?"

What the officers thought of it did not transpire, for, without another word, they rode off towards London.

"Well," said Job, as he watched them disappear, "that was done to rights; but now there's this letter to give the young woman."

CHAPTER VIII.

MOTHER CLIFFORD—THE WHITE CAT—THE VISION OF THE INN—WHERE THE WILL WAS CONCEALED.

THERE was a hollow in the Winterleigh Wood.

A secluded, out of the way, wild spot, where few dared enter and where few dared stay.

In this hollow was situated the cottage of Mother Clifford.

In days gone by, but many long years ago, before Farmer Clifford died so suddenly, and left his wife and daughter so badly cared for, the hollow in the wood was deemed a pretty and desirable spot, but when the Baronet of Winterleigh gave the widow the keeper's lodge, situated therein, and she made it her place of abode, the spot began to bear an ill-name, which increased with years, and finally became possessed of a most unenviable and ghostly notoriety.

Mrs. Clifford had never borne a good name in the county.

As a girl she was said to possess dark passions, and to be accursed with the evil eye.

She was beautiful, but she was evil. An unearthly lustre shot from a great black eye; a satanic curl marked her otherwise beautiful lip, and her voice, when raised in anger, made people shudder, for it was a dismal, shrill, and unearthly voice, and resembled that of the raven when driven off from its meal of carrion.

Nevertheless, good, genial, respected young Farmer Clifford married her, and for a while appeared proud of her, but rumour said that in his choice of a wife he had not acted of his own free will.

According to the village gossips the lass had thrown the glimmer of her eye upon him, and he struggled in vain against her fascinations.

The tale ran thus:—

The young farmer met this singular being for the first time on a May-day revel.

He was at the time sweethearting with the daughter of a neighbouring farmer, the girl who had been on this occasion chosen as the May Queen. Young Clifford followed in the train of his lady-love, and appeared the happiest of them all. Men envied him as he tripped along with his fair girl, whose heart was his own, and the youth was full of joy.

On the green of Winterleigh was raised the times honoured May-pole, and about this centre the rustic capered in the most unrestrained glee.

Young Clifford danced the first dance with the Queen of the May; but, after this, as was the custom, he had to resign her to the crowd of less fortunate but expectant swains who coveted the honour of her hand in the merry caper.

Finding that his chance of again dancing with the Queen was very small, Clifford, who had no heart for the other damsels, walked away, and awaited the sports about the May-pole. At a slight distance from the festive scene he encountered a tall, and remarkably beautiful girl, who had attracted universal attention, but who resolutely refused to take part in the merry-making.

She was dressed as a peasant, and her contour was that of a superior rustic, but her skin was remarkably white for one of her condition and station, and there was a singular reserve and haughtiness in her behaviour, which rendered her more conspicuous.

Her hair was raven black, and fell unrestrainedly down her back to her waist. A small knot of blue ribbons was the only ornament she wore; her eyes were of a lustrous blue-black, and her teeth were of pearly whiteness. In repose, her face was marvellously beautiful; in moments of excitement and anger it was terrible, for her eyes wore an awful look, and her mouth wore that satanic expression already alluded to.

Such was the woman young Clifford encountered.

He raised his hat respectfully to the beautiful stranger, and she returned the salute with a low curtsey.

They immediately entered into conversation, and, ere an hour had passed, became so absorbed in each other that they wandered heedlessly from the green, and left all traces of the revel far behind them. What they found to converse about during the hour we know not; but, at its expiration, young Clifford suddenly remembered that his sweetheart would be expecting him, and that he had done wrong in straying so far away, and in such company.

"I must return," he said.

"And wherefore," asked the beautiful unknown.

"Because I have left one on the green who expects my return."

"You refer to the May Queen?"

"Yes. She is—."

"Your betrothed."

"Yes."

"I knew it. I saw it directly you came to the green."

"Then you observed us?"

"Yes; and I said to myself they love one another."

"We do."

"Believe it not," said the girl; "you have no love for the pale-faced chit who apes the Queen to-day. There is no love in the case."

"But my heart——"

"Hearts; believe not in them. They are liars, flatterers, and deceivers. If you married this girl you would not be happy."

"I think I should."

"And I say you would not, for I know better."

"Then mine is an undesirable fate, for I must wed her."

"You will not."

The young farmer started back in amazement.

"I repeat, you will not marry her."

"And wherefore?"

"Because I love you."

"Good Heaven!"

"An unmaidenly avowal, no doubt; but still a true one. I love you—I love you, and you will be mine."

Clifford looked fixedly at the beautiful being before him, but he could discern neither jest nor madness, one or other of which he thought to discover in her face.

"You love me?" he said. "Can it be possible?"

"It is so; and I say you will love me, and be my husband."

The spell was perfect.

The mysterious girl held out her arms, and Clifford threw himself into them.

Pressed to her bosom, all thought of the May Queen fled, and he felt a new kind of happiness.

How different was this girl to the cold, impassive Queen of the May.

Yes; she was right; he had been mistaken; he did not love "the pale faced chit," after all. His heart had deceived him.

He gazed into the wild, dark eyes, and therein read a tale of bliss and love.

"I love you—I love you," rang in his ears, and the past was as a dream.

He lived in the present only.

He returned not to the village green.

"Let them dance," he cried; "I am not for such disports. I am better away from them"

He remained with her alone until it was dusk, and then she left him, promising to return to him on the morrow.

Clifford went home in a delirium of joy, and dreamt that of mortals he was the happiest and most to be envied, and through his wild dreams rang the words "I love you—I love you;" and his transport almost drove him mad.

Next day Annie Ness, the little pale-faced May Queen, sought out her truant love, and, with tearful eyes, asked why she had been so cruelly used?

But Clifford had no ear for her sorrow; he had no eye for her distress; for the magic words, "I love you—I love you," rang through his brain, and deadened him to the pitiful sight his old love presented.

He sent her from him. He told her the past must be forgot: that he loved her not; and that it was best they should part.

And they parted!

He to meet the wily girl who had enslaved him; she to weep and wail in the solitude of her own chamber.

They parted to meet no more!

Six months passed, and young Clifford married the mysterious girl who had so enslaved him.

Six months passed when it was whispered in the village that young Clifford was about to be married, Annie Ness, who had been pining away since the evil May-day, drooped and died.

And on the morning the wedding party left the little church of Winterleigh a corpse was borne into it.

Annie had died of a broken heart.

And people shook their heads, and said that it was an ill-fated union, and that no good would come of it.

They were married, and for a time lived happily together.

But at last the young farmer lost the happy expression of face that had so long characterised him. He seemed to have some secret sorrow, and he neglected his farm for the public-house of the village.

And things went ill with him, and at last he died.

People said of a broken heart.

From that time the evil repute of the woman Clifford had married grew more terrible.

She appeared to grow prematurely old, and her beauty feded and faded till she became perfectly hideous.

Then came the stories of her two daughters. The one married to, and divorced from, the young baronet of Winterleigh; the other the ill-fated mistress of the younger brother.

And with each of these misfortunes the woman seemed to grow more diabolical, and yet older, until she was truly hideous, and people shunned her.

At last Mother Clifford was the curse of Winterleigh, and the hollow in the wood in which stood her little cottage became the most dreaded spot for miles round.

Nevertheless the hollow was full of beauties.

The cottage was perched upon the side of the slope, and over it hung in artistic confusion a mass of trees of every growth and variety.

In the hollow was a little stream, and here the herd of deer came to repose and drink.

The solitude was seldom disturbed, and with the birds and wild animals it was a favourite spot.

In the winter it was, of course, desolate and sad, but even then it had its peculiar charms for the lover of nature.

It was the day after the death of Sir Lascelles Winterleigh, and the wood wore a peculiarly sombre appearance.

Through the trees whistled the mournful blast, stirring up the dead leaves and sending them along the ground.

A thin wreath of smoke curled upward from the cottage of Mother Clifford, but this was the only sign of the place being inhabited.

It looked the picture of desolation and decay, and bore but slight vestiges of being the habitation of a human being.

Above the cottage towered an ancient oak tree, the lower branches of which almost touched its roof.

In the tree was chirping a little robin, and on the roof, watching it with hungry eye, was a gigantic white cat.

At last the animal made a fierce spring into the branches, and the chirping suddenly ceased.

Then the white cat sprang from the tree to the roof, and from the roof to the ground, and in his mouth he held the poor fluttering bird.

With his prey the cat ran into the cottage, wherein by the side of the grate, cowed Mother Clifford.

The white cat dropped the poor robin at the feet of his mistress, and then looked up into her face as if expecting some signs of approval.

And he was not disappointed; for the old woman patted her cat on the back, and said,

"Good cat—good cat. Poor old Melvin. Ah! kill all the feathered screech owls—kill them all. Why should they mock our misery with their happiness? Why should they sing when we wail? Kill them all—kill them all."

The cat mewed in approval, and fixed its cruel pink eyes upon its mistress.

"Tear it to pieces—tear it to pieces," cried the hag

The vehemence with which she uttered these words startled the cat, and it jumped backwards, withdrawing its paw from the bird. Feeling itself released, the poor little thing flew from the ground, but, in its blind flight, it rushed headlong into the fire blazing on the hearth.

It uttered a long and piercing cry, and endeavoured to extricate itself, but all in vain.

In a few moments it was burnt alive.

"Ha! ha!" screamed the hag, "a good sign—a good sign, by my soul an excellent sign. Ah! Melvin, it's no use to look for it now: it's burnt—burnt, blood, bones and all. Burnt, mark ye. It's a good sign. A very good sign."

The old woman had sat chuckling over the fate of the robin some few minutes when a knock at the door aroused her from her reflections.

She rose and opened the door.

Before her stood the young baronet of Winterleigh.

"Oh, it is you, is it?" she said, eyeing her visitor. "I am not surprised to see you. Enter."

Lewis stepped into the cottage.

As soon as he placed his foot within the threshold the great white cat fixed its glearing eyes upon him and drew itself up as if for a leap at the young man's throat.

Observing its motion the old hag waved her hand and uttered some unintelligible words, the effect of which was to make the animal slink away into a distant corner, as if suffering acute agony.

Lewis marked this, and in the act saw confirmation of the reports of unnatural powers possessed by the woman in whose presence he stood.

He, however, made no observation on what had taken place.

"And now that you have found your way to the old hag's cottage what is it you demand of her?"

"I demand nothing. I but come to tell you what has taken place."

"A useless trouble."

"How?"

"I know all that has taken place."

"You do not."

"I say I know all."

"But you cannot yet have heard of the flight of Evelina."

"I have."

"Indeed."

"Yes, and I know more than that. I can tell you why she fled the house."

The man bowed his head and spoke not.

"You are surprised at this," said the old hag; "you are surprised because you know not my power, but you will know it ere long. Yes, boy, I tell you I know of the flight of the girl you would have ruined. I know that she escaped the fate of your mother by nothing short of a miracle."

"Knowing this much," said Lewis, "you can tell me to whom she owes her rescue?"

"Yes."

"His name?"

"All in good time. Now, you say you came here to tell me all that had occurred since yesternight, but I tell you to your face you lie. You came here for no such purpose."

"Can you then read my thoughts?"

"Yes, and I can see that you came but for the purpose of getting some clue to the missing will, in order that you may secure it and thus firmly establish yourelf at Winterleigh. I tell you it was for that purpose and that purpose alone you came hither. You do not answer. I am right!"

"I can hide nothing—not even my thoughts—from you."

"No, your thoughts are as easily understood as your spoken words; but I forgive them. I can afford to do so, for through you I shall rise to wealth and power."

"Through me?"

"Yes; through you. Whilst you enjoy that which is not yours I shall share with you. Have I not the right? Who so fit as the woman who has been so wronged to share in the luxuries left by the spoiler? You would grasp all, but I shall be at your side evermore. I can thrust you forth at any moment, for you are an impostor. The dwarfish idiot that haunts these woods would have been the real heir, had there been no will, and I can prove it, but there *is* a will and it is in my possession, so I have you at all points."

"But he to whom the property is bequeathed may be dead?"

"He is alive and already on the scent. He was here yesternight."

"Here?"

"Yes, here."

"Great Heaven! Am I then placed in so precarious a position?"

"Heed it not. I am your friend, and all shall yet be well."

"But this person; this heir. Tell me who he is."

"The man to whom you are indebted for bearing off Evilina."

"He?"

"Yes   The son of my daughter, the wife of the seventh baronet Winterleigh."

"How will this end?"

"I cannot foresee the end, but we have much to battle against. But I am on your side. You are the child of the daughter I loved best. She was like myself, of no common nature, fierce in her hate, intense in her love, skilled in the mysteries of the stars and possessed of a thorough contempt for the whole human race. My other child, the wife of the Baronet, more resembled her father. He was a true Saxon, forbearing, loving, and gentle; fair as a lily, trusting as a dove. For these qualities I hated her. I love self-reliance and power, such as was possessed by your mother. Oh, she would have avenged herself nobly had she lived, but she was thrust forth one night into the frost and snow and came to this spot dying and broken-hearted. I took her in and chafed her cold hands. I warmed her frozen heart and restored animation to her stiffened limbs, but it was too late, too late, she only opened her eyes to say 'avenge me.' She only lived to hear me swear to do so. She left me you, and snatching you from her icy body I rushed with you madly to the Hall, intending to dash you in the face of your unnatural father, and leave you to your fate. But chance favoured me : in his cradle lay the bantling of Norman, but an hour born. I snatched it from its place

and substituted you; taking the deformed brat with me and exposing it as the child of Lascelles Winterleigh. Ha! Ha! the trick succeeded and I triumph. I liked the noble face of the young Norman. I gloried in his deformity, so I reared him and tortured Lascelles with his presence. I made his life a long drawn out scene of torture, and I cursed his death bed, my daughter's bastard inherits all his treasures and thus I triumph, I triumph."

Lewis was dumfounded at this passionate outburst and held his peace.

He could scarcely realise the picture painted by the old hag, and yet there was so much of truth and reality about it, and so much in accordance with the nature of the woman that Lewis was convinced, and he trembled as he thought of the awful position in which he was placed ; being under the power of one so malignant and capable of evil.

Thoughts of freeing himself of one so terrible crossed his brain ; but he reflected on her power and he remembered how she had served him on the previous night, and reflected that violence could produce no good effect.

After a pause Mother Clifford looked into the face of her grandchild and said:

"Would you like to know who your cousin really is ?"

"Yes," replied Lewis, eagerly.

"Then I will tell you. He is no other than Paul Clifford, the thief and highway robber."

"Indeed?"

"Aye, indeed. You now know into whose hands your Evelina has fallen."

"Powers of earth! She had better been my mistress than his."

"Not so. He is your superior in all things. Robber as he is, he has what is called a good heart, and is kind and generous to women."

"But in the power of a robber—a common thief."

"Better thus than to be the dishonoured mistress of the master of Winterleigh."

"But what can be her fate? can he love her ?"

"He can and does, and she loves him."

"How know you this ?"

"Would you like to be made acquainted with the secret ?"

"Yes."

"And your heart would not fail you ?"

"No."

"Are you sure ?"

"I am confident."

"Then I will show you how I know these things. Take my hand."

Lewis did as he was desired, and as he clutched the bony fingers of the old woman, she rose and muttered the following words :—

> "Through the earth, and through the air,
> Spirits of darkness and spirits fair,
> Take us hand-in-hand to where
>   The fugitive is hiding.
> Bear us swiftly as through the brake,
> Bear us over hill and lake,
> Through dark space a flight we'll take,
>   And trust t ） thy guiding.

"Save me !" cried Lewis, "I tremble—I loose my eyesight—I fall—my brain reels—I am mad !"

"Fear nothing," he heard a voice whisper in his ear. "A moment and the flight is ended."

"What sensation is this? Where am I ?"

"Hist! Seeing but unseen. You are in the presence of the man you have most to fear. What do you see ?"

"I am in an old chamber. The light fails, and the glare of the fire fills the room. In a chair at the table sits a man preparing to write. Ah ! it is he who bore away Evelina."

> He is deaf, and he is dumb,
> Speak on now, and clutch my thumb,
> Pain you feel, like adder's bite,
> But power thou hast to see him write,
>   What says he?

"He hesitates ; he asks what shall he write ?"

"THE TRUTH!"

"It was the voice of the old hag. And the words were those that so startled Clifford as he unconsciously asked this question.

What ensued the reader is already acquainted with.

"What do you now see?" demanded the hag.

"I see another chamber, but similar to the one I have just quitted. At the window sits Evelina. She weeps. And now she shudders, and gazes wildly about her, as if she knew I was present. Let me clasp her to my heart!"

"Fool!" cried the hag, "you are but dreaming."

"My brain!—my brain!" cried Lewis, clasping his hands over his head. "What horrible feeling is this?"

* * * *

The next moment he was sitting in the old woman's cottage, gazing vacantly at the hag, who stood before him, with outstretched arm and face distorted.

"Was it a dream?" cried Lewis, "was it in reality a dream?"

"You know now whence I get my information."

"Great powers of mercy! Have I then really witnessed these things? Was I in those chambers? Did I see them?"

"Think what you will. Enough you know my power."

"Too well!—too well!"

"And now begone. I have no more to say to thee, and would be alone."

"But Evelina! Shall I see her no more?"

"I know not."

"But will not your arts bring her to me? Can you not force her here?"

"I have no power over her."

"Then she is lost to me."

"As you deserve. Begone!"

"I will obey you. May I return?"

"No. In a few short hours we shall meet again."

"Where?"

"At the Hall."

"Why there?"

"Because I am coming there to remain forever. When you go this place will be reduced to ashes. I have done with it."

Lewis turned from the cottage, and, cursing his fate, took the path to the Hall.

"And now," said Mother Clifford, as she saw him disappear from the wood, "and now for the will."

She drew from her bosom the deed executed by the old baronet, and for a few moments regarded it fixedly.

"I will not destroy it," she said, "for I may yet require it to remind this boy of my power over him. I will bury it here, and in an hour the ruins of these walls shall fall upon it, and hide it from all eyes. I alone will know where to find it."

She went to a drawer in an old chest, and drew therefrom a short bar of iron.

With this she returned to the hearth, and stooping, proceeded to raise the large stone on which the embers blazed.

It was a work of time, and to effect it she had to exert the whole of her great strength.

At length, however, the task was accomplished, the stone moved from its bed, and revealed a small cavity, into which the will was thrust.

Then the stone fell once more into its place, and all trace of its having been moved was wiped away.

"There," she said, "there lies the will of Lascelles Winterleigh, and no one but myself has clue whereby to trace its resting place."

Had Mother Clifford turned at that moment, she would have seen the form of the dwarf stealing away from the door.

Had she not been so much pre-occupied, she would have heard the frightful being chuckling to himself and muttering.

"Buried, buried, but I know where," whispered it.

In a few more minutes the old woman issued from the cottage, and at a distance regarded it fixedly.

"It is the last time," said she, "it is the last time I shall ever see it. Home of misery for many and many a year, adieu."

A volume of smoke issued from the open door, and anon came forth sheets of angry flame which licked the walls and roof, and in half-an-hour made all a charred and unshapely ruin.

It was night now, and as Mother Clifford hobbled away, accompanied by her great white cat, the snow fell, and the bitter blast shook the wood of Winterleigh.

CHAPTER IX.

EVELINA RECEIVES CLIFFORD'S NOTE — HER DETERMINATION TO FLY—DOUBTS AND FEARS—THE MESSENGER AND THE JOURNEY BY THE STAGE COACH—CLIFFORD'S TERRIBLE MISTAKE.

JOB certainly did not like to convey to Evelina the note he had received from Clifford.

He divined that its contents would be distressing to the lady; for his kind heart told him that there was a bond between the two that linked them together more closely than could the ties of friendship.

He tapped gently at the door of the young girl's chamber.

"Come in," she said, without rising from her seat.

Job entered, and found his guest seated at the window, her head resting on her hands, and her eyes fixed on the gathering darkness.

"I hope the noise did not distress you," said Job, awkwardly twisting the note between his fingers.

"What noise?" demanded Evelina.

"The noise in the yard."

"I heard nothing."

"I am very glad of that; for there was rather a serious disturbance between some gentlemen awhile ago, and I was afraid you would be alarmed."

"No," said Evelina, sorrowfully, "I have been too deeply buried in thought to mark what has been transpiring without; but I trust nothing serious has occurred?"

"Nothing at all," said Job—"nothing."

"Where is Mr. Everton?"

"Who?"

"Mr. Everton."

"I don't know anyone of that name."

"I mean the gentleman with whom I came to this place."

"Oh!" said Job, "I beg pardon, ma'am; Mr. Everton; oh—yes; just so."

"He appears to be a stranger to you. I thought by the manner you received him that you were acquainted with him."

Job was puzzled.

"Ah, yes," he said, "you are right, ma'am. I know Mr. Everton very well, but I am such a bad 'un at remembering names."

"Where is Mr. Everton?" again asked Evelina.

"He's gone."

"Gone!"

"Yes, ma'am! he's gone on some little business. The fact is he had some pressing engagement; I don't know exactly what it is, or where he is gone, but he left this note for you, which may explain all."

Job hurried out this speech as if he would be glad to rid himself of it; and immediately he had finished he ran to the door, and hurried away.

"A pretty fellow I am," he said to himself, as he descended the stairs! "a pretty fellow to jerk out what I had to say after that fashion. Poor young lady! My speech must have fallen upon her like a thunderclap, instead of having the soothing effect it ought to have had. But it's no use; I ain't up to that sort of thing, and always make a mull of it. What a pity it is the world couldn't have been made up of men only; for, hang the women! there's no knowing how to deal with 'em. They're as shy as fawns, and as skittish as two-year-old fillies."

Job was a bachelor, or he would never have made that speech.

Evelina paused some moments before she opened the note left for her by Job.

"Dark forebodings of something terrible creep upon me," she said, "and I fear that all is not well with this Everton."

She reflected a short time, and then, holding the

scrawl to the light, she read the hasty message of her protector.

She could not comprehend its tenor. There was something in it that correspouned with her own mind. The lines were in harmony with her own thoughts, and she became more and more distressed in mind.

At first she did not notice the signature, but at last her eye fell upon it, and her mystification and misery were complete.

The singular appearance of Clifford at Winterleigh, the false name, and his sudden disappearance from the inn, accompanied by the hint dropped by the landlord of a disturbance in the yard, and then his marked agitation, at last convinced the girl that she had only fallen out of one trouble to light upon another.

"Oh, what a fate is mine!" she cried; "what an untoward, unaccountable fate! And the worst has not yet transpired; I feel well assured of that."

Again she perused the lines.

"I am left alone in this place," she said; "who knows to what purpose? He may never return, and after awhile thay may thrust me forth, and I shall not know where to go. What can be his motive for leaving me? Ah! I can see it now. He dared not leave me in the power of that terrible man, so he bore me away to a place of comparative safety, and then reflected on the burthen I should be to him. He dared not meet me again and tell me this, but has fled from me, and left me to find out the dismal truth for myself. Oh! what shall I do!"

Evelina reflected on the courses open to her. She concluded that she was deserted by Clifford.

Having determined on that point, it only remained to her to decide on some immediate course.

"I am within ten miles of London," she said, "and to London I must go In the great city I may find protection and a means of earning bread; if I remain here I may fall into some unforeseen trap, or at least expend my little all. Yes, I will fly at once."

Acting on the impulse of the moment she ran to the bell, and rang it violently.

Job answered it.

He regarded her nervously, and with all the anxiety he felt expressed in his face.

"What can I do for you?" said the landlord.

"Nothing, but tell me what I am indebted to you."

"Indebted to me?"

"Yes, to you, for the use of this room and the refreshment I have had during the day."

"I don't understand."

"Am I not sufficiently explicit? I have used your house during the day, and you have supplied me with food and drink; I wish to know in what sum I am indebted to you for this."

"Nothing whatever, ma'am. Mr. Clif — that is, the gentleman—would break every bone in my body if I took anything from you. Besides, why should you pay me now, if you had to pay me yourself?"

"Because I am going."

"Going! Where?"

"To London."

"What, lady, to-night?"

"Yes, at once"

"It is absurd to think of such a thing, ma'am. The night is dark and foggy, and I have not a conveyance to send you in."

"I want no conveyance; I can walk."

"Walk! Good heavens, you know nothing of the road, ma'am, or you would not dream of such a thing! Walk to London! Why the way is besieged by highwaymen and footpads, and it is possible that you would not progress a mile before you would be robbed, perhaps murdered."

"Oh, say not so! for I dare not remain here."

"And why not remain here, ma'am? No harm can come to you under the roof of Job Winchurst."

"But I am ill at ease. I know not the man who brought me here, and I fear, although he is a gentleman

well behaved, that he is one with whom I dare not associate. He gave me a false name, and by his note has betrayed himself. His real name is Clifford."

"So I have been given to understand."

"And his calling—will you tell me that?"

"He is A GENTLEMAN."

"Indeed! I feared he was an adventurer, if not something worse than that"

"You may be mistaken, ma'am. Mr. Clifford has always behaved well at my house. He is generally admired as a man of address and high respectability, and I don't think you will ever find him any other."

"I trust not; but my heart misgives me on the subject. I fear the worst."

"Bear up, lady, and trust for the best. The devil himself — saving your presence, ma'am—isn't half so black as he's painted."

Plain, outspoken Job thought this a very consoling and admirably conceived speech; but it certainly did not convey with it the comfort intended.

Evelina hung her head, and after a pause said —

"Your words are those of sympathy and consolation rather than of assurance, and if I do not quit your roof to-night I shall go to-morrow."

"Think of it again before you decide, ma'am. I hope, for my part, that you won't go until you hear from Mr. Clifford – unless you have some friends to go to, and some purpose in view. A young girl in London, alone, and without friends, has such trials to go through as are seldom overcome. I wouldn't hurt your feelings by saying that you'd come to any harm, ma'am; but it's an awful place is that great, busy city; and there's so many traps laid for the unwary that, somehow they tumble in, and then, heaven help 'em! It's a downward path after the first false step—down, down, down, until the depths of degradation and suffering are reached."

Job warmed into true eloquence as he pictured the trials of an unfriended female in the great city of London Unfortunately the outburst frightened himself, and he thereupon relapsed into his old, awkward silence.

"You are right," said Evelina; "I feel you are right; but I believe this gentleman will never return again, and I may as well go first as last."

"Did he say he would return?"

"He said he would either come or send for me."

"Then he ll keep his word. I'll stake my life on his truth."

"I will, then, stay until to-morrow; and if he should not send—"

"Remain until the next day, or the next, or the next. You're welcome to all the accommodation I can offer."

"Thanks, friend; but my purse is a slight one, and I had best go before it is exhausted."

"It will never be exhausted here, ma'am for when old Job Winchurst offers his poor fare to any one he don't often turn round and demand money for it."

"You are too good, but I cannot take advantage of such generosity."

"Oh, nonsense; there's no generosity in the case. It's a mere matter of course, and I hope you won't hurt my feelings by going away until you hear from Mr. Clifford."

"I have no hope of seeing him again."

"But I have."

"And if I should wait, and wait, and he should not come?"

"Give him a reasonable time, and he will come."

"I will, then, wait over to-morrow."

"And the next day?"

"Yes."

"And the next day?"

"I dare not."

"But to oblige old Job?"

"Well, I will wait three days."

"And if Mr. Clifford isn't here or doesn't send some one before then, I'll eat—" Job reflected on the something he should find himself to eat, and, after a pause, said, "my old hat."

With this he left the room.

"Three days," thought Evelina ; "if not then I shall never see him more."

Never more !"

Was the thought a painful one?

"Never more," she repeated "never more ! What a sad, sad sound there is in the words never more. Shall I regret it ? A voice within answers 'Yes.'"

Job soon returned with lights, and threw a large log on the fire.

"There," he said, "now we'll close up the shutters, and make all snug. Well, that's a little more cheerful, I'm sure. See the sparks flying up like a—like a—like a lot of blessed —" Job was about to say angels, but he thought the simile too strong, and simply said "sparks," which took all the sentiment out of his rhapsody, and reduced it to a very common-place remark.

"It's a bitter night," he continued, after a slight pause, "a very bitter night, and the fog's rising at an awful rate, and to think that you should have thought of going to London on such a night ; lawks ! lawks ! what a go that would have been. Ah ! my dear young lady, you had better stay with old Job, and try his nice cakes and preserves for tea."

A brisk servant girl here entered the room with a steaming urn and a tray set out with a nice tea.

"There," said Job to Evelina. "that's the sort of thing I like to see on such a night as this—the red-hot urn, the smoking cakes, the tempting ham, and the nice preserves, looking as sweet and as bright as—" Here, again, Job's faculty of comparison failed him, and he had to say "preserves."

He felt that this was not quite the thing to say, but he passed the matter off by bustling about and arranging the tea tray."

"Indeed," said Evelina, "indeed you are very, very kind, but I cannot eat."

"Can't eat? oh! nonsense, you must eat. Nobody ever heard of anybody as couldn't eat. You *must* eat. It's the only way people can live. Eat, drink, and be merry, for to-morrow *we die*. Hey? No, I didn't mean that. Die, nobody dies, now-a-day ; we all live and get jolly. And you must get jolly : there's some nice books in the other room. I'll fetch 'em, and then you'll be happy as a dove all the evening."

Job drew a chair to the table, and then gently drew his guest into it.

He next poured out a cup of tea for her, and then set the tempting viands before her.

Seeing that the kind-hearted old fellow would feel hurt if she did not at once attack his good cheer, Evelina made a tolerably hearty meal.

"There," said Job, as he stood by, respectfully watching her, "there, my dear ma'am, there, don't you feel better after that?"

"Yes," said Evelina, "I thank you much sir ; I *do* feel much better."

"Of course you do," said Job, "but don't call me sir. I'm Job, plain old Job, and never want to be anything else—not I. Job Winchurst is only a poor victualler, and he knows it. But there, I'm chattering like—like anything, and you want some more tea."

"No," said Evelina, "no, I thank you ; not another drop. I did not think I could have done so well."

"Of course not ; no one knows what they can do till they try ; but if you are sure you won't have anything else I will take away the tray, and leave you to yourself."

"I could not touch another morsel."

"Well then, it only remains for me to go, but first I'll fetch the books for you."

Job went into an adjoining room and soon returned with a parcel of books.

"There," he said, "there's some nice reading for you, I'll leave you till supper time. My dear eyes! how the does blow, to be sure."

The door slammed violently as Job went out. A piercing gust of wind made the logs crack again, and sent the curtains waving to and fro, with the greatest violence.

As Evelina listened to the wind, she felt glad in her heart that she had not sallied forth.

"It is a dreadful night," she said, turning to the books brought there by Job. "A dreadful night ; dark as a grave, and bitter cold. Yes, he was right, and I was wrong. It would have been an unwarrantable temptation of Providence to go forth on such a night. I am glad now that I listened to reason."

She took up a book, and attempted to read.

It was an odd volume of Shakespere, and with every word of which Evelina was quite familiar ; she nevertheless fixed her eye dreamingly on the page and read on and on, but her thoughts were far away from the book.

At length it fell into her lap, her head drooped, and she fell into a light sleep.

Nature was exhausted, and required repose.

But there was none for it.

Evelina had not slept long when a dark vision disturbed her rest.

She thought she beheld herself dragged through Winterleigh Woods by the old hag she had seen in the corridors of Winterleigh Hall.

On she was pulled through the wood towards the hall, and at last she found herself in an old chamber, in which she saw a great white cat that glared at her and appeared ready to spring at her throat at any moment.

She was thrust into a chair, and in a few moments, Lewis Norman entered, and confronted her.

"You here again," she thought he said.

"Yes," she returned, "here again."

"And you will stay here now, and be mine."

"No—never yours ! never yours !"

"Mine, I say, mine for ever. You cannot resist me now."

"I will, by Heaven !"

"You dare not, by hell !"

Evelina thought that she rose, and attempted to fly. She was at the door and was about to turn, when the great white cat flew at her throat and pulled her to the earth.

With a shriek Evelina awoke.

Was she still dreaming?

Or was it a reality?

Could that be the great pink eyes glaring at her out of the darkness? What was the shadow that flitted between her and the light?

What sound was that like the croaking of the raven that rang in her ears?

She clasped her hands over her eyes for an instant, and then looked round.

All was still once more. The room was tenantless.

"Horrible !" said Evelina, "how horrible ! Oh, I shudder with fear. I dare not stay here another moment."

She flew from the room, and descended the stairs.

The house was free of customers.

Job sat in his little parlour behind the bar, and the ostler and the servant girl hung over the kitchen fire, and slept soundly.

Pale and terror-stricken the girl stood before the ruddy-faced Job.

"Hey, bless me, what's that?" cried the host; "what's that, hey? My dear eyes, what's happened?"

"I do not know," said Evelina ; "indeed I do not know ; but I think I have seen some things not of this world in the old chamber above."

"Hey? Ghosts in the Harvest Home? Ghosts, I can't believe in it. I can't; it's no use to tell me. I could no more believe it than—than nothing."

"I don't think it was a dream, it was too palpable. Oh, had you but seen those cruel pink eyes staring at you out of the gloom !"

"Cruel pink eyes out of the gloom, hey? That's serious."

"It was terrible."

"Come, come," said Job; "haven't you been sleeping and dreaming?"

"Yes, yes!"

"I thought so."

"But what terrified me was that which I saw on awakening."

"Hillo! That was still more serious. And what did you see?"

"The figures of my dream."

"Hey?"

"Yes, a shadow, as of an aged woman, pushed passed me, and great eyes glared at me out of the darkness, and an awful voice rang in my ears. Oh, I shall never forget that voice!"

"And I shall never forget what you say. Ghosts in the Harvest Home! Ghosts! Oh, dear; oh, dear me. It's too bad—too bad. I can hardly believe it."

"I do not know what I have seen. I am not superstitious, and I do not dread being alone; but I have seen that in the chamber above which I would not see again for worlds, so pray let me sit here with you until you retire to rest."

"Yes," said Job, "and happy shall I be to have your company, ma'am. There, sit near the fire, and don't get in the way of the draught of the door. Now you're quite snug, I'm sure. Lawks, it's so pleasant to have some one to talk to on these dull evenings!"

"And have you no one to talk to?"

"Not a soul, unless its Bob and Milly. But they're such sleepy-headed beggars. I've had 'em in here night after night, and tried to make something out of 'em, but its no manner o' use. Five minutes talk, and they're off as sound as churches. But there, it's quite supper time. Now, what shall I get for you?"

"I could not eat."

"But try one little mouthful of chicken, it's so nice and tender, and it's safe to do you a world of good."

"Indeed I could not eat."

"Well, you musn't go to bed without having something. I'll make you a nice glass of mulled port, that's a good thing to sleep upon."

Job would take no refusal.

In spite of the earnestness with which Evelina had spoken, Job thought that what she had seen in the chamber above was but the creation of her fancy, or some idle dream, and he determined that she should go soundly to sleep, and wear of the effects of her excitement.

He therefore mulled, over his bright fire, a glass of good old port, and flavouring it like a true artiste, he insisted upon every drop being swallowed by the fair guest.

Job had the satisfaction of seeing his prescription duly taken, after which he closed up his house, and then the four inmates retired to rest.

No more dreams troubled Evelina that night.

* * * * * *

Another day passed.

On the third day, soon after noon, a large travelling chariot, drawn by four splendid horses, drew up at the door of the Harvest Home, from the London road.

"My stars," said Bob, as the equipage dashed up; "if that's not a brilliant turn-out, why I never seed one, that's all. By George, it's a beauty."

On the outside were two men.

One drove the four splendid horses; the other was seated in the rumble.

There was no other occupant of the carriage.

The man in the rumble jumped to the ground and motioned the coachman to drive into the inn-yard.

He of the rumble at once proceeded to the inn, and demanded to see the landlord.

He was not a very enticing man in appearance, and had a rough and discordant voice.

This personage was none other than Bill Waters, the friend and admirer of Gentleman Clifford.

"Hillo, landlord," shouted Bill, as he entered the house; "hillo, here—look alive, will ye?"

"What can I do for you, sir?" demanded Job, looking quite surprised at seeing so common a looking individual step from so elegant an equipage.

"What can you do for me? Why, let me have a few words in private, that's all."

Job led his visitor into the little bar parlour.

"And now," said Job, "what is it?"

"It's just this. You've a lady here.!"

"Well, I didn't want you to come here for the purpose of telling me that."

"I suppose not, but you've a lady here whom I want."

"Do you?"

"Yes. Don't you understand me!"

"Not quite, my friend."

"Well, then, to be a little clearer. I'm sent here for the lady left in your charge by my pal, Gentleman Clifford."

"Oh, oh; that's it, is it? Now I am opening my eyes."

"I thought you would."

"Well, and if you're from Clifford, where's your credentials?"

"My what?"

"Credentials."

"Whose them?"

"Whose them?"

"Whose them? Why I mean your letter of introduction to be sure. Clifford wouldn't send a stranger here without giving him some sign by which he'd be made welcome."

"You don't doubt my word, I s'pose."

"Not in the least; but if the king himself came and asked me to hand over the lady, and didn't bring Clifford's handwriting with him, he'd go back empty-handed,"

"Ah, you're an old soldier."

"I am."

"Well, I like ye all the better for it. I hate the fellow who'd give up like a lamb anything that the first stranger demanded; it's a bad policy. But I'm fortunately able to deal with ye, old careful—here's a scrawl from the captain."

Bill handed over to Job a small paper, on which was written—

"The bearer hereof will bring to me the lady I entrusted to your keeping. I cannot come; the neighbourhood of your house is too hot for me. You will understand this. "Yours,

"PAUL."

"It's his fist, safe enough," said Job, as he perused the scrawl; "I'd swear to it in any place, and under all circumstances."

"Yes, it's his fist; and ain't it a stunner? Ah, he's a genius, is Gentleman Clifford! It's a pity he wasn't born a great lord—although, I don't know! It's a pity such a knight of the road should have been lost to the world. He's the greatest of 'em all. Ah! put 'em all together, roll 'em into one—do what you will with 'em—you won't make another Clifford."

"Hear, hear," said Job approvingly. "I believe that; but I must see the lady about this note. She'll be glad enough to know its contents, though I'm precious sorry it's come—for I don't like to spare my fair guest. She's a regular good 'un, and I wish she'd stop here for ever."

"I say, she's not down to the captain's game, is she?"

"No."

"I thought not, for he told me to be dark. Though why he should hide his profession from her beats me hollow. It's good enough for any lady; that's my opinion."

"Yes; but, fortunately, that's not the opinion of the world. Now I wouldn't have the lady utter such an opinion for twice as much as I'm worth. What you and I think may be all very well, but it would be a pity if we all thought alike—an awful pity, to be sure. But it's no use talking."

Job motioned the new-comer to be seated, and taking

up the note and carefully putting it in his pocket, he went up stairs to the chamber occupied by Evelina.

She was reading when he entered.

"I'm right, after all," said Job, at once breaking into his subject; "I m right, and you're wrong."

"What—is he come?"

Her face brightened with hope.

"No.' replied Job, "he's not come."

The brow of Evelina was shadowed once more.

"He's not come, but he's sent."

"A messenger to me?"

"A messenger *for* you."

"For me? Then he has not deserted me."

"Deserted you! As if he could do such a thing! Bah! it's an absurdity!"

"I'm so glad," said Evelina.

"Yes—and I'm so sorry."

"Sorry that I am glad?"

"No; only sorry to lose you. Why I'd grown to look upon you as something belonging to myself. In fact, in my humble way, I d grown to love you as a father—only, I suppose it's nothing like the sort of love your own father would have for you. We common folk couldn't, like you would; but I was saying—you've got to be a sort of daughter to me, and I shall miss you sadly these long nights. I feel already as if I'd lost something which I should never recover. Ah, ma'am, I wish I'd found out earlier in life how good it is to have something to love. I should have been a better man if I had married, and could now have the company of a good wife or daughter to cheer me."

"Never mind, Job Winchurst," said Evelina, "you will soon forget me."

"Never, never It isn't often as Job takes a fancy, but when he does it is a fancy, and no mistake. Not a touch and go affair—a here to-day and gone to-morrow sort of thing; but a good solid liking. Such a one I took for Mr. Clifford, such a one, only stronger, deeper, I've taken for you; and if you should ever want a humble friend, which I s'pose a lady like you never will—and Heaven save you from that!—you'll find a good and true one in old Job. Come when you will you shall be as welcome as the flowers of spring, and I shall be as proud to see you as—as a peacock."

"I know you are good and kind, and if ever I should want a friend I *will* come to you. I am all but alone in the world, and Heaven only knows what may befall me."

"True, but you have a good friend in Mr. Clifford. Believe no ill of him, let the world say what it will. Disbelieve even your own eyes if you think they are leading you to doubt him, for he is a good man. I have proved it so, or I would not say so to you of all others in the world."

"I know you would not. But why all this mystery, why this secresy, and why, of all things, did he conceal from me his real name?"

"I do not know, but his motives must be good."

"Would that I could think so!"

"Do not doubt it."

"I will strive not to."

"And now will you prepare for a journey?"

"Whither am I going?"

"To London."

"And shall I see my preserver there?"

"Undoubtedly."

"I do not know whether I should go or not. My heart misgives me, and I feel that I am doing wrong."

"There, you're giving way to those old fears again. Let me beg you to banish them; they're not of any solid foundation."

"I do not know that. I am sorely afraid that no good will come of this. And, again, am I not thrusting myself in the power of a man who may presume upon my defenceless position, and treat me as I most dread to be treated?"

"Whatever he may be guilty of," said Job, warmly, "no one will ever say that Mr. Clifford presumed upon the defencelessness of a lady's position to take advantage of her. He's too much of a man and a gentleman to dream of such a thing."

"Oh! how sincerely I trust so."

"You may take my word for it."

"Then I will go fearlessly. But still—oh! but still this misgiving is at my heart."

"Then shake it off, for it has no right there."

In an hour Evelina was prepared to start on her journey.

Bill Waters received her in the bar of the Harvest Home with the profoundest bows, and introduced himself as the humble agent of Clifford.

So completely did he assume the servitor that Evelina was blind to his real character, and took him for some over-officious but well meaning steward.

The carriage was at length brought to the door, and Evelina stepped into it.

She bade adieu to Job. Bill Waters took his place in the rumble, and the vehicle moved away.

Job turned disconsolately into his house as the carriage turned down a bend of the road, and was lost to sight.

"Oh, dear! Oh! oh, dear," he said, as he walked into his bar. "I've only known two happy evenings in all my life, and that's the two that's just passed over my head. Ah! I was after all a fool not to have married I see it now—I see it now."

"The governor's cranky," said Bob, looking after Job, "I wonder if he's in love with Paul Clifford's young woman?"

On the evening of the day Paul despatched Bill for the purpose of bringing Evelina to town. He felt very unsettled in his mind, and determined to ride out a few miles into the country; more for the purpose of attempting to settle his disturbed spirits, than for aught else.

No sooner thought of than done.

As soon as the shades of evening began to fall, Paul mounted his darling White Mare, and rode from London.

As fate would have it, he took the very road Evelina was to come; but it never occurred to him, and had it done so; the possibility was that he would have still gone towards Banford Wells, for he imagined that Bill would have returned before nightfall.

It was a favourite haunt of his, and he was oftener seen in that direction than any other.

Out into the country he went.

He regarded not the bitter wind, and paid no heed to where he was rushing.

His Mare was surefooted, and could traverse the road blindfolded with the greatest ease.

His brain was full of excitement, and dashed on regardless of all things.

There was but one thought in his head, and that was Evelina.

"I love her," he said; "I love her; but she is far above me, and I ought not to think of her. She is good and pure, and I am evil and a highway robber. Ah! let them flatter as they will, the brand of *thief* is on me, and nothing will take it off. Still I love her: does she, can she love me? I hope not. Bad as I am I would not have her fix her affections on one so utterly worthless as myself. But she knows not of my doings. To all my career she is blind. Could I not fly from this spot with her? could I not go where we are unknown, and where I could forget the past? could she not love me as Paul Everton, never having known me as Clifford the Highwayman? I think she could. But it is a wild dream; I will think no more of it."

He adhered to this resolution for no greater space of time than ten seconds.

Do as he would the recollection of her voice and her face *would* return to him, and with it the feeling of love —deep, deep, unquenchable love. And as he saw how hopeless his case was, he became more and more gloomy, and thus time passed with him.

He rode on until at last the sounds of wheels fell upon his ear.

"A carriage," he said, "and drawn by four horses, if my ears do not deceive me. Shall I stop it? Why should I not do so? The time has not yet arrived for reform. She may not love me, after all, and it is only for her sake that I would throw up my way of life. Yes, I will stop this carriage, just to convince myself that I am not grown weak and childish."

The carriage was descending a tolerably steep hill leading into an avenue of trees.

"Hurrah!" shouted Clifford, as he beheld the approaching carriage, drawn by a noble team of horses. "This must be some one worth stopping."

Another minute and he galloped to the carriage.

"Stand!" he cried, presenting a pistol at the head of the coachman, "stand! or I'll blow you from your perch."

He then turned his attention to the interior of the carriage.

He found that its occupant was a lady.

She was cowering in a corner, and her face was turned from him.

"A lady!" he said, raising his hat, "I am sorry to disturb you, but you really must—"

"That voice!" Clifford heard some one exclaim from the rumble of the carriage, "that voice! I'll be kicked if it ain't the Gentleman himself!"

"Good God!" cried Clifford, "what have I done? It is Bill, and I am lost!"

He glanced once more at the figure in the carriage, and saw that the eyes of Evelina were turned full upon him.

She turned ghastly pale, and then sank back and hid her face.

"Heaven protect me!" cried Evelina, "*He is a highway robber!*"

"Lost! lost!" cried Clifford, dashing his spurs into his Mare, and galloping away.

CHAPTER X.

WHERE EVELINA WAS TAKEN—THE INTERVIEW AND SEPARATION.

As soon as Clifford moved away, the carriage was once more set in motion and sped onward towards London.

Evelina would have risen and demanded that she should be put down from the carriage, but the pace at which the horses went placed this beyond her power.

She fell back in her seat, and gave way to a wild outburst of tears.

"It is terrible," she said, "too terrible to reflect upon. Oh! God! what—what have I done that I should be thus punished?"

On, flew the horses, on, and on, and at length the green trees and fields were left behind, and the jolting of the carriage assured its occupant that she had entered London.

It was about eight o'clock, and still many of the shops were open, and the streets were full of life and bustle.

As the carriage rolled on it would ever and anon pass some brilliantly illuminated house, and sounds of mirth and music fell upon the young traveller's ear.

At length the vehicle stopped at a house in one of the great squares in the west end of London.

The steps of the carriage were lowered, and Bill descended.

"Where am I?" asked Evelina of her conductor.

"Have no fear," whispered Bill, "you are at the house of a good and true man, and your will will be the law here."

"I fear to dismount."

"You are safe. If you don't choose to remain after you have entered you will find yourself at liberty to go. You are mistress, and no one will attempt to act in opposition to you."

Evelina hesitated no longer.

"There can be no harm in entering," she said, "be he what he may. I do not think he would harm me."

The words of Job occurred to her, and she immediately banished what remaining fears clung to her.

The house was approached by a flight of steps, and on mounting these Evelina found herself in a magnificent hall, tastefully and brilliantly decorated.

Several servants in plain but superb livery stood on either side of the door, and a few paces down the hall stood a well-dressed elderly lady, who bowed respectfully to Evelina, and handed her a small billet.

She at one recognised the hand.

It was from Clifford.

She tore it open, and read the following words:—

"Welcome to the home I have prepared for you until the will is found. The lady who will give you this is one in whom you can repose all confidence. I have selected her for your companion during your residence under my protection. Forget not that you are in your own home, and fail not to use it as your own. Nothing will give me greater joy than to find that I have been instrumental in making you forget the past, and in making the present tolerable. I have left this with Mrs. St. Henry because I may not be here to meet you.

"I am, yours sincerely,
"PAUL EVERTON."

She refolded this, and looked once more at Mrs. St. Henry.

The face of that lady re-assured her.

There was truth and goodness marked in each feature, and Evelina knew that she had found a true friend.

The fair young girl extended her hand to the lady, and said with all sincerity—

"I am glad to know you, madam."

"And I," said Mrs. St. Henry, "shall be proud of your friendship."

"Alas!" said Evelina to herself, "I shall not know you long enough to secure that to you."

She had even then determined to quit this gorgeous house as soon as she had seen Clifford.

The chamber into which Evelina was conducted by Mrs. St. Henry was furnished with all the elegance art could devise or money secure.

The room opened on a sleeping apartment, and both were fitted with furniture covered with rich satin of a rare pink hue.

Large mirrors ran the whole height of the room, and the floor was covered with velvet carpet, into which the feet sunk noiselessly.

Rare articles of the toilet stood on marble and gilt tables, and scattered here and there were sculptures of great beauty and value.

Evelina gazed about her in astonishment.

Everything at Winterleigh had been so sombre and dreary that the blaze of brilliancy into which she had come completely mystified her.

She walked as one in a dream.

"Whose mansion is this?" she asked.

"Whose but Mr. Everton's?" replied Mrs. St. Henry.

"Indeed!" said Evelina; "and does he reside in so costly a house?"

"No, he does not reside here; his home is in the country."

"Have you known Mr. Everton long?"

"I have never seen him."

"Indeed!"

"It is so. A gentleman acting as his agent came to me yesterday, and arranged with me to fulfil the position of companion to you. Since the death of my husband my circumstances have been but poor, and I gladly grasped at the princely offer of Mr. Everton to act as your guardian and humble friend."

"Do you know me?"

"I only know that you are an orphan, who has been cruelly wronged by some schemers, and that Mr. Everton has undertaken to see you righted. But I have not yet learnt whether you are related to him or not."

"No, he is simply my friend. We met but recently, and, on learning my story, he determined to assist me. But I never anticipated that he would have placed me in such an establishment as this. I cannot and will not remain in it; I could not sanction such outlays on myself, when I can see no hope of being able to make the slightest return."

In spite of all she felt, Evelina dared not hint to Clifford's real character to the lady in whose presence she stood.

At a glance she could see that the tale of Mrs. St. Henry was the truth. She knew not the real nature of her employer's mode of life.

Hers was a mind that could not stoop to participation in a deceit, and Evelina readily comprehended how deeply she would feel her position should the occupation of her employer transpire.

"Besides," said Evelina to herself, "why should I expose him? Why should others know what I know? He has done me no harm, and the secret I have learnt shall be preserved in my bosom. He shall have no enemy in me."

Evelina had seated herself on a couch, and fell into a profound reverie.

For some moments she moved not, forgetful that another was present.

At length Mrs. St. Henry advanced to her side, and taking her hand, asked her if she would not change her attire.

"Change my attire," said Evelina; "how am I to do so?"

"Every preparation is made for the purpose, if you will but step into the adjoining room."

"But my wardrobe —"

"Is left in the country. I understood so, and by the direction of Mr. Everton have selected a few dresses for your present wear. Will you look at them?"

"No, thank you; this will do well enough."

Evelina would fain have changed her dress, but the thought of *how* those dresses had been procured kept her from doing so.

"The very gold that furnished this room," she thought, "may have been torn from some dying wretch whose blood stained the hand that took it. Oh! God preserve me from touching anything in this place!"

"Since you will not change your dress, will you eat or drink?"

"Thank you, no; and if you will do me a favour, my kind friend, you will leave me for a little time. You know not how much I have been distressed of late, and the agony of mind I have endured. I would have a few moments to compose myself, and then I shall be better able to speak to you."

"I will do anything you can desire. Pray ring when you would have me come, and I will hasten to attend you."

"Thanks."

Mrs. St. Henry withdrew.

"In love," cried Evelina, in a passionate flood of grief, as the door closed upon her companion, "in love, and perhaps beloved by a terrible criminal—a man of darkness—a man of blood, and a hunted felon. Oh, power of mercy, what a fate is mine!"

She wept long and bitterly.

"I will fly," she said, after a pause, "I will fly at once. I will escape unseen, and not risk a meeting with that man. I dare not remain here, or something evil will be the result. I tremble with fear, and I shudder with an unaccountable horror. Yes, if I can gain the streets I will fly far away, and nothing shall ever bring me into his presence again."

She rose to her feet, and was about to walk towards the door, when a servant entered and announced—

"Mr. Everton!"

Evelina staggered back, and sank on a lounge.

For a few seconds she neither moved nor spoke, but at length she was brought to a sense of her position by the servant asking what message he should convey.

"It is better to see him," said Evelina, "it is better to see him, and end all at one stroke. The interview over, I am free to go, for he will not attempt to detain me. "Tell Mr. Everton," she said aloud to the servant, "that I will see him."

The man withdrew.

"Courage!" murmured the girl; "courage, Evelina, and be firm."

There was a pause, during which her heart ceased to beat, and a choking sensation arose in her throat.

The blood seemed to rush to her head, and her sight failed her.

She pressed both hands to her brow, and awaited the coming of the man who swayed her thus powerfully.

The door opened again, and a servant ushered Clifford into Evelina's presence.

The robber was dressed to perfection.

His garments were of the richest material, and fitted to a miracle.

His dark hair and moustache rendered him most conspicuous, for, at the period of which we are writing, it was the fashion to wear the white peruke, and the moustache had died away in England.

Clifford looked more like a cavalier of the time of Charles II. than a gentleman of 1748."

He was, however, as singular in his dress as in all his actions.

His magnificent face was ashy pale, and his limbs trembled violently.

"I am come," he said, "for the first and the last time. Perhaps I ought not to have come at all; for after what has happened to-night I should not have sought your presence again. But I could not resist this one visit. I am here to beg your forgiveness, and to say farewell."

"I am glad you are come," said Evelina, with low and choking accents; "I am glad you are here, for I should not like to leave this house, after your great kindnesses, without expressing my deep gratitude."

"Leave this house!" repeated Clifford. "You will not do so?"

"How can I remain?"

"Why not? I promise never to come near it again."

"That is not my reason; but you forget that I cannot receive even house-harbour from —"

She paused.

"I know what you would say," said Clifford, "a robber and a felon!"

"I would not say so."

"No, your good heart would not let you use the words, but they are the only ones you can associate with my name—use them."

"Never, I would tear out my tongue first!"

"You are all goodness," said Clifford; "and would that God had made me worthy to assist you. But I see that it is not to be. Evelina Courtenay can be under no obligation to Paul Clifford, the highway robber."

"Oh, it pains me to refuse your kindness! Believe me, I am grieved to the death to have to do so. But I can only gaze about me, and think that all this magnificence has been purchased by violence and bloodshed. It is too terrible for contemplation, and I must fly the scene at once."

"At once?"

"Yes, this moment."

"No, no, that must not be; something must be done for you—something shall be done. I cannot allow you to walk into the streets on such a night, without a guide and protector."

WHAT THE DWARF DID WITH THE BODY OF WILFRED BARNARD.

"I dare not stay here."

"Oh! Heaven! what a wretch am I to be thus punished. I could, in my frenzy dash my brains out, and end my miserable life. Just as a better career was dawning for me, the vision of future happiness is torn from me, and I can see nothing but sorrow and misery before me. A life of crime, and the doom of the felon!"

"Say not so. It is not too late for repentance and amendment. If such thoughts have crossed your brain, let them not fly from you now. Pray for strength to develope them, and let the vision of a better career lead you on to its ultimate enjoyment."

"Alone, and uncared for?"

Evelina hung her head, and answered not.

"With some one to love me I might have thought of reforming, but I cannot give up my friends and my mode of life to embrace such a future as would be open to me. I should have to quit this place for ever; I should have to seek some foreign land, and without a voice to cheer me—without a face to smile upon me—struggle on and live apart. Such a life would drive me to the grave."

"But is not such a life preferable to that which you now lead?"

"To you it may appear so, but to me, who have known no other, it is too terrible to contemplate."

"You may find some one to love you in some far off land, where your career is not known, and where the past can be entirely buried. You will find some one who can love you for yourself, and feel no pain at reflecting on your past life. You will be loved, and you will be happy."

"It is not so; I cannot delude myself with such hopes. I am alone for ever."

"Why should that be so?"

"Oh! dare I tell you?"

"Why should you not tell me? Anything that affects you is of interest to me."

"Then know that I love you. Nay, stare not, lady; it is a hopeless love; there is presumption in it. I know my position, and shall not presume upon your sympathy. I love you as man never loved woman. I love with all the devotion of a wild and wayward nature, that never has known, never can know control. I love you, and I could not live without telling you this; but having spoken, I shall say no more. You know now why all hope is for ever closed against me. Had it pleased heaven to have shut out from your knowledge the secret of my real character, I should have, perhaps, won your regard; and then the future of which you spoke might have been realised. But now that I see how contemptible a thing I am in your eyes, now that I see you shudder at my presence, I can only go on and on in the old path, looking back upon the memory of the few hours we have spent together as the one bright spot in a career otherwise utterly dark. And so we shall part."

"Not so. Learn, Clifford, learn that I love you."

"Lady!"

"Speak not, but listen; I love you deeply, sincerely; but fate has decreed that we are not for each other. If the knowledge of my true affection be of any consolation to you, receive it."

"You love me, and I may hope?"

"Hope for nothing, Clifford. I love you, but that is all. We part this moment, and for ever."

"Oh, heaven, this is worse than all."

"No, Clifford. if yours is the true and deep love you imagine it to be, my words will be a consolation to you. It will lead you to brighter deeds. It will blot out the past—it will make the future worth living for."

"There is hope in your voice—in that future of which you speak."

"There is nothing that I can promise you. We part now, and may never meet again. Still, time, the worker of wonders, may bring us together in after years; and then, if you are altered, and I am the same as now, we may be linked together, but there must be an awful probation before that be thought of."

"Then, I am again hopeless. If you would name a period, say five or ten years, I could be happy and strive to be a better man, but in the hopeless and indefinite time you speak of——"

"I should not be doing my duty to you and myself if I held out hope more clearly defined. Go, Clifford, and do better."

"Nay, hear me, Evelina, my own Evelina, hear me!"

"Sir, you have heard me. Let me pass."

"Evelina—oh, God, I shall go mad!—hear me, hear me!"

"I have no more to hear, no more to say, save that I am deeply grateful to you. I must go."

"But not to-night? Not into the cold, desolate streets at such a moment?"

"Now, Clifford, now! Farewell, farewell."

"Evelina! Evelina!"

She threw herself into his arms, and their lips met.

Next moment she was gone!

Stupefied with amazement, Clifford stood on the spot where Evelina had left him.

His eyes were fixed on the floor, and his hands were folded over his heart.

He looked like some statue of despair.

He was at length called back to his senses by hearing the voice of Mrs. St. Henry.

"Sir! Mr. Everton! Pray, pray, what has happened? Miss Courtenay!—where is she?"

"Gone—gone!"

"Gone—whither?"

"I know not, madam; I know not. I can only tell you that she has fled from me."

"Sir; will you explain this?"

Clifford looked about him wildly for a few moments, and then closed the door of the apartment.

"Yes," he said; "I will tell you all."

He seated the lady beside him on a lounge, and then poured forth the whole of his tale.

Mrs. St. Henry listened in astonishment to all she heard, and at last Clifford rose and said,

"And now, madam, you have heard all. Will you, too, spurn me?"

"Heaven forbid that I should do so; you are more an object of pity than contempt; but I cannot, after hearing your story, remain here another moment."

"Alas! it is the same cry by all. You fly me as if I bore a plague about me."

"Heaven help and pity you!"

Mrs. St. Henry was now following in the direction taken by Evelina.

"What!" cried Clifford, "am I deserted by all?—am I, then, friendless?"

"Friendless!" he heard some one say, "friendless! what the bold Captain Clifford? Why, he's more friends and admirers than any other gentleman in the world. Friendless! Why you don't call such *things* as them as is gone friends, do you? Bah! come with me to Mrs. Greville's, my boy, and then I'll show you friends of the right sort."

It was his admirer, Bill Waters, who spoke.

"Yes!" cried Clifford; "yes, it must be so. The honoured and the good spurn me; then there is nothing for it but to cling to the bad."

"Don't use hard names, Captain, we ain't so bad, after all. A little rough, perhaps, but that's all. I've seen and heard how these fine birds have treated you; but now come home with me and make up for it. I'll find you the glass and the lass that'll cheer your heart."

"I want excitement. I cannot bear this inward torture. Yes, Bill, I'm with you; and since it must be so—since she's pitched my love back into my teeth, why I'll even seek those that love me, and—"

"Hurrah for the road."

They left the house.

Next day Mrs. Granville took possession, dismissed the servants, sold the gorgeous furniture, and closed the doors.

Thus ended Clifford's dream.

CHAPTER XI.

CLIFFORD FINDS WILFRED BARNARD'S PAPERS—THE FIRM OF WILSNICK, WICKLES, AND WILSNICK, SOLICITORS— THE REPOSITORY OF THE PAPERS.

THE apartments of Wilfred Barnard were in the house of Mrs. Greville.

He had ever been a great favourite with the old lady, and the intelligence of his death caused her great trouble.

The facts connected with the melancholy affair were, however, in part suppressed by Clifford, for he dreaded to make known anything in connection with that secret Wilfred was desirous of having kept in its integrity.

The day after his departure from Evelina, Clifford repaired to the chamber of his friend, with the intention of opening the iron chest alluded to by him on the night of his terrible and mysterious death.

"Now," said Clifford, as he stooped over the iron chest in the now deserted apartment; "now for the secret."

He applied the key to the rusted lock, and the heavy lid opened under his touch.

The chest was nearly filled with the spoil of many a long year of crime and bloodshed.

Mementos of numberless deeds of violence and daring were spread out before the gaze of the searcher.

Trinkets, jewels, and plate of all descriptions were there, and money was thrown in carelessly, and wedged up the spoil.

Carelessly Clifford threw all this on the floor, and at last came to a small packet carefully wrapped in a piece of silk.

He opened it, and found it contained papers.

Clifford discovered that this was what he sought. He at once bundled all the rest back again, and closed the box. Drawing his chair to the window, he commenced the perusal of the papers.

The first was a certificate of marriage, in which was wrapped a wedding ring.

The old parchment told of the marriage of Adolphus Winterleigh, of Winterleigh, with Agnes Clifford, of Winterleigh.

Paul trembled as his eyes fell upon the words.

Next he read a number of old papers, chiefly law documents, all of which touched upon the progress of a case before Parliament in which Adolphus Winterleigh prayed for a dissolution of his marriage with Agnes Winterleigh, neé Clifford, on the ground of adultery and the practice of witchcraft.

Clifford then found the certificate of his own birth.

Born long after the marriage had been declared null and void, the boy bore the name of his mother.

Clifford then examined a sealed packet, directed to him by Wilfred.

He found that it contained a short note from his friend, enclosing a voluminous letter in the hand of his deceased mother. The note written by Wilfred ran as follows:—

"MY DEAR CLIFFORD,

"When your eye lights upon this scrawl I shall be no more. When your mother parted from me, she made me swear that until the last you should know nothing of your parentage. She had such a horror of her own, and the family of her husband, that she preferred you should go through the world nameless and a vagabond, rather than you should meet them and be under any obligation to them. I loved your mother, but she did not return my passion. You will best learn her feelings towards me by a perusal of the enclosed letter, which contains the history of her life.

"Heaven help you, my boy. Let me entreat you to bear in mind the injunctions of your mother, and to avoid those nearest to you by the ties of blood.

"Your friend to the last,
"WILFRED BARNARD.

The letter of his mother next engaged the attention of Clifford, and it was not without deep emotion that he perused the following words:—

"DEAR BARNARD,

"You have been good to me, and Heaven only knows how much I appreciate that goodness. No words of mine could ever convey my sense of your kindness.

"Coming to London a poor, houseless, stricken wanderer, I lighted upon you, a fine, open-hearted, well-to-do medical practitioner.

"Sick, weary, and desponding, you took me to your home, and, by undeviating care, brought back to me health and strength, and when I told you that I never could repay your wondrous goodness, you said the debt could be wiped off if I would give you myself.

"My God! Give you myself! The thought was a terror to me. Bind myself, a woman branded with the crime of adultery, spurned by all, and bearing in my womb the child of the man who had accused me—bind myself to you, a young and rising man, well to do in life, and well respected by all who ever crossed your path! Could I do this, and for ever blight your prospects by coupling your name with one so tainted as my own? No, Wilfred, I could not do this, and I thank God that he gave me strength to withstand the temptation.

"Years have passed since then, and yesterday we met again.

"Would that we had never met, for a glance told me of the ruin I had effected.

"I needed not to be told that you had been stricken down—that your health and strength gave way under the pangs of an unrequited love. All this I could see.

"But then came the terrible story of your having turned your back upon the usages of society, and your having set at defiance the laws of your country.

"Oh! that in Wilfred Barnard—the good—the gentle Wilfred—I should have lived to recognise the infamous robber and highwayman known throughout the length and breadth of the land."

"And then, Wilfred, then to think that all this was my doing.

"It is too much for me to bear, and it will turn my poor brain.

"You know not what it has already borne—you know not the trials I have undergone, or little as you now care for me, you would not have put this additional weight upon me.

"I have told you much of my history; I will now complete the tale.

"I do so in order to justify my refusal of your hand—which you now, doubtless, deem to be a caprice, and nothing more.

"Hear, then, my tale, Wilfred; and then, for my sake—for the sake of the woman you once loved—turn from the path you are following, and seek by honesty to find the bread of life.

"Of my parents I have already told you.

"Of my unhappy home, and the dark and terrible character of my mother and sister, you also know.

"I will now tell you the story of my love, in order that you may not think I had insufficient reason for the refusal of your hand.

"I was but a mere child when first I met Adolphus Winterleigh.

"He was always my friend and companion, and to each other we entrusted those childish griefs and cares which appear so ridiculous to the man and woman, but which have, nevertheless, immense import for those who experience them.

"As years progressed our friendship warmed into love, and from an early period of our lives we were betrothed to each other.

"Adolphus was delicate, and promised not to be long of this world.

"He was a sad and gentle youth, whose life was made unbearable by the younger, though stronger, brother, Lascelles—than whom a greater villain ne'er drew the breath of life.

"Adolphus was, however, blind to the majority of his faults, and bore with him beyond even the limits of Christian endurance.

"At length the old baronet died, and Adolphus was lord of Winterleigh.

"After twelve months of mourning, the Hall was blithe and gay once more; for the young baronet was about to wed his first and only love—myself.

"I will not trouble you with the details of that event. Suffice it to say that it occasioned much joy in Winterleigh, the only persons who appeared discontented being my mother and sister, and Lascelles Winterleigh. Though they uttered no remark on the event, it was easy to understand, by their behaviour, that it pleased them not.

"But Adolphus and I were happy—oh, how happy I cannot tell you; for we loved one another—loved more deeply than words can express.

"We were one in mind and soul; morn, noon, and night we were inseparable.

"My darling was, however, fading fast. Medical men did their best to patch up his health, and they smiled, and said, under my care he would soon grow better again. But they could not deceive me. I saw he was to die.

"I saw it, and I prayed that it might please heaven to take me with him.

"Day and night, night and day, I never ceased to watch and tend him.

"His lightest wish was my law, and if they had said to me, 'Lay down your life and it will save his,' I would have gladly done so.

"Mine was not love—it was wicked idolatry, and God punished me for it. Oh, how terribly has he punished me; but I have not yet complained, and I never will.

"A month passed, Wilfred, a month of bliss; for, in spite of the hectic flush on his cheek—in spite of the hollow cough, and unnaturally brilliant eye, which spoke of death only too plainly, we were happy. He was happy in having me to attend him, and I was happy in the thought that I was his, and that when he was called away I should follow him.

"So passed the month.

"Then Adolphus grew worse, and the doctors separated me from him.

"They told me I must have a regard for my own health, and that his touch was contagious. As if I did not pray that this contagion might attack me, and lay me low with him I so madly loved!

"But this was wicked, and I dared not give utterance to such words, and so we separated.

"I had my own apartment, but it was seldom occupied, for I could not quit the sick man's chamber until exhausted nature forced me to do so.

"About fourteen days after my separation from Adolphus, the dark event occurred in which my future wretchedness had its origin.

"I had been in the chamber of my husband the best part of three nights, and only quitted it at his request, which was made at the earnest solicitation of the doctors.

"I retired to my own chamber, leaving the door of my room open, in order that I might catch the lightest sounds from that of my husband.

"I was much exhausted, and almost before I had disrobed myself a drowsiness came over me, and I knew no more.

"This was at about seven in the evening.

"At four in the morning I was awakened by the buzz of many voices.

"I started up in bed, and gazed wildly about me.

"Before me was an array of faces, all marked with the expression of disgust and anger.

"What was it?

"I could not understand the meaning of this.

"I clasped my brow, and endeavoured to recal my senses.

"'Shame! shame!' was the cry that rang in my ears.

"I turned my eyes from the light, and they fell upon *the form of a man*.

"Yes, Wilfred, in my bed, lying by my side, was a man.

"With a wild scream I threw myself from the couch, and ran into a corner of the room, and hid behind the tapestry.

"They mistook my terror and anguish for an expression of shame, and I was universally condemned.

"What then passed I know not, for my brain reeled, and for days I was delirious.

"They told this to my husband, and it broke his heart.

"I never saw him again, but they told me of his anguish—they described his horror, his frenzy, and his groans of anguish.

"They told me this, and I prayed to die, but that mercy was not extended to me.

"Gradually I heard it whispered that the man found in my bed was one Reuben Cardnell, a dissolute young squire of a neighbouring village, the friend and boon companion of Lascelles.

"I heard also that he had said I was his concubine, and that he had often visited me since my marriage, and shared my couch.

"Need I say that I was turned from the doors as soon as the doctors pronounced me out of danger.

"Yes, they thrust me forth, unheard—undefended; and he died believing me guilty.

"As I quitted the house I met Lascelles, and although he spoke not, I read in his face that it was to him I was indebted for the diabolical plot that drove me from my worshipped husband and my home, and that deprived me of my honour.

"I turned upon him, and I said, 'You triumph now, Lascelles Winterleigh, but you will live to undergo an awful repentance.'

"He sneered, and motioned me to the door, and weak and suffering, not knowing where to turn for shelter, I left the home in which I had passed my brief dream of happiness.

"I came to London, and I met you.

"You were good to me, beyond the bounds of human goodness, or I should have died.

"You saved me, but then, Wilfred, you committed the fatal error of asking me to love you. Would that I had had the courage then to tell you all I have now written, but I could not do so. I could only turn and fly from your presence.

"Anywhere, anywhere, beyond the reach of your goodness.

"Far away, where those eyes, so full of love and tenderness, could not gaze so sadly, so reproachfully, into mine.

"I fled your roof.

"You do not know what I have suffered since.

"I could rest nowhere. It appeared to me that I must wander.

"I could not breathe in the towns and cities I entered, and it appeared that the open country was too confined for me.

"I was constantly walking.

"On, on—anywhere, anywhere—change, change, to drive away thought.

"It was thinking that maddened me.

"At length I had to enter some village workhouse, and there I was confined.

"A few months passed, a very few, and then the old restless spirit was on me again, and one day I caught up my child and started forth.

"For five years I have subsisted by vagrancy. I have

sung at village alehouses, I have danced and acted at village fairs, and now Fate has brought me back again to London.

"And I have seen you!

"My tale is now finished, Wilfred. You now know all, and can you find it in your heart to blame me, knowing all?

"Had I been less scrupulous I should have married you, and secured a home and a competence, if not comparative happiness, by dragging you into misery unutterable!

"I have struggled on, God knows how; sometimes I have wanted bread! Sometimes I have existed for days on a hard crust that had been thrown to a dog! Sometimes my senses have left me, and I have been incarcerated as a vagrant or a sorceress, and I have wandered over the country with aching heart, and feet that left blood marks on the road! I have gazed into the face of my poor boy, and he has fixed his eyes upon mine and cried pitifully for food—and I have had none to give him!

"Oh! you know not what we have suffered, and you cannot think what we may yet suffer, for the weary pilgrimage is to be resumed, and it can only end when death comes, and I am called to my husband, who now knows of my truth.

"Wilfred, Wilfred, once more let me entreat you to turn away from your present mode of life, and to devote yourself to better things.

"This is the prayer of

"The heart-broken, dying

"AGNES."

Pinned to this letter was the following lines, written by Wilfred Barnard:—

"*I saw her after she wrote the foregoing letter. I saw her, and I wept bitterly, as I gazed into her once beautiful, now melancholy and pinched face.*

"*She was still lovely to me, and I could have worshipped the very ground on which her foot fell.*

"*I followed her through the streets at a distance. I saw her stagger, as if from exhaustion. I then approached her, but a stranger had anticipated me, and he supported her.*

"*' What ails you?' he asked.*

"*And she replied, 'I faint from weakness and want of food.'*

"*Oh, God, how my heart bled then.*

"*This stranger gave her some silver coins, and then left her.*

"*I flew to her side, and offered the support of my arm, but she drew her boy to her bosom, and waved me off.*

"*' Agnes! Agnes!' I cried, 'do not break my heart by this conduct!—Oh, do not, do not drive me mad! If you cannot love me—if you will not be mine—at least allow me to offer some assistance. Let me not see that you have died of neglect whilst I have the means of alleviating your anguish.'*

"*Still she waved me off, and in a faint, almost inaudible, whisper, said, 'Not your assistance, Wilfred, not your's. There is blood upon the money you earn!'*

"*Her words had an unspeakable terror for me, and I fled and saw her no more.*

"*Time passed, and then I heard that she had died in the house of Mrs. Greville.*

"*I sought out her boy, and have since kept watch over him. He has followed in the evil path, but he is not evil. I would have prevented his straying from the right course, but I had not the power. I could not do more than I have done.*

"WILFRED BARNARD."

Tears coursed down the cheeks of Clifford, as he read the history of his ill-starred mother.

Visions of the sweet, sad face he could remember seeing years and years ago, flitted across his mind, and opened up a well of sorrow.

The discovery he made concerning his parentage had no interest for him now.

He could only think of his unhappy mother.

"Oh!" he cried, "oh! that it had pleased God to have revealed this secret before this Lascelles Winterleigh died. He should not then have quitted the world without that reward which was his due. Vile dastard! that such a being should have been permitted to crawl the earth!"

At length Clifford governed his rage, and gave himself up to thinking on the chain of incidents that had revealed to him his true name and position in the world.

"Had not that will been stolen I could have claimed my own, and thrown over my evil ways. Had the will been preserved, I should have been able to win Evelina, who now despises me. But thank God that I know so much of my history. For the restitution of my rights I must trust in Providence. But the will—the will. For *her* sake, as well as my own, I must find that. Meanwhile, these papers must be deposited in a place of safety."

Where or with whom Clifford did not quite know, but after much reflection he determined on having an interview with the Messrs. Wilswick, Wickles, and Wilswick, solicitors, of Clements'-inn.

This firm had not a very enviable reputation, the practice of its members being principally confined to the lowest law courts of London, and in business of a not very praiseworthy nature.

The principals of the firm were Erasmus and Windington Wilswick. The second partner was Mr. Wickles, once a clerk to the firm, now raised to a third share of the business in consequence of his uniform good, or, rather, bad conduct.

He still did all the dirtiest of the dirty work of the firm, and was an invaluable member thereof.

He seldom attended consultations, but confined his attention to the desk, and in sifting out evidence that would not bear the light of day being let in upon it until it was in an advanced state of completeness.

Mr. Wickles was a sort of human ferret, and seemed to imagine that every man's home was a rabbit's hole, into which he must, perforce, enter, and draw forth one or more of its occupants, for the mere gratification of fastening on to their throats and tasting their blood.

He was fierce and ungovernable, and whenever he thought fit to carry out the ferret simile, he would hold on until he had succeeded in making his teeth meet.

He was a little man, and dressed in the most disreputable of rusty black.

His head was small and his features sharp.

His eyes were under the average size, and their colour was a piercing grey. His mouth was large and cruel, and when open displayed a row of very small but even teeth, that had once been white. His mode of speech was as snappish as his whole contour.

Erasmus Wilswick was a tall, thin individual, of the parrot type.

He had small round eyes, a retreating forehead, and a large hooked nose.

He seemed to be afflicted with snuffles, for he was constantly sniffing and drawing up the corners of his proboscis and mouth.

He spoke like a parrot, too—shrill sounds came from his throat, and his neck sank into the depths of his anything but white neckerchief, as he gave utterance thereto.

He wore a dingy suit of black, but it was less dingy, although more dilapidated, than that of the firm or partner.

The third partner, the brother of Erasmus, was the youngest of the three, but what he was deficient in years he made up in weight, for he was much larger than the other two would have been united together.

He was elephantine in appearance, thought, and action.

There was a ponderous air about all he did, that involuntarily reminded one of solidity and heaviness.

His words fell roundly and convincingly on the ear; his step was slow and sure, and his whole bearing massive and weighty.

Thus this firm of lawyers was made up of individuals possessing the peculiarities of the ferret, the parrot, and the elephant.

He who escaped the ferret, had to undergo the ordeal of the parrot's sharp beak, claws, and voice; and if this was passed through safely, there was the smashing trunk of the elephant, and his massive foot to wear him down and annihilate him.

Altogether that was a very delightful firm to do business with.

Clifford did not, however, reflect very deeply on the peculiarities of the individuals when he took his papers to them. He had before had dealings with them, and Mrs. Greville was their constant client.

When Clifford visited the office of these worthies he found them seated in solemn conference, poring over some musty old deed with the greatest avidity.

They looked up as our hero entered, and each greeted him after his own peculiar fashion.

"Well, Clifford, in trouble, eh?" cried the ferret; "Ah, you'll follow the rest of 'em one day, and swing at Tyburn, or some such place, you will!"

"Mr. Clifford," said the parrot, pulling up the corners of his nose, "Mr. Clifford, how d'ye do? Take a seat, take a seat; we will attend to you presently." Here the neck and a part of the chin disappeared in the neckerchief, and a snuffle was emitted from the nose expressive of anything the hearer chose to imagine.

"We won't keep you long," said the elephant, "not —a—great while—my friend."

He coiled an imaginary trunk about Clifford's body, placed a mental foot of ponderous proportions upon his neck, and assuring himself that he had his man safe, resumed the perusal of the deed.

"There's no doubt of it," said the ferret-like man, pouncing upon all parts of the deed at once, and bringing to view many legal rabbits, the main points, and only leaving his hold of them when they were safe in the sharp beak of Erasmus, who in turn placed them in the keeping of his mammoth brother.

"There's no doubt of it, sir; there the male line ends, and the estates then go to Diana Montville and her heirs, administrators, executors, and assigns. It's as clear as daylight; anybody can see it."

"Yes," said Erasmus, "anybody can see it, but nobody can prove whether the said Diana left any heirs or executors. Who was Diana? who was Diana?"

"I know more of this than you think," said the ferret, "I have found a man who did know Diana Montville."

"He knows a man who did know Diana Montville," echoed the parrot.

"Explain," said the brother.

"Well, last night a fellow turned up who knew the lady. She married an officer of the army, and at the expiration of about two years both died, leaving one child, a daughter."

"Leaving a daughter," said Erasmus; "leaving a daughter, and she died."

"No she didn't."

"No she didn't," said Erasmus, turning to his brother: no she didn't."

"Well, she didn't," said the brother, securing the fact under his foot.

"Well, if she didn't die," said Erasmus, "what became of her?"

"She fell into the clutches of a rich baronet of Bucks, who adopted her, and reared her as his own child."

Clifford opened his ears.

"His own child," said Erasmus, "well?"

"This baronet is now dead."

"Now dead. Well, and you know where to drop upon the girl?"

"No. She disappeared in a most mysterious manner as soon as the breath quitted the body of the old man."

"Whose name was —?" asked Erasmus.

"Whose name was—no matter."

The ferret fixed his eyes upon Paul Clifford, who was listening with breathless attention to every syllable.

"Some other time," said the elephant, gathering up the deed, and securing it in a drawer.

"Curse my stupidity," said Paul to himself; "if I had feigned indifference or sleep, I might have heard all."

"And now," said Erasmus, "what can we do for you?"

He turned to Clifford, and fixed his cruel, grey eye upon him attentively.

"For me?" said Clifford. "Oh, yes—of course."

Clifford came to the lawyers with the full intention of allowing them to peruse the whole of his papers, and to accept their advice upon them, but from what he had just heard he thought this a most imprudent thing.

"If they should be speaking of Evelina —if they should be referring to Sir Lascelles Winterleigh," he said, "it will never do for them, just now, to know of my case in that quarter. I had best keep silence."

This was hastily resolved upon, and Clifford formed his plans accordingly.

"I will thank you," he said, "I will thank you, gentlemen, to witness that I seal up these papers, and I will thank you to place them in safety until I call upon you to open them, or hand them over to me."

"A mystery?" said the little ferret.

"Yes, a mystery," said Clifford; "at least, for the present."

"Well, it is not our business to penetrate mysteries unless we are called upon to do so by our clients, so we will seek to know nothing of your's. Here is a parchment cover, and here sealing wax."

"Thanks," said Clifford, drawing forth his packet, and placing it in the parchment cover. "That will do very well."

He took from his finger a large ring, and therewith sealed his packet.

"Now, how shall we endorse the packet?" asked Erasmus.

"Simply papers, the property of Paul Clifford," answered our hero.

"Papers, the property of Paul Clifford," repeated Erasmus, writing the words on the parchment. "There," he continued, "that is done. And now are there any further demands?"

"Nothing," said Clifford, throwing some gold pieces on the table, and preparing to go; "nothing, gentlemen; and so I will say good day."

"Good," said the three lawyers in a breath; "good day, Mr. Clifford!"

Clifford withdrew.

"I should like to know the secret of that document," said Clifford, as he left the office of the attorneys.

At the same moment the attorneys were saying to each other—

"How much I should like to understand the mystery of this packet."

There was no more *said*, but it remains to be seen whether the lawyers and Clifford had not secretly determined to probe the secrets of each other.

CHAPTER XII.

THE FUNERAL OF THE EIGHTH BARONET OF WINTERLEIGH
THE DESOLATE HOUSE—MOTHER CLIFFORD AND HER
CAT—THE DWARF AND THE BODY OF WILFRED—THE
YOUNG HEIR AND HIS AMUSEMENTS—THE ORDEAL BY
WATER—CLIFFORD ON HIS WHITE MARE RESCUES ROSE
FROM HER PERSECUTORS.

ON the seventh day from that of his decease the remains of the eighth baronet of Winterleigh were taken from the Hall, and conveyed to the final resting place in the the village church of Winterleigh.

The funeral cortege was but small. A few of the tenants were asked, and some distant relatives of the deceased came from different parts of the county to attend the ceremonial.

Lewis was among the number, but he exhibited no more grief at the sombre ceremony than did the others, who viewed the whole proceeding with marked indifference, if not with contempt; for Lascelles Winterleigh was generally disliked, and those who followed his remains to the family vault did so rather as a matter of course than from any other prompting.

The coffin and pall were very gorgeous in their emblazoned arms, and heavy trimming of silver.

The hired mourners were also elaborately decked out in the most extravagant and sumptuous trappings of woe money could procure; but beyond this, one would look in vain for any sign of grief.

There was no tearful eye—no face marked with an expression of genuine grief.

All were cold, impassionate, and indifferent, and the great baronet of Winterleigh sank into the grave unregretted and unmourned.

The church bell tolled dismally as the procession moved from the Hall and threaded its way to the church, and, save for this, there would have been no sign of sorrow.

The village pastor hurried nervously through the funeral ritual, and thus closed the last scene in the career of Lascelles Winterleigh.

He had been a bold, bad man in life, and his death bore the impress thereof.

Lewis seemed delighted to think the ceremony over, and hurried back to the Hall, where a splendid collation awaited the party.

The feast and the partakers thereof would have been more in keeping with a wedding ceremony than that of a funeral.

People appeared to think they had got well over a disagreeable duty, and enjoyed themselves accordingly.

Young Wilfred was in high glee, and did the duties of host with a singular grace.

He dispensed his hospitality so largely that ere the day was ended two thirds of his guests had followed his example, and got beastly drunk.

He talked of the sports of the field, of horses, dogs, and badgers, and his guests took considerable interest in his discourse.

They were all, more or less, addicted to the sports of the field, and found no difficulty in adapting themselves to the tastes of their host.

Accordingly sport was the current topic, and in its exciting details all the funeral party shut out the grave from their thoughts, and enjoyed themselves.

But the house was desolate.

Through the whole of the vast building an air of solemn and mysterious silence pervaded.

The servants stole about the corridors noiselessly, and did their missions with an air of dread and grim stateliness that could not fail to strike the beholder.

All the servants of that wretched house were poor superstitious people, and the death of the baronet was sufficient cause to oppress them in the most dismal manner.

But when this cause was augmented by Mother Clifford taking up her quarters in the house without dispute they became doubly fearful, and cared not to remain in the place.

They had whispered consultations in all manner of odd corners, but none of them possessed sufficient courage to speak out and assert their intention of quitting the house.

Fear fascinates us very often; and when we would most readily fly a spot, we are compelled by some unaccountable feeling to remain.

So it was with these poor silly people. They dreaded their position, but had not the courage to fly, and leave it behind.

And so they stayed, and stayed, and wondered at the awful stillness and the mystery by which they were surrounded.

Above all did they wonder at the impious conduct of the new baronet.

Their simple minds could not comprehend such a terrible bearing at such a moment.

Meanwhile Mother Clifford made herself thoroughly at home in the Hall.

She commanded with an imperious air, and awed everyone into submission.

The servants said that all night strange unearthly sounds emanated from her chamber.

Sometimes it appeared to them that these sounds resembled shrieks of agony, at others they would be the plaintive moans of grief, and then again would come roars of diabolical laughter.

Singular smells, too, stole through the house at night.

Sometimes they were those of flesh burning, and at other times they were those of many herbs.

But no one had seen anything. The chamber was always empty, and bore no trace of being disturbed when it was entered by those of the household.

On the hearth would be reposing the great white cat, and in her great chair Mother Clifford, either buried in thought, or reading some old book from the library.

Altogether, however, the house was a truly melancholy one, and, bad as its repute had ever been, it now grew worse, and was more avoided than ever.

* * * * * *

There had been one being at the burial of Sir Lascelles Winterleigh who had not been noted by any of the mourners, and that was the hideous dwarf, Cackalo.

The shocking being had hid himself in one of the quaint old galleries of the church, and from that spot had watched the progress of the ceremony.

After its conclusion, and all the mourners had left the church, he descended from the gallery, and stole towards the marble tomb.

"Dead!" he cried, "dead! I know, I know; dead, dead; but I'll tear him out, I will!"

He applied his strength to the vast marble slab that closed the vault, but he could not succeed in moving the ponderous weight.

Dashing himself against it many times, and at last exhausting himself, he found that his efforts were useless, and, with a yell of disappointment, started off.

"If he won't come, I know where to find one. I know where a dead man is to be found. Ha! ha! On a tree—on a tree!"

Repeating these words again and again, he started off through the wood of Winterleigh, and hence to the marsh.

It was an unfrequented spot. Strangers seldom had occasion to traverse it, and the villagers, knowing it to be the haunt of the dwarf, always avoided it, therefore it was not to be wondered at that the body of Wilfred remained for the space of seven days hanging undiscovered to the limb of the willow tree overhanging the water.

There it dangled in all the hideousness of decay; there it hung in the bitter blast until the day of the funeral, and then the murderer cut it down with the knife that had let out it's life's blood!

The dwarf, filled once more with ideas of death, sped to the marsh, and sprang into the tree.

He was mad with brutish excitement, and drawing his great knife, severed the neckerchief by which the body hung, and then, swinging it to the ground, descended the tree after it.

Catching it, despite its palpable horrors, in his arms, he ran as swiftly as possible with it to the wood of Winterleigh.

Dropping it here, and then dragging it along the ground by the scarf about the throat, he proceeded with it to the brook in the hollow of that part of the wood where Mother Clifford's cottage stood.

Seating himself on a stone at the brink of the water he thrust the body in, and then sat grinning at it.

Ever and anon it rose to the surface, and the dwarf would thrust in his great foot, and press it down; screaming with joy at the amusement thereby afforded him.

After continuing this for some time, he went to the ruins of the cottage, and treading on the hearth stone, cried—

"There, there buried paper; I know, I know, buried by old woman. Hugh! bad woman—make me cry. Cut me hard, and cat tear me. Hugh!"

He did not appear to care about staying longer in this spot.

He looked about fearfully, and then slunk away amid the trees.

*   *   *

Evelina had left behind her a very pretty and really good girl, who had served her as lady's maid, for some five years.

Her name was Rose Andrews. Rose grieved terribly at losing her young mistress, and had it not been that she did not wish to quit Winterleigh until after the funeral, nothing would have induced her to remain under the roof a moment after the departure of her well-loved mistress.

But Rose respected Sir Lascelles for his uniform kindness to her young mistress, and in respect to his memory she desired not to quit the house until after he had been laid in the vault of Winterleigh.

As soon, however, as the ceremony was over, and she could get to speak with Lewis, she hastened to the apartment to which he had returned, to shake off the effects of his carouse.

"Can I speak to you Sir Lewis," she asked, stepping into the room.

"Can you speak to me, my pretty Rose, of course you can; what is it?"

"I came, sir, to say farewell and to thank you for your kindness to me."

"What! are you going?"

"I've no further business here now, Sir Lewis."

"No further business. Oh nonsense; you mustn't go."

"But indeed, I must! My mistress is gone, and there are no ladies in the family who require my services."

"But there's a gentleman who does, Rose."

"I do not understand you, sir!"

"Well, you women do bother me so about speaking plainly."

"Don't you understand what I mean? I wish you to stay."

"But *you* have no occasion for my services."

"No, I only want your company. Come and sit down beside me, my pretty Rose."

"Indeed, Sir Lewis, I dare not."

"Oh! nonsense; what a shy little devil you are."

"Then, Sir Lewis, I will not sit down. I know my place better."

"Nonsense. Look here, Rose, I've always had my eye upon you, but when Sir Lascelles was alive, and your mistress was here, I didn't dare to say what I meant. The plain fact is that I'm deuced fond of you, Rose, and if you like to live with me here you can do so. D'ye understand that?"

"I understand that you offer me a deep and terrible insult, and that I will not submit to that from you or any one else in the wide world. I am poor and lowly, but virtue has not deserted me. Sir Lewis, I wish you a good day."

"What—you jade—d'ye mean to pitch my offer back into my teeth?"

"Yes, Sir Lewis. I spurn it and you."

"Beware!"

"I've nothing to fear from you. Thank Heaven I am independent of you."

"Beware, I say; you do not know me."

"And you do not know *me*."

"I honoured you beyond your deserts by the offer I made, and which I was a fool to make, for I didn't mean it, so think not that I'll submit to any of your nonsense."

"Wretch!" cried the indignant girl; "wretch! too contemptible, too pitiable, to waste words upon; I despise and loathe you. I will not stay another moment in your presence!"

"Won't you? Well, we'll see about that!"

Lewis sprang to the door, and held it in his hand.

"Now," he continued, "you'll have to alter that tone, or it'll be the worse for you!"

"You will hear no other words from me!"

"Mind, I am a desperate man, and I promise to effect your ruin if you do not lower that haughty tone. By hell! you shall not quit this apartment until I am avenged!"

He was fired by drink, passion, and excitement; and his eyes glared wildly into those of the terror-stricken girl.

She well knew it was useless to cry for help, for the voice of Lewis would send back those who might, perchance, hear her.

She knew not what to do, and was about to throw herself at the feet of the libertine, and cry his mercy, when her eye fell upon the open window.

It was but a few feet from the ground, and, without hesitation, she rushed to it, and sprang into the garden.

With a cry of pain she fell to the ground.

She had sprained her ancle.

Seeing Lewis about to follow her, she rose to her feet, and flew away, although the agony she endured was beyond expression.

Before her lay the wood of Winterleigh, and thither she hastened as fast as she could fly over the ground.

Lewis would have fellowed, but a voice arrested him.

Turning, he beheld Mother Clifford.

"What is the matter?" she asked.

"Matter," he cried; "enough to make a man mad. Foiled, scorned, jeered at by a serving wench."

"She showed her taste."

"By Heaven I'll pay her for it if I catch her again."

"If you catch her again. Why not? Poor stricken deer; see how she limps. Jumping from such windows will not agree with such dainty ancles."

"I will follow."

"What will you do?"

"I know not; but she shall be forced to return."

"Good. Bring her back, and punish her. A saucy minx. She is the only one of all the household who has dared dispute my will, and set me at defiance. Punish her; punish her."

"That will I."

Lewis sprang through the window, and running round to the stakes bellowed lustily for his men.

Meanwhile, poor Rose, sickened with pain and exhaustion, and shuddering with terror, entered the wood.

Chance led her to the little brook near the ruins of the cottage, and, arrived here, she could go no further.

The pain in her foot was unbearable, and sinking down by the water, she slipped off her shoe, and prepared to bathe her foot in the stream.

Just as she was about to do this a horrible sight met her gaze.

There, in the water, swaying slowly to and fro, was the body of Wilfred.

The girl could scarce believe her eyes. She started to her feet, and then again gazed into the stream.

"No, no," she cried; "I must be mistaken; it cannot be a reality."

She looked again.

But there it was, the terrible features of the dead man staring up through the water, seemingly into her very face.

In her fright she ran to and fro, and waving her hands above her head, cried—

"Woe, woe! what a sight is this—what a sight is this! Woe, woe!"

She was maddened with terror, and knew not what she did.

Behind the ruins of the cottage were several men observing her.

It was Lewis and his servitors.

"What is she doing?" asked Lewis.

"She's a witch, or clean demented," said one of the men.

"I never saw such antics. What can she mean?"

"See! she looks into the water."

"Ah; there's more in this than appears at first sight. Come, let us see what she is doing."

Lewis and his men started off to the water, and before the girl knew of their presence she was in their power.

"Now, wench, I have you; you thought to escape me, did you; but I'll be even with you, for all those insults. Now we'll see what you were up to at the side of that bit of water."

He went to the water and looked in, and there his eye fell upon the sight that had so frightened Rose.

"Look here," cried Lewis to his men, "look here—there's murder been done—she's killed a man."

They all gazed upon the body, and they all condemned her.

"Yes," they said, "she's murdered some one. Pull him out."

"I murder a man," cried Rose, in bewilderment, "I murder him!—no, no, it cannot be that you suspect me of such a crime."

"Oh! you're very innocent, you are," said Lewis, "it's as clear as the light of day. She has killed this poor devil, whoever he is, and come here to perform some evil ceremony or other.

"Yes, that's so. She's a witch; she's a witch!"

"A witch!" cried Rose; "a witch! Oh, do not say so, gentlemen; or they will torture me. I am no witch, indeed—indeed, I am not. I never did any one harm in all my life."

"Bear her to the village. I'm lord of the manor, and will see the truth of this affair. Bear her to the village, and let us tell the people what has occurred."

They seized the girl by the wrists, and were about to obey the cruel order of Lewis, when Rose fell fainting to the ground.

"Ah, that's a very good sham," cried the brutish Lewis, "a very good sham; but it won't do for us. On with her!"

They seized her again, and were roughly raising her to her feet, when the pain she endured brought back animation, and, looking at her tormentors, she cried—

"Oh, spare me—spare me. I cannot walk. I am far too ill to walk, and my foot is very, very painful."

"Oh, curse your foot. You're a witch, and can bear pain."

"Oh, Heaven, protect me. I cannot endure this pain."

"On with her."

They obeyed, and pulled her roughly after them.

At each step the poor girl took, her frame quivered in agony, and a piercing shriek rang through the woods, but it failed to touch the hearts of those who held her.

They were determined to force her to the village, and on they rushed.

The perspiration stood on the girl's brow, and her face bore traces of the quintessence of torture she underwent; but still on they went, and she had to use her lamed foot in scrambling over the rough road that led through the wood to the village.

The beauty of poor Rose was no preventative against the anger of the mob that gathered, as her tormentors dragged her through the village.

"A murderess and a witch!" was the cry uttered by the followers of Lewis; and the brutal superstition of the rustics led them to glory in the poor girl's agony, and to assist the torture.

The poor girl was past protecting now.

She was only partly aware of what was now being done with her.

She was conscious of a violent pain in her foot; but this became but a secondary consideration compared with her agony of mind.

On they bore her, limping and crippled, and moaning bitterly.

On they rushed with her to the village, where, for a time, they made a halt, and related what they had beheld in the wood.

"Beat her down," cried some; "stone the witch to death!"

"Hang her! hang her!"

"No," cried Lewis; "let us have some fun with her."

"What shall we do, then?"

"Float her in the river," replied the young baronet.

"Aye; float her, float her—and hang her afterwards!"

"Spare me! spare me!" cried Rose.

"Spare ye—spare a witch? Not likely. To the river with her!"

"Oh! will no one heed me? will no one save me?"

"Nay, nay," cried the mob; "no one will help thee. If thee art a witch, help theeself!"

"I am no witch! indeed I am no witch!"

"We'll see, wench; we'll see."

"Now, then," cried Lewis, "come on to the Holywell meads. Let us try what effect water will have upon her."

Fainting, and weak as an infant, the poor young martyr was once more set in motion—the whole pack of rustics at her heels, hounding her on.

The meads were at length reached, and the preparations for floating the girl proceeded with.

It was now near sunset, and, for the time of year, the evening was calm and beautiful.

The river ran placidly through the verdant meads, and all was still and beautiful before the wild yells of the brutal gang of torturers disturbed the scene with their yells and imprecations.

Down to the bank of the stream they came, and in a few moments all was prepared for the ordeal the unhappy girl was to undergo.

A strong cord was borrowed, and with this her hands and feet were bound, the knot being drawn until a cry of unendurable anguish was uttered.

Still the plaintive cry for mercy was uttered.

Still the little hands were extended in supplication; but not one eye expressed sympathy, not one heart relented.

All were imbued with the notion that she was a thing of evil, and her torture was, to her tormentors, a source of extreme gratification.

Just as all was prepared, one ruffianly clown advanced to the group more immediately engaged in superintending the preliminaries, and catching the poor girl's soft arm between his great hard fingers, pinched her brutally.

"Ah," he cried, seeing that this awakened no animation in the victim; "ah, it's but little use o' floating her, I see."

"Why? why?"

"Because she can't feel aught you'll do. The devil has stood her friend."

"You don't say so!"

"I do."

"Let us keep her till she do recover, then."

"Nay," said the man, "I'll try and bring her about. Hast any o' ye got a pin?"

A woman hastily came forward from the group, and proffered a large pin, with which she had fastened her shawl over her shoulders.

The man took it, and with a diabolical grin, said—

"This is the way to try if she can feel."

He took the pin between his finger and thumb, and plunged it violently into the bosom of poor Rose.

With a yell she sprang up and confronted her torturer, and then, quivering from head to foot, fell back insensible.

"Aye, she feels well enough," they shouted; "in with her! let her float for it!"

"Now, then," said Lewis, taking Rose by the shoulder, and lifting her; "Now, then—in with her!"

Two or three ran forward and lent him their assistance' and the next moment the inanimate girl was floating in the river.

Gradually her clothes soddened, and then the almost freezing water sent a chill to her very heart, and restored animation.

She plunged and dashed about her arms, but the cruel cords cut into her wrists, and made her cease.

She rolled over, and, with eyes strained towards the people on the bank, screamed madly for help.

"I shall drown!" she cried, as the weight of her clothes bore her down. "I shall die! Help me!—help me!"

Still they laughed, and mocked her agony.

"Nae fear o' you dying," they cried; "nae fear."

"No, let her float," said Lewis; "the cold water will do her good. Besides, the more she gets of it the less she's likely to feel the hanging, so let her swim."

It was a terrible sight to see, those pale, terror-stricken features turned imploringly to those who felt not for the agony that occasioned the sad and heart-rending look.

It was an awful picture of brutality and gross super-stition, but one which not unfrequently disgraced our country at the period of which we write.

There was the poor, bruised, half-dead girl, guiltless and pure as God made her, tortured for the gratification of a set of brutes, who had not one spark of humanity in all their composition.

She sank—down—down—down! The water bubbled into her ears and filled her mouth as she attempted to repeat her cries for help, and there was not one hand stretched forth to aid her.

She looked beseechingly in all their faces, and she could only see therein malignity and wild satisfaction.

All the crew indulged in every kind of grim antic expressive of satisfaction, and cried gleefully, or mocked her terror with shouts of laughter.

As the stream slowly bore her on, so they followed, continuing their savage delight with unabated strength.

At length the girl disappeared beneath the surface of the water.

It was, however, but a second, and then she rose again, and cast one more glance at those who had it in their power to save her.

"She's a dead woman if she's not pulled out at once," said one man to the young baronet.

"Oh," he replied, "she's only feigning; there is no fear for her."

"If that's feigning," said the man, "I never saw any realities in my life. She's drowning as fast as a woman can drown."

"We had best take her out," said one of Lewis's men, respectfully.

"Fools!" shouted the young man, in a great passion; "fools! I'm the best judge, I should think. Let her stay, and if so be she drowns, why let her; it'll be a d——d good riddance, that's all."

"There! she rises again," said another. "Look how her face swells and her eyes protrude. She ain't no witch."

"Dare you contradict me?" said Lewis. "If you open your mouth again I'll pitch you in after her."

The man slunk away, and no one dared say another word on the subject, although it was palpable to all that the girl was sinking.

Again and again Rose appeared above the surface, and struggled to save herself, but each time her efforts became weaker and weaker, and then her head fell back, and she ceased to move.

Slowly, slowly, she was disappearing.

"It's all over with her," cried the people; "she's dying now."

"Then the sooner she will be with her friend the devil," said Lewis.

There was now some more murmurs in the crowd.

The test of witchcraft was supposed to be the floating of the body.

Therefore, as soon as it became palpable that Rose was dying, the men were convinced that she had been wrongly suspected, and desired to see her punishment ended.

"It's time she was out," they cried; "it's too bad to kill her like that. If she's done aught wrong, try her and hang her."

"Silence," screamed Lewis, still further enraged at these manifestations; "silence! I say she shan't be taken out, and I'll be the death of the first that dares help her; so now you know with whom you're dealing."

"But she will die!"

"She shall die, since you put me to it. I'll have my way, and now let me see who will dare dispute it."

There was a hurried sound, as of a horse at full speed

A loud snort, and a shout of defiance, and then a horseman dashed to the spot.

Without hesitating a second, he drew from his holster a pistol, and with the butt end dashed to the earth, by a series of terrible blows on the head, Lewis and his men, and next moment were plunging into the river and swimming towards the fast-sinking body of Rose.

His gallant horse obeyed his lightest touch, and mate-rially assisted him in catching the body.

Wetting himself to the skin in the task, he at length succeeded in holding the body above water, and giving his horse the rein, the gallant brute struggled out of the river on the opposite bank.

He cast one glance behind at those from whom he had rescued the victim of superstition and malice, and then rode away.

All this was effected in much less time than it has taken to describe it, and even before the rustics could re over from the appearance of this daring horseman, he had vanished from their sight.

"Who was it?" they asked each other, after awhile; "who could he have been?"

"I know him," said one; "or, at least, if it's not the man I think him, I'll never believe my eyes again."

"Well, who was it?"

"Why, Gentleman Clifford, the highwayman."

The man was right.

It was Gentleman Clifford.

CHAPTER XIII.

ACCOUNTS FOR CLIFFORD'S APPEARANCE AT WINTERLEIGH — THE OATH TAKEN BY LEWIS — HIS INTERVIEW WITH MOTHER CLIFFORD — PLANS FOR THE DESTRUCTION OF THE HIGHWAYMAN.

AFTER he had read Wilfred's papers, Clifford became totally wretched. It appeared to him that his life was an entire blank.

Something within whispered him that he was for ever an alien from that branch of the community to which he belonged by right of birth, and another voice seemed to warn him away from those with whom he had hitherto associated.

He was alone.

"Oh! had she but loved me," he would say "what a different fate would be mine!"

In spite of what Evelina had uttered at the time of her parting, Clifford could not bring himself to believe that she had any true affection for him.

"For," he would repeat over and over again, "if she loved me, would she not have clung to me, bad as I am?"

He could not even yet divest himself of the romance of his dangerous and evil career.

He could not yet see its black realities; and he had the misfortune to think that others looked with his own eyes.

There is some self-love, some conceit, in us all; and Clifford was not different to others.

There was some inward chord that had become unstrung—some sensitive part wounded; and at times he would think himself more of the martyr than he had a right to imagine himself.

"What would I not have done for her, had she asked me?" he said; "what would I not have given up for her sake? And had she loved me, she would have taken my word, and allowed me the chance of reforming."

In spite of his determining to rejoin the companions so earnestly recommended by Bill Waters—in spite of the burst of enthusiasm with which he started from the house in which he had learned his fate—he exhibited no marked signs of hilarity on entering the charmed circle that so honoured him.

Bill took him direct to the public house in which we were first introduced to him; and he was received with all the honours usually accorded him when he came thither.

There were the usual shouts and cheers, and for a moment Clifford seemed to take pleasure in them; but the smile cleared from his brow, and he grew sad and silent.

"You see," said Bill, in explanation of the captain's melancholy, "he ain't quite well to-night. A little disappointment, and all that sort of thing, d'ye see."

"Aye, we understand; missed a good haul, or had a near shave with the limbs of the law."

"Hey? Oh, yes, somethink of that kind," said Bill; "leastways that's near enough. Here, landlord, bring the captain a dozen of wine, the best; and a bottle of brandy for me. I can't come the thin wash, myself, but the Gentleman and the ladies will get through with it."

By *the ladies* Bill meant several not unhandsome but vulgar and be-painted damsels who were distributed over the apartment, and to whom he winked to close about the Captain, and divert him to the best of their ability.

The wine and the brandy were brought in and quaffed, and Clifford made some attempts at mirth, but they were signal failures.

The ladies, on their part, did their best to amuse him, and by many of those little artifices known only to the sex, strove to win his smile; but after a while Clifford rose suddenly to his feet, and calling on Waters sharply, rushed from the room and out of the house.

"Hillo," said Bill, "what's up now?"

"Don't ask me!—can you not see?"

"I can see nothing; I'm sure we were jolly enough, and all the women were mad about you."

"Bah! speak not of them, they excite no other feeling within me than the deepest disgust."

"Hillo, that's warm for the ladies, and they ain't such a bad lot, neither."

"They please me not, and therefore I will not keep their society."

"But I thought you was a coming round again, and going to forget those as turned round upon you and served you so shabbily."

"I thought I could, but it is impossible."

"More's the pity."

"Oh! Waters, Waters, where is she—where is she?"

"What, the young she?"

"Evelina—Evelina."

"Well, I'm sure I don't know, and I'm sure I don't much care, such ungrateful birds don't suit Bill Waters."

"Speak not disrespectful of her, or I shall force the words back into your throat. Her name must ever be sacred in my presence."

"Oh, well, if you're a going on like that I'll shut up. I don't want to say anythink agin' the young 'ooman, but—"

"No more, no more, or we may become enemies on the instant."

"Very good, Captain, I'm done: not another word will I say about her without you gives the cue."

"Would that I knew what had become of her. Fool

that I was not to force her to remain beneath that roof. Fool—fool!"

"You want to know where she is?"

"I would give the world to know."

"Well, it's easily done. I'll go on the track, and find out. It's not the first job of the sort I've been on."

"Thanks—thanks," said Clifford. "I will trust to you."

It mattered not to Bill what "the Captain" required him to do. In his service he was always happy, and so he accepted this office with a great deal of pleasure, although he could not rid himself of the thought it was all a waste of time, and that the individual about whom such a stir was made was entirely unworthy the trouble.

They separated—Bill to at once commence his mission, and Clifford to roam about and try to dispel the gloom gathering about him, in rest.

Next day, as already stated, he found and perused the papers of his friend's box, but this only added fuel to flame, and set his mind more than ever on the rack; more particularly as what he had heard in the lawyer's office seemed to bear directly on the mystery surrounding the birth and parentage of his beloved Evelina.

The lightning wings of time soon brought round the seventh day since that on which the journey into Buckinghamshire had been made.

On this day our hero could find no rest; he was astir with the dawn, and could not find peace at home or abroad.

An idea possessed him.

He would ride to Winterleigh.

There was no possible reason that guided him in this decision.

He could not have found an excuse for so singular a determination; but go he would, and go he did.

Acting on that impulse which so often and so furiously swayed him, he ordered his mare to be saddled, and in less than two hours after the dawn of day, he was riding out of London.

He passed the house of his old friend Job Winchurst, and paused not to bait his steed.

On, on; he felt he must go on without delay.

Forward, on the aimless errand.

The result of this long ride is already before the reader.

Hearing at the village inn that all the people, headed by the young baronet, had crossed the meads to swim the maid of Miss Evelina—as she was commonly called at Winterleigh—on the supposition of her being a witch and murderess, Clifford determined to follow.

The name of Evelina was sufficient to interest him in one who had been connected with her, in however remote a degree, and pricking on the gallant mare, he reached the river just as poor Rose was disappearing, to rise no more.

To snatch her from the water and disappear, as we have related, was but the work of a moment.

Again had he to ride from Winterleigh, within seven days, bearing with him a persecuted female.

It seemed as if fate had designed him for the champion of the oppressed, the upholder of virtue, and the avenger of vice.

But for the stain—the deep, dark stain—on his name, he would indeed have been the Admirable Crichton of his time.

Away he rode, back again on the well-remembered road, back again towards the great metropolis.

The gallant steed, with the swiftness of the wind, bore him on bravely, and he did not draw rein until far from the village, and night had thrown its mantle over the earth.

At length he felt that it was safe to stop in the wild flight, and dismounting from his mare, he took the inanimate girl in his arms, and laid her gently on a sloping bank by the wayside.

Drawing his knife he severed the cord that cut so roughly into her injured foot, and released it from the shoe that now tortured it so much.

The cords had slipped from one of her wrists in her last struggles in the water, and her hands were free; but they were much swollen and discoloured.

At first Clifford thought that he had been too late; for there was no sign of returning animation in the poor persecuted girl.

Her eyes were closed, her lips livid, her face cold and pale, as if death had done its work. There was no pulsation of the heart—no breath to speak of life, and give hope.

Clifford tore from his pocket a flask of *eau-de-vie*, and forcing it between the teeth of the girl, poured the greater part of its contents down her throat.

He next tore off the heaviest of her soddened garments, and threw them away, replacing them with his own warm cloak.

Gently he enveloped the maiden in its voluminous folds, and then, once more taking her in his arms, he sprang on the back of Brilliant, and bearing his burthen as if she had been but an infant, close to his heart, he pillowed the poor inanimate head on his shoulder, and thus resumed his journey, but slower than heretofore.

"Gently, old girl; gently," he said to Brilliant; "we must have no hurry now, or. if the life still lingers in this poor frame, we shall drive it out. Gently, gently."

The mare needed no admonition.

She cantered slowly and lightly along, as if she had been a ladies' hack for years, instead of the high-mettled charger, used to bear so rough a rider as Clifford.

"I must seek Job's hostelry once more," was Clifford's thought; and in spite of himself he could not suppress a smile at the idea.

"He will think that I have naught else to do, but ride into Bucks, and rescue distressed damsels."

While he pursues his journey, we will return to the bank of the river, and mark what took place after Clifford disappeared.

As soon as the servants had recovered from the surprise into which they had been thrown, they turned their attention to the prostrate Lewis, who had received a tremendous blow on the head.

They assisted him to rise; but all the life appeared to be knocked out of him.

Lifting him on their shoulders they bore him slowly to the Hall.

The women, and the majority of the villagers, followed, awe-stricken behind.

On entering the Hall they were met by Mother Clifford, who ordered them to bear the wounded man to her chamber.

She did not seem at all agitated at seeing the senseless man borne on the shoulders of his servants.

She looked at his bloody head, and then bade them hasten with their burthen to her room.

She turned and dismissed the gaping villagers, and then slowly mounted the stairs at the heels of those who bore Lewis.

Arrived at her chamber, she bade the men sit the wounded man in her own great chair.

They obeyed her, and she then bade them leave the room.

They would have lingered, but she stamped her foot impatiently, and then they were gone.

They knew her well, and did not dare disobey her will.

Slinking down the stairs to their own apartment, they wondered what the old woman would do with the insensible victim to Clifford's just anger.

Mother Clifford poured some water from a ewer into a basin, and then washed the wound made by the butt end of Clifford's pistol.

After this she annointed it with an ointment, and plastering it over, proceeded to recall the animation that had so long fled.

She damped his lips with a greenish-coloured liquid she took from a stopped bottle, and which perfumed the room with a faint and sickly smell.

She then applied strong salts to his nose, and in an instant he was on his feet, as free from pain, as if nothing had happened.

"Are you any better?" asked the man,

"Better! What has happened? How came I here?"

"Is your brain so dull?"

"I begin to remember now. The river, the ordeal, the rescue!"

"Yes, and the blow that split you skull and laid you to the earth."

"Aye! the day will come when I pay him for that."

"You remember your assailant?"

"Remember him! I shall never forget him."

"They have not told me his name, but I can guess it. There is but one man who could and would have done this."

"It was Clifford!"

"Yes, Clifford, our natural enemy! As soon as I saw you borne into the house, I said, that is his work."

"It is, it is. Oh! I owe him a heavy debt, and I will pay him in full."

"Unless he should acquit you of it, by dashing out your brains!"

"He would have good fortune to be enabled to do so."

"Has he not nearly accomplished the deed? Beware, lest it be done effectually!"

Lewis shuddered.

"He is a braver, stronger man than art thou, so mind how you play with him."

"In a trial of skill on terms of equality, you would be the victim. I know it, and I warn you not to allow your vanity or your passion to mislead you into any false position. If you would cope with him, play the fox, not the lion; the part will become you best and be more effective, for his ingenuous nature knows no deceit, and cannot foil clever trickery."

"But I am no trickster."

"True, you have not brains enough to plan an effective scheme wherewith to baffle an enemy. I see I must take the initiative."

"You may lead me in this matter."

"Yes, and in all others."

"I know not that."

"But I do. Deceive not yourself, Lewis, you are completely in my power. You are but my passive tool—my puppet, that moves when I pull the strings, and then only. Assume no false position, lest I bring you to your bearing with a rudeness that will not prove acceptable to you."

Lewis would fain have rebelled, but a glance into that awful face, a gleam from that terrible eye, spoke but too plainly of her unlimited power—of his own helplessness.

"As you will," he said; "as you will."

"Yes, it must be as I will. Now listen to me."

"I am prepared."

"Yes, and mark well my words. In the first place, this man must die."

"Yes—we cannot live, we cannot breathe, until he is disposed of."

"Having determined thus, it remains to mark out the mode by which he is to meet his fate. We cannot trust your own arm, and the dagger of the assassin is objectionable; fortunately, there is another course open to us, which relieves us of the responsibility of crime, and saves us from the grasp of the agent we should have to employ. This man is a lawless vagabond, a price is set upon his head, and the executioner awaits him on the scaffold."

"Yes."

"Well, it remains for us to drag him there. The law is a tortoise, that creeps and creeps when it should fly: it is the eagle, that outdoes the wind in swiftness, when it should be motionless. In our case it is the tortoise, and we must transform it into the eagle."

"Yes—yes! But how is this to be done?"

"How is this to be done? Fool! does not your poor

dull brain comprehend that gold is the talisman to effect this change? Gold—bright, shining, gold—will do it.''

"I begin to comprehend."

"It is time you did."

"Tell me what you would have me do, and I will do it."

"You must go to London.''

"Yes; I imagined as much."

"You must find the man they call Jonathan Wild."

"The thief-taker?'.

"Yes; he has a liking for this same boy, and will not, therefore, interfere with him until forced. You must seek him out, and pander to his cupidity. You must feed him with gold, and make him interest himself in you. Having once done this, a bloodhound on the scent is not more relentless—more implacable. He will bring this rash boy to the scaffold, and then we shall be in safety.''

"I will obey you to the letter."

"You had best do so; and, mind, no shrinking from the task. I know you well, and dread lest, when you reach the metropolis, you may become dazzled by its glittering and brilliancy, and in drunkenness and debauchery forget the purpose of your journey, and let opportunities slip by unheeded.''

''You may trust me. In all my hate, thrust on by a longing for revenge, I shall not forget myself. Believe me, I am to be trusted now."

"I hope so."

"I am, indeed; and to-morrow sees me engaged in my task."

"Not to-morrow. A week or two must elapse ere you are fit to undergo the fatigue and excitement in store for you. For a few hours the wound in your head is painless, but the effects of the drug I have administered will soon wear off, and then you will become prostrated, and incapable of moving from your couch. I could do much for you, but it is best to let nature take her course. My drugs are too potent for so weak a brain."

"You do not mean to tell me that I shall suffer illness."

''Yes; it may be a long and trying one. Such blows as you have had leave their effects behind them a great while."

'' But you will help me ?"

"I would rather not."

"You will not let me suffer; look upon me, I am well now. Why should I return to weakness, and become again the victim of pain?"

"I could restore you with a touch, but *I dare not*."

"And wherefore ?"

"Because there is that in the touch for which you would not care to pay."

"I do not comprehend you.'

"Indeed! Am I unintelligible? I mean that I derive my power from one who does not dispense favours gratis. You would not care to become a slave of—"

"Hush, hush! I comprehend you. Look—look at the cat! Good God, how terrible."

The white cat, that had been lying at full length on the hearth, now rose to its feet, and, arching its great back, glared at Lewis out of its terrible pink eyes, and gave utterance to such cries as drove the colour from the man's face, and set his heart violently palpitating.

"Down," cried Mother Clifford to the animal, " down, I was wrong to speak at all. Begone," she said, turning to Lewis, " begone: this is no place for thee !"

Lewis was only too glad of the chance to fly, and made a precipitate retreat to the entrance.

He paused awhile, and applied his ear to the door.

From within came sounds of mourning, and low cries of pain and distress.

There was another sound, as if another person were speaking.

Could he be deceived?

He listened again.

Two voices!

"Yes, two voices," he said; " and yet I left but the woman in the chamber."

He thought for a moment.

A shudder crept through his frame.

"Powers of mercy," he said, rushing from the spot; " the cat—the cat must be some awful familiar."

CHAPTER XIV.

JOB AND BOB PREPARE FOR REST AND GET DISTURBED— A DROWNED WOMAN—JOB TURNS NURSE—BETWEEN LIFE AND DEATH.

IT was near midnight.

The "Harvest Home" was wrapped in silence, and a gloom overhung the house.

All the lights, save that in Job's bar, were out, and there was no sign of life in the little wayside house.

Job sat in his little bar parlour, smoking a pipe before a waning fire; at his elbow was a stiff glass of pine-apple rum and boiling hot water.

In the kitchen, sound asleep over the fire, were Bob and the maid.

Save this trio the house was empty.

Job was reflecting.

"It's bad times," said Job to himself, " awful bad times; nobody seems to come this road now. I s'pose all the business of the world goes on on some other road. Here I sit all day long, and smoke my pipe and drink my rum like, like—anythink, and never a soul comes. If it warn't for the little sum in the Bank of London I should go to smash, and become a precious bankrupt—that's what I should become. and then the "Harvest Home" would go to some other feller; and if he wouldn't have it, it would go to, to—the devil ! and a werry good job too. Aye me ! I wish as how I'd a got married back in the good old days, and, then, I wouldn't a been sitting here, a lonely old codger, a smoking my pipe and drinking my rum like, like a— like a lonely old codger ! It's a cussed bad line I've got into, thinking about getting married. and so on. Ever since that Clifford came here, and brought his young lady with him, I've done nothing but curse my fate that I hadn't got married, and had some one to share my troubles, my money, my rum, and—"

He took out his pipe, and glanced at it. He was about to add, " my pipe," when the thought struck him that the gentler sex were not addicted to the use of the fragrant weed, and so he dismissed the idea in disgust, and substituted therefor,

"And my everythink else. I s'pose I should ha' been a happier feller then; but it's no matter. What's happiness? What's women? What's *anythink*? Why *anythink !* that's what it is."

Job continued his philosophising until his pipe was burnt out, and then he turned his thoughts to his rum and water.

He swallowed the spirit of the pine-apple apple flavour with extreme gusto. and finding that he had nothing else to do he looked at the clock.

It struck twelve.

"That's it," said Job; " twelve of 'em—bed-time. Now, to wake up them heavy heads in the kitchen."

The heavy heads did not require his assistance in waking.

The clock had informed them that they could retire to rest, and, rising with one accord, they yawned in concert, shook themselves. yawned again, and, from some inexplicable cause, said,—

"Oh, dear !"

After this the girl seized two small lamps, which she lighted. Taking one in her hand, she nodded to Bob, and said,

"All right.'

In reply to which he said,

"Go it, then."

This probably meant "Go to bed," for it was no sooner uttered than the girl was gone.

"Hillo, there !" shouted Job.

"Now, then, governor."

"Come along, Bob. Close up the yard gates, and then rake out the fires; it's bed-time.'

"So it is," said Bob, advancing to the bar ; "so it is, governor, and a precious cold bed-time it is."

"By which you mean to say that a dose of rum and hot water wouldn't come amiss afore you go out into the cold to close them 'ere gates ?"

"Which them's my sentiments to a T, governor."

"Bob," said Job, with great gravity : "Bob, ain't you getting addicted to rum."

"Not as I knows on, governor.'

"I thought you was."

"Not a bit. Why, what could a put that into yer head ?"

"Well, it struck me that your nose was becoming more pine-appley in appearance, and that there was a stronger essence of Jamaica than ever about yer."

"No."

"Yes."

"Ah, you're only a-goin' on."

"Bob, I'd scorn to go on, and I only spoke as a Christian, so that you mayn't go off."

"Why, I don't drink 'arf what you do."

"No, but you see we're different in the constitution line. You're a little 'un, and a wiry 'un, and the rum ain't got much to eat through in you, but in me it's different—I've got a substance—a substance, Bob."

"Which means paunch."

"Which means corporation, Bob, and rum will only reduce my fat. Now don't you see ?"

"Well, there's somethink in yer argyment; 'spose I take to best brandy ?"

"If you do, Bob—now I don't want to be a blackguard, and go a swearing, but if you do, I'll be d—d ! What d'ye think of that?"

"I'm cussed if I know what to think, only I must drink somethink, and if it ain't rum it's some other liquor, so you may take yer choice."

"Well, Bob, stick to rum—stick to rum. Brandy ain't good for yer. Besides, it's awfully dear."

Bob now swallowed his rum, and was rubbing his hands preparatory to going out to shut up the yard gates.

"Well," he said, " I 'spose I must shut 'em up again—only devil a horse in the stable, and it do look queer to go shutting up gates to keep in nothink at all."

"What ! d'ye call my cob and my trap, and my property nothink ? '

"Well, no, but you know what I mean "

"I'm cussed if I do."

"Well, I mean it's a sort o' sham to shut the yard as if it contained all the world, when there ain't nothink but our own machinery in it. It don't look the cheese, and it grieves me so, you can't think ; for I looks back, and I thinks to myself, thinks I, five year agone I've seed a dozen cobs and spanking chargers in them stalls ; and many's the morning we had a pound afore breakfast from them as is now absent, and gone some other road. Blest if I know what is come to 'em, I don't."

"No more do I ; but it'll take a turn, Bob, it'll take a turn."

"I 'spose is will."

"And if it don't, we won't break our hearts."

"No, governor. I think as how we're both pretty well off. Thanks to you and the travellers five year agone, I can put my hand upon a goodish penny ; and so it's no use caring about dull times. Besides, it do seem ungrateful, after making a pile o' money, to fret for more. I will shut up the gates, and go to bed contented."

"Here, here !"

Bob applied a light to the caudle in his horn lantern,

and, closing the gates, made three paces towards the door, when sounds fell upon his ear that at once arrested his attention.

"A hoss at full gallop, or Jim's a Dutchman," he said, turning, and looking Job straight in the face, as if defying him to contradict his statement.

"What, a hoss at this time o' night?" said Job ; "that's singular."

"Hark !"

They both listened, and the ringing sound of a horse's hoofs fell upon their ears.

"You're right, Bob," said Job ; " you're right again, my boy ; it is a hoss."

Another moment and the horse was stopped at the door, and a voice without was heard crying—

"Hillo, within there ; lights, lights !"

"Hey," said Job ; " I know that voice.'

"I'd swear to it among a million," said Bob, rushing out ; "it's the Gentleman !"

Job was advancing to the door to meet the late arrival, when Clifford entered the house, bearing in his arms the inanimate form of Rose.

"Hillo, Job," said Clifford ; " have you a fire ?"

"Yes ; come in the bar parlour. What's this ?"

"A poor girl whom I have rescued from cruel persecutors. Assist me with her.'

Job lent a willing hand in bearing the inanimate form into the bar, while Bob took the mare to the stable.

"My eyes," said Job, glancing at the mangled feet and wrists of the poor sufferer, "but she has been served bad."

"Served bad ! fiends could not have inflicted worse torture. Good God ! That such beings should be called men, and be permitted to crawl the face of the earth without incurring the reward of such crimes as they are guilty of !"

They laid Rose before the fire, and adopted every measure of which they could think to restore animation, and set the blood once more flowing through its channel.

After a while their efforts proved successful, and they had the satisfaction of beholding the girl move once more.

The slight motion, however, appeared to occasion her exquisite pain, and was beyond endurance.

She sank back into the arms of her preserver.

"She is better now," said Clifford ; " much better. She will recover from the effects of the drowning, but it is these bruised and sprained limbs of which I think. What can be done for them ?"

"Sprains ; my dear fellow, leave 'em to me. I know all about 'em. I believe I've sprained every joint in my body. I can treat 'em better than any doctor in the kingdom ; but it's no manner o' use talking. Just hold up her head and bathe her temples, whilst I go up stairs and rouse up that girl, if she is to be roused up ; and I've serious doubts on the subject, knowing her weakness is sleep.

Job trotted off with the lamp that was lighted by the girl for Bob's use, and was soon banging away at the door of the girl's room.

"Hey, hey," he shouted. "I say, Milly, Milly, wake up, will you ?"

No reply.

"Milly, devil take it—Milly ; here, wake up."

Still no answer.

"It's what I'd rather not do, seeing as how I never face a 'oman in her night-dress, but there's no help for it ; in I must go."

He opened the door of the girl's room, and entered.

Milly was hid away somewhere under the bedclothes, and her snores alone spoke of her whereabout.

"Milly," shouted Job ; " Milly, why the devil don't you wake up ?"

But Milly was too sound asleep to answer.

Job advanced to the side of the bed and reiterated his shouts, but there was still no reply.

Milly declined answering.

Job became petulant.

He pinched the heap under the bed-clothes, and then shook it roughly, but this would not do.

Job then pulled off the clothes, and applied his fist more vigorously than ever to the region of Milly's head.

This had the desired effect.

Milly turned on her side, and said—

"I knew it."

"You knew it—what the deuce did you know?"

"It was the brindled cow that calved the black steer they sold in Smithfield market."

"Oh, d—n the black steer! She's dreaming. Milly!"

"Hey?" cried Milly, starting up in the bed, and confronting her master. "Hey? Yah! Murder! Fire! Robbers!"

"What the devil do you mean you lunatic!"

"Get out—get out! I ain't the master, and I've no money."

"What the devil d'ye mean?"

"Hey?" said Milly, rubbing her eyes, and staring at Job. "Oh, measter, measter! I did'nt think it o' you!"

"What the deuce didn't you think?"

"Why, that you would take advantage of a poor young girl."

"Me! Advantage! Oh, curse your foolery! Here we've been banging away at that door, to make you hear, for over an hour, and then I came in and banged away at you; but it was no go; you wouldn't wake; and it was nothing but the cold air that brought you round. Come, turn out."

"What, is the house on fire?"

"No, it isn't a fire, neither, and ain't agoing to be, as I knows on—leastaways it ain't at all likely; but there's a poor young girl below as has been nearly drowned, and I want you to help her to her bed—that's all. *Now* will you open your eyes.

Milly was a good sort of a girl, and became much concerned at hearing of the misfortune to one of her own sex.

"I'll be there as soon as I can," she said, as Job left the room.

"Very well," said Job; "don't go to sleep again—that's all."

He quitted the apartment, and strode along the little gallery to the stairs.

As he approached the landing, he almost fell over a *great white cat.*

The animal spat at him, and after showing some symptoms of spite, disappeared in the gloom.

"Curse the cat!" said Job, "it almost broke my leg."

Beyond the surprise of seeing a strange animal in his house, Job heeded not the apparition of the cat.

Had he, however, but dreamt of its owner, and suspected that its home was at Winterleigh, he would have experienced some other sensations.

He descended to the lower apartments, and bustled back to the bar parlour, where he found Clifford and the fair-girl he had brought to the inn.

"It's all right," said Job, "all right, my boy. Nelly *has* woke up, and will be here directly. She's a fine girl, when she's awake, and I think she's all right now."

Rose now drew a heavy sigh, and opened her eyes.

She stared wildly at those who held her.

"Where am I?" she asked.

"With friends," said Clifford; "with friends, fair one; have no fears."

"Oh, the pain, the pain I endure!"

"Do you, though?" said Job. "Well, never mind my dear, Milly will be here presently, and then I will find something that will soon dispose of the pain. Oh; we will. Milly's a clever girl when she's awake, and if we get her to rub in the oils I'll give her, you will be out of pain in less then no time, and as happy as—and as happy as—and no mistake about it."

"But where am I?"

"Briefly," said Clifford. "Heaven directed me to you aid when you were in the power of your cruel persecutors. I snatched you from the water, and bore you away to this place."

"The Harvest Home, ten miles out of London; well known house of call for all respectable travellers; good accommodation for man and beast," said Job.

"Ah," said Rose, "I can remember all now; that terrific scene in the hall—the flight to the wood—the dead body—the torture they made me endure in dragging me to the river—the cruel ordeal—and then all is a blank."

"And a good job too," said the host, "a very good job, my dear. It's a pity such a poor young thing as you should remember any time of the suffering you have undergone. You know enough now to make you disgusted with all mankind."

"Except those about me," said Rose, "oh, gentlemen; how can I thank you?"

"Thank me," said Job; "I've done nothing to be thanked about. It's this gentleman as is to be thanked if anybody is. Oh, he is a kind-hearted one, he is. He would'nt see a poor young woman put upon, he would'nt. No, no; he's the real sort, and no mistake; and it's proud old Job always is to have him beneath his roof."

"Nonsense, Job, nonsense," said Clifford, who never could bear praise; "don't talk such utter stupidity."

"It ain t stupidity," said Job; "and them as knows you'll bear me out. You're always a doing some good or other, and you knows it."

"Heaven will bless you for your goodness," said Rose, looking up into Clifford's face with tears in her eyes; "the good never go unrewarded."

"There is comfort in those words," said Clifford, "much comfort. Perhaps Heaven will yet look upon me with compassion.

Milly here arrived, and Job signalled to Clifford to raise the sufferer.

With as much care as if she had been an infant Rose was lifted into the arms of her new-found friends, and carried to the chamber hastily prepared for her above.

A fire burned brightly in the grate, and in a few minutes Rose was laid on her couch, and left in the care of Milly, who did her best to relieve the sufferer of her garments, with as little pain as possible.

Job returned to the bar-parlour, and commenced preparing with great alacrity, a glass of mulled port wine, which he averred was the finest thing in the world for the women.

"They're poor, soft creatures, sir," he said to Clifford, who stood by the fire, moodily observing his movements; 'poor soft things, sir, and you can't be too delicate with 'em. Once I had a notion that they were fed solely upon sugar and jellies, and all that sort of thing; but I got to know better in the course of time, although I still think that the more delicate the food supplied the better they get on.

Clifford smiled at this theory, but still said nothing.

Job for some moments busied himself with the wine, and then, suddenly looking up in Clifford's face, said—

"I say, sir—how d'ye manage it?"

"Manage what, my friend?"

"Why, picking up all these wonderfully handsome girls, and scampering all over the country with 'em in the dead o' night? One would think you had nothing else to do but to run about and rescue damsels in distress. You put me in mind of a feller I read of in an old poetry book, written by a cove as did'nt know how to spell correct. His name was Spencer. Well, he was always at this sort of game; but I thought the time had gone, and all the damsels had been rescued, married, and buried many years ago."

"I know not how to answer you. Some men are ordained for special purposes. Place them in what position you will, the predilection for some peculiarity will show itself in the most unmistakeable manner. Fate has much to do with it, as I think; for certainly fate is ever throwing me into contacts of this kind. It was fate, and

no seeking on my part that earned for me the title of the Ladies' Highwayman. I have sought to change this order of things, but the effort has been in vain. Do what I will, I seem thrust into positions that force upon me, as the necessity, the maintenance of my character for gallantry."

The wine was now quite ready for the patient, and Job poured it into an old-fashioned silver cup, and then carried it to the chamber of the sufferer.

He knocked softly at the chamber door, and, after a little while, Milly came out to him.

"Here, give her this," said Job; "give her this, and it will do her good. How is she now?"

"You can see for yourself."

Job entered the room, and found poor Rose on the couch. She was thoroughly exhausted, and pain had told its tale upon her.

Her head lay on the great pillow of the old-fashioned bed, and her face rivalled in whiteness its snowy covering.

Her little mouth was extended, and her lips were all but colourless.

There was, moreover, a pinched expression about the nose that spoke of pain and suffering.

Her breathing was quick, and very low, and, save now and then, when a sharp twinge of pain awoke her to consciousness, she lay still and inanimate as one in a trance.

"What d'ye think?" asked Milly.

Job shook his head.

"She do look bad, don't she?"

"She does. She's weak, she's weak, that's all. If she could only swallow this."

Milly went to the bedside, and took the hand of the sufferer within her own.

A moment, and poor Rose opened her eyes.

"How are you now?" asked the girl.

"Ill, ill, and in sad pain. Who is there?"

"It's only the measter; he's brought you some nice wine. Do 'ee think 'ee could swallow it?"

"No, no, I am too weak."

"That's it," said Job; "that's it, my dear. You want some new life put into you, and this is the stuff to do it. Don't tell me of physic, and such like. This is the kind o' thing. Now, have a good drink at it, and in ten minutes you'll be as right as—as—you'll be right again."

Rose smiled faintly, and shook her head, but Job was not to be put off thus.

He advanced with his miraculous draught, and held it close to the lips of the girl.

Milly lifted her head, and the beverage was sipped.

A very little of it would have served Rose, but Job would not be denied.

He held the cup to her lips again and again, and at last the girl dropped back on her pillow in a profound slumber.

"That's the sort of thing, Milly," said Job. "Now, if she would but sweat."

Milly threw two extra blankets on the bed, and in a few minutes the watcher had the satisfaction of seeing the perspiration break out on the brow of the sufferer.

"She'll do now," said Job; "there's nothing like sweating it out."

Job was right to some extent, and she certainly benefitted under his treament, but she was dangerously ill. Until daylight they watched her with unceasing care, and each time Clifford came to the door of the chamber to ask for the sufferer, the answer given was, 'She lingers between life and death."

CHAPTER XV.

WHAT BEFEL EVELINA—THE KIND FRIEND AND THE NEW HOME.

For some minutes after leaving the gorgeous home prepared for her by Clifford, Evelina continued to walk rapidly through the streets.

She flew onward, until at last the conviction of her position came forcibly upon her, and she suddenly stopped.

"Where am I flying?" she asked herself.

An echo answered:

"Into the jaws of danger!"

She looked about her in bewilderment.

She was at the bottom of Pall-mall and now gazing at St. James's Palace.

For the first time she felt that she had been premature.

"Heaven help me!" she cried, "whither am I going? whither shall I go?"

It was late now, and save in those houses where revelry was being held, the streets were silent as the grave; the only sound heard being the voice of the night watch calling the hour.

All was strange to the young girl, and she could not comprehend her position.

She reflected.

"Shall I ask some one to direct me?" she said, and then a moment's thought assured her that this would be the very height of folly.

"I had best take my chance!" she said, "and leave all to fate."

She stood on the spot where she had first come to a standstill, and appeared spell-bound.

The fact was, that in the great terror that had seized her she found her strength and power of action give way, and knew not what to do.

Leaning against a wall opposite the palace, she fixed her eyes vacantly on the grim old building, before her mind gave way to thoughts.

How long she thus remained she could not say, but it appeared a great while.

She was recalled to consciousness by a burst of loud laughter, in her immediate neighbourhood.

She started and would have fallen, but her limbs refused their office, and she stood motionless as heretofore.

In a few moments their issued from the opposite side of the way, a party of young officers of the King's Guards.

It was from thence the merriment proceeded.

It so chanced that they crossed the road at the very spot where Evelina stood.

The moon mounted from behind a vault of clouds, and threw its rays full upon her, revealing her exquisite form, to the group of astonished gallants.

"Hillo," cried one, " a lady, by all that's beautiful."

"Why, my sweet one," said another, " what brings thee here, gazing so sorrowfully at the palace yonder?"

"Ask no impertinent questions, Danvers: can't you see that the fair one awaits her gallant spark, who doubtless lingers too long within the precincts of the palace?"

"Bah!" cried another, "there is no one in the palace now but lackeys and clerks of the stable or kitchen. I'll wager the lady was anticipating the coming of some such individuals as ourselves. She appears a wench of taste."

It was evident that the whole party was heated with wine, and mad with excitement.

They spoke incoherently and seemed to have no particular guard over their tongues or demeanour.

Poor Evelina was sorely terrified.

"Now," said one of the party who had not yet spoken, "you may be all in the wrong, so the best way is to allow the lady to speak for herself. Madam, pray explain your presence."

Evelina essayed to speak.

At first her tongue clove to the roof of her mouth.

She, however, after an effort, conquered her terror, and said in a low tone,

"I pray you, gentlemen, pass on. I am terrified at your presence, and would fain be alone."

"Oh," said the one who had been addressed as saucily, "that's a most uncomplimentary speech, young lady. To order us forward is cruel, but to say that our presence terrifies you is positively galling in the extreme."

"Do, pray leave me. I am unused to such language; indeed I am, and I sink with fright."

"Nonsense, that will not do for us," they said. "We are used to the wiles and pretty tricks of your amiable sex, and more particularly of that class of which, as a matter of course, you are a member; so save yourself the trouble of being so coy and gratify our curiosity by explaining your presence in the precincts of St. James's at this hour of the night, or rather morning."

"I cannot."

"You must."

"Since you press me," said Evelina, "I can only tell you that I have rushed thoughtlessly from the home of one who shielded me from harm, and who would, had I so willed it, have been a kind friend to me."

"But you did not care about him, or had a quarrel and so rushed away from his arms and thought St. James's the most likely place in which you might find one with whom you could live in more comfort."

A suspicion of the meaning of the words flashed across the brain of the poor girl.

"Good God," she cried, "that I should be subjected to an indignity like this. Are you men, I will not say gentlemen, for your tone, your language, and your bearing tell me plainly that you can have no claim to such a title. Have you no feeling of pity and no power of discernment in you? If you have, for the love of God leave me."

"Hillo! Danvers has touched our fair friend's pride," said one of the party. "His tongue is always too quick. Now, I should use a more conciliatory tone, and take good care not to refer to a past evidently obnoxious to the lady."

"Let me pass!" cried Evelina.

"Oh, no," they cried, "not under any circumstances. We cannot afford to lose you thus."

"I will go."

"Now you are positively rude, and shall not go. You must stay with us, or, at least, with one of us. Now, which do you choose?"

"I choose to pass, so you had best not molest me."

"Our fair friend is in a passion; but no matter. Women, as a rule, always look best when in a decided passion, and so we must not grumble."

"Gentlemen," cried Evelina, "indeed you mistake me. Pray, pray, allow me to pass."

"Under no circumstance."

"I will cry for aid."

"Such cries will be useless. We are supreme in this quarter, and if the watch should be silly enough to venture an interference, we flatter ourselves he would only come off second best, so let us have no more nonsense."

"Let me entreat you to permit me to pass on."

"Threats and entreaties are alike in vain," said Danvers. "Do you not see how desperately we are all smitten with you, and how anxiously we await for your decision, Look at us—one, two, three, four, five—five gay, good-looking, rich, devil-may-care soldiers of the King's Own Guard; we are all desperately smitten with you. Those eyes have fascinated us—that thwart has bewitched us—that voice has enslaved us—that form has driven us to the verge of desperation; but as we cannot all hope for your favours, we must ask you to select one individual, and I assure you all the others will honourably retreat."

"Honour!" said Evelina, "Dare you use the word?"

"And why not? What is there opposed to honour in my proposition?"

"I cannot argue with you, and demand that you will allow me to pass."

"Nonsense—choose,"

"I will not. Oh! will no one release me from this persecution?"

"Come, d—n this mock-modesty, select one of us, or we will toss who takes you."

Evelina attempted to fly, but two of these villains caught her by the arm, and held her against the wall.

"Come, young Miss Modesty, make your selection."

"I will cry for help. Oh! this is unbearable."

"There's nothing for it, fellows, but to toss. Now, out with your coins."

Laughingly the officers drew coins from their pockets, and commenced tossing.

A few minutes was thus passed, and at last the tossing was confined to Danvers and another.

"Now then, Walton," cried Danvers, the very first time. I will cry to you."

Walton covered his coin, and Danvers cried "Head!"

"Head it is," said Walton. "Devil take it, I've lost, and she's yours. Much pleasure may you have, but my impression is you have caught. Tartar."

"Good night, Danvers," cried the others in a chorus, "good-night, and joy be with you."

"I say," said Walton, "let us have all fair. I propose a kiss all round to console us for our loss."

"Bravo," cried his companions.

"Hillo," said Danvers, "no nonsense. I shan't allow that, my boys."

"You won't?"

"No."

"Very well, then, we will go; but you are a stingy old humbug."

They took their arms, and went laughingly away.

"Now, my pretty bird," said Danvers, "you see fate has thrown us together. They are gone, and so we can now throw aside all reserve. Don't you think we were designed for one another? Why, we shall be as happy as turtles."

"Sir," said Evelina, "you see I am weak and ill, and incapable of taking care of myself. I am alone, and unprotected, and therefore I appeal to you to take no advantage of my position. I charge you by your manhood."

"Now, young lady, why continue this farce? Do we not yet understand one another? I like you, and will be a good friend to you, if you behave well. You say you are friendless and unprotected, and, as a matter of course, I understand what that means. Well, I am willing to protect and be a friend to you, so pray place your arms in mine and come along with me to my quarters, without more ado. A little show of modesty is all very well. A little resistance lends a piquancy to an adventure like this, but both can be carried too far. I think you have gone beyond the limits, so now be a little more cosy, and hasten on with me, for the night wanes and morn will be with us ere we can count a hundred."

"Dream not that I will move a step in company with you," said Evelina; "I tell you I am not what you take me to be."

"Well, I am all the better pleased to hear it. But it matters little to me what you are, I like your face, and so your condition and your position is nothing to me. Come on."

He caught her by the arm and attempted to drag her away.

"Help, help!" cried Evelina.

"Hold! Just cease, or I shall use you roughly."

"Help, help!" Evelina continued to scream.

"Devil take you!" cried Danvers, catching Evelina in his arms and lifting her off her feet; "this won't do. Come along, and if there is any more of that squalling I'll make you repent it!"

Heedless of his threats, Evelina continued to cry loudly for help, and attempted to struggle from the arms of her persecutor.

He was, however, far too powerful for her, and, after

some resistance, she gave up her endeavours to free herself and fell across his shoulder, faint and exhausted.

"Oh, you have given in, have you?" said Danvers; "I thought you would. Now for the quarters."

He was about to start off with his victim when a man, habited in the dress of the King's Guards, sprang across the road and, catching him a severe blow between the eyes, felled him to the earth.

He supported Evelina in his arms, and endeavoured to bring back animation once more.

He succeeded.

The girl opened her eyes, and saw at a glance what had occurred.

"I have rescued you from a villain, lady, said the officer, who proved to be a young and remarkably handsome man, with light brown hair and of fair complexion. "He is one of many in the King's Guards who regard not persons, and serve all as you have been served, should they have the misfortune to be as you have been tonight, in the neighbourhood where they can act the blackguard with impunity, without a protector."

"I know not how to thank you for your timely aid."

"Mention it not," said the officer, raising his cap, "I am well repaid in having been fortunate enough to save you from such a wretch."

Danvers now rose to his feet, and Evelina clung to the arm of her new found protector.

"So," said the young libertine, "so, St. Henry, I am indebted to you for that blow, am I."

"To me."

"Very well. I shall take an early opportunity of calling you to account for it."

"You know where I am to be found when wanted."

Danvers answered not.

Cowed and beaten, he, after flinging a glance of rage at Evelina stalked away.

"Poor, contemptible cur," said St. Henry looking after him, "he has not the spirit of a worm, which will turn when stepped upon."

"I fear you have incurred trouble on my account," said Evelina.

"Oh, no, lady; there is no danger, such things as that can only attack defenceless women. He will not molest me."

"But his words —?"

"Mean nothing. In the morning he will send an abject apology, pleading drunkenness as the the excuse for his folly. I know him and his companions of old."

"I trust you are right."

"Be well assured of it."

"And now let me repeat my thanks, and say good night.

"Stay, lady, we must not part thus. In the streets of the city at this hour there are many who will treat you as you have been treated by the scoundrel from whom I have been fortunate enough to snatch you. I must see you to your home."

"Alas!"

"What means that sad ejaculation?"

"I dare not say! Let me bid you good-night; I must hasten away."

Evelina made a step or two in the direction of St. James's Park.

St. Henry followed her.

"It is evident," he said; "it is quite palpable that you are a stranger to this locality, and know not where to go. The park gates are closed, and there is no passage that way. Pray allow me to conduct you to your home."

"Sir, sir," cried Evelina, "if the truth must be spoken —I have no home!"

"How?"

"I will not trouble you with my sad story, for it cannot be of interest to you; and your time can, doubtless, be better occupied than in listening to me. Once more, good night."

"Think me not presumptuous. Think not that I would force from you that which you would conceal; but I must know more before we part. I have a sister of your age, and you remind me of her. Should she be placed in a situation similar to that in which I find you, how thankful should I be for some one to assume the part I am now playing with you. Whatever may be the nature of your misfortune, it is clear you have sought it not; and be you who and what you may, it is a man's duty to offer you the protection he has it in his power to afford; and, therefore, you must explain to me so much as will give me the opportunity of doing you the service of which you evidently stand in need.

Thus pressed, Evelina could not but relate to the young officer the story of her life.

This she did as briefly as possible, concluding her narrative by saying that he who had rescued her proved to be one whose protection she could not accept, but the motive that guided her to this course she studiously concealed.

"What is the name of this gentleman?" asked the young officer, thoughtfully.

"Everton is the name he gave me."

"Indeed."

"Yes. Do you know him?"

"I do not; but the lady who received you on your arrival in London was my mother."

"Mrs. St. Henry your mother?"

"Yes. Unhappily we are, by the death of my father, reduced to something like poverty. My pay is barely sufficient for my own support; my sister has to teach music for a livelihood; and my mother accepted this engagement to relieve me of the weight she but too well knew she was to me."

"Your mother!"

"Yes, my mother, lady. Oh, Heavens!" he cried, "I trust no ill has befallen her with this man whose protection you could not accept."

"I will answer for her safety under his roof. Whatever he may be, she is safe with him."

"But what can this man be that, for a single night, you could not accept his protection?"

"Do not ask me. You will, doubtless, know all from your mother, and now—now leave me."

"Not so. You will come to my mother's house with me, and there, at least, await the light of day."

"I could not be so great a trouble to you."

"My sister will be delighted to make your acquaintance, and I shall esteem this the happiest chance of my life. Pray, pray come with me."

He did not await her reply.

Drawing her arm within his own, he hurried her through the streets in the direction of Westminster.

*   *   *   *   *

St. Henry stopped at a small, but neat-looking, house, near the Abbey of Westminster. and, knocking at the door, was soon admitted by a woman servant.

"My sister has, of course, retired to rest?"

"No, sir," said the domestic, "she's alone with your mother."

"My mother here?"

"Yes, sir; Mrs. St. Henry returned some three hours ago."

"That is, indeed, fortunate," said St. Henry. "Come, lady, let me take you to my mother."

They mounted the stairs, and in a few moments stood before the astonished ladies.

"There, I have brought you a lady with whom you are already acquainted, mother," said St. Henry.

Mrs. St. Henry appeared bewildered at this unexpected apparition, and demanded an explanation on the instant. It was soon given.

The young soldier related all that had passed at St. James's, and Mrs. St. Henry folded the poor young girl to her heart.

"Heaven has been merciful to you," said the lady.

"Very merciful, for it has preserved you from a fearful fate."

St. Henry now demanded to know the reason of his

mother's unexpected return to her own house, and with the consent of Evelina, the lady related the whole of her extraordinary adventure.

"I have before heard of this extraordinary being who, whilst following the vocation of a common thief, has the education and breeding of the most perfect gentleman, but I never anticipated that it would be the fate of one of my family to have come into so close and extraordinary a contact with him."

Evelina found in Adelaide St. Henry a sweet girl of about her own age.

She was as graceful and fascinating as a Hebe, and of a most angelic disposition.

Sincerely did she sympathise with the unhappy position into which Evelina had fallen, and many and deep were the expressions of consolation she uttered to the fair wanderer.

It was near morning before the conversation between the quartette ended and then it was arranged that Evelina should retire with Adelaide, and in sleep try to banish from her mind the recollection of her sufferings.

"I will claim your hospitality for the night," she said, "and in the morning will seek a home in keeping with my position, but Heaven only knows how short may be the period I may have a roof to cover me, for my store is but small, and when it is expended I have no further resources."

"You shall never leave us," cried Adelaide. "It is true we are not rich, but still we can find sufficient for your wants. You shall live with me and be my sister."

Evelina shook her head sadly.

"I could not be such a burden to you," she said.

"You will be no burden," said Mrs. St. Henry, "and we shall be only too delighted to receive you; as Adelaide says, we are not rich, but there is enough for you."

Tears streamed down the face of the young girl as she listened to these kind words, and it was with the deepest gratitude impressed upon her heart that she uttered her thanks to Heaven that night for the blessings it had bestowed upon her in casting her lot among people so good and generous.

CHAPTER XVI.

LEWIS HAS AN INTERVIEW WITH JONATHAN WILD—WHAT IT LED TO.

At the period of our tale the reputation of Jonathan Wild was at its height.

The thief-taker had, by his wonderful deeds of daring in the cause of justice, and by his no less wonderful association with and participation in the doings of thieves and villains, spread his repute over a vast area, and in the then constitution of society he was, by universal consent, acknowlenged the chief actor in the drama of justice.

Reforms have swept away all vestiges of the days in which Wild flourished.

We, who enjoy the protection of an excellent police system, can form but little conception of the days when to a few old and infirm men was intrusted the guardianship of the peace, when railways were little anticipated, and the electric telegraph not dreamt of.

These were the days when roguery held full sway in England, and such men as Wild made gigantic fortunes by plundering society, and casting their protecting influence over thieves and murderers.

Wild is a character in the historical drama of our country, and his portrait is as familiar as that of any individual in this or by-gone eras.

He was, at the time of which we write, just past the prime of life, but only just making his vast power felt.

Universally feared and hated, he held the sceptre over the realm of crime, and through him the majority of London thieves and cut-throats met their fate.

He was peculiar in the manner in which he dealt with criminals.

He would calculate their value to him whilst their health was unimpaired, and their faculties in full play.

He had a ledger, in which was inserted the doings of all with whom he was acquainted. What they brought him was regularly entered to their credit. What their capture and death was worth to him was set against them. Their lease would run out, a balance was eventually struck, and if found against them, they were handed over to the hangman with as little compunction as if they had been so many mangy curs, of which it was desirable he should rid himself.

Personally, Wild was a most revolting man. He was of the middle height, coarse and brutal in bearing, and possessing a head and face whose hideousness could not fail to strike the least observant of men.

His face was marked in every part with old scars and wounds; his nose had been smashed into his face, and his mouth much disfigured with blows. His eyes were those of a cat, and his brow was low and retreating.

Over the greater part of his skull was a massive silver plate, which protected the brain, the major portion of its natural covering being slashed off. This terrible sight was, however, screened by a full bag-wig, which also covered most of his terrible face.

He was of great strength, and his muscular development was astonishing.

To describe his costume would be a task we have no wish to engage on, as by the number of disguises he was constantly assuming, his original style of dress would be very difficult to hit upon.

Such was Wild.

His house, near Newgate, was in itself a formidable prison, resembling, in detail, the construction of the Italian Inquisition.

On all sides were mysterious passages, sliding panels, and trap-doors, used in Wild's transaction of business.

The room he called his office was a perfect marvel of construction, built, as it was, for the purposes of his dangerous calling.

There were places in it where witnesses might lay concealed, and overhear all that passed, without being seen.

There were holes used for the identification of criminals.

There were traps in the floor, acted upon by springs, which precipitated victims into the cellarage of the house, and there were places for the concealment of a whole troop of subordinates, who could rush to the assistance of Wild on the slightest signal.

The walls of this singular place were decorated with various weapons used by the thief taker.

In one corner was a large glass case, which Wild called his museum.

It contained some memento of every noted criminal with which its owner had had dealings, not the least conspicuous being a number of human skulls, all labelled and marked with scrupulous care.

Such was the house of the thief-taker.

It was about a week after Clifford had sent Lewis Norman Winterleigh to earth with a broken skull, that that individual, pale and emaciated from the effects of the punishment he had received, walked into the office of Wild.

He found that celebrity seated at his desk, his eyes fixed upon a book before him.

He was introduced by a little withered Jew, who said,

"A shentleman from the country to speak vith Mister Vild."

The thief-taker raised his eyes, and, finding a stranger before him, rose from his seat, beckoned the Jew to retire, and offered Lewis a chair.

"What may be your business, sir?" asked Wild.

"It is of a very urgent nature," replied Lewis, "a very

urgent nature. I desire the capture of a criminal of whom I stand in bodily fear."

"Humph!" said the thief-taker, "that is the usual cry of gentlemen who come to me. Who may be the man you desire to rid yourself of ?"

"One well known to you. His name is Paul Clifford!"

"Paul Clifford!"

"Yes, I know, or rather I have been informed, that this man is a favourite of yours ; or, at all events, that you hold him high in your estimation. I am, therefore, prepared for whatever objections you may urge against his capture and condemnation."

"Ve-ry good," said Wild, slowly. "What is your name ?"

"Lewis Norman Winterleigh, Baronet, of Winterleigh."

"Lewis Norman Winterleigh, Baronet, of Winterleigh," repeated Wild, as he wrote the name in a book. "Yes, good ! What more have you to ask ?"

"I should rather ask, what have you now to ask, having heard me ?"

"Very little ! What has occasioned this hatred on your part, for hatred must be the motive that prompts this act ?"

"You are right, I do hate him."

"And the cause ?"

"He has crossed me."

"In a love affair ?"

"Yes."

"I anticipated as much, he is always doing such things. Is that all ?"

"Yes."

This was said slowly, and with a reluctance that told the shrewd thief-taker that the answer was a lie.

"Well then, Sir Lewis, I am bound to tell you that I cannot hang Clifford simply because he has robbed you of the affections of a pretty girl. I only act on strong motives. I can discover no motive at all."

"Indeed ! but I can."

"That may possibly be the case ; but I cannot. If you choose to conceal from me the real motive that prompts you, I must at once dismiss you."

"Dismiss me ! I am no beggar. I can pay you for your services."

"Your presence here is sufficient to assure me of that fact. I do not doubt your ability to pay."

"You decline to assist me ?"

"Hark you, Sir Lewis, there stands the case ; if you say you know Clifford to be a favourite of mine, I admit the fact. I admire the man. Well, being my favourite is it just to suppose that I would sacrifice him to your jealousy ? Particularly as my reward for putting away a rival would be in all probability a thousand pounds."

"I never dreamt of so large a sum."

"Of course not ! Just as I anticipated. Now, Clifford is worth to me full fifty thousand pounds, so you comprehend how loth I am to part with him, and how small a temptation is your offer."

"Confusion ! I never anticipated this."

"Of course not. People commit sad errors sometimes. You're wrong in supposing that I value human life so cheaply. Good morning."

"Nay ! I dare not go thus. I tell you this Clifford must be destroyed."

"And I have told you my feelings on the subject."

"But we must not part thus. There is more in this than I have spoken."

"I thought as much."

"Oh, that I could tell you all."

"And why should you not do so ? I am the repository of a whole volume of secrets, and no one can say that I have betrayed one."

"I have a mind to reveal mine to you."

"Do so ; you cannot place it in better hands."

"Listen, then. I suspect—mind, I only suspect, that this highway robber is the real heir —"

"To the estates you hold? Well, I always thought Clifford well born."

"The heir under a will made by Sir Lascelles Winterleigh, on his death bed, and which has been lost."

"But which might be forthcoming, to your entire discomfiture. I comprehend you better now."

"Well, now you know the motive that actuates me. What do you say to my proposition ?"

"Stay, stay ; I must know more before we settle upon anything. What do you know of Clifford?"

"Very little beyond what has been related to me by his grandmother, Mistress Clifford, of Winterleigh."

"What, the old hag of the wood?"

"The same."

"I know her well ; but this story grows mysterious. Explain."

Lewis here related the whole history, as clearly as he was able.

From time to time the thief-taker made notes of what fell from his client, and, after he had finished speaking, said :—

"Well, Sir Lewis, the case stands thus :—Clifford is your successful rival, and the heir to estates you hold. A will has been made, and is in existence, bequeathing all the Winterleigh property to him, and when this document is forthcoming, the highway robber has but to establish his identity, in order to thrust you into beggary and misery. Now if you wish me to stir in this matter on your side, you must pay ten thousand pounds down ; and give me security on your estate for, say, thirty thousand more, on the death of the man you want me to dispose of."

"Forty thousand pounds ! Absurd !"

"You think so ! Very good ! very good ! There is no harm done, you keep your money, and are satisfied ; I make use of my information, and am equally pleased ; good day."

"You do not mean to say you would betray me ?"

"I don't say anything of the kind ; but I leave you to judge of what I shall do. Clifford is my friend, and I shall delight in serving him, if I cannot better serve myself by rendering you assistance. I am a man of the world ; and not governed by any Quixotic or chivalrous notions. I serve those best who pay me best. In your case I ask but a fraction, taking into consideration the great good I am doing you, and the magnitude of the estates you have at your disposal ; wherewith to realise the sum required. In your calmer moments you will see that I am right."

Lewis, like most of his class, was a niggard, and grieved to part with a penny, save on himself.

He did not therefore very readily agree to the terms of Jonathan Wild.

"Oh ! that I dared stir alone in this matter," he said, "fool—fool that I was to entrust my secret to another's keeping."

He was silent for some moments, during which Wild regarded him attentively.

"Well," said the thief-taker, at last, "on what course have you decided ?"

"There appears but one open to me."

"And that is to decline my offer ?"

"No ; to accept it."

"Ah, I see you are growing more reasonable. I am glad you see the folly of declining so moderate an offer as mine."

"And for this sum," said Lewis, without heeding Wild's words, "and for this sum you promise to rid me of Clifford ?"

"I promise."

"Then I am satisfied."

"You have reason to be. The work is dirt cheap."

Lewis looked inclined to doubt this assertion, but did not venture on a reply.

"Now," continued Wild, "perhaps you will oblige me with the sum I demand ?"

"What ! before you have done aught to deserve it ?"

"On the instant. I am always paid in advance for such business as this."

Lewis saw that he had nought to do but comply with the request of the thief-taker, and, drawing from his pocket a book, wrote an order on his banker for £10,000.

This he handed to Wild, who folded it carelessly, and tossed it on the desk without, as far as Lewis could see, as much as glancing at it.

"I presume you have no more to say?" said Wild, "and so I will wish you good morning."

"Good morning. When shall I hear from you?"

"Call here to-morrow at this time, and then I may have news for you, but I can make no promises."

"Very well. To-morrow I will be here."

They separated, the Jew showing Lewis to the door.

"Ha, ha!" roared Wild, as he got rid of his visitor, "this is a glorious morning's work. Ten thousand pounds without an effort, and thirty thousand—ah, perhaps ten times thirty thousand in perspective. It is hard if I, who have dealt so successfully with all the rogues of my day, cannot bleed this young baronet to death. And if not him, there is Clifford to fall back upon. Clifford—he's to die at last, is he? Poor devil! So good-looking and clever, too. Well, I don't know about his dying just yet. I think I can so plan matters as to make both these fellows my tools; however, time will reveal the right course. Could I but gain the will of the old baronet, and the proofs of Clifford's identity, he would be my man! I could make most out of him. The proofs, the proofs! Devil take it, what a muddle this affair will put me into if I don't look out. The proofs—well, they may yet be forthcoming."

They were certainly much nearer than Wild anticipated, for at that moment the Jew put his head in at the office door and announced, "Mr. Wickles."

"Of the firm of Wilsnick, Wickles, and Wilsnick, attorneys-at-law," said the ferret, popping his head into the office of Wild.

"Ah, Wickles," said the thief-taker, "walk in, old fellow, how are you?"

"I'm jolly. I may say I'm very jolly. And how's my noble Wild?"

"Oh, as usual."

"As usual is very well. My noble Wild is very well."

"Yes."

"That's pleasant, very pleasant. And how's business?"

"As usual."

"As I remarked before, as usual is very well. Business is, then, very well?"

"Yes."

"That's also pleasant."

"Oh, d—n your pleasants, it isn't after my health and business that you came here, is it?"

"Partly, partly."

"Well, you might have saved yourself the trouble."

"Not a bit of it. Always go about business politely is my motto; it has a better effect, and takes the rough edge off anything unpleasant you may have to say."

"I don't see it. Do you think the prey of the boa-constrictor is any the more pleased that it gets licked all over before being swallowed?"

"Sir! Mr. Wild! I never was the prey of the boa-constrictor, and I'm sure I don't know. I'm referring to humanity, and you descend to comparisons to the brute creation, of which I know but little."

"I know you are a sort of legal cannibal who feeds on human flesh, in preference to aught else."

"That sounds very like a crock accusing his mate, the kettle, of being smutty."

"No matter. I've no time to lose in argument. What is your business?"

"Well, Mr. Wild, I've made a discovery."

"I make fifty every day."

"That's no business of mine. I've made a most important discovery."

"Does it concern me?"

"It all depends upon whether you choose to concern yourself in the matter."

"Well, I may do so if it is worth my while. What is in the wind?"

"Heaps of money."

"Through whom?"

"Now who do you think?"

"I never guess at anything."

"Well, then, through Gentleman Clifford."

"Paul Clifford?"

"The same individual."

"Well, man, can't you speak?" said Wild, impatiently, and all attention to the lawyer. "What is this concerning Clifford?"

"Simply this: He is the son of a late baronet, of Winterleigh?"

"Well?"

"Well, arn't you astonished?"

"Not in the least. Had you said he was the son of the king I should not have been astonished, for Clifford bears about with him the air of a noble of the first water."

"So he does."

"Well, how did you hear of this?"

"I don't mind your knowing, because, of course, you don't split."

"Oh, of course not."

"Well, then, Clifford himself lodged with the firm the proof of his birth."

"Yes; and you, I suppose, broke open his papers and gleaned his secret?"

"Yes."

"I thought as much."

"Well, you would have done the same."

"I don't know that."

"But I do. However, the affair is not worth canvassing."

"But the papers?"

"What are they like?"

"Letters: reports of divorce between Clifford's father and mother, a wedding ring, and certificates."

"Indeed! What is it you propose?"

"I don't know what to propose."

"Or you would not have come to me?"

"I did'nt say that."

"But you mean it, and that's much the same kind of thing."

"Well, well, we must all live, and, to do so, must assist one another. Now, what do you think can be done?"

Jonathan paused.

"It will not do," he said to himself, "to allow this fellow to know of the will, and the real state of the case, or I shall shut myself out."

"Well," he continued, aloud, "I can't advise you to any course. It is clear that Clifford is the son of a dead baronet, but the fact of the marriage being annulled is sufficient to shut out his connection with the family."

"Just so! Then you see nothing to be made out of this business?"

"Nothing. Do you?"

"No. But I want you to put your men on the scent and see if anything can be sifted out in connection with the affair. If the papers were valueless, *Clifford would not have sealed them so carefully and placed them under our charge.*"

"There is something in that and I will see what can be done. Meanwhile keep the papers close."

"I will. But what if he demands them of me?"

"No matter. Give them up. There are ways to regain possession of such things without much bother."

"Oh, you're a genius, Mr. Wild, you are indeed. I'm really charmed to hear you talk."

"Well, I can't say as much for you, and as I'm busy you had best get out."

"And you won't forget to make the inquiries?"

"No."

" And you will communicate with me as soon as you learn anything ?"

" Yes."

" That is good ; very good. And now I must be walking, for I've other fish to fry. By the way, there is another piece of business I wanted to speak to you about, but that is not ripe enough for discussion."

" What business is it ?"

" I shall want you to find for me a lost heiress.'

" Will anyone do?"

" I don't quite know yet, but I think anyone would do, provided she comes to our terms ; however, that is a matter for future cousideration."

With this they parted.

*   *   *   *   *

"Moses," said Wild to his Jew, on the evening of the day of his conversation with Lewis and the lawyer, " Moses, I want to see Clifford."

" Vot, the shentleman "

" Yes."

" Vell, shall I find him ?"

" Do, by all means, and at once. I've business for him."

" Vot sort ?"

" No matter to you. Do as I bid you."

" Vith all the pleasure in life, master. I'm off at vonce."

In another hour Clifford stood before Wild.

" Well," said the highwayman, " you sent for me ?"

" Yes, there's work for you to do."

" Of what kind ?"

" Oh, quite in your own line, I asssure you. There's a ball—a masked ball—to-morrow night. You must attend it."

" To what end ?"

" To make money."

" Wild, I am sick of this, and I did intend—"

" To turn honest ?"

" Yes."

" Oh, indeed. Well, hear me. The moment you take to honesty I turn you off, and that means that the hangman may follow my example. Do you understand that ?"

" I fear only too well."

" No more nonsense! The fact is this work must be done. I know that the Duchess of Lakemont has sent to her banker's for all her diamonds. They are the handsomest in England, and I have long wished to have them in my possession."

" And you put me to steal them ?"

" Of course! Who's so capable of doing the job neatly as yourself. I must have them, and as there is sure to be a magnificent reward offered for them, you will make a good thing out of it.

" Wild! Wild! I cannot do this!"

" I will take no denial. You do this, or go to prison."

" Are you then relentless ?"

" As destiny."

" Then I am lost."

" What do you mean? Am I not your friend ?"

" Yes ! If I get the diamonds, if not—"

" If not, you take the consequence. The diamonds I will and must have ; so no more on the subject."

" Where is the ball ?"

" At Lord Belmore's !"

" And how am I to obtain admission?"

" I have obtained it for you. Here it is !"

" I see, I am to personate the Count de Aramis.

" Yes ! a French count; you can do that well enough."

" Too well !"

" Psha !"

" Oh, did you not know how weary I have become of this life; how sick of its varied phases; how tired of its terrible monotony you would pity me."

" No cant here, Clifford, I can't and won't stand it, you know."

" Well, I will do your bidding, but if I fail ?"

" If you fail! when did you ever fail ?"

" Never! but that is no reason why the time is not come."

" Get from my sight ! I can't stand such croaking ! and mind you bring the diamonds."

Clifford, without another word, left the room.

" Now," said Wild, when he was gone, " now I shall have him. If he attempts to take the diamonds, he is lost. He will be detected, and sent to prison, and I shall have him in my power, either to kill, or hold secure, as I may deem best."

CHAPTER XVII.

THE MASKED BALL—MEETINGS AND RECOGNITIONS—THE MYSTERIOUS FOREIGNER—THE DUCHESS AND THE DIAMONDS.

A MASKED ball was a great rarity in England.

Such entertainments were novelties only rarely introduced into the mansions of the great.

On the Continent they were of course a rage, and an established fashionable institution ; but at home the age of mummery and disguise had died away, and no trace of it remained in its original form.

Lord Belmore was the leader of fashion. Young, rich, and handsome, he was sought for in all quarters, and admired beyond measure.

He had a vast estate and a tremendous fortune, and he was spending it with no niggard hand.

His splendour was the theme of conversation in all quarters, and his entertainments were as much sought after as introductions to the Court itself.

The friend of Lord Belmore had a passport to all sections of fashionable society, and it is not, therefore, to be wondered at that his name was upon the lips of all, and that his house should, throughout the season, be the centre of attraction.

On the night of his masked ball, strings of carriages, conveying the first notables of the land, flocked to his mansion in Pall-Mall, and completely blockaded the road.

Many court carriages were discernible in the crush, and rank and fashion in all their degrees were adequately represented.

His lordship bore a commission in the king's guards, and to all the officers of that brilliant regiment he extended a number of invitations to the ball.

St. Henry, a special favourite with the young nobleman, was invited with his family, and the little circle made great preparations for the festival as soon as it was determined that all were to go.

At first all manner of objections, founded upon the expense that would be incurred, were urged, but St. Henry would not listen to them.

He had, he said, determined that his family should be present, and participate in the great treat of the night, and, after a struggle, he overruled all objections.

Appropriate costumes were thought of and adopted, and the time between the receipt of the invite was expended in making them.

Evelina would have chosen the simple costume of a flower girl, but against this Adelaide strongly protested.

" It is not in keeping with your character or your appearance," she said ; " and, therefore, some other must be thought of. You have been educated in the country, practised rural sports, can follow the hounds, or fly the hawk. You must be Diana."

" Diana ! I should not personate the character."

" Indeed you must," said Mrs. St. Henry; " I agree with Adelaide. The part of the goddess is the one you can best sustain."

It was thus decided upon, and without delay the costume of Diana was purchased, and shaped to the fair girl's lovely form.

No one could deny that it was admirably adapted to

her. Her nobly-proportioned limbs were shown to the greatest advantage in the garb of the huntress, and the taste of Adelaide in selecting it for her was universally praised.

Adelaide adopted the character of Starlight, and wore a wondrous blue gauze dress, sprinkled with stars of silver. On her brow glittered a large star of diamonds, a family treasure, belonging to her mother.

St. Henry wore a Venetian dress, and his mother was habited as became her age and position.

Thus did the little party, fluttering with excitement, set out for the great mansion in Pall Mall.

Had Evelina but dreamt of the being she was fated to meet at this entertainment, she would have thrown off her dress and remained in the quiet of her own home.

Among the foremost of the invited was Sir Lewis Winterleigh.

On arriving in town he had at once fallen into the clutches of Danvers, who, being a gamester and *roue*, found in Lewis a pigeon whom he could easily pluck.

He, therefore, fastened upon him, and made him bleed freely.

Lewis was but too glad to see life, under any circumstances, and looked upon the patronage of Danvers as a complete god-send.

He did not mind paying, and Danvers was never tired of showing him how to expend his cash.

In short, they became inseparables.

"Here Winterleigh," said Danvers, as he broke open the envelope containing Lord Belmore's invite. "I say, here is fun; Belmore gives a fancy dress and masquerade ball to-night, and has sent me an invite for self and friend. You'll go, of course?"

"But I have no dress"

"Nonsense. I can easily procure one for you."

"But why have you but now received the invite? Is it usual to delay so long?"

"Oh, some oversight of Belmore's, but it's no matter. He knows I'm always prepared for such scenes, and so left me till the last. But you will go?"

"I really do not know what to say."

"Say, why say yes. It's awfully jolly. Under your mask you can do as you please, and no one a bit the wiser. I like such games beyond everything."

"Well, I do not mind going, but what shall I wear ?"

"A dress of mine. I have a Spaniard's costume that will suit you, and you can wear a domino. That will hide all objects."

"Very well, then ; I will go."

"That is right. You've no idea of the number of pretty girls you will find there, who, under their masks, will prove agreeable companions. Oh, I love a masked ball ! It is a scene wherein the old restraint of England is thrown on one side, and wherein one breathes a freer atmosphere.

The scene was a brilliant one.

Men and women, habited in every imaginable costume, paraded through the brilliant suite of rooms, and mingled the many beauteous hues of their costumes in one harmonious and continuous stream of colour. The jewels flashed in the myriad of lights, and sweet music sounded without intermission.

It was growing late, when the servants handed from one to the other the name of the Count de Aramis.

The name was repeated to a great number of the guests as Clifford entered the grand saloon.

"The Count de Aramis ! Who is he ? Who knows him ?"

These questions were buzzed about by the fashionable mob. But it appeared that there were but few indeed who had ever heard the name, and none who had ever looked upon the man who bore it.

Curiosity being raised to fever point, Lord Belmore was appealed to.

"Who is your friend, the Count ?"

"I really do not know. Lord ——, of the Foreign-office, asked me for a card of invitation for the Count. I presume he is some diplomatist, or illustrious incog., who, under a mask, wishes to obtain a glimpse of English society."

Clifford, in the guise of a troubadour, walked through the rooms with a listlessness that displayed but little interest in the scene in which he was taking part.

After a slight acknowledgment of the courtesy extended to him by Lord Belmore, he mingled with the crowd, and appeared to take no further interest in the proceedings. At length he seated himself in a recess at the extreme end of one of the saloons, and there gave way to the gloomy thoughts that had agitated him since his interview with the relentless thief-taker.

His reverie was at length interrupted by the voices of a knot of masqueraders near him.

"Bah," cried one, tearing off his mask, "what a relief it is to get this thing off for a while. Were it not for the fun of the thing, I should discard mine entirely."

It was Danvers.

His companions followed his example, and, throwing off their masks, revealed themselves to be the same knot of officers that had assaulted Evelina. With them was Lewis Winterleigh. As that individual unmasked, Clifford raised his eyes. They fell on that cruel, never-to-be-forgotten countenance.

"You here," he thought. "Well, there will be rioting before the night's out, or I know you not."

The officers and their new-found friend commenced a scrutiny of those who formed the principal feature of attraction in the saloon, and, as may be supposed, their remarks were less complimentary and refined, than coarse and emphatic.

Clifford listened to them until he sickened of their talk, and then he again occupied himself with his own thoughts.

After awhile, the voices, or rather the pronunciation of a name by one of them, once more rivetted his attention.

"By jove !" cried Danvers, "here is St. Henry."

"Yes, and with him his mother and sister—and, as I live, the girl we tossed for outside St. James's Palace."

"Hush," cried Danvers, "replace your masks."

They did so.

"Hillo !" cried Lewis. "Am I dreaming, or is that Evelina ?"

"Who the deuce is Evelina ?"

"Look, look, that is she, habited as Diana."

"Do you know her, then ?"

"Know her—I ought, considering we were brought up—I may say—in the same cradle together."

"The deuce !"

"How came she wandering at midnight about the streets of London here, and without a protector ?" demanded Danvers.

"I don't know. She left my roof with some lawless vagabond on the night of Sir Lascelles' death, and I have never seen her until this moment."

"Indeed ! What a romance."

"No matter. Let them pass ; but I am glad I have a clue to her."

Evelina was leaning on the arm of the young officer, to whom she was conversing in a strain of cheerfulness which had not characterised her of late.

But the brilliancy of the scene, the excitement, and the music made her forget the gloom of her life, and awakened a new joy in her bosom.

And so she smiled, and was, to all appearances, happy.

"Thank God for that !" said Clifford, looking after her. "Oh ! I am, indeed, happy to know that she has found friends—such friends as Mrs. St. Henry will be to her. That is a weight from my mind."

He glanced at her again, and a shadow crept over his brow.

"Yes," he murmured, "yes, it must be so. There is no deceiving oneself. She does, or will love him, and I—oh ! I shall die of misery. But I have no right to complain. A thief—a felon—why should I raise my eyes to an angel ? It is the height of presumption, and I will strive to forget her, and learn to bless him she loves."

Once more the voices to which he had previously listened arrested him.

"By the God above us," said Lewis, "it is maddening to see her thus happy !"

"What, are you, then, smitten with her ?"

"Smitten ! Well, I once loved her, and she, in return, spurned me. One can scarcely be smitten after such treatment as that ; but I hate to see her look happy. I would give the world to drag her back again into wretchedness."

"Well, I've a small spite against her, and should not mind taking her from that cub, St. Henry. It is worth thinking of."

"An abduction !" cried one of the others ; "how delightful !—quite a sensation for us blaze fellows, and we'll assist. Danvers won her fairly, and ought to have her, but if he likes to forego his claim in favour of Winterleigh, I have naught to say in the matter. But anyhow I'll lend a hand in serving out St. Henry."

"Agreed," said the other ; "we'll play the poverty-stricken upstart a trick. But how shall we manage ?"

"Come this way," said Danvers, "there's a fellow on that lounge who appears to be listening to us."

They moved away.

"I must warn this man, St. Henry," said Clifford, to himself, as he started to his feet. "I may be powerless to aid him, but forewarned is forearmed. I will seek him."

He rose, and wandered through the rooms, and ere long found St. Henry conversing with a group of persons in a recess of the grand saloon.

"May I claim your attention in private for one moment ?" said Clifford.

St. Henry started and looked puzzled, for he could scarce understand being thus addressed by a mysterious mask.

Clifford spoke with a strong foreign accent, the more perfectly to escape identity.

"I do not think I have the pleasure of your acquaintance," said St. Henry, bowing to his friends and following theTroubadour.

"You do not know me," said Clifford, "but I am acquainted with you."

"Indeed! Here, I think we may talk without interruption."

He pointed to a deep window shaded by heavy curtains of velvet.

"Yes," said Clifford, "that spot will do as well as any other. Come, sir."

He took St. Henry by the arm and led him behind the curtains.

"Now," said the officer, "What is your business?"

"It is soon told; you passed a group of gentlemen just now in the further saloon. One of them wore a long domino of blue velvet; you could not have failed to remark him."

"I did notice such an individual."

"I presume you know the history of the lady who hung upon your arm?"

"Perfectly well, sir," said St. Henry, looking at Clifford in amazement.

"Well, you will understand my reason for asking that question when I inform you that the owner of the blue domino is Sir Lewis Winterleigh."

"Indeed!"

"I speak the truth. He has recognised the lady, and is even now concerting with his friends, men into whose grasp it appears the lady fell, outside the Palace of St. James', a plan to carry her off. I am powerless to assist you, but I beg you to heed my warning."

"I will do so. And I thank you sincerely for placing me upon my guard."

"You are welcome, sir. And now I must be gone."

"But you may, at least, tell me what course I had best pursue in this matter?"

"I will readily do so. Order your carriage and drive home immediately. Warn your servants, and give information to the authorities that they may place the necessary guard about your house."

"I will follow your advice to the letter."

"You cannot do better, and now I must take my leave."

"May I not ask to whom I am indebted for this kindness?"

"You may. I am the Count de Aramis."

"A Frenchman?"

"Yes."

"This only makes confusion more confounded. How you could have known aught of——"

"No matter. Suffice it that I have warned you.

Next moment the troubadour was gone.

St. Henry for a few moments gazed after him in astonishment; he then turned and walked hastily through the rooms in search of his mother and her charges.

He found Mrs. St. Henry and his sister seated together, but Evelina was not with them.

"Where is Evelina?" he asked.

"She is dancing."

"With whom?"

"An officer of the King's Guard, who was introduced by Lord Belmore."

"Indeed! I must seek her."

"Wherefore? What has occurred to discompose you thus?"

"Nothing—that is, nothing serious. All will be well as soon as I find her."

He wandered among the groups of dancers—he sought her throughout the whole of the rooms, but without success.

Evelina was gone!

St. Henry returned to his mother.

"Show me with whom she danced—show me the villain!" he cried, in wild excitement.

"What mean you?" cried his mother; "oh, what mean you? Tell me what has happened."

"I tell you to point out the man to me. She is gone."

"Gone!"

"Aye, gone. She has fallen into the hands of her worst enemy."

"Clifford?"

"No; would that he was her worst enemy! I mean Sir Lewis Winterleigh."

"Great Heaven! can this be true?"

"It is—it is! Can you show me with whom she danced?"

"I cannot; he has left the saloon."

"Yes, and they have taken her with them. Villains—villains!"

"What is to be done?"

"I know not. Get you home without delay; I must seek her out."

"My boy, my boy! pray control yourself. There may be some error: you may have been mistaken. Reflect."

"How can I reflect when I know she is in the power of that fiend in human form. Get you home, I say, and leave me to seek her."

Seeing that it was useless to remonstrate with her son, Mrs. St. Henry rose to leave the ball room.

She took her terrified child by the arm, and walked away, whilst St. Henry ran off in an opposite direction.

* * * *

"Having warned him," said Clifford; "I can do no more, for the hour has come for the performance of my hateful task. My life depends upon its prompt execution, or nothing should tempt me to the crime. But life is dear to me, wretched as I am; and to save it—above all, to prevent my being dragged to an ignominious death on a public scaffold—I must do the bidding of Wild."

His eyes wandered over the saloon and at length they rested upon the Duchess of Lakemont.

He had no occasion to inquire, for the individual upon whom his glance rested, was in reality the one he sought.

A glance at the marvellous gems that encircled her brow, throat, and arms sufficed to assure him of her being the veritable duchess.

Her Grace of Lakemont, was more famous for her beauty than for her moral worth, which, truth to tell, was a somewhat doubtful commodity with her.

She was a woman who had seen some five or six-and-thirty summers, and was in the full bloom of womanly beauty.

The duke was some thirty years her senior, and, being a martyr to rheumatic gout, was seldom seen in public.

He had married the present duchess in order that he might have a being near him who could maintain the splendour of his house, and wear with a grace his world-famed diamonds.

As may be supposed, love was out of the question between such a pair; but, as both followed their own inclinations, to their full extent, they agreed remarkably well together.

The duke liked giving riotous dinners to men of his own stamp every day of the week, and detested to have females about the house.

The duchess liked to have the admiration—perhaps adulation would be the better word—of men younger than herself, and chose to go into society to meet them.

As the duke knew nothing of this objectionable fancy, and as they never clashed in any way at home, the Lakemonts were cited as marvels of domestic bliss; and, although some wondered how a woman so young and beautiful as the duchess could tolerate one so old and decrepid as the duke, the majority paid little heed to them, and so they went their several ways in peace.

Clifford approached Lord Belmore, who stood talking in the immediate vicinity of the duchess.

He bowed to Belmore, who, seeing he was still alone, turned from his friends, and opened a conversation with the supposed foreigner.

"How are you—enjoying yourself?" he asked of Clifford, in French.

"Very much," replied Clifford in the same tongue: "very much, but I am a stranger, and know no one."

"Why did you not seek me out before, I would have introduced you to many delightful people."

"Oh, I feared to trouble you. I am not known to you and I, of course, knew that there are hundreds here who have more claims on your attention than I can have, so have endeavoured to amuse myself."

"My dear Count," said Belmore, "you are by far too retiring. Who can possibly have more claims on my attention than a stranger? The politeness for which your countrymen are conspicuous should have taught you this much."

"I feared to intrude."

"Nonsense! But I will make amends now. See. There is the Duchess of Lakemont. Do you mark her?"

Considering that Clifford had pulled Belmore firmly, but at the same time imperceptibly, in front of that lady, it was but right to suppose that he did mark her; but it was Clifford's will to be blind to her presence, so he turned his eyes in a contrary direction, and fixing them upon a young girl, who sat some ten yards from the Duchess, he said,

"Ah! she is very young and fair."

"No—no," said Belmore; "you do not see whom I mean. I called your attention to the lady who wears the rose-tinted robe."

"Ah, she with the glorious black hair and eyes."

"Yes."

"She is lovely."

"Are you smitten?"

"Could I be otherwise?"

"Well, it's all a matter of taste. She will be charmed with you. Come, I will introduce you."

"You are all goodness."

"Oh, nonsense."

They approached the Duchess, and an introduction was effected.

Clifford poured forth a whole stream of high-flown compliments, after the style of the country, a native of which he was personating.

The Duchess was delighted, more especially as Clifford pulled off his mask, and revealed his strikingly handsome face, which at once rivetted her attention.

She made room for the supposed Count at her side, and that individual hesitated not to avail himself of her courtesy.

Seeing that he was likely to get on very well with his new found acquaintance, Clifford was left to her by the host, who at once turned his attention to other guests.

It required but a very short time to reveal to Clifford the nature of the woman with whom he was seated in converse.

Discovering her love of admiration, he kept up a volley of strong but marvellously well-timed flatteries, with which it was evident she was fascinated.

Time passed. They danced together, walked in the conservatories together, supped together, and, in short, were inseparable.

At length the hour for breaking up the ball arrived, and people began to separate.

The carriage of the Duchess was ordered.

"Before I go you may take me to one of those retiring rooms, and get me a glass of wine. I declare I am quite exhausted."

Clifford offered his arm, and, the Duchess accepting it, they walked to one of the many little bowers leading from the saloon.

As chance would have it, there was no servant at hand.

"It is of no consequence," said the Duchess; "you may see me to my carriage."

"Gladly; but not until you have had some wine. I will be your attendant."

"I could not think of troubling you."

"You could not do so if you were to try for ever."

"Go away, flatterer."

"I speak the truth."

"I am forced to doubt you."

"Ah, madam, it is clear you know not the power of your own influence. I fly to bring you the wine."

Clifford left the bower, and as soon as she was alone, the Duchess rose and glanced at her own beautiful face in one of the many mirrors.

"And why should he not fly to serve me? There is not a wrinkle yet—there is not a charm faded. But I am older than he by many years. Nay, not so many; perhaps five. And what is that? But does he love me? Can he love me? Oh, Count, Count, I fear you have turned my brain!"

She turned from the mirror.

At her feet was Clifford!

The Duchess started back in terror.

"Pardon me," he cried, "Oh, pardon me, madam! I heard you speak, and I was spell-bound. I could not choose but listen. Can I love you? Do I love you? Oh! why should you ask yourself that?—Is it possible to live in the same atmosphere you breathe? Is it possible to see your angelic form, to drink in the accents of your voice and not love you? I swear I madly worship you!"

"You forget, Count, I am a wife."

"That name cannot quench my passion. I will not ask you to return it. I will go away from you, and love you at a distance. My passion is far too holy to obtrude itself upon you without your leave; I am to be dismissed with a breath."

"Rise, rise! You must not heed my words. I was mad to speak thus—I did not dream of your presence."

"But you spoke your thoughts."

"I may have done so but I knew not what I said. Do not resume the subject."

"I will have my tongue torn out rather than it should offend you by a word."

He tendered the wine he had brought, and the Duchess placed it to her lips.

Clifford watched her eagerly.

She drank and set the glass upon the table.

"Now I will go," she said.

Clifford again offered his arm, and they left the saloon together.

They found the carriage at the door.

As soon as the cold, night air fanned the cheek of the Duchess she grew faint, and staggered.

"You are unwell," said Clifford.

"Yes," she replied, "very unwell; I cannot think what ails me."

"I will ride home with you; you need help."

"Thanks—if I do not trouble you."

"I shall be glad to render you what poor assistance lays within my power."

He assisted her into the carriage, and in a few moments the Duchess was laying insensible in the arms of the highwayman.

"The potion works," he cried; "it works, and I shall be enabled to rob her. Wretch that I am. Oh, how I feel the misery, the degradation, of my position."

He gazed upon the being he held in his arms.

He would have given the world if she had recovered her senses, and thus baffled his scheme, but she lay as still as death.

No movement, no sign of life. The opportunity was all his own.

The iron will of another forced him to seize it.

Hastily he snatched the whole of the diamonds from the Duchess; they came off but too readily.

Everything appeared to favour him. There was no hitch, no baulk. He was possessed of the glittering treasure!

"Now to escape," he said, as he hastily concealed the gems about his person, and laid the insensible woman back on the soft cushions of her carriage. "Now for the attempt."

He quietly opened the door of the carriage.

The footman, as well as the coachman, sat on the box, and so the act was not noticed.

With alacrity he sprang to the ground, and, running a few paces, reclosed the door without a sound.

He then stood in the road, and the carriage passed him.

As it drove out of sight he turned into a bye street, and fled as if for life.

"Fiend! fiend that I am!" he cried wildly. "Oh! who, save the devil, could have devised so damnable a plot?"

CHAPTER XVIII.

THE INTERVIEW WITH JONATHAN WILD.

CLIFFORD'S first thought was to rush to his home; but this intention soon gave place to another.

"I must see Wild at once," he cried. " Yes, this very hour, and rid myself of these gems. If I do not dispose of them they will drive me mad. Their glitter is in my eyes now. Their sparkle blinds me. I must rid myself of them."

On he rushed through the streets, thinking of nothing but the possibility of ridding himself of his ill-gotten treasure.

On, on, regardless of the cold blast of morning that pierced his garments, and cut into his very heart; heedless of the quaint costume he wore, thinking of nothing but ridding himself of the diamonds.

On, on, and at length the house of the thief-taker was reached.

He knocked hastily at the door, and, obedient to his summons, came the old Jew, Moses, who appeared to be ever at his post, morn, noon, and night—never tiring—never sleeping—always alive to the slightest sound at that door.

At first the Jew started back in amazement, as Clifford's singular costume met his gaze, but he soon recognised him, and dragged him into the passage.

"Ah! ah! my tear, I didn't know you, ma tear, indeed, I didn't. Vy, vot a queer dress you have got on, to be sure. I never seed sich a rum turn out. And vot is this," he continued, handling Clifford's lute, "my, my, von vould think the shentleman had turned street mourner."

"Would to God I was something half so honest!"

"Vhy vat a queer speech; vhy, a peautiful shentleman like you. The prince of all the prigs, to use such talk; it's past believing, it is! it is! Its enough to make you weep; it is! it is! it is! I declare I could cry."

The Jew was about to oblige Clifford with a specimen of his abilities in the tearful line, when, that worthy stopped him by demanding an instant interview with Wild.

"Vy, mister Vild aint out of his precious ped yet, ma tear, can't you vait a pit in the peautiful office, and look over the curiosities."

"No! no! I must see your master at once. At once, I say! Why do you not fly?"

"It's all very vell to say, ' vy do you not fly!' put you jist go to wake up Jonathan yourself ven he's had put two hours sleep in forty-eight."

"Will you go, or shall I? I will see him at once."

"Oh, I'll go. He never allows anybody but me to enter his bed-room, so I'll go and do your bidding. Maybe he von't be cross ven he knows who it is as vants him. I'll go."

The Jew walked slowly up the stairs, and Clifford entered Wild's office.

He waited some five minutes, and the Jew returned, holding his head with both hands, and howling piteously.

"I knew how it vould be. I knew how he vould serve me, ven I valked into his bed-room. Oh, my head!"

"What has he done to you?"

"Only broken in my skull, that's all. It's of no conse-

quence ven you're used to it, but it's gettin used to it; that's the devil of it."

"I am sorry to have occasioned you this inconvenience."

"Oh, don't mention it; it's all in my day's vork. You see, this is how it is: he pays me to be half killed, and so I'm not allowed to complain. I knew vat a dreadful temper he vas ven I took the sitevation, ma tear, and so I can say nothing at all, nothing at all. It is'nt the fust time he's served me in that vay. Vell, I valked into his room, and says, quite gently like, ' Mr. Vild, you're vanted.' He took no notice; then I screamed a bit louder—'Mr. Vild! Mr. Vild! you're vanted;' but he snored on. Then I knew how it vould be, so I vent over to the side of the ped, and caught him by the shoulder, and gave him a shake. In a moment he was upon me, and, before I had time to tell him who I vas, he had knocked me down vith his pistol, caring no more apout preaking a poor old feller's head than nothink at all, ma tear. Then I told him who it vos as vanted him, and all that kind o' thing, and he said I should have called to him, not have shaken him—as if I hadn't screamed myself as hoarse as a raven vithout his taking any notice of me."

In spite of himself Clifford could not help smiling at the comic agony of the old Jew, but his mirth was of short duration, for almost as the Jew ceased speaking Wild entered the room.

"Now, then, Clifford," he said, springing on his stool; "have you been to the ball?"

While the Jew was telling his story, Clifford had pulled off the garments of the troubadour, and assumed an ordinary coat, of which there were many in Jonathan's rooms: so that the thief-taker may have been pardoned for asking the question.

"Yes," said Clifford, pointing to the dress he had cast off.

"And how have you succeeded?"

"As well as you could desire. Behold!"

He drew from his bosom the diamonds, and placed them in the hands of Wild.

"My, my!" screamed the Jew, " if ever I seed anythink so peautiful!"

"Begone!" cried Wild, savagely; " begone, I say! What business have you here?"

The Jew slunk out at the door without a reply.

He was used to such rebuffs.

"So," continued Wild, " you have succeeded. Very well, you are a clever boy; I don't think there's another like you in the world. I'm really growing to love you as if you were a child of my own."

Clifford replied not, but his cheeks were dyed crimson.

To be loved by such a man!

The thought was maddening.

"Heaven and earth!" he said to himself, "am I, then, reduced to this?"

"Now," said Wild, " just tell me how you did the brimer—cleverly, cleverly, I'll bet my life."

Clifford briefly related his story.

"Ah, I thought you would manage it without a bungle, you're always so clever. I never heard of anything half so neatly done. And to think that the duchess should have been smitten with you. Ho, ho! that in itself is an excellent joke."

"It is that which maddens me."

"Don't be a fool," cried Wild. "Maddens you! Why, it'll be a fortune for you if you manage things properly."

"Do you think me capable of taking an advantage so mean, so despicable?"

"Well, I don't understand any of that high flown nonsense. But I do think you an ass if you don't make capital out of a passion so marked."

"I would not do so for worlds."

"We shall see. You forget you are not yet your own master."

Paul looked up into the stern iron face of the thief-taker, and he read there that hope would be madness, and he was a doomed man.

"Oh, spare me!" he cried. "What have I done that you should turn upon me thus? Never before have you behaved in this manner to me."

"Doubtless; but I am a man of the world, and well know how to act the character. I am all self! There is no mawkish sympathies, no drivelling affections, clinging to my nature. I use my fellow creatures to shape my own ends. They are but my tools; to-day it serves me to fawn upon them, to-morrow to assist them, then to persecute them, and *sometimes to hang them!* Do you comprehend?"

"Yes, yes; I comprehend your meaning."

"Do not forget, then, and, above all, remember that I am not to be played with, and that my will is law. Should I order you to again play upon this woman's affection for you, you must do it."

"I dare do all but that."

"You shall do that, and nothing but that, when it suits me; and now no more on the subject."

"You dismiss me?"

"Not yet."

"What further commands are there?"

"But one. You must dispose of these diamonds."

"I dispose of them?"

"Yes, you must dispose of them. Take them, and bring me three thousand pounds for them."

"Three thousand pounds!"

"Yes, three thousand—one for you and two for me."

"But where am I to take them? Detection would be a certainty."

"Nonsense, nonsense! You know where they are to be sold."

"I do not."

"You do not? Have you forgotten Hawkins, the pious fence?"

"Hawkins, of Oxford-street?"

"The same?"

"Must I, then, take them to him?"

"You must; he will make the purchase."

"Yes, and hand me over to justice as the robber."

"No fear of that."

"There is everything to fear. In a few hours the news of this robbery will be noised over London, and a great reward offered for its perpetrator."

"There, you show how little you know of the world. The course that will really be pursued will be the very opposite one. The affair will be hushed up and placed n my hands on my vowing the utmost secrecy. I shall get the reward that the duchess will offer for her lost gems, and old Hawkins will be some three thousand pounds the worse off, without the power of retaliation."

"How?"

"He is in my power. I could crush him at any moment, and will do so if he betrays from whom the diamonds were purchased. Trust me, I know what I am about."

Clifford was astonished at the marvellous tact of this man.

Not content with the great reward that would sure to be offered for the recovery of the jewels, he contemplated extorting a further sum from this man Hawkins, whose cupidity would doubtless induce him to buy the diamonds, and whose helplessness would force him to relinquish them when called upon to do so by the authorities.

"Take them," he said, placing the gems back into Clifford's hand; "take them, and make the best bargain you can."

"I hear you."

"And see that you obey me. If you do not, you know what you have to expect."

"I will obey you."

"Adieu then, my brave Count. Ah, ah! may you frequently make such excellent work in masquerade."

Clifford flew rather than walked from his detested presence.

*   *   *   *   *

As soon as the highwayman was gone, Wild called to the jew.

"Moses! Moses!" he cried.

"Yesh, Mr. Vild; I'm here, sir."

"Where, is Harmer, and Adfield?"

"Down stairs."

"Send them to me on the instant!"

The jew vanished.

The next moment two men, habited in the usual style of thief-takers entered the office.

"Now you, fellows, have you anything in hand?"

"No!"

"Well, then start for Hawkins' shop, in Oxford-street."

"What to do there?"

"Clifford will be there in the course of the morning."

"Well?"

"He must be arrested."

"As he enters?"

"No! as he departs. He will have money about him. Three thousand pounds at least. Take it from him and then carry him to Newgate."

"On what charge?"

"One of the thousand there are already lodged against him; but say nothing of his visit to the goldsmith's."

"All right,"

The men took their leaves, and Jonathan returned to bed to resume his nap, which he did as composedly as if nothing uncommon had transpired.

CHAPTER XIX

HAWKINS, THE PIOUS FENCE—CLIFFORD AND THE DIAMONDS—THE BARGAIN—THE ARREST.

At the corner of one of the innumerable turnings out of Oxford-street, was a large and fashionable-looking jeweller's shop, over which swung the name of Hawkins.

The proprietor was a middle-aged man, of highly respectable appearance, and *naïve* manners.

He was a religious man, and was an Elder of the body of Roaring Psalm Smiters, whose chapel stood in the vicinity of Oxford-market.

The Roarers, as they were briefly called, were a very respectable body of persons, presided over by the Reverend Obadiah Snaggs, a gentleman who had taken holy orders late in life; the early part of his career having been devoted to the less respectable pursuit of butcher.

The Roarers were a comparatively modern body; not having been established over ten years.

The father of the sect was one, Drinkwell Lushington, who had been turned out of the church for hard drinking, and who avenged himself on the Church by mounting a tub in the market-place every Sunday and holding forth to the disparagement of the body that had scouted him.

"Throw mud enough, and some of it will stick."

So says the proverb, and believing in its truth, Drinkwell Lushington threw his faith in handfulls on each sabbath evening, and at length he got an audience who sympathised with him, and thought the Church a very disreputable institution.

This audience at length made a subscription; Snaggs, the butcher, headed it with a good round sum. The list swelled, and a respectable amount was shown.

With this a large loft was hired by the year, and the audience became a congregation.

On the opening day, the congregation, aided and assisted by some forty old men and women and little children, listened with wrapt attention to the eloquence of Obadiah, which was now not so much directed against the Church as against the poor old men, women, and children.

He told them that they were all sinners.

That they were to prepare for death at that moment, and that they were to expect no peace there or there-after.

He called the world a vale of tears, told his friends that all within it was vanity, and that the devil had got his eye upon them, and was sure to have them sooner or later.

He raved like a lunatic, and terrified the old men, women, and children into hysterics and fits; and then con-cluded amidst universal praise; of course, not loudly expressed, but, nevertheless, very palpable.

Lushington was a success.

People liked to be frightened; they choose to be terri-fied, and, in nine cases out of ten, would rather be miserable than happy; and so Drinkwell secured a congre-gation, which extended each week in size, and which, at last, raised over the ranter's head a very respectable chapel.

The butcher from the first acted as clerk to Drinkwell, and when that worthy man quitted the world in a fit of *delirium tremens*, Obadiah was selected, by universal con-sent, to fill the vacant pulpit.

The clerk's desk then fell to the lot of that highly-intelligent and dear, pious brother, Hawkins, who had, from the first, exhibited a great esteem in the welfare of the Roarers. Hawkins assumed the habits of the Church. He was always dressed in a neat suit of black, and wore the most elaborate of clerical scarfs.

He was a fat man, and had a very white face, and dazzling white hands. His hair was jet black, and he allowed it to grow very long, and wore no wig.

He was also possessed of a remarkably white cage of teeth, which he was very proud to exhibit on all occasions. Such was Hawkins.

People who did not belong to his sect—they must have been naughty, worldly, disreputable people—said that Hawkins was a humbug, and expressed an opinion to the effect that he and the Reverend Obadiah were a miserable pair of scamps, who fattened on the folly and incredulity of the frequenters of their chapel.

But this, as a matter of course, was only the outpour-ings of splenetic natures, who envied them their respecta-bility and reputed wealth.

It was morning, and Hawkins was to be seen behind his counter, his white hands twisting and twining among silver spoons and forks, and arranging golden chains and rings.

By his side was a tall and thin young man, his assistant, who was also pale, and who also had white hands, and who rejoiced in the name of Smawkins.

To them entered an old lady, a member of the Roarers, who seated herself, and with a groan said it was a fine morning.

Hawkins groaned again, and said,—

" It was."

And thereupon the long assistant groaned louder than either of them, and said,—

" It was beyond dispute."

Then the old lady groaned again, whereupon Hawkins turned up the whites of his eyes, and moaned pitifully.

And the long apprentice, taking up his cue very neatly, turned up his eyes until only the whites were visible, and fairly howled.

After this delicious performance, the old lady said she wanted to purchase a small diamond brooch.

" For a sister or a brother ?" asked Hawkins.

" For a brother."

A case of diamond brooches was placed before the old lady.

" Do you require a very handsome one ?"

" Yes, brother! rather a tolerably handsome one. I did promise such a toy to our Reverend brother and pastor, Obadiah; and I would fain give him one that will be worthy of him."

" Here is one the reverend gentleman hath often ad-mired," said Hawkins, taking up a very third rate brilliant, and showing it to his beloved sister.

" And hath he admired this ?"

" Yes, that very brooch."

" Then that one shall it be ; although there are others I would fain select in preference."

" Doubtless ! but our brother hath a keen eye for a diamond ; the one I have shown thee is of the finest water."

The old lady believed him, and made the purchase ; but she was miserably taken in.

In the height of his brotherly affection, Hawkins asked about twice the real value of the brooch, and thus served himself, and swindled both his dear sister and be-loved pastor.

The money was paid, and the brooch was wrapped up, and placed in the purchaser's hand.

The old lady then entered into a conversation of religious subjects.

Brother Hawkins was immensely entertained, and a half hour slipped over before he was well aware of the fact.

At least he pretended such was the case, although a close observer might have noticed a restlessness in his manner that but ill-accorded with the assertion.

The half-hour passed and still the old lady talked.

It was evident that she considered herself entitled to her say, having expended a tolerably large sum in the establishment, and so she exhibited no signs of moving.

At length Hawkins was relieved.

The tall assistant informed him that a gentleman who had entered by the side door wished to see him on par-ticular business.

Turning over the old lady with a sigh of relief to Smawkins, he quitted the shop, and entered a small room at the back, which was designated his private office.

Entering this apartment, he found it tenanted by a young and handsome man, dressed in the very height of fashion.

Hawkins bowed low, and assuming his usual cant whine, asked what he should have the pleasure of doing for the gentleman.

The young man raised his eyes, and revealed the face of the highwayman Clifford.

He looked long and earnestly at the goldsmith, and then said he had some things to dispose of.

" Thank Heaven !" he said aloud; " he does not know me."

" Gentleman Clifford," said Hawkins to himself at the same moment, but exhibiting no sign of recognition.

" Some things to dispose of," continued the jeweller, with a smile, " really, sir, I am not in the habit of buying —selling is more in my line."

" I know it; but still I believe you make purchases on an occasion."

" I have done so."

" And will again, I have no doubt."

" It entirely depends upon the nature and quality of the article, my dear sir."

" Diamonds."

" I purchase them occasionally."

" Look at these, and say if you will purchase them."

Clifford drew forth the glorious gems of the Duchess of Lakemont, and placed them on the table before the gold-smith.

That individual appeared fascinated by their glitter.

He fixed his eyes upon them, and stared in extreme astonishment.

" They are glorious," he cried, in an ecstacy, and then remembering himself, added, " that is, they are very tolerable—very tolerable, but nothing wonderful."

" They are the finest in the world, and you know it."

" They are pretty good, there is no denying that; but —but I don't think I can purchase them; I have too little money."

" I want but little for them."

" Then they are not honestly come by."

" No matter how I came by them ; they are mine, and I wish to sell them. Is not that sufficient ?"

" Well, you see, sir, I like to be well assured that the seller has a perfect right to the goods he offers for sale before I make a purchase."

"Indeed !' Time was when you were not so over scrupulous."

"Then live and learn, young sir; and blessed are they that see the evil of their way, and turn therefrom.'

"Psha! that is hyprocrisy, and I am in no humour to listen to that."

"Sir! I am a religious man, and, I trust, a conscientious man.''

"And I am a hasty man, and, I trust, a man of few words. Do you desire to buy these diamonds ?"

"I am afraid of the price."

"What do you offer ?''

The goldsmith took up the gems one by one, and appeared to examine them minutely.

"They are not all alike," he said.

"I care not—your price."

"I think—mind, I do not say I can do so—but I think I can give you a thousand pounds for them.

Clifford, without another word, gathered up his diamonds, and prepared to depart.

"Stay, stay," said Hawkins, "why are you so hasty?"

"I am not inclined to be trifled with, so I wish you good morning."

The face of the goldsmith became gloomy.

" Nay;" he cried, " I meant not to offend you ; pray resume your seat and allow me to see the diamonds again. I may be enabled to offer you a little more "

"Before you look upon them again," said Clifford, "I tell you candidly, I will not accept anything like the price you have offered."

"Let me look at the diamonds."

Clifford again handed them to the fence, who once more examined them.

"Come," he said after a while, "I will double my offer."

"You must treble it."

"Indeed I cannot."

"Very well; we cannot deal."

"Stay—stay; you are the quickest tempered man I ever met. Will you take two thousand five hundred ?"

"No."

"Seven-fifty ?"

"No."

"Then I do not think I can go another penny beyond that figure.''

"There are others who will be glad to get them at thrice the sum, so I will trouble you no further.''

"There, there, wait one moment; let me get another look at them. Well, I suppose I must give the three thousand, but I make an awful sacrifice."

"It is I who make the sacrifice, you well know that; they are cheap at fifteen thousand.''

"Oh, how you do magnify their value."

"I know full well their real worth."

"Well, here is your money. Will you have notes or a draft?"

"Notes.''

The jeweller handed the robber three notes, each one thousand pounds in value.

"And now I wish you good morning," said Clifford.

"Good morning, *Clifford*," said the goldsmith, glancing up from the diamonds.

"You know me ?"

"Yes; I knew you from the first moment."

"No matter."

"Not the slightest. All's right with me."

"I believe so, or I should not have come here."

"Once more, good morning."

Clifford bowed and withdrew.

"Deuce take it." he said, as he left the office, "I flattered myself that I was unknown. If those diamonds are wrested from the old villain, he will be my bitterest enemy for ever."

"A nice morning's work," said Hawkins, rubbing his hands in great glee, " I never saw such diamonds in all my life. I wish these fellows had such hauls every day, the trade of a fence would be worth something then, and as to the Roarers, they should all go to——blazes for me. But I musn't run them down, or undervalue them; they certainly gave a man an air of respectability, and keep the pot boiling when better business is slack.''

*   *   *   *   *

With the air of a languid dandy, Clifford strolled into the street and glanced in at the shop window.

He walked a few paces down the street towards Holborn, when two men advanced and, ere he had time to turn or defend himself, a pair of handcuffs were upon his wrists, and he was a prisoner.

"Well, Gentleman," said one of his captors, thrusting him towards a vehicle that drew up at his signal, "well, Gentleman, you've had a tolerably long run, you have, but it's over now. You're booked, d'ye see."

They thrust him into the carriage and, springing in after him, ordered the man to drive towards Newgate.

"What is it? what is it?" shouted the bystanders.

"Oh, nothing particular," said some one who appeared to know the parties interested in the scene, "nothing particular. You see it's just two thief-takers in the pay of Mr. Wild walking off Gentleman Clifford, the highwayman, to Newgate. That's all."

CHAPTER XX.

THE ABDUCTION OF EVELINA—WHERE "DIANA" WAS LODGED—BOB THE OSTLER SMELLS A RAT—JOB SMELLS TWO—ROSE TRIES A PLAN—HOW JOB AND BOB DETERMINED TO TURN CHAMPIONS OF INJURED INNOCENCE—THEIR SUCCESS IN THAT LINE OF CHARACTER.

THE officer with whom Evelina danced was one of those who tossed for her on the eventful night of her quitting Clifford.

She did not, however, recognise him through his disguise, and in all probability would have failed to do so had he been unmasked for she was by far too terrified at her first meeting with him to note his countenance or that of either of his companions save Danvers, whose features were indelibly impressed upon her memory.

She found this young man, whose name was Norrington, a very pleasant companion, and by his easy and genlemanly behaviour, he hid the unmanly scheme against the happiness and liberty of the lady, in which he was engaged to play so prominent a part.

"The rooms are very sultry," he said to Evelina, "will you take any refreshment?'

"I thank you, no; but I should like a little air."

"There is a conservatory close at hand, will you rest there awhile?"

"Thank you, but I do not care to leave my friends.''

"Let me conduct you to the bower, and I will at once return to the ball room, find your friends, and bring them to you."

"You are very good, but I fear I am giving you a great deal of trouble.''

"I take a pleasure in attending one so beautiful."

Evelina blushed, and said no more.

Placing her arm within his she left the saloon with him.

They walked to the grand conservatory that opened upon the garden facing into St. James's Park.

Here the officer placed her on a rustic bench, and retired.

To all appearances the place had no other tenant save herself.

The cool breeze of the night—or, rather the morn, for it was long past midnight—played upon her fair brow, and soothed its throbbing.

In the silence the old trouble came upon the young girl again.

JONATHAN WILD'S VISIT TO GENTLEMAN CLIFFORD IN NEWGATE.

Her thoughts wandered back to Winterleigh, to the old house, the solemn chamber of death, to Lewis, and thence to Clifford.

In a few moments she was very wretched.

"Would they were come, would they were come," she cried.

But the velvet curtains that concealed the entrance to the ball-room stirred not, and all was still as death.

"I will seek them," she cried.

She sprang to her feet, but a weight appeared to press upon her brow, a cold, clammy touch was upon her shoulder, and she sank back powerless and in terror.

A dark shadow fell before her eyes, and casting up her glance she saw before her the dreaded form of Lewis Winterleigh.

"You have evaded me," he said, "you have escaped my vigilance a long, long while, but I have found you again, and now we part no more."

She would have screamed for help, but her tongue clave to the roof of her mouth, and she could neither speak nor move.

The clammy hand was on her shoulder, the weight was on her brow, and she was completely in his power.

"You are mine now, and must submit to your fate. Nothing can snatch you from me. A spell is upon you, and you are inanimate. Come, come, I have a vehicle in waiting, and, ere long, you will be once more in the Hall of Winterleigh."

He threw a heavy cloak over her as he spoke, and, catching her in his arm, disappeared with her through the shrubs and into the garden with the rapidity of lightning.

As he rushed away the heavy curtains moved, and the young officers rushed into the conservatory, and, giving vent to a loud burst of laughter, congratulated themselves on the success of their scheme.

*   *   *   *   *

A vehicle was in readiness in St. James's Park, and very soon Lewis and his victim were dashing along the road in the direction of Winterleigh.

For a time the poor girl was powerless and speechless, lying as one in the embrace of death.

But, after a while, she recovered; and, her position revealing itself to her, she burst into tears, and, burying her face in her hands, gave way to her grief.

Her companion endeavoured to enter into conversation with her, but she would not speak, and kept her face buried in her hands.

The journey was pursued at a great speed, and an hour and a half scarcely elapsed when the postilions checked their horses at the door of Job Winchurst's hostelrie.

The horses were quite blown by the fearful pace at which they had been going, and were covered with a perfect lather, whilst foam dropped from their mouths and nostrils, and their loins literally quivered from exhaustion.

It was necessary to rest them at this point, for they were not in condition to go on without sustaining great injury, and as they were hired horses the postilion naturally declined to kill them in the interest of the stranger who had engaged their services.

As a matter of course the little house was closed, and its occupants at rest, but Lewis hesitated not to spring from his carriage, and summon them from their beds.

It was, however, some time before he could make Job hear his summons, and then he turned impatiently to the post-boy, in order to induce him to continue the journey, but the boy shook his head, and pointed to the condition of the cattle.

Thereupon Lewis angrily beat at the door, and at length Job's head popped out of window.

"Who is there?"

"A traveller requiring assistance for his cattle. Be quick."

A traveller in such a vehicle, at such an hour, was a most unusual thing to see, and caused Job a great deal of excitement.

He hurried on his clothes on the instant, and rushed to Bob's chamber, and conveyed to him the information.

Bob was quite excited at the intelligence, and in a few moments was following his master down the stairs of the house.

The postilion had dismounted, and, with the assistance of Bob, released the horses from the carriage.

"A roll in the straw, a rub down, and a little corn after it, will be all they'll want," he said, to Bob, who led the animals quietly to the stable.

"They've set out on this journey in an awful hurry," thought Bob, "or they would have had a change of horses awaiting 'em somewhere's, that's certain."

Meanwhile, Job was attentive to Lewis.

That individual had drawn rein at the door as he proceeded on his journey to town, and Job recognised him again. Rose, who had not yet quitted the inn, was out of the way when he paused at the door, or the possibility would have been that his reception would have been less warm, for Job had conceived a great liking for the young girl chance had thrown under his protection, and the name of her persecutor to him was a bugbear of the worst possible description.

"Will you not come into the house?" asked Job of the young baronet, who stuck with singular pertinacity to the door of the carriage, and seemed most anxious to cover the window, so as to exclude all view of the interior.

"No," said Lewis, shortly; "I will stay here."

"Can I bring you anything?" said Job; "it is but cold work, travelling on such a night."

"I require nothing of you," said Lewis, "but attention to the horses, and the sooner you get them into condition for going on, the better."

"Oh," thought Job, "you're a nice civil sort of gentleman, you are. But stay there, and welcome."

Having nothing better to do, Job stared at the costume of the traveller, and for the first time was struck by its singularity.

Lewis was dressed in a cavalier hat, with a long, sweeping feather hanging over his shoulder. He wore a domino which covered his fancy costume, and on his arm was still hanging the mask he had worn at the ball.

"Hillo," said Job, "if that ain't von of the rummiest coves as ever vos, I'll be kicked. What a dress! why, he looks like a play-acting man. I never did see sich a rum one in all my life!"

The possibility was that that was the fact, since Job did not live in an era of history when cavalier hats were in vogue, and that his knowledge of the adaptation of fancy costumes to the English ball-room, was remarkably limited.

Job continued to regard him curiously, and could not comprehend the pertinacity with which he clung to the door of the carriage.

This behaviour fairly puzzled the host.

"There must be somethink in that carriage as he don't want anybody to see," thought Job, "and, therefore, that somethink ought to be seen. Suppose he was a running off with a lot of stolen property, or a *young woman!* A nice name the 'Harvest Home' would get, when it was known that here he got assistance, and a shake down for his hosses. It's a dooty I owe somebody, somehow, to see into that carriage, and see into it I will, and no mistake. But Bob must lend me a hand; he has a stunning nose for smelling out a rat."

At this point Bob and the postilion approached the door of the inn.

"Get what you require," said Lewis, to the man; and then, in an undertone, he continued: "but keep your mouth closed. On your silence depends the amount of remuneration you will get."

"I'm dumb, sir," said the man, touching his cap, and following Job and the ostler into the house.

The two entered the bar, and Job lighted up his candles, and made the place look lively.

"I'll light the fire if you want anything warm," said the host.

"No," said the boy; " a glass of old ale and a dash of rum in it will do for me very well."

"And I'll take the same," said Bob, who was always anxious to indulge in stimulants late at night or early in the morning.

"I dare say you will," said Job, "you're one of them sort of chaps as is always ready to go in for anythink."

"Well, governor," said Bob, " you ain't a man as looks with disgust at a stiff glass of grog when the cold has to be kept out."

"I've told you afore, Bob, that I'm differently constituted; what's one man's bread is another man's pisen; and what'll fatten and do me good, will bring your grey hairs with sorrow to the grave."

"Seeing as how I haven't never a grey hair in my head," said Bob, "I don't know how that can well happen."

"Don't you?—then I do. It'll come about like—like—anything—that's how it'll come about."

"No odds," said Bob, "let it come about—only let's have the old ale and rum."

Although he offered strong objections to Bob's ever indulging in the free use of spirituous liquors, Job never absolutely refused them to him, and so, with a sigh, he now proceeded to the taps, and mixed the stimulating beverage.

Bob winked, and poured the draught down his throat with a deep-drawn sigh of satisfaction.

"That's what I call a reg'lar warmer," said the ostler, looking affectionately at the empty glass; " next to pine-apple rum punch, which the guv'nor can specially recommend, give me the pure Jamaica in old ale—that's the way to tell what it's made of."

"You're right," said the London postilion, " I see you fellers know what's good, although you do live so far out of town."

"Aye," said Job, "it ain't they as lives in town as knows the most, I'm thinking. I've generally found that if you take them out of their own element, they're as soft as soft can be, and flounder about like fish out of water, which isn't a lively sight to behold."

"Not at all," said Bob, " and I agrees with the guv'nor, who's as downy a one as can be."

The glasses were replenished, and then Job ventured upon a slight pumping process with the postilion.

"The gent don't appear to be over and above amicable," said he to the man.

"He ain't one of the best-tempered in the world," said that worthy.

"Don't care about facing the light," continued Job.

"I don't know," answered the man, shortly.

"Oh, you don't know?"

"No; I never saw him before to-night."

"He travels in a rum costume."

"I s'pose it's a fancy he has."

"So I should say. Well, he seems like a post at the door of the chaise. Got something particular inside I should say."

"P'rhaps so."

"You don't know?"

"I don't know."

"I suppose you know who and what you took up?"

"I s'pose so."

"And that was—?"

"Yes, it was."

The postilion emptied his glass, and walked out of the room.

"That's a cool 'un," said Job, looking after the man, with something like blank astonishment depicted on his countenance.

"He don't appear to be of a talkative character, neither," said Bob.

"No; he's, in all probability, too well paid to open his mouth."

"Aye; there's a mystery about that carriage that I should like to see into."

"Well," said Job, "I'd give something to know what's there."

"I shall try and find out."

"How will you do it?"

"Never you mind; but I will do it."

"That's a brick! It ain't often I feel any curiosity of this sort, but when I see a feller, togged out as that one is, going as he is, and sticking at the door of that carriage instead of walking in and taking refreshments like a Christian traveller, I knows that there's something as isn't right a goin' on, and I'd like to see into it, that's what I should."

"And that's what I will do."

Bob seized a lantern, with an air of deep determination on his face, and lighting it, slammed home the door with a bang, and stalked out into the yard.

Job was about to follow, when Rose, still pale, and apparently still suffering from her recent severe treatment, stood before him.

"Hillo, Poppets," he said, " what ever roused you at this hour in the morning?"

"I heard the carriage," said Rose, " and finding that you were called out of bed I felt anxious to know what was going on, for I have been very nervous to-night."

"Oh! there's nothing going on, my dear," said Job, "at least, nothing as I'm aware of; a carriage at the door, and there's a gentleman with it as won't come inside while the horses is resting a bit, but who will stick at the side of the carriage, as if to shut out a view of what's in it, and that's the only suspicious part of the business."

"You do not think there is anything wrong going on?"

"Oh, no."

"You are sure?"

"Quite sure, Poppets; but Bob has gone out with the lantern to get a peep into the carriage, and he'll be back presently, and tell us what's in it; for he's an awful downy customer, my dear, and does such things as you'd scarcely think anybody could do, however great might be the amount of downyness they possessed."

"It's a strange thing," said the girl; " a very strange thing."

"So it is, my dear: I never saw a stranger—but here comes Bob."

Bob the ostler now entered the bar.

"Governor," he said, "I smell a rat."

"Do you though?"

"I do."

"And what is it like?"

"It's like a rum 'un."

"Is it though?"

"That's what it's like, governor."

"Tell us all about it."

"I will."

Job and Rose drew close to the ostler, and listened in breathless anticipation of his recital.

"Well, you know," said Bob, " I goes out into the yard with this 'ere blessed lantern in my hand, and I looks about. The post-boy was a-gone into the stable, and the swell was a standing against the side of the carriage nearest the house. 'Well,' says I to myself, 'there's two sides to every question, my boy.'"

"So there is, Bob, so there is."

"Well, I knows it, and that's why I said it to myself. 'Well,' says I, 'there's two sides to every question, and, consequently, there's two sides to every carriage; so here goes for the other side.'"

"See how downy he is," said Job, nudging Rose, "oh, ain't he awful?"

"Be quiet," said Bob, but he said this in a tone that told as plainly as possible he was not adverse to the compliment. "Well," he continued, "I went round to the other side, looking as if I didn't expect to find anythink, you know, and whistling just to make believe that I was doing the most casualist thing in the world, and when I gets close agin the carriage what did I do but raise my lantern to the window, and peep in."

"And what did you see?"

"Ain't I a telling of you, old patience on a mony-ment; I seed a voman."

"I knew it," said Job; "I knew he had a woman there."

"Yes, but that ain't all."

"What! he'd got two there?"

"No he hadn't, he only had one, but you never see sich a one in all your life."

"Why, is she good looking?"

"I don't know about that, for she took care to bury her face in her hands, and not look up."

"Well?"

"Well, guv'nor, although she is a young 'ooman, you never saw such a rum dress as she had got on."

"Law!"

"You never did."

"What's it like?"

"Well, I don't know *what* it's like, only it ain't Chris-tian, I know *that* much."

"You don't say so?"

"I do."

'She may be a foreigner, Bob?"

"P'raps she is."

"And she's dressed more peculiarly than he is."

"Ever so much. She's got on the rummiest gown as ever was! On her forehead there's a great star, and at her back there's a golden bow, and an awful lot of silver arrows."

"P'raps she's an Indian princess?"

"I shouldn't be surprised; but she's a queer one whatever she is, and maybe she ain't crying at all."

"Well, *that* don't look well. What's making her cry, I wonder?"

"I can't think."

"No more can I; but it's suspicious, and ought to be looked after."

"So it did, and I votes as I ask her."

"Nonsense!"

"I do."

"What, in the face of the gentleman?"

"To his very teeth!"

"There," said Job, in admiration, "I told you he was a queer one. My eyes! there's no getting at the bottom of him. He'll do something or other yet that'll frighten somebody, for certain. I know he will; I'm sure of it, and so I tell you."

Bob nodded his head in approval of this speech, but seemed to take the compliment as a matter of course, and a thing to which he was justly entitled.

"Poor woman," said Rose; "he may be ill-using her. Perhaps carrying her off against her will! It is a pity that some assistance does not reach her."

"Look here," said Job, "if there's anything queer going on I can't put up with it. I'll have it out with the fellow, and he shan't take any young girl out o' this place without giving an account of her, or leastwise without letting her give an account of herself."

"That's the sort," said Bob, delighted at the enthu-siasm of his master; "them's the sentiments I likes to hear, and no mistake. Go it, governor, and I'll help you out."

There was a consultation as to what was to be done, but Bob would only hear of a direct appeal to the young lady through himself, and so that course was determined upon.

"And you shall come and see fair play," said Job to Rose, whose curiosity was certainly much excited, and who appeared by no means loathe to see what was going on in the court-yard.

The three went to the door of the house together, and Bob tripped into the yard.

The light of his lantern revealed the form of the traveller, and, as the flare fell upon him, he turned round and uttered a loud imprecation.

"What the devil do you want here again?" he asked of Bob. "Quick! see to the horses; I'll not remain in the place another moment."

Before Bob had time to reply, Rose uttered a faint shriek, and ran back into the bar, Job following her.

"What is the matter?" he asked.

"Oh! it is he—it is he!" she cried.

"He! what he, my dear?"

"The man of whom I have so often spoken to you—the young baronet."

"What, that d——d scoundrel of Winterleigh?"

"Sir Lewis, Sir Lewis," she replied. "Oh! let him not come near me!"

"I'll take good care of that," said Job, "but are you certain? Is there no mistake?"

"Not the least."

"Then I'll make him give an account of himself, and no mistake."

"No, no; pray let him go. I fear there will be danger in interrupting him."

"Nonsense, my love. There can be no danger in having to do with such a reptile as that, I can assure you."

Job hereupon went to the door, and, stepping up to the carriage, said to Sir Lewis—

"I want a word with you."

"What do you mean, fellow?"

"Don't fellow me, for I won't stand it. I know you, Sir Lewis Winterleigh, and your big words won't frighten me."

"Known! The devil!" cried Lewis, "what is it you want?" he continued, turning to Job, and looking the per-sonification of anger.

"I want to talk with you on a subject of some import-ance—your own bad heart."

"Fellow!"

"Not that word again, or, baronet as you are, I'll make you eat it."

Lewis was, at heart, a most abject coward, and, mark-ing the determined manner of Job, he thought it best to follow him.

Meanwhile, Bob slipped round to the opposite side of the carriage.

Job led Sir Lewis into the house, and, taking him into the bar, said to him—"Do you know that poor girl?"

He pointed to Rose, who cowered in a corner, shrinking within herself, from fear at the man who had served her so badly.

Lewis started back in amazement.

"I see, you do know her; and I want to know why you dared to treat her as you have done?"

"She is a witch, and, perhaps, a murderess."

"You are a liar and a villain to say so; and you know that such accusations were only prompted by your own malice."

"How dare you use such language to me?"

"I'll use whatever language I think proper in my own house, and to such a thing."

"You had best beware, or I will punish you. Mark me, I accuse that girl of being a witch, and I suspect her of murder. Harbour her after that at your peril!"

"And who are you that you should talk so loud? What if I accuse you of attempting the life of this poor girl, because she would not gratify your lawless pas-sions? Perhaps I should have less cause to fear results than you would. But it is not to lecture you that I have brought you here."

"I presume not."

"You can presume what you please. I have called you in to make you give an account of your-self."

"Insolent!"

"I've no manner of doubt that you think so, but it

doesn't trouble me in the least. Now tell me who is the lady you have in that carriage."

"Tell you! By what right do you ask me?"

"By the right every honest man has to inquire into the character of villains, and by the right a publican has to know who his guests are, in order that he may not be trapped into doing aught that is wrong and illegal. By doing you a service, in resting and feeding your horses, I may be a party to some crime; and I demand to know who that lady is, and whether she is in that carriage of her own free will. I tell you there's something deuced suspicious about it, and I'll see into it."

"You are a meddlesome fool, and shall know nothing from me. I have a right to keep my own business to myself, and that I will do, you may depend."

"And I have a right to perform my duty, and from that course you won't frighten me, so you had best say who the lady is."

"I will not."

"Then I shall inquire of her."

"Dare to approach that carriage, and I will run you through."

"Dare to draw a sword upon me, and I'll split your head with the poker."

"For God's sake do not quarrel, Sir Lewis! Mr. Winchurst, I pray of you desist."

"Go down, my dear, and take no notice. That gentleman knows better than to strike me, or any one capable of defending himself."

Job picked up his large poker and twirled it in his hand.

"This weapon," he said, "has frequently served my turn against greater odds, so beware."

Lewis did not attempt to draw his sword, and stood gazing at Job, with fear and rage mingled in his glance.

"Now, are you going to tell me the name of that lady, and whether she is in that carriage of her own free will?"

"No."

"Then I'll go and see."

"No occasion, guv'nor'" cried Bob, walking into the room with Evelina resting on his arm. "Look—here's the lady, who will tell you all about it herself."

The astonishment of Job and Rose at the apparition of one so well known to them, in that quaint costume, may be well imagined.

Evelina rushed forward and caught her humble friend around the neck.

"Do not let him bear me away," she cried. "Oh! have pity on me, and protect me."

"I'll stand by you through thick and thin," said Job; "and if anybody attempts to interfere with you let him look out."

Lewis was for a while quite speechless, but at last he burst out with a loud command to Job to release the lady and allow her to resume her journey.

"Not if I know it," said Job. "She says she'll stay, and stay she shall, whatever you may think about the matter."

"Release her, I say, or it will be the worse for you."

"It's likely to be the worse for you, if you stand there going on with such talk."

"Yes," said Bob, putting in a word, "we ain't going to stand this sort o' thing at the 'Harvest Home,' more particularly when we knows the lady, and has rather a fancy for her."

"Fools!" cried the once-more baffled villain. "Fools, you shall rue this."

"If we do, we'll tell you of it," said Job.

"Yes," said Bob, "we'll write you a kind letter, and give you all particulars."

"And now," continued Job, "the best thing you can do, is to get out."

"Yes, hook it," said the ostler, "you see you ain't wanted any longer."

"Oh!" cried Lewis, grinding his teeth with rage, "I will have an awful revenge for this."

"Much good may it do you," said the imperturbable Bob.

"A time will come when you will wish you had not done this, for I never forget an injury."

"And the time is precious near at hand when you'll get put under the pump, if you ain't off," said Job, "so go at once. The postilion is putting to your horses, and the sooner you are out of my house the better. Don't offer to pay for the accommodation you have had, for I should only shy the money at your head. So go, and don't be many seconds about it."

With a look of baffled rage Lewis turned on his heel, and walked from the house.

The postilion had linked the horses to the carriage, and stood awaiting orders.

Lewis sprang into it, and closed the door.

"Go on," he cried.

"And is the lady coming?" asked the man, in a respectful manner.

"No. Go on."

"To Winterleigh?"

"Furies and the devil, no! To London."

And thus terminated the abduction of Evelina.

CHAPTER XXI.

WILD'S INTERVIEW WITH CLIFFORD IN THE CELLS OF NEWGATE—PROPOSITIONS—WILD'S PLANS BAFFLED—THE THREATENED DOOM.

ON his arrival at Newgate Clifford was at once conducted to the darkest and dreariest cells of the prison.

The place chosen for his confinement more resembled a series of cellars than the dungeons of a prison in a great metropolis.

The one set apart for Clifford consisted of three damp and murky chambers far underground, and only receiving their light from a grating in the roof, through which a dull glimmer poured from the passage above: that passage being the one in which was situated most of the ordinary cells.

This particular place had been purposely selected by Wild for the reception of Clifford.

It was the worst place in all Newgate, and was chosen in order to break the spirit of the young highwayman, as its filth and loathsomeness were of the very worst description.

"If he can stand that," said Wild, "he can stand anything."

"Yes,' said the Governor, to whom Wild's word was law; "yes, it's a devil of a place, and I don't know of a better for making a fellow sick of prison life, and inducing him to come to any terms to get out of it, which I presume is your game."

"No matter, my friend," said Wild, "it won't do for us to inquire into the secrets of each other—no particular turn can be served by that course."

"You are right, and I don't want to know what's in the wind, I assure you. My own business is enough for me."

With this they separated.

In a short time Clifford came, and was conducted to his noisesome den.

So suddenly was his capture effected, and so short the time that had elapsed between his leaving the shop of the jeweller and his being ironed to the wall of the cell, that he had scarcely recovered from his surprise, when he found himself alone and in darkness.

The blow was a heavy one for him to bear, and bitterly did he curse himself for being trapped into this position by a plot so palpable as that laid for him by Wild.

"Villain, villain!" he cried, in the bitterness of his heart. "Oh, villain to treat me thus. But I will be avenged. *I swear on this spot that, should I escape, I will know no rest of mind until I have hunted Jonathan Wild into a prison, and thence to the scaffold!*"

The hours passed heavily, and the day seemed as long as three passed in liberty.

The prisoner could but glance about the limits of the cell.

He could only contemplate the dark, dank walls, and watch the puddles of filthy water that had settled in the crevices of the stones, and in the corners of the cell.

A ponderous chain bound him to the wall, and he could not move beyond its limits.

He became sadly oppressed, and towards the noon of the day after his capture he thought he should go mad.

He had seen the gaoler but twice, when he brought him water and some coarse bread, and he began to long for the sound of human voices and other signs of life.

Again did the hours go on slowly—more slowly than ever the prisoner thought, and towards mid-day he began to heed time no longer.

He could only reflect, and his thoughts maddened him.

Had he possessed a weapon he would have doubtless attempted his own life, but fortunately he could not effect any such dreadful purpose.

One thought occurred to him.

He could dash his brains out against the wall, and this form at first appearing too revolting to be thought of again, was at last a fixed idea with him, and he said,—

"In my desperation I shall do this!"

Time passed on, and at length the door of the dungeon opened and a man entered.

Clifford imagined it to be a visit from the goaler, and did not lift his eyes.

But at last a well-known voice rang in his ears, and he looked up to find himself confronted by Wild.

"Well," said the thief-taker, "what are ye thinking of; suicide? Yes, I can see it in your face; well, the old cells of Newgate are certainly the very place for engendering such thoughts."

"Villain!" cried Clifford; "oh, villain! release me from this place. What have I done to you that you should treat me in this manner?"

"Nothing."

"Then you are a double villain."

"That's hard words to a visitor who came for the purpose of comforting you."

"Comforting me!"

"Yes; comforting you. I suppose you want some consolation in your trouble, don't you?"

"Not yours."

"Ha! that's a pity. But what's the matter? What have I done to be served in this manner—I, who am so fond of you, and who have always been your good friend? It's rather too hard upon me, this is."

"Do not mock me," said Clifford, "oh, do not mock me thus. Am I not suffering enough without that?"

"How do I know what you are suffering? I came to bring you consolation, if not hope—and you turn upon me, and revile me."

"Because it is to you I owe this. To you—and you alone."

"Not to your own deeds?"

"No."

"Then stealing the diamonds from the Duchess is not a crime for which the perpetrator should be incarcerated in Newgate?"

"Who made me steal the gems? Who has benefitted by the theft? You, or I?"

"So far, I!"

"Then how dare you turn upon me thus for what has been your own act?"

"I am not turning upon you; I am merely engaged in my own business matters, and bringing you here is a part of a plan I have in hand. One day you will thank me for the interest I take in your welfare."

"Never."

"You will, though you do not know it."

"Never."

"We shall see; and now let us talk business, for I hate bickering and quarrelling."

"What other devilry have you in hand?"

"No devilry, my boy, as we shall see. But come, let us understand each other. I know you."

"There is no doubt of it."

"Oh! you think I am referring merely to the life you have led since I have had the honour of your personal acquaintance; but I was referring to your whole life—from the moment of your birth till now."

"Indeed!"

"Yes, indeed."

"I know you are a Winterleigh—that your mother was wronged by her husband's brother, and that that brother, on his death-bed, had sought to wipe out the wrong by making you his heir."

"How know you this?"

"No matter."

"I also know that it is possible to establish your identity, and to find the will you think lost for ever."

"Well?"

"Well; on the other hand, I can destroy the identity, and I can secure the will, or place it in the hands of Lewis Norman, falsely called Winterleigh, should I think proper to do so, instead of lending you my aid."

"Well! man, well?"

"Do not be impatient. You now know what I can do, and I must act according to the manner in which you elect to receive my propositions, which will be moderate enough."

"Name them."

"You are a prisoner."

"Yes."

"You have committed crimes that will send you to Tyburn."

"Yes."

"And without my assistance you have no hopes of life."

"That is true."

"Well, you shall see how generously I can act, although you have placed upon me the stigma of villain."

"Name your terms."

"I will save your life; will give you liberty, and secure you from further molestation on this one condition. You make over to me the whole of the Winterleigh estates."

"Is that *all?*" asked Clifford, in a sarcastic tone, that made Wild wince.

"That is all."

"Then I fling your offer back into your teeth, and will die!"

"Then your property is irrevocably settled upon Lewis Norman, and he, in consideration of my despatching you, will give me the very thing I am now asking you for."

"Liar!"

"You are most complimentary to day. I'm sure I scarcely know how to receive your flatteries, and were it not for the pleasure I shall feel in seeing you dangle from a gibbet, I should reward you with this."

This was a life-preserver, which he drew from his pocket and exhibited.

"If you have any mercy in you, despatch me with your weapon: you could not do me a better turn."

"No, my bold lad, the scaffold—the scaffold is for you, unless you think better of my offer."

"I decline it altogether."

"You do?"

"Yes, in the most decided manner."

"Take time to consider. I will not only see you out of your difficulties, but will provide you with twenty thousand pounds to take you to another country, and start you afresh in life."

"I decline your offer. I will have nothing whatever to do with you, and bid you begone!"

"Fool! I will give you a minute to think. Remember what is staring you in the face."

"Death! I have lost all fear of it."

"Think upon what I can do for you; think of the happy life you can lead in France or Italy with the money with which I will provide you."

"I will not think of it, I am resolved."

"Then I will leave you to your fate."

"Do so. I shall be too happy, under any circumstances, to be rid of you."

"You will tell another tale ere long, and will be glad of the chance I now offer; but know that when I quit this cell it will be all over with you. I shall return no more, and your doom is sealed."

"Leave me."

"For the last time I ask you to pause and reflect."

"For the last time I bid you begone; if you remain another hour you shall not force another word from me."

"Curses upon you for an ass! I leave you, and may you die a dog's death on the scaffold, to which I have doomed you."

He paused a moment, but Clifford spoke not, and, then muttering half-suppressed oaths, he left the cell.

At seven o'clock the gaoler came with more water and bread for the prisoner.

He had been in the habit of placing the things he brought on the floor of the cell, and quitting it immediately.

Now he paused, and looked long and anxiously at the prisoner.

Clifford raised his eyes, and returned the look given him. For a while the man spoke not.

Then he shuffled about uneasily, and, at length, said—

"This ain't a nice place to be in, is it?"

Clifford looked at the man to see if he was speaking in ridicule, but the face into which he gazed was stolid, and had rather a nervous, anxious look, which little corresponded with irony of feeling and thought.

"Oh," said Clifford, "a most miserable place."

"And you're very wretched, I suppose?"

"Yes; very wretched."

"And would give your life to quit it?—at least, not your life, but everything else in the world?"

"Yes."

"I supposed so. I'm a new jailer, I am, and thought when I came here that I shouldn't mind the work, and I did'nt till you came, for those in the prison are a bad set, and seem as well lodged as they deserve to be. But you are of a different sort, and it does seem hard to put you away down here, along with the rats, when some of the greatest wretches in the world occupy cells as snug as drawing-rooms in comparison with this. I'm downright disgusted with it, and I can't help thinking it downright spite on the part of old Wild."

"You are right; it is spite."

"I thought so. Now I suppose you wouldn't mind making your escape?"

"Indeed I should not," said Clifford smiling at the manner in which the question was put.

"Well," continued the man, "I think I know how it could be managed."

"Do you?"

"Yes; these irons off, and that door open, there wouldn't be much to stop you."

"Perhaps not; but the irons are not off, and the door is not open, so it is useless to talk of the matter."

"Perhaps not altogether useless. Now, if I were to help you, I suppose you would keep the thing secret, wouldn't you?"

"I would, indeed," said Clifford.

"Well, then, I shouldn't mind it, but you must keep it very dark."

"I will."

"Here's something for you; use it to-night, to-morrow it may be too late."

He handed Clifford a small file, of the very finest tempered steel.

"You must cut through the irons, and then serve the lock of the door in the same manner."

"Thanks," said Clifford, grasping the man's hand.

"Oh, don't mention it," he said, "Will Bennett don't mind doing any body a good turn when they deserve it, and he's sure you do."

"I will endeavour to convince you of that, if I but escape from this terrible place."

"Oh, you'll be off right enough if you only work with a will. Such a file as that is good enough to go through anything."

"I will use it carefully," said Clifford. "Fear me not."

"I don't: and now good-bye. I shall expect to find you gone when I come down in the morning, and, my eyes! won't there be a stir throughout the prison, and how I shall enjoy it."

Without another word the man left the cell.

"There is not a moment to lose," said Clifford to himself, "for there is work for some hours before me."

Feeling about for the iron ring that encircled his waist, he at last commenced the task of sawing it through.

CHAPTER XXII.

SHOWS HOW WILD CONDUCTED HIS BUSINESS—THE DUCHESS AND HER DIAMONDS.

WILD, on quitting Newgate, after his visit to Clifford' returned to his office, and, on being admitted by the ever-watchful Jew, was told by that worthy that there was a lady in the private office waiting to see him on particular business.

"Who is she?"

"I don't know, but she looks like a real lady, and no mistake, Mister Wild."

"A real lady, hey? Well, I suppose I had better see her."

Wild walked into the room indicated by his man, and there found, awaiting his coming, a lady closely muffled, who rose on his entrance.

"I was told you would be back within the hour, and I have waited to see you," she said.

"Whom have I the pleasure of addressing?" asked Wild."

"The Duchess of Lakemont."

"Indeed! And to what am I indebted for the honour of this visit?"

"I am come to you on an affair of the greatest importance, and on which the greatest secrecy must be observed. I have had the misfortune to lose my diamonds."

"And under what circumstances?"

The Duchess, with the greatest possible candour, told the whole tale of her adventure with the French Count.

"And do you really suppose that you were robbed by a Frenchman?"

"Yes."

"I can scarcely credit it. I should rather say the act had been perpetrated by some clever scamp of an Englishman."

"I do not think I could be deceived."

"I am sure you might be, and that very easily, too, by some of our expert rascals."

"But this was such a gentleman."

"Ah, many of them are gentlemen, and that is how

many singular robberies come about. The general impression is, that thieves are a band of low, ill-bred ruffians, and that they bear the mark of their nefarious trade upon their brows, but nothing can be further from the real facts. Many of our best thieves are the best-bred men in England; but will you describe these diamonds to me?"

The Duchess entered into a minute description of her lost gems.

"Ah," said the thief-taker, "they must be of immense value."

"They are, indeed, of great value, but it is not on that account alone that I would repossess them."

"So, I presume—they were lost in a very awkward manner?"

Wild leered at the Duchess, and she blushed crimson.

"I will reward you handsomely if you will but find them for me," said the Duchess at length.

"Well," said Wild, "I will, you may depend, do the best I can, but I shall require some slight assistance from you. Pray describe this man to me."

The Duchess entered into a marvellously minute description of Gentleman Clifford.

So well was the portrait drawn that Wild fairly smiled. It was done with a truth and perfectness which love, or a passion very near akin to it, could only accomplish.

"Upon my word," said Wild, "I really think I know the man who robbed you."

"Indeed?"

"Yes, indeed; if your description is a true one I can only think that you were robbed by Paul Clifford, the highwayman."

"I cannot credit it."

"But I assure you I am right."

The Duchess looked confounded, and said nothing.

"I see," said Wild, "you are chagrined to find that you have been so much imposed upon; but it is a matter of every day occurrence with that fellow. He is the most talented man and best thief in all London, and it really seems a pity to put an end to his career, but it must be done. This last crime must about settle him, and it is fortunate that he is already in prison."

"In prison!"

"Yes madam, safe under lock and key, and likely to remain so."

"I much regret that, for it is a pity that one so skilled should meet with such a fate."

"It does appear a pity, but society must be rid of these pests, and we are bound to clear them off with as little delay as possible."

"I suppose so," said the Duchess, absently.

There was a pause, and then Wild said—

"I will not detain you any longer now, madam. If you will call again to-morrow, I think I shall have news for you."

"And should you recover the diamonds, what reward do you expect?"

"The absolute charge will be a couple of hundreds, but I must leave the reward to you."

"I will make the two hundred a thousand, if you but save my gems."

"I will do so if possible, and I believe that there is a possibility of doing so."

"Thanks, thanks; you ease my mind very much by those words, and now I will go."

She rose, and left the office.

"Four thousand pounds for that little job," said Wild, as the lady left; "four thousand pounds, and through Clifford! Well, he'll be a great loss to me! But there's no help for it; I would have saved him if he had only agreed to my terms. But he was too doggedly obstinate, and must suffer for his folly. Yes, it is all over now—he must die."

There was a silence of a few minutes, and there came a knock at the door of the office.

"Come in," said Wild; and looking up, his eyes rested once more on the face of the Duchess.

"Well, madam," he said, "what brings you back?"

"Listen to me one moment," she said. "You told me that Clifford, the man whom you supposed robbed me, was in prison. If you find that you are right, I pray you spare his life; I would not have him die. You say he is talented, and the world says he is good. Therefore spare him, and you will not repent it."

"Madam," said Wild, "Clifford must die. I have it not in my power to save him."

"But they say you can do as you will with these men. The world says you have unlimited power over them, therefore you can save Clifford if you but wish to do so."

"But I have no wish to do so."

"I can make it worth your while."

"Indeed, madam, you cannot."

"I will double, treble, the reward I offered you for the diamonds, if you will but let him escape."

"Madam," said Wild, "his doom is sealed, and all the gold of the Indies would not tempt me to stir in his behalf."

"Think again; I pray you, think again. I cannot hear that he shall die; it is too sad to contemplate, far too sad."

"No one will regret it more than myself, but there is no alternative. Madam, I wish you a good day."

The Duchess saw that further parley with this man would be but a waste of time, and so she turned from the office.

But now her face was overcast and dejected.

*   *   *   *   *   *

"Humph!" said Wild, after a long reverie into which he had fallen when the Duchess quitted him—"humph! I must go and see after that mad woman's diamonds now. She's madly in love with that fellow, Paul, and the ass might have made a fortune out of her; but there, it is no business of mine, and so I'll go, and leave it alone. She must have her diamonds, though; I promised them, and I must, and will, keep my promise, under all considerations; besides, I owe that fellow, who has bought them, a good turn, and it will be a pleasure to me to make him hand them over again, so here goes."

He put on his hat, and seizing his great stick, with which he always walked, he set out on his expedition to the shop of Hawkins the money lender. Being in *propria personæ* everyone knew him, and as he walked through the streets he was recognised and accosted again and again.

At length he was in Oxford-street, and then he turned into the private office of the goldsmith and fence.

He had been there often, and knew his way thoroughly.

Entering without knocking, he somewhat surprised the man of psalms by his sudden and unexpected appearance.

"Well," he said, seating himself before the jeweller, "Well, Hawkins, how are you?"

Mr. Hawkins turned very pale, and replied not. He half suspected the errand on which he was come.

"How are you? I asked," said Wild, louder than before.

"Oh, I'm very well I thank you, brother," replied Hawkins.

"Don't brother me. I'm no brother of your's, so don't use the word. I hate your d——d religious cant."

"You shouldn't run down religion, Mr. Wild."

"I don't! I only run down those who profess it, and don't act up to their own preaching."

"Which does not apply to me."

"Which *does* apply to you."

"I hope you don't mean that."

"I do mean it; but that is not my business here."

"No? Then what can I have the pleasure of doing for you?"

"Nothing more nor less than handing me the diamonds of the Duchess of Lakemont."

The fence turned ghastly pale.

"The—the diamonds," he stammered.

THE FIGHT IN THE INN YARD.

"Yes, the—the diamonds. You know the ones I mean."

"Indeed, I do not."

"Indeed, you do. The ones brought you by Gentleman Clifford, now in Newgate, and for which you were fool enough to give him three thousand pounds."

"There must be some mistake."

"No mistake."

"But—"

"But, don't make a fool of yourself by contradicting. I say the diamonds are in your possession, and you know best whether it will answer your purpose to give them up or to go to Newgate."

The old man was clearly confounded.

"Well, friend Wild," he said, "supposing I have them, what are you going to hand over if I give them up?"

"Will you trust to my generosity?"

"I will."

"Give me the gems then."

The sanctified fencer went to a safe in the room and drew forth, with evident reluctance, the whole of the diamonds he had paid so dearly for.

"Here they are."

"Give them to me."

"Take them. And now what am I to have?"

"Nothing; and think yourself well off that I haven't walked you into Newgate."

With this he rose and quitted the room, leaving the old man utterly speechless with amazement.

CHAPTER XXIV.

SHOWS JONATHAN WILD IN A NEW CHARACTER.

ON leaving the shop of the fence, Wild suddenly determined to pay a visit to the Duchess of Lakemont, in *propria persona*.

With this thought uppermost, he strode away in the direction of Cavendish-square, that being the locality in which the Duchess resided.

Such an ill-looking vagabond had never, in all probability, before darkened the doors of the mansion of the old Duke, and great was the consternation of a remarkably aristocratic footman when Wild ascended the steps of the house, and accosted him.

"Is the Duchess within?" he asked.

"Why—ye—yes," said the man, and then he looked at Wild with an expression that seemed to ask, in very plain words,

"But what on earth can you want with the Duchess?"

Wild noted this, and rather gloried at it. He liked to puzzle people, and the expression on this man's countenance gave him complete satisfaction.

"Now, then!" he cried, "just stir your stumps, and, as quickly as convenient, inform your lady that the gentleman at whose office she called a few hours ago is here, and has a wish to see her."

"But I'm afraid the Duchess is engaged."

"Your fears are nothing to me, my fine fellow. Deliver my message, and reduce the size of your eyes to that generally seen in human beings. Your glims look positively hideous, and, moreover, it's rude to stare so."

It was quite evident that the man could make nothing out of his strange visitor, and, with a last long look at him, by way of seeing if there was any chance of making any further discovery that might lead to the satisfaction of the doubts he felt, he turned and set about the execution of the mission given him by the thief-taker.

During his absence, Wild took a minute survey of the hall in which he stood.

It was a splendid place; elaborate in architectural design, and glorious in its embellishments.

Wild examined every nook and cranny with the eye of a connoisseur, or, perhaps, with that of a professional thief; both have a strong inclining to be particular in the survey they make of places and things in which they feel any marked interest.

"Yes," he said, speaking to himself, "a very nice house, and *very easily entered*."

He glanced behind the door.

"No bolt," was Wild's mental remark; and his eye gleamed with pleasure.

In truth, there was but one ponderous lock that secured the door.

There was also a niche in the wall, and here hung *two keys*.

"They belong to the lock," said Wild; and then he took a glance at the hall porter.

That gentleman was sound asleep.

Wild sneezed.

No movement of the porter.

"Ah!" said Jonathan; "he seems fast enough."

And then his eye wandered once more to the keys.

"Surely *one* is sufficient for their purposes," he said, mentally.

He waited a moment, and listened.

No movement of the porter—no trace of anyone approaching.

"Now's the time," thought Wild.

He darted to the niche in the wall, and in a second one of the great keys was transferred to his own pocket.

He retired to the position in which the servant had left him, and commenced to whistle carelessly, beating time, meanwhile, with his great stick on the floor of the hall.

The servant was not long absent, and on returning wore a more puzzled expression of countenance than before.

"Well," said Wild; "what says the lady?"

"You're to go up," answered the servant.

"Oh, I am, am I? Well, that's considerate on her part. Show the way."

The man tried to assume his wonted aristocratic and starchy bearing, but the attempt turned out a lamentable failure. His wonderment reduced him to a very ordinary individual indeed, and all the training he had undergone went for nothing on this occasion.

He had all the appearance of the vulgar, inquisitive lout he was before leaving the plough tail in his native Dorset.

Wild tripped lightly after this man up the stairs of the house, and in a short time was landed in a magnificent drawing-room, which fairly glittered with the glorious golden plate and trophies of the Lakemonts, all arranged with true artistic taste and care.

The sight did not, however, at all startle Wild.

He appeared to be quite as much at home in that drawing-room as he would be in the cells of Newgate; and advancing to the Duchess, who sat in a chair at a window, commanding a view of the gardens, said, with the greatest *nonchalance*—

"We meet sooner than you anticipated, my dear madam: but good fortune has attended me, and I am enabled to quiet your natural anxiety before the promised time. Dismiss your servant."

"Retire," said the Duchess, waving off the footman, who remained with the door in his hand.

As soon as this fellow had taken his departure, the Duchess rose hurriedly to her feet, and in a tone of anger addressed her visitor.

"How dare you come here?" she said, throwing a look of fury at Jonathan.

"Hoity-toity!" cried that individual, "why all this rage? I thought I was doing you the greatest possible favour; but if you take my visit in this manner I will retire at once."

"Stay, you said something of being successful. Have you the diamonds?"

"I have; and it appears that my thanks for the expedition I have used are frowns and high words."

"Pardon them. I am angered at your coming, for it will make people talk. Your manner, your appearance, is strange—so—"

"So disgusting—that's the word! Use it, you won't hurt my feelings."

"No, no ; I meant so entirely different to what my people are accustomed, that this visit will give rise to gossip that might find its way to the ears of the Duke—"

"No fear. I am not one who would commit myself by an act or word. You may rest satisfied."

"Then to the matter that occasioned your coming—the diamonds."

"They are here."

Jonathan produced the glittering gems, perfect and unsullied, as when taken from the Duchess. He threw them on the table carelessly, and rose.

"I succeeded, you see, but the next time I may not use so much care over a matter in which you are connected."

The Duchess looked confused.

"Pardon me," she said at length, "pray pardon me. I meant not to offend you, but I am ill, sick at heart, and scarce know what I say. Give my words no heed, and be assured that I am grateful."

"Well," said Wild, "that's more the style of thing I like, and, as I don't bear malice very often, I'll say no more of what's past."

"You are good," said the Duchess. She then went to a splendid *escritoire*, and, opening it, drew forth an immense sum of money, from which she selected notes to the amount of one thousand pounds, and, placing them in the hands of Wild, she resumed her seat.

"Whew," thought Jonathan ; "this would be something like a crib to open. The swag that could be brought away would be worth something, and no mistake."

"And now," said the Duchess, blushing crimson as she spoke, "once more, touching this unhappy man, Clifford. Is there not a ray of hope for him ?"

"Not one, madam ; on that point I am adamant."

"I would give all I am possessed of to effect his release. The contents of that drawer (she pointed to the one from which she had taken the notes) shall be yours ; only release Clifford."

"The contents of that drawer will be mine without doing so much to earn it," said Wild, to himself ; but aloud he merely said he was sorry—deeply grieved, to think that he could not comply with the lady's request.

"And now," he continued, "our business is over, madam, and I will take my leave. Should you again want me, you know where I am to be found."

"Yes," said the Duchess, while mentally she added, "God forbid."

"Good day, madam," said Wild. "If there's any message to convey to Clifford, I don't mind taking it."

"Enough, sir," said the Duchess, indignantly ; "our business is over."

With a rude laugh Wild left the room, and, descending the stairs, was soon out of the house.

Tossing the discomfited servant a guinea as held the door open for his departure, he walked away, leaving behind him a better impression than he had made on his appearance.

CHAPTER XXV.

WILD FOLLOWS UP AN IDEA—THE SELECTION OF CRACKSMEN—THE BURGLARY.

"I LIKE to dabble in my old ways," said the thief-taker, as he stood with his back to the fire in his own office. "There's something prime in cracking a good crib, and the sight of a good sack of swag is more congenial to my tastes than any amount of gold earned by other means, acceptable as that may be."

He reflected for over an hour, and then called his Jew.

"What is the hour ?" he asked.

"Shix."

"Who's here ?"

"About a 'af dozen."

"Name them."

"Carrotty Ned."

"Yes."

"Bodger Backley."

"Yes."

"Washy Patkins."

"Humph !"

"Bill Hawkes."

"Yes."

"Snipey Villiam."

"Good."

"And Squally Stocks."

"Pah !"

"Which means that Squally isn't vanted ?"

"Just so."

"Nor Washy Patkins ?"

"I don't know about that fellow ; he's a clever area sneak, and at this he's handy in a big cracking game. He steals about like a snake, and being about as thin, can get into places that an ordinary man could not enter."

"Oh, he's a werry handy poy, is Vashy, and if he only had more heart he'd put some of 'em to shame ; put the poy's vhite livered, and don't care about a rough job."

"I know it. Nevertheless, he may come up with the other fellows."

"Shall I call 'em ?"

"Yes, all except Stokes. I don't want him under any circumstances."

The Jew vanished, and in a few moments returned in company with five of the most disreputable-looking villains it was possible to conceive.

At a glance any neophyte could distinguish the man referred to as Washy Patkins.

He was a lean and lank individual, with red or gingery hair, and his face was a dirty white ; and from this he, in all probability, received his cognomen of Washy.

He was very dirty, and had small eyes, that betrayed, by their constant blinking, the cur he was at heart.

The others were all sturdy villains, of the true type of burglars ; low, beetle-browed, flat-nosed, heavy-jawed, and high cheek-boned. There was no mistaking them.

"Well, governor," said Backley, "what's in the wind now ?"

"Much."

"Any business to do ?"

"Yes ; a crib's to be cracked."

"Then we're the boys to do it, only say where it it is and name the captain, and we'll be there, and do the work like true cracksmen."

"It's the house of the Duke of Lakemont, and it's situated in Cavendish-square."

Wild looked into the faces of the men, and enjoyed the look of surprise marked on all their countenances.

"You seem rather discontented," he said.

"Well, governor," continued Backley, still acting as spokesman for the others, "you see, we didn't think it was so big a job as that."

"I suppose not. It's magnitude and danger somewhat daunts you."

"Well, governor, there's no use in denying of it. The square's devilish well looked after ; the house is full of servants, and we may get ——"

"The worst of it. I should say that was more than probable. But you'll attempt it ?"

"Well, Mr. Wild, for my part I don't mind, but, I must say, I should not care much about acting unless there was a first-class captain at the head of us."

"You shall have one."

"That's another thing. Name him, and I've no doubt we shall get on all right. Do we know him ? Have we worked with him before ?"

"You do know him, and you have worked with him before."

"His name ?"

"Is *Jonathan Wild*."

"What ; the governor going at it again ?"

"Yes; just this once. It's a matter I don't care to trust out of my own hands."

"And perfectly right, too, for if there's one man in the world better able to pull through a job of this kind than another, it's Jonathan Wild."

"Enough! You are all prepared to follow me to-night?"

"Yes," they shouted in a chorus, "any time you like to name."

"To-night be it, then. At twelve."

"We'll all be ready."

"But what say you," said Wild, turning to Washy Patkins; "this is a little out of your line. Don't you shake at the chance of getting blown to the devil by some clever officer?"

"Not I," said Washy, looking very valiant indeed; "such trifles don't bother me."

The others burst into a loud roar, and the grim visage of Wild was lighted up with something like a smile.

"That's good language," he said, after a pause; "I like it, and I'll make you my lieutenant on the spot. You shall share all the danger with me, and all the glory afterwards."

The others again roared, but Washy looked remarkably pleased at the eminence he had so suddenly and unexpectedly attained.

"Now, begone," continued Wild, "and let me see you at twelve, in Cavendish-square. Mind, don't be all of a heap and attract the attention of the Charleys. I suppose you know better than to do that?"

"Trust us."

"It will be time enough to meet when you hear my whistle, and that will be given from the door step of the Duke's house."

"At twelve, then."

*   *   *   *   *   *

It was a splendid night, and there was but the faintest sign of clouds obscuring the brilliancy of the moon, as Wild, roughly clad, stepped from his house into the streets, and made his way towards Cavendish-square.

The thief-taker gave a rapid glance at the heavens, and uttered a loud curse.

"It's always so," he said, "want a fine night, and you'll never get it. Pray for a dark one, and it won't come."

He strode on, highly indignant with the weather and made rapid progress towards his destination.

It was a long walk, but Jonathan did the distance in a comparatively short time.

He had calculated the distance to a nicety.

As he stepped towards the Duke's house the clock struck twelve.

He paused and looked about him.

"Too soon, too soon," he muttered; "but I must give the signal."

There were lights in the house, and the shadows of figures were observable on the blinds; nevertheless Jonathan applied his whistle to his mouth and blew a loud shrill blast.

In a moment the five ruffians were at his side.

"Too soon, too soon," he said. "There are people within, and in all probability there is a party. If so, all the better. Be here again at two o'clock, sharp to the moment."

As if they had sunk into the ground the men disappeared, as silently and mysteriously as they had come.

Wild, too, walked away.

*   *   *   *   *

Two hours soon passed, and once more Wild was within the square. As he entered it a watchman was passing through.

"Two o'clock, and a fine moonlight morning," cried the old man.

"Oh, yes," said Jonathan, "d—n ye, we know all about that, you needn't wake the people to tell 'em so."

He kept under the shadow of the houses until the watch had passed. Then he glided rapidly to the door of the house.

All was silent now.

No lights —no sign of animation.

"This is something like business," cried Wild, in delight. "And now for the boys."

He applied the whistle to his mouth, and in an instant 'the boys' were around him.

"Now for it," said Jonathan, "steady all!"

He advanced to the door, and drawing the great key from his pocket, he applied it to the lock.

Without trouble the door opened.

"Well, that's neat," said Backley; "how the devil did you manage that?"

"No matter. It's enough that we're in without bother."

"Well," said Washy, "the Captain is a wonder."

CHAPTER XXVI.

THE SPOIL—THE BURGLARS AND THE MURDER.

On entering the house, the door was carefully re-closed and locked, and then Wild drew from his pocket a lantern, with which he completely illuminated the passage to the stairs.

"Where do we commence?" asked Backley.

"Up stairs," was the reply of Wild.

They trod softly along the hall, and as silently wended their way up the stairs.

Wild led, and soon had his men in the drawing-room.

Here two more lanterns were produced, and in a brief period the treasures of the apartment lay exposed to the view of the lawless band.

Wild pointed out the work each had to do.

"Stow as much as you can, but don't overload; too much is worse than too little."

The men were soon ransacking the room in all corners, whilst Jonathan applied himself to the escritoire.

He thirsted for the immense heap of money he knew to be concealed there, and drawing a large clasp knife from his pocket, he applied it to the drawer to which he had seen the Duchess go.

It did not take him a great while to force the lock, and then the treasure lay under his hand.

"What's there?" asked Backley.

"No matter to you; attend to your own business."

"Oh, all right, captain; no offence in asking, I suppose."

"Not in the least, only don't do it again."

The man directed his attention to some plate near at hand, and with no further heed of Jonathan, who, without delay, filled his pockets with the treasure of the Duchess.

"Kind soul!" he said, "how considerate of her to leave all this good money here for my especial use. So it was to be mine for the liberation of Clifford, was it? Ha! ha! it's mine without that bother; without that foregoing of vengeance. All, all—every penny."

"What's the matter, captain," asked Backley, alarmed at Wild's manners.

"Nothing, nothing—attend to your work."

"It's all very fine to say attend to your work; but p'raps you'll tell us what other work we've got to attend to. The sacks are as full as they'll hold, and we think as how the best thing to do is to be off."

"You're right, boys; enough's as good as a feast. Come along."

They rose to their feet simultaneously, and were making for the door, when an incident occurred that somewhat checked their progress.

In the doorway stood the footman to whom Wild had given the guinea in the fore part of the day.

As may easily be comprehended, the man's face now wore a more puzzled expression than ever.

He fixed his eyes upon Wild, and started back.

"Stop," cried Wild, "stop, or I'll blow you to the devil!"

"Help! help!" shouted the man, rushing down the stairs. "Help!—help!—robbers!—thieves!—help!—help!"

Jonathan sprang after the man like a tiger, and, drawing a pistol, prepared to let fly at him, but the man was beyond reach.

Flying down the stairs, he sped across the hall, and, dashing open the door, ran into the streets, and screamed aloud for help.

Jonathan followed him to the door of the house.

He heard a great springing of rattles, of answers to the call of the alarmed footman from the by-no-means-distant watchmen.

He saw that to follow him from the house would be to run into the very jaws of danger; so he rapidly re-closed the door, and ascended the stairs.

On the landing he found his fellows, pale with fear, and trembling from head to foot.

"Steady," he cried, "steady, or all is lost."

"What's to be done?"

"Keep quiet."

"Hark! I hear a footstep."

In another moment a light was seen approaching, and a voice reiterating the cries of the footman.

On through the corridor came the light, and the men stood at bay, ready to follow the command of the Captain who led them.

"Let us see what this fellow is made of," said Wild.

He left his men, and advanced to meet the approaching figure.

In a moment they were together.

"Villain!" shrieked the man, who proved to be no other than the old Duke, "villain! robber! what do ye here? I'll have ye all hanged!"

"Silence, you old ass," cried Wild; "does not the little sense you have left tell you that your best plan is to keep silent?"

"Villain! I'll call my servants! Miscreants, I defy ye all! Help! help!"

"Silence, I say; or this moment shall be your last!"

"Help! help!"

"You will not cease?"

"Help! help! I say; why do ye linger? I am beset. Help! help! John!—Alfred!—Thomas!—Char—!"

"Curse ye, you drive me to it," cried Wild, placing his hand on the old man's throat.

"Help!—hel—Char—!"

"Will ye cease?"

"Help!"

"Then Heaven have mercy upon you."

Wild opened his great clasp-knife with his teeth, and next moment the blade was buried deep in the old man's throat.

With a moan the poor old Duke fell to the ground.

"He's done for," said Wild; "but it was his own look out. I gave him all the chances I could."

"What's to be done now?"

"What's to be done? why, escape, to be sure."

"How?"

"That's to be considered."

The men seemed to have complete confidence in Wild's every movement, and they followed his every plan with the docility of dogs, feeling sure that he could conduct them in safety.

As the chief was planning an escape from the threatening danger, a loud knocking at the door disturbed the whole party.

"Do you hear that, Captain?"

"To be sure I do; I'm not deaf."

"Yes, but—but," said Washy, "this is getting—"

"Well?"

"Well, it's rather a teaser, ain't it?"

"No; it's one thing to knock, but it's another to get in, I can tell you. I've taken care of the door."

"What have you done?"

"I've placed that in the lock that it would take the devil himself to get out, if he were the most expert of locksmiths; so you may consider the door tolerably safe."

"Oh, what a glorious creature the Captain is," said Washy, elevating his eyes.

All this time there was no heed paid to the dying man. The thoughts of that group of evil ones were solely bent upon self-preservation, and, had fifty men lain dying around them, they would have heeded them not.

"Come," cried Wild, "there is but one thing left us, and that is, to reach the top of the house. There is sure to be some trap in the roof serving as a fire-escape. We must go there at once."

Springing over the prostrate form of the Duke, the men mounted the stairs, and in a short time reached the attic of the house.

Just over their heads, on the landing, was a trap door, apparently leading to the roof.

"I thought as much," said Jonathan, looking up.

"Lor, Mr Wild," said Washy, "it's my opinion that you know everything."

"Produce the light!" said Wild, without heeding the compliment paid him by the pale and fearful Washy; "Look about for the ladder!"

"Here it is, secured to the wall," said one.

"That's right, boys. Have it off; we shall do. Act with care and caution."

Another terrific burst of knocking at the door now resounded throughout the house, and, at the same moment, one of the doors of the mansion's attics opened, and a man looked out, crying—

"Goodness, gracious! is it fire?"

"No," cried Wild, as he hit the man a tremendous blow on the head with a short club, that sent him flying back again into his room; "No, it's thieves, old fellow."

This was another footman, and the only one who, despite the great disturbance, dared to show himself.

Servants are not, as a rule, a very valiant order of men

"Now for the ladder," cried Wild; "quick—quick I say. That will do—follow me. Don't crowd, though for there's time enough for all."

The ladder fitted into the ledge of the trap-door, and, no sooner was it adjusted, than Wild mounted it, closely, perhaps too closely, followed by his anxious comrades.

Then it was that a series of heavy blows upon the street door let them know the officers had discovered that any attempt to get it open, short of using main force, was out of the question.

"They've got a crow-bar," said the lowermost on the ladder.

"Very likely," said Wild.

"The door won't stand long against that."

"Not a minute."

"There it goes."

"I told you so," said Wild, "and now it's our turn to follow the example at this door."

He drew back the bolt in the little trap-door, and then it opened.

Another moment, and he scrambled through into the dark space between the inner roof and the tiles.

Wild was in perfect darkness.

"Hand me a light," he cried.

"Here's one."

"That will do."

He shaded the light with his hand, and then he saw the opening in the outer roof that led out on the leads of the house. One thrust of his disengaged hand flung it over on its hinges, and the rush of wind blew out the light.

The darkness was profound.

"No fear of daylight yet," said Wild.

"I don't know about that," said Washy; "its always darker just before daybreak than at any other time."

"Come on; tumble up," said Wild; "daylight or not, there's no time to throw away. Come on, one and all of you. There's lots of room here on the roof; and mind that the last man closes up the small trap-door in the ceiling."

"All right, Captain."

Washy was the first to follow Wild.

Fear made him exceedingly agile, and he was at the elbow of the captain at a moment's notice. He was followed by Bill Hawkes and Backley.

The two still below called out in frantic accents—

"The officers are coming! Get out of the way, and let us come! We can hear them coming up the stairs."

"On—on!" cried Wild; "but no hurrying."

They just contrived to get through the trap-door between the roofs, when the foremost of the officers presented himself on the top of the stairs.

Wild lay at full length on the roof, and placed his ear so that he could listen to all that was said.

"Hillo!" said one of the officers, "I'll bet my life that they're on the roof."

"So will I," said another, "but here is a ladder."

"All's right. Hoi, hoi! come up here. You will have the game rather *high* though. Ha! ha! that's not bad."

"Bad," said Wild to himself, "that's very clever: I didn't think that there was so much wit in the whole bundle of Newgate birds."

There was a scrambling and scampering of feet on the stairs, and Wild began to feel that the situation of himself and his friends was anything but pleasant.

"We are done for now, as safe as possible," said the chicken-hearted Washy.

"Who said that?" asked Wild.

"I—I—did," said Washy.

"Then you had best be quiet, for the way to be done for is to insist upon it before it happens."

"If you can save us, Mr. Wild—"

"If? Stuff!"

"You cannot!"

"Who says cannot? Hark you all, now, once for all! I have undertaken to lead you through this affair, and intend to do it, at all risks. I never yet deceived a comrade, and I don't mean to begin with you. All you have to do is to follow me obediently."

"There is no fear of that."

"Hush, now," said Wild, "they come, they come. They don't seem, though, to be able to manage the trap-door very well."

"It's not likely they will," said he who came through last, "for as I shut it down I felt it jamb after me, in an awkward fashion, and I jumped upon it to fasten it."

"If they will have the goodness to remain below just five minutes more, I will send them down the ladder quicker than they shall come up it."

"How do you mean?"

"You," said Wild, turning to one of his band,—"you are a strong fellow; follow me."

"Yes, captain."

This man, who was familiarly known as Carrotty, possessed more strength and courage than all the others united, and, knowing this, Wild selected him for his lieutenant, in place of Washy, who did not at all like this preferment.

Carrotty scrambled on to the roof after Wild, who looked through the trap, and said to the others,—

"Don't stir; don't stir till I come for you, if you value your lives."

"No, no."

"Come this way, Carrotty," said Wild: "it is a good foothold along this drain, and we have both clear heads, I think."

CHAPTER XXVII.

THE WAY IN WHICH WILD TREATED THE OFFICERS—THE ESCAPE FROM THE DUKE'S HOUSE.

WILD and his man crawled along the drain that ran by the ridges of the tiles, and in a few moments they came upon a stack of chimney-pots.

"Carrotty."

"Well, capt'n."

"We can reach the chimney easy enough."

"Oh, yes."

"Well, I have been upon the tops of many houses in my time, and I never yet touched a chimney-pot that you could not lift out of its place with a very small amount of force."

"Nor I."

"Well, there's no direct occasion why these should prove an exception to the rule."

"I think not."

"Well, I want one of these gentlemen."

"Very good."

"Lay hold of this one. Ah! it moves, of course. Have you a good hold?"

"Yes."

"Then lift. Gently with it. It is heavier than it looks. Now, can you guess what I want it for?"

"Yes."

"Ah! you can?"

"I can; you want it to send down upon the heads of the officers directly they show themselves above the trap," said the assistant, with a grim smile.

"Ah! you're a fellow of discernment, come along."

It was a perilous task to carry that massive chimney-pot along the slippery, narrow gutter, but Wild and Carrotty were both men of great strength and nerve, and they moved along under their great burthen with comparative ease and rapidity.

When they reached the trap-door they found that their friend had scrambled through.

"Good Lord! what's that?"

"It's a body," said one.

"No, it's a chimney," said another.

"Silence, all of you," said Wild. "What are the officers about?"

"They're working away at the trap-door like mad; they seem to think that we are holding it."

"Then keep your heads out of the way, or a bullet may find its way through directly."

"But what are you going to do with that chimney-pot, Captain?"

"You will see. There."

Wild adjusted his chimney-pot so that by a slight push he might tip it through the aperture in the roof, and so down upon the opening in the ceiling below.

The whole gang at once saw the plan the chief intended to pursue.

"That will do beautifully," said Carrotty, "we shall get the better of the rascals this time."

"Yes; Wild managed this affair capitally," said Washy.

At this Wild laughed heartily, but he forbore to make any remark.

Meanwhile the officers worked away at the trap door, which had got a little awry, and was thus jammed tight in such a way that made them think the burglars were holding it down as a last resource against capture.

With this idea, one of them spoke,

"Hillo!" he cried, "it's of no use up there, my boys, it won't do, you're as good as nabbed, and you know it; come, now don't be foolish."

Not a sound was heard in reply.

"Now then," he continued, "curse your obstinacy; let go the trap and hold your hands; it's the best way when you're at this pass."

No reply.

"Oh, you won't speak, won't you? If you won't be

civil, why, you'll have to take the consequences, that's all."

Again no reply.

"Hey? Did you say anything! Hey? Now then above there, I know you're holding that door, and I mean to fire a brace of pistols through it, each of which is loaded with a couple of slugs; why, the best thing you can do is to get out of the way.

All were silent.

"Oh," continued the officer, "you will have it, will you? Now I shall count three before I fire. I'm sorry to swindle the hangman, but if you will have the slugs, you know it's no fault of mine, and I'm only doing my duty."

There was a pause of a moment, and then they heard him say,

"Push now."

A vigorous effort was made to force the door, but it still resisted their efforts and remained fast.

"Very good," said the officer. "One—two—do you hear, you asses? I am going to say three."

"Keep out of the way," said Wild to his men.

"Yes, Captain."

"Three."

Bang—bang.

Two pistols were discharged in rapid succession.

The shock of the bullets going through the trap loosened it, and it no longer stuck fast as it had done.

"Come on, comrades," said the foremost of the officers "I must have hit some of 'em, I'm quite sure, for the trap is loose enough now."

"All's right."

"Follow me, quickly,"

The officers now rushed in a body up the ladder, and one of them was partly through the trap, when Wild put his mouth in the hollow of the chimney-pot, and cried—

"Ha! ha! Meet the doom you seek!"

"Oh, d—n the doom. D'ye think we're children, to be frightened by that row?"

"You're dead men!"

"Come on, my boys!"

There was a struggle to get through the trap; but, as the first man got on to the roof, Wild gave the chimney-pot an impetus downwards, and away it went, crashing through the orifice in the roof, and then fell, with terrific force, straight on the trap-door in the ceiling.

The consequence was that the officers were swept, like an avalanche, before it; and, the ladder being shaken from its position, the whole of the men were laid prostrate on the landing, at the top of the attic stairs.

Wild smiled at his ghastly work; and the others looked on with something like awe depicted in their faces.

There was a shriek and a groan, and then the thief-taker turned to his companions, and said—

"That's done for them. We can go on all right now."

"Go on," said Washy; "it's all very well to say 'go on;' but where are we going on? What's the next move?"

"Let all follow me: I know the way to get out of the scrape. All these houses are alike in construction; and, as I prefer going down the next trap-door instead of this one, you had all best stick to me, and bring along the swag. Don't leave that behind."

"We will follow you, Mr. Wild."

"Not that name! Fool, don't whisper it! You know not what ears may be open, and I've no wish to appear at the Old Bailey to-morrow. All powerful as I am, I might find it a tough job to pull through such a slaughter-house job as this."

They carefully closed the door in the tiles, and then scrambled along the narrow ridge, dragging the plunder after them.

In a few moments they were at the trap-door in the roof of the next house.

"Now then," said Wild, "you have the way all right?"

"Oh, yes, Captain."

"Take care of it."

"We will."

"It would be galling to lose it after such work to get it."

"As you say, Captain, it would be galling; but have no fears."

"Oh, I'm satisfied. Now, follow me, and understand that we want to get out of this house without noise, so use all your discretion, and try and emulate the mouse in quickness and lightness of foot."

"All's well; we understand."

It was now close upon five o'clock, and daylight was at hand.

In their elevated position they could see the long streaks of light begin to show themselves in the east, and every object was becoming more and more distinct each moment.

In the event of any early risers getting a glimpse of them on the top of the house, their detection would be a matter of certainty.

Wild did not, however, exhibit any sign of fear, for he knew that he was in a neighbourhood where early rising was not, as a rule, indulged in.

Nevertheless, he made his men all crouch down while he tried the trap-door.

"It strikes me, Captain, that the sooner we are out of this the better," said Washy.

"I know it," said Wild.

"You have your hand on the trap."

"Yes, and it is conveniently open for us, but we may have more trouble below."

Wild lifted the trap.

"Now, gentlemen," he said, "you will see that all you have to do is to follow me."

As he spoke, he let himself through the opening in the roof.

They all went after him in perfect silence, and then, to his satisfaction, he found that the lower door was open, and yielded to his touch.

All was darkness there in the house.

"Hush," said Wild, "let me listen for a moment or two. It won't do to drop into an ambush."

They were all as silent for the space of a minute as if death had suddenly seized upon the whole party.

That minute appeared to be ten at the very least, but they did not interrupt Wild, who peered through the trap door, and listened with breathless attention.

At length, to the relief of the men, he looked up, and said, in a low tone—

"I don't think there's a mouse stirring in the house."

They felt much delighted at this, and appeared satisfied that they should get out of the adventure with nothing more than their fright to remind them of it.

"Follow me one by one, and very silently. There's no steps to aid you, but you'll not find any difficulty in dropping this small height. It is a mere nothing, as you will find."

With great skill Wild dropped to the landing-place.

"The swag," said Wild.

"Yes, Captain, all right."

"Hand it down."

It was pushed through the trap, and the whole of the men followed it.

"Is there anything to be done here?" asked the carrotty one.

"No, delays are dangerous; besides, we've enough."

As he spoke, the sound of voices fell upon his ear.

"Hush."

They all listened, but could not make up their minds where those sounds came from. Then they were convinced that they came from the street, and this assured them of the danger they would run into in attempting an exit under the circumstances.

They looked at each other in doubt, and with some little appearance of dismay.

Wild listened.

"What's to be done ?" asked the carrotty one, after a smile.

"I don't quite know. We must wait, although each moment is fraught with more and more danger to us."

It was quite evident Jonathan was rather at a nonplus. No doubt many plans of operation flitted through his fertile brain, but which to adopt puzzled him, as it might have done a more far-seeing and acute man than Jonathan.

If they remained where they then were they saw a chance of some one coming up and discovering them, and so giving the alarm at once, and, besides, the daylight was indeed making rapid strides.

Then, again, if they should descend to the lower part of the house and attempt to emerge into the streets, all the probabilities were in favour of the supposition that the officers and the people of the house they had plundered could at once disarm them, and make a desperate effort to effect their capture.

After a while, Jonathan turned sharply to his companions, and said—

"I have concluded that there is less danger in going than in remaining."

"I think so," said the carrotty one.

"I'm glad you agree with me. Let us go, then, at once."

"But—but," said Washy, " are we to make a rush out of the house ?"

"No ; we must go as quietly as possible, and take our chance of being stopped. We are all well armed, and if any of the officers stop us, we must fight our way off. I think that the possibility is we shall get a good way down the street at once, and without obstruction ; and then the principal force of the officers will be behind us at the next house."

"Yes."

"You are all prepared to follow me, I suppose ?"

"We are !—we are !" they all murmured.

"That is well ; come on, then."

Jonathan coolly led the way down stairs, walking with as much confidence as if he had been descending the stairs of his own house. But the party were not doomed to get far without something in the shape of an adventure.

The moment they reached the landing of the second floor, upon which the principal bed-rooms of the house were situated, some one there sleeping opened a door, and a nightcapped head projected out, while a voice called—

"John, John; what is that noise ?"

Wild's companions drew back in alarm, but Jonathan himself stepped up to the door, and placing his hands upon the shoulders of the old gentleman, for such it was, he said—

"Sir, do you want your throat cut ?"

"Eh ! Oh, no—no—no—murder !"

"Silence ! I am an officer, and am here for your protection. The house is full of thieves, but I and my men are on the look out : we can't miss them."

"Can't you ? That's very gratifying to my feelings."

"My advice is," said Wild, "that you do one of two things : either dress yourself and come and aid me, so that you may share in the glory of the capture of the villains, and probably die some awful death in the defence of your property, or go into your room and lock the door, and don't appear until it is all over."

"I think the latter course would be the most gratifying to my feelings."

"Very good, sir ; that is the course I should have advised you to take. By the bye, what is the time ?"

"I will look at my watch."

"Bring it here at once, then."

The old gentleman at once brought a watch to the door, and Wild took possession of it, saying,—

"This will be handy to me, and you may depend upon my returning it as soon as this shocking affair is over."

"But, sir, such a course is not gratifying to my feelings."

"Ah ! I hear them. Perhaps it would be best, after all, if you come and join us."

"No, no, no. Such a course would—"

Wild heard no more. Without delay, he closed the door, and disappeared from sight.

"Come on, now," said Wild, with a laugh. "I don't think we shall be interrupted again."

They now ran down the staircase as fast as possible, and reached the hall in a moment or two. Just as they entered it though, and as Wild was making for the door, there came a loud rat-tat at it, and he drew back.

"Who the devil is that, now ?"

The others looked at each other in gloomy silence.

Rat-tat-tat came the knock at the door again.

"It's the officers."

"Not a doubt of it."

"They are knocking for leave to get on the roof of the house."

"They are," said Wild.

"What can we do."

"Just nothing. Let them knock again."

The officers, for such they really were, did not pause long between their knocks, but at length the tattoo they played on the door resounded through the hall like thunder.

There came with a shuffling step down a back staircase of the house to the hall, a man who was hastily pulling on a pair of yellow plush smalls and a livery coat' and who looked very wild and only half awake.

"Oh, lord !" he cried, as he caught sight of Wild and his gang, " there's something the matter I do believe."

"There is," said Wild, approaching the fellow, who stood stock still, "stop."

"Oh, don't; I'm only a poor fellow who never hurt anybody in all my life, so don't do me any harm."

"None is intended you."

"I'm so frightened,—fire ! thieves !"

"Now, my good fellow," said Wild, " if you continue that noise you will compel me, however much it may go against my feelings, to blow your brains out. Do you see that pistol ?" Wild presented one at his head ; " well it is loaded with slugs, and, if you say another word they will lodge in your skull. Will you attend to me ?"

"Ye—ye—yes ! Oh, spare my life ! I'm only a poor man, with twenty pounds a year, sir ; and find my own tea and ale, sir."

"Poor devil ! Talk of the badness of the world ! My only wonder is that there are half so many honest men in it ! Now, listen to me."

"Yes, sir."

"Are you the footman ?"

"Yes, sir. Footman to Mr. Barjoribanks, if you please."

Bang ! bang ! bang !

"Do you hear that ?"

"Yes, sir."

"Go to the door," said Wild.

"Yes, sir."

"And, if you follow my instructions, you may save your life."

"Yes—yes, sir."

"Those who are now knocking are officers. They want leave to go on the top of your house to look for some suspicious characters. You will open the door for them."

"Yes, sir."

"And let them pass up stairs to execute their duty."

"Yes, sir."

"We will stay in the dining-room here, and you will not look towards that apartment."

"No, sir."

"Nor by word or act signify that it has occupants."

"I wont; indeed, I won't, sir."

"If you do, I shall blow you to the devil !"

"Yes, sir ; you are very good, sir."

"You comprehend me now ?"

"Couldn't mistake you, sir."

"Well, here's a couple of guineas for you; so do your work properly. No nonsense, or you know the consequences."

The man evidently had a better opinion of Wild the moment he clutched his gold, and went to the door without any further hesitation.

Jonathan gave a sign with his hand to his companions to follow him, and they all went into the dining room, the door of which Wild kept just a little open, so that he could both see and hear what passed in the hall between the officers and the footman.

In a moment there were half a dozen men in the presence of the terrified servant.

"We are officers," said the new comers, "and we want to get on the roof of this house, so get out of the way."

"But—but——"

"Oh, we lose no time to talk to you. The magistrates in the morning will satisfy your master about why we came, so get out of the way, do, and don't impede us."

The footman was pushed aside, and some half dozen officers at once dashed through the hall, and made their way up the stairs at great speed.

"That will do," said Wild, as he stepped out into the hall, "you did that very well, John."

"Lor, sir, how did you know my name was John?"

"I guessed it—good morning, John. You may now sleep in peace, you may depend, for we will consent that you live as long as you possibly can."

"You are very kind, sir."

"I say," said one of the officers, at this moment returning quickly down the stairs, "be so good, Mr. Footman, as to keep the outer door fast, and——The devil!"

He just saw Wild and his party standing on the door step, and for about half a minute the two opposing principles of thieves and thief-taker regarded each other in silence.

The officer then rapidly drew a small, thick holster-pistol from his pocket, and pointing it at the group in the hall, cried out—

"I'll have one of you at all risks; so here goes."

Bang! went the pistol.

"Fair play all the world over," said Wild. "It's my turn, now, old fellow, so here goes."

Bang! went Wild's pistol, and the officer fell headlong down the stairs to the hall below.

"Who is hit?" said Wild to his party.

"None—none," they all cried.

"Come on, then, there is not a moment more to lose. Those pistol shots will give an alarm to the other officers, and we shall have them all upon us. On, on, after me!"

They sallied from the house, leaving the dead officer in the hall, and the scarcely less dead footman lying on his back, half fainting from fright at the rapidity with which two shots had been exchanged in such dangerous proximity to his person.

Wild turned to the left when he got out of the house, and rapidly walked down the street.

The others followed him, and in a few moments they met a watchman, who held up his lantern for a moment, and then evidently thought it the best and wisest plan to say nothing, so he turned his back to them, and called out in a loud voice—

"Past five, and a fine morning!"

"It's a lie, for it rains," said Wild.

"Yes, sir," said the watch. "Past five, and it rains!"

Wild laughed to himself, and then seeing a hackney coach coming swinging along, he turned to his companions, and said—

"I am going in that coach. Now, give me the swag. I know where to part with it before to-morrow night, or rather to-night, and you can have your shares at the old ken."

"All right, Captain. We can depend upon you."

"You may; and you may so far depend upon me, too, as to feel assured that I know where to get double the money for the swag that any of you could, and so your shares will be all the greater, and you will lose nothing by my taking half."

"That's right enough, Captain. All's right"

"Hoi!" called out Wild, and the coach stopped.

"Coach, yer honour?"

"Yes. You needn't get down—we can manage."

"Lor, but I can't take all on you, you know, for the regular fare, gents."

"No, we are not all going; and as for the regular fare, I don' mean to give it."

"You don't?"

"No. When I hire a coach, I hire a sensible coachman with it, and I give him a guinea."

As he spoke, Jonathan Wild handed a guinea to the coachman, who, after placing it between his teeth to assure himself that it was genuine, said—

"You is a gent, and no mistake. That's how a coachman ought for to be treated, and no how otherwise. Get in all on you if you like, and I'll drive you anywhere."

"That will do,' said Wild, as he flung the booty into the coach. "Now, remember, at twelve o'clock I will be with you. Good-bye for the present."

"Good-bye, captain."

Wild sprang into the coach, and the others separated and went by different routes to where they knew they could rest during the hours of daylight, which did not at all suit gentlemen of their complexion.

"Where to, yer honour?" said the coachman.

"Oxford-street," said Wild. "Ha! ha! I'll give that pious fellow a really good turn now, for he deserves it, after the scurvy manner in which I served him over the diamonds."

———

CHAPTER XXVIII.

THE ATTACK ON THE INN BY SIR LEWIS AND HIS FRIENDS — PERIL OF EVELINA AND ROSE—THE STARTLING RESCUE.

IT may be presumed that the state of mind in which Sir Lewis returned to town after his unexpected defeat at the little inn was far from being an enviable one.

At first he intended rushing without delay to his friends, the officers of the King's Guards, and laying before them his troubles, but after a while he quite abandoned this plan for the present, being too much humiliated to carry it into effect.

So he went quietly to the quarters he occupied in St. James's-street, and skulked to bed.

Two days passed over without his once quitting the house, and then he perforce went forth again, and, as a consequence, sought the young men in whose society he found so much pleasure.

They received him with open arms, for he had money, and they had comparatively none; and then there were numbers of inquiries after the lovely "Diana."

At the mention of the lady he had so grossly persecuted, the young libertine hung his head in shame.

"I suppose," said his friend Danvers, "you have her snugly hid away down in verdant Winterleigh?"

"No."

"No? How is that? Changed your mind, and taken her somewhere else?"

"No."

"What the devil have you done with her, then?"

"Nothing; but she has done a great deal with herself."

"Explain yourself."

"That's readily done, but don't laugh at me too much, or you will add to the humiliation I already feel."

He then briefly explained to his friends the circumstances that occurred after his quitting them at Lord Belmore's."

Despite his request to be spared, the young men could not contain their mirth at the revelation of what they were pleased to term his softness.

They laughed long and loudly, and called the young country baronet by all the epithets expressive of contempt that they could think of.

After which they began to debate on what was to be done.

"Do you want to continue the game?" asked Danvers.

"I do," said Lewis. "I would give my right hand to humiliate her, and bring her once more within my power."

"Then it must be done."

"How?"

"I presume she is still at this little inn?"

"Not a doubt of it, although three days have elapsed since the rescue."

"Well, we must lay seige to the place, and bring her off."

"But is there not some danger in this?"

"Psha! who thinks of danger in such a matter? We will serve you if you like to trust to us."

"I shall be only too glad of your services."

"Then say no more about it. Ere night has closed over us, we will down upon this country inn, and bring forth the damsel—both of them, if you desire it."

"Very well, both of them. It is only one trouble."

A plan was soon arranged by which action was to be commenced forthwith.

Lewis was left with two of the officers, whilst Danvers went to see after the preliminaries.

"First," he said, "there are the horses to be saddled, and made ready, and excuses of illness, or some other preventitive from attending duty, to forward to head quarters. I must see after Bolter.

He went into the kitchen of the house, and calling a man who sat there, walked towards the stables.

"Bolter," said the officer to this individual, "saddle three horses immediately, one for myself, another for Captain Sharper, and the other for Sir Lewis Winterleigh."

"Troop horses?"

"No, my own private hacks. You appear to be a jolly sort of a fellow, and I've taken a fancy to you, although you have only been in my service two days, and I don't mind telling you the game. This young milksop, Winterleigh, has carried off a girl at Lord Belmore's ball, and then had her taken from him by two boors at a country inn. The damsel is still there, and we're going in a body to seize her, and bring her off; isn't it fine fun."

"Splendid," said Bolter, dryly.

"In ten minutes I'll have some letters for you to take to head-quarters; see that they are delivered at once, as they are to excuse Sharper and myself from duty to-night; and now," he continued, "look sharp with the horses."

"I won't be long, sir," said Bolter, touching his cap.

The officer walked away.

As soon as he was left alone, the features of this Mr. Bolter began to assume a remarkable likeness to those of Clifford's staunch friend and admirer, Bill Waters.

"Well," said that individual, "I have been and gone and entered this here service for something, I have. The Captain, he gave me the office—and it were the last the poor Captain ever did give me—to look after this young woman; and I've been a doing of it. I have watched her and watched her, until I seed her agoing to the ball dressed up anyhow, and then I lost all trace of her until this precious moment. But I guessed these coves had something to do with it, and so I've stuck to 'em, and to good purpose, by the look of it. But what's the odds now? Ain't the Gentleman in Newgate? Ain't it all up with him, and ain't I going to turn honest and stick to this service and never go on the road agin? Well, even let 'em take her—but no, d——n it, that won't do; the Gentleman mustn't say, Bill Waters gave up his gal 'cause he was shopped. No, that won't pay at any price; so I'll go to the old quarters and think on it, and try if something can't be done."

Having come to this determination, Mr. Bill Waters, late highwayman and thief, now servant in livery to a pair of vagabonds of his own calibre, walked off to saddle the horses.

* * * *

In high glee two out of three horsemen left London *en route* for the hostelrie of Job Winchurst.

They were Danvers and his friend with the ominous name.

The third was by no means in an enviable frame of mind, and appeared disposed to linger behind. He was Sir Lewis Winterleigh.

The road to the inn lay through pleasant lanes, and by the finest scenery to be found in the neighbourhood of the metropolis; and cantering onward gaily, the distance

appeared a mere trifle to those bound on the errand of mischief.

It was the third hour after midday when they drew rein at a small distance from the village inn.

They saw the old-fashioned little house, nestling in the sunny vale in which it was embosomed, and simultaneously they all drew rein, and gazed upon it.

"A suitable nest for so pretty a dove," said Danvers.

"Yes," said Lewis, "the nest is well enough, but you know not what a set of vipers it contains."

"No matter; we are capable of depriving them of their sting."

"I hope so."

"Be assured of it."

"All my assurance has vanished lately."

"Psha! Don't act the fool, man, but pluck up some kind of courage. if it be only Dutch courage."

"How shall I do that?"

"Here; pull at this flask."

Danvers handed to his friend a flask filled with brandy, and Lewis, applying it greedily to his lips, took it not therefrom until he had all but emptied it.

"Well," said Danvers, looking at the diminished fluid, "you seem to like that sort of thing, and I don't blame you, for it's the finest brand France could produce; but you might have left a decent mouthful for your friends."

"It does me good, it revives me."

"Poor fellow," said Danvers, "you certainly must be much distressed and fatigued by the exertion of riding ten miles through such a beautiful country."

"I am not so used to adventures of this kind as you appear to be."

"So it seems; for you have more the appearance of being dragged to a slaughter, than into the arms of a lovely woman."

"No more jesting," said Lewis; "but let us on, while I'm in the humour."

"By all means," said Danvers. "Don't let the opportunity slip. If you mean fighting, let us begin while your courage keeps at the sticking point. Ha! ha!"

They moved forward again, and in a few moments were in the yard of the inn. All was still!

Job and his right-hand man were enjoying a snooze: the former in his little bar parlour, the latter on a bundle of sweet hay in the stables.

There were two persons, however, who witnessed the advent of the horsemen. They were Evelina and Rose.

Seated at a window, engaged in some feminine occupation, were the two girls, radiant in loveliness, blooming in the bright spring sunshine, that poured upon them through the open casement.

"Here is custom for Job," said Rose, looking at her young mistress: "see, what gallant cavaliers!"

Evelina turned her eyes into the yard, and then sprang to her feet as if stung by an adder.

"See, see," she cried, "do you not recognise *him*?"

Rose looked out of the casement with anxious eyes, and her gaze lighted upon the upturned face of the young baronet.

Uttering a cry, she sprang back.

"They are come for us," said Evelina; "there can be no doubt of their intent. What shall we do?"

"Do not be distressed," said Rose, "I will act for you, and for our mutual welfare. Remain where you are."

The brave-hearted girl sprang from the side of her mistress, and descending the stairs with great speed, flew without hesitation to the door of the house, and closed and barred it.

She then ran into the bar, and awakened the slumbering Job.

"Job, Job, dear Job," she cried, "rouse ye, we are in danger."

"Hey—what? Danger? Who talks of danger in the Harvest Home? What d'ye mean, Rose?"

"I mean that Sir Lewis and two others are at the door,

evidently with the intention of bearing us off. What shall we do?"

Job, by this time thoroughly aroused, shook himself, and stared at his fair guest.

"D'ye mean it?" he said.

"Yes, yes—see for yourself."

"All right," said Job, "get you upstairs, and lock yourself up with Miss Evelina, and leave me to deal with these blackguards."

"But you will not let them take us—you will not deliver my sweet mistress into the power of that scoundrel?"

"Never, as I'm a living sinner!" cried Job. "I shouldn't be able to think of such a thing. It's like—it's like—d—n—its like anythink. I couldn't do it—I couldn't do it."

"Thanks—thanks."

"Get away, girl, don't give 'em a chance. I'll defend the stairs with my life. If they force an entrance, and try to mount 'em, it will only be over my body."

Rose ran quickly up the stairs, and followed the advice of Job, while Danvers, who appeared to lead the other two horsemen, advanced to the door, and knocked loudly.

Job walked into the kitchen, and opening the window, popped out his head, and demanded to know who was there.

"Gentlemen!" cried Danvers in reply; "gentlemen; so open at once."

"What is your business!"

"Our business," said Danvers, "why refreshments, of course; what other business could a traveller have at an inn, this time of the day?"

"Ah," said Job, "that will apply to ordinary travellers; but, there is one of the three who is in the habit of turning inns to other account; and, I should particularly like to know, what *his* intentions are *now*, before I open the door? You see, gentlemen, we know each other."

"Curse your impudence?" cried Danvers, "open the door."

"Again I ask, to what purpose?"

"Well," said the officer, "since you will be told, know that we are here to liberate a lady, whom you unlawfully retain. Her legal protector and guardian is here to bear her away."

"And, her legal protector and guardian is *here*, and says he'll see you d——d first."

"No insolence, fellow, but open, or it shall be the worse for you."

"And if you ain't off," said Job, "you shall find to your cost, that it shall be the worse for you. No man ever yet annoyed Job Winchurst with impunity."

"Oh, you're one of that sort, are you?" said Danvers, "but we'll soon teach you manners. Now, will you open?"

"Not if I know it."

"I give you fair warning, that we shall dismount and force an entrance."

"And I give you fair warning, that if you attempt it I shall dash the brains out of the first man that shows himself on this side of the threshold."

"Psha!" cried Danvers' friend, "he is but one, and unarmed, let us have no more parley with such a boor."

"All right," said Danvers, "one man is not much to engage; so come on. Now, Winterleigh, let us see what sort of stuff you are made of."

They drew their swords, and were about to dismount, when a horseman galloped into the yard, and facing the invading force, demanded to know their business.

"Who are you, who dares ask?" cried Danvers.

"I will tell you," said Lewis, raving with excitement; "it is Clifford, the highwayman."

"Yes," cried Clifford—for it was he; "I am Clifford, the highwayman, and I demand your business here."

"Devil take your impertinence!" cried Danvers; "do you mean to attempt to rob us in broad daylight?"

"No," said Clifford, with a sneer; "I am above robbing such things as you. I merely want to know from you why you are here."

"Can we not stop at the door of an inn without being subjected to questioning from you?"

"Certainly—if your business is legitimate; but if it is of the nature I suspect it to be, you have no earthly right here, and it is the duty of every man who possesses a spark of honour to defend the house and its inmates against you."

"Indeed!"

"Yes, indeed."

"And you are a man possessing the requisite spark of honour, I presume."

"I trust I am."

"Psha! This interchange of words is mere folly. Stand from our path, or we will cut you down, and trample upon you."

"You had best try, if you think yourselves capable. For my part, I have my doubts of your ability."

"You are a fool. Remember, we are three to one."

"I care not. If you were thirty to one, I would still stand here and defy you."

"Away, I say," yelled Danvers, growing each moment more furious; "away! or we will have no mercy."

"I am still here."

"You will not move?"

"Not an inch."

"You know the consequences?"

"Yes; and am prepared to brave them."

"You are only one."

"That's a lie," cried Job, springing through the casement; "at all events, the odds shall only be three to two, for I'm here likewise."

The landlord ran to the stable as fast as his legs could possibly carry him, and rousing Bob, bade him seize a prong, and come to the assistance of Clifford.

"Hillo!" said the ostler; "what's the matter? Eh, —what's up now?"

"Just this. Clifford is in the yard attacked by three fellows, who are going to break into the house, and carry off the girls. Do you intend to lie here snoring, and let 'em do it?"

"Carry off the girls," cried Bob, springing to his feet, and seizing a stable prong,—"I'll tell 'em about it."

Job followed the example of his courageous man, and each with a formidable prong in their grasp, rushed into the yard.

They noticed Clifford engaging the three horsemen, and immediately rushed to his assistance.

Clifford was a splendid swordsman, and kept his adversaries at bay with great skill.

He parried and thrust with great strength and determination; but although the odds were too great for him to make any successful point, he yet had the satisfaction of knowing that they gained nothing.

On the arrival of the host and his man Bob, the invaders felt somewhat embarrassed, and knew not how to act.

"In the rear, Bob, "in the rear," cried Job; "stick 'em well behind."

Job, in obedience to this command, ran behind Lewis, whom he looked upon as a mortal foe, and raising his great stable fork with two steel prongs, sent it flying into a very tender part of the body of that worthy.

With a yell, Lewis dropped his sword, and at the same time received a great blow over the head from the sword of Clifford, and he tumbled out of the saddle and lay sprawling in great agony on the stones of the yard.

Job repeated this successful manœuvre on the person of Danvers, and Clifford was at the same moment and in the same manner ready to deal the finishing stroke and thus number two was disposed of.

The third gentleman, deeming the best part of valour to be discretion, turned his horse's head and fled, receiving as he did so a most vigorous application of the awkward prongs of Job and Bob, that made him bound forward in his saddle with a yell of mingled pain and rage.

He did not, however, stop for retaliation. Appearing

quite satisfied, he raised himself in the saddle, and, lashing his horse, galloped away as if pursued by ten thousand fiends.

"The next business," said Job, "is to dispose of these blackguards. Lead their horses out of the yard, Bob."

Bob did as desired, and then Job motioned to Clifford to lend him a hand with the fallen great ones.

Clifford, no ways loth, picked up Lewis by the collar, and Job did the same office for Danvers. They dragged them into the open road, and thrusting them under their horses' heels, left them.

"There," said Job, as he stood contemplating his work, with evident satisfaction; "I don't think they will trouble the Harvest Home again for some time. Such a lesson isn't forgotten in a hurry."

"I believe you," said Clifford; "but I have no time to stay now, Job. Good bye."

"Eh?—what? You don't mean to say you are off?"

"Yes," said Clifford, gazing up at the window at which Evelina sat. "Yes, I have no business here. I must go."

He nevertheless stayed, and continued to gaze upon the pale face that looked down upon him.

"But you musn't go," said Job; "I insist upon you're coming in and taking something to revive you. Come on."

Clifford did not offer any very vigorous resistance, and so was taken into the house, whilst Brilliant was walked by Bob to a comfortable stable.

CHAPTER XXIX.

CLIFFORD RELATES TO JOB THE HISTORY OF HIS CAPTIVITY IN NEWGATE—HIS ESCAPE AND SUBSEQUENT OPPORTUNE APPEARANCE AT THE HARVEST HOME.

JOB dragged Clifford into the little bar-parlour, and there regaled him with the best the house afforded.

After a while he said—

"Won't you go up stairs and pay your respects to the ladies?"

"No," said Clifford; "they have no wish to see me. I will not go."

"Wherefore?"

"I dare not face Evelina," he said; "she knows me."

"And thinks the worse of you?"

"Yes, undoubtedly."

"I wouldn't have believed it if you hadn't said so."

"And why not? Why should she think well of me—a villain, a robber, and a hunted felon?"

"Oh, that's nonsense," cried Job; "we can't stand that, you know."

"It's the truth, and, therefore, should be spoken."

"It's not the truth, and should not be spoken. But we'll drop the subject, and go to another. Where have you been all this time?"

"In Newgate."

"How! Newgate?"

"Yes! in its deepest dungeon."

"And how did you get there?"

"By the treachery of Wild."

"Ah! you were a fool to trust that scamp."

"I never did; but my mode of life placed me in his power; I could not fight against the influence he had over me."

"Well, tell me all about it."

Clifford related the history of the diamonds, and how he had fallen into the trap the thief-taker had set for him, and then continued:—

"I should not have been here now, had it not been for a good and true friend, who generously placed in my hand a file, by which I effected my escape."

"A file!"

"Yes; a common file."

"Tell us all about it?"

"It is a brief story. No sooner was I left alone after receiving the little instrument Providence sent to me, than I commenced cutting through my chains. Strong as they were, they could not stand against the well-tempered steel of the file, and ere long I freed my body from the incumbrance.

"The next work was to cut through the lock, and this, thanks to the ravages of time, and the dampness of the dungeon, proved no severe task; indeed, I accomplished it without difficulty."

"But the peril was to thread my way through the barriers of doors and officers of the prison."

"But caution and courage brought me through, and at length I stood at a window overhanging a wall, by which I could descend into the street.

"Into this room I entered, and found a little rod of iron, used as a poker.

"This I bent into the shape of a hook, and fastening a rope made of the blankets I laid my hands upon, threw it to the wall, the top of which it caught.

"I then stretched it, and fastened the other end to a nail in the wall of the room: thus I was furnished with a bridge, by which I could gain the wall.

"The next difficulty was to get from the wall into the street.

"I hunted about for material to make a rope, and this I found after a diligent and careful search.

"It was almost daylight, and I dreaded detection.

"But life and liberty depended upon immediate action and I hesitated not.

"Binding my rope about my body I trusted myself to the frail bridge between the wall and the window.

"If the nail or hook gave way nothing could save me from death; but I reasoned, 'it will be as well to die thus as by any other means, so I will attempt it.'

"I felt the blanket stretch and give under my weight as I clung to it, but still I did not shrink from my work.

"On I went, and in a few seconds had the satisfaction of clutching the wall.

"Dragging myself to the parapet, I loosed my rope, and, by means of the bent iron, fastened it to the wall.

"The other end dropped to the ground.

"Fortune favoured me; there was no sound—no step—no sign of a human being, and silently I glided down the rope and into the street.

"You may depend I did not stop to see if I was followed.

"With lightning speed I rushed away, and ere long was in the arms of the good woman who has reared me and treated me as her own son.

"I ate and drank, but so overpowering was the sense of freedom I enjoyed, that I called for my bonny mare and rode away. I knew and cared not whither.

"Chance led me towards Holborn, and when on the hill I saw a carriage approaching.

"A most mysterious impulse induced me to walk my mare towards that carriage.

"I did so, and gazed in at the open window.

"There, with his head bowed upon his breast, sat Wild.

"I could not resist speaking; I told him what I thought of him. I told him what I meant doing with him, and passed on.

"I could have killed him where he sat, but I preferred allowing him to live until my plans were ripe for drawing him to the gallows.

"After a long gallop on my bonny mare I returned to my lodgings.

"It was long after midday, and Brilliant was tired.

" I sent her to the stables and entered the house.

" Ere long they came to my room, and told me that I was wanted.

" I inquired who desired audience of me, and learned that it was my old friend Bill Waters.

" I desired that he should be instantly admitted, and on coming into my presence he gave way to a wild outburst of joy, and evidently could not contain the delight he felt.

" ' Hurrah, governor !' he cried ; ' hurrah ! I little thought to find you, but it's a glorious thing to think that I have done so. Hurrah !'

" Why this wild delight, Bill ?"

" Why ? Ah, why ! Only wait till you know all, and then you won't ask why. I've been at your games, I have."

" What mean you ? "

" You remember the job you gave me when we parted."

" I do ; it was to seek for Evelina."

" ' Yes,' he said, ' it was, and a nice time I've had of it.'

" ' What mean you ? '

" ' Why, I mean that I've been a hunting London all over for her.'

" And with what success ?" I asked.

" With what success ? Oh ! the very best. I tracked her to the house of Mrs. St. Henry, I followed her to a fancy ball—and, then I lost her.

" And is that all you have to say ?"

" No, it ain't ! I suspected *why* I lost her, and stuck to those upon whom my suspicions fell. I was with 'em night and day, but without effect, until this very morning, when they came to me, and told me of a plan to drag from a little inn, in the country, the very lady I was after."

" Bill now aroused my attention to the full, and I listened eagerly to the remainder of his tale.

" You may readily guess the remainder ; and, can see why I am here so opportunely."

" Yes," said Job, when Clifford ceased speaking, " I can see it now ; and a precious good job that I can see, or I don't know what would have become of us all."

" I am glad that I have been of service to the ladies, and now I must go, for my presence can only be distasteful to them and dangerous to you."

" Dangerous to me ! Oh, hang the danger—I care nothing for it."

" No ; but I would not willingly bring disgrace upon you—so I will go."

" Well, as you will ; but I'd rather you'd stay."

" I've no doubt of it ; but must go. Remember, that I am prepared to defray all the expenses of the ladies while they are here. I cannot hope to induce them to leave the place with me, but all I can do for them I will gladly do."

" I know you will, Captain ; but nothing is required, for as long as they please to remain here they are welcome. Old Job will only be too pleased to have their company."

" Thanks, Job ; and now, farewell !"

" Farewell !"

Clifford was about to leave the house, when a gentle hand was laid upon his shoulder, and a sweet voice rang in his ears.

" Stay," it said, " stay ; and at least let me thank you."

He did turn, and found the eyes of Rose fixed upon him.

" No," he said, " no ; I dare not receive your thanks. I deserve them not."

" You do ; you do, indeed."

" I am not deceived," said Clifford ; " I know the true estimate of my own services. They are beneath thanks."

" I do not think so—my mistress does not think so. Believe me, she is grateful."

" I know the full bent of her gratitude, and I appreciate it."

" Come, then ; and receive thanks from her own lips."

Clifford sprang from her side.

" No," he said, " no ; it is better we never meet again. Such another interview as our last would kill me,"

" Do not go—do not leave us ! If they should return ?"

" Fear nothing. They will not return."

" But what—what are we to do ?"

" Ask me not, ask me not, for I cannot tell you. I will aid you if *she* will accept my aid ; if not, I am powerless.

He ran from the house, and mounting his white mare, rode away.

———

CHAPTER XXX.

WILD LEARNS THE ESCAPE OF CLIFFORD—HIS RAGE—THE THIEF-TAKER SEES THE CHASM WIDENING AT HIS FEET.

DISMISSING his charioteer, Wild entered his own house.

Before him stood the Jew,

" Well," he said, " what has happened—anything ? "

" Nothing here ; but there's been a feller round from the prishon with news for you—dreadful news—dreadful news."

" Why, what the devil do you mean ? "

" Oh, Misther Vild, of course it isn't my fault—of course I could'nt help it."

" What do you mean ?" cried Wild, his brow darkening each moment.

" I mean that somebody's got out of Newgate, that's all."

" What ?" screamed Wild, " what ?"

A dreadful suspicion flashed dimly across his brain— the face at the carriage window—the fearful voice in his ears !

" Speak," he continued, " speak ; give me your message, or I'll tear it from you ; I will—will."

Wild was fearful to behold ; his eyes started out of his head, and a foam dropped from his lips.

" It washn't my fault, my dear Mr. Vild ; it washn't my fault, but the shentleman, the shentleman has escaped !"

" Ah, I knew it, I knew it. Tell me all, or I'll choke you !"

" I don't know much about it, shir, indeed I don't ; they shent round to say that on entering the ' shel ' they only found a few pieces of broken irons. The door vas proken and forced, and on searching it was found that the prishoner got out from a vindow on to the vall, from vich he escaped by plankets cut into ropes."

" Is that all you know ?"

" That's all shir, that's all."

" Devil seize them all !" cried Wild, " they must have been conspiring against me, to allow him to escape ; I'm ruined, ruined.

" No, Misther Vild ; no, shir, that can't pe."

" Silence, fool ! I know what I say."

" Oh ; it's shad, shad ; perry shad ; I don't know vot ve shall do, I'm sure. To think that the shentleman should ha' pen aved *so bad*, after all you've done for him. Oh ! it's dreadful, dreadful."

" Leave me," cried Wild, " leave me, fool ; you know not what you are saying."

The Jew well knew that in this humour his master was dangerous, and so without delay, strode from his presence.

Wild once more sunk into a fit of thinking.

He saw that he was gradually falling into an abyss.

He beheld a trap set for himself, but struggled from it in vain.

It appeared to him that he must go on—must fall into it.

The thought maddened him.

"Alas!" he cried—"alas, that I should have been fool enough to perpetrate last night's business, and thus throw myself into the power of that thief of a canting silversmith! and Clifford, too! *He* is free, and my deadly enemy. I know full well what that means, for he is a desperate man, and when he means mischief will assuredly perpetrate it. I must think—I must think—or I shall be nabbed, and have no chance of freeing myself."

He thought and pondered over his position for a full hour, and then started up, and thrusting on his hat, walked off to the prison.

Without a word to any one, he entered the cells of Newgate, and descended to that in which Clifford had been incarcerated.

He looked at every hole end corner, and soon saw how the escape had been effected.

"I can see, I can see," he said, "some one must have given him a file; it s my business to find out who did it, and woe betide the one I find to be guilty."

He was mumbling this when the jailer who had proved to be a great friend to Clifford entered the cell.

"Well," said Wild, "what do you know of this?"

"Nothing."

"Oh! that's what I thought you'd say; you fellows never do know anything of a mess like this."

"What should we know?"

"Everything, if you did your duty: nothing, if you keep your eyes obstinately shut. I suppose that's what you've done."

"I can't have eyes everywhere, and the man didn't escape in my turn."

"No! so much the worse for you. I would'nt accuse the man on duty for a moment; I know too much of these affairs to think that he had a hand in it."

"Then whom do you suspect?"

"No matter. I may suspect whom I please; as long as I don't speak."

"Ah! you are trying to make me angry, and think I shall say something to commit myself; but, I'm not such a fool."

"You may not be—but it's my opinion that you're an infernal rogue."

"Thanks."

"Oh, no thanks! I mean it, and don't hesitate to say it"

"Mr. Wild, I care not whether you mean it or not. I shan't come to you for a character."

With this the jailor walked away.

"Ha!" said Wild, "I'll keep my eyes upon him, for I strongly suspect it is to him that I owe the escape of Clifford; and if I'm right—if I'm right—it will be better for him had he never been born."

With this Wild left the prison, and walked away, brooding on the terrible position in which he stood.

CHAPTER XXXI.

GOOD MR. HAWKINS RATHER DISCONCERTS JONATHAN WILD, WHO ALSO RECEIVES ANOTHER SHOCK, BY WHAT HE THINKS MUST BE A GHOST.

It was very early for a visit to good Mr. Hawkins, but Jonathan had a perfect knowledge of the habits of that gentleman, and hesitated not to pull up his hired coach at the door, and take therefrom the plunder he had made during the night.

Of course the shop of the respectable and very sanctified goldsmith was closed, and the unsuspecting would not have known how to proceed in order to effect an interview with the gentleman at that hour in the morning; but Wild was acquainted with his habits, and thus went to work.

Next door to the shop of the silversmith was the establishment of a milliner, of the name of Majopoline. But one remarkable circumstance always occurred in connection with this lady's business.

When any one called to give an order or to look at any millinery, there was a quiet, ladylike looking person in deep black, who replied that Mrs. Majopoline was very dangerously ill, and not able to attend to them.

Now, one would have thought that such a state of things for a continuancy would very materially have interfered with the exertions of Mrs. Majopoline to obtain a living.

But it was no such thing.

Mrs. Majopoline had been at No. 99, and Mr. Hawkins had been at No. 100, for nine years and more; and what was strange enough, too, was that both the houses belonged to Mr. Hawkins, so that he was Mrs. Majopoline's landlord, and he said, that he found her a very worthy woman, and remarkably punctual with her rent.

Mrs. Majopoline must have had some very serious indisposition indeed to be always ill—never doing any business, and so punctual with her rent.

But, then, as folks did not compare notes together, nobody knew that she was always ill and always unable to attend to business, or else the curious affair might have been talked about, which it certainly was not, or if it was, it was only in a very limited sort of way indeed.

Now, as soon as the vehicle by which he came was out of sight, Jonathan seized his swag, and rushed with it to the door of the milliner's establishment.

He gave the latch a push, and it yielded to his touch.

In a moment he was in the passage leading to the shop, but in that direction he did *not* turn.

On his left was a door, and this he pushed open, and found himself in the next house—that occupied by the good silversmith.

The door closed after him with a loud snap: but this did not at all disturb the old thieftaker, who well knew the peculiarities of good Mr. Hawkins.

"Now," said Wild, "will he know me, or will my disguise be sufficient. It ought to be, for I shouldn't care about being recognised in this business; but the swag must be got rid of *at once*. If a suspicion but fell upon me, I should be a ruined man. Psha! This is a touch of folly. Let me seek the old fool; he will fail to trace a feature."

Muttering this, Wild walked into the private office of Hawkins, and found that individual sitting at a desk, and making entries in a book by the light of an oil lamp that burned before him.

It was evident that the silversmith was an early riser.

"Mr. Hawkins," said Wild.

"Well, sir? Anything in my humble line to-day?"

"Yes."

"The Lord is good. What can I do for you, sir?"

"He don't know me," thought Wild; and then he said aloud—"Hawkins, my old buck, I have some swag."

"Oh—eh?"

"Don't you know me?"

"No," said Mr. Hawkins. "Are you Bill Snaggs, from Bermondsey?"

"No, I am a new hand from Bristol."

"Oh—indeed. And who sent you here?"

"Harry White, the Long Knight of the Road. You know him, I suppose?"

"I did."

"That is right. He is a by-gone."

"Yes; he was hanged last June, I think."

"You are quite right. But I suppose you do business in the old way, Hawkins?"

"Oh, yes—the Lord willing; that is, I mean of course I do, and no mistake. But I don't like now to be bothered about trifles, and Long Harry ought to have told you that I took nothing but plate, and jewels, and watches, or articles of great value in small compass."

"He did; look at them."

"Ah," said Hawkins, as he viewed the treasures placed before him by Wild: "they are grand, and, as I live, from the Duchess of Lakemont's."

"Why, how the devil did you know that?"

"Oh, any fool can know that. Look at the crest."

"Oh—ah—I forgot. Well, what d'ye think of it?"

"Humph! ha! very good indeed! very pretty, indeed, —upon my life—yes. Well, I should hardly have thought it, do you know. You mean to sell, I suppose?"

"I do."

The goods had all been turned out of the bags, and lay upon the desk between Wild and Mr. Hawkins, and then the latter, in rather a startling manner, cried out—

"Hush! Is that some one at the door?"

"No—no."

"Look!"

Wild started round. There was a slight jingling sound, and when he turned to the desk again, every vestige of the plate and other articles of value that he had laid upon it had disappeared.

"Hem," coughed Mr. Hawkins. "How much did you say you wanted for them?"

"I did not say any sum; I leave that to you."

"Well, let me see. There's a good bit of it. Suppose we say a thousand."

Wild did not like to haggle about the matter. He had a goodly sum in cash in his pocket, unknown to his companions; and the thousand offered by Hawkins he thought sufficient to divide among those with whom he was connected in the robbery.

"Well," he said, "I don't object, as long as we close at once."

"I never make two bites at a cherry," said the pious one; "and as *I'm convinced* Wild *won't* be after *this*, I come down handsome, and at once."

"How dy'e know that Wild will not get a scent of this robbery?"

"Oh, he can get scent enough of it, and no man will know better than him where to put his hand on the stuff; but he won't raise a finger."

"But I don't see why."

"Here's your money," said Hawkins; "count it. Good, crisp, bank notes; count them."

"Thanks; there's no occasion; but concerning Wild and this robbery. What makes you so sure that he'll not interfere with us in the matter."

"*Because Wild is the principal thief.*"

Wild started back, and looked completely floored.

"Ha! ha!" roared Hawkins; "you thought I didn't know you, eh? Well, you did come the Bristol bumpkin very well, but you don't get over me."

"So it appears," said Wild, with a desperate attempt at a laugh, which, however, turned out a lamentable failure. "Of course," he continued, "of course I should have told you all about the matter, and revealed myself, before I left; but I—I wanted to see how my disguise told."

"It's a very good disguise, Jonathan; but it's not good enough for me; but I'm square."

"Oh, *of course* you are."

"You need have no fear as long as you go on like this, and bring me really good bargains; but no more tricks like that of the diamonds, or, by God! you and I come to squaring accounts pretty sharply. It's my turn now. I'm up and you're down. Dy'e blame me for kicking?"

"No."

"It's all the same if you did, I should still do it. However, I'm expecting somebody you needn't see, so go away and be pleased with your work."

Wild stood aghast.

At length he repeated his awful attempt at laughter, and broke out into a rigmarole of explanation and apologies, and said,

"Of course I never tried to let you in. I said to myself, 'If Hawkins knows me not, no man can ever attempt to say he has seen me before.'"

Mr. Hawkins coughed.

"And that," added Wild, "you see was all about it, and the whole and sole reason."

"Oh, yes, I know."

"Hawkins, of course I am quite aware that I may trust you as I would trust myself."

"Mr. Wild," said Hawkins, gravely, "you are a little chagrined at my finding you out, and I think, with all due deference to you, that you are very foolish to be so; for you know your secret is safe with me, and, as far as I am at all concerned in the matter, I am very glad to find that you are going into business again in the old line."

"Well, I am, you see."

"So I find. You will ever be welcome here; but I should advise that you go nowhere else. I must have the full benefit of your talents, or you shall see what will follow."

"Oh," said Wild, "I'm not the man to desert an old friend."

"Perhaps not."

"You may always rely upon me."

"I hope so."

"Hope so! Why have we not known each other long enough to be assured of that fact?"

"We have, as you say, been acquainted some time; but as to relying upon *you* after that last little game of yours, I do not much care about it."

"Pshaw, man! Don't bear animosity. It was all in the way of business."

"Business or no business I do not like to be treated in such a scurvy way."

"Well, anyhow you've returned the compliment this time."

"True, and if you do not keep faith with me, you'll find me a more formidable enemy than you imagine."

"Tut—tut, man; let us be friends. Forget and forgive, as I do."

"So be it."

"That's the way to do business, my boy; so I will now wish you good morning."

"Good morning."

Boiling over with rage, at the manner in which he had been played upon and duped, the great thief-taker turned from the office, and stepped out of the house; muttering to himself the most terrible oaths, as he went.

"Ha! ha!" roared Hawkins, "Wild's in *my* clutches now, and it's strange if I don't make something out of him. It's good to have so great a pigeon to pluck; I would'nt have missed this for half a million; that I would'nt."

*   *   *   *

Wild turned away.

He walked towards Holborn, *en route*, for the City.

Baffled and beaten, he felt in no enviable humour; and hailing a passing coach, he sprang inside, and told the driver, to go to his house, as fast as possible.

Giving way to his gloomy thoughts, Wild buried his head in his bosom, and looked not up for some minutes.

At length they were descending Holborn Hill, and the man was driving at a very slow pace, when a voice rang in the ears of Wild, and looking up, he obtained a momentary glimpse of a pale, worn face glaring in at him through the window.

"Jonathan Wild!" said the voice, "I, Paul Clifford, am free, and I have sworn a great oath to be even with you. Beware! I am your deadliest foe, and before I die I will see you perish on the scaffold."

An instant and the vision was gone.

"Good God!" cried the terrified thief-taker, "it must have been a ghost!" and after a pause, he continued, "Psha! what an ass am I! It was but a fancy of the brain I must have dropped off to sleep; yes, that was it."

Was it? We shall see!

CHAPTER XXXII.

CONCERNING THE RESOLVE OF EVELINA AND ROSE TO
BE NO LONGER A BURTHEN ON JOB WINCHURST—
THE POOR STROLLERS — SHADOWING OUT A NEW
CAREER.

EVELINA was very sad and gloomy when she heard
that Clifford had so abruptly left the house.

It was now impossible for her to conceal from herself
the fact that in spite of herself she loved him, and,
although she felt wretched at the line of policy Clifford
pursued towards her, she could not deny that he was acting
in strict conformity with the laws of honour, and manhood, and as she had desired him to act.

"He is a very impetuous and altogether too proud a
man," said Rose to her young mistress; "I do not think
he can care much for you or he would not have refused
my request to stay and see you."

"You judge him harshly," said Evelina, "he acts for
the best. He is prompted by the purest motives, and it is
as well that I have not seen him, for we know what the
result of the interview would have been. Nevertheless,
I would fain have heard from him what I had best do
in the future. He could have advised me."

"His advice would have been that you placed yourself
under his care."

"That could never have been."

"Then it is as well you did not meet."

"I think so. But I know not how to act. I would
that there was one kind friend to advise me."

"Mrs. St. Henry," suggested Rose.

"No, no," said Evelina, "I feel that I could be but a
burthen to her. I know that I should but diminish an
income already too small for the requirements of the
family. I am resolved to go to them no more. But
you, my poor girl, it is of you I think. What will you
do?"

"What you do," said Rose.

"No, no," cried Evelina, "that may not be. I am too
poor to retain your services, and I would not do you the
injustice to chain you for an hour to one who would be so
helpless in furthering your welfare. It is right you
should be told this now, for the hour is at hand when we
must part. This good man, whose roof now shelters us,
must not be clogged with our maintenance another day.
We must go from here. You can seek and find employment congenial to yourself, and, I have no doubt, I shall
push through the world without much difficulty."

Evelina said this with great briskness and with a
forced smile upon her face, but there was a sadness in
her voice that brought tears to the eyes of the faithful
attendant.

"No," she cried, "no, I will not hear of it. I will
never leave you. Where you go I will go. I can starve
in your service, but I cannot live in comfort while you
may be in trouble. I could not rest apart from you, so
we will go together. I can work for you and will work
for you, but without you I should die."

Evelina could urge nothing against this; she was too
overcome to speak, and grasping the hand of poor Rose,
she held it to her bosom and wept long and silently.

After a while they conversed again, and then they arranged to at once seek Job and communicate to him their
intention to forthwith leave the house to seek their
fortunes.

This was done, but Job protested loudly and emphatically against the plan. He could not see why the girls
could not live there with him until such times as "something turned up," as he expressed it.

But the girls were not to be convinced that his plan
was a good and practicable one, and they declined to
accede to it.

Job was almost frantic, and Bob sank into a gloomy
silence and smoked his pipe with a savageness very
seldom exhibited by him.

"You *can't* go," said Job, breaking out suddenly,
after a rather long pause; "I say you *can't* go. You
haven't a penny between you, and not a change of dress
to your name. Why, hang it! you'd die of starvation
by the roadside, or worse. I won't hear of it."

"Indeed, it is but right that we go," said Evelina.

"Indeed it's all wrong, and it musn't be."

"Good, kind friend," said Evelina, taking Job's rough
hand between her own; "I must go. It would be un-
generous, unwomanly in me to remain here, and be a
burden to you. I must go hence, and seek my fortune,
so do not think me unkind—do not misunderstand me—
for that would break my heart."

"Ah," said Job, "I know what you mean; I know—
I know. And you are right, I've no doubt of it; but I
can't bring myself to think of it. I don't like it; besides,
you *musn't* go forth to the world without money."

"Then we will receive a little from you, just to give us
a start in life. I may, at least, borrow a small sum from
you."

"Ah," said Job; "that you shall, if you've really made
up your mind to go."

Evelina, by a movement of her hand, signified that
such was her intention.

"Well, then; I'll make you up a little parcel that will
be of service to you."

"Oh, thanks," said Evelina; "I trust I shall soon be
able to repay your generosity."

"Don't mention it—don't mention it. I don't want
any payment, I only want to serve you."

He shook hands with the two young girls, and walked
away.

He was absent some time, and when he next met his fair
guests he carried a bulky and weighty parcel, which he
placed in the hands of Rose.

"That's old Job's parting present to yourself and mistress," he said. "Don't open it here, and take it with
this understanding: If you ever alter your mind, and
think better of it, come back to me. Here's my hand,
and here's my heart; they're both big enough for you two
ladies. Will you promise to share 'em."

Rose could not speak. She could only clasp the hand,
and, by a pressure, express the gratitude she felt.

"Will you mention what I say," said Job; "and, before
you go, bring me the promise I want? It'll be a comfort
to me when you're gone; for I shall know, if you do not
come, you're not in want."

Rose hurried away.

The scene was too affecting for her to bear.

* * * * * *

Hawford Wells was frequently enlivened by the presence of public entertainers, and, as may be supposed,
the presence of such parties on any occasion created in
the bucolic mind no small excitement.

Now it chanced that, on the day of the occurrence of
the incidents just related, a band of poor strollers set out
from London to share in the festivities of certain fairs
about to be held in the counties of Buckingham and
Kent, &c., and, as a matter of course, the first halt was
made at Hawford Wells.

The mummers, as they were termed, consisted of a
troop of tumblers, conjurers, dancers, and clowns, and
being dressed in the wild, fanciful costumes usually
adopted by them, they attracted the greatest attention,
and as they passed along, managed to congregate a tolerably large audience, which concentrared in the neighbourhood of the little inn, and then an entertainment
took place, to the admiration and bewilderment of the
rustics.

This lasted some three-quarters of an hour, and then
the troupe entered the inn yard for the purposes of obtaining rest and refreshment.

"Beer, my noble host," cried a little man, who appeared to act as leader of the troupe. "Beer, to quench
our excessive thirst." He was a quaint little fellow, and
appeared to be possessed of extreme eccentricities.

His costume was not unlike that of a field officer, but

he wore enormous pantaloons, and carried an eyeglass and umbrella of absurd proportions. Of these he divested himself without delay; and assuming the ordinary garb of a wayfarer, stalked up to the door of the house and contemplated Job's comely figure.

His companions were four in number. Two of them were lank and lean, men given to the consumption of spirituous liquors, and appearing to think tobacco smoking the prime object of life.

They were bedaubed with paint, and wore an attire similar to that of the man we have described; only that tights, instead of pantaloons, stuck to their thin limbs, and their coats were of a less gorgeous description.

Two females; one, a little woman, habited in a costume popularly supposed to be adopted by a Circassian princess; the other, a child of tender years, " made up" in the tinsel and muslin tradition has established as the costume of fairies.

They led an old grey horse, which had evidently done the state much service, and now carried the slight baggage possessed by the party.

" I'm Adolphus Fitzfizzlegig Bolster," said the little man to Job; " and having in my time tasted of the ales procurable in every county of England, declare thine to be the best."

As he uttered these words, he replaced to his lips a mug he had but then taken therefrom, and took a second long and hearty pull.

" Hillo," said one of his companions, " that ain't fair, governor; pull and pull all round is my fashion."

" Dobson," continued the little man, turning to him who addressed him, " pull and pull all out is mine, therefore your health."

A third application to the mug served to empty it, and turning it upside down, he let a few drops of froth fall to the ground.

" Replenish," said Dobson.

" Which means," said Bolster, returning the mug to Job, " which means fill up again."

" And next time hand it to me," said Dobson.

" Or me," said the third man, " for I'm famished."

" Nonsense, Hipkins," said Dobson, " the pipes afore the drum. If you'd been a-blowing as I have you'd say first pull."

" And if you'd been a-dancing as I have," put in the woman, " you'd say, if you were men. ' she requires it most; let her quaff the flowing bowl.' "

This lady was Mrs. Dobson. She had in her time personated the heroines of melodrama, in a canvas theatre, but growing too stout for the business, had to relinquish it for the dowagers, a line of parts she was successfully representing when chance threw her in the way of Dobson, who proposed, was accepted, and lifted her from the stage into the mud.

Dobson did not rank high in the profession. He had never appeared on the stage—it is not even recorded of him that he ever performed on sawdust.

This fact induced the high-souled and talented lady, who had taken him for better for worse, to treat him with a contempt warranted by her superior position in the world of entertainers.

Truth to tell, Dobson was a snubbed man, and the only person who looked up to him, or offered him any sympathy was his little daughter, a pretty child of about ten years of age, who clung to the poor crushed mountebank with a fondness beautiful to behold.

He used to tell her that she was his only pet, and that in all the wide world she was the only one who ever looked kindly on him; and, feeling this, the child strove to make her little store of love doubly dear—doubly valuable—and she succeeded.

In the course of this history we shall see how.

Return we to the inn yard.

Job, liking his customers, soon returned with a couple of mugs of ale; presented one to Mrs. Dobson, and the other to her spouse.

" There you are," he said; " drink, and much good may it do you."

" Hillo!" said Adolphus; " here's extravagance—here's luxury. Who's to pay ?"

" That shall be my treat," said Job; " drink man, drink; and be not troubled about paying."

" I won't," said Adolphus, snatching the measure quickly from Dobson; " here's your good health my noble host."

He was about to apply the mug to his mouth, when Hipkins tore it from his grasp.

" Fair is fair, all the world over," said that worthy; " you've had your innings—now comes mine."

He drank deeply.

" You'll excuse him," said Adolphus; " it's a way he has. It's constitutional, and he can't help it. Let him drink, although I blush for him. Such greediness can only raise in honest breasts the utmost indignation."

Adolphus looked very big and important, and pretended to be immensely shocked at the behaviour of his companion, a proceeding which set Job off into a roar of laughter."

" Well," he said, " you are a funny lot."

" We are," said Adolphus, " we are; it was born in us and we can't get rid of it. It's a family complaint, and I'm the greatest sufferer of the whole lot."

" At all events you are the greatest fool," said the dignified Mrs. Dobson.

" Such language, madam; such language to a man of my position. It's disgraceful and not to be tolerated. I shall have to reduce your salary immediately."

" Get out," was the reply of the lady. To which the facetious Adolphus answered that he would esteem it a favour if she would show him how to set about it.

A half-hour passed in talk like this, during which the troupe rested.

From the window of her room Evelina watched these people. She had been preparing for her departure, and the noise occasioned by the new arrivals had drawn her from her employment.

She looked at them long and attentively, and then called Rose.

" Look at those people," she said, pointing down into the yard.

" Yes," said Rose, " I see them."

" What think you ?" continued Evelina, " What think you of leading a life like theirs ?"

" Miss Evelina !"

" Ah, I see you are startled at the proposition, but I have long contemplated it. In fact, I can see no better prospect before me."

" Oh, Miss Evelina. To hear you talk so ! For myself I should not mind—but for you ——"

" Why not for me. Penniless, nameless, without a friend ! Is not this life the very one for me ?"

" But you have been so delicately reared, so fondly treated. It would kill you."

" No, Rose, I have long contemplated this. I have thought that, failing to find other employment, this would be what I should of my own free will select. I know not why, but my inclination tends that way, it is in keeping with my real position in the world. But think not that I will drag you after me into a course of life that may be distasteful to you. I would scorn to do so. Your path and mine, dear Rose, lay separately, and once more I bid you pause ere you jeopardise yourself by following the fortunes of one unable to help herself."

" Where you lead," said Rose, " I will follow. I will never quit your side until you drive me from you !"

" Then have your own way. I will not separate myself from you, for there is still sufficient selfishness in me to make me long for one who loves me to be near me, and share my sorrows with me."

" That one I will be," said Rose. " It would be cruelty to me to drag me from you."

" Then again I ask, what think you of leading a life like that followed by the people below."

"It is not distasteful to me."

"Are you sure ?"

"Quite sure."

Evelina paused a while.

"Do you think," she asked, "do you think those people would object to our joining them ?"

"I can question them if you desire it."

"Do so."

Rose was about to leave the room.

"Stay," said Evelina, "I will speak to them myself. Come with me."

They descended the stairs, and passing Job, who looked on in astonishment, entered the court-yard.

For a moment Evelina hesitated.

She then singled out Adolphus, and beckoning him, drew him on one side,

"What can I do for you, my lovely lady ?" asked the polite Adolphus.

"I would ask a favour of you, a great boon, and I trust you will grant it."

"If it lays in my power I will do it," said Adolphus; "but I am only a poor stroller, and not like to be able to in any way assist you."

"Thanks for the promise; it is, indeed, within your power to render me assistance. I am poor beyond description, and need help even from one so familiar with poverty as yourself."

"Then what is the favour you have to ask ?"

"It is, that you will allow myself and a friend to join your troupe."

"To join the troupe ?"

"Yes."

"And—and go about with us ?"

"Yes."

"You can't know what you say."

"Oh, yes; I have a perfect knowledge of what I speak."

"But you're not used to the thing; you—"

"Understand nothing whereby we can earn our bread —is not that what you would say ?"

"Well, it is something like it."

"But we shall be willing pupils, and will soon learn."

"Can you dance ?"

"Yes."

"That will do, then ; a good dancer, who has a pretty face, is always a welcome addition to any troupe. And your friend ?"

"You behold her."

Evelina pointed to Rose, and the mountebank scanned her from head to foot.

"Yes," he said, "she is pretty enough for anything. And you really intend to join us ?"

"We should esteem it the greatest favour you could grant us."

"Well, I see no objection."

"Oh, thanks, thanks."

What objection there possibly could be to such an arrangement no one could see, for two more beautiful and attractive girls could scarcely be found.

The mountebank well knew this.

He foresaw that the two girls would be a perfect treasure to him could he but secure them, and as the certainty of this dawned upon him his eyes dilated, and a broad smile of pleasure spread over his face.

He rubbed his hands, and pictured to himself a picture in which he stood the central figure—an envied man, and the possessor of a fortune accumulated for him by the two beautiful girls.

"Hurrah !" he cried, rushing towards his friends; "hurrah! here's a treat! By Jove, Bolster's troop will be the most envied in all the world. Look at 'em—look at 'em! Arn't they beautiful! Won't they make a stir in muslin !"

He soon explained the occasion of his delight, and the two girls were scanned with anxious eyes by the remainder of the troupe.

"Why, how's this ?" said Job to Evelina; "what does this mean ?"

"It means that we have joined the troupe of strollers," said Evelina.

"No," cried the astonished Job.

"Yes," said Evelina, "it is true, my good and generous friend. It is thus I quit your hospitable roof."

"Good gracious," said the astonished Job, "what ever will you do? It beats—it beats—there, it beats cockfighting—that's what it does! But you don't mean it? You can't mean that you're going to turn up long skirts, and take to them things ?"

"Them things," was the dress of the stroller's child.

Evelina smiled sadly and answered not.

"It's too much to believe," said Job, in continuation, "I couldn't and wouldn't have credited it. Here, Bob! Just think of this ; the ladies ; our ladies, Bob, are off with the mummers."

"No !"

"Yes !"

"I'll kill their old white hoss first."

With this awful threat Bob was about to walk away, when Job caught him by the arm and dragged him into the house.

"It's best to talk it over in quietness over a glass of pineapple rum," was the philosophical speech of the landlord; "these things do puzzle so when they come upon one all of a sudden like."

The pineapple rum-and-water was soon mixed, and the affair was being talked over, when Evelina and Rose entered the bar, and catching Job by the hand bade him adieu.

"Good-bye, best of friends," cried Evelina, "good-bye, and may God bless you for all you have done for us."

"Adieu !" said Rose, "think of us as we will think of you."

Before the astonished Job could reply, his favourite guests had again vanished from his presence.

Not daring to trust themselves to take a long and trying farewell, they adopted this course ; and before Job could open his mouth were gone.

In the same yard the mountebanks were preparing to resume their journey ; and ere many moments had elapsed, Dobson had seated his little child on the old horse, and the troupe was in motion.

Evelina and Rose, trudging on beside Adolphus, who appeared very proud of his fair companions.

"Put the best foot forward, ladies," he said ; "for it's a good seven miles to the village where we shall next halt."

And as the poor girls strode onward, Job and his faithful servant stood at the bar window, and watched them until they were out of sight.

CHAPTER XXXIII.

WILD'S PLANS TO RUIN CLIFFORD — A FIEND TO FIGHT AGAINST — HOW THE THIEF-TAKER PERSONATED THE HIGHWAYMAN.

WILD knew that Clifford was gone for ever from his control.

The words uttered by the highwayman rang in his ears, and he knew he had a bitter enemy to fight against.

"He is safe among the devils at Mother Granville's, and I darn't go there for him. My influence won't touch him now, so I must e'en make the country too hot for him. He has a reputation that is dear to him, I'll get at him through that means. I'll blast his good repute. Yes, that is my plan."

He thought this matter over and over, and after three days thinking he matured a plan which he flattered himself would succeed to the full bent of his high expectations.

He called the jew to his aid.

"I want a white mare," he said.

"A vhite mare, Misther Vild. Vot shall you do vith a vhite mare?"

"No matter, get me one. You know Clifford's Brilliant?"

"Who doesn't?"

"Well, then, let her be as much like her as possible."

"Vy, such a mare vill cost no end o' monish."

"I care not how much, I must have one. Send Nobby Tom to purchase her."

"Against ven?"

"To-night."

"Very goot."

"And now I want clothes cut as fashionably and made of stuff as good as that worn by Clifford. Can you get them?"

"Yesh, Misther Vild, a frent of mine, a shentleman of the Hebrew persuasion, puys all Misther Clifford's old clothes. He's got sheberal suits by him now."

"Very good, get me some of the best of them at once."

"I'll do so in no time. I begin to see now vot they're vanted for."

"Do you? Then I'd advise you to say nothing about it."

"In course I vouldn't. Don't I know pishness petter than to do that?"

"I hope so, for your sake."

"Vell, I suppose you're a going to personate the shentleman?"

"Yes, but it's no matter of yours, so ask no more questions."

The jew left Wild alone.

"Yes," said the thief-taker, when his man was gone, "I'll personate the gentleman, and to some tune. I'll make England ring with the acts I'll do in his name, and then let him escape the gallows if he can!"

*   *   *   *   *

That night, as dark spread over London, Wild had merged himself into a fair resemblance of our hero.

Externally he was Clifford.

There was the same clothes, the same pointed beard and moustache, the same walk, the same voice, the same air, and there was, moreover, a tolerable counterpart of Brilliant.

Wild, when he had made up for the character he was about to play, suddenly summoned the Jew to his presence; and on encountering his master, the man started back in amazement.

"Enough," said Wild; "I need not ask if the thing will do—I can see it will. Ha! ha! Now for work."

"Oh, my!" cried the Jew, his eyes dilating with wonderment; "however you do it I can't think. It's marvellous! it's vonderful! it's—it's—the very shentleman himself."

"Very good," said Wild, evidently pleased with the effect he created. "Very good; and now to be off. Is the mare ready?"

"Yes."

"Pistols in the holster?"

"Two pairs of peauties."

"Plenty of ammunition in the pack?"

"Lots."

"That will do."

"Vhen shall I expect you pack agin?"

"Don't expect me at all. To all inquiries answer that I'm gone into Lincolnshire on urgent business."

"I understand."

Wild left his house, and springing on the back of his new purchase, rode away.

He had no settled plan in his mind, but he trusted in chance to throw good opportunities for the furtherance of his object into his way.

The night was rather a dark one.

Jonathan Wild looked up at the sky, and appeared for a few moments to be ruminating upon it, and then he said—

"It will do. It will be one of those dark but clear nights in which the air is keen but pliant. The darkness will wrap one up like a mantle—for there is no moon to-night, and it is all the better for me."

He rode on with a gentle trot till he came to Tyburn gate, and then he pretended to take no notice that there was a toll to pay, till the man ran out and cried—

"Hillo, sir! Threepence, if you please."

Wild pulled up.

"Oh, yes, certainly—I—a—that is—dear me, I have left my purse, I fear, at home. My name is Clifford; you will trust me?"

"Not a bit of it."

"Oh, you won't?"

"Not a farthing."

"Well, you are rather uncivil. I am glad I have found a sixpence with which to pay you. Here it is; but I think my name ought to have sufficed."

"That will do," said Wild, with one of his old hideous looks, as he trotted down the Western Road. "That will do, I think; for now will that fellow be ready at any time to take his oath that a Mr. Clifford, upon a white mare, passed through his gate at a quarter past eight on this, I hope, eventful evening."

Thus, then, had the villain Wild made, as he thought, an auspicious beginning in the persecution of Paul Clifford.

We shall soon see what further steps he took for the purpose of vilifying his character.

Jonathan Wild fully intended to perpetrate some act of crime in his assumed character, which should make Clifford amenable to the highest punishment of the law; and so he hoped that there was even a possibility of driving Paul to such a condition by depriving him of sympathy, and by supplying the only possible motives that he could have for the commission of offences.

This was the rascally project of the prince of plotters, Jonathan Wild, against Paul Clifford.

The night, as we have stated, was a dark one; and it was, indeed, just such a night as suited Wild.

If it had been positively bad weather—which it was very far from being—he would have felt that such a state of things was against him, inasmuch as it would have kept people at home.

But such was not the case, and the night was not one to deter anybody from going out in it, whether on business or on pleasure.

But Jonathan Wild was too near to London yet to commence operations, so he put his horse to speed, and trotted as far as Ealing Common before he thought it at all wise to look about him for anything in the shape of an adventure.

"Now," he said, "I have the road pretty well to myself, I reckon, and we will see what we can do."

Hardly had Wild uttered these words, when he became aware of a strange light flashing across his path, and on glancing about him he found that it came from a lantern that some one was holding up at a gate in a garden wall, a good distance from where he then was.

Wild did not by any means wish to be seen, so he took a round course to shift out of the way of the direct rays of the lantern, and then he slowly and cautiously walked his horse in the direction of the house to which the garden wall appertained.

By the aid of a clump of trees that grew close at hand, Wild was able to get so close to the door in the garden wall that he could see a man, in the sort of undress of a gardener, standing at it.

In a few minutes a female figure, with something on her head to keep out the cold air, came to the door.

Wild could hear their voices in the silence of that spot quite plainly; for at that time Ealing Common was very considerably more in the country than it is now.

"Do you see the chaise, John?" said the female.

"No, ma'am."

"But it is nearly nine?"

"Yes, ma'am, it is."

"Then they really ought to be here. Dear me—dear me! I objected to her going."

"Yes, ma'am."

"Hold up the light higher, John."

"Yes, ma'am."

"It is a very dark night."

"Well, ma'am," said Jonathan, with a mocking kind of voice, "I suppose we may say that it is a dark night, ma'am, and no mistake."

"I wish you would go out on the common, John, and look for them. There is the black ditch, you know, that people are so very apt to drive into."

"Yes, ma'am; I should say they were."

"Then do you go out with the lantern, and if you hear the sound of wheels, you can call out."

"Yes, ma'am."

John did not appear to be the very brightest specimen of domestic servants in the world, but he sallied out with the lantern in his hand, and kept looking about him as far as the halo of light which the lantern shed about the spot upon which he was, as a kind of centre, would permit him.

In this way John approached pretty close to Jonathan Wild, without knowing it.

"Hoi!" cried Wild.

"Hillo! who is there?"

"A gentleman," said Wild. "I am afraid, though, that I have lost my way on the common."

"Oh, have you, sir?"

"Yes. What house is that opposite? Is it called the Cedars?"

"Lor, no, sir. I don't know of such a place as that about here, sir. That house opposite is Mrs. Brown's school for young ladies, sir."

"Oh, indeed."

"Yes, sir; and as for the Cedars, I don't know of such a name of a house, sir."

"You are looking for some one, I presume, as you have your lantern with you, my man."

"Yes, sir, I is."

"Some scholar, I suppose?"

"Yes, sir, I is."

"Ah, I know her very well; it is Miss—a—tut, tut, I shall forget my own name next. Miss—Miss—"

"Weston, sir."

"Oh, yes, Weston."

"Miss Annie Weston, sir; and she has been up to town to see her uncle, you know, sir, who is very ill; and our boy, Bill, as works in the garden with we, and is a sort of page, too, to missus, is with her in the pony chaise, and is, I suppose, a bringing of her back."

"Of course he is; I know now all about it. Here is a guinea for you to drink my health."

"Oh, Lord, sir? A guinea?"

"Yes."

"You are jesting, sir, with a poor fellow."

"Not at all."

"Why, I only gets six pounds wages and my keep, sir, in all the year, I assure you."

"Never mind that; take the guinea, and mind you drink my health with it in something good."

"Yes, sir; but I don't know your honour."

"My name is Clifford. That will do. Good night to you, my good fellow. I think Annie Weston is about the prettiest girl in the school."

"And so do I your honour."

Jonathan Wild trotted slowly off, leaving the gardener, upon whose dense stupidity he had worked so effectually, in quite a state of delighted amazement at the reception of the guinea.

"I think," said Wild, "this will do. By now affecting a passion for this girl, Annie Weston, whom I certainly never saw in all my life, I will make this night the first effort to compromise the fame of Paul Clifford. Ha! We shall see—we shall see."

It was now an object with Jonathan Wild to look out for the approaching chaise himself, and he did not at all wish that his encounter with it and its occupants should take place near to the house of Mrs. Brown, or even within sight or hearing of the stupid gardener.

With this view, then, he kept across the common, every road and path of which he knew so well, towards London, and just as he got in the rather narrow part of the road that leads towards Acton he heard the grating sound of wheels approaching him from London.

"This must be the chaise," he said, "and our boy Bill with the young lady."

Jonathan Wild had a strange sort of reputation as regarded his eye sight, and that consisted in the belief, on the part of many people, that he could see in the dark.

There is very little doubt but that the rascal had found it to his interest to promulgate such notions concerning him, as the more extraordinary and out of the common way his powers were thought, the greater power he really acquired.

Jonathan Wild seemed to give himself some sort of credence to the idea that he could see in the dark, for he placed himself close to the hedge in a very dark part of the road.

The chaise came on at a very creeping sort of pace, and, to the surprise of Jonathan, it stopped just at the spot that he had chosen to halt at.

A young and pretty voice then said—

"Why, Will, won't Lightfoot go on?"

"Yes—oh, yes," groaned another voice. "I stopped him."

"Then don't stop him again, I beg of you, but go on at once; you know I promised Mrs. Brown to be home by nine o'clock at the latest, and it has struck that hour, as you yourself heard."

"Oh—oh—oh!" said Will.

"Why, what is the matter?" said the female voice.

"Oh, Miss Weston, I've stopped Lightfoot, the pony, on purpose at this here quiet spot, miss—yes I've stopped him on purpose, because, miss, I've got something to tell you."

"To tell me?"

"Yes, you, miss."

"Impossible."

"That's very likely, miss, but it's true for all that."

"Then, Will, I will listen to whatever it may be to-morrow, if you please, and not now."

"Oh, but it won't do to-morrow."

"Yes, it will, I daresay. I insist upon going on, Will, at once. If you don't, I shall complain of you to Mrs. Brown."

"You may, Miss Weston, you may, and your Will will be gone miss, I can tell you but, oh—oh—oh!"

"Are you ill, Will?"

"Yes, that's it."

"Then give me the reins, and I will try and drive Lightfoot home. If you had said at first that it was illness that had possessed you, I should have known what to do."

"Yes, but it isn't the regular sort of illness, Miss Weston. Only look at everything all about you. The waving trees, miss, as you can't see; and the blue sky as is now black, miss—only look at nature, miss."

"I think, Will, that the illness that possesses you is in your brain. I cannot and do not understand you."

"Then I—oh—I—I—"

"You what?"

"I can't say it."

"Give me the reins, directly. If you do not I will get out of the chaise, and try to make my way on foot to the school."

"Then, miss, I love you."

"You what?"

"I love you! Oh, Miss Weston; from the first day—the first hour—the first minute that your Will saw you, he loved you—he adored you, and he said to himself—'Oh, ye heavens; that's the gal for me!' Yes, I have said it now. I love you."

Miss Weston laughed so she could not speak.

"Oh, don't laugh—don't. This is just the opportunity—"

"So I think, Will."

"Do you, though?"

"Yes, I am sure of it; and so I can't help laughing."

"Oh, but I didn't mean for that."

"Then what did you mean for, Will."

"For running off to Gretna Green, Miss Weston. Only look here, now. Here we is. I have got one pound fifteen in my pocket, and here is a chaise and a pony, and here is you, and here is me. Now, what, miss, is to hinder us driving off all at once to Gretna Green, and getting married, and being happy for ever after?"

"Oh, nothing in the world, Will."

"Then, let's come."

"But one little objection."

"Objection?"

"Yes. I won't go."

"You—won't—go?"

"No."

"Then you don't love Will?"

"Certainly not."

"Then I'll go and list for a soldier to-morrow, that I will."

"There is one little objection to that, too, Will."

"Oh, lor!—is there?"

"Yes. You are not big enough."

"Well, no, I ain't; except for a drummer-boy."

"And now, Will, listen to me. Upon one condition, or rather, I should say, upon two conditions, I will keep secret this folly of yours. One is, that you never presume again to speak to me at all upon any subject whatever; and the other is, that you drive to Mrs. Brown's this moment, without any further delay."

"Oh—oh!"

"Don't make a greater fool of yourself than you are, my good lad, but be thankful that I am not disposed to relate your conduct to your mistress, which would not only produce your instant discharge from your situation, but without a character, too."

Will got really alarmed. With a deep sigh he jerked the bridle of the horse, and it had made two or three steps forward, when Jonathan Wild darted out from the shadow of the trees, and cried—

"Hold!"

Will pulled up in a moment.

"Another step and you die," said Wild.

"Oh, murder! It's a highwayman, with a pistol as long as a rake!" cried Will.

"Silence!"

"Yes, sir—yes, your worship."

"On, then!" cried Miss Weston. "We are close to home. Drive on, Will, or you risk your life and mine."

"If he attempts to move an inch," said Wild, "I will shoot him dead upon the spot. I only want to ask a question of you, that is all, and I will ask it."

"What is it?" said Miss Weston, assuming a boldness that her heart was in reality a stranger to. "What is it? If in my power, and a proper question for me to answer, I will do so at once."

"I think, as well as I can see, that this is the pony-chaise belonging to Mansion House Academy, kept by a Mrs. Brown."

"It is."

"Are you going there?"

"I am."

"You are one of the establishment, perhaps? It is so dark that I cannot see who or what you are, but you seem to be a lady."

"I am one of the establishment. What then?"

"Then I want you to take a letter for me to a young lady there of the name of Weston."

"Weston?"

"Yes, Miss Annie Weston. I have seen her, and I adore her. She is to me all perfection; and now that I have a little time on my hands, I am anxious to let her

know of the existence of the secret flame that consumes me. I am a gentleman, and can soon satisfy her of my position in life. Will you take the letter?"

"No."

"No, say you?"

"I do say no."

"Then you drive me to despair."

"Oh, lor!" cried Will, who was unable to hold his tongue any longer. "Oh lor! why this is Miss Weston!"

"Oh, Will?" said the young girl, "why did you speak?"

"This Miss Weston!" cried Jonathan Wild, with affected enthusiasm. "Oh, why did not my fond heart tell me so? Oh, Miss Weston, I admire, I love, I adore you! My name is Clifford; I do not know if you have heard of me or not, but ——"

"Sir, I will not listen to this!" cried the young lady, and then raising her voice, she shouted out, "Help!—help!—help!"

"Do you wish to bring destruction on me?" said Wild; "your cries will do so. If I love it must be in secret, for I am so situated that I am compelled to appear to be the devoted of another, who——"

"Hilloa!" cried a voice, "what cry was that?"

A horseman galloped up to the spot.

"Protect me," cried the young girl; "protect me, sir, if you be a gentleman. I am going to Mrs. Brown's, and this man will not let me proceed. Oh, protect me, sir."

"I will soon do that," said the stranger. "Who are you, sir, I should like to know?"

"Find out," said Wild.

"Very well, we can do that at the moment. Look you, I can take you to prison. I suspect you are a highwayman."

The mounted man made a dash at Wild, but from the tone and manner of the stranger, Jonathan perceived that he was a patrol, and that it would be quite as well not to get into a personal scuffle with him; so he made an effort to get away, being pretty well satisfied with the fright he had given to Will and to the young lady, which fright, he felt certain, would be associated with the name of Clifford, that he had so freely used.

Giving his good horse, then, an impulse with the spurs, Wild, who was a good horseman, and had taken care to be well mounted, dashed off across the common.

But the stranger was well mounted too, and he was not at all disposed to let Wild escape him so easily, so off he went after him, calling out—

"Stop! stop? I will send a bullet after you if you do not."

"Oh, indeed!" said Wild, pulling up.

Bang went the pistol, and Wild heard the hissing whistle of the ball as it went past his face, much too closely to be at all agreeable.

"Oh, that's the game, is it," he said. "Two can play at that."

This prompt use of firearms at once convinced Jonathan Wild that he had come across one of the horse patrol, then quite a new institution, and which he had not been, until then, aware was extended so far as Ealing common.

Turning in his saddle, and stooping down so as to bring his eye on a level with the pistol he had taken from one of the holsters of his saddle, he levelled it at the dusky figure of the approaching man.

Another minute and Wild had fired.

There were few men who, in the dark, could fire a pistol so correctly as Jonathan Wild could. When he meant to kill he certainly could, in the ingenuity of malice, succeed; and, at all events, he generally hit the object

The distance on the present occasion was not great, and Jonathan Wild thought he heard a cry mingle with the report of the pistol he had fired.

In another minute a horse without a rider passed him at full speed.

Then Jonathan Wild knew that he had shot the patrol, and that he had fallen from his horse, and was lying dead or wounded on the common.

It did not appear to Jonathan at all necessary to inquire into the condition of the man whom he had thus shot down. He felt quite satisfied with the night's work, so he rode on to Henwell with quite a feeling of satisfaction, and when he got into that rather primitive-looking village he heard a clock strike ten, so that the night was still quite young.

Wild drew up at a little inn on the left-hand side of the way, that had a light placed at a pane of glass that looked up the London road, with a reflector behind it, to let every one see that it was an inn that they were approaching.

"Hilloa!" he cried. "House!"

"Here you are, sir," said a fat looking man, in a white apron, rolling out at the door.

"Have you any wine?"

"Wine, sir? Yes, sir—that is—a—elder-wine."

"Bah! I mean foreign wine."

"Well, I don't think we have, sir."

"Then I can't drink anything else, my good friend, so good night to you."

As he rode off, Wild purposely dropped a glove that he had in his pocket on the ground at the inn door. That glove was one that had really belonged to Paul Clifford.

He considered that it would do him good service, in establishing the seeming fact that Clifford had passed that way.

The fact was, that Paul's initials, P. C., were on the inside of the glove, as Wild had ascertained.

CHAPTER XXXV.

WILD PURSUES HIS ADVENTURES DISGUISED AS CLIFFORD.

It was far into the night when Wild again drew rein. This time he paused at a little inn by the road side.

He was now at a considerable distance from London, and began to be less careful of not exposing himself to view on the highways.

He knocked at the door of the little inn, but it was a long time before anyone made answer. At length, however, the door was partly opened and a head protruded.

"Who's there?" was demanded from within.

"Who should it be at this hour but a traveller?"

"Then you can't enter here. The house is closed for the night, and there's no admittance."

"That's a nice tale to tell a poor devil who has been on the road all day, that is. I must enter."

"You shan't."

"Curse you! I'd make you say something else if you were out here."

"Would you? Then it's fortunate that I'm in here. So get on with you, and don't disturb honest people at this hour."

"What's up?" demanded a voice within.

"It's a fellow calling himself a traveller, demanding admittance," said the one who had conversed with Wild.

"What's he got to say for himself?"

"Much," said Wild, "much for himself, but very little for a set of devils who won't open the door at this hour to a tired traveller."

"Hillo," said the one whom Wild could not see, "hillo, that's a voice I know very well, let's get a glimpse of the owner."

The first man now retired, and the other pushed his head through the partly-opened door.

"Hey," he said, looking out at the figure standing in the moonlight, "it's the form and dress of Clifford, but the voice is that of Jonathan Wild."

"It is Jonathan Wild, so open the door, Master Perry, since it is you who are here."

"With all the pleasure in life," said Perry, withdrawing the bolts, and admitting Jonathan; "enter, and let us have a look at you."

"There's the mare to be seen to."

"Why, it's Brilliant!"

"No it's not, but it's a very good excuse for her, isn't it? Get her pushed into the stable for me, and I'll feel obliged."

"Here, Bill," said Perry, "put the mare into the stable, and look sharp about it."

Bill was the man who had treated Wild so cavalierly, but, on beholding how well acquainted he appeared to be with the man called Perry, he ran out with extreme alacrity, and, taking the panting steed by the bridle, took her to the stables without further delay.

Meanwhile, Wild entered the inn, and confronted Perry. The man answering to this name was a burly ruffian of Wild's own make and style.

He motioned the thief-taker into a room near at hand, and then closed the door.

"Now, governor," said Perry; "just tell us what the game is. How came you down here, and in this make-up?"

"Can't you guess?"

"I'll be hanged if I can."

"Know, then, that I am personating your old friend Paul."

"To what end?"

"To bring him to the dogs."

Wild then briefly related the history of his adventures with the highwayman, and wound up with his work on Ealing Common that night.

"So you see," he said, "you see how I am working the oracle against him. What think ye of the plan?"

"It's worthy of the devil himself, and, next to him, of Jonathan Wild."

"I should think it was," said Wild; "at least, it shall be, before I've done. I've not begun yet. And now confidence for confidence. What's your game in these parts?"

"A rum 'un. I've got a body to bury to-night in the ruins of the Old Abbey, yonder."

"Hillo!" said Wild: "that's a queer game. What's in it?"

"Blest if I know. You see, it's a job I'm doing for some swells in London, and I was told to ask no questions."

"And you haven't?"

"And I haven't."

"What about the people of this house?"

"They're the right sort."

"Friends of yours?"

"In my pay."

"And they know of this burying match?"

"Yes; and the fellow who is taking your horse round to the stable is going to lend me a hand in the matter."

"Oh—oh! And who is he?"

"The ostler."

"Where's the landlord?"

"In bed. Sensible man; he never interferes with the work of his guests."

"Sensible indeed."

"And now that you're here, you'd best follow his example, if you're not off again."

"I've no great business on hand just yet, but at the same time, I don't want to go to roost. Can I lend you a hand?"

"Well, you may if you like, and I should be obliged to you; for I'd rather have your assistance than that of the fellow who's looking after your nag. You're more in the line."

"I believe you."

"Well, then, d'ye care about a walk to the Old Abbey?"

"With all my heart. I'd go, not only to serve an old friend, but for the sake of satisfying a curiosity I feel in the matter. What's the body like?"

CLIFFORD'S INTERVIEW WITH THE DUCHESS.

"Well, it's a woman."

"And is that all you know ?"

"That's all."

"Can't you let slip the name of your employers ?"

"You're richeous ?"

"Don't you kuow I am ?"

"Well, then, I'm doing this for old acquaintances of yours—*three lawyers !*"

"What, the—"

"Hush ! there's no occasion for repeating names; it ain't polite, you know, and there's no occasion for it."

"But what can they have to do—"

"There you go again.   What do I know or care about what they have to do ?   I never asked them, and you needn't ask me."

"All right; but I say, Perry, there's more in this than you and I can see just now. Mark me, there's some devil's work on with those three fellows that you and I would do well to look into."

"How dy'e mean ?"

"Is the corpse in a coffin ?"

"Well, an excuse for one ; it's a rough box."

"Have you opened it ?"

"No."

"Then you must."

"Why ?"

"To see the contents, and take from the body any-thing that may lead to its identity."

"Do you suspect anything ?"

"A great deal.   Will you do as I bid you ?"

"Yes."

"Then lead the way to the place where your precious dead 'un lies, and let me overhaul her."

"Come along ; follow me, and don't make any noise."

They left the room together.

Traversing a dark passage they at length reached a door which, on being opened, led them to a small yard, in which stood an outhouse of mean aspect.

This building they entered, and, by the light of a lantern carried by Perry, Wild discovered a long deal box, which he at once divined to be the receptacle of the dead body.

"Now let us see," he said, taking a small wrench from his pocket and applying it to the lid of the box; "no screws, I see. That saves trouble. Now for it."

Applying some force to the instrument he used the lid gave way, and with a loud crack flew partly open.

"Do you see anything ?" asked Perry.

"No," replied Wild ; " nothing at all. Do you?"

"There's a small gold cross about the neck," said the man.

"Well, then, have it off," said Wild as he moved towards his companion.

Next moment he pretended to lose his footing, and, stumbling against Perry, knocked the lantern from his hand, and they were left in utter darkness.

"Devil take you," cried Perry ; " what made you do that ?"

"'Twas an accident."

Had Perry been able to see what Wild was doing in the dark, he would not have been so easily convinced that there was so much of the accidental as the intentional in the movement.

The hand of the thief-taker was plunged into the coffin, and it was drawn forth clasping *a something* which was instantly thrust into the pocket of his coat.

"Now then," he said, after completing this manœuvre, "get that candle relighted, and let us set to work."

*   *   *   *

An hour later two men might have been seen lowering a dead body into a shallow grave beneath the shadow of a grim old ruin. They were Wild and Perry.

"There," said Perry, glancing down on the corpse, "there you are my beauty ; snug enough."

"Yes," cried Will, drawing a pistol, and firing it at the head of his friend, "and there *you* are, my fine fellow, to keep his company. You'll lay snug enough together."

With a yell the poor wretch fell forward a corpse, and ere the life's blood had ceased flowing, Wild had buried them both in that one unhallowed grave.

CHAPTER XXXVI.

CLIFFORD MEETS THE DUCHESS ONCE MORE—HE ALSO HEARS OF WILD'S EXPLOITS IN HIS ASSUMED CHARACTER—THE FENCE PROVES A FRIEND.

NEXT to his cares for Evelina and her young companion, Clifford was principally concerned for the Duchess of Lakemont, and his aim was to return to her, if possible, the diamonds of which he had robbed her.

At length he determined on resisting the step of Hawkins, and endeavour to repurchase them ; being, of course, unaware of the fact of Wild's having anticipated him.

Clifford had heard, with pain, of the robbery and murder committed in the mansion of the lady he had served so ill, and was filled with fear lest she should suspect him of having a hand in that terrible enterprise.

He knew full well that his identity had been revealed to her, and he naturally argued that nought was so reasonable as that she should suspect him as the chief actor in the awful drama that had made all London shudder with horror.

His plan of action was to endeavour to regain the diamonds, and return them to their owner, accompanied by a letter, asking pardon for his offence, and disavowing, on oath, all knowledge of, and participation in, the terrible robbery and murder.

It was about a week after Wild had perpetrated the outrages in the character of Clifford, that the latter, elegantly dressed as usual, went forth from his lodgings, and bent his steps in the direction of Hawkins's establishment, in Oxford-street.

No one would have suspected the calling of that elegantly-attired, gentlemanly man, as he tripped through the streets to his destination.

To all appearances he was a gentleman of the first water.

In deportment, in dress, and in language he was one.

It was only in a moral point of view that he was found wanting.

The great black stain on his character was the only instance in which, if tested, he could possibly be found wanting.

It was two o'clock in the afternoon when Clifford reached the shop of the fence.

It was the fashionable time for shopping, and Oxford-street was filled with fashionables hustling one another in entering the great marts of the West-end.

When Clifford reached the door of the shop, he found that Hawkins was engaged with many customers, so he turned and strolled about in the locality until he saw that the jeweller was disengaged.

Then he entered.

His appearance seemed to surprise Hawkins, who started back on seeing him, and regarded him with a fixed stare most unusual to him.

After a moment, however, he recovered his usual coolness and suavity of manner, and invited his visitor into the private office, into which we have more than once introduced the reader.

As soon as they were within and the door closed, Hawkins fixed his hands behind his back and, looking Clifford straight in the face, said—

"Well, this is cool."

"What mean you ?"

"What do I mean. Why I mean that to show up in Oxford-street, after perpetrating within the week such acts as you have done, denotes an impudence of which I could not have suspected you possessed."

"Such acts as I have done within the week ! Really you confound me. What can you refer to?"

"Why, to the adventures on Ealing-common, and the murder of your pal over the funeral business."

The look of bewildered surprise that spread over Clifford's face as he heard the fence speak thus convinced that worthy that there must be some mistake somewhere.

"You speak in riddles," said Clifford, "and I should really like to know what you mean ?"

"It's soon told," said the jeweller, and without delay he rehearsed the tale with which the reader is already acquainted.

Clifford looked amazed as he heard what fell from the lips of Hawkins.

"I cannot conceive what all this means," he said ; "on my oath, I have not left my house for three days, and since my escape from Newgate I have been but once in the saddle, and then for a very different purpose to that to which you allude. It's the most singular affair I ever knew."

"At the first glance it does appear so, but I think I can comprehend it."

"If so, pray explain to me, for I am sorely puzzled."

"Do you suspect nothing ?"

"Nothing."

"Then I do. I can see the hand of Jonathan Wild in all this."

"How?"

"It strikes me that this is but part of a plan for rendering your name infamous. He suspects that if you stood a trial you would be one too many for him, and so he takes this mode of ridding himself and the world of your presence."

"I begin to understand."

"I should think so. What so simple? He has but to purchase a good suit of clothes and a white mare to become Gentleman Clifford. His wonderful power of assuming character makes all the rest easy."

"I see it, I see it. Good God! it is an awful scheme, and I have no means of combatting it, no means of counteracting its influences."

"Don't be too sure of that."

"Sir?"

"No matter. What is your business with me?"

"I wish to repurchase the diamonds I sold you on the morning of my introduction to Newgate."

"Ha, ha! Repurchase them—that's a good joke! Repurchase them! Do you come here to mock me?"

"Not I. Can you not see that I am in earnest?"

"Then you do not know that what you would repurchase was demanded from me, torn from me in the name of the law by Wild?"

"You surprise me!"

"Ecod, it surprised me! I can tell you."

"Then Wild has the diamonds?"

"No. I believe he returned them to their owner; but, as a matter of course, made her pay a precious price for them."

"Then he is still more my enemy than ever."

"Ah, and mine too, for I was a loser of three thousand pounds over that bargain!"

"The loss has been but a temporary one," said Clifford, putting his hand in his pocket and drawing forth a note-case, "here is the money with which I would have repurchased the gems. Take it, it is yours."

"Hillo!" said Hawkins, "you must be jesting."

"Not I. Count out your notes."

"Well, that is something like honour, and I respect you for it. But in a more recent transaction with Wild I had the best of him to some tune, and so I can afford to knock off something, Clifford. I'll take *two thousand* and leave you *one*. I'm always generous, I am, when people act on the square by me, so take back the money."

There was nothing so very magnanimous in the act of the fence, seeing that he made a tremendous haul over his bargain with Wild. But he liked to parade his generosity on every available occasion; and there were so few that, when one came, he always made the most of it.

For a few moments there was not a word spoken on either side; but, after a while, Hawkins broke the silence by bursting into a loud laugh.

"Ha, ha!" he roared, "to think that I should so nicely trick the cunning Jonathan. Ha, ha, ha! He never was so taken aback in all his life."

"To what do you refer?"

"To the bargain I made with him."

"What was it?"

"Ah, that's my secret. You know I'm not in the habit of blabbing about business."

"True; I have no right to ask."

"No, you have no right to know; but still, as I like you so much, and hate Wild so intensely, I don't know but what I'll tell you. The fact is that he has had swing enough; but there's only a few who dare pull him up. The matter that I have against him would do the trick, but I dare not be seen in it; for I'm in the swim, and, what's more, my little game would be up if it came out that I, in the remotest particular, had dealings with men of his and your stamp. So, if I tell you what I know, you will have to swear to me, by all your hopes of salvation, never to mention from whom you have gleaned your information."

"If you can tell me aught that will tend, in any way, to assist me in bringing Wild to the scaffold, I will not only hear you thankfully, but will bind myself, by my soul, to keep your secret. I have registered an oath that Wild shall die on the scaffold, and that I will drag him there; so you may be assured that, if there is a man breathing to be trusted with your secret, whatever it may be, I am that man."

"I think so, and therefore will not hesitate to put you in the way of the work to be done. The robbery and murders done at the mansion of the Duchess of Lakemont were the work of Jonathan Wild and his associates."

"How?"

"The Duke and the officers fell under his hand, and the swag was brought to me by Jonathan himself. Cunning devil! He thought I should not know him; but he could not deceive me. No sooner did my eye light upon him than I knew him; but I feigned ignorance of his identity, until I had him in my power, and then I spoke, and he left me crushed and humbled—for he knew the weapon he had placed in my grasp. Had he but suspected how I would use it, he never would have made so hazardous a venture; but the best beat themselves sometimes, and Wild has proved no exception to the rule."

"You indeed surprise me."

"I have no doubt of it. My secret is a matter of surprise; but you will swear to hold me harmless?"

"I swear by my soul! May the bitterest curse Heaven can put upon me, now and hereafter, light upon me if I, by word or deed, attempt your betrayal!"

"It is well. I know that I can trust you; and now that our business is over we will part. Act as you will, but be cautious."

"You need not warn me. I am too painfully conscious of the power and cunning of the man against whom I move my hand not to be wary how I attempt to strike the blow."

"You ought to be. My advice is, do not make yourself too public, and trust no one, or a pistol ball through the brain, or a knife through the heart, will inevitably be your fate."

"Thanks! I am conscious of my peculiar position, and will avoid the chances against which you warn me."

"Then that is all I have to say, save that I hope you will come here to report progress, and always comand my assistance when I can with safety afford it."

"I will not fail to do so."

"Then we will say good-bye."

"Good-bye. Once again a thousand thanks!"

They parted.

"Now," said Clifford, as he walked into the street, "now, Wild, I have you! If I could but raise the Duchess against you! If I could only find the means to make her exert her great power in avenging the death of her—"

"Clifford!"

Our hero had moved some twenty paces from the door of the goldsmith's shop, and was passing a large silk and milinery establishment, when a hand was laid upon his shoulder, and a voice rang in his ears—

"Clifford!"

He turned.

Before him stood the Duchess of Lakemont.

He turned crimson, stammered, and would have fled, but her appearance reassured him.

She approached nearer.

"Not a word," she whispered, "not a syllable. You see I know you, *and I do not despise you.* Come with me."

Her carriage awaited her.

The door was held open by a servant in livery. She entered, and Clifford followed.

Next moment they were rolling away towards the mansion of the Duchess.

For many minutes Clifford sat in mute surprise.

The words of the Duchess still rang in his ears.

"I know you, and do not despise you."

What could it mean?"

It was vain to think, and he had to wait until his fair companion spoke.

He stole a glance at her.

There she sat, with her eyes fixed on his, beautiful as when he first saw her.

She was pale, and the sombre hue of her dress lent her an air of sadness he had not marked in her before. Otherwise she was the same.

"I am glad to meet you," she said, "I cannot tell you how glad. I never expected to see you again after what fell from the lips of that terrible man."

"Wild?"

"Yes. I begged for your life. I tempted him by every means in my power; but he was relentless. He would not listen to me, and I thought you were doomed to an ignominious death."

"And you cared for me—you tried to save my life, and after what had passed. Oh! can there be such goodness in the world?"

"Hush! let the past die. I have no wish to refer to it again. Let it go now and for ever."

"But—"

"Silence, the carriage stops. We will speak again anon."

The carriage now drew up at the mansion of the Duchess, and she and Clifford alighted.

The door of the house swung open, and the highwayman, with the lady on his arm, passed through the grand hall, up the splendid staircase, and thence into a magnificent apartment.

"Stay here," said the Duchess, "and I will return in an instant. I have but to change my dress, and give a few orders to my servants."

Bewildered, and as one in a dream, Clifford sank into a seat pointed out to him by the Duchess.

Without another word she left him.

While she was absent Clifford was plunged into a perfect chaos of thought.

It was all dream-like and unreal to him.

A short time ago, under an assumed name, he professed love for this grand lady. He sought by every art to make her return the passion. He drugged her wine, robbed her, left her in a situation which might have blasted her reputation, and after a short lapse of time, he hears from this woman's own lips that she does not despise him, that by every means in her power she had tried to save his life, and now he was actually sitting in her apartment, awaiting her coming, and without dread.

What was he to think of all this?

What interpretation could he put upon such conduct?

Common sense suggested only one, and that one was *love!*

As the thought occurred to Clifford he battled it down manfully.

He crushed it as it rose; stamped it out, as if he had been fighting with a devil within him.

"If it should be that," he said to himself—"if it should be that, I am the most unhappy of mortals. I am unworthy her pity. I love another, and yet she has an affection for me. God help me!—I am distracted—I do but dream—this is unreal. My brain must be affected —I see not these things that surround me—they are but the creatures of a disordered fancy. It cannot be."

"Why not?"

Again that voice!

He looked up, and there, with the great lustrous eyes beaming down on him again, was the Duchess.

She was ravishingly attired in the most *neglige* of costumes. The sorrow seemed wiped away from her radiant countenance, and she stood before him a very vision of loveliness.

Clifford started to his feet.

"Once," continued the Duchess—"once it was your

chance to overhear me—now it is mine to have caught you in self-communion."

"You heard?"

"But little. Unfortunately I did not arrive soon enough."

"Thank Heaven!"

"Amen!—if you said aught that I should not care for hearing."

"I know not what I might have said," continued Clifford, "this is so unexpected—so strange—so unreal."

"It must appear so, but calm yourself. A few moments will assure you that after all there is nothing so strange about it."

"But that fatal night! Could I hope that you would again honour me with a thought, save one of bitterness, after that awful night?"

"The memory of the first part of the evening," said the Duchess, evidently striving, though at the risk of appearing unwomanly in her demeanour, to restore the confidence of Clifford—"the memory of the first part of the evening obliterated that of the unfortunate *contretemps* at its termination."

"And you know me for what I really am?"

"Yes. Wild told me all."

"And you do not despise me?"

"Can a woman despise one who has professed to love her, and whose professions have been listened to with pleasure?"

"Lady, pause," said Clifford, "I am not so great a villain as to take you, or the humblest of your sex, at a disadvantage. Pause, I say, and reflect on whom and what I am."

"I have reflected and still—"

"Yes, lady, still—"

"Clifford, robber, outcast, felon though you are, I love you."

She threw herself into his arms, and buried her beauful head in his bosom.

Our hero stood as one petrified: had not his limbs refused their office he would have turned and fled.

A moment passed, and he still pressed her to his heart.

It was a trying position for him.

He felt the danger he was in, but had not strength to fly from it.

A vision of Evelina rose before his eyes, but vanished on the instant.

The real was too powerful for the ideal. Besides, had not Evelina despised him? had she not flown from him? did she not refuse to allow him even the happiness of assisting her in her utmost need? And here was a lady, high born, marvellously beautiful, and rich, whom he had betrayed, imposed upon, and robbed, with her arms about his neck; with her heart, full of love, beating against his, and her whole soul filled with one thought— and that of him!

It would have been a man cast in a more angelic mould than that in which the majority of mankind are formed to withstand this, and it is not a matter for wonder that Clifford's arms gradually tightened about the fair Duchess, that his heart should have roamed towards her, and that he should have repeated in earnest the words he uttered at the masked ball in jest, and for the purpose of facilitating a vile plan of robbery.

It will avail nothing to depict the scene that ensued.

The reader will understand, had Clifford related his own history, how he revealed the authors of the murder of the old Duke, and the great robbery, and how the Duchess swore to assist him in his scheme of vengeance.

"I can," she said, after all these things had been rehearsed; "I can sway the Home Secretary, and bind him to my will. He is old, and not very strong-minded, and, moreover, he *loves me.* I can so work upon him as to make him grant you a free pardon for the past, and, in spite of Wild's power, we will hurl him from his position, and bring him to that scaffold with which he threatened you."

"You are all goodness," said Clifford.

"Would I not do this, and a thousand times as much, for you?"

"Thanks, thanks! I can never repay such kindness."

"Yes," she said, "yes, Clifford, you can by giving me your love—your whole and sole love! With that I shall be amply repaid."

Clifford could not reply in words. His conscience told him that, as yet, there was no love in his heart for this woman, so he held her in his arms, and imprinted a kiss upon her lips.

She was answered: and, feeling that Clifford was indeed her own, she was happy.

Such is life, and *such is woman!*

CHAPTER XXXVII.

THE END OF WILD'S POWER — THE DOWNFALL — THE PURSUIT AND THE ESCAPE.

IT was several days after the events recorded in the last chapter that Wild returned to London.

Changing his clothes, and disposing of his steed at a well-known spot, he walked leisurely, and with evident self-satisfaction, towards his own house.

It was night, and he was unnoticed by the crowds that flocked through the streets; but just as he was about to turn towards Newgate a hand was laid upon his shoulder, and, turning, he beheld the countenance of the Jew bent upon him with a look of anguish he could not account for.

"Well," said Wild, "what is the trouble now?"

"Oh! Misther Vild, the vorst poshible trouble. You are betrayed—you are undone; the house is full of officers, and this time they vant you."

"Me! Why, you old idiot, you are either drunk or dreaming:"

"No, no, I'm not indeed, indeed, Misther Vild. They've turned me out and taken possession of all your peautiful treasures. Oh, it vas sad, very sad, to see vat they did vith 'em! I thought I should have proke my heart."

"I think I shall break your head if you don't speak out plainly what you have to say."

"Vell, sir, you're betrayed—you're undone. It vos that little bit o' bishness at the Duchess's that did it. Oh! sir, read this, read this, and convince yourself."

The Jew drew from his pocket a placard and placed it in the hands of the thief-taker.

Wild walked quickly to the nearest lamp and by its somewhat dubious light read the following :—

£1,000 REWARD.

"WHEREAS on the —— of —— 17—, several atrocious murders and an extensive burglary were committed within the mansion of the Duchess of Lakemont, in the parish of St. James's, and whereas it has been satisfactorily proved that in the commission of these crimes one JONATHAN WILD, and several others, unknown, were engaged, the above reward will be given to any person or persons who shall give such information to the authorities as shall lead to the apprehension of the said Jonathan Wild. And further, the said sum of £1,000 will be given to any person or persons who shall produce within one calendar month from the date hereof the person of the said JONATHAN WILD, *dead or alive!*

"A further sum of £200 will also be paid for the appre-hension of those persons implicated with the said JONATHAN WILD in the above-mentioned murders and burglary.

"Signed
"——— ———."
"—— day of ———, 17—."

"Hell's fury!" cried Wild, as his eye fell upon this document; "betrayed!—ruined!—who could have done this?"

"Can you not guess?"

"No."

"Vell, then; it's no other than the Shentleman."

"Clifford?"

"The same."

"Impossible!"

"I know I'm right, sir. I can prove it to you; but, hush, there's some one coming."

Wild and the Jew quickly separated, and the former walked on with an air of indifference in the direction in which the persons alluded to by the Jew were coming.

The approaching parties were three men who had just quitted his house.

They passed them.

But suddenly one of them turned.

"I tell you it's he. Come on."

The man made after Wild, and the others followed.

Wild heard them approaching.

To fly would be to raise an alarm that would insure his own destruction.

Calmly he put his hands into his pockets, and awaited the coming of the men.

The foremost of them was upon him in an instant.

"Jonathan Wild," he cried, "I apprehend you in the King's name."

"And I send you to the devil, in my own name," he cried, turning upon his man and braining him with the butt of his pistol.

In a few seconds the others were upon him with drawn staves, and he had as much as he could do to defend himself. But he was a resolute and powerful man, and in a shorter space of time than it takes to record the fact the men were all laid low.

It was now the time for flight, and ere the men could recover their senses he was many hundred yards in advance.

On he flew, with the velocity of wind; but they came after him with no less speed.

On they went, he reserving his strength, and running with the greatest swiftness; they yelling his name, and crying on the passers-by to stop him.

But no one dared lay hands on him.

There was that in his face that told them such a proceeding would be indeed dangerous.

On, on, they dashed through the streets of London.

On, into the suburbs; the speed of the officers relaxing each moment, and Wild continuing his own bravely. On they went, and without a change in the position of affairs—the open country was reached; but still, in the calmness of the night, the fugitive heard the terrible voices of the awakened multitudes roused to fury, bent on vengeance at the sound of his hated name.

Still he knew that he was pursued.

Still he found the relentless bloodhounds on his track.

At length he reached Cricklewood, and deeming it advisable to leave the main road, dashed through a hedge, and disappeared.

It was now daylight.

*   *   *   *   *

THE Edgeware-road, at the time of Jonathan Wild, was a very different place to what it is now. It is a road, and always, no doubt, will be, and as far out as Cricklewood, even now, things will grow, and the trees will look as if they really had some truth about them.

But, in the days of Jonathan Wild, and of Paul Clifford, Cricklewood was quite in the country.

The stillness about Jonathan Wild, and about the

field into which he had sprung through the hedge, had nothing at all unusual or exceptional about it.

The birds sung upon the tall trees in the hedge-row close to him, and he heard the two ducks in the road cackling and routing about in a little muddy water-course that was close at hand.

Wild lay in this way for about half an hour, or perhaps more.

After that he looked about him a little, but without getting up.

"Well," he said, "this is better than swinging on the gibbet at Tyburn!"

"Yes," he said, "this is better after all."

Dark and horrible thoughts then began to take possession of his soul.

"I may yet," he said, "have vengeance upon all my foes. They thought that they had so very nicely hunted me to death, but they may be very much mistaken, after all. No, no, it won't do yet—Jonathan Wild's time is not yet come."

"Hilloa!" cried a voice.

Wild very nearly uttered a cry of alarm, but he just had presence of mind enough not to do so.

The voice came from some one in the road.

"Hilloa!" it cried again, "is that you, Judkins, old boy?"

"Well, Samuel Fay," said another voice, from some garden or meadow right on the other side of the way, "what's the news, lad?"

Wild was more careful; he felt that as yet, at all events, he was not compromised in what was going on, but he thought that his position there in broad daylight was rather hazardous.

Gently rolling over, he got right down into a hollow that had once been a water-course, and was still damp, just at the foot of the hedge.

Then he found that he was about the level of the field, so that any one even looking after him would hardly be at all likely to see him.

The conversation went on between the two countrymen, one in the road, and the other in a ploughed field, on the opposite side of it to that on which Jonathan Wild was now concealed.

"I say," said one, "they're down upon that thief-taker, Wild, at last, and they're after him as he has been after many a poor devil in his time."

"Found out?"

"Yes; and there's a matter of a thousand pounds offered for him dead or alive."

"No?"

"Yes it is. Oh, lor', wouldn't that be a good day's work, Judkins?"

"It would, lad—it would."

"Why, a fellow might take a Uphill Farm, and be a squire all the days of his life."

"He might, lad, he might."

"But there isn't no chance for the like of us, is there, Judkins?"

"No, lad, there isn't. I only wish as there was, that's all."

"So do I."

"Have you took them tares down to Farmer Anderson, lad?"

"No, but I am a-going."

"Do, do, and be quick about un. Only to think, now, that if we could only lay hands on Jonathan wild, we might take to the Uphill Farm, and be squires. Lord! lord! what chances there are in the world, but he's far enough off by this time, I take it."

"No doubt about it, Judkins."

"Well, well, take the tares, and you might as well, lad, take the taturs, too, they come to three and ninepence, you know, lad."

"Ay, ay, all's right."

The voice ceased.

"Indeed," muttered Wild to himself, "you would like to nab me, no doubt, and take a farm with the money, but

I'd eat your poor stupid brains with a wooden spoon first, idiots that you are. You little suspect that I am so near to you."

Wild began to feel though that his present place of refuge was, in reality, anything but a safe one, and that it was a very desirable thing to make some effort to procure a better.

Glancing about him, he saw, at no great distance off, a large hay-rick.

That gave him an idea.

"Ah," he said, "that may do; I have known many a worse hiding-place than that before to-day. It may do well—at all events it shall be tried."

With this he made his way towards the hay-rick.

It was his intention to get right into it, if possible. He well knew that his position was one, now, of the greatest danger.

That the Government would make every possible endeavour now to capture him, he was well aware.

In fact, he knew that it would, so far as the officials were now concerned, become quite a point of honour with them to get him hanged according to law.

Of course, he likewise knew one great and important fact connected with his position, and which made it differ with many others.

The important fact consisted in the great truth that, notwithstanding that he was a hunted criminal, he had no comrades—he had no one to sympathise with him. There was no party in his favour—none to try to shield him from the arm of the law.

Who cared for Jonathan Wild?

Not one.

Had he ever made a friend in the whole world during his whole career of crime?

Not one.

Such, then, was the degraded situation of that bold, bad man. Deserted by the Government that had made an unscrupulous tool of him for so long, he was thrown upon the wide world alone.

Therefore, like Cain, was Jonathan Wild a wanderer in the world, with his hand raised against all men, and the hands of all men raised against him.

But we cannot pity him for all that, because we cannot help considering that he is but reaping that which he has sown, and that he has but now a small taste of the misery and the suffering which he did not scruple to inflict by wholesale upon many others.

But he is crawling along towards the haystack now.

Oh! what a different position was Wild in now to that in which he was, so to speak, the arbiter of life and death to all around him!

Why, time was—and that only a very short time ago, too—when he, Jonathan Wild, actually and truly had, in London, more power than any judge in the land, and when his favour was far more sought after than that of the very Secretary of State himself.

But all that was changed now. There he was, a poor, houseless fugitive, with a heavy price upon his very head!

Fearful if he let even so much as the top of his head be seen above the level of tall weeds that grew in rank luxuriance about that spot, Jonathan Wild still, like a great snake, wriggled his way towards the hay-rick.

If there were, now, anything more than another that he wished for, it was night to come.

Yes, while the broad, open eye of glorious day was upon him, Wild felt all his danger, and what a fearful thing it was to be at such open war with all his fellow-creatures.

For he was, in good sooth, at open war with them all.

It took him a good ten minutes to get close to the hay-rick, but when he did get there he thought that the time so consumed had not at all been ill-bestowed; for he felt a sensation of safety from that moment.

But still, some one might come into the field, and see him.

One-half of that danger did occur, even at the moment that the probability of it occurred to him.

Some one did come into the field.

It was a country-looking boy and a young girl, and they seemed to be having some sort of quarrel and discussion about something that very much interested the boy, if it did not the girl.

" But I tell you, Sue, master says he will give I seven shillings a week when my time is up," said the boy.

" I don't care," said the girl.

" Then you won't marry I ?"

" No."

" Oh—oh—oh !"

" Hold your noise, and don't be moaning like a bull in that way."

" I can't help it. I'm the most out-and-out miserable miserable fellow as never was in all the world, I is."

"Then, Sam, you must just remain so ; and I can tell you one thing, and that is—what do you think ?"

" I don't know, I never was good at thinking, Sue."

" Then I'll tell you."

" Yes, do."

" I never will marry any one who can't keep a cow."

" A cow ?"

" Yes, a cow ; because I have set my mind upon a dairy, you see, and so there is an end of it ; and it is of no use your bothering me any more about it, so good-by."

" Oh—oh! when am I to get a cow ? Why cows just now fetch a matter of eight pounds a-piece."

" I know it."

The girl walked off with great speed, and the country lout, her admirer, after uttering some howls that rather resembled the tones of some wild animal disappointed of a meal than anything human, likewise left the field.

"Curses on them both !" muttered Wild, " they gave me a fright ; for if they had only seen me, I suppose there would have been such an alarm as I would hardly have escaped from."

This circumstance only, then, made him still more solicitous to conceal himself effectually in the hay-rick ; and he set to work for that purpose.

He began, about three feet from the ground, to pull out handfulls of hay, and he scattered them at some distance from the rick, and in such a way, too, that the light morning air took them and carried them for the greater part over the meadows in the immediate neighbourhood.

By working in this way for some time, he made quite a large and deep opening in the hay-rick ; and then he began to force himself into it, feet foremost.

This was, to say the best of it, anything in the world but an easy job to do.

Perseverance, however, combined with the dread of capture, effected wonders, and in the course of a quarter of an hour—during which, luckily for him, he was not at all intercepted—Jonathan Wild managed to conceal himself in the hay-rick.

When he had got so far into the very body of the rick that only the top of his head was about an inch or two from the outside of it, he pulled down a portion of the hay, and so covered that opening, and then he was buried in hay.

There was no obstruction at all to his breathing, for he was very close to the surface of the stack on the side that he had got in at.

But yet his situation was more snug than pleasant.

A painful sensation of weight was upon the whole of his limbs, and he began to get seriously apprehensive that the hay-rick was collapsing down upon him.

All this, though, was but the apprehension of an excited fancy.

After a time such feelings subsided, and Jonathan Wild became rather more accustomed to his situation.

The idea, though, of having to stay there so many hours, till nightfall, was not a very pleasant one.

He began to try and come to some sort of consideration as to what the time was, so that he might make a

mental calculation as to how long he would have to wait in his then present position.

While he was thus calculating how long it had taken him to get through the mob at the execution—how long he had been with the two men in the cart, and how long a time had elapsed since then, he fell asleep.

Yes, this villain yielded to the soft influence of sleep.

Nature would assert her supremacy, and after the fatigues, the excitements, and the terrible exertions of the last four-and-twenty hours, Jonathan Wild slept as soundly as an infant at its mother's breast.

But what made Jonathan Wild sleep so well for a time was the fact that his frame was thoroughly and completely exhausted.

So soon as that effect had passed away, although the sleep still continued, it was in a very different fashion.

The brain, no longer lulled to oblivion by intense excitement, began to exert itself in its old fashion.

The most terrible dreams then commenced to exercise their sway over Jonathan Wild.

This was the curse of conscience—this was the peculiar kind of moral retribution for his crimes which of late years, notwithstanding all his successes, he had never been able to free himself from.

No sooner used he to lie down to sleep than he became tormented by the most terrible images.

Then it was that the victims of his passions that he had with his own hand murdered, or brought to death by the many means at his disposal, rose up spectre-like before his mental vision, and drove him to the very verge of madness.

And now some such a vision of the over-wrought brain began to oppose him as he slept in the hay-rick.

Legions of gory skeleton forms appeared to be crowding about him.

He fancied he was forced into some deep pit, and at the bottom of it held down by bleeding spectres.

The pit appeared to be so deep that the mouth of it, as he looked up to it, only revealed a small portion of the mid-day sky.

He thought it mid-day, because that was the best real impression of time that was made upon his waking senses.

But, in reality, Jonathan Wild had slept on uninterruptedly in the hay-rick for many hours, and the evening had fairly set in before he awakened.

Then he thought that skeleton forms, each one of which was so dripping with gore that it seemed as though they had all come out of a sea of blood, sprang down upon him.

He thought that, with mad and hideous glee, they piled themselves one upon another upon him, seemingly intent upon filling up the pit while he should be at the bottom of it.

This was too much, even for his sleeping brain to bear.

With a strange, half-stifled cry, Wild awoke.

For the first few moments, now, of his waking existence, he really thought that his dream was a reality, for he could move neither hand nor foot.

The hay closely compressed him, and, in the agony of his dream, he had grasped at a mouthful of it, and was half choked by so doing.

" Help, help !" he gasped.

And then, as though the sound of his own voice in the pronunciation of an articulate word had had the effect of at once dispelling the delusion under which he had laboured, he recollected where he was.

He was still in a moment.

" A dream !" he muttered—" only a dream after all—one of the old dreams that were wont to drive me nearly mad before."

He cleared the hay from before his mouth, and looked out.

All was darkness, and the cool night air was blowing around the hay-rick.

That revived him a little.

" If I had but some brandy now, he said to himself, " I should be all well again. Oh ! for some brandy."

But that stimulant was, in his present circumstances, not to be had ; so he was compelled to do the best he possibly could without it.

It was, though, a great gratification to him to find that the day had passed away—that day he had so much, and with such reason, dreaded.

" I shall do now," he said ; " oh ! yes, I shall do now. It is night, and I have a thousand chances in the night to one that I had in the day."

But so sudden, so unexpected, and so actually surprising and impromptu-like had been his escape from the scaffold that he had no plan of operations matured by which to profit by.

So he felt, now that there did, indeed, seem to be a something in the shape of a chance of his ultimate escape, that it was time to settle in his own mind what he meant to do.

Leave England !

Yes, that was now the first project. He felt that England was too hot to hold him. No longer, after all that had occurred, could he be safe on English ground.

" I will go to France," he muttered to himself, " and from there possibly to America. The state of society there may suit me well."

His idea now, as he matured his plans, was to proceed on foot, or on horseback if he could get a horse, to some sea-port.

From there he considered that he would not have much difficulty in reaching some part of the Continent where he would be safe from the operation of the English laws.

There was one little circumstance which would have been rather a serious obstacle to most people in the carrying out of such an enterprise.

That was, that he had no money with him for its exigencies.

But that was hardly an obstacle to such a man as Jonathan Wild.

He could rob for the means of proceeding. He did not give himself the least concern upon that head, for he meant to avail himself of the first well-filled purse that any lone passenger had upon the highway.

And so, having settled that much in his own mind, and feeling very much cramped in all his limbs, in consequence of having been in one position for so long in the hay-rick, he thought of getting out of it.

" Oh, that I could know the time," he said to himself. " It would be quite an useful piece of information for me now if I could but know the hour."

There did not appear any ready way, as yet, by which his curiosity on this point could be at all gratified, so he gave up complaining about it.

And now he was on the point of making his first movement to get out of the hay-rick when he fancied he heard the sound of feet near at hand.

It was a strange sound, too, for it was like feet moving in regular marching order over the fields.

Wild listened.

On came the sound towards him, and just as he had made up his mind that he was listening to the march of soldiery, he was confirmed in that opinion by hearing a loud voice cry out—

" Halt !"

The sound of feet ceased on the moment.

" Troops?" muttered Wild, " what do they do here ? Oh, they are only on the march to some place or another, that is all."

He said this, but he did not think it, As in every bush the thief fancies he sees an officer of police, so in every sound Jonathan Wild now fancied that he found food for the suspicion that some one was taking some cunning steps towards his capture.

He was right in this case.

In a straggling sort of way now several footsteps approached the spot where the hay-rick was.

Jonathan thought himself deceived.

" Well, Mr. Thornton," said a voice, " you, as a magistrate of the county, have asked for my services, and the services of my men, but I don't think we shall be of much use to you."

" Oh yes, Captain Holmes," replied some one, " oh yes, you will."

" Very good, sir."

" I am sure you will, captain, and I am very much obliged to you for your readiness in the matter."

" Oh, don't mention that, sir."

" Nay, but it should be mentioned to the Secretary of State, who is particularly anxious to take that rascal, Jonathan Wild."

" So I hear."

" Dead or alive."

" Ah, and perhaps, between you and me, Mr. Thornton, the former would be the better and more acceptable state in which to present him."

" Well, captain," replied the magistrate, lowering his voice, " I should not be at all surprised but that you are right in that idea."

" No doubt of it."

" Curse you all !" thought Wild, " I have no sort of doubt of it myself."

" Well, Mr. Thornton," added Captain Holmes, as the magistrate had named him. " Here am I, and here is a party of my dismounted dragoon guards at your service."

" Many thanks for them. I assure you I shall need them, for there is not an officer to be found who cares about the task of attempting the capture of this villain after the manner in which he served the fellows who started him last night, near Newgate."

" I presume that that will be the case, independent of the fear they may entertain for the man's prowess in a personal encounter, I should be much surprised if they are not so mixed up with him as to dread his capture, and what will follow."

" Ah, that is so."

" But why is the Secretary for the Home Department so anxious for the capture of this man."

" I really cannot say from personal knowledge, but I am given to understand that a certain Duchess has a hand in it."

" You mean the Duchess of Lakemont ?"

" I am not inclined to mention names, but you are at liberty to make what guesses you please."

" And so the Duchess is anxious for his capture ?"

" Rumour whispers as much."

" But why ?"

" Have you ever heard of Gentleman Clifford ?"

" The highwayman ?"

" Yes."

" Very frequently."

" Well people do say that the Duchess acts less from personal motives than at his instigation. Wild and the highwayman are at daggers drawn."

" And is it possible that the Duchess can take an interest in one so base as this robber ?"

" Why not ? The Duchess is a peculiar woman, and Clifford is a remarkably handsome man."

" Ah ! I divine your meaning. But it is a strange affair."

" It is, indeed."

Well, now, Captain, to business. Hark ! did you not hear something move ?"

" Not I."

" I thought there was a sound of a human voice somewhere near."

" I heard nothing."

" It is strange."

" Nonsense. I begin to think that you are as frightened of Wild as all your men. Where do you suppose he could be—in that hay-rick ?"

" Ha ! ha ! A curious place for a fellow to hide."

" Yes, indeed. But if he is not there he is nowhere."

WILD HIDING FROM THE DRAGOONS.

No. 14.

"And yet I could have sworn I heard a voice."

"Mere fancy."

"So it appears."

"Well, then, let us begone."

"With all my heart, for this fellow must and shall soon be in my power."

Wild heard them departing.

He breathed more freely.

CHAPTER XXXVIII.

THE DUCHESS AND THE MINISTER—AFFAIRS OF THE HEART — JEALOUSY — AN UNEXPECTED MEETING AND THE RESULT.

THE Duchess had acted like a thorough woman of the world in the affairs of Wild and Clifford.

The minister, in whose hands was placed the power to pardon or condemn these men, had been played upon with the greatest tact, and the result was that the first was deposed and hunted to the death, and that the second received a full pardon for all the acts of which he had been guilty.

How was this done?

The process was a simple one.

The Duchess, leading the not over-wise old minister to suppose that she entertained some affection for him, and that at no distant date she might become his wife, assured him that to Jonathan Wild could be traced the murders and robbery committed in her mansion.

"And," said she, "I demand but justice. This man must and shall be brought to the scaffold."

"But," urged the old man, "whatever may be the crimes of this man he has proved a marvellously useful thief-taker, and to turn upon him would be to arouse the indignation of my colleagues and disturb the tranquillity of the public."

"Then, because this man is an useful officer, he may, with impunity, commit the most heinous crimes, and I, who am the sufferer, can obtain no redress?"

"I did not quite say that."

"But you infer as much."

"I am afraid that we must wink at the acts of this man, but if you can trace the crimes to his door he shall make ample reparation."

"Reparation! Can he give me back my husband?"

The old man held his peace, but to himself he said—

"Heaven forbid that he should!"

"Can he restore a life as dear to me as my own? and can he draw forth the bitter sting he has planted in my breast?"

"It is, indeed, much to be regretted."

"But you do not answer my question."

"My dear Duchess, the case is a painful one, and I am afraid no *adequate* recompence can be offered you."

"Farewell, then. It is best we should never meet again."

"Eh? What? No, you cannot mean that!"

The Duchess rose to depart.

The old minister saw determination in her eye, and trembled.

"I do mean it," said the lady; "I can never bear to look in the face of the man who has it in his power to grant but refuses me justice."

"But stay a few moments; the thing may yet be arranged."

"Yes; by dragging Jonathan Wild to the scaffold."

The old man winced.

"Surely some milder——"

He was about to proceed, but the Duchess interrupted him imperiously.

"Farewell," she said; "I see I but waste time."

"Indeed you do not. Let us talk the matter over."

"I demand the life of Wild. Any conversation that has for an aim the driving me from this idea is but time occupied fruitlessly. I had best begone."

"One moment."

"Do you consent?"

"Give me a day to consider."

"Not an hour."

"Yes, yes, my dear Duchess; one hour."

"I require your answer."

"You demand Wild's life?"

"His life."

"And nothing but his life will appease your anger?"

"Nothing."

"Consider the position in which you place me."

"I will consider no more. I have thought and thought, and I have said the man who has any regard for me would not hesitate one moment."

"I know not *how* to act."

"I have shown you how to act. Do you consent?"

"I have no alternative. I must—"

"Hang him?"

"Yes."

"That is well!"

"Now, am I in better odour?"

"You are indeed."

"Ah, but the sacrifice is an awful one."

"I doubt it not, but I am firm."

"Then Wild dies, and now that I have done all you have to ask of me, are we friends again?"

"Yes; but you have not quite done all I have to ask of you."

"Indeed!"

"No, indeed."

"What next?"

"The next and last request I have to make will, I trust, occasion you less trouble in granting."

"I trust so, too."

"Without further prelude, let me say that I require a free and unconditional pardon for the highwayman Paul Clifford!"

The minister staggered back in amazement.

He paused as if to catch his breath.

Then he looked at the Duchess.

"You surely jest," he said after a while.

"Jest! Not I, forsooth. I am in no jesting humour."

"But the absurdity of your request."

"I do not consider it absurd."

"But I do."

"Because you do not know why I ask it ——"

"That may be."

"Well, know that my request for vengeance on Wild arises from the same cause that makes me ask for mercy to be extended to the highway robber."

"How?"

"It was Clifford who revealed to me the name of my husband's murderer."

The minister muttered—

"And the devil take him for his trouble."

But aloud he merely remarked—

"Indeed."

"Yes, sir; Clifford put me on the track of the villain, and as a reward I have promised to exert the small influence I have with you in his favour."

"Should I grant you this request just upon the other, the public would say that I had assuredly taken leave of my senses."

The Duchess probably thought, had the public arrived at that conclusion, it would not have been far wrong, but she only said—

"The opinion of the public will not affect you in any way, and if you think proper you can grant me this request without hesitation. Indeed the act will but appear a graceful acknowledgment of the man's exertions in dragging to justice the greatest villain that ever crawled the earth."

The minister saw the affair in a very different light, but he saw that there was an iron will opposed to his and that all argument would be useless, and so he waited for the Duchess to speak again.

After a pause she continued—

" Am I to take your silence for acquisition ?"

" Indeed, lady, you press me hard."

" I have no doubt, but I require a definite answer."

" Ah, me !"

" That is no answer."

" I see that you are determined to ascertain how far my admiration for you will carry me."

" I have no such thought. My requests are based upon no idle caprice. I feel that in procuring the destruction of the one man and the pardon of the other I am performing an act warranted by the circumstances of the case."

" I wish I could see with your eyes."

" If you had a desire to oblige me you would."

" I suppose I must."

" You are not necessitated."

" True ; but how can I refuse a request of yours ?"

" Ah. You would flatter me."

"Not I, by Heaven!"

" But this pardon. We are wandering from the point."

" It shall be granted."

" Thanks."

" And now I must leave you. Urgent business tears me away from your side. Ah, what punishment."

" But the pardon ?"

" I have said, it shall be granted."

" Oh ! but that will not do. Even now the officers of the prison from which he has escaped may be upon his track and done their best to drag him back to his noisome dungeon. I must take the pardon with me."

" Dear me, what haste !"

" No matter. It may be a whim, but you will grant it."

" I ought to consult my——"

" But *you* have the power."

" I have, but courtesy——"

" May prove fatal to the man I wish to save, so the pardon, the pardon I pray you."

" Well, since it must be so, I can urge no more. Ah, my dear Duchess, you may be assured that this morning's work is a great and incontrovertible proof of the esteem in which I hold you."

"I feel it to be so."

" And you appreciate my concessions. You admire my courtesies, and will one day make me happy—"

" This is not the time for such conversation. Remember, the grass has not yet grown over the resting-place of the Duke."

" True ; pardon me, but my feelings got the better of me. I knew not what I said."

" I readily excuse you."

The minister sat at a desk, and, drawing forth a sheet of paper, wrote on it very rapidly, and then affixed his seal.

" There," he said, " that is the warrant for the apprehension of Jonathan Wild ; and now for the pardon of Clifford."

In a few moments a second paper was written, and sealed, and this was placed in the hands of the Duchess.

" That," said the minister, " will secure the safety of the man whom you wish to save from the gallows."

" Thanks, thanks ! a thousand thanks ! and now adieu. I shall see you soon ?"

" Yes. May I call ?"

" At your earliest convenience."

" At what hour have you most leisure ?"

" I can always find leisure to receive one who has so far obliged me. Adieu."

The Duchess took her departure.

The above conversation took place in the private residence of Sir Lawrence Totterly, the aged and extremely silly Secretary for Home Affairs.

He was a man entirely unfitted, bodily and mentally, for such an office, but he belonged to a family that somehow managed to find a place in every Whig administration, and could not well be shaken off, having an immense amount of local influence.

It generally happens that the most important offices fall into the hands of men who are so constituted as to have no manner of appreciation for them, and this was the case with Sir Lawrence Totterly.

Instead of being placed in some snug sinecure, where his failings could not be perceived, he received the most critical and important office that can possibly fall to the lot of the statesman.

Foreign affairs are difficult enough to manage, but to preserve the nation in internal peace and order—to command, as it were, the arrangements whereby Englishmen maintain their pride of place among nations, whereby they present to the eye of the foreigner so perfect a picture of joy, comfort, wealth, and independence, is a task for a gigantic intellect, a will of iron, a nerve of steel, and a heart brimming over with human kindness.

Such was not possessed by Sir Lawrence.

He was open to aristocratic influence.

He was a man swayed like a reed by every petty breeze.

He had no mind of his own, and hesitated to be guided by those who could think.

In exercising the prerogative of mercy he made some awful blunders.

At one time the most notorious of criminals escaped scatheless, and at another a man whose innocence was marked and proclaimed by all the world went to the scaffold to be judicially murdered.

Truly, this peculiarity in the Home Secretary seems to have descended with the traditions of the office to the present time.

But with such matters we have no right to deal in these pages, and must quit the subject now that we have accounted for the incidents detailed in the last chapter.

* * * * *

The Duchess hurried home.

With hurried step, and face flushed with excitement, she rushed up the stairs of her mansion and soon stood in her own *boudoir*.

As she entered a man rose from a chair in which he had been seated, and stood to receive her.

"Joy," she cried, drawing from her bosom a paper, and placing it in his hands. " Joy ! Here is your pardon !"

" Have you, then, succeeded ?" cried Clifford, for it was he. " Am I, then, once more at liberty to walk abroad without fear of being dogged for the purpose of being dragged to a prison, and thence to a scaffold ?"

" You are, indeed ! See ! the writing of Sir Lawrence."

" How obtained ?"

" No matter."

A shade of sadness passed over the brow of Clifford, for as he looked into the face of the Duchess she hung her head.

Did he love her, that he should feel thus.

We shall see.

Every effort that could be made for the apprehension of Wild had been made, but, as we see, without avail.

It was two days after the escape of the notorious thief-taker, that an awkward scene took place at the house of the Duchess. That noble lady had now begun to re-issue invites, and many were the visitors that flocked to the house, to pay their regards to the magnificent and wealthy widow.

As the Duchess had, since the dreadful murder of the Duke, become a town talk, it was not surprising that the majority of people who had not the *entre* to his house should now desire it, and that in consequence his personal friends should be much vexed to introduce them.

The noble widow was in reality quite a centre of attraction, and her house, during the hours for visiting, was always crowded with the *elite* of society.

Among those who called her friend was the unscrupulous Danvers, of the King's Guards.

By his interminable rattle and agreeable manners, he had found his way into the regards of the Duchess, and was ever a welcome visitor at her house.

Now, as soon as this man heard that the Duchess was once more receiving friends, he determined on a visit, and, as a matter of course, Sir Lewis Winterleigh, was to accompany him. Accordingly on the morning we have mentioned they strolled together as far as the widow's splendid mansion.

They were instantly admitted.

On entering the drawing-room, they found the Duchess in company with Sir Lawrence, who had now snatched a few minutes from his official duties, to make his first visit since the kind invitation he had received on granting the requests made by the lady of his love.

The Duchess received her visitors very gracefully, and extended towards Danvers an amount of favour that did not make old Sir Lawrence feel particularly well at ease.

Time passed in pleasant conversation, and at the expiration of half an hour Lewis and Danvers rose to take their leave.

They were about to take their departure, when a servant entered, and announced—

"The Count de Aramis."

"Admit him instantly."

"The Count de Aramis," repeated the minister, "who is he? I never heard that title before."

Doubtless you have not; the Count is a stranger. I met him at the ball of Lord Belmore. He is the most perfect gentleman I ever met. But stay; you shall judge for yourself. See—he is here."

Paul Clifford entered the room.

The surprise of Danvers and Lewis Winterleigh may readily be imagined.

Clifford saw that they recognised him, but by a wonderful effort of self-control did not give vent to the slightest expression of alarm or surprise.

Advancing easily to the Duchess, he took her hand, and, saluting her in the continental fashion, underwent an introduction to those he knew so well.

There was an awkward silence. At length Clifford found an opportunity to whisper in the ear of the Duchess—

"Have you forgotten the name? My young friend is Lewis Winterleigh."

The Duchess had forgotten the name, but on hearing it thus recalled to her memory she entirely lost her self-possession, and turned ghastly pale.

Clifford noticed her agitation.

"Be firm," he whispered, "and they shall not notice aught."

Marvelling at the self-possession of the man, but filled with admiration at his coolness and daring, she essayed to follow his advice.

But the attempt was futile.

She tried to converse with Sir Lawrence; but the words died away upon her lips, and all she could do was to turn again and again to Clifford, and whisper in his ear.

This proceeding struck the three guests with amazement.

Whilst Danvers and Lewis were perplexed, Sir Lawrence was dumbfounded.

"This woman cannot know the man with whom she is conversing," said Danvers. "I must put her on her guard."

"Do so," said Winterleigh.

The friends rose to take their leave.

"You certainly are not going?" asked the Duchess.

"Yes," said Danvers, "we can stay no longer; but before we take our leave we should esteem it a favour if you will grant us a moment's conversation in private."

The Duchess started.

"Be firm," whispered Clifford; "grant the request, and be sure and not betray yourself."

The Duchess rose, and, with a slight bow to Sir Lawrence and Clifford, left the room with the young men.

She opened the door of an apartment near at hand, and beckoned them to follow her.

They did so.

"Now, gentlemen," said the Duchess, "what is this matter that you can only communicate in private?"

"We wish to ask whether you are acquainted with the real name and character of the man with whom you have just been conversing?"

"Certainly; he is my very good friend, the Count de Aramis, and the most accomplished gentleman of his time."

"Indeed, you are mistaken."

"Oh, nonsense."

"But we assure you. The man is no other than Paul Clifford, the most notorious *thief* of his time"

"Ha! ha! ha!" laughed the Duchess, "you are really extremely droll."

"We are only speaking from personal experience of the man, having met him more than once, and not under circumstances that would be likely to leave so slight an impression as would lead us astray in the matter of his identity."

"Ha! ha! This is really too absurd. Why, I have known the poor, dear Count these five years, and am not likely to make a mistake on that score; and as to Paul Clifford, the robber, I am also able to identify him, having a slight acquaintance with him. You may have heard that it is to him I am indebted for the discovery of the murder and robbery perpetrated in this house."

"Are you certain you are not labouring under a false impression? Are you convinced that you are not the victim of this designing robber?"

"Will you allow me to say that I am not a child, to be led away by every designing wretch I meet. I tell you, again and again, that my good friend from whom I have just parted is the Count de Aramis."

"It is useless to say anything more on this point," said Danvers, much piqued at the firmness of the Duchess, "but I trust your grace will not find yourself mistaken. Having put you on your guard, my friend and I will retire."

"It is the most advisable thing you can possibly do," said the Duchess, haughtily; "and if you only come here to render yourselves so painfully ridiculous, I think it is well that your visits should be as few as possible."

With this the Duchess touched the bell, and swept from the apartment, leaving the visitors to quit the house in the most chop-fallen and ignominious manner.

At the door of the drawing room she met Sir Lawrence.

"Ah," she said, "whither away?"

"I like not my company," said Sir Lawrence, gruffly, "and am quitting it as hastily as possible."

"What mean you?"

"Simply that I don't care about being insulted by your guests."

"Insulted?"

"Yes, insulted. The man whom I have just quitted has offered me the greatest possible insult."

"How?"

"*He has been teaching me my business.*"

"Ha! ha!" laughed the Duchess. "My dear Sir Lawrence, you cannot possibly be insulted by that?"

"I am. To be told what I ought to do as Home Secretary, by an impertinent young jackanapes of twenty-five is too much to bear."

"Ho! ho! The poor dear Count."

"Poor dear Count, madam. Poor dear devil. That fellow and I never meet under the same roof again. If he continues his visits mine cease."

"Sir," said the Duchess, assuming all her *hauteur,* "you can observe your own opinion. I shall not consult your taste in the choice of my friends, so I pray you begone."

"Do you mean that?"

"Shall I ring for a servant, or can you find your way to the door?"

"Madam, you shall repent this."

"Dare you use threats to me?"

"I threaten nothing; but I say you shall repent this. There is Wild——"

"Yes! A proclamation offering a thousand pounds for his apprehension is already spread over the kingdom. What can you do in that matter now?"

"Confound it, nothing. But there's that villain, Clifford, in whom you take so warm and incomprehensible an interest——"

"Just so: he has his free pardon! that cannot be recalled."

"And—and—," stammered the minister, "you have no affection for me: it was for this you used me."

"You are quite right, and now adieu."

"The devil take me for an old ass," cried Sir Lawrence, rushing down the stairs, as the Duchess returned to her expectant lover.

* * * * * *

At the door Sir Lawrence encountered Danvers and his friend Winterleigh.

"What so soon after us, Sir Lawrence," said Danvers, "how is this?"

"Sir," said the fussy old minister, "I could not stand being talked to by that impudent foreigner."

"Foreigner! Ha! ha!"

"Yes, sir, foreigner. Is there anything extraordinary in that?"

"There would be if your friend really happened to be a foreigner, seeing that the place of his birth happens to be London."

"What do you mean?"

"Simply that the Minister of State for the Home Department of the Government has had the extreme felicity of spending a morning in company with Paul Clifford, the highwayman."

To say that you could have knocked Sir Lawrence down with a feather would be but to convey but a faint notion of the wretched state of prostration produced by the intelligence conveyed by the dashing young Guardsman.

At a glance he saw the real state of things.

He had been cleverly fooled in order that the Duchess might save the life of a notorious criminal in whom she took so mysterious an interest.

One thing was certain.

Although Sir Lawrence had granted a free pardon to the great highwayman, he made up his mind to spare neither influence nor money in bringing Clifford to that very scaffold from which, in his blindness, he had snatched him at the instigation of a clever, designing woman.

CHAPTER XXXIX.

THE GERMAN PRINCESS—HER CAREER—WILD AND HIS PLANS—THE MEETING WITH THE PRINCESS—A CHANGE OF EMPLOYMENT.

THE dragoons went their way.

Would night never come?

This was the question Wild asked himself a hundred thousand times as he lay in the hay-rick, half-suffocated and wholly exhausted, mentally and physically.

The longest lane has its turning, and the longest day its end, and at length the clouds changed from blue to grey, and from grey to black, and then the stars shone out brightly, and the long-wished-for, prayed-for night was come.

Wild left the hayrick with the greatest caution.

He knew that the whole country was aroused against him, and he dreaded to move lest from every post should start a dragoon to send a bullet crashing through his brain.

What was to be done?

He did not know where to go, nor where to seek for aid or shelter.

He was quite assured that for some time the country would be too hot for him to walk abroad with impunity, and he felt that with such a reward as one thousand pounds hanging over his head it would be useless to trust to any living being for help.

"Unless I have twice that sum wherewith to bribe them," he reasoned, "it is useless to seek aid, or I am lost. And yet this want of rest—this awful gnawing pain within—is killing me. Ah! there is but one thing for it, and that is to remain here about until some traveller passes, and then I may procure money and a disguise. If I can but dash out a fellow's brains on the quiet, and get his horse from him, I am as good as saved; but these soldiers, these soldiers!—it is their infernal carbines I fear."

He crawled, serpent-like, through the field into the ditch, from which he had overheard the conversation we have already given, and thence to the hedge through which he had dashed on leaving the main road.

"Yes," he continued, "here I must take my stand; thus must I wait until chance sends me a victim."

It was wearisome work, and in the stillness of the night Wild went almost mad.

In every sound he imagined he heard the approach of an officer.

In every rush of the wind and murmur of the trees he conjured up the breathings of a horse and the rattle of a mounted soldier.

Many hours passed, and hope was fast deserting the breast of the criminal, when the sound of carriage wheels fell upon his ear.

He listened again and again.

Yes; there was no mistaking the sound.

A carriage was fast approaching.

"Now or never!" cried Wild, dashing through as the vehicle came up.

It was a small, though elegant, vehicle, driven by a coachman seated on a high box.

Singular enough there was no other servant.

All this Wild beheld at a glance, and, making a spring at the man, he dashed him to the earth in an instant.

He lay there insensible, and, with the rapidity of lightning, his assailant rushed to the door of the carriage, and tore open the window.

To his great surprise he found the occupant to be a young and beautiful woman, who met him by levelling a pistol full at his head.

"Not this time," she said, as Wild started back.

"Drop that toy, or it will be the worse for you," cried Wild.

"Hillo!" said the woman; "surely I know that voice."

"And you. I certainly know your voice, although I can't see your features."

"I'm the Princess, and you are Wild, are you not?"

"Yes, yes."

"I thought I knew you. And so, Mr. Wild, you would serve an old friend in this way, would you? That is too shabby."

"Ah, my dear Princess; I didn't know it was you."

"I presume not, or you would not have risked a meeting of this kind, eh? You know my style, and you may thank your lucky stars that you have not a bullet in your brain by this time."

"I do."

"But what brings you here?"

"Have you not heard?"

"Heard what? I have just returned from Cologne,

and know nothing of what has passed in England during the past five months."

"I forgot. Well, Princess; you must know that things have changed of late, and the once all-powerful Jonathan Wild is now a hunted felon, with a reward of a thousand pounds upon his head."

"Whew! But that is hot work."

"It is."

"What are you doing here?"

"Waiting for the chance of blowing out some one's brains, in order that I may get the wherewithal to fly the country."

"A bad look out."

"So I am afraid."

"Well, it is bad to hear of an old friend's distress, and I'm not the one to have money and see another want. Here's my purse."

"Thanks. I'll repay the favour one day, you may take your oath of that."

"I know you will. No thanks; I don't want any. But have you hurt my coachman?"

"I will see."

Jonathan left the carriage door, and approached the spot where the coachman was toppled off his box.

He was now picking himself up, and rubbing his eyes.

"Any bones broken?" asked Wild.

"No," said the man, jumping to his feet; "all's right."

"That's well. Hark! Do you hear anything?"

"Hear anything! Well, unless there's something wrong in my ears I should say that that's the sound of horse trappings."

"Yes, yes," cried Wild, excitedly, running to the door of the carriage; "it is the dragoons," he cried, gazing piteously at the woman within the carriage, "it is the dragoons. Will you save me?"

"How?"

"Allow me to hide in the bottom of your carriage; it is my only chance."

"Jump in. Quick! I hear them approaching. See! they are at hand; a whole squad of them. See, they have sent their lights down upon us, and are cantering now."

Wild leapt into the carriage, and in a moment was at the feet of the Princess, and completely concealed from view.

"Hold your tongue," said the woman to her servant, as the party of dragoons came up.

In a moment the lady threw herself back in her carriage, and assumed an air of terror.

The dragoons surrounded the carriage, and the officer in command came to the door and peered in.

At the sight of him the woman screamed.

"There is no occasion for fear, lady," said the officer, in a respectful voice; "I am a soldier, and merely want to know why you have stopped your carriage here, and if I can render you any assistance."

"I have been robbed," said the woman; "shamefully robbed, and my servant brutally ill-used by a footpad."

"Indeed! How long since?"

"Not half an hour."

"Can you describe the man?"

"Oh, yes; a thick-set, burly ruffian, with a face seamed and scarred all over. He wore a rough wig that jutted awry, and his clothes were much soiled and stained."

"Enough," cried the man; "it was Jonathan Wild himself. Which way did he take?"

"He ran in the direction from which I am going."

"Ha, ha! then he will not proceed far before he falls in with a squad of our party.

"Are you, then, in chase of him?"

"That we are, lady, and a troublesome chase it has been. On this very spot the officers who pursued him on his flight from London lost sight of him; and he must have been in that confounded ditch to the right, or the hay-rick yonder ever since. But this mad trick of his has betrayed him into our hands. Ah, madam, your

information is indeed of value to us, for it will lead us in the path of this villain; and fear not that your property is lost, for within the hour we must have the thief, and then all you have missed shall be restored to you."

"It was but a purse of mean value, and if you recover it, I pray you share it among your brave fellows. Will you oblige me by seeing if my coachman is sufficiently recovered from the brutal attack made upon him to proceed on our journey?"

"He is even now on the box, madam."

"Many thanks. Give him the word to proceed."

The officer told the coachman to drive on, and with a courteous salute to the lady the dragoons and the carriage parted company.

This was indeed a narrow escape for Wild.

*   *   *   *   *

It is well now that we see into whose company we have fallen.

The heroine of this adventure was a notorious thief and courtezan, who was at the zenith of her fame at the time of this tale.

She was known as the German Princess, a title given her for reasons that will hereafter transpire.

We will now give a brief outline of her career up to the point of her introduction into these pages.

She was about eight-and-twenty years of age.

Of glorious appearance, being possessed of a form of rare symmetry, and a face of exquisite proportions and marvellously chiselled features.

She was fair; her complexion being the purest pink and white that could be conceived.

Her disposition was extremely lively, and being possessed of considerable gifts in the shape of musical and artistic skill, was just the woman to attract universal attention in all grades of society.

Singular enough, although of low origin, her father being a poor chorister of Canterbury Cathedral, she early imagined herself to be a princess, and this idea either really possessed her, or was assumed by her throughout her career, in order to appear conspicuous and create a sensation as a "character."

But in her marriage she lost sight of her exalted conception, and united her fortune with a journeyman shoemaker. She resided with him until she had two children, who both died in their infancy.

The industrious shoemaker was unable to support her extravagance, so that she at last left him to seek her fortune elsewhere.

A woman of her figure, beauty, and address, was not long before she procured another husband.

She went to Dover, and married a surgeon of that place.

She was apprehended and tried at Maidstone for having two husbands, but by some dexterous manoeuvre she was acquitted.

She now embarked for Holland, and travelled by land to Cologne; and, having a considerable sum of money, she took handsome lodgings at a house of entertainment, and cut a dashing figure.

As it is customary for the gentry in England to frequent Epsom or Tunbridge Wells in the summer, so it was then customary for those in Germany to frequent the Spa.

The Princess went thither, and was addressed by an old gentleman who had a good estate in the vicinity.

With the assistance of her landlady she managed this affair with great art.

He presented her with several fine jewels, besides a gold chain and costly medal, which had been given him for some gallant action.

He at length began to press matrimony with all the keenness of a young lover; and, unable to resist the siege any longer, she consented to make him happy in three days.

Meanwhile he supplied her with money in great profusion, and she was requested to prepare what things she pleased for the wedding.

The Princess now deemed it high time to be gone, and, to secure her retreat, acquainted her landlady with her design.

Having already shared largely of the spoils that the adventurer had received from her old doting lover, she, in hopes of pillaging him a little more, encouraged and aided her flight.

She requested her to go and provide her a seat in a carriage which took a different road from that of Cologne, as she did not wish that her lover should be able to trace her route.

When the Princess found herself alone she broke open a chest in which the good woman had deposited all her share of the spoil that she had received from our heroine, as well as her own money.

Madam made free with all, and took her passage to Utrecht; from hence went to Amsterdam, sold her chains and some jewels, and then passed into Rotterdam, from whence she speedily embarked for England.

She landed at Billingsgate one morning, and found no house open until she came to the Exchange Tavern, where, in the following manner, she attained the rank of a German Princess.

In that tavern she got into the company of some gentlemen whom she perceived were full of money, and, these addressing her in a rude manner, she began crying most bitterly, exclaiming that it was extremely hard for her to be reduced to this extreme distress who was once a Princess.

Here she repeated the story of her extraction and education, and much about her pretended father, the Lord Henry Vandwolway, a Prince of the Empire, and independent of every man but his Imperial Majesty.

"Certainly," said she, "any gentleman here present may conceive what a painful situation this must be to me, brought up under the care of an indulgent father, and in all the luxuries of a Court, to be reduced thus low, But, alas! what do I say? Indulgent father! Alas! was it not his cruelty which banished me—his only daughter—from his dominions, merely for marrying, without his knowledge, a nobleman of the Court, whom I loved to excess? Was it not my father who occasioned my dear lord and husband to be cut off, in the bloom of his age, by falsely accusing him of a design against his person—a deed which his virtuous soul abhorred?"

Here she pretended that the poignancy of her feelings would allow her to relate no more of her unfortunate history.

The whole company were touched with compassion at the melancholy tale, which she related with so much unaffected simplicity that they had not a doubt of its authenticity.

Compassionating her unfortunate situation, they requested her acceptance of all the money they had about them, promising to return again with more.

They were as good as their promise, and she ever after went by the name of the unfortunate German Princess.

The man who kept the inn, knowing that she was come from the continent, and seeing that she had great riches about her, he was disposed, more than ever, to believe the truth of her story.

Nor was madam backward to inform him that she had collected all that she possessed from the benevolent contributions of neighbouring princes, who knew and pitied her misfortunes.

"Nor durst any one of them," continued she, "let my father know what they had done, or where I was, for he was so much more powerful than any of them that if he understood that any one favoured me he would instantly make war upon them."

The innkeeper, being convinced of her rank and fortune, his brother-in-law no doubt receiving proper information from him, became enamoured of the Princess, and presumed to pay his addresses to her.

She was highly displeased at first, but, from his importunities, she was, at last, prevailed upon to descend from her station, and receive the hand of a common man.

Poor Carleton thought himself the happiest of mortals in being thus so highly honoured by an union with such an accomplished and amiable princess, possessed of an ample fortune, though far inferior to what she had a right to expect from her noble birth.

But during this dream of pleasure the landlord received a letter informing him that the woman who resided at his house and was married to his brother-in-law was an impostor; that she had already been married to two husbands, and had eloped with all the money she could lay her hands on—that he said nothing but what could be proved by the most unquestionable evidence in a court of justice.

The consequence was that a prosecution was instituted against her for the crime of polygamy; but, from insufficient evidence, she was acquitted.

She was then introduced as an actress among the players, and by them supported for some time.

Upon her account the house was often crowded, and the public curiosity was excited by a woman who had made such a figure in the world, and received great applause in her dramatic capacity.

She generally appeared in characters suited to her habits of life, and those scenes which were rendered familiar to her by former deceptions and intrigues.

But what tended chiefly to promote her fame, was a play called "The German Princess," written principally upon her account, in which she spoke the following prologue in such a manner as gained universal applause:—

"I've pass'd one trial, but it is my fear
I shall receive a rigid sentence here:
You think me a bold cheat, but 'case 'twere so,
Which of you are not? Now you'd swear I know,
But do not, lest that you deserve to be
Censured worse than you can censure me;
The world's a cheat, and we that move in it,
In our degrees do exercise our wit;
And better 'tis to get a glorious name,
However got, than live by common fame."

The Princess had too much mercury in her constitution to remain long within the bounds of a theatre when London itself was too limited for her volatile disposition.

She did not, however, leave the theatre until she had procured many admirers.

Her history was well known, as well as her accomplishments and her gallantry, and introduced her into company.

She was easy of access, but in company she carried herself with an affected air of indifference.

There were two young beaux in particular who had more money in their pockets than wit in their heads; and from the scarcity of that commodity in themselves they the more admired her wit and humour.

She encouraged their addresses until she had extracted about three hundred pounds from each of them, and then, observing their funds were nearly exhausted, she discarded them both, saying she was astonished at their impudence in making love to a Princess.

Her next lover was an old gentleman, about fifty, who saw her, and though he was acquainted with her history, yet he resolved to be at the expense of some hundreds a year, provided she would consent to live with him.

To gain his purpose, he made her several rich presents, which, with seeming reluctance, she accepted.

When they lived together, as man and wife, she so accommodated herself to his temper and dispositions that he was constantly making her rich presents, which were always accepted with apparent reluctance, as laying her under so many obligations.

In this manner they continued, until her doting lover, one evening coming home intoxicated, she thought it a proper opportunity to decamp.

So soon as he was asleep, she rifled his pockets; found his pocket-book, containing a bill for a hundred pounds, and some money.

She also stripped him of his watch, and, taking his keys, opened his coffers and carried off everything that suited her purpose.

She next went and presented the bill, and as the acceptor knew her, she received the money without hesitation.

Having thus fleeced her old lover, she took up her lodgings in a convenient place, under the character of a young lady with a thousand pounds, and whose father was able to give her twice as much; but, disliking a person whom he had provided as a husband for her, she had left her father's house, and did not wish to be discovered by any of her father's friends.

Madam continued, at the same time, to have different letters sent her, from time to time, containing an account of all the news concerning her father and lover.

These were left carelessly about the room, and, her landlady reading them, she became confirmed in the belief of her story.

That woman had a rich nephew, a young man, whom she introduced to her acquaintance, who became enamoured of her, and, to gain her favour, presented her with a gold watch.

She was hardly prevailed upon to accept of that present. Her lover already thought the door of Paradise was open to him, and their amour proceeded with all that felicity that young lovers could wish.

But in this season of bliss a porter knocked at the door with a letter.

Her maid, as previously directed, brought it in to her, which she had no sooner read than she exclaimed—

"I am undone!—I am ruined!" and pretended to swoon away.

The scent-bottle was employed, and her enraptured lover was all kindness and attention.

When she was a little recovered, she presented the letter, saying,

"Sir, since you are at last acquainted with most of my concerns, I shall not make a secret of this; therefore, if you please, read this letter, and know the occasion of my affliction."

The young gentleman received it, and read as follows:—

"Dear Madam,—I have several times taken my pen in hand on purpose to write you, and as often laid it aside again, for fear of giving you more trouble than you already labour under.

"However, as the affair so immediately concerns you, I cannot in justice hide what I tremble to disclose, but must in duty tell you the worst of news, whatever may be the consequence of my so doing.

"Know, then, that your affectionate and tender brother is dead.

"I am sensible how dear he was to you, and you to him; yet, let me entreat you, for your own sake, to acquiesce in the will of Providence, as much as possible, since our lives are all at his disposal who gave us being.

"I could use another argument to comfort you, that with a sister less loving than you, would be of more weight than that I have urged; but I know your soul is above all mercenary views.

"I cannot, however, forbear to inform you that he has left you all he had; and, farther, that your father's estate of £200 per annum can now devolve upon no other person than yourself, who are now his only child.

"What I am next to acquaint you with may perhaps be almost as bad as the former particular.

"Your hated lover has been so importunate with your father, especially since your brother's decease, that the old gentleman resolves, if ever he should hear of you any more, to marry you to him, and he makes this the condition of your again being received into his favour, and having your former disobedience, as he calls it, forgiven.

"While your brother lived he was every day endeavouring to soften the heart of your father, and we were but last week in hopes he would have consented to let you follow your inclinations, if you would come home to him

again; but now there is no advocate in your cause who can work upon the man's peevish temper; for, he says, as you are now his sole heir, he ought to be more resolute in the disposal of you in marriage.

"While I am now writing, I am surprised with an account that your father and lover are preparing to come to London, where they say they can find you out.

"Whether or not this be only a device I cannot tell, nor can I conceive where they could receive their information, if it be true.

"However, to prevent the worst, consider whether or not you can cast off your old aversion, and submit to your father's commands; for, if you cannot, it will be most advisable, in my opinion, to change your residence.

"I have no more to say in the affair, being unwilling to direct you in such a very nice circumstance.

"The temper of your own mind will be the best instructor you can apply to; for your future happiness or misery, during life, depends on your choice.

"I hope that everything will turn out for the best.
            "From your sincere friend,
                        "S. E."

Her lover saw that she had good reason to be afflicted, and, while he seemed to feel for her, he was no less concerned about his own interest.

He advised her immediately to leave her lodgings, and added that he had very elegant apartments, which were at her service.

She accepted of this offer; and she and her maid, who was informed of her intentions, and prepared to assist her, immediately set out for the residence of her lover.

When introduced to their new apartment they did not go to bed, as they resolved to depart next morning, but lay down to rest themselves with their clothes on.

When the house was all quiet, they broke open his desk, took out a bag with a hundred pounds, two suits of clothes, and everything valuable that they could carry along with them.

Her numerous and varied adventures would far exceed our limits.

It is sufficient to observe, that rather than her hands should be unemployed, or her avaricious disposition unpractised, she would carry off the most trifling article; that, according to the proverb, "All was fish that came into her net;" and that, when a watch, a diamond, or piece of plate, could not be found, a napkin, a pair of sheets, or any article of wearing apparel would suffice.

She one day, along with her pretended maid, went into a mercer's shop in Cheapside, and purchased a piece of silk to the value of six pounds.

She pulled out her purse to pay the merchant, but, to her surprise, found that she had no money except some large pieces of gold, for which she had so high an esteem that she could not think of parting with them.

The polite merchant could not think of hurting the feelings of a lady so elegantly dressed, and accordingly dispatched one of his shopkeepers along with her, to receive his money.

They went all three into a coach which was ready to receive them.

Arrived at the Royal Exchange, Madam ordered the coachman to stop, when, upon pretence of purchasing some ribbons that would suit the silks, her maid carried out the parcel, and went along with her, leaving the shopman in the coach to wait their return.

The young man waited in the coach until he was impatient and ashamed, and then returned home to relate his misfortunes, and the loss of his master.

The transfer of invention and of villany was easy to the next adventure.

Madam waited upon a French weaver in Spitalfields, and purchased goods to the amount of forty pounds.

He went home with her to carry the goods, and to receive his money.

She desired him to make out a bill for the whole goods, as one-half belonged to a lady in the next room.

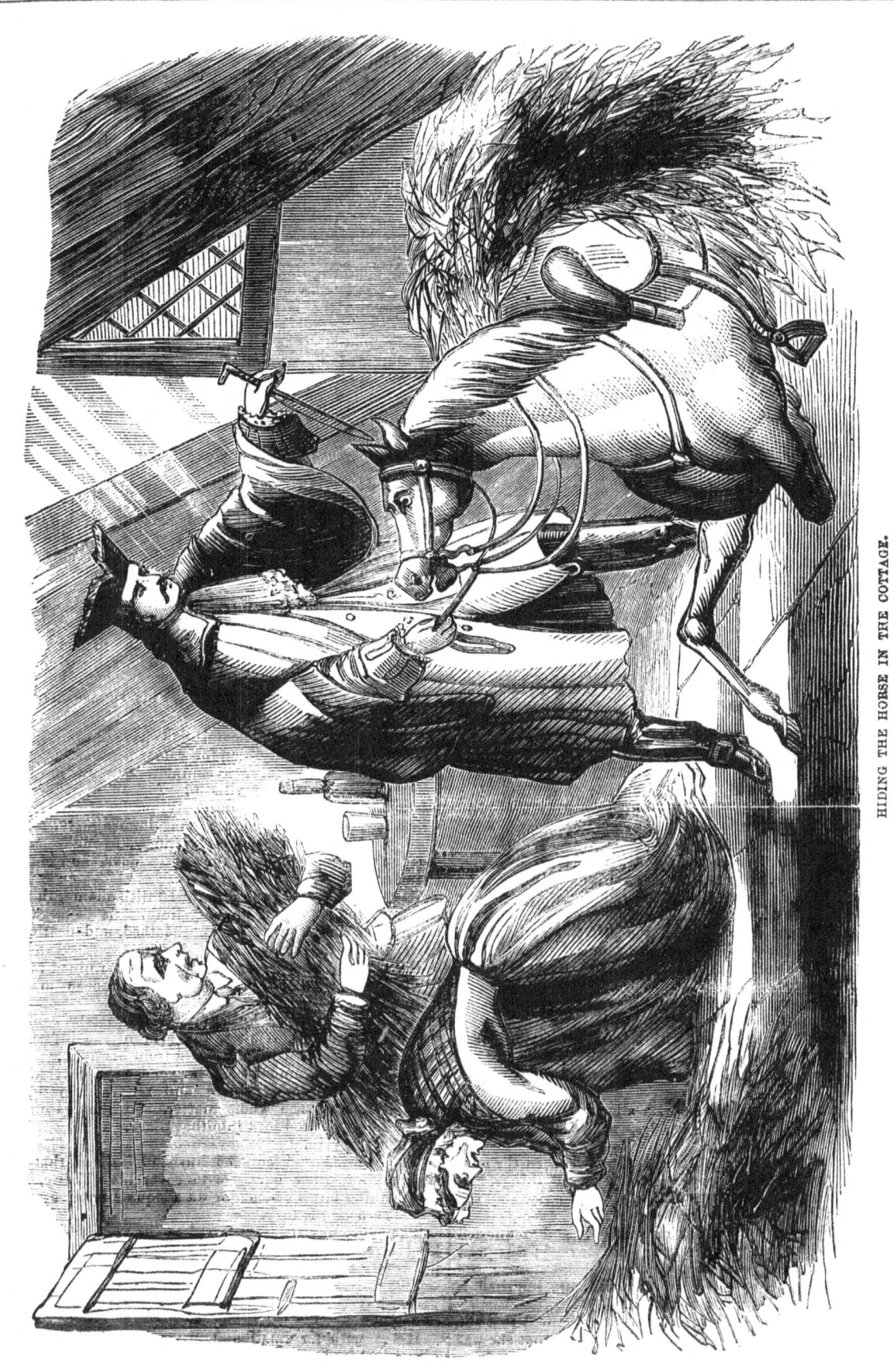

HIDING THE HORSE IN THE COTTAGE.

With all the ceremony natural to a Frenchman he sat down to write his account, while she took the silk into the adjacent room to show it to her niece, to whom the one-half belonged.

By means of a bottle of wine that Madam had placed before the French weaver, one-half hour passed over without much uneasiness.

At length his patience was exhausted, and, having called up the people in the house, he inquired for the lady who came in with him, and who told him she was only gone to the next room.

To the utter confusion and disappointment of poor Monsieur, he was informed that his lady was gone, and would, they believed, return no more to that dwelling.

The Frenchman was instantly in a violent passion, and quarrelled with the people in the house.

To calm his rage, and to convince him that they were not confederates in her villany, they conveyed him to the next room, and showed him that the proper entry to her room was by a back stair; adding that she had only taken their room for a month, for which she had paid them, and that, her time being expired, they knew not where she had gone.

Determined to collect her contributions from householders, instead of travellers, she next took lodgings from a tailor.

As it was natural for a generous, good-hearted lady to promote the prosperity of the family where she resided, Madam employed the tailor to make the goods she had procured from the mercer and the weaver.

Convinced that he had got an excellent job, as well as a rich lodger, the tailor, with mirth and song, sat down to make Madam's dresses.

As she acquainted him that, upon a specified day, she was to have a large party, the tailor called in several journeymen to his aid, and had them all finished by that time.

Meanwhile she gave her landlady one pound, to purchase what things she deemed necessary, promising to pay her the remainder the following day.

The day arrived, the guests appeared, an elegant entertainment was served up, and plenty of wine drank.

None were without their due portion.

The tailor had his glass served so plentifully that his wife had to lend him her assistance to his bed-chamber.

This answered the designs of the Princess.

She and all her company departed one by one, carrying away a silver tankard, or salt, or knife, or fork, while the maid carried off all the clothes that were not upon their backs.

The moment they reached the street, the maid was placed in a coach with the booty, and the rest of the company took different directions, and none of them were discovered.

Thus a merry night brought a sorrowful morning to the poor industrious tailor.

Madam being attacked with a fit of mourning, sent her confidential maid to a shop in the New Exchange, where she had purchased a few articles the previous day.

The woman of the shop, with all possible expedition, selected the best of her articles, and hastened to her lodgings.

Madam was so very much indisposed when the milliner arrived that she could not look at the things, and desired her to return after dinner, when she doubted not but they should agree as to the price.

The obliging milliner was satisfied, and requested liberty to leave her goods until she returned; a request which was readily granted.

At the hour appointed she returned and inquired if the lady up stairs was at home.

To her great mortification, she was informed that she was gone, they could not tell where, and that she was not to return.

But before her departure she had conveyed away the valuable part of her effects.

Thus, both her landlady and the milliner were left to regret her absence, and to reflect upon their own easy credulity and loss.

But the adventures of madam increase in magnitude as they increase in number.

Being arrayed in her sable robes, and having taken lodgings in Holborn, she sent for a barrister of Gray's Inn, and informed him, that, by the death of her father, she was sole heir to his fortune, but being married to an extravagant husband he was resolved to secure her property to himself.

Here she poured forth a torrent of tears, and the most grievous lamentations, the more to interest the young barrister in her favour.

But while the lawyer was squaring his features to the occasion, and talking of the matter in a learned and eloquent strain, a woman runs up stairs, crying—

"Oh, madam, we are all undone, for my master is below! He has been asking after you, and swears that he will come up to your chamber. I am afraid the people of the house will not be able to hinder him, he appears so resolute."

"Oh, heavens!" exclaimed madam, "what shall I do?"

"Why?" said the lawyer.

"Why," quoth she, "I mean for you. Dear me!— what excuse shall I make for your being here? I dare not tell him your quality and business, for that would endanger all. And, on the other side, he is extremely jealous. Therefore, good sir, step into that closet until I can send him away."

Surprised, and at a loss what to do, the lawyer complies.

The closet is locked, and the curtains of the bed are drawn; then she opens the door to her husband, who was loudly demanding admittance.

The moment he entered he gave his spouse the most opprobrious language.

"Oh, mistress, I understand you have a man in the room! A pretty companion for a poor innocent woman, truly!—one who is always complaining how hardly I use her. Where is the villain? I shall sacrifice him this moment. Is this your modesty, madam? This your virtue? Let me see your gallant immediately, or, by the light, you shall be the first victim yourself."

Upon this he made to the closet door, and burst it open like a fury.

The young lawyer was discovered with shame, though innocent, and trembling in every limb.

The husband's sword was unsheathed, and death was before the barrister's eyes.

But madam interposed, and seemed determined rather to die herself than suffer the blood of an innocent man to stain her chamber.

A companion of the husband also fortunately came to her assistance, and, seizing the arm of the infuriated man, struggled to wrest the sword from his hand.

But the discernment of a lawyer soon discovered the deception; and to exculpate and relieve himself, he candidly related the whole matter, and the reason for which he was introduced into that place.

But all in vain.

The injured and enraged husband insisted that this was only a feigned narrative to cover his villainy, and that nothing but his blood, or an adequate remuneration, would assuage his fury.

The cause was at last referred to the arbitration of the kind stranger who had interfered and aided Madam in protecting the young lawyer.

Five hundred pounds was proposed as a proper recompence, but that was far beyond the power of the lawyer to command.

It was with no small difficulty agreed that he should give a hundred pounds rather than be found exposed to the consequences of detection in a situation where he was unable to vindicate his innocence.

He sent a note to a friend for that sum, the confederates being careful to examine it before it was sent away, lest it should have been for a constable instead of a hundred pounds.

Upon payment of that sum the lawyer was liberated, and went off with the bitter reflection that, instead of receiving a good fee for writing a deed of settlement, he had paid a hundred pounds only for a few minutes' lodging in a closet, but consoled himself with the hopes of seeing this amiable widow speedily *exalted* to merited honour.

This gentleman was not at all satisfied with himself until he had driven the Princess out of England—a feat he accomplished after some trouble and expense; but the term of banishment she limited to five short months, returning at the end of that time to resume her old occupations, and seek fresh adventures in a sphere peculiarly her own.

Her first adventure on approaching the metropolis was that of her encounter with Jonathan Wild; and we have already seen how cleverly she brought him through that trouble.

They had not proceeded a great distance when the Princess touched Jonathan on the shoulder, and bade him sit up and listen to her.

"Now," she said, "in all probability you are, for a time, quite safe. What do you mean to do? Use the money I have given you in escaping to the Continent, or will you remain with me, and see what sort of fortune may befal us in a partnership?"

"I shouldn't mind the latter course, my dear Princess," said Wild; "but the fact is, your partnerships are generally such one-sided affairs that I dare not trust myself to join you."

"What do you mean?"

"Simply that you generally contrive to secure all the booty, and leave your mate to come in for all the reward of the acts in which you have mutually engaged."

"Ha, ha! I certainly have played some of them some nice tricks; but I should be clever to beat Jonathan Wild at such a game."

"My dear Princess, you are clever enough for anything."

"I've been clever enough to save your life, and you owe me something on that score; but I'm willing to forget all that, provided you accede to my terms. I've been thinking during the last ten minutes what a fine thing we could do together, if we were so minded."

"In what line? Surely not as the German Princess and Jonathan Wild?"

"No, but as a lady of title and her valet. Listen! Whilst at Cologne I induced a foolish old Englishman whom I found there endeavouring to restore his shattered health to make over to me the house called the Willows, only a mile or two further on this road, and nearer London. He died in my arms *very soon after he made his will,* and here I am to take possession."

"What! Do you mean to say that, with a fine property to live upon, you will again turn to your old habits and risk your neck when you can live in peace and affluence and without a care?"

"I mean to say that the passion for my mode of life is still strong within me, and that I will continue it at all risks."

"Then you are, indeed, an extraordinary woman."

"I am—I know it. But that's not to the point. What say you to my proposition?"

"I'm almost inclined to accept your offer."

"Why hesitate?"

"Because my life is in danger while I remain so near London."

"Is that all? Psha! As the footman of a lady of rank and great wealth, who is to suspect you? Have you lost all your old cunning—the way of disguises? Can't you

now make up for a character as I have seen you do a thousand times before?"

"Yes; but I believe all my nerve is fast going. The fact is, Princess, that fellow, Paul Clifford, has sworn a great oath to bring me to the gallows, and by Heaven I believe he will keep his word. Be that as it may, I have a superstitious dread of the fellow, and would fain be hundreds of miles away from the land he inhabits."

"Ah! this is not the Jonathan Wild of old."

"It is not. No one knows it more surely than myself, but I cannot help it. I am breaking down, and that's the truth."

"Tush! tush! When did you last taste food?"

"Not for many, many long hours."

"And you have had no brandy lately?"

"Not a drain."

"So I thought. It's that which makes you dull and stupid. Here, man, take a long pull at this, and tell me if it does not do you all the good in the world."

She handed a small silver flask to Wild as she spoke, and he eagerly placed it to his lips.

It was not removed until every drop was quaffed.

"You seem to like it."

"It is rare stuff."

"It is. I brought it over with me. How do you feel now?"

"Better."

"Much better?"

"I think so."

"And Clifford! Have you quite so much fear of that poor, beardless boy now?"

"Not quite. In fact, did we meet now—"

"You would tear his heart out, and make him eat it! You see I have not forgotten your favourite expression."

Wild smiled.

The brandy had warmed up his heart, and had, moreover, mounted to his brain.

"What say you," said the Princess; "will you join me?"

"Yes; and the devil take all the fears and dreads."

"That's well said, and now for the future you are Henry Brownlow, and I am Lady Belle Harringcastle. Will you remember?"

"Ha, ha! I'm not likely to forget."

"'Tis well. Here we are at the Willows. See the lights burning in the avenue and at the old house. You see they expect their young mistress. Now hide your face and follow me closely when we quit the carriage. I must smuggle you away, and get you into a livery before you are to be seen."

"'Tis well. Upon my soul this is an adventure."

"It is rare fun; but mind, no forgetfulness of your new character."

Here the carriage drove through an old lodge gateway, and a loud cheer marked the coming of the new mistress of the Willows.

Had the servitors known who they were shouting at it is just possible that their enthusiasm might not have been so strong.

CHAPTER LX.

JONATHAN WILD DOES NOT AT ALL LIKE THE WILLOWS— COMMUNICATES A TALE OF HORROR TO THE PRINCESS— THEY REMOVE FOR A TIME TO LONDON—LADY BRAZEN —A DARING ROBBERY AND MURDER—PAUL CLIFFORD ON THE TRACK OF WILD.

WE must suppose a week to have elapsed since the occurrence of the event narrated in the last chapter.

During this period Wild had been studying his new character, and, it must be confessed, managed it with peculiar skill.

His tact for disguise and the assumption of character

was indeed marvellous, and in these few days he became a footman "to the manner born." At first he rejoiced exceedingly in the turn his affairs had taken ; but this satisfaction was of but short duration, for there appeared to be a gloom over the old house, and in its loneliness the disturbed mind of the robber found ample material for pandering to the awful fancies that haunted him, so that at the expiration of a week he was entirely dissatisfied with himself and the position he was occupying, and longed for a change.

Anything to break the gloomy monotony of the Willows.

He spoke to the Princess on that score, but she merely laughed at his fears, and taunted him with his increasing feebleness and faintness of heart.

It was after a conversation with his supposed mistress, just before her retiring to rest for the night, that Wild beheld a sight in the old house that filled him with horror and made him long for the opportunity of leaving it.

He was in the grim old hall, and was wandering about with his mind reverting ever and anon to Gentleman Clifford, when, overcome with a peculiar drowsiness, he sat himself in the great chair of the hall porter and tried to fix his mind on one distinct train of thought.

"There is a sort of crisis in my destiny," he said, thinking aloud ; "what shall I do ? My fate, in the person of Paul Clifford, seems to be upon my track. If I now flinch I at once allow him to become the Destroying Spirit of my existence."

There was too much yet of the spirit of active exertion in the mind of Jonathan Wild to suffer this.

After a time he spoke with vehemence through his clenched teeth, saying—

"No—no ! I will not, and I cannot suppose it. I will fight him to the very last. He shall not find that I am cowed before him, and that I hourly fear to be crushed. I will kill him, or he shall kill me ; but I will fight him on the best terms I may."

This was just the sort of determination that such a man as Jonathan Wild was likely enough to come to, and he felt all the crimes in his own mind when he had cause to.

The how and the when he was to carry on the war against Clifford had now to be most fully and amply considered.

Jonathan had no sort of idea, when he had once made up his mind to such a state of things between him and Clifford, that it was death to one or the other of them to wait for the attack to be made upon him.

From that moment he resolved in his own mind upon the necessity of seeking his foe, for that would give him all the advantage which, if he waited for the presence and the attack of that foe, would be decidedly the other way.

It was, then, in deep thought of this kind that Jonathan Wild, sitting in the hall of the Willows, resting his head upon his hand, lapsed into a profound reverie.

How long he had thus sat in such a frame of mind he could hardly say, but he was suddenly aroused by his taper burning more brightly than it had hitherto done, and, upon looking up hurriedly, the blood almost paused for a fearful moment at his heart as he saw a human form upon the grand staircase leading to the upper part of the old mansion.

Jonathan Wild tried to utter an exclamation, but the sound died away upon his lips.

He tried to rise and fly from the spot, but his limbs refused to aid him, and there he sat, condemned to be a spectator of all that might occur in that old haunted house.

The taper burnt brighter still.

Down the grand staircase came two persons now ; but, although they did not come quicker than a person might descending at an ordinary pace, it seemed to Jonathan Wild as though they glided down without at all moving their feet in walking.

One of these persons was an old man, very richly dressed, and wearing on his head a skull cap.

The other person was a young lady all in white satin, and her right hand was in that of the old man's.

As they came down the stairs, floating from stair to stair in the strange fashion that we have recorded, Jonathan Wild saw that the gentleman held a handkerchief pressed very closely to his breast with his disengaged hand.

He was very pale.

And, so far as that went, nothing could exceed the paleness of the young lady. Her face was as white and as pure as alabaster.

As the man came down with her in this way gently to the hall, he every moment turned and turned the pocket handkerchief that he had pressing with his disengaged hand over his bosom, and, as he so turned it, it seemed to become redder and redder, and, in fact, to be gradually saturating with blood.

It was an awful sight.

And now the old man and the beautiful young lady reached the hall, and there they paused, and Jonathan Wild heard the young lady say to him—

"Yours in life, dear one ; yours in life, and so yours even too in death ! I shall rejoin you soon."

The face of the old man lit up with a strange expression of joy, and he spoke in reply—

"My own, my best, but to be regretted love ! blessings on you for ever and ever."

"And so on," said the young lady, "for ever and ever."

"He comes !" said the old man.

Then from the far end of the old hall, where everything was in gloom and shadow, there came a man dressed in a dark-coloured suit, with a sword in his hand, and as he advanced the old man cried out in doleful accents,

"Mercy ; oh, mercy—mercy !"

The old man then dropped the handkerchief, and showed a sword wound right through his chest, and the young lady, with a cry, clasped him in her arms.

Then there appeared, as though coming through the air, a perfect shower of sword blades, and they all pointed at the heart of the old man, and in another moment they all plunged into his body.

With a shriek he fell to the stones in the old hall.

It was that shriek that seemed to awaken Jonathan Wild from the fascination of the strange lethargic condition into which he had fallen.

He sprang to his feet.

"Help, help," he cried. "No—no ! Don't drive me mad, spirits of another world. I had nothing to do with your acts and deeds in this—eh ? Oh, God !"

He looked around him in surprise.

The hall was deserted.

The little bit of taper had burnt quite out, and a broad gleam of daylight came in through the glass at the upper portion of the old hall door.

"What is this ?" said Wild. "Is it possible that it was but a dream ?'

He sank down on to the chair again, and looked aghast.

He wiped from his brow the heavy drops that intense fear had established there, and he looked about in something of the fashion of a man who is not yet thoroughly awake to the reality of life.

This sort of weightiness of the soul though that had been upon the spirit of Jonathan Wild soon fled. The one gleam of daylight that he saw, and which kept on increasing in brightness, did wonders for him.

Drawing a very long breath, he rose to his feet again, and staggered to the hall door.

"It was a dream," he said, "only a dream. How foolish I am to allow myself to be terrified by a dream."

He flung open the hall door, and let in the daylight in a broad flood into the old house.

The sun was shining on the lawn, and the birds were

singing sweetly upon the branches of the old trees, and so Jonathan felt each moment more and more himself again.

"It is very strange, though," he said, as he looked about him in some trepidation. "Was it a dream, or not?"

This was a question which Jonathan Wild felt at once that he would never be able to answer to his own satisfaction, were he to think of it for the next twelvemonth; so he gave it up.

"I care not," he said. "It may have been that I became the accidental spectator of a scene in which I had no sort of concern, so my best plan is to forget it. But I do not think I shall like to stay here."

Of that there could be no doubt at all. After what he had seen, or thought he had seen, the Willows was about the last place that he, Jonathan Wild, thought he would like to fix upon as a place to which to repair upon any very special occasion.

"No—no," he said; "before the sunset of this day I will bid adieu to this house for ever."

He shuddered every time he looked about the hall as though he expected again to see some one, if not all, of the three spectres of the preceding night.

But there was not the slightest trace of such ghostly visitants.

He looked down upon the stones of the hall where the wounded man had stood stanching the blood that had evidently been oozing from the wound in his breast with his handkerchief, and then Jonathan Wild felt terrified to see no less than three spots of blood.

It was not fluid blood, but blood it was, and the colour and general appearance were quite unmistakeable.

This was a sort of confirmation of what had taken place that was anything but agreeable to Jonathan Wild; and, after looking at the spots some short space of time, he said—

"No, I will not stay here even till sunset, as I thought of doing; I do not like the place at all."

He had some slight idea now of making a hasty tour through the upper rooms of the house, and he had advanced about six steps up the grand staircase.

But his courage failed.

"Poh!" he said, "what is the house to me that I should take the trouble to go through it? It is but a waste of time to do so."

This was a very good excuse to make to himself, but it was not the real reason.

Jonathan Wild was, to all intents and purposes, afraid to explore the house.

"No," he said, "I will seek the chamber of the Princess, and tell her what I have seen."

Acting on this impulse, he rushed up the stairs, and groped his way to the sleeping-room of the adventuress.

There was a taper burning.

By its light Wild saw that the woman was sleeping uneasily.

He advanced, and, catching her by the shoulder, aroused her.

She awoke with a scream.

"Ah!" she cried, recognising Wild; "is it only you? That is well. I have had awful dreams."

"And I have seen awful things."

"What mean you?"

"Listen to me, and then say if I decided wrongly in making up my mind to leave this place without delay."

He related the history of the vision in the old Hall.

"Is this true?" she cried as Wild concluded, "is this true, or have you wormed into my secrets, and take this mode of rehearsing them?"

"What mean you?"

The Princess looked at Wild attentively.

"No," she said, "no, you can know nothing of it, but listen to me. What you have seen to-night is in reality the very scene that occurred at Cologne. The old man was the late owner of this house—the young girl was I; the other figure that of the assassin hired by me to kill

him. I told you he died in my arms, but I did not relate the manner of his death, nor should I have done so had you not seen this awful vision. The old man, failing fast, he wanted to be taken into the air, and I led him down the stairs of the villa in which we lived, and at the foot gave the signal for his death. Now you know all."

"I do indeed, and the revelation fills me with horror. But think not—dream not that I will stay here another day to see again such sights. If you remain you may enjoy the fruits of your crime alone. I'd rather rush into Newgate and die the death I so much dread than pass another night beneath this roof."

"I will also go," she cried; "yes, it is no place for me. We will go to London together."

*   *   *   *   *

In a few hours the Princess and her *quasi* footman had taken up their quarters in elegant apartments in St. James's Street.

It was not long before the young heiress of the Willows became quite the attraction.

Her magnificence soon attracted universal attention, and, being fond of society, her house soon became the fashionable lounge.

No one recognized the once famous Princess, and in his disguise Wild passed unobserved.

In a short time the Princess formed the acquaintance of one Lady Brazen, a rich young widow, who was at the time attracting the attention of all London.

It may readily be conceived what was the aim of the Princess and her ally in seeking the society of this young lady of fashion.

They saw at a glance that she was unprotected, and that by one bold stroke the property of her ladyship might be conveyed to the lodging of the Princess.

To effect this, Wild began to organise a plan whereby a robbery could be successfully perpetrated.

Without making himself known, he engaged the assistance of many of his old companions, and choosing the night of a grand ball at Lady Brazen's, he put his scheme into execution.

He succeeded but too well; the robbery was effected, but not without violence, for the Lady was disturbed, and on attempting to open the door of her chamber was rewarded with a bullet, which crashed through the panel and lodged in her brain.

The amount of pelf carried off was enormous, and next morning all London was literally in arms about the matter.

So impudent and terrible a crime had not been perpetrated for years.

But most mysterious as it may appear, there was no trace of the perpetrators. Clifford heard of it, and the more he thought the matter over, the more he felt that Wild must have had a hand in it.

Imbued with this notion, he went to a magistrate, and, without conveying his suspicions, asked to be allowed to proceed in the matter, with a view to the discovery of the perpetrators.

The magistrate referred him to the Home Office.

Sir Lawrence was not to be found, and the Under Secretary, acting on the plan that it was most desirable "to set a thief to catch a thief," gave Clifford the necessary authority, and set him to work.

Paul hastened to the scene of the crime.

There he found two magistrates, and on showing them his authority, they expressed their satisfaction at having him as an ally.

Paul requested the magistrates to step with him into a private room and talk the matter over; and, after hearing all they had to say, he spoke calmly but decisively.

"Gentlemen," he said, "do you suspect any one in particular of this affair, I would like to know?"

"No," was the reply. "It is involved to us in the greatest possible mystery. The boldness and the cruelty with which the whole affair has been carried out stagger us. Have you any idea about it, Mr. Clifford?"

"Yes, I think I have."

"We shall pay every attention, sir, to any suggestion of yours upon the subject, quite independent of the large powers which you have shown us you are entrusted with by the under Secretary of State."

"Gentlemen," said Paul Clifford, "Jonathan Wild is at liberty."

The magistrates looked at each other.

"You do not mean to say that you suspect him, sir?"

"I do."

"Oh, that is scarcely possible. It is not at all likely that Wild, with a reward of one thousand pounds out against him, would show himself in London."

"That is just it."

"What, sir?"

"Why, you think it the most improbable place for Jonathan Wild to be in?"

"We do."

"Then you may depend, gentlemen, that that is the very place in which to look for Wild. My own opinion is that he is in London, for he knows well that it is in London will be found the most effectual- hiding places."

"And, sir, do you really then think that he was here last night?"

"I do."

The magistrates looked very serious, and one of them said—

"If it be so, it is quite clear that he has got about him, in a very short time, a fearful gang."

"That is likely enough. There are those in London who belong to the ' family,' as they call themselves, who, notwithstanding they hate Wild, and have the very worst opinion of him, as a man, may still, from a knowledge of his ability in planning and carrying out robberies and disposing of the proceeds, join him in any nefarious transaction for the time being. I don't think that he would have the slightest difficulty in getting together a gang of twenty persons in twelve hours in London."

"You don't?"

"I really do not."

"Why, with such a force, Jonathan Wild could levy a contribution on every house in the metropolis."

"He could; and so you see the necessity for his being effectually and for ever put down. I make no secret of it to you, gentlemen, that that is my mission."

"Upon my word, Mr. Clifford," said one of the magistrates, "we wish you every possible success."

"I must succeed, sir."

"If anybody does, you will, Mr. Clifford."

"So I think; self-confidence does not look very amiable on some occasions, I grant, but upon this it is an absolute requisite for success, and I think that the more I have of it the better it will be for me, and for the end I have in view. And now, gentlemen, will you favour me with your assistance to thoroughly search the house, and particularly the route taken by the thieves."

"Most certainly."

The feeling thus freely expressed by Paul Clifford had a very great effect upon the magistrates, and it was evident that they now viewed the whole affair with a much more serious and alarmed aspect than before.

The investigation that Paul Clifford requested, however, was at once undertaken, and it led to rather an important result.

Lying in a corner, between the roof of the house and the lower ceiling—that is to say, between the outer and inner trap-doors, through which Jonathan Wild and his party had made their escape from the house of Lady Brazen—Paul found a small memorandum-book, with a lead pencil fitted to it.

There were only a few memoranda on the first page, and those were far from being at all intelligible; but the handwriting was rather peculiar, and Paul at once said—

"I think that in the Secretary of State's office they have specimens of the handwriting of Jonathan Wild in abundance—for he was in the habit of forwarding reports to the Government, in his police capacity, upon every topic; and if this should turn out to be in his handwriting, I presume you will then be quite satisfied that he was here last night?"

"Yes, Mr. Clifford, we shall indeed be much more satisfied than pleased at such a discovery, we assure you; but you may depend upon our hearty co-operation in anything you desire and recommend for the capture of the rascal."

"I must think about it," said Clifford. "Whatever is done must be done with care and with caution in the matter. I will now go at once to the Home Office, and I will write you a line to let you know the result of my inquiries."

The magistrates expressed their obligations to Clifford for his help, and he then said to them—

"I shall be obliged to you, gentlemen, if you will confine to your own breasts, as a profound secret, the fact that I am on the track, so to speak, of Jonathan Wild. Do not let any of your inferior agents know of it, for if you do, it will assuredly reach him."

"We will be careful, sir."

"Do so. And now good day; you will hear from me in the course of the next few hours."

Paul went direct to the Home Office, and there he was at once shown specimens of the handwriting of Jonathan Wild.

There could be no doubt for a moment, after one glance, that the handwriting in the memorandum-book was the same. This was no surprise to Clifford, for he had fully made up his mind that the robbery and the murder at Lady Brazen's were the handiwork of Jon a-than.

Paul Clifford concluded that now he was fairly on the track of Jonathan Wild, to follow it up became the object, just then, of his existence.

But Paul knew well the sort of person he had to deal with, and consequently he was not at all too sanguine of success in the matter, and he knew that if he was successful at all it must be from one of two causes.

Either he must, by untiring perseverance, track Jonathan Wild and so hunt him down by patience, or some fortunate and not to be calculated upon accident must have the effect of throwing him in his way.

Clifford did not allow his imagination to dwell on the likelihood of such an accident, but yet he felt that it was possible.

After thoroughly satisfying himself that he was right as regarded the handwriting of Wild in the little memorandum-book, Paul, instead of writing to that effect to the magistrates, called at the house of one of them to let him know the result.

The magistrate resided in Queen Street, Westminster, so after calling at the Home Office, which was then in Abingdon Street, it was not very much out of his way to drop in in Queen Street on the magistrate.

The moment he appeared in the private room of the magistrate, that gentleman cried out—

"Oh, Mr. Clifford, I am so glad to see you, for I shall have something curious to communicate to you."

"Indeed?"

"Yes, Mr. Clifford; allow me to introduce you to Sir Adam Brown."

Sir Adam Brown bowed to Paul, and Paul bowed to Sir Adam Brown.

The magistrate now said—

"Mr. Clifford, have I your permission to let Sir Adam Brown know the object that at present occupies your thoughts?"

"Certainly, sir. That object is soon told."

"Yes," added the magistrate, with a nod to Sir Adam Brown, "and it is the same that occupies yours."

"Is that possible?"

"It is so. You are now thinking of Jonathan Wild?" I am, indeed."

"And so is Mr. Clifford."

The magistrate then told Sir Adam that Paul had quite devoted himself to the destruction or capture of Jonathan Wild, and then turning to Paul he said—

"Mr. Clifford; just before you came in Sir Adam Brown had concluded the relation of, to my mind, one of the most singular circumstances connected with Jonathan Wild that I ever heard, and I am sure he will now, as he has told it to me, tell it to you in his own words."

"With pleasure," said Sir Adam Brown; "and if what I have to say will in any way tend to aid you, sir, in your pursuit of such a ruffian, I shall be very happy."

"Sir," said Paul, "I am grateful for any information I can get, for we never can tell the value of it till circumstances give a colour to it, sometimes quite unexpected."

"Just so. Then, Mr. Clifford, I was at Lady Brazen's party on the night of the robbery at her house and her murder, and, as I am a living man, I saw Jonathan Wild there, in the guise of a footman."

"Jonathan Wild?"

"Yes, Mr. Clifford: I had my doubts, but they have gone now, and I feel certain of it."

"You astonish me."

"I expected I should; but he was there, sir."

"But, Sir Adam, why did you not seize him?"

"I was not quite certain. Every circumstance tended to make it very doubtful, and I went for an experienced police officer who knew Wild well to come, and, if he recognised him, apprehend him at once. I was not gone more than twenty minutes, and when we returned he was not the same person."

Sir Adam then gave a minute description of the livery worn by Wild.

Paul Clifford listened to all this with the greatest attention, and at its conclusion said—

"Sir Adam Brown, the information you have rendered to me is very important, for it all tends to confirm what I suspected—namely, that the robbery and murder were the works of Jonathan Wild."

"You really think so?"

"I do, on my life."

"The villain!"

"He is worse than villain, but let us hope that his career is now nearly at an end, and that the time is fast approaching when he will have to render up an account of his many crimes at that tribunal from which there is neither escape nor appeal. I feel it to be a duty that is incumbent upon me to place him in the hands of justice, and I will do so if I can."

"You will be a public benefactor, sir, if you do really succeed in bringing such a man to justice."

"I am afraid," said Paul, with a slight smile, "that I shall not be able to lay claim to such public gratitude upon the occasion though."

"Indeed, sir; and why not?"

"Because folks will be apt to say that it was from personal motives I acted, and I am free to confess that it is so."

"Never mind that, Mr. Clifford," said the magistrate. "The police are but too glad, I can assure you, to have your aid and assistance, let it come from what motive it may."

"Be it so, then," said Paul, as he rose to go. "The question as to whether or not Jonathan Wild was the person who took the life of Lady Brazen and robbed her house is quite settled, I presume?"

"Oh, quite, sir."

"Then I will, with the clue you have given me to his appearance, Sir Adam Brown, set to work and try and ferret him out in London, and it shall go hard with me; but I will, before many days are over, give you some sort of news concerning him."

"I sincerely hope you may, sir, and that in the pursuit of him you may run no mischance."

"Sir, I thank you for that wish," said Paul, as he left the house of the magistrate on his mission in search of Jonathan Wild, which mission he now considered, after what he had heard from Sir Adam Brown, was very much facilitated and simplified indeed.

By now carefully placing every circumstance connected with Wild that he knew of in regular order in his mind, Paul came to the conclusion that the villain was playing some very deep part in London.

There was one rather important piece of intelligence, too, that he had gained from Sir Adam Brown, and that was rather a particular description of the livery which the supposed Jonathan Wild was dressed in.

This was the clue which Paul Clifford thought would, if well followed up, enable him to come to something like an idea of where Wild was to be found.

*   *   *   *

The day after the incidents just detailed had taken place, Wild, with all the daring of his nature, was out with the Princess doing duty behind the carriage with a coolness worthy of his reputation.

They were in Oxford-street, and the supposed lady of title had been shopping.

An assistant placed the goods she had purchased in her carriage; the door was closed, and Wild sprang up behind as the vehicle rolled away from the shop.

The Princess ordered her coachman to drive home.

Jonathan Wild was in rather an elevated situation, and he had a good view right along the Oxford-road; but little did he expect that that view would be sufficient soon to show him something that made him wish himself anywhere but where he then was, notwithstanding all his faith in his disguise.

We must suppose though that that faith had been to some extent shaken by the recognition of him by the keeper of the receptacle for stolen goods some time previous.

As Jonathan Wild looked over the roof of the carriage right along the Oxford-road, he saw a gentleman on a very beautiful white mare coming along at a trot.

The beauty of the horse and its exterior make first attracted the admiration of Jonathan Wild, for he was a tolerable judge of horseflesh, and then he glanced at the gentleman.

That one glance was enough.

The gentleman was Paul Clifford!

It would be a difficult matter, indeed, to define the various emotions which Jonathan Wild experienced at this most unexpected meeting with the man who of all others he had most occasion to dread.

Rage—fear—revenge and terror took possession of him by turns; and there he stood at the back of the coach, crouching down till nothing but his eyes were just above the level of the roof of it, and glaring at Paul Clifford.

If a look would have smitten poor Paul to the earth a corpse, he would not have lived to get past that coach.

Clifford was plainly attired in a suit of grey cloth, and he wore a hat without any ornament whatever to it. A short horseman's cloak was hanging from his shoulder, and Jonathan Wild could see that a sword was by his side, and that his saddle was a military one, with pistol cases by each side of it.

But what alarmed Jonathan as much, if not more than anything, was to see a couple of men, on good steeds, following Paul Clifford closely; and when he, Paul, got somewhat near to the coach, he paused, and turned his head, upon which the two men rode up to him.

They touched their hats, and otherwise showed that they looked upon him, Paul, as their head and superior.

Jonathan Wild would have given all his share of the booty from Lady Brazen's at that moment to have heard what Paul said to the two men. He could see his lips move, and then the men touched their hats again and turned their horses' heads in another direction and rode off.

Paul Clifford advanced along rather slowly, and quite alone.

Oh, what was Paul thinking of now that he did not cast a glance at the back of that coach, and in the cowering, trembling wretch there recognise his great foe, Jonathan Wild, and at once seize him and hand him over to be dealt with according to the law.

Perhaps it was the sweet image of Evelina that filled his mind at that moment, but certain it is that to the immense relief of Jonathan Wild Paul Clifford let his horse slowly pass the carriage.

The danger was over.

Paul had never even glanced at the back of the carriage, or even at the carriage at all.

And yet Paul was upon a mission that should have induced him to see everything and everybody on his route. He had broken up, so to speak, the happiness and the serenity of his home to try and rid the world of Jonathan Wild, and so he should have turned his whole attention to that one object.

There was a faint gleam of a smile upon Paul's lips as he rode on. Ah, yes! he was thinking of Evelina, and it is probable enough that if Jonathan Wild, without any disguise at all, had crossed his path, the fair image of Evilina would have blocked out all his ugliness from the perception of Paul Clifford.

If Fate had tried how in the best possible manner, so as thoroughly to alarm him, it could inflict a blow upon Jonathan Wild, it could not have hit upon a better plan than the letting him see that Paul Clifford was after him.

There was not another man in the world that he really and truly dreaded.

CHAPTER XLI.

A MYSTERIOUS VISITOR AT THE HOUSE OF THE PRINCESS—
AN INTERVIEW—NO TRACE OF WILD—CLIFFORD STILL
ON THE WATCH.

Two days passed.

Clifford and his emissaries never ceased in their efforts to find Wild.

He was indefatigable; but, unhappily, his efforts were not yet crowned with success.

Clever as he was, Wild was still more cunning; and having once got scent of what Clifford was after, contrived to keep completely in the dark.

Recognising the horseman in Oxford street had been a fortunate chance for him.

On arriving at home, he related to the Princess what had occurred.

"Ah," said she, "the young man may be clever, but it is not difficult to outwit your amateur thief-catcher at any time, and we will do him."

"I hope so, but I do not see how."

"Can you trust in me?"

"I must do so, for my ingenuity has entirely deserted me."

"Listen, then, to what I propose. There is no doubt that this fellow has a clue to your whereabouts, and will follow you. The only thing, therefore, that can be done is to lead him on, and let him find you."

"What?"

"Let him find you."

"Are you mad?"

"Not that I am aware of."

"Do you think I would risk a meeting with him?"

"Certainly not; and yet my servant must do so."

"I do not understand."

"The plan is a simple one. I know a man who is the very image of you. I will engage his services for a while, and you may lay by. This Clifford shall see him, and it shall go hard, but I'll sorely puzzle him."

"I begin to understand you now."

"All you have to do in the matter is to cast off your livery and remain quiet. Leave the rest to me."

"When is this farce to begin?"

"At once."

"And I am to be *non est* ?"

"Yes."

Wild disappeared, and ere a couple of hours a man who looked his twin-brother was in his livery, and in attendance on the Princess.

Followed by her new servitor, the Princess ordered her horse and went into the parks.

Ere long she saw that Clifford had his eye on her.

This assured her that the highwayman really had an idea that the veritable Wild was in her service.

Having paraded herself, and, what was better still, her servant, she turned to go home.

Again she encountered Clifford.

This time she greeted him with a winning smile.

Clifford, convinced that this woman was some vile wretch, of whom Wild was the accomplice, determined on the instant to return the smile, and strike up an acquaintance.

He eyed the servant.

Yes, he could not be mistaken.

Although admirably disguised, there could be no mistaking Jonathan Wild.

And yet the supposed thief-taker sat on his horse, immovable, statue-like, evincing no sign of recognising the highwayman.

Finding that the lady drew rein, Clifford walked to her side.

He raised his hat, and she greeted him with a smile of encouragement.

"It is a sweet day," said the Princess.

"It is, indeed," said Clifford, endeavouring to appear at ease.

"Are you fond of horses ?"

"Very."

"So am I. Ah! methinks life would be a blank without them."

"You are an enthusiast in these matters."

"Yes, indeed, I am."

"So am I; I own the most beautiful horse in the world!"

"Indeed! You must be proud of the animal."

"I am."

"Mine are but poor beasts, for I have no one to guide my choice, and those horse dealers take every opportunity of imposing on the unprotected."

"They do, indeed."

"I should be delighted to make some new purchases under the direction of a good judge.

Here she looked slyly at Clifford.

"If I could direct your taste," he said, again raising his hat," I should esteem it a happy chance."

"Oh, I could not think of troubling you."

"It would be a pleasure to me."

"May I really so far presume ?"

"May I hope for the honour ?"

"Oh, indeed, you are too good."

"Not at all."

"Then may I ask you to call upon me at home."

"You will do me great honour by giving me your address."

"It is here," said the Princess, drawing forth a small card, "when may I expect you ?"

"When may I come ?"

"At once if you will."

"The earlier the better."

"Then I will ride home and prepare to receive you Shall I give you an hour ?"

"Within the hour I will be with you."

"It is well. I am charmed to make your acquaintance."

"Either this woman is playing a deep game with me, or she is ignorant of the character of her servant. Bah! she is some vile courtesan who has Wild in her pay, and this is a trap to lead me off the scent. Nevertheless, I am convinced the man who follows her is Wild, and if I get within her doors, he is my prisoner."

An hour passed.

CLIFFORD MEETS JONATHAN WILD AT THE WILLOWS.

On presenting himself at the doors of her ladyship, Clifford was instantly admitted.

He found the cunning Princess seated in her neat little *boudoir*, toying with her pet birds, and awaiting his appearance.

"You see," he said, "I was so anxious to renew our conversation that I am here at the moment."

"Thanks," said the lady. "You do me great honour."

"Nay, the compliment comes from you."

"I choose to think otherwise."

"Ah! a wilful woman."

"Will have her own way. You are perfectly right, but I trust I am not quite a wilful woman."

"I trust so too, and unless appearances greatly belie you, you are not."

"Well, let us drop the subject. Have you lunched?"

"I have not."

"Will you join me?"

"With pleasure."

"Then I will ring for the servant."

Clifford's eye flashed!

"You do not mind dispensing with ceremony?"

"I would rather."

"Then we will have our little meal in this cosy place, and *tell a tale*."

"I shall be charmed."

The Princess placed her arm about Clifford's neck, and imprinted a kiss upon his lips.

"You are a dear, obliging fellow," she said, "and I quite love you already."

If Clifford had had a doubt on his mind respecting the character of his companion it was now dismissed.

The Princess rang the bell.

Next moment the servant was in the room.

He had his hat off now, and Clifford eyed him narrowly.

"Bring luncheon," said the lady, and the man took his departure.

"It is he," said Clifford to himself, "and the next time I will have him ; there shall be no mistake next time."

He waited a few moments, during which the Princess toyed with his raven locks, and ran her little white finger over his face.

Then the servant re-entered with a tray containing luncheon.

As he was setting it on the table, Clifford rose to his feet and, springing to the door, presented a pistol at his head.

"Move !" he cried, "and I blow your brains out."

"Why, what means this ?" cried the Princess.

"It means that that man is Jonathan Wild, and that I apprehend him in the King's name for highway robbery, and murder, and burglary."

"Psha ! That man Jonathan Wild ! Why, he is my very old and tried servant Peter Morris."

"I am not to be deceived."

"I be Jan Wild," laughed the servant ; "he ! he ! That be foine joik, that be."

"You do not deceive me," cried Clifford, rushing at the unfortunate servitor, and dashing his wig off. I know you."

To his surprise he found under the wig of the servant a full crop of short black hair, such as had not graced the head of Wild for many a year.

Where was the gashed and scarred skull ? where was the well-known silver plate ? where the low-retreating brow ?

There were none of these to be seen in the man who stood before him, and whose throat he clasped.

Starting back as if stung by an adder, Clifford released his hold, sank into a chair, and gazed upon the fellow who had so deceived him."

"I see you are convinced of your folly," said the Princess, haughtily.

"I am, indeed," said Clifford ; " how could I have been mistaken ?"

"How, indeed !"

"The likeness is wonderful, yet I should have known Wild better than to have made this mistake."

"No matter ; say no more about it, and let us resume our luncheon. Mistakes, you know, will happen in spite of every precaution."

Clifford could not but think so.

Yet this adventure had entirely destroyed his appetite, and he cared not how soon he could beat a retreat.

But the Princess had not yet done with him.

CHAPTER XLII.

TAKES US ONCE MORE INTO THE SOCIETY OF MESSRS. WILSNICK, WICKLES, AND WILSNICK, AND GIVES US AN INSIGHT INTO A MYSTERY HERETOFORE BUT DARKLY HINTED AT.

LORD ALGERNON was, perhaps, the most brilliant, if not the most notoriously dissolute, noble of his day.

Young, handsome, witty, and wealthy, he flitted about in the most reserved circles, and was generally esteemed and sought after.

But, nevertheless, his moral reputation was not what it should have been.

He was, moreover, connected with a gang of people of notoriously suspicious character.

He had married young—very young ; but his wife had suddenly disappeared. He said she had died in Spain,

but report darkly hinted at foul play, and gossips' tongues wagged of the subject until they ached.

Nell Lavender, the name by which the beautiful but rather dissolute woman who had linked her fate with that of Lord Algernon was known, was certainly loved by the boy lord to distraction, and as certainly was it in his power to have made her a good and happy woman.

But the infatuation that led him to marry her soon died away, and she became a loathsome burden of which he would fain have rid himself.

All the world *knew* this when, under the plea of failing health, he sailed with her for Madrid.

He was absent twelve months, and he came back alone.

She was dead, he said—carried off by a malignant fever —and, in the absence of evidence to the contrary, society had to believe him.

Ever gay and full of life before quitting England, it was observed that on his return a settled gloom had stolen over him against which he tried in vain to combat.

It was also then observed that he was seen frequently in the low haunts of vice, and also that he had certain dealings with the firm of Wilsnick, Wickles, and Wilsnick, solicitors, which, to say the least of it, had a most suspicious air, for men of his standing but seldom sought the advice and services of Old Bailey pettifoggers.

But then Lord Algernon was rich, and this, like the cloak of charity, covered a multitude of sins ; and society winked or altogether closed its eyes to the suspicious acts and failings of this young man.

Lord Algernon had not returned from Spain many months when, in passing through the Mall, he suddenly encountered a form that brought the perspiration in large drops to his brow, and made his legs totter under him as he contemplated it.

It was a woman, young and beautiful, but pale as death, that thus distressed his lordship.

It was, in fact, no other than his supposed dead wife.

She fixed her eyes upon him, and, as if drawn towards her by a magnet, he approached.

"Algernon," said Nell Lavender, "Algernon, you have served me ill—you have been a villain ; but I love you madly—devotedly. I escaped the assassin's knife, and have come back to you. Take me—take me to your heart again, and let the past be buried for ever in the deepest oblivion."

What was he to do ?

He stood on the brink of a precipice.

Here was his wife, who was reported dead *by him.* Here she stood, once more to accuse him—to brand him, and drive him from the circles in which he moved—to crush out all his hopes if he spurned her, and to destroy his dream of love if he acknowledged her.

Yes, Algernon loved !

Ada Loraine, the companion and humble dependent of Lord and Lady Storks, was now the idol of his heart, and he was just on the eve of proposing to her.

Ada was beautiful—marvellously beautiful, and, although poor, was much sought after by the scions of noble houses.

But she had eyes only for Algernon, and he knew that he had but to ask her hand to receive it.

This, then, was the state of affairs when Nell again appeared on the scene.

Algernon hesitated but a moment.

He hailed a coach, and in a few moments the wretched wife, happy in his false oaths and protestations, blinded by his plausible excuses, was pillowing her head on his bosom, and being carried along to his seat at Kingston.

There he determined on keeping her a prisoner until something could be done.

In this awful emergency he sought the advice of Wilsnick, Wickles, and Wilsnick.

We will follow him to the office of these worthies.

He entered, and found the three men seated, as usual, in solemn conclave, discussing the merits of a case in which the firm had a deep interest.

"Ah, my lord," said Wickles, rising as the young man entered, "ah, my lord, what brings you here so soon? Tuesday next was the day appointed, and here you are three days before your time."

"We have no news yet," said the elephantine Wildnick; "no news. We have looked over the document again, and we have also consulted the other papers with which you furnished us, and we have not yet altered our opinion. You are no more the heir of Algernon Manor than we are.

"No," said Wickles, "no more than we are."

"Are you sure?"

"Quite; the matter is beyond a doubt. The male line is clearly ended, and to the females of the family the estates undoubtedly should have passed; and had you not have turned up at the right moment, there is no doubt but that the affair would have been in the hands of the Lord Chancellor."

"The devil!"

"It's a solemn fact."

"Yes, a solemn fact," said the other two, in a breath.

"Well, then, you mean to say that I am—"

"A beggar! Just so."

"But these women; there is no evidence to prove they are not all dead, and that I am not in reality the real heir."

"Oh, isn't there?" said Wickles. "We thought there was."

"Oh yes," said the other two, in pretended astonishment, "we thought there was."

"Do you mean to say that you can trace any of them?"

"We mean to say that we have traced the succession in a straight line to your great aunt, Angelica Mouldsley."

"And she—"

"Is dead."

"I breathe again."

"Yes, but you need not breathe too freely. This Angelica married."

"Whom?"

"We don't know."

"How, then, do you know that she married?"

"No matter. On Tuesday next you shall be in full possession of the particulars; we are preparing our opinion for your perusal."

"Well, did she leave issue?"

"One daughter."

"And she—"

"Is not to be traced! But we are not without hope."

"And if she is found?"

"She will undoubtedly claim, and the law will award her the estates, unless—"

"Yes, unless—"

"You make it worth our while to put her quietly out of the way."

"Have I not before told you that, in the event of any such improbable contingency, I would do so?"

"You have."

"Well, then, until you find your impossible heiress, the matter had best rest."

"So we think. We did not open this conversation. We appointed Tuesday next for an interview, and yet we find you here to-day."

"Just so; but I am not here on that subject."

"What! some other trouble?"

"Yes, and a serious one, as I think."

"What is it?"

"My unhappy wife has turned up again."

"The deuce!" said the three, in a chorus.

"Yes; she is here, and I know not what to do."

"Then the malignant fever did not carry her off?"

"Curse her, no."

"And she comes back to find you laying siege to the heart of another."

"Yes."

"And she will, in all probability, spoil sport?"

"Yes."

"That is unfortunate."

"It is; but she must be stopped. I must rid myself of her."

"How?"

"I came to you to know how."

"My dear sir," said the parrot like Wilsnick, "what can we possibly know of such matters?"

"You know all, and you must give me your assistance."

"Must?"

"Yes, must."

"We can see no must in the matter."

"Perhaps not; but if I make it worth your while——."

"To send her again out of the country?"

"To send her out of the world!"

"Sir! do you think we could engage in such a matter? The firm of Wilsnick, Wickles, and Wilsnick engaged in a murder!—a cruel, bloodthirsty, shocking murder! It could not be done—it could not be done."

"Psha! I know you for three desperate pettifoggers. I know you as the employers of the most desperate wretches in the universe, and the concoctors of such plans as that by which I wish to rid myself of this woman; so deal plainly with me."

"Ah! you're a passionate, wild young man, and say things that you should not. Nevertheless, Mr. Wickles will attend to you; and if we can give you any little assistance in this desperate matter, we will do so; we can say no more."

There was an interview with Wickles, and his lordship left the offices with a lighter pocket, but with a lighter heart.

* * * * *

Meanwhile Poor Nell had found the means of making several secret excursions from Kingston to London, and had struck up an acquaintance with the very woman to whom her husband had been paying his addresses!

Such is the intricate workings of fate!

On one of her visits to Ada it so chanced that Algernon had given out that he had business in Suffolk that would take him out of town for three days, and supposing that he had departed from London Nell willingly accepted the invite of Ada to pass the night with her in the mansion of Lord Storks.

Now it so happened that Algernon had delayed his Suffolk business, and had staggered into his Club in Pall Mall, where, meeting Lord Storks, he was invited by that nobleman to sup and sleep at his house.

"I will gladly do so," said Algernon, "more particularly as many people believe me to be gone into the country and will not be prepared for my sudden appearance among them."

Perhaps the real secret of this ready acceptance of the offer was his desire to pass the night under the same roof as the woman he loved; but be that as it may, he went home with Lord Storks.

"I'm quite a bachelor," said his lordship, "her ladyship is at Tunbridge Wells, and I'm left alone."

"Alone?" said Algernon. "Scarcely alone with your sweet protege under the same roof with you."

"Sweet protege," said Storks; "ah, that is, to say the least of it, strong language! Ah, I see! you are somewhat stricken in that quarter?"

"Nonsense!"

"Ah, I see you are, so don't deny it! But I tell you it's no use, it's no use, my dear fellow; her heart is gone."

"Gone?"

"Yes, given to another."

Then Lord Storks simpered and wriggled about with a self-satisfied air that said, as plainly as actions could speak—

"And I'm the happy man."

But Algernon was too busy with his own thoughts to notice this.

* * * * *

The two young girls had retired for the night, before Lord Storks and his friend entered the house.

The two noblemen supped in silence.

They were both occupied with their thoughts ; and, strange to say, those thoughts run in the same direction.

Algernon, actuated by he knew not what mad impulse, determined to seek the chamber of Ada that night, and Lord Storks thought the present a very good opportunity for attempting the same purpose.

Brooding on these evil thoughts the two men separated, and sought their respective chambers.

At length the house was wrapped in stillness.

* * * * *

Ada and Nell took a very long time to disrobe themselves that night, for they had an immense deal to say to each other, and it was all to be said before they laid their heads on their pillows.

Nell related to her new-found friend the story of her trials, and the effect of the tale on Ada may be imagined.

She, on her part, revealed to Nell the fears she felt of Lord Storks, and gave several instances of his marked attentions that had distressed her very much.

"I fear him," she said, " and I should be thankful to leave this place for ever, but I am only a poor dependent, and dare not throw myself out of such a home, perhaps to starve."

"Just so," said Nell ; "I could not advise you to do so. Bear with it, and by every means in your power endeavour to suppress his familiarities, and in time he will discontinue them."

"I hope so."

"Believe it. Coldness is fatal °to the warmest love, and a frown is capable of damping the fiercest flame. In time you will see that he will discontinue the annoyance."

It was at this moment that a very soft and quiet knock came at the chamber door of Ada.

They both started, and the low suppressed tone in which their conversation had been carried on was on the moment suspended, and they listened with breathless attention for a repetition of the tap on the panel of the chamber door.

That repetition did come, but, pending its coming, we may as well leave the chamber for the purpose of accounting for it.

It had occurred to Algernon to try the effect of a guinea upon one of the domestics in getting precise information of where the sleeping chamber of Ada was situated, but there was so much risk in such an attempt that he gave it up in despair, after looking into the face of the servant who had lighted him to his own chamber, which had been done with all imaginable respect.

Algernon then was quite abroad.

With the exception of the grand fact that all the bedrooms were upon one floor, and that the men seemed to occupy exclusively the rooms upon the right-hand side as you entered the corridor from the grand staircase, he knew nothing.

Such a positively mad infatuation, though, as that which now possessed Algernon was not likely to be set aside by any ordinary or even extraordinary difficulties, and after waiting about an hour, and hearing nothing move, he ventured to take a peep into the corridor.

All was still, and all was very dark.

Algernon, upon the whole, was rather glad of the absence of the light, for he felt more confidence, as the guilty are apt to do in the dark.

Thus, then, did he start out of his chamber, with his head inclined to a listening attitude, and all his senses thoroughly awake to the least disturbance of the stillness of the place, to make his way to the chamber of that young and innocent girl, for whom he had conceived so sudden and so perfectly bewildering an attachment.

There was but one course that he could now pursue with the least chance of success in finding Ada, and that was to tap gently at the doors of the different chambers on the left-hand side of the corridor till he was answered by Ada.

"I shall know her voice," thought Algernon. " Her faintest whisper would at once come direct to my heart, and I should know it among a thousand."

Taking long and cautious steps then, Algernon reached the first door and tapped at it.

There was no answer. That one was vacant.

The second—the third—the fourth were vacant, but the fifth, as he reached it, he fancied must be the right one, for he could faintly hear the hum of a voice.

"Is she saying her prayers ?" thought Algernon.

As this supposition came across him, he trembled so excessively that he could hardly remain upon the spot, and the idea, then, of abandoning the guilty enterprise upon which he came for an instant flashed across his mind ; but the image of Ada, in all her beauties, rose up to his imagination, and he was, we may truly say, mad again.

After anxiously endeavouring to make out the voice that he had heard within that room, Algernon tapped at the door of it in the way we have mentioned, and so startled Nell and Ada.

After that one tap he felt so terrified at his own temerity, and so full of fears a'sto what Ada would say to him, if she should open the door, that he was ready to sink through the floor of the corridor.

Strange to say, now it was the totally innocent and unsuspicious nature of the young girl that he seemed to dread more than all.

After a time, though, he did gather courage to tap again at the door, and then, with a desperate feeling of resolution, he nerved himself to go through with an adventure that could bring him nothing but woe—nothing but sorrow—nothing but repentance !

"Who can that be ?" whispered Nell to Ada. "Did you expect any one at such an hour ?"

"Oh, no—no !"

"Perhaps, your maid."

"No. The girl sleeps at another part of the house, and she never comes to me till I ring for her in the morning."

Nell felt chill and terrified.

The few words that they had spoken together were uttered in so low a tone that it was quite out of the question they could reach any ears out of the room, especially through the thick panelling of the rather massive door.

They both now, as the tap upon the panel came a third time, looked at each other with faces of undissembled alarm.

"Is it possible," said Nell, " that something is amiss in the house ?"

"Oh, no."

"Why do you say no ?"

"Because alarms never come with so gentle a tap as that. Oh, no—no. It is not an alarm," and then she faintly continued, " It is Storks."

"Do not say that, Ada. On, how glad I am that I am here to protect you. The villain ! If he dare to set foot within the sanctuary of this apartment, I will shoot him dead upon the threshold of it."

Nell, as she spoke, took from her pocket one of the small pistols she had always carried about with her since quitting Spain. and the use of which she knew so well, and looked to the priming of it.

"Oh, you terrify me," said Ada.

"Nay, I will protect you. Providence has surely sent me here this night to stand between you and all harm. With my life I will protect you, Ada."

The tap upon the panel came again.

Nell looked calm and collected, and, laying her hand upon the arm of Ada, she said in a low but clear tone of voice—

"Now, Ada, attend to me. I am older than you are, though not much—that is to say, in years. In experience and knowledge of the world I am, I expect, a perfect patriarch in comparison to you ; so you will permit me to act in this matter for you, will you not ?"

"Oh, yes, I will."

"Very good. Whoever is knocking at that door, no doubt, has not the smallest idea that I am here, or, indeed, that you are otherwise than alone. I will step aside, but keep on the alert; and I would advise you, lest afterwards suspicion should unjustly light upon the wrong head, to ask who is there, and to assure yourself of the intention of the person who comes at such an hour.

"Would you have me open the door?"

"I would, and then depend upon it I will be by your side at the proper moment; but do not too hastily take alarm. You can afford to be patient with the knowledge that you are perfectly safe."

"With you with me," said Ada, "I do, indeed, know that I am safe; so I will do as you direct me to do."

With these words Ada approached the door of her chamber, and said gently—

"Who is there?"

Nell retired to the farther end of the room, so that, although she heard that some response was made to this question, she could not hear what it was, nor the voice in which it was uttered.

"Who is there?" repeated Ada.

"A friend," said a voice; "a friend. Pray, open the door."

Ada thought at the moment the voice was not that of Lord Storks, and she was quite surprised at that fact, for both she and Nell had in their little conversation concerning the visitor fully made up their minds that it could be no one but that nobleman.

Oh! how little Nell suspected who it really was.

"I pray you, Ada, to open the door," said Algernon, "I must speak to you, if it be only for a moment or two."

Ada was now more alarmed at the idea that something was amiss in the mansion than from any other cause, and she hastily opened the door, and stood pale and bewildered upon its threshold, attired in the snowy drapery which she had put on to retire to rest with.

The shawl had fallen from her shoulders, and lay at her feet.

Algernon could just see the dazzling whiteness of her neck and bosom, and trace the delicately beautiful contour of the girlish figure beneath its thin covering.

"Oh, what is it?" said Ada. "Who are you?"

"Do you not know me?" said Algernon, speaking as though he were half-choked; "do you not know me?"

"Algernon!"

"You are alone?"

"What do you want?" said Ada, evading the last question.

"Hush! Not so loud."

Algernon stepped across the threshold of the room, and laid his hand upon the door and closed it.

"Alone!" he said,

It was from that one word, now that he was fairly within the room, that Nell knew him.

The conviction that it was Algernon came across her like death, and she sunk into a chair, half-fainting.

No—no!

She recovered a little. A happy thought had darted through her brain.

He had, of course, come to warn Ada of some danger —to protect her!

Oh, there could not be a doubt of that, and all would be well again.

Poor Nell!

As Algernon advanced into the room the young girl crept back towards where Nell was hiding behind a pretty screen, and in a tremulous voice she said—

"Oh, sir; you have not come here without some object. Tell me at once what it is. Has anything happened in the house? Is there any danger? Of what would you warn me?"

"Oh, yes," thought Nell, as she drew a long breath; "that is it. He comes to warn her; that is it."

How Nell hugged this delusion to her heart, feeling at the same time that it was but a delusion after all.

Algernon was silent for a few moments. He felt hot and cold by turns, and, then sinking on to his knees, he said—

"Beautiful living angel of excellence; oh, do not despise me. Do not cast me from you when I tell you that I love you."

Ada started back, and laid her hand upon the screen.

Nell felt as though her senses were going, but she did manage not to faint.

"You—love—me?" said Ada.

"Ah, yes, with all my heart—with all my soul. Oh, Ada, Ada! I thought I did, but in good truth I never did know what love was till I looked upon you. Henceforth I shall live but for you alone. Love you, do I say? Oh, how weak a word that is to express my feelings towards you, Ada! I adore you."

"Oh, no—no—no!"

"Yes, a thousand times yes. Does not your glass tell you that you are beautiful? Are you not aware that there never was, and never will be, one who can compare to you in loveliness? I have struggled against this passion, but it is all in vain. It is my fate, and I cannot resist it. I am impelled by an uncontrollable destiny to tell you how much I love you."

At the words so passionately spoken by Algernon poor Ada was so alarmed that she cried out—

"I shall be protected—I feel I shall be protected!"

When Nell heard this, she felt what she was there for, and she nerved herself to go through a scene of, to her, perfect misery; for with the declaration that Algernon had made to Ada all her own hopes of happiness had at once and for ever fled.

There was something sublime, though, in the conduct of Nell now—for it was in the midst of her own terrible, heart-breaking misery that she thought of the duty she had undertaken to protect Ada.

It was a duty that she did not shrink from, although she had to exercise it against a very different person from what she had expected.

"I will protect you," said Algernon. "I will protect you, Ada, against all the world; but you must let me love you."

"No, no! Oh, why have you, by this one act, scattered all the kindly feeling that I had towards you? I would rather have perished than that you should show yourself to be so base."

"Base do you call me?"

"I do."

"Is it base to love excellence and beauty? Oh, recall the word. In me the voice of nature speaks, when I tell you that I love you—that I adore you!"

"No—no, you must not! This is a lesson to me, for I find that there may be in the same mind the motives to do sudden acts of greatness, and daring, and generosity, and deliberate acts of villany. Go, sir. Let me never look upon your face again. I pray you to leave me."

"Ada, I cannot—I dare not leave you; I should go mad were I to do so. You have no conception of the extent of my love for you. I have battled with it and tried to conquer it, but I could not. Oh, do not frown upon me! All I ask of you is one tender look—the privilege of holding you to my heart for a moment, and I will then go."

"Never!"

"Oh, do not drive me frantic!"

"This, sir, is great baseness. How dare you say that you love me? What have you to offer me but disgrace and misery?"

"I have to offer you a heart that will know no change— a love that will be eternal."

"False—false! You have already made such offerings to another, and you have broken all your vows."

Algernon looked aghast.

"Ah! you tremble. Do not force me to say more, but go at once, and only hope for my forgiveness. Let it suffice for you that I know you. Do not force me to tell you how very base you really are."

"I can guess," said Algernon, rising, "who told you; but it is false; she is no wife of mine."

"Another word and I call for aid."

"Nay, Ada, you would not be so cruel. What if all the house were alarmed, and found me in your chamber, why what would be the supposition? Just that I had come here with your good will, and then that we had had a quarrel—a foolish lovers' quarrel. Come, come, I will not leave you. Let me but kiss that gentle, vermilioned cheek."

"Off, villain! Advance another step and my cries shall arouse Lord Storks."

"You would arouse him to danger, dear Ada. I tell you I madly love you, and now that I am here—"

"Help!"

"Hold!" said Nell, stepping out from behind the screen, and pointing, with a firm, unshaking hand, a pistol towards the head of her husband, while she placed her left arm round the waist of Ada. "Hold! Begone, villain—begone, midnight ruffian, or you shall have the reward of your rascality! Begone, I say!"

If the apparition of one whom he had long since known to be dead had suddenly risen up before Algernon he could not have been more completely petrified with fear and astonishment than he was by the appearance of Nell in that chamber as the defender of Ada. He staggered back till he could get no further for the wall, and then he ejaculated—

"God of Heaven! she here?"

Nell's attitude was a fine one.

There she stood, her taller figure than Ada's making her, indeed, appear the defender of the young girl, who was struck down, and clasped her round the feet.

There was a fine flush of colour upon Nell's face, although her eyes were brimful of tears, and she looked gloriously beautiful as she there stood in defence of outraged innocence.

Oh, what a contrast was Algernon to her!

Cowering down till he did not look one half his natural height, his arms extended as though to keep off some dreadful spectacle, and his eyes cast down and abashed, he trembled before the gaze of those two beings who must for ever regard him with mingled feelings of reprobation and contempt.

For a brief moment he hoped that it was all a dream. What would he have given that it had been so.

Nell, after the first outburst of passionate feeling, was still, and apparently calm.

She could not just then have uttered another word to the indignant philippic she had uttered if her life had depended upon so doing.

It took some moments for Algernon now to rally sufficiently to be able to say—

"You here? You—you?"

"To save me," said Ada, tremblingly. Oh, go at once from this room, I implore you! Let it suffice that upon this night you have done and said enough to embitter my recollection of you, and I think yours of me."

"Go," said Nell.

With a crouching step Algernon went towards the door of the room. His brain felt as though it were on fire, and he turned when he reached the threshold.

"Nell," he said—"Nell?"

She did not answer him.

"Nell, I say—follow me."

"Never," she replied. "Time was when your slightest gesture of command would have received my ready obedience. But the bond is broken between us. Go!"

"You dare not disobey me."

"We shall see."

"Leave this room, then, at once. I must and will speak to Ada alone. Leave this room, I say!"

"Oh, no, no!" cried Ada. "Do not leave me, I implore you! Do not leave me to the mercy of this man's passions."

"My poor girl, I will not," said Nell. "You need not be afraid. I will not leave you while I have life; and I do not think that even he dare kill me."

"Kill you? Oh, no—no!"

"Silence," said Algernon; but although he strove to put on a look of stern command, he trembled in every limb, and his teeth chattered so together that he could scarcely articulate the words. "Silence, I say! Nell, I command you to leave this room at once."

"I will not."

"Beware how you tempt me too far."

"Tempt you? Alas, poor wretch! you have, it seems, been already too far tempted, and you have fallen. Was it not possible for this young girl—this all but child in years—to be beautiful, and innocent, and angelic as God has made her, but you must look upon her with unholy eyes, and strive to be her destruction? Oh! shame—shame upon your manhood! I did think better of you. Nay, Ada, do not tremble. There is no danger."

"There is danger!" cried Algernon, advancing with a menacing attitude towards Nell and Ada.

"Then be it to you," said Nell, as with a firm hand she held the pistol towards his head. "Hear me, Heaven, while I swear that if you do but lay a hand upon this young girl, or even move one step forward with the seeming intention to do so, I will kill you!"

Algernon staggered back, thunderstruck at this calm and cool speech of Nell's.

"You do not mean—you cannot mean," he gasped, "that you would dare to fire at me?"

"I would, so help me, Heaven. I am here to protect this girl, and I will do it, let the life be whose it may that falls in the performance of that sacred duty."

"You are mad!"

"No, Algernon, it is you who are mad. Leave this room, the air of which you pollute by your presence. Leave this room. It is I who command you so to do, for it is my turn to command. I stand here upon a pinnacle that you can never hope to reach. I feel the strength of many persons in my heart. I feel that I am doing the holy work of Heaven; and so, with all your evil passions—with all your disappointed rage, I defy you! I tell you to your face that I defy you! Keep off, if you are wise—keep off, I say, for you know me well enough to know that I will keep my word!"

Who is there, however abject might be his condition, would change it for that of Algernon at such a moment as that—a moment when he could not but feel the sense of a degradation that there was no emerging from in this world?

Even if what had passed were to be, by some rare act of generosity upon the part of Nell, forgiven, would it, could it ever, be forgotten? Oh, no! Was it now possible that he could ever be the same to her, or she to him, as they had been to each other? No, no!

A man may struggle against adversity, poverty, pain—ay, he may go calmly to meet death itself; but degradation, the contempt of those who have been accustomed to know him, the disgust of those whom he cannot but exonerate, will haunt him even to the grave.

Algernon, as he stood trembling before those two young girls—for Nell was but a girl in years—felt all this, and more than this; for such agony of the heart and brain as came over him cannot be well expressed in any words.

Much at that time would he have wished to say, but found that his power to say it was all too limited to permit him so to do. He only stood and trembled.

"Go," said Nell, "go. We wish to hear no more."

"Not another word," said Ada, with a shudder. "Oh, we have heard too much already!"

Algernon was still inclined to speak, but, like the celebrated "Amen" of Macbeth, his words appeared to stick in his throat, and he fairly turned and fled from the room.

What must have been the humiliating feelings of Algernon as he was thus forced to effect an ignominious retreat before those whom he had so deeply injured?

There was another person, though, who upon that night was about as intent upon making a fool of himself as Algernon was.

That other person was Lord Storks.

Now his lordship was full of the idea that he was beloved by the fair and really spotless Ada. He considered that he had but to speak to make her fall at his feet, and consent almost to anything in the world he might propose.

Lord Storks set about, like Algernon, only in a different way, to convince Ada how great a rascal he could possibly be.

With his lordship, though, there was less excuse than with Algernon; for notwithstanding some rigid moralists take upon themselves to tell us that there is no excuse at all for crime, we are of a different opinion.

In the first place, Algernon struggled very hard with himself against the grievous temptation that he fell into on account of the charms of the young and artless Ada, and when he gave way to that temptation we must recollect that it was not for the mere pride of conquest, it was not for the mere love of change, or that fickleness which is incidental to some minds, but it was because he felt himself beaten down and overpowered by the master-passions of human nature.

All along, too, from the moment that he left his chamber in order to seek that sanctuary of innocence in which reposed the young girl, he had felt sick at heart, and ashamed of the part that he was acting.

Even when he fled from the chamber, dismayed by the presence and reproaches of Nell, he showed that there was some good and proper feeling still in his bosom.

The case as against Lord Storks was different in several very essential particulars.

In the first place, Lord Storks was not capable of that feeling of overwhelming love for any one which breaks down the bounds of all reason, and induces the most extravagant actions. Lord Storks was very fond of himself, but it is doubtful if his affection for any one else ever got so far.

Still, my Lord Storks was human, and he could not look upon the beauty of the fair Ada without acknowledging it; and as he had been brought up with the vicious idea that it is a great thing, and as he himself expressed it, quite delicious to get the better of female innocence, he coveted such a triumph over his young *protege*.

A false pride, a foolish vanity, and a defective education induced his lordship to act as he did.

It was genuine admiration, boundless devotion, that made Algernon play so mad a part.

Now, his lordship would have been quite satisfied if Ada had yielded to him through fear.

Algernon, on the contrary, would have scorned such a triumph.

If she could not love him she was not for him. He would have thought it base to owe his triumph to any other feeling.

Having thus drawn the proper line of distinction between the two, in appearance, similar proceedings of Lord Storks and Algernon, we proceed to give an account of his lordship's proceedings upon the eventful night in question.

Lord Storks waited rather later than Algernon before he made an attempt to improve upon the circumstances that had seemed, as he thought, to give him such a signal opportunity of placing poor Ada in a serious predicament.

Immediately Algernon left the chamber of the young girl Lord Storks left his, and with a great flowered dressing-gown on he issued forth to conquer, as he thought.

Creeping along by the wall of the corridor, the first thing that alarmed Lord Storks was to come against something that threw him at full length to the floor.

He had stumbled over Algernon.

In a moment, however, he was again upon his feet.

A glance at the open chamber door of Ada told his lordship how matters stood.

He had cunning enough to take advantage of the situation.

"So," he said, shooting an angry glance at Algernon; "so, my lord, this is the way you abuse my hospitality."

Algernon was as speechless as he had been on facing the pistol of his wife.

"What means this?" continued his lordship, with increasing warmth.

"I will tell you," said Nell, rushing from the room; "that man is a villain, and would have destroyed the poor innocent girl under your care."

"And who are you?"

"There was a pause."

Algernon glanced beseechingly at his wife.

"I cannot answer that question," said Nell, after a while; "suffice for you to know that I am the friend of Ada."

"Yes," cried Ada, "she is my friend, and she is the wife of—"

"Hush, Ada," said Nell; "do not betray him. Let not his downfall be attributed to me."

Ada was silent.

In an outburst of virtuous indignation Lord Storks said he thought the whole three no better than they should be, and gave them to understand that the sooner their backs were turned his house the better he should be pleased."

"You will not surely turn Ada from your door?"

"Yes."

"But she has done nothing to merit your displeasure."

"Psha! I have eyes, and I can see. Begone, the three of you! My house shall no longer be contaminated with your presence."

Without pausing to hear more he rang violently for the servants, and in a few moments the two poor women were shivering in the streets, and Algernon had fled.

"What shall I do?" said Nell; "what shall I do for you? For myself I care nothing, but to bring this misery upon you!"

"Say not that," said Ada; "do not upbraid yourself thus, for it is undeserved. You could not prevent what has occurred. God knows, that had you not been with me it might have been worse for thee. Better a wanderer in the streets, penniless, homeless, desolate, than the dishonoured thing I might have been but for your opportune visit."

They went away from the neighbourhood of Lord Storks' house together, the one friendless and homeless, the other friendless, but with a home that she would not enter again.

*　　　*　　　*　　　*　　　*

Lord Algernon repeated his visits to the firm of Wilsnick, Wickles, and Wilsnick on three successive days.

Each day found him a poorer man, but on the last visit he was told that Nell should be no longer a trouble to him.

"We have tracked her," said Wickles; "there's a man on the scent, and to-night she will be hunted down."

"And killed?"

"And killed!"

"Can I depend upon you?"

"You may rest assured that by to-morrow morning your wife will be in the grave."

"And Ada?"

"Of her I can tell you nothing."

"But is she not with Nell?"

"Perhaps."

"But—"

"Silence!"

Lord Algernon could get no more out of the cunning old lawyer, and had to leave him.

But the next day Algernon had convincing proofs that poor Nell was now really dead.

*　　　*　　　*　　　*　　　*

We want our readers to turn back a few pages and contemplate that scene in which Wild, a certain friend of his, and a great, unsightly box, containing the body of a poor woman, are represented.

The corpse was that of the unhappy Nell Lavender.

CHAPTER XLIII.

THE GERMAN PRINCESS FORMS AN ALLIANCE, OFFENSIVE
AND DEFENSIVE, WITH THE NOTORIOUS " COLONEL
JACK."

THE Princess had not long parted with Clifford when
Wild entered the room.

"Well," he said, " that was nicely done I should say."

"Yes," said the Princess, "nicely done, but don't be
deceived ; he's not at all a fool, and, though baffled, he's
not defeated. We shall have more trouble with him yet."

"Curse him, yes ; he's one of those bloodhounds that's
only disposed of when their throats are cut."

"Ah ; it may come to that yet."

"It must!" said Wild, and his eyes gleamed with fiery
malignity. "It must—it shall, if I can't drag him to
the scaffold. *That's* the place where I want to see him,
for there my vengeance will be complete."

"Be careful, be careful, I say ; there's danger in the
man, and I bid you be on your guard."

"I am."

"I am glad to hear it, but I doubt you. There is that
in your eye which bids me repeat my caution again and
again. I fear your intemperate passions, and I tremble
lest you may blindly rush into that danger you so much
dread."

"You may trust me."

The Princess did not reply, but she smiled in a manner
that forcibly expressed her doubt.

A servant now entered.

"Well," said the Princess, as Wild assumed an attitude
of deep respect, and appeared as if he had been receiving
some commands from the lady, " well, what is it now?"

"If you please, my lady, there is a gentleman below
who bade me bring this card and say that he was anxious
to see you as soon as you were disengaged."

The Princess took the card.

A glance revealed the name of COLONEL JACK!

"Admit him instantly."

The servant retired.

"Colonel Jack!" said Wild; "I certainly know that
name. It seems to be associated with some early reminiscences in my career."

"I should say so, but he's a gentleman now, and must
be treated as such."

"There's no occasion."

"Is he to be trusted?"

"Oh, yes."

At this moment an elderly, well-dressed, firm-set, and
not ill-looking man entered the apartment, and advanced
to the place where the Princess stood.

"Ah, my dearest friend," said the Colonel, " this is a
great pleasure. I did not anticipate the satisfaction of
meeting you in England."

"Perhaps not ; I am, like yourself, only a recent
arrival."

"And who is our friend?" asked the Colonel, looking
at Wild, who stood leaning over the back of a chair,
eyeing the Colonel with an impudent stare.

"That, allow me to say, is the most famous of his
class ; no less a man than Jonathan Wild."

The Colonel advanced and took Wild by the hand.

"I'm proud to know you *now*," he said, " although
once your name was a complete terror to me."

Wild smiled his grim smile, but said nothing.

There was half an hour of small talk, and then the
Colonel broke out with—

"And now I suppose it's time for me to reveal the
cause of my being here, for you may imagine that I do
not come without a motive."

"I presume so."

"Well, the fact is I am rather inclined to recommence
on a grand scale my old work. Returning and recognising you in the park, I at once knew that a splendid
game was afloat, and made up my mind to seek an inter-

view and ask to be taken into partnership ; but then I
was not aware that you had so powerful a partner as Mr.
Wild. I presume that *my* little assistance would, under
these circumstances, be scouted?"

"I don't know," said Wild; "I don't know. How are
you connected ?"

"Excellently."

"Have you the *entree* to the best circles?"

"To the Court itself."

"*That's* well."

"And I'm busy taking notes for some stupendous
enterprises."

"Are you ?"

"Yes ; and I've the means of shipping the stuff, getting out of the country, and finding a good market for
it."

"That's better."

"Yes ; I think I could open your eyes to a few
tricks."

"Perhaps so. But before you reveal any of these plans,
I should like, if it won't be a trouble, to hear you run
over the principal events of your life. I always like to
know something of the antecedents of the people I am to
work with."

"Very right and very praiseworthy, and I've no objection to rehearse my little tale for your edification."

"Thanks."

"I'm all attention," said the Princess, seating herself,
and pulling the chair of the Colonel nearer to her own ;
"pray be quick. The life of Colonel Jack must be worth
hearing."

"I don't know that," said the Colonel, with a smile.
"To such people as you, whose existence has been an undeviating scene of excitement, my poor tale must appear
flat and tame, but such as it is you are welcome to hear
it."

"Now, then," said Wild ; " let me ask you to go on
without further preface."

"My life," said Colonel Jack to Wild and the Princess,
"has been a chequered scene, and will, perhaps, repay
your attention if you grant me whilst I rapidly relate it.

"For anything I can tell my descent may be as dignified as that of any person ; for my mother often asserted
that she associated with her betters.

"But that belongs more to her history than to mine.

"The only facts that I could glean were from my
nurse, who told me that my mother was a gentlewoman,
and my father a man of quality.

"She further informed me that herself had a considerable sum of money given her to relieve them from the
importunities of having a child to keep which should
neither be seen nor heard of.

"It seems that my father gave my nurse more than
was stipulated for, upon the express condition she would
use me well, send me to school, and, when I grew up to
the years of understanding, to inform me that I was a
gentleman born.

"My father said that this was all the education he
wished her to give me, because he was confident that if it
was once impressed upon my mind that I was a gentleman I would then act as one.

"It was not my fortune, however, that my miseries
should end as soon as they began.

"As the great ascend to the summit of grandeur by
slow and imperceptible degrees, so the unfortunate
descend by gradual steps through a continued series of
disasters to the depth of their misery.

"My good nurse was as honest to her engagements as
could be expected, or as she had it in her power.

"She trained me carefully with her own son and
another in similar circumstances with myself.

"She told me that my name was John, but I was left
to find a surname for myself.

"Her own son was also called John, who was about a
year older than myself.

"About two years after she accommodated some other
loving pair as she had done my father and mother.

CLIFFORD HAS A DOSE PREPARED FOR HIM BY THE PRINCESS.

" The name of that boy was also John.

" But the nurse was not destitute of ambition ; therefore, to distinguish her son, because he was the oldest, she would have him called Captain.

" Upon this my high-born spirit began to swell, and I cried, and told my nurse that I would be called Captain too, for she had told me that I was a gentleman.

" Anxious to maintain peace in her dwelling, the good woman told me that I should be called a Colonel, which is higher than a Captain.

" This for the present satisfied me, and the more so as I heard her inform her son that as I was a gentleman, he was to call me colonel.

" Here John then began to cry, and would be called a colonel likewise.

" Thus Jack showed how deeply ambition is implanted in the human mind, and that the meanest boy has his own share.

" To present a full picture of the family, I shall give you a sketch of the characters of my companions before proceeding farther in my own history.

" Captain John, the eldest, was a stout-made boy, but not tall, and promised to be a well-built, strong man.

" He was an original rogue ; and, to gratify his own depraved dispositions, he would perpetrate the most nefarious actions.

" He was of such a thievish turn that he even stole from his fellow-rogues, a thing generally unknown among the pilfering race.

" Major Jack was a merry, facetious boy, and had a gentle turn of behaviour.

" He was truly bold and courageous, feared nothing ; but, when he gained the superiority, he was as meek and gentle as a lamb.

" In short he wanted nothing but honesty in order to be a complete gentleman.

" With regard to my own character, my companions esteemed me a bold, active, resolute boy.

" I, however, made a different estimate of my character, therefore shunned boyish war as much as consistent with my honour.

" I was cunning and dexterous in my trade, and not so often detected as my fellow rogues ; nay, though I have been in the trade twenty-six years, I have never been detected, and I am still unhanged.

" I was near ten years old, the Captain eleven, and the Major eight, when the old nurse took her leave of t his weary world.

" Her husband was drowned a little before, in a ship going to Scotland.

" The industrious nurse died so poor that the parish was at the expense of her funeral.

" After her death we were thrown loose upon the world, rambling about all three together.

" The people in Rosemary-lane and Radcliffe knowing us very well we were easily provided with victuals.

" Shop-doors, or the foot of stairs, or any convenient place, during several summers, served us for lodgings.

" In the winter season we slept in the ash-holes and nealing arches in the glass-houses.

" This was a rendezvous for several youngsters equally destitute and profligate.

" Some of them persuaded the Captain to go a kidnapping—a trade at that time much followed.

" It was usual to catch children in the evening, stop their mouths, and carry them to certain houses, where there were rogues ready to receive them, when they put them on board ships bound for Virginia, and sold them for slaves.

" This gang were at last detected and sent to Newgate, and Captain Jack among the rest, although he was not much above thirteen years of age.

" On account of his youth he was ordered to be three times whipped, the Recorder of Bridewell informing him that it was to save him from the gallows.

" He had no sooner regained his liberty than he returned to his companions, and remained among them as long as that continued.

" The misfortune of the Captain made a strong impression both upon the Major and myself.

" About a year after, the Major, who was a flexible boy, was enticed by two rogues, to pick pockets at Bartholomew fair.

" The Major was ignorant of the trade, and was therefore to do nothing, but was promised a share of the booty.

" The two rogues managed so well that they returned to our quarters at the glass-house, and, sitting down in a corner, they began to share their spoil by the light of the glass-house fire.

" The Major delivered up the goods, because, as soon as they stole any article, they delivered it to him, that so, if they had been caught, nothing might be found upon them.

" It was a lucky day to them, and calculated to entice a young adventurer.

" The money, and the splendid articles that were brought home from the fair, quite captivated the heart of the Major, and he wakened me early next morning, and showed almost his handful of money.

" The sight surprised me not a little, and, putting his money into his pocket, he gave me a shilling and a sixpence, which made me think myself a rich man.

" As I had never before a shilling that I could call my own, I was very intent to learn how he came by this wealth ; he told me the whole story, and that he had for his share seven shillings and sixpence in money, a silver thimble, and a silk handkerchief.

" We went to Rag Fair, and purchased each a pair of shoes and stockings ; then to a cook-shop in Rosemary-lane, and dined, like lords, upon boiled beef, pudding, a penny brick, and a pot of strong beer ; and, as we were disposed to be gentlemen once in our lives, were greatly surprised when sevenpence was the amount of our bill.

" The Major exulted in his good fortune in being introduced to such an easy and elegant mode of life, and went to his usual place and enjoyed a sound repose, undisturbed by dreams of poverty or want.

" The next day the Major and his commander took another walk, and were equally successful.

" Success stimulated their invention, and increased the desire of the Major, and, in a short time, he not only became an operative man, but more dexterous than those who had initiated him into the mysteries of picking pockets.

" Nor did any disaster occur to damp their ardour, or to alarm their fears.

" In this manner success perfects and matures villany.

" But I must relate my own adventures, and not those of the Major.

" The silver and the silk handerchiefs dazzled me, and, the entertainments of Rosemary-lane pleasing my palate, I was overcome by the persuasion of the Major, and, without hesitation, entered into the new society.

" With one of my new associates, who had the charge of my education, I went down to Billingsgate, which was crowded with masters of cook-shops, fishmongers, and oyster-women.

" Our eyes were first directed to the latter.

" My orders run in the following terms :—

" ' Go you into all the alehouses, as we go along, and observe where people are telling money, and, when you find any, come and tell me.'

" So he kept sentry at the door, and I went into the houses.

" It was not long till I brought him word of several.

" He went in and made his observations, but found nothing to answer.

"I at last informed him that I saw a man receiving sums of money from different persons, and that it was all before him upon the table, and he was counting it, and putting it up in bags.

"'Is he?' exclaimed he; 'I'll warrant I'll have some of it.'

"In he walks, and, as there were several empty tables and boxes, he listened to learn the name of that man.

"Then he makes up to him, and, after a long story, tells him, 'that there were two gentlemen at the Gun Tavern sent him to inquire for him, and to tell him they desired to speak with him.'

"The collier master had got all his money before him, put up in little black dirty bags; and, as it was duskish, my companion contrived, while he was speaking to him, to put his hand upon one of these bags, and carry it off undiscovered.

"When he came to the door he pulled me by the sleeve, saying—

"'Run, Jack, run for our lives.'

"We ran as if pursued, until, coming into the fields, we turned into a bye corner to examine what we had got.

"He pulls out the bag.

"'You are a lucky boy, Jack,' says he; 'you deserve a good share of this job, truly, for it is all owing to your lucky news.'

"As I had now a hat, he poured all into it.

"It was a matter entirely beyond my comprehension how it was possible to steal money from a man before his face and in his full senses.

"We found in the bag no less than seventeen or eighteen pounds.

"I received one-third, and was well pleased.

"We would no longer lodge in the glass house, nor walk naked and ragged.

"According to his directions I purchased two shirts, a waistcoat, and a great coat.

"The latter was the most necessary part of dress to men in our profession.

"We now lodged in a little garret.

"After diminishing our stores, and recruiting our spirits, we went out again to try our fortunes.

"It was agreed to act separately, and I soon displayed my dexterity.

"I observed two gentlemen upon the Exchange talking together in a warm and interested manner, while one of them pulled out, and thrust into his pocket, a pocket-book, so frequently, that my covetous eyes were captivated.

"I moved softly forward, and stood close beside him, and, in the alternate pulling out and throwing into his pocket, it happened that the lap of the book was suspended over his coat pocket, which I slipped out, lodged in my own, and ran for Moorfields.

"Hearing the bustle upon the Exchange, my companion was there as soon as me.

"Upon examining the book we found several goldsmiths' and other notes, and in one of the folds several diamonds.

"The owner was a Jew, and dealt in these brilliant commodities.

"My partner returned to the Exchange to receive intelligence, and there heard a reward of an hundred pounds offered to the person who would return the pocket-book.

"The next day he went to the Jew, and informed him that he knew the person who had his book, and, for the reward, would return it upon being secured from danger.

"After many preliminaries, it was agreed that Will, for that was the name of my companion, should bring the book, and all the articles it contained, and receive the reward.

"Nor was he less faithful in giving me the share which belonged to me than I was dexterous in procuring the booty.

"Our next adventure was in Smithfield, upon a Friday.

"A country gentleman, from Sussex, had been selling his bullocks, and, having received the money for them in a tavern, he came out with a bag, containing the same, in his hand.

"He was immediately seized with a fit of coughing, and rested the hand with the money upon a post, to support him during the struggle with the violent cough.

"We went both behind him.

"Will says,

"'Stand ready!'

"He stumbles, falls upon the man coughing, and down he tumbles, while I pulled the bag out of his hand, and fled like an arrow out of a bow.

"Will recovered himself, and followed my example.

"The violence of the fall increased the corpulent gentleman's cough, so that he could neither recover himself, nor, for a considerable time, utter one word.

"At last, however, he obtained strength and breath sufficient to say,

"'The rogue has got away my bag of money!'

"In the meantime, the people around could not understand who he meant by the rogue.

"Will was soon at the place of rendezvous, and, upon examination, we found that the cough of the Sussex grazier had just cost him eight guineas, and five pounds in silver.

"The spoil was instantly divided, and we went to work immediately, but frugal Fortune had no more to bestow upon us that day.

"But she was generous enough not to allow us to go to bed without supper.

"In the dusk of the evening, in Greenchurch-street, we observed a young apprentice to a woollen-draper with a large sum of money, going to pay an account to a goldsmith in Lombard-street.

"We traced his footsteps, saw the money paid, but a bag was still reserved, which he carried below his arm; and, in a dark court, where he had to turn a corner to go into Gracechurch-street, Will came behind him, and gave him a violent push that drove him to the ground: the bag fell out of his hand; and, whilst he attempted to recover himself, I snatched up the money, and ran off.

"Will soon followed; the poor young man was not a little injured by the fall.

"His master was thankful that the whole of the money was not lost, and made no great bustle to recover that which was in our possession, but cautioned his servant not to venture himself in the dark in future with money about him.

"The bag contained fourteen pounds eighteen shillings for each of us; my stores now rapidly increased, but I was too covetous to entrust my property to the care of any person.

"In a short time after my tutor introduced me into the company of other two young fellows.

"We formed our plan, and embraced a large extent of ground, to observe what flying shot we could discover.

"The watch-word, at which we were all to stand at proper distance, was:

"'Mark, ho!'

"Will and another met a single gentleman.

"Will approached him, saying,

"'Sir, your money!'

"Seeing him alone, the gentleman struck at him with his cane, but Will rushed in upon him, struggled, and threw him down.

"The gentleman begged for his life.

"Will told him, with an awful imprecation, that if he spoke, or made the least resistance, he would instantly cut his throat.

"Meanwhile, a coach comes up, and one of our company cried,

"'Mark, ho!'

"Two were, in a second, at the coach, in which was a doctor of physic and a surgeon.

"Their fees, watches, rings, and silver instruments were the reward of our active exertions.

"Will still kept down his prize, and when he heard the

noise cease, and the coach proceed, he tied his hands behind his back, assuring him, upon his word of honour, that if he lay quiet he would return and relieve him; but, if he made the least noise, he would return and kill him.

"Will took fourteen shillings and sixpence from him, which was his all, and carried it to his companions, congratulating them upon their better luck.

"Meanwhile, I was stationed upon the side of the Pindar of Wakefield, and I also cried,

"'Mark, ho!'

"What I saw was two poor women, one like a nurse, and another like a maid servant, moving toward Kentish-town.

"Will, knowing that I was a young hand, came flying to me, but seeing that it was smooth work, cried,

"'Go, Colonel, fall to work.'

"I went up, and accosting the nurse, said,

"'Don't be in such a hurry.'

"She seemed frightened.

"'Don't be afraid,' said I, 'a little of the money that s in the bottom of your pocket will put all right.'

"By this time Will appeared.

"Both the women screamed aloud.

"'Be quiet, and do not force me to murder you against my inclination: give me your money presently.'

"Upon this the maid pulled out five shillings and sixpence, and the nurse a guinea and a shilling, weeping and bewailing, and crying out that it was all she had in the world.

"I found my heart beating and aching for her, and only asked her name, which, she told me, was Smith, and that she lived in Kentish Town.

"In a few minutes we were all together, and it was agreed to suspend our toils for the present.

"'But hold!' exclaimed Will; 'I must go and untie the man.'

"One says, 'Let him lie.'

"'No,' says Will, 'my word must be kept.'

"He returned, but the man had either untied himself, or some other person had done him that kind office.

"We all now hastened from the scene of plunder.

"But Fortune was not yet contented with what she had lavished upon us.

"On entering Hyde Park a coach appeared with a single gentleman, and a Cyprian damsel that he had brought from Spring Gardens.

"We made free with the gentleman's money, watch, and silver-hilted sword; but, when we demanded a contribution from the lady, she scolded us, saying, that she had not a penny, and we had not left the gentleman one to give her.

"This adventure being ended, we retired to our respective lodgings.

"As I had now a room of my own, in two days Will waited upon me, and I made an appointment to meet him at a certain place.

"Will was not there, but his associates were.

"They had committed a robbery near Hounslow, wounded a gentleman's gardener, and robbed the house of much plate and money, with which Will had decamped.

"The neighbourhood was alarmed, the rogues pursued, and one of them taken.

"Will, hearing that one of our party was taken, who had informed upon the rest, hastened to my lodgings, wrapped all his booty into his great-coat, and put it below my bed, leaving word to me, 'That he had left the great-coat that he borrowed from me below my bed.'

"I was at a loss to understand the import of this message, but going up stairs found the parcel, with about an hundred pounds in plate and money.

"I sold the plate to a broker, but heard nothing of brother Will for several days.

"But, some days after, going upon the stroll, I met brother Captain Jack, who came close to me, and, in his own blunt manner, said,—

"'Do you hear the news?'

"'What news?' said I.

"He told me that my old comrade and teacher was taken, and that morning carried to Newgate; that he was charged with a robbery and murder, committed somewhere beyond Brentford, and that the worst was he was impeached.

"I thanked him for the information.

"Next morning, when going across Rag Fair, I was surprised with the cry of 'Jack!'

"I looked behind, and saw three men making towards me.

"I was soon surrounded, and informed that they were in search of one of the Three Jacks of Rag Fair, who was charged with being partner in a robbery.

"I shall not trouble you with the dialogue which passed between me and the justice before whom I was carried.

"It is sufficient for you to know that I recovered my liberty, while poor Will was suspended, in three weeks' time, for his activity.

"I next went in search of the Captain, and informed him of all that had happened.

"By his surprise and agitation, I discovered that he was concerned.

"He told me, 'That it was all true, that he had engaged in the robbery, and had the greatest part of the booty in keeping; but what to do with it, or with himself, he did not know.

"'That he thought of flying into Scotland,' asking me if I would go with him.

"I consented.

"The next day he produced about twenty-two pounds, and I about sixteen.

"We set out upon foot, and travelled to Ware.

"At an inn, while we were drinking a mug of beer in the gateway, a countryman had hung his horse's bridle over the gate, while he went in to refresh himself in the inn.

"We asked the way to Scotland of the hostler, who desired us to ask for Royston.

"'But,' said he, 'there is a turning just here a little farther; you must not go that way, for that goes to Cambridge.'

"We paid our beer, and continued to rest our wearied limbs, when a gentleman's coach arrived.

"In the bustle, the hostler says to the Captain—

"'Young man, pray take hold of the horse, and take him out of the way, that the coach may come up,' meaning the countryman's horse.

"The Captain did so, and winked to me to follow.

"'Do you step before, and turn up the lane, I'll overtake you.'

"In a few minutes he was at my heels upon the horse, requesting me to get on behind him.

"As the hostler had directed us a different route, we went towards Cambridge, passed through several towns, took two shirts off a hedge, and got safe to that city.

"At that place I also purchased a horse, and being both well mounted, prosecuted our flight to Scotland.

"But nothing could restrain the Captain from his favourite employment.

"During divine service at Stafford he stole a watch from a lady's side, and though ten guineas reward was offered we were afraid to hazard a discovery.

"We prosecuted our journey, and arrived safe in Edinburgh without meeting with any accident, except the horse of the Captain falling down in fording a river, when he was almost drowned.

"But the proverb, that the gallows must not be robbed by the water, saved his life on this occasion.

"We remained in the capital of Scotland about a month, when all of a sudden the Captain and his horse disappeared without leaving me the least intimation whether or not he was to return, or where I was to find him.

"This was the more distressing to me, as I was in a

strange place, and my money very nearly exhausted. Thus circumstanced, I was under the necessity of selling my horse.

"Being freed of the expense of maintaining this faithful companion, and having nothing to do, I began seriously to look out for some honest employment, and resolved to be a thief no longer.

"I now applied myself to learn to read and write for six months, and then got into the employment of a custom house officer.

"My work was only to pass and repass between Leith and Edinburgh, and he left me to live at my own expense, and by this means my money ran short.

"I had indeed a reserve in a friend's hands in London, but I was unwilling to lessen that sum.

"It unfortunately happened that, just about the time when I was to have received twelve pounds, my master, on account of some misconduct, was not only turned out of his place, but under the necessity of taking refuge in England.

"In this case I and other two servants were left to seek employment where we could, without a penny for our support.

"I therefore resolved to return to England, a shipmaster being willing to take my word for ten shillings until I arrived there.

"But just as I was about to embark Captain Jack appeared.

During his absence, he had been actively employed at Glasgow, and in the West of Scotland.

"He had also passed over into Ireland; but, not being successful there, he was constrained to leave that country, and passed over into the North of Scotland.

"Misfortune still attending him, he was constrained to enlist in a regiment belonging to Douglas.

"In this capacity, with his musket upon his shoulder, he again appeared to me at the port of Leith.

"In the reduced circumstances in which I then was it appeared to me that the best thing I could do was to enlist also.

"Thus the Captain and Colonel were both joined together as private men, with a musket upon each of their shoulders.

"I was highly pleased with the life of a soldier, and almost at once learned to handle my piece.

"The sergeant who was employed to teach us, finding me so ready, asked me if ever I had been a soldier before.

"To which I replied, that I had not.

"'Then,' replied he, 'they called you Colonel, and I believe you will be a colonel, or you must be some colonel's bastard, or you would never handle your arms as you do, at once or twice showing.'

"My ignorance of my father, and my nurse assuring me that I was a gentleman, came forcibly into my mind upon this repartee; but I kept my secret to myself.

"In a short time, however, my musket became heavy for my shoulder, and I became uneasy in that station.

"About six months after we had entered the service we were ordered for England, in order to be shipped for Flanders.

"Poor Captain Jack had so conducted himself when he was last there that he could not walk as a recruit through the streets of Newcastle; and it occurred to me that it was a hard matter for me, that had a hundred pounds in London, to go over to Flanders in the character of a private soldier, to be shot at for three shillings and sixpence per week.

"While I was daily ruminating upon the hardship of my situation, and the danger of poor Jack, he one evening waited upon me, and said he wished me to take a walk in the fields, as he had something to converse with me about.

"During our walk, the various turns of our fortune, and the pressures of our present situation, were discussed.

"The result was a determination to desert that very night, as the light of the moon favoured our route.

"Jack also informed me that he had a comrade equally disposed for a private march, who knew the whole of the country; and that, when we were safe upon English ground, we would take shipping from Newcastle for London.

"In the morning we reached the Tweed, and overtook two men who had deserted from the same regiment at Haddington.

"They supposed that we had been sent in pursuit of them, and were determined to stand upon their own defence, having their swords; for we were not to receive our clothes until we joined the regiment in Flanders.

"They were, however, soon made to understand that we were in the same condemnation; so we became confederates.

"These were Scotchmen, and so very poor that they had not one penny in their pockets.

"Our money was also nearly exhausted, but we arrived at Newcastle, and contrived to get into that place in the dusk of the evening, and went down to the waterside.

"Here we knew not what course to pursue.

"To remain gazing at an element upon which we could not walk to London was doing nothing.

"Accordingly, with the best face we could, we went into an alehouse, and called for a pot of beer.

"The woman in the house conversed very freely, and conducted herself with such civility that we were emboldened to reveal our circumstances to her, and to entreat that she would procure us a passage from some of the collier-masters.

"In the kindest manner possible she lamented that we had been a day late; that a friend of her's had just fallen down to Shields, and that she would have had sufficient influence with him to have taken us all to London.

"'But,' added she, 'he is not yet, perhaps, gone; he sometimes waits after the ship, and follows her in the boat.'

"We entreated her to send to inquire.

"To our great satisfaction he was not gone, and would call in a little time at this house.

"Our countenances began to brighten, and in an hour in the captain comes.

"'Where are those honest gentlemen soldiers that are in such distress?'

"We stood all up, and in a submissive manner paid our respects.

"'Well, gentlemen, and is all your money spent?'

"'Indeed it is, and we will be infinitely obliged to you, sir, if you will give us a passage. We will be very willing to do anything we can to the ship, though we are not seamen.'

"'Why,' says he, 'were none of you ever at sea in your lives?'

"'No, not one of us.'

"'You will be able to do me no service, then, for you will all be sick. However, for my good landlady's sake, here, I shall accommodate you. But are you all ready to go on board? for I go on board myself this very night.'

"'Yes, sir, we are ready to go this very minute.'

"'No, no, we'll drink together. Come, landlady, make these honest gentlemen a sneaker of punch.'

"Conscious of empty pockets, we stared at one another.

"'Come, come,' said the captain, 'don't be concerned at your having no money: my landlady and me, here, never part with dry lips. Come, goodwife, make the punch as I bid you.'

"Our hearts were full with the generous captain's goodness, and we thanked him, praying God to bless him.

"While we were drinking the punch he told the landlady that he would go home, and order his boy to bring the boat at high water, and in the meantime ordered some supper.

"In less than an hour he returned, and frowned that we had not drunk out the punch.

"'Come, don't be bashful; when that's out we can have another. When I am obliging poor men I wish to do it handsomely.'

"The bowl was emptied, and another brought, then a good leg of mutton.

"We ate heartily, and were pressed by our kind captain, assuring us that we should have nothing to pay.

"After supper the captain inquired of the landlady if the boat was come. She brought word that it was not yet high water.

"More punch was called, and something more somniferous than liquor put into it.

"It circulated very speedily; we were all intoxicated, and I fell sound asleep.

"At last the boat came; I was aroused, and, along with the rest, staggered into the boat, and off we went with the captain.

"When the boat was stopped we were told that she had arrived at the vessel.

"Care was taken that none of them should tumble into the water in moving into the ship, and the captain cried—

"'Here, boatswain, take care of these gentlemen; give them good cabins, and let them turn into sleep, for they are very weary.'

"We were carefully lodged, and enjoyed a sound repose until the middle of the following day.

"When we came to move on deck we saw land at a very great distance.

"Thus we thought we were on our way to London, exulting in our good fortune.

"In this pleasant turn of mind we remained during three days, supposing that by this time we were nigh home.

"We now asked if we were not yet near the shore, and about to enter the river.

"'What river?' said one of the sailors.

"'Why, the Thames,' said Captain Jack.

"'The Thames! What d'ye mean by this? What, han't you had time enough to be sober yet?'

"Jack said no more, but looked sheepish.

"The same questions being repeated, the sailors began to 'smell a rat,' and, turning to the other Englishman who came along with us, said—

"'Where do you fancy that you are going that you ask so often about it?'

"'Why, to London,' replied he; 'where else should we be going? We agreed with the captain to carry us to London.'

"'Not with the captain, poor men; you are all deceived. I thought so when I saw you come on board with that infamous, kidnapping rogue Gilliman. The ship is bound to Virginia.'

"We were like madmen, drew our swords, and raged liked furies.

"We were soon overpowered, and brought before the captain.

"He expressed his sorrow at our situation, declared that he could not help us, and that he had no hand in the matter; and that we were put on board his vessel as servants, to be delivered to proper persons in Maryland.

"He added, that if we behaved quietly we should be civilly treated, but if not, put in irons.

"Captain Jack lost all temper.

"'What! no hand in it? Is he not a confederate in the villany? Would any honest man receive innocent people on board his ship, and carry them off without inquiring into their characters and circumstances? Why does he not set us on shore again? I tell you all that he is a villain. Why does he not complete his villany, and

murder us? Then he'll save himself from my revenge, but nothing else shall deliver him from my hands; and I am honester in warning him than he is in deceiving me!'

"All was of no avail.

"It was necessary to submit.

"We had a pleasant voyage.

"When we came on shore Captain Jack said, 'I have something to say to you, captain. I have promised to cut your throat, and, depend upon it, I'll be as good as my word.'

"He delivered us to the merchant to whom we were consigned, who disposed of us to the best advantage.

"Captain Jack had an easy, good master.

"It soon happened that he and another were sent in a boat to carry provisions to one of the plantations down the river.

"They ran off with the boat, and, leaving it, wandered through the woods, arrived in Pennsylvania, and from thence the Captain sailed to England, where, joining his former companions, and pursuing his old courses, about twenty years after he was executed at London.

"I was sold to Mr. Smith, a rich planter.

"Hard labour and solitude gave time for reflection, and, though my understanding did not enable me to form a proper estimate of my past conduct, yet I was filled with remorse at my folly and guilt.

"My industry and sobriety recommended me to my master, who in time made me an overseer.

"He also sent home my note to London for my ninety-nine pounds, which I received.

"He at length informed me that he intended to give me my liberty.

"I told him that I was very happy, and did not wish to leave his service.

"Then he gave me a paper, containing my discharge from his service, and full liberty.

"I replied that I would be his servant as long as he would keep me.

"He said that he would retain me in his service upon two conditions.

"First, that for managing his plantation he would give me thirty pounds of yearly wages; secondly, that he would purchase me a plantation near his own, that I might begin and do something for myself.

"He added, smiling, 'Jack, though you are but a young man, yet it is time that you were doing something for yourself.'

"These arrangements being made he purchased me three hundred acres of ground near his own plantation.

"Nor was this all: he supplied me with necessaries, or gave me credit for what was required to enable me to manage my property.

"I was soon provided with materials to build houses, with cows, horses, hogs, and two servants.

"Meanwhile I managed my kind protector's estate.

"The first produce of my estate was sent over to a correspondent of my old master's, and the goods in return faithfully shipped.

"But to my sad loss the ship was damaged in coming into the harbour.

"The nails, iron, and tools were saved, but the soft goods were greatly injured.

"This threw me into the utmost concern, as I was so much indebted to my friend, and had now no view of repaying him.

"He consoled me, saying that I might soon make up for all.

"In that hour of despondency I exclaimed that I had no hopes of that, and that I should never be out of debt.

"He generously added, 'Well, you have no creditor but me, and remember I once said that I would make a man of you, and I will not disappoint you.'

"I supplied him with such part of my iron as I could spare, and took some linen and clothes in exchange.

"I by this time had a large quantity of my ground cleared of timber, and the view of an excellent crop of tobacco.

"I got three servants more, and one negro, and all things succeeded to my sanguine wishes.

"But there is a void in every situation, and I found a great one in mine.

"This was, indeed, the beginning of a new scene to me, but it was not that kind of life which suited my expectations and wishes.

"Honesty and virtue alone exalt a man, and not riches or power.

"While I was in Scotland I had begun to read and write, so that I now sought after books and information.

"Fortunately I procured a number of books which belonged to a planter who was dead.

"Though I was then thirty years old I looked upon this period as my youth, and would have gone to school to learn.

"It happened, however, that one came into my service from Bristol who had been well educated, but, in consequence of his improper conduct, had been transported for several years.

"He continued to increase in my esteem; and, as he was active, and a good scholar, I asked him if he could teach me the Latin.

"He replied, that if he had books he could in a short time.

"I told him that a book would better become him than a hoe, and that, if he would instruct me in the Latin, and any other languages that he knew, I would give him his liberty.

"He fulfilled his engagements, and I received a fund of knowledge more valuable than the price of many slaves.

"I continued in this manner of life for twelve years, and, by a correspondent recommended to me by my friend, my goods were regularly sent to the London market, and goods or money returned.

"Meanwhile my good friend died, and left me to manage his affairs.

"Now I was disconsolate; indeed, there was none with whom I could freely converse and unbosom myself at all times.

"And though I was now in a station that enabled me to carry on my plantation without pecuniary aid, yet the loss of his company, counsel, and conversation, was irreparable.

"In these circumstances I formed the resolution of returning to England, and was determined to see more of the world.

"It was three years before I could arrange matters so as to leave Virginia.

"I relieved my tutor, and would have taken him to England with me, but, to my sad mortification, his term of banishment was not ended: I therefore made him my overseer, and, under a certain plan of management, committed all things to his care.

"Having settled this matter, I next was anxious to provide such a quantity of goods as might enable me to provide my plantations with proper utensils, and to afford me money for my expenses.

"At length I embarked for England in a stout vessel, having shipped my goods on board different vessels.

"The weather was at first very stormy, and the ship was so much damaged that some leaks were found.

"The men, however, got them stopped without any injury, and we proceeded on our voyage.

"But when we had arrived in the British Channel, about the dawning of the morning, a French privateer of twenty-six guns appeared, and crowded all sail to come down upon us.

"Our captain exchanged several broadsides with her, but the Frenchman was too strong for us, and we were obliged to surrender.

"I was detained on board the privateer, and our vessel, also manned by Frenchmen, was carried into Maloes.

I, however, heard that she was retaken, and carried into Portsmouth.

"The privateer continued to cruise in the channel, and took a rich prize homeward-bound from Jamaica.

"She was carried into Maloes, and from this place I was conducted to Bordeaux.

"Here the captain asked me whether I would be delivered up a state prisoner, get myself exchanged, or pay three hundred crowns.

"I requested time to consult my correspondent in England, and I was exchanged for a merchant who was prisoner in England.

"Having got a certificate, I arrived safe on the English shore at Deal.

"When I came to London I was welcomed by my correspondent, who had managed all things in the best manner to my advantage.

"I also found that my overseer in Virginia had made regular remittances of the crops of my plantations, and had acted in the most industrious, skilful, and honourable manner.

"My principal concern was now to conceal myself from all my former acquaintances.

"Nor was this difficult: I was so altered that they could not identify me, and they were equally changed.

"I have already related what was the fate of Captain Jack, and as to Major Jack, I learned that he was daring as ever, and so dexterous a rogue, that, continuing his former depredations, he was thrown into prison and condemned, but that he had relieved himself of his irons, and escaped to France.

"Nor could he refrain from his old pranks, even though he had so narrowly escaped the gallows.

"In France he practised his calling until he was at last detected, and broken upon the wheel.

"This was, indeed, rather ungrateful, as my friend had taught the French gentlemen of the road the English generous mode of robbing politely, and without committing murder, which had, almost universally, been the practice formerly with French robbers.

"Thus was I, by the kindness of Heaven, spared, the last of the Three Jacks, who had made such a figure in their native country, and in other places.

"Now arrived at the summit of my fortune, I assumed the name of a rich merchant, and kept a French servant, because I was desirous to learn the French language.

"In this situation I continued about two years.

"Previous to this time no woman had deprived me of a moment's repose; nor had I the least partiality for the fair sex.

"But there was a beautiful and highly accomplished lady who lived in the house opposite to mine that attracted my attention.

"She sung admirably, and at times she was careful to make me hear the sound of her fine voice from my window: she was equally careful to present herself frequently at her own window, so that I must have been callous and blind not to be smitten with her accomplishments.

"In a neighbouring house, where I sometimes visited, I had the felicity of seeing and conversing with her.

"But no sooner did she perceive that I was captivated, and sought an opportunity to declare my sentiments to her, than she dexterously shunned my company, or, at least, was careful that I should have no opportunity to slip a note into her hand, to whisper in her ear, or ask a private interview.

"She was, indeed, more *knowing* and *versant* in the ways of the world than I was, though I had seen many different faces and some foreign countries.

"She at last, however, granted me a hearing, and, to avoid the speculation of neighbours, and the expense of a wedding, we were privately married.

"Scarcely was the ceremony over, and this fair lady introduced into my house, than she threw off the mask.

"Her charms were obscured by frowns.

"Her elegance became extravagantly expensive.

"Her vanity was nourished by an expense to which I was a stranger, and which even my funds, though great, would not have long sustained.

"In the course of a twelvemonth she bore me a fine boy, and her expenses on that occasion amounted to no less than one hundred and thirty-six pounds.

"Such jarrings took place betwixt us that at length a separation was proposed, and she insisted upon having three hundred a year settled upon her.

"This, however, made me look better into her conduct, and, by means of two trusty agents, I was enabled to detect her infidelity, and to sue her before an ecclesiastical court, and obtain a divorce.

"Thus circumstanced, I resolved to fly from the strife of tongues and the breath of calumny, and to retire to France.

"Arrived in that country, I became acquainted with some Irish officers of the regiment of Dillon, bought a company, and joined the French army.

"Our regiment was ordered to Italy, where I experienced some pretty sharp service.

"Having served in several campaigns, I received *brevet* for a colonel to raise a regiment in Great Britain.

"I accordingly sailed for Leith, but, as our fleet was anchoring, Sir George Byng with the English fleet appeared.

"Upon this surprise the French admiral set sail, and run to the north of Scotland, and, with the loss of one vessel, got safe to Dunkirk.

"I was truly glad to set my foot once more upon land, for my imagination was filled with terror at being taken, tried, and hanged, for bearing arms in foreign service.

"This alarm made me abandon the army, and I went to Paris, a place full of mirth and gallantry.

"Here I was so unwise as again to try the game of matrimony; and, if I was unhappy before, I was no better now.

It was not long before I discovered a marquis doing me the honour of supplying my place; I fought him next day, and left him for dead.

"In this dilemma I set sail for Virginia.

"We had a pretty good voyage; but we fell in with a pirate, who plundered us of all that suited his purpose. I was, however, indifferent to that which I had lost, as I had plenty before me on land.

"I found all my plantations in good order, and in a flourishing state.

"My old tutor had acted entirely to my satisfaction, and was transported with joy at seeing me again, and so were all my slaves and domestics.

"Not long after my return, I married a white servant, who, for some time, proved a very affectionate and faithful wife.

"She, however, in a short time played the fool, and not long after died from the fruits of her own imprudence.

"This circumstance being the subject of no small conversation among the planters, I sent for a copy of the king's general pardon, and finding that I was most certainly included, I resolved again to visit England.

"Having arranged all my affairs, and, committing them to the care of my overseer, whose fidelity and skill were formerly proved, I set sail for my native country, and here I am.

"'Good,' said Wild jumping up and seizing the hand of the Colonel, 'you are one of my sort, and I like you.'

"Then you agree to allow me to join you!'

"What says the Princess?'

"With all my heart."

"I echo the words."

"Then all is right, I am one of you."

They joined hands in silence, and the interview terminated.

The Colonel rose and took his leave.

On his face as he left the house was playing a particularly bright smile.

Wild and the Princess took it to be indicative of *satisfaction!*

Closer observers of physiognomy would, however, have set it down as an expression of *triumph.*

We shall see.

CHAPTER XLIV.

CLIFFORD RECEIVES INFORMATION OF WILD—LEARNS HOW HE HAD BEEN TRICKED BY THE PRINCESS AND STARTS FOR THE WILLOWS—WHERE THE WHITE MARE WAS CONCEALED.

BILL WATERS had particular business with Clifford.

He set off in haste to find him, and came upon him in the West-end.

Clifford had not yet recovered from the disappointment he had experienced in his wild-goose chase, and was not in the best of humour.

"How now?" he said roughly, as Bill came up to him.

"Well," said Bill, pausing for breath, "*he's* been back."

"Who do you refer to?"

"Who but him as you jist vanted to see."

"What, do you mean—?"

"Of course I do."

"Well."

"He's a downey one, and is a doing matters to rights."

"Well—well."

"He has information."

"Has he *found* him?"

"Yes."

"Where, then, is he?"

"In the very house you tracked him to."

"Nonsense. I have not been deceived. That servant fellow is not Wild."

"Perhaps not; but Wild's in the house."

Bill Waters related with great precision the manner in which Clifford had been tricked by the Princess.

Paul stared in amazement.

Wherever Bill got his information from it was certainly very accurate, and Clifford could scarce credit that he had been so duped.

"It's been a neat thing," said Bill, "but the card we have played has about done 'em, and no mistake."

"And he is still in that house?"

"No."

"Where then?"

"At the Willows by this time."

"Their country house?"

"Yes."

"I must follow."

"Mind, its dangerous work follerin' lions into their dens."

"What care I? I have sworn to drag him to the scaffold, and all the danger in the world shall not baulk me. He shall die, and, come what will, my hands shall wind the noose about his throat."

"Oh, you're a good 'un," said Bill, looking at Clifford with great enthusiasm; "I always said you was a stunner, out and out; but it was a bad day for the pershun ven you gave it up and took to this mean business. By the king's big toe, if you vos after any other cove but that Wild, I'd never look yer in the face again; I couldn't do it—I couldn't upon my word."

"Enough! You tell me Wild is at this place you call the Willows. There I will follow him."

"And now I'll tell you something more: Wild has gone to the Willows with the Duchess of Lakemont."

"The Duchess of Lakemont?"

"Yes. I thought this would startle you."

WILD ATTACKED AT THE FOOT OF LUDGATE HILL

"Is this the truth?"

"True enough."

"Then why did you not tell me at first? The Duchess borne off by Wild! Heaven and earth! what can this possibly mean?"

"Come with me," said Bill; "I'll walk towards the stable with you, and then I'll explain how this affair came about."

Leaving Bill to satisfy Clifford, we will turn to the Duchess and see what had occurred to her.

*   *   *   *   *

On the advent of the Colonel, Wild felt more than ever inclined to rid himself of Paul Clifford.

He saw before him a life of profit—a career of brilliant exploits.

But Clifford, like a dark shadow, hung across his path and defied him.

He pondered day and night how he was to rid himself of this terrible enemy, but it appeared to him that Clifford was invulnerable.

He took Colonel Jack into his confidence, and related to him his own story and that of the highwayman.

Colonel Jack listened with attention to all Wild had to say, and when he ceased speaking shook his head gravely.

"It appears to me," he said, "that this fellow is not to be touched. Did it never strike you that you could render him powerless through a third party?"

"What do you mean?"

"Briefly this. You say he is either in love with or is beloved by the Duchess of Lakemont?"

"Yes."

"Well, she is easily reached, is she not?"

"I begin to see what you mean."

"I thought you would."

"Yes," cried Wild, springing to his feet, and gleaming like an amiable tiger down upon Colonel Jack; "yes, I see my way clear now. By Heaven, before to-morrow morning the Duchess of Lakemont shall be in my power!"

"Ho! ho! You are an apt scholar."

"Yes; I can take a hint as quickly as most persons, and I thank you for yours. Ah, my beautiful Duchess; by twelve to-night I will have you in my power."

"By twelve?"

"Yes. I know the house. I know its ways. At midnight I'll enter, and it's much if I don't secure the lady."

"Without assistance?"

"Yes; I must be alone in this business."

"Good."

The Colonel went his way, leaving Wild to mature his plans for the abduction of the Duchess.

"Yes," he cried; "if I get her down at the Willows I'll keep her there until I can either kill or subdue that devil."

*   *   *   *   *

An hour after Wild had arranged his plans, the following mysterious billet was placed in the hands of the Duchess:

"*A friend advises her grace the Duchess of Lakemont to absent herself from home to night, and place a strong body of officers in the apartments used by her grace, at midnight, as at that hour an impudent attempt will be made to carry off her grace, in order that Paul Clifford may be induced to abandon his oath to track to the death the murderer of his grace the late Duke.*"

The Duchess failed not to act upon this friendly though mysterious warning.

At dusk that evening she quitted her mansion, and proceeded towards Kew, to pass the night at her villa on the Thames, but she did not fail to give information to the authorities, and to demand that some officers might be placed in the house at midnight.

This precaution was, however, useless, for Wild had changed the hour of his attack from midnight to ten o'clock.

*   *   *   *   *

Now it happened that on this particular day there arrived at the mansion of the Duchess an old Scotch woman, a very distant cousin of her late husband, who, on coming once a year from her house in the Highlands to London, always invited herself to spend her brief season of dissipation at the house of her relative.

This was her first visit since the death of the Duke, and the old lady, always crabbed, was now positively unbearable.

She was full of complaints and running over with ailments, and nothing that the Duchess could possibly do added in the least to her comfort.

Driven to desperation, the Duchess had just made up her mind to abandon her house to this old woman during her stay in London, and seek some more enjoyable locale, when the mysterious billet was placed in her hands. Truth to tell, she was by no means loath to embrace this excuse for getting away.

It so chanced that Lady Bumbozen had, on her arrival, taken a strong fancy to the set of rooms occupied by the Duchess, and had had a serious tiff with that lady, in consequence of her having refused to resign the rooms to her.

On hearing from her maid that the Duchess had quitted the house for the night, the idea of taking forcible possession of her rooms came full upon the old lady.

She forthwith ordered her boxes to be taken to the bedchamber of the Duchess, and at nine o'clock retired to bed, gloating over the *coup d'etat* she had effected.

At ten she was aroused.

A well-dressed, soldier-like man was standing over her couch. It was very dark, and she could but barely catch sight of the glimmer of the lace on his coat.

In an instant a handkerchief was over her mouth. A few things were thrown about her person, and she was in the arms of the intruder.

"Hush!" cried Wild, for it was that worthy; "hush, or I'll cut your throat."

"What are you going to do with me?" groaned the poor old lady from beneath the voluminous folds of the handkerchief.

"Do with you," said Wild in a jeering tone; "I'm going to take you to see a dear young baron whose dying with love for you."

The old Scotchwoman was amazed.

A dear young baron in love with her.

This was a glorious sunshine, and she submitted to be carried off in perfect contentment.

She was half conscious of being hurried through passages into a coach, and then of dashing along the roads for some considerable time at a great pace.

At length the carriage stopped, and Wild sprang out and ordered her to alight.

They were at the Willows.

"Come," he cried, as he pulled her through the principal entrance of the old forsaken premises. "This is the way, and you will soon be under a roof."

"Stop!"

"No—no! I cannot stop now."

"Murder."

"Ah! have you come so far as this in partial submission to your fate, and are you so foolish as now to attempt to anger me, or to do any good to yourself by your cries?"

"I will go no further."

"Indeed?"

"No. I will know now who it is that is so fond of me."

Wild was a little staggered at this speech from the supposed Duchess, and he paused for a moment.

"It is possible," he thought, "that the sudden fright of my presence in her chamber has evidently turned her brain."

After the pause of a moment he said aloud—

"What did you mean by your last remark?"

"Just what I said, that is all. You are an officer."

"An officer?"

"Yes. I have caught a sufficient glimpse of your apparel to know that you are an officer in the army."

"Ah," thought Wild, "she does not recollect me, then, after all, but thinks me some very different person from what I am in reality. I will favour this idea. Hem! Yes, as you say, I am an officer."

"I know you are."

"But how came you to think that I, an officer, should mix myself up in this affair?"

"Oh, I don't know. You officers are such wild sort of people at times."

"Wild sort of people," thought Jonathan. "Is that a play upon the word Wild, and does she really know me, after all? Well—well, we will soon see when we get into the house."

"I can hardly make out," he said, "what you mean. But we will not converse further in the damp, open air. Follow me, and you will soon be free from it. The house is close at hand."

"What house?"

"Oh, it is the house of a gentleman, and is one of some size and distinction, I can assure you."

This explanation appeared to have some effect upon the prisoner, for she followed Jonathan with alacrity. He took his route exactly to the window by which he had, upon his former visit to that house, made good his entrance to it.

A very trifling amount of examination soon convinced him that the window remained in precisely the state in which he had left it, and that no one had had the curiosity during the brief interval that had elapsed between his first and his present visit to the Willows to come near the place.

"All is well," he said. "This way."

He opened the window sufficiently wide to let his prisoner come into the room; and then he thought that it would not b prudent to go further into the house before he indulged either himself or the Duchess with a light.

"Follow me," he said; "and you may do so in perfect confidence, as far as your safety is concerned. You are now under a roof, and I impart to you my assurances that I only keep you as a hostage for the good behaviour of another, with whom I hope, for your dear sake, to be able to make such terms as I will."

"Oh, indeed."

"Yes. It is not difficult for you to guess, of course, who that other is?"

"Yes, it is, though."

"Eh?"

"I say it is, though."

"Oh, impossible. You know who loves you better than all the world beside?"

"I only wish I did."

"You only wish you did?"

"Certainly. And I only hope you will be as good as your word, sir."

"As good as my word? Why, what on earth are you talking about?"

"About the promise by which you induced me to come away from London so quickly. You spoke of some young nobleman who was fondly attached to me; and what conclusion could I draw but that you were about to take me to him?"

Wild was puzzled.

"Listen to me," he said.

"Well, I do."

"What induces you to alter your voice so? Have you a cold?"

"A cold? No."

"Then, perhaps it is the handkerchief over your mouth that makes your voice sound so odd to me."

"Perhaps it is. I am reckoned to have a good Scotch tongue in my head."

"A what?"

"A good Scotch tongue in my head; and I rather think that will carry anybody all over the world."

"Good God!"

"Why, what is the matter now with the mon?"

Jonathan Wild felt cold at his very heart at a terrible idea that had come across him of the possibility that, after all his schemes and all his trouble, he had made some awful mistake.

Was it or was it not the young and beautiful Duchess that he had with him in the room at the Willows adjoining to that one which he had entered by the window from the lawn?

This question once arising required an instant solution, and he cried out, in frantic accents—

"Be still!—be still! Stir not, on your life, while I get a light!"

"Hoity-toity! what's the matter with the mon?" said the prisoner again. "Stir not on my life, indeed! What do you mean by that?"

Wild uttered a couple of terrible groans, and hastily felt in his pockets for the phosphorus matches he always carried about with him in a little tin box. He soon found them, and then, hastily igniting one, he produced, from another division of the same tin box, a bit of wax taper, which he stuck, by its own adhesive qualities, to the corner of the box, so as to form a kind of temporary candlestick.

Lighting the taper, he held it up in his hand, and glared at his prisoner.

It took both his hands, though, to get the silk handkerchief from her face, and so he placed the light upon the marble chimney-piece of the room, which he could now perceive was close at hand.

"I will soon come at the truth of this seeming mystery," he said. "Stand still."

In a moment he stripped the silk covering from off the head and face of his captive, and he saw the large coarse, repulsive features of a woman of some forty-five years of age or more, who evidently owed the colour on her nose to the rather liberal indulgence in ardent spirits.

Wild staggered back till he fairly reached the wall; there he stood glaring at the female he had taken so so much trouble to bring from London as if she had been some horrible apparition.

"What's the matter with the mon?" cried the prisoner. "Why what is he staring at?"

"At you—at you! The devil!"

"Go to the deuce, mon! What do you mean by that, I should like to know?"

"Woman! Witch!"

"Witch yourself, you bundle of ugliness and deformity, What do you mean by speaking to me in that way?"

"In the name of all that's abominable, who the devil are you?"

"Who am I?"

"Yes, who are you, woman?"

"Deeil, then, and you know well enough I am Lady Bumbozen, and I have got good Scotch blood in my veins, and a good Scotch tongue in my head."

"Wild nearly fell to the floor. He struck his head a blow with his clenched fist, as he cried—

"Oh, fool! fool! fool!"

"Well, I dare say you are a fool," said Lady Bumbozen.

"Beast! impostor! how came you here?"

"How came I here, you great bundle of dirty ugliness? You know well enough. Where is the young baron you said was dying in love with me? Let me ask you that, you brute. How dare you promise a lone woman a young baron, and then bring her here only to abuse her?"

The shrill tone of defiance in which our old acquaintance, Lady Bumbozen, spoke to Jonathan went through his head, and he merely looked at her for some few moments now in silence, during which he made vain efforts to collect his scattered thoughts.

At length he roared out—

"Silence! Silence, woman, or I will make you."

"You make me, indeed! Deeil, then, it would take a

great many like you to make me; and I should have mighty little spirit if I let you, you ugly-looking rascal."

"Fiend!"

"Fiend and Beelzebub yourself!" said Lady Bumbozen, advancing and clapping her hands together so close to Jonathan Wild's nose that he thought she had clawed it off.

For once Jonathan Wild had met with his match, and he staggered back in dismay.

"Deeil, then," said the lady, "I'll soon let you know who I am. To come into a lone and defenceless and delicate female's chamber, and to carry her off in this way, and then to do nothing in all the world but abuse her! It's a shame and a disgrace to you, mon, it is."

Clap went Lady Bumbozen's hands together again in such dangerous proximity to Jonathan's nose that he roared out at the top of his voice—

"Keep back, she-devil, or I will blow your brains out for you as sure as you are alive!"

He took a pistol from his pocket and pointed it at her, and that had the effect of frightening Lady Bumbozen a little, so that she retreated and said—

"And what have I done that you should threaten to take my life? I did not ask you to bring me here."

"I know it—I know it."

"Then what do you mean by it?"

"My brains are in a mist."

"Faith, then, I think they are."

"Stop—stop! I want an answer to some questions that I must put to you. How came you at the house of the Duchess?"

"How came I there? Why she's a friend of mine, you see, and so——"

"That will do: that is a sufficient answer to that part of the matter. And now how came you in the apartments that I am told were in the possession of the Duchess?"

"Eh?"

"I say, how came you there?"

"Is it possible? Well I never. Oh, the hussy!"

"What on earth do you mean by all that?"

"Now did you take me for that young hussy?"

"I took you for the Duchess of Lakemont."

"Eh? I see it all."

"So do I."

"Why what an escape you have had."

"Escape?"

"Yes; you might really have taken her, and instead here you have me, a respectable person of mature years, and with a good Scotch tongue in my head."

"Curse you! How came you in the room of the Duchess? that is what I want to know."

"Weel, she went out d'ye see, and when I heard, late at night, that she had left the house, I went and took possession of the room, you comprehend; and when you came and I saw you had the uniform of an officer, and you said that a young baron was dying in love with me, I came away with you willingly enough, as I was thinking for some time past of altering my state and taking a husband, and a young baron would do very well indeed, you see, now."

"Oh—oh—oh!"

"What do you mean by Oh, oh, oh?"

"Oh, horror!"

"What?"

"Here is a dreadful mistake. But I must be plain with this horrid old Scotchwoman."

"What?"

"Madam, I took you in mistake. I hate the sight of you! You are an emetic to me, and there is nobody in love with you, and nobody ever will be, unless, previously to that circumstance, he is a candidate for Bedlam; so you will be so good as to find your way back to London again by yourself, and as soon as you can conveniently."

"To London?"

"Yes, or to the devil for all I care."

"Mon!"

"Well—well?"

"I am here, and I mean to stay here till you bring me the young baron who is in love with me."

"There is no one in love with you, and I tell you that you are a useless encumbrance to me, and you must be got rid of in some way or another. If not by fair means, you must by foul. Do you comprehend that?"

"I comprehend that I am to get a husband."

"Then you won't get one."

"Yes, you must just marry me yourself."

"I?"

"And why not, pray? You are an officer, and so that will do very well; and I will introduce you to my forty-fifth cousin, the Laird of Coaldstairs, in the highlands."

"Go to the devil," cried Wild. "You are mad, madam. Will you be off?"

"No I won't then."

"Then I will take your life, and bury your body in the softest bed I can find in the garden—not that I care a straw about its being soft for you, but it will on that account be all the easier to me to dig a hole in."

There was an air of such calm and cool villany now about Wild that poor Lady Bumbozen began to think that he might be as good as his word. She, however, made but one last effort to move him.

"Eh, mon," she said, "only consider that if you have made a mistake, it is on the right side."

"As how?"

"Why, you might have got the brazen hussy in whose bed you found me, and that would ha' been a misfortune."

"To the devil with you!" roared Wild.

"I'll no stir a step."

"Then I will."

With this Wild took to his heels and fled.

*   *   *   *

Meanwhile a horseman had ridden hard from London.

He rode a dashing white mare, and was, to all intents and purposes, as dashing a cavalier as could be found on the road.

He arrived at the Willows soon after the carriage containing Wild and the ancient lady from the Highlands had entered the old house.

It was evident that he was a stranger in that locality, for he pulled up at the lodge of the old place and reconnoitred with the deepest attention.

After a while he dismounted, and approached the wretched hovel that did duty as the dwelling-place of the lodge-keeper, and knocked for admission.

"A carriage has not long since passed to your house," said Clifford, for it was our hero; "am I right?"

"Quite right," said an old man, who opened the door and peered at the stranger.

"Who were its occupants?"

"Henry Brownlow, the footman to Lady Harringcastle, and a dame whose face I did not see."

"Is the house tenanted?"

"No; my lady lives in London, and never comes down here now. There is only one servant in the house."

"Now listen to me," said Clifford, as he stepped over the threshold of the cottage; "that man is no other than the notorious criminal, Jonathan Wild, and I am here to effect his capture. The lady with whom you saw him was no other than the Duchess of Lakemont, whom he has forcibly brought to this place for reasons best known to himself. See here," he continued, producing a paper, and holding it up to the light, "this is the warrant for his apprehension, and I command you to assist me in my task."

"Lord deliver us!" cried the old man, clasping his hands, and looking at his wife, who had just joined him.

"And save us from all sinners," muttered the old dame, apparently frightened out of her wits.

"If you hesitate," said Clifford, "I shall have to apprehend you as aiders and abettors, so choose. There is a reward of £1,000 hanging over the head of this man, and if you act as I desire in this matter the money may fall into your pockets. The alternative is a cell in Newgate!"

"Don't mention it," said the old woman; "we take the £1,000 without hesitation."

"Very good. Now the first thing to do is to conceal my mare. Have you a convenient place?"

"There is no place but the cottage, and but one room in it, as you may see. Will you bring her in?"

"Yes. Brilliant will be quiet anywhere, and will cause you no disturbance."

"Quick, then."

"Come!" said Clifford, to his mare, and in an instant the beautiful creature followed him into the room.

"She must be concealed," continued Clifford, glancing about the room.

"Concealed! Save us, how will that be done?"

"Easily," said Clifford, and, turning to the mare, he pushed her gently into a corner, and bade her lay down.

With the docility of a trained dog she obeyed.

"Now," continued her master, addressing the lodge-keeper, "bring some faggots of wood and furze, and throw them upon her."

"And she will stand it?"

"She will lay as quietly as a lamb."

The old couple looked surprised, and hustled about to fulfil the order given them.

In less than a minute there was no trace of the white mare Brilliant.

"I am going towards the house," said Clifford, "and shall call to you if I require your assistance. Leave the door of the cottage open, or, on hearing my voice, Brilliant will beat it down. Now, remember my injunctions, and be wise and obey them."

The lodge-keeper promised obedience, trembling with excitement, watched Clifford, as he stepped forth in the moonlight, and walked deliberately up the avenue leading to the house.

He had not proceeded many paces when a turn in the path brought him suddenly face to face with the man he was seeking.

Wild was rushing from the hateful presence of the old Scotchwoman, and before he could bring himself to a standstill was in the arms of his deadly foe.

There was a mutual recognition in an instant, and swords were drawn as quick as lightning.

"Well met," cried Clifford; "now we will settle old scores."

Wild uttered not a word, but glared at his enemy with the look of a tiger.

He set his teeth firmly, and prepared to act on the defensive.

He well knew Clifford's skill as a swordsman, and dreaded the result of what he knew to be an unequal contest. Nevertheless, he trusted to fortune for the presentation of some chance by which he could obtain an advantage.

Their weapons met, and in a few moments they were thrusting and cutting with the malignity of fiends.

Clifford attacked, and Wild, with his heavy hanger, acted solely on the defensive. He made no effort to dash at his opponent, for he feared lest he should leave open his guard, and receive a mortal wound for his pains.

At length Clifford, by a marvellous turn of the wrist, wrenched the weapon of his antagonist from his grasp, and it fell at some distance from where they stood.

Wild's first impulse was to fly, but the next second he determined to stand his ground without flinching. He knew that Clifford's aim was *to take him alive,* and so he awaited the movements of his foe.

Clifford rushed upon him with the intention of beating him to the earth, but Wild, with cat-like agility, sprang on one side, and Clifford stumbled forward.

Next moment Wild's hand was on his throat, and his own sword at his breast.

"Help!" screamed Clifford, as his fearful position became apparent. "Help! help! The lodge, there, Brilliant!"

But before a hand could be raised in his defence Wild had thrust the sword through the ribs of the poor young fellow and had fled.

CHAPTER XLV.

THE PURSUIT—THE DRAFT PREPARED BY THE PRINCESS —AWFUL POSITION OF GENTLEMAN CLIFFORD.

As Wild rushed off a figure sprang from the bushes, and sent a couple of pistol bullets after him.

But without effect.

"Look to Clifford," cried the mysterious man who had thus suddenly appeared on the scene; "look to Clifford and his mare, and as to Wild. I will track him."

Another instant, and he was in full pursuit of the flying figure.

Wild sped with might and main towards London, and his pursuer stuck to him in a manner that proved the race would be an equal one.

*　　*　　*　　*　　*

But we must pause on the scene of the disaster that had befallen our hero.

With gentle care the lodge-keeper and his dame raised the bleeding and inanimate body, and bore it into the cottage.

Poor Brilliant followed, with her head bowed low, as if she fully understood the position of her unfortunate master.

"Poor gentleman," said the good dame, as she layed Clifford on her rough couch, "poor gentleman, how pale and ghastly he looks. I'm afraid it's all over with him."

"He do look mortal queer," said the man, pulling open the coat and waistcoat of the wounded man, and searching for the wound; "I never seed anything so death-like."

In a few moments the wound was laid bare, and an effort made to stay the bleeding.

Fortunately the sword had struck a rib, and had glanced off, making a triangular cut which, although deeply serious in its character, did not appear to have touched any vital part.

"I'll do the best I can for him," said the man "but thee had'st best run as hard as thee can to the nearest village and fetch a doctor, for this wound seems beyond my skill."

"I'll fly," said the old woman, throwing a hood over her head and running from the cottage; "I'll fly, Simon, but do 'ee try to save the poor gentleman. Lord-a-mercy! do but look at the poor white horse! I declare the poor brute do look quite as if it understood the peril of its master."

"It do, dame, it do; but don't 'ee stop to talk. Run as fast as thee legs will carry thee."

The dame ran from the cottage, and the lodge-keeper was alone with his patient.

By bandaging the man had contrived to check the great flow of blood, but he could not by all his rough efforts bring back animation to the poor broken frame before him.

Time passed but slowly, and he counted the hours before his wife could possibly return with the required aid, and feared lest, in the meanwhile, life should fly and leave him watching over a stark and bloody corpse.

But ere his wife had been one hour gone the sound of wheels fell upon his ear, and soon a carriage halted at the lodge gates.

The bell summoned him, and he went out.

Before him was his mistress, the German Princess, or

to give her the title by which he was known to him, Lady Belle Harringcastle.

"Oh, my lady," he cried, as his mistress dismounted and discharged the postilion, "oh, my lady such bloody doings ; such awful work."

"What mean you ?"

"I hardly know what I mean, but Mr. Brownlow, your ladyship's servant, or Jonathan Wild, as the stranger called him, came here a few hours ago in a carriage with a lady and conveyed her to the house, when up rides a handsome gentleman on a white mare, and declares Brownlow to be Jonathan Wild, and commands me to assist in his capture."

"Well," cried the Princess.

"Well, my lady. the gentleman goes up the avenue to find Brownlow, or Wild, which ever he may be, and in a minute we heard the clashing of swords and then a cry for help, and on reaching the spot found the gentleman bleeding to death, and Brownlow flying, with another man shooting at him and running after him as fast as his legs could carry him, and that's all."

"And did Brownlow escape ?"

"That I can't say."

But where is the man with whom he fought ?"

"In my poor cottage, my lady. Oh, such awful work ! That ever I should have lived to see such goings on at the Willows, where I've lived man and boy these forty years."

"Silence, and lead the way into your cottage ; let me see this man."

"Yes, my lady," said the man, and walking before her, and bowing her into the cottage : " yes my lady, this way, my lady."

The Princess entered and stood gazing for a few moments in deep silence at the form before her.

"You do not know who went in pursuit of Brownlow ?"

"No, my lady."

"Where is your wife ?"

"Gone for a surgeon, my lady."

"Humph! Was there any one but yourself and wife who beheld this riot ?"

"No my lady."

"I can't understand it," said the woman, appearing to be much perplexed ; "it is evident that some slight resemblance between Brownlow and Wild, the robber, has led to this *contretemps* ; for, of course, it is absurd to think that Wild and Brownlow are one and the same person."

"Just so, my lady."

"Brownlow I brought with me to England, so, of course, I can swear that he and Wild are two distinct individuals."

"Just as I thought, my lady, only the poor gentleman would be so certain."

"He must be mad !"

"Very mad, my lady."

"And so your wife has gone for a surgeon ?"

"For a surgeon, my lady."

"How long will she be ?"

"Another hour."

"Ha! Well, do you think you could carry this poor fellow ?"

"I'm sure, my lady."

"Well, take him in your arms and bear him to the house ; he must have a softer couch than that."

"You're very good, my lady."

"Yes ; now do not delay, my good fellow."

"I won't, my lady."

"Can you tell me where is the lady with whom my servants came here ?"

"She is in the house, my lady"

"Very good. Now, be careful of your brother, and follow me."

In a few minutes Clifford was laid on a couch in one of the gloomy apartments in the Willows, and the Princess seated herself by his side to enact the nurse, but not before she had found the apartment wherein sat the lady Bumbozen, and turned the key upon her.

    *   *   *   *   *

"Ha! Humph! Ha!" muttered the doctor, who had been sent for, as he viewed his patient. "Humph! Hem! Yes, just so !"

"What think you of him ?" demanded the Princess.

"Bad case, bad case, my dear Lady Harringcastle ; never saw a worse."

"Will he recover ?"

"Recover! my lady ? *I* am his doctor ; he must recover, although there's no hiding the fact of its being an ugly case. A duel ?"

"Yes, yes," said the Princess ; "a duel, I believe. I really do not know the sense of the matter. I arrived long after the affair had taken place."

"Bad job ; very bad job."

"Yes ; and one that, for my sake, must be kept as quiet as possible. The scandal—"

"Just so, madam ; the scandal—I comprehend. Although, on second thoughts, I do *not* comprehend ; for your servant said something about Jonathan Wild."

"Psha! A mad assertion. How could Jonathan Wild be *here*, fighting with my intimate friend the Count de Aramis ?"

"Just so ; absurd ! absurd !"

"What do you propose to do ?"

"I'll just bind up the wound, and leave a draught for him to take as soon as his eyes open. You will, perhaps, administer it yourself, for it's bad trusting to servants, and I regret that I cannot stay. In fact, I left the bedside of a lady in the interesting way to fly here. If you will leave the room, I'll do my task, and when I require your attendance, I'll call."

The task was soon completed, and the Princess resummoned.

"He will do now," said the doctor. "I fear nothing but inflammation, and that the draught will tend to allay. Be sure and give it him as soon as his eyes are open."

The doctor took his leave, and the Princess was alone with the wounded man.

"So," she said, "this draught is to save his life, is it ? Well, he shall have it ; but I may be excused if I mix with it a decoction of my own, the effect of which, I think, will startle the doctor."

So saying, she took a small cup from the table, poured therein the doctor's draught, and then let fall into it several drops of a liquid from a small red phial, which she drew from her bosom.

CHAPTER XLVI.

THE CAPTURE—THE TRIAL—THE SENTENCE—"YOU HAVE
NOT YET SEEN THE LAST OF JONATHAN WILD."

WILD led his pursuer an awful chase.

He bounded over the roads with the agility of an antelope, and slackened not his speed until he arrived in the suburbs of London.

It was then early morning, and there were a few persons moving in the streets, but Wild turned and took a glance at his pursuer.

He found the man rushing after him as if life and death depended upon his haste.

"So," said Wild, "this fellow hangs on like the bloodhound, but he must be beaten by cunning."

He started off again, and in about five minutes entered a hackney carriage, which he found rumbling along Cityward.

"Drive as if the devil was after you !" he cried, to the astonished coachman.

"Where?"

"To the Minories, or across Blackfriars—anywhere, as long as you baffle the fellow who is following me."

"And the reward?"

"Twenty pounds!"

"All right."

The coachman lashed his horse into a gallop, and then set about reaching the city by a circuitous route, calculated to baffle the pursuer, upon whom he kept his eye with the greatest vigilance.

They speeded on, and at length St. Paul's was reached. Here Wild put his head out of the window of the vehicle.

He saw that, at that moment, his pursuer had overtaken and engaged another hackney-coach, and well knew that now he was not to be shaken off.

Without hailing the coachman, he opened the door of his coach, and sprang lightly to the ground.

The act was, however, observed by the party in chase, and he performed a similar piece of dexterity.

At the same moment he discharged a pistol, and the report was answered on all sides by the rattles of the watch, and the officials of the old Fleet Prison, who rushed into the street to see what was the matter.

A glance sufficed to reveal the state of affairs.

They beheld Wild flying, and a man in hot pursuit.

They stationed themselves at the foot of Ludgate-hill, and Wild had no option but to face his foes.

He was defenceless, and they were at least five to one, but he hesitated not.

On he rushed, and in a few moments was in their midst.

Snatching a bludgeon from the hand of the nearest, he belaboured his assailants right and left, and in a few moments had mastered the whole gang.

They had done their best, but Wild appeared to be invulnerable, and their blows had no effect.

The whole of them lay writhing on the ground in the deepest anguish, and the desperate cut-throat was about to rush forward when another pistol report rang in the clear air, and the bullet lodged in Jonathan's shoulder.

With a yell of agony, he fell to the ground senseless.

Other watchmen came up, and the thief-taker was at length a prisoner.

But the man who had pursued him so unrelentingly— the being by whose hand he had fallen, was nowhere to be seen.

*   *   *   *   *

Next morning, Wild, weak and faint from loss of blood, was carried before a magistrate.

Without pausing, the functionary committed him to take his trial on the charges of murder and burglary, and thought it expedient that he should be tried at once, as his marvellous powers of evading punishment were well known and appreciated in the metropolis.

The sessions were on at the Old Bailey, and accordingly Wild was, within forty-eight hours of his capture, placed at the bar, to take his trial.

The court was, as might be anticipated, crowded to excess, and the interest in the case nothing short of intense.

Wild suffered acutely from the bullet wound in his shoulder, and was to all appearances unconscious of what was proceeding in the court.

The trial was a long and tedious one, but never once did Wild raise his head until after sentence of death had been passed upon him.

At the words:—"And may the Lord have mercy upon your soul," which were uttered in a deep and impressive voice by the judge, and then he stood up, sneered disdainfully at the bench, and cried in an insolent tone—

"Thanks for the prayer, my lord judge, but you might have kept it for those that stand in need of it; *I do not*, for *you have not yet seen the last of Jonathan Wild.*"

CHAPTER XLVII.

ON THE ROAD TO TYBURN.

St. Sepulchre's clock had just struck nine, and a drizzly shower was falling, as such a motley assemblage as London rarely saw turned from the Old Bailey into Snow-hill.

There was a party of mounted officers of police, with cutlasses in their hands, and formidable, thick holster-pistols stuck in their girdles.

One of the sheriffs of London, looking anything but delighted with the business he was upon, rode, pale and agitated, after the police, and then came a cart drawn by a thick-set, powerful horse, blind of one eye, and of very doubtful vision with the other.

By the stolid indifference with which this horse proceeded, despite a ringing shout that arose from the throats of about five thousand people, one might conclude that deafness likewise was among his infirmities.

By each side of the cart rode men armed to the teeth, and it was followed by another party of police, so that, take it for all in all, the escort was unusually strong.

But it is to the occupants of the cart that we would direct the most special attention.

First, there was a coffin with a double row of rather glaring white nails down each side of the lid.

It was placed right across the front part of the cart, so that its ends projected some half a foot each way, and it was a prominent object above the heads of the crowd.

In the cart was a brawny-looking, thick-set man, with red hair, without his coat.

His sleeves were tucked up, and he was in the act of lighting a short pipe as the cart turned out of the Old Bailey into Snow-hill.

That man was the public executioner.

He cared as little for the wild yelling of the mob as did the horse with the doubtful external senses.

With a prayer-book in his hands, and in full canonicals, the chaplain of Newgate steadied himself by one arm against the side of the cart, while, amid the din, he read some prayers to a man, who, if the truth must be told, paid more attention to the thousands of upturned faces around him than he did to the words of the divine.

That man stood in the middle of the flooring of the cart.

His hands were folded across his chest; he swayed gently to the movements of the cart, as a practised sailor might do upon the deck of his vessel to the pitching and tossing of the waves.

As we have said, the clock of St. Sepulchre's struck nine as this cortege hurried from the Old Bailey into Snow-hill, and slowly took its way towards Holborn.

The yell that the mob uttered was positively hideous.

It was on Monday, and Smithfield had poured forth all its crowds to witness the procession.

Field-lane, and the frightful rookeries beyond it, and upon each side of it to Gray's-inn-road on the one hand, and right away to St. Bartholomew's on the other, had supplied a strong force; and Fleet Market, too, had contributed its hundreds to swell the assemblage.

But, in addition to all these, parties had come from all parts of London and its suburbs to witness the march to Tyburn of one whose exploits had been in everybody's hearing.

St. Giles's had sent its swarms of the idle, the dissolute, and the dishonest, to make up the crowd; and by the time the head of the procession reached Holborn Bridge it was forced to come to a dead stand.

The yells and other cries, shouts, shrieks, and every variety of noise or execration which the human voice was capable of giving utterance to, now transcended all description.

The officers pressed more closely round the cart.

The clergyman dropped his book in trepidation, and the hangman withdrew his pipe from his mouth.

The prisoner stood with his arms still folded across his breast, unmoved, or apparently unmoved, by all the riot and racket that was taking place around him.

That man was Jonathan Wild.

He was on his way to Tyburn.

" Push on," cried the sheriff, turning almost a shade paler than was the prisoner who was to be taken to death. " Push on—this won't do."

The man who had the care of the horse was on foot, and now that he saw the sheriff was determined to make way he proceeded to use his whip; and holding the horse by the bridle, the cavalcade again moved on slowly through the throng of people up Holborn-hill.

The mounted officers used their cutlasses flatwise; and after something of a scuffle with the more forward of the crowd, and some half-dozen broken heads, a way was cleared, and the cavalcade moved slowly past St. Andrew's Church.

The most ticklish spot was now considered to be past; for it was where Field-lane on the one side, and Fleet Market on the other, sent forth their streams of rabble, that the officers feared that an attack on the prisoner would take place.

That something of the sort was apprehended was sufficiently evidenced by the unusual strength of the police force sent with the party on the occasion.

The mob now appeared to be more inclined upon cheering the prisoner on his route to death than upon stoning him.

It is rather a remarkable circumstance that in not one solitary instance did the immense mobs collected upon the occasion of popular favourites being taken to death at Tyburn really rescue any one; and yet in twenty cases, at the least, the populace assembled in force enough to have walked over the escort.

" Keep up," cried one.

" A stout heart, old feller," would shout another.

" Not dead yet," screamed a third.

And with such like cries and vociferations ringing in the air, and occasionally some immense shout at nobody knew what, the procession reached the head of Gray's-inn-road, then as now anything but a very choice thoroughfare, although, then as now, from its situation it might have been made one of the best outlets from Holborn.

At this point the mob acquired fresh power, for some three or four hundred people were stationed at the head of Gray's-in-road to join the procession, and another stoppage took place as they all made a rush to take the lead of the dense throng that had accompanied Wild and his guards from the City.

One of the horses belonging to the officer fell, and, instead of helping the man to rise, the mob rolled over him and a *melee* began, that at one time threatened to be of rather a fearful character.

The screams of women and children, the shouts and outcries of men, and the clatter of the horses' feet made up such a medley of sounds that was fearful to listen to.

By a vigorous charge, heedless of the amount of mischief they did, the officers brought off their comrade from amid the mob, but his clothes were torn to tatters, and he had been so mauled that they were fain to place him in the cart, where he lay upon his back looking much more like a fitting candidate for the coffin than Wild.

" Oh, this is very dreadful," said the clergyman to the condemned man. " You ought to feel that it is you who are the real author of all this riot and mischief, and it is truly shocking to find you so hard of heart, even yet, when you are at each step approaching death."

Wild waved his hand and slightly smiled.

The mob did not know what it was at, but they saw the action, and raised a shout of—

" Bravo, Wild! Hurrah—hurrah!"

It was in the lull after this ringing shout—such a lull that was sure to follow it—when every one who had joined his breath to it as if stopped to rest from the exertion that one clear note from a bugle horn struck upon the ear.

Nobody knew where this note came from, and yet every one heard it, and looked around for the author of the sound; but the effect that it produced upon Wild was manifest to all.

The moment the sound of the bugle struck upon his ear, a vivid flush came over his previously pale face, and his eyes lighted up with a brilliancy that, for a moment, was dazzling.

It was only for a moment, though, that the condemned man suffered any one to see how deeply he was interested in the bugle note.

" What's the meaning of that ?" said the sheriff to the officer who rode the nearest to him.

" I don't know, sir, but I don't like it. It sounds like a signal of some sort."

" A signal ? Then it can only be a signal that Wild is going to be hanged at Tyburn."

" I hope so, sir."

" You hope so ? Well, that is a good idea, when you see him the cart, Mr. Officer. There will be no attempt at rescue, much as it was threatened by I don't know how many letters to Newgate. People who mean to embark in such a course don't look so much beforehand."

The officer grinned acquiescence in the sentiment, and then with a nod, he said—

" If they try on anything, sir, it will be by St. Giles's Church, but it ain't at all likely."

" Certainly not. Now, come on quicker, will you, there, with the cart. Are we to be all day reaching Tyburn ?"

A groan from the mob, levelled at the sheriff, showed how they appreciated his services on the occasion; and a pebble was thrown into the cart, and struck the executioner on the arm.

" Ten guineas reward for the man who threw that," cried the sheriff.

" How much for the woman ?" cried a shrieking female voice in the crowd.

This produced a roar of laughter at the expense of the sheriff, who, although he thought he actually saw the virago from whence the words came, did not deem it prudent to attempt her capture, but upon the maxim of always finishing the business you have on hand first, before you begin anything else, he rode on now in gloomy anger.

The appearance of Wild now was rather strange.

He had again, after his brief gesture to the chaplain, by way of reply to his exhortation, folded his arms across his chest, but although he kept his head rather down, it was tolerably evident that he was scanning the outskirts of the crowd with rather a keen eye.

The officers who were upon the watch for his slightest movement did not fail to notice the change of demeanour, but what it portended they had no possible means of guessing.

Contrary, however, to all supposition upon that point the cavalcade passed through St. Giles's without any demonstration in favour of the prisoner, beyond the usual yelling and shouting which had acccompanied him all the way from Newgate; and when once the procession had turned into Oxford-street it got on at a much better pace, for the majority of the mob, feeling now apparently convinced that the execution would really take place without any doubt, set off at a race, to get to the place appointed by Tyburn-gate, and secure the best place before the prisoner could arrive.

" Well, Wild," said the hangman, " it's all up with you, I take it now; I hope you won't feel any malice, as you go out of the world, to a poor fellow who only does his duty. You know, if I didn't do the job, there's plenty that would."

AN ENEMY IN THE CAMP.

"Wait till it's done," said Wild.

"Wait till it's done ? Umph ! it won't matter, I take it then, Jonathan."

"Silence !" said the chaplain. "How dare you, at such a time as this, indulge in unseemly talk ?"

"There it is again," cried the sheriff, as once more the bugle sounded on the damp morning air, for the rain still fell. "There it is, again ! Where did that sound come from ?"

This time Wild just caught his breath at the moment, and then he subdued every appearance of unwonted emotion, and looked calmly around him as though he was as much puzzled as any one to know where the bugle sound came from.

The officers looked rather perplexed, but, although they raised themselves in their stirrups and took long and wistful glances about them, they could not see any one who seemed at all likely to have made the sound.

"There's more in this than meets the eye, or the ear either, sir," said one of the mounted men to the sheriff.

"Ah, what does it mean ?"

"Why, I don't know, sir."

"Indeed ; I could have told you as much as that ; but pass the word among your comrades for them to look to their pistols. I don't know yet what may happen, but this I do know, that if Wild sees twelve o'clock again in this world, I will never ride as sheriff to a hanging again."

"What will you take for the bay horse ?" said Wild, as he looked calmly in the sheriff's face, for the speech of that functionary was addressed to him.

"This horse, do you mean ?"

"Yes, to be sure, Mr. Sheriff, for if you never ride to a hanging again I don't at all see what you want with him."

The sheriff shook his head.

"You carry it off boldly," he said, "my fine fellow; but perhaps when you get a hempen cravat round your neck, instead of that silken one, perhaps we shall hear you sing a different tune."

"Don't make too sure of that, Mr. Sheriff," said Wild. "Over-confidence is the ruin of many."

"Well, we shall see. Just look ahead, Wild, and tell me what you can see now."

Jonathan did not look ahead. He knew quite well to what the sheriff alluded without looking at all; but he said, with something of a heightened colour—

"I know well that from first to last, from my capture to my condemnation, I have had your bad word; and I don't know why, for I never took a pennypiece from you or yours. I am of a forgiving disposition, Mr. Sheriff, but there are times and seasons when people go a trifle too far with me. Mind you don't do so."

"That for your times and seasons!" said the sheriff, as he snapped his fingers close to Wild's face. "I don't mean to deny but that you are a daring rascal, and that if you and I were on Hounslow Heath I should pay some attention to what you might say; but your career is over now. Look about you, and take a last glance at London."

"Very good," said Wild.

"Ha, ha! it is very good. Push on, will you, with the horse there! What do you mean by crawling in such a way, sir?"

The man who had charge of the horse's head was one of the under-turnkeys of Newgate, or probably he might not have taken the rough reproofs of the sheriff quite so meekly as he did.

As it was, however, he gave the horse two or three savage cuts with the whip, and the whole cavalcade went on at a kind of trot that was so distressing to the chaplain that he was fain to call out that it should be moderated to a walk again, which was done accordingly.

Notwithstanding that a great portion of the crowd had certainly gone on in advance of the cart, yet the mob that followed it, and still surrounded it, was very great.

Itinerant ballad singers chanted quite close to the officers the exploits of Wild in verse, and one mendicant, in stentorian accents, had the gross impertinence to offer, for one halfpenny, his dying speech and confession, which certainly was, upon the whole, rather a premature production.

From Soho a great throng, too, joined the procession, that neighbourhood being then, as it is now, not very choice in its morals; so that, by the time the gallows had actually appeared in sight, towering above the densely-packed throng of persons who surrounded it, there were as many people accompanying the procession as there were waiting for it by Tyburn Gate.

Perhaps, even with all his courage, Wild did not like the sight of the gallows, for he resolutely kept his back to the horse, so that he saw nothing of it until one tremendous shout from the dense crowd around it warned him that he must be close at hand to it.

He then turned with a sharp jerk, and faced it.

"All's right," cried the sheriff. "Clear the way, officers—clear the way for the cart! In good time, too."

The sheriff looked at his watch, and gave a grim sort of smile, for he did not now entertain the shadow of a doubt of the execution taking place according to arrangement.

Wild's face was now a little flushed, and he had never in all his life looked so decidedly jolly as he did at that moment when death appeared to be before him, and when every one in that vast assemblage fully believed that it would have been no great effort of arithmetic to have counted his mortal life in minutes.

The officers who were foremost made themselves into a kind of compact wedge, and began to fight and push a path for the horse and cart through the closely-packed throng of people.

It seemed marvellous how, by any possible amount of violence, a passage could be at all procured for the cavalcade; but it was, after a time, so procured, and at the expense of fewer broken heads than any one would have supposed.

A mob, after being squeezed as tightly as you would fancy it possible for it to go, will yet bear a little more compression; and so, in a tortuous way, Wild was led to the spot where so many had perished before him.

The vociferations of the people were perfectly deafening during the slow progress of the cart.

Some called upon him to die game; others shouted, they knew not why, but that they had heard the saying somewhere, that he was worth fifty dead ones yet; and one or two stones that were thrown at the police gave some indication that there were many in the crowd who only wanted a little egging on to make a regular riot of it.

The officers who were struck began to handle their pistols, but the sheriff cried out to them—

"Wait a bit, my lads—wait a bit. Let us get business over first, and then, perhaps, we may not take things quite so easy."

The officers understood him, and nodded their satisfaction at the idea of having a gallop among the mob after the execution was over, which they fully understood, from the manner of the sheriff, that they were to be indulged with.

Another minute, and the cart halted under the gallows.

With an adroitness that practice and a total heedlessness of the consequences to any one might be in the way had given them, the officers now, with their drawn cutlasses, formed round the cart and the gallows, and the last hour of Wild appeared to have arrived.

The hangman rose up, and from round his waist proceeded to uncoil the rope which was to do the work of death, and the chaplain, with his hand upon Jonathan's arm, earnestly spoke to him.

"Let us all hope, now," he said, "you hardened sinner, that you will see the error of your ways, and repent before it be too late. You now stand upon the brink of that eternity into which, when you have plunged, you will find—"

"Yes," said Wild, "I know all that, but do you think you can reconcile a man to death by such talking? I tell you, as I told the judge when he condemned me to death—and he was well pleased to do it—that, although I was guilty of many things, I was innocent of the charge that I was condemned upon."

"Oh, do not say that, you hardened man!"

"Indeed! Why not?"

"Because the law has decided otherwise."

"Oh! and so the law makes facts, does it? Well, I never knew of that before. But, come, I dare say, now, that in your way you mean well by exhorting me as you do, so I thank you for it, and if I must die, I die in peace with all men."

"That is something," said the chaplain; "but it is nothing unless you die in the faith of the Established Church, by law set up, and kept up, in this country."

"Come, come," said the sheriff, "all is ready."

"Die game, Wild!" shouted a voice from the crowd. "Give him a cheer, lads, and let him go off with it in his ears. Hip—hip—hip—hurrah! One cheer more for Wild! Hurrah!"

Amid the deafening roar of the people the hangman intimated, by holding up one end of the rope to the sheriff, that he was quite ready for his part of the job.

The other end he had fastened fairly to the cross beam of the gallows, and, by hanging his whole weight upon it for a moment, had satisfied himself that it was firm.

The mob saw these proceedings of the executioner,

and began groaning at him, while various peices of friendly advice were shouted to him as to the best mode of testing the strength of the rope.

" Put your neck in it, old boy," cried one, " and we will pull your legs."

" Try it yourself," said another, " and hang the consequences."

" Let's hang the sheriff," said a third.

This suggestion was greeted with a roar of laughter, but the sheriff did not seem at all to see the fun of it. He looked scowlingly about him, and muttered—

" Just wait till this job is over, my fine fellows, that's all, and maybe you will get a kick or two from the horse's heels."

Wild was evidently, with some anxiety, looking far away towards the outskirts of the crowd. There was now upon his face an aspect of intense expectation ; but what it could mean, no one but himself had the least idea, or could hazard the smallest conjecture.

" Now, Mr. Executioner," said the sheriff, " what are you waiting for ?"

" For me," cried Wild. " You surely don't want to hang a man out of the world so quickly ! I believe it is usual to let a poor fellow say a few words of warning to the people before you turn him off ?"

" Oh, pho ! pho ! what can you want to say ?"

" That's quite impossible for you to know, till you hear me, Mr. Sheriff. Of course, I shall do what's right. But I never heard of a poor fellow being turned off at Tyburn till he had had his say."

" Be quick, then, about it. You set yourself up for a brave man, but it seems to me that you wish to keep out of the noose as long as you possibly can, at any rate, Wild."

" Which is very wonderful," said Wild. " I believe you intend to do the same thing."

" The same thing ? What do you mean ?"

" Why, keep out of the noose as long as you can. Is that to be made a matter to stare at, eh ? But get out of the way, Mr. Jack Ketch. If this is to be my last hour, let me say my say to those who have come to see me die."

" The hangman shrank back to the other side of the cart, and Wild, with one foot upon its edge, looked at the sea of heads before him, and held up his hand as an indication that he was going to speak. For some few moments the most uproarious demands for silence were made in every variety of tone.

" Hats off !" cried a hundred voices. " Hear—hear ! Bravo ! Wild ! Hold your row ! Stop that fellow's bawling ! Go it, Jonathan ! Hurrah !"

These, and a thousand other discordant noises, made up such a tumult that it was some minutes before Wild began to speak ; but when he did, the great anxiety to hear him kept the multitude tolerably quiet, and it was a strange sight to see the man who was waiting for death addressing that enormous mass of people, who, with one movement, could have saved him, and who really did wish to save him, but for want of some directing hand remained inert.

In a loud, clear voice Wild spoke, and to the furthermost margin of the crowd, now, every word he said was audible.

" Friends all—you have come here to see me die. I can't say how much obliged to you I am for the compliment, but I know it is not to see a man take leave of his breath that you crowd round the gallows, but it is to have a last look at Jonathan Wild, whose name is familiar to you all."

" Bravo !" yelled the mob.

" Bring him away !" cried the sheriff. This won't do."

" Hold yet a moment," said Wild, " I am going to confess."

" He says he is going to confess," said the chaplain. " Let him do that."

Go on—go on ! Let him go on !" shrieked the mob.

Wild raised his hand, and all was still again.

" I confess," added Wild. " I confess, my good and kind friends, that many a time I have robbed to the utmost your oppressors."

" Hurrah !—Hurrah !"

" Proceed with the execution," said the chaplain. " I now very plainly perceive that this man is quite incorrigible. Proceed at once with the execution."

" Nay, hear me out," said Wild. " I have a friend in Parliament, who was to make an application to the Secretary of State, to get me a pardon."

" What ?" cried the sheriff.

" A pardon. Don't you understand what that is ?"

" Yes, Mr. Wild, I do. But if the Secretary of State pardon's you, I'll eat the gallows, that's all, my fine fellow. I won't hear any more of this. Swing him off. Let there be an end of the affair. I tell you, Wild, this is your last minute. It's of no use your dallying with your fate. This is what you and such as you, know well, you must all come to sooner or later."

" Hold !" said Wild, " you will let me finish my speech, and after that who knows but I may be inclined to listen to what the chaplain has to say for a few minutes or so."

" Obdurate man, !" said the chaplain ; " you have had the most complete opportunity of listening to me, and you never would profit in any way by my exhortations. Now, I very much doubt your sincerity, and would rather not have any more to say to you.

" Come—come, that's not Christian-like, said Wild. " I confess, as I tell you, to many crimes, but not to the one of which I have been tried and found guilty ; so I naturally object to being hanged upon that account. Fair play, you know, is a jewel, and ——"

The hangman, now, in obedience to a signal from the sheriff, laid hold of Wild by the arms, and proceeded to place them behind his back so as to tie his hands together, but the highwayman resisted, and suddenly turning upon the hangman, he, with the greatest ease, tilted him out of the cart. Half-a-dozen officers sprang upon Wild in a moment, and prevented him from taking any sort of advantage, if he had attempted to do so, of the temporary defeat of the hangman.

" Hold him !" cried the sheriff, " hold him tight! This comes of bringing a prisoner to Tyburn unpinioned ; but my colleague would needs have it so, to show that we were not afraid of him. Hold him tight my men. Don't shoot him. Don't kill him. Hanged he came to be, and hanged he shall be."

At that moment it is likely enough that if any leader had started up in the mob, such was the state of popular excitement, that Wild would have been rescued ; but although the dense mass of people swayed to and fro, and groaned and hissed and yelled their disapprobation of the proceedings of the authorities, not one hand was actually raised to resist them.

The hangman was severely bruised by his fall, and with a face as pale as death, save where a streak of blood from a wound on the left temple came across it, he was helped into the cart again by the officers.

He shook so, that it was quite evident he was, for the next few moments, incapable of performing his repulsive functions.

The roaring yell with which he was greeted, too, by the people, seemed for the first time to appal him, and he shrunk back while his lips moved convulsively.

" To your work," said the sheriff. " What are you afraid of a yelping rabble ? Pho ! pho ! man, to your work. They have all come to see the hanging, and if it were not to take place, they would be as much disappointed as we should about it."

Thus encouraged, the hangman plucked up a little courage ; and as the officers kept a firm hold of Wild, and such another tumble as he, the hangman, had had was not likely to ensue, he pounced upon his victim with a savage earnestness.

"That's the way to do it," cried the sheriff. "Now you will have him. All's right. How do you feel now, Wild."

The very lips of the highwayman were white now, and he did not reply to the sheriff's taunt. His eyes were wandering far away over the outskirts of the mob. Every eye in that vast assemblage was fixed upon the scaffold. The cord that was to tie the condemned one's wrists was in the hands of the executioner, when the crowd suddenly heaved and swayed to and fro like the ocean in a storm, and far off appeared a horseman, with something white fluttering at the end of a stick. Then, with a voice that had a most startling effect, the multitude shouted out—

"A reprieve!"

CHAPTER XLVIII.

RESCUED!

WITH what a pleasant tingle that one word, reprieve, came upon the ear of Wild.

Had he expected it?

Yes; but the time had gone past when he thought it would be there, and despair had begun to settle round his heart; but when he heard the joyous shout of the mob new life appeared to get possession of his frame, and the warm blood darted to his cheeks and lips again.

"A reprieve! a reprieve!"

"Hurrah!" cried Wild. "Didn't I say it would come?"

"It has not come yet," said the sheriff.

"A reprieve! a reprieve!" still shouted the people—and all eyes were bent upon the horseman, who was making his way through the crowd as best he could, carrying a white handkerchief at the end of his riding-whip.

The people made way for him right and left, and many a voice greeted him as he came along with words of congratulation and welcome.

"A little more," cried one, "and you would have been too late."

"I couldn't help it," he said. "I had a fall from my horse, and that delayed me ten minutes. I am bruised and hurt, but I am in time, after all, and Wild is saved this time."

"Where do you come from, old fellow?" cried another of the mob to the man who bore the white handkerchief, as the horse nearly trod upon his toes.

"From the Secretary of State's office," he replied.

"Hurrah! Hip—hip—hurrah!"

What a ringing shout it was that the people set up, and how the sheriff bit his lip, as the man on horseback came nearer and yet nearer to the scaffold, and waved the white emblem of peace and of mercy.

The executioner looked amazed.

The chaplain shut up his book, and with an abstracted jerk of his head, as much as to say, "Who would have thought it?" waited to hear what would happen next.

The sheriff raised himself in his stirrups, and looked rather angrily at the man who came with such a word as reprieve in his mouth for a condemned highwayman.

"I thought it all along," said Wild. "I knew I had some friends at court, who would not let me die like a dog, without a struggle. It is a reprieve, after all."

"If it really is," said the sheriff, as he pointed to the cord that dangled from the beam, "that is cheated of its due."

"Thank you, Mr. Sheriff," said Wild, as he bent his brows for a moment upon the man in authority. "You have pursued me in all this affair with a relentless rigour that you might have left alone; you have said things of

me, and to me, that had been quite as well unsaid. You and I may meet again."

"Yes, I hope so—upon another such occasion as this, Wild."

"We shall see," said Jonathan.

The man on horseback reached the foot of the gallows.

He was dressed in a suit quite in the prevailing fashion. His own hair, which was of a handsome brown, hung in curls down upon his shoulders, and, but for a certain white and red kind of complexion, that was not very manly, he looked like a young man who might be supposed to hold a clerkship in the Secretary of State's, or any other public office.

"Well, sir?" said the sheriff sharply, when the horseman came within speaking distance. "Well, sir?"

"Oh, yes," said the horseman, speaking, and displaying as he did a brilliant set of white teeth. "It is quite well. Wild, you are reprieved."

"How do we know that, sir," said the sheriff.

"Oh, I have a letter addressed to Thomas May, Sheriff of the City of London, Esquire. I had it—where can it be? I am sure I had it here, somewhere. It is from the Secretary of State himself. It was here, somewhere—oh, in this pocket—no, in my hat—no—"

"Oh, this is too absurd—this is a cheat. You have no letter, sir. Officers, take this person into custody, and let the execution proceed."

A startling yell from the mob followed these words, and the sheriff looked rather alarmed.

"Ha, ha!" said the young handsome horseman, displaying all his brilliant teeth again right in the face of the frowning sheriff. "Here it is—here it is, after all. I knew I had it somewhere; but when I found I was late, you see, I slipped it into the first pocket I could get at, and hoisted the white flag at the end of my riding-cane."

As he said this the young horseman handed to the sheriff an epistle, upon which there was rather a massive seal.

The sheriff took it with evident reluctance.

He had begun to hope that the letter either really had no existence, or was lost by the carelessness of its bearer.

"Who are you?" said the sheriff, holding the letter in his hand, and feeling angry to recognise the proper seal of the Secretary of State's office upon it. "Who are you?"

"Oh, I'm a clerk in the place; so when they wanted some one to mount and be off with the reprieve, I offered, and here I am."

"Bravo!" shouted the mob. "Bravo! You are a fine fellow! Bravo! Three cheers for the young clerk! Hurrah! Hurrah! Hurrah!"

"Oh, indeed," said the sheriff; "you have made yourself very busy—very busy indeed, young man. I shall remember you, I am sure. Umph! Let me see. Perhaps this is a mistake, after all."

The sheriff dashed open the letter, and read, in a mumbling voice, the following brief announcement of Wild's pardon. Every word was like a blow to him, he had so set his mind upon Wild's execution:—

"Sir,—

"I have to inform you that his Majesty is graciously pleased to grant a reprieve, during his royal pleasure, to Jonathan Wild, convicted of murder and burglary, and to request that you will cause the said Jonathan Wild to be forthwith liberated from custody.

"I am,

"Sir,

"Your obedient servant,

"LAWRENGE TOTTERLY."

The sheriff turned the letter over and over two or three times. It seemed as if he hoped to find in some obscure corner a postscript that might contradict the substance of the epistle. He even held it up to the light, and looked through it; but there it was, staring him in the face, a reprieve, signed by Sir Lawrence Totterly, Secretary of State for the Home Department, and there was the clerk with the fine teeth. The sheriff bit his lips, till the yelling of the people aroused him to a sense of his position.

"Oh, very well," he then said, in a high, cracked tone of voice. "Very well: it is nothing to me. He is reprieved. Of course the Secretary of State can set him up again. Ha, ha! It's no business of mine—none in the least. Ha, ha!"

"It's funny, though, ain't it?" said the young clerk. Ha, ha!"

"Oh, very," cried Wild. "Ha, ha!"

How the mob roared again. The sheriff dashed the letter into the breast-pocket of his riding coat, and cried out—

"Come back to Newgate, then, Wild, and you will be released in due form. Close round him, officers, and bring him back.'

"I beg your pardon, Mr. Sheriff," said Wild. "I am reprieved, and I don't intend to go back to Newgate at all. The Secretary of State has sent me the King's pardon; and who will drag a man back to prison, when the King has said let him be free, I should like to know?"

"But you shall come back," roared the sheriff, glad of some point upon which to vent the rage that he dared not launch forth at the letter of the Secretary of State. "You shall, I say. There are certain forms to be gone through, before any malefactor, pardoned or not, can leave Newgate, and you shall go through them."

The clerk turned to the mob.

"Oh, is not this too bad!" he cried. "Here I have brought Wild his pardon, and yet the sheriff wants to drag him back to Newgate again. It's a shame and a disgrace, it is, to the poor fellow. Has he not suffered enough already, I should like to know?"

"He shan't go back!" cried a stentorian voice among the crowd, and the sentiment was immediately echoed by a thousand.

"He shall!" shrieked the sheriff, and he made a dart at Wild's arm, but the reprieved man eluded him; and then, by one impulse, the mob made a rush forward, and cart, and gallows, and officers, and sheriff were all whirled along in mad confusion, and, in the course of a few minutes, were inextricably mixed up with the crowd.

It was in vain that the officers tried to rally and to get together.

The fate of two or three who struck at the people, and who were on the moment dragged from their horses and trampled under foot, was a warning to the others.

As for the sheriff, he kept bawling out—

"Let him go!—let him go! I wash my hands of the affair! Let him go!—I don't hinder him! Do you want to murder a man for trying to do his duty? Clear away, there!—clear away!"

The sheriff was really in such an agony to be off, now, and to escape from the fury of the people, that his air and manner were completely altered.

His face got red and white by turns, and at times there is very little doubt but that he gave himself up as a lost sheriff.

"Let's hang the sheriff!" shouted a voice.

It's a good thing that the voice was rather a comical-toned one and made the people laugh, or else, in the wayward humour of the mob, who shall say what might have been the consequences of such a startling suggestion?

As it was it only chanced to be greeted by laugther, and the sheriff, whose heart had sunk within him as the words fell upon his ears, plucked up a little courage, and made a wretched effort to join in the general laugh.

"Oh, it is very funny—very!" he said. "Allow me to pass, good people. You know I am here only because I am obliged, and that this is one of the most decidedly disagreeable duties of my office."

The people seemed more inclined to have some sport

with the sheriff's fears than to do him any real injury; but it is to Wild and the young man who had brought the reprieve that we would now draw attention, as they behaved in a very odd way.

When the rush of the people was made, and the cart, and the gallows, and the officers, and the sheriff, were all swept along in the general *melee*, the horseman who had brought the pardon kept close to Wild, and cried out to him—

"Jump on the horse, Jonathan! — jump on the horse! All's right. That will do!"

Wild had only just time to spring upon the back of the horse as the cart was carried away, and the mob, seeing how very kind the young clerk from the Secretary of State's office was to the reprieved man, were quite enraptured with him, and cheered him wonderfully.

It was then seen that Wild laid hold of the good-looking clerk's hand, and was shaking it furiously, while the clerk showed all his white teeth, and looked as pleased as possible.

"That's the thing!" cried the people. "Take him away! Hurrah! That's right!"

"Thank you," said the clerk. "I pray you make way for the horse. You know, for you have seen as much, that the sheriff and the officers don't like this affair at all; and if they should get any assistance Wild might still be dragged to a prison. Let us get clear, now—oh, do!"

Upon this appeal the vast throng opened to let the horse make its way through it, and what a magnificent creature was that horse!

It was of the darkest bay that you could imagine, and its coat was as glossy as satin itself. In its action there was a majesty and gentleness that was surprising; and, although hemmed in by such thousands of faces, it showed no alarm. It carried the two persons upon its back—Wild and his deliverer—with the greatest ease.

But now the people were rather surprised to see the young clerk from the Secretary of State's office surrender up the reins of the horse to Wild, who, stretching his arms past the clerk's, took them, and guided the horse onwards.

Ever and anon the glittering smile would come across the face of the handsome young clerk, and there could be no mistake at all about his being well pleased with the aspect of affairs.

It was towards the Edgware-road that Wild now urged the horse, and at each step that it took the crowd got thinner and thinner, and he was still further away from the authorities, who yet might make an attempt to rally and attack him.

If the constables had but kept together in a compact body they would, no doubt, have been able to resist the people; but the sudden rush of the mob had been so totally unexpected that they had got scattered, and were perfectly helpless before they knew exactly what was going on.

That they would endeavour to retrieve their position was probable enough.

But now Wild and the young clerk had got quite to the straggling to the outskirts of the crowd by the Edgware-road, and then, as he glanced behind him, and saw how far off he was from the officers, he cried—

"Saved!—I am saved!"

"Yes, Wild," said the young clerk. "Yes, you are saved; and did I not say that I would save you."

"Make way!—make way!" cried a voice. "Down with everybody who opposes you! Push on!—push on!"

Shrieks, and cries, and groans, began to issue from the mob, towards the right of where Wild had paused for a moment, and, upon casting his eyes in the direction, he saw three mounted officers, with their drawn cutlasses in their hands, making towards him, and recklessly cutting down every one who opposed their progress.

"It won't do, Wild," cried one of them. "You are our prisoner, and we will have you now. Clear the way, there!"

"Perhaps you will wait till you have got me," said Wild.

"And some time after that!" cried the young clerk, as, plunging his right hand back into the breast of his apparel, he produced a pair of pistols, one of which he handed to Wild.

Upon this sight, for the officers were not twenty paces from them, and saw it well enough, one of them cried—

"It's a take in! Fire upon them both!—fire upon them!"

"No—no!" cried Wild. "Cowards!—no!"

The people then saw how he swayed himself in the saddle so as, as much as possible, to cover the young clerk from the shot if any should be fired at them, and at the same moment he gave the horse an impulse forward, and off it went at a tremendous gallop up the Edgware road.

Two of the officers fired after him, but the shots were far too much by random ones to be of any effect.

The officers, however, cleared the way for themselves, and in another moment off they went in pursuit of the fugitives.

The people seemed to have a pretty good idea as to the capabilities of Wild's horse, and to make up their minds pretty well in whose favour the race would be, for they gave the officers a derisive cheer as they started after Wild and the young clerk.

The Edgware-road at that time did not bear the remotest resemblance to its present appearance.

The long rows of houses that now extend for some two miles into the country had then no existence, and, save a few mansions of the nobility close to the Oxford-road, there were no houses until you got to the little village of Kilburn, which then was a village in reality, if we except a stray public house or two by the roadside.

The road, as now, though, was one of the best out of London, and Wild's horse went along it gallantly, although he had a double burthen to carry.

That he should distance his pursuers Wild did not entertain a doubt, but just as Kilburn came in sight a new danger presented itself, in the shape of some mounted men coming in the opposite direction. This was a malapropos occurrence which Wild had not calculated upon, and if these men, who were rapidly meeting him, should take it into their heads to be troublesome, his position would be anything but satisfactory.

They might, however, take no notice further than a passing glance at him; and with that hope he kept on the side of the road farthest from them.

If the officers who were in pursuit of Wild had just continued that pursuit, it is probable enough that they and the fugitives might all have passed the men upon the road without anything occurring: but they had already seen enough of the power of the horse that Wild rode to begin to be very doubtful, indeed, of the result of the chase; and therefore was it that, with loud cries, they shouted to the men upon the road—

"Stop him—stop him!"

The men were four in number, and when these cries met their ears, they drew up, and looked rather doubtful as to what to do.

Every moment was precious to Wild, and he gave the horse a further impulse that increased its speed.

"Stop him!" cried the officers, again. "Stop him!—stop him!"

Upon this, the horsemen showed an inclination to block up the road.

The young clerk gave a cry of dismay, but Wild called out—

"All right; let who will take his chance of stopping me!"

With his left hand he guided the horse, and with his right he held a pistol to the level of the heads of the horsemen, and on he went.

This was a state of things that those who were upon the road by no means seemed to relish, for they cleared out of the way with wonderful expedition, and one of them ducked his head right down to his horse's mane.

CHAPTER XLIX.

OUT OF DANGER.

"COWARDS!" shouted the officers, as they passed the four rather bewildered horsemen on the road. "Cowards, you might have stopped him. It is Jonathan Wild!"

"It may have been anybody," said one of the horsemen to his companions; "but it ain't very agreeable to be shot through the head by an infuriated highwayman. There they go. Oh, he will beat them hollow."

Before the man had got these words fully uttered, Wild and the officers were nearly half a mile off.

Kilburn was dashed through at a terrific pace, to the great detriment and terror of a regiment of geese, that happened to be waddling over the road at the time.

Wild slackened his pace just a little as he got through the village, for he had not quite made up his mind whether to make a dash into the green lanes to the left that led to Wilsden and Marshdown, or go right on.

There was not much time, however, for the making up of his mind on the subject; and, after a moment or two given to thought, he determined upon keeping straight on, until, at all events, he had distanced the officers more than he had already done.

The young clerk had pretty well, having nothing else to do, kept one eye upon the foe who lay half turned in the saddle, and he now suddenly cried—

"Down, Wild. One of them is down!"

"A fall?" cried Jonathan.

"Yes, his horse has gone over with him, and one of the others has stopped to help him. There are only two on our track."

"Then warrant me for settling two," said Wild, and gradually pulling up the horse, he turned him on the road, and faced his pursuers.

This was a manœuvre that the officers evidently so little expected that they were quite taken by surprise by it, and they made an effort to pull up, in which they were so far successful, that they succeeded in stopping at about twenty or thirty yards from Wild and his horse.

"Give up, Wild," cried one of them. "We must have you, and it's no use trying to fight it out with us. We must, and will have you."

Jonathan saw that this man who was speaking was trying to cover his companion, who was taking aim at him with a holster pistol.

Such a sinister mode of attacking him was not exactly one that Wild was likely to put up with quietly; and, accordingly, he levelled his pistol at once, but before he could take anything like an aim, the officer fired.

Jonathan could hear the bullet or bullets whistle past his head in much too close proximity to be at all pleasant.

"A miss is as good as a mile," he cried. "I'll try my luck, now, if you can have it."

With these words, Wild fired without taking any very particular aim, but the officer who was foremost certainly had the worst chance.

As fate would have it, though, the bullet passed him, and hit his companion, who was cringing behind him, and who, with a loud roar, fell off his horse, on to the middle of the road.

"Oh, I'm hit—I'm hit!" he cried. "I'm a dead man at last. Oh, I'm done for."

"A good job, too," said Wild, as he turned his horse's head again to the north, and set off at a gallop.

The officer who had escaped the shot did not seem to be at all anxious to follow, and after Wild had gone a mile, he pulled up, saying—

"We are free from the bloodhounds at last, I think. They have had enough of it by this time; and now, thank you, my dear Princess, for you have saved my life this day, and wonderfully well you made up in those clothes?"

"Do I?" said the sham clerk, with a smile; "and you really think they never suspected that I had no right to dress as I do, and that it was a girl who had the courage to save you?"

"No, they do not suspect it. But what can I say to you, and how can I thank you for thus snatching me from death?"

"Say nothing to me, Wild," she replied. "You know that I am bound to save you; therefore, what I did was little enough, since it succeeded so easily. Ah, they little suspected that my heart was beating ready to burst its bonds, while I kept a smiling face. Little did they fancy that I was almost mad as I came through that throng, and saw you so near to death."

After a pause, she continued.

"Let us proceed. We are far from safe now in this public road; and, besides, the authorities will soon discover the trick that has been played upon them, if they know it not already; and then every possible exertion will be made to take us."

"Not a doubt of it, Princess; so it must be a case of keeping close for a time. The worst of it is, that I have no money."

"And I very little."

By this time the little conversation was over, they had trotted on for a considerable distance, and had reached the head of a lane that led to the right.

There was a direction-post at the corner of this lane, signifying that it led to Hendon, so Wild felt very much inclined to go to that village, as he knew there was a public-house in it, the landlord of which was rather disposed to be friendly to the gentlemen of the road, and Wild wanted a rest somewhere to arrange his ideas, as they had been rather confused by the day's proceedings.

"Let's be off to Hendon," he said. "It can't be above a few miles to the right here, and I think we shall be as safe, if not safer, in that district than anywhere else. What say you?"

"Yes," said the girl.

"Then come on. Hold on firmly, and we will put the horse to a canter, and soon get over the ground."

This was done.

The horse did not appear to be in the least fatigued by the work he had already performed, and went on the canter for the next three miles as willingly as possible.

Then they saw a stone by the roadside, which let them know they were in Hendon parish, so they went on still at the same rate until they reached the little village, and halted at the door of an inn called the King's Head.

It was a very old-fashioned house, was the King's Head at Hendon.

It was built of wood, and was evidently inclined to have a great affection for the street, as it nodded towards it for a considerable distance, and upon some future day would, no doubt, tumble right into it.

In fact it had rather a stumbling look.

"Shall we be safe here?" said the Princess, as she glanced at the old house.

"Yes," said Wild, "I think we shall. But how do you mean? Is it as regards the place or the people?"

"Why," said the Princess, "if the people betray us I hope the old house will betray them, and fall into the road; but if they do not it shall have my best wishes that it may keep up for all times to come. It is very old, is it not?"

"Yes, but here is the landlord."

The landlord of the King's Head, now hearing the sound of horse's feet, came out to the door, but when he saw Wild, he lifted up his hands, and starting back, he cried—

"The Lord deliver us! It's the ghost of Wild, as I'm a sinner. He was hanged an hour ago at Tyburn, and here he is at my door!"

"Silence!" cried Wild, "don't you give way to such ridiculous fancies. It is absurd. I'm Wild, but as to the hanging part of the business, that did not come off as we expected, and here I am, without anything of the sort having happened to me. If you can let us put up here for a time I shall be obliged."

"Can this be possible?"

"Yes, and true as well, so don't make a fuss about it. All's right enough. I was reprieved; but caution is the word, landlord. Who have you in your house at present?"

"Not a soul."

"That's all the better."

"Is it though? You will permit me to say, Wild, how much I differ from you there. That's a state of things that would not do long. Who is the young spark you have with you?"

Wild and the Princess had dismounted by this time, and this question of the landlord's was put in a whisper.

"Oh, that," said Wild, "is a friend of mine, upon whom I can fully rely, and who has placed me under the greatest obligation. I hope that you will pay him every possible attention."

"That I will, for many a guinea you have spent at the Old King's Head."

"And many more I mean to spend," said Wild.

"That's good news enough for me," said the landlord. "Go in, both of you"

"But the horse," said Wild; "mind where you place it. You know I like to have the power of getting hold of the bridle at a moment's notice."

"I know that, Wild; you will find it in the stable by the corner of the meadow, and you know you can cross that same meadow in a few moments, and get upon the high-road, when you may chance to please to do so."

"All's right; that will do."

Wild and the Princess entered the old inn, and the landlord soon provided them with a hasty repast, consisting of ham, grilled over the coals, and new-laid eggs, which, together with a few glasses of pure humming ale, made up a very hearty kind of lunch indeed, and one which Wild enjoyed with very considerable relish.

"I shall remain here until midnight," said Wild.

And then there ensued a long silence.

CHAPTER L.

FEARS FOR GENTLEMAN CLIFFORD.—FRIENDS HOLD A COUNCIL.—NED BONNET AND BILL WATERS VOLUNTEER A SEARCH.

As day after day passed and no tidings were heard of Gentleman Clifford, Mrs. Granville and the frequenters of her house of entertainment grew much alarmed for his safety.

One evening the common room was full, and it was determined by those present, at the head of whom we might name Bill Waters, to set off to the Willows in search of him.

"Bill will, of course, go," said Mrs. Granville; "but he will want some stout hand to help him."

"Well, let him take me," said a tall, fierce-looking fellow, standing up and glancing at Bill; "what say you, mate?"

"I'm agreeable," said Bill.

"All's right then," said the man, who was no other than the noted Ned Bonnet.

Before proceeding further with the discourse in the hostelrie, we must formally introduce Mr. Ned Bonnet to the reader.

He was born in Ely, and received a decent education, but turned it to an indifferent use.

When ten years of age he was sent to the prison with the spare rib of a hog, wrapped up in a cloth in a basket. Ned knocked with some degree of importance at the door—a servant answered, inquiring his business.

"I want to speak with your master."

The master came.

"Well, my dear, what is your business!"

"Why, only my father has sent you this," says young Ned; and gives him the basket without moving his hat.

"O, fie, fie, child! have you no manners? You should pull off your hat, and say, 'Sir, my father gives his service to you, and desires you to accept this small token.' Come, go you out again with the basket, and knock at the door, and I'll let you in, and see how prettily you can perform it."

The parson waited within, until his impatience to receive and examine the contents of the basket incited him to open the door.

But Ned was at a considerable distance, walking off with the present.

"So ho, so ho, sirrah! Where are you going!"

"Home, sir," replied Ned, in an equally loud voice.

"Hey, but you must come back, and do as I bade you first."

"Thank you for that, sir, I know better than that; and, if you teach me manners, I'll teach you wit."

The father smiled at the story, and retained his spare rib.

At the age of fifteen he was sent an apprentice to a grocer, served his time with honour, was afterwards married to a young woman in the neighbourhood, and continued in business until he had acquired about six hundred pounds.

Unfortunately, however, he was reduced to poverty by an accidental fire.

Unable to answer the pressing demands of his creditors, he left the place and came to London.

He soon became acquainted with a band of highwaymen, and began with them to seek from the highway what had been lost with fire.

Nor did he long continue in the inferior walks of his new profession, but, providing himself with a horse which learned to leap over ditch, hedge, or toll-bar, and to know all the roads in the country, whether by day or by night, he quickly became the terror of Cambridgeshire.

Upon this horse he one day met a Cantabrigian, who was possessed of more money than good sense or morality, in a calash, with a dashing courtesan.

Ned commanded the student to stand and deliver.

Unwilling to show his cowardice before his companion, he refused.

Without any respect to the venerable university to which he belonged, Ned, by violence, took from him about six pounds, presented a pair of pistols, constrained the hopeful pair to undress themselves of every rag, bound them together, and, giving the horse a lashing, he went off, at a full trot, with them to the inn to which he belonged.

But no sooner did these Adamites enter the town than men, women, and children came hallooing, shouting, and collecting the whole town to behold such an uncommon spectacle.

The student was expelled for disgracing the University, and the courtesan was sent to the correction-house.

Humorous Ned next met with a tailor and his son, who had arrested him for five pounds.

He commanded him to surrender, and received thirty-five in place of his five.

"I wonder," said the son, "what these fellows think of themselves? Surely they must go to hell for committing these notorious actions."

"God forbid," replied the tailor, "for, to have conversation with such rogues there would be worse than all the rest."

Ned's next adventure was with an Anabaptist preacher, whom he commanded to deliver up his purse and his scrip.

He began by reasonings, ejaculations, and texts, to avert the impending evil.

Ned was soon in a great passion, and replied—

"Pray, sir, keep your breath to cool your porridge, and don't talk of religious matters to me; for I'll have you to know that, like all other true-bred gentlemen, I believe nothing at all of religion; therefore, deliver me your money, and bestow your laborious cant upon your female auditors, who will never scold with their maids without cudgelling them with broken pieces of Scripture."

Thus, taking a watch and eight guineas, he tied his horse, and let him depart.

Upon another occasion, Ned, and a few associates met a nobleman and four servants in a narrow pass, and accosted them in his usual style.

The nobleman pretended that he supposed they were only in jest, and said if they would accompany him to the next inn, he would give them a handsome treat.

He was soon informed that they preferred the present to the future.

A sharp dispute ensued, but the nobleman and his men were conquered.

He was robbed of a purse of gold, a gold watch, a gold snuff-box, and a diamond ring.

They were conducted into an adjacent wood, and bound hand and foot.

When the robbers left them, they said "that they would bring them more company presently."

They increased the number to twelve, on which Ned cried—

"There are now twelve of you, all good men and true; so, bidding you farewell, you may give in your verdict of us as you please, when we are gone, though it will be none of the best; but, to give as little trouble as possible, we shall not now stay to challenge any of you. So, once more, farewell."

Ned and his companions then went to a solitary inn, to make themselves happy with what they had thus honestly acquired.

A traveller who was benighted, entered the same inn, and, while conversing with the landlord, Ned introduced himself, and not long after another of his men, who pretended to be an old acquaintance of the stranger's.

He, however, did not recollect him, nor was he without strong suspicions of the quality of the house into which he had come.

They insisted upon him supping with them, which he agreed to.

By pretending to treat him, and he insisting to pay his share, it was at length agreed to throw for the payment of the whole, amounting to more than three pounds.

The stranger had the supper to pay.

He went to bed, barricaded his room door with all the moveable furniture of the room.

His caution was necessary, but unavailing; for the thieves entered by a secret door, carried off his clothes, and bound him.

The noise alarmed the house; Ned, his companions, and the landlord all rushed into the room, and bewailed his case, saying that they would have the rogues if they remained upon the surface of the globe.

The stranger was perfectly convinced that they had not far to search for them; but, lest his life should have been taken away by those who had taken away his clothes, he was silent; and borrowing some old garments of the inkeeper, he was under the necessity of returning home, having no money with which to prosecute his journey.

One day, having the misfortune to have his horse shot

ADA SEEKING HER PROPERTY AT THE HANDS OF WILSNICK, WICKLES, AND WILSNICK.

under him, Bonnet embraced the first opportunity to take a good gelding from the grounds of the man who kept the Red Lion Inn.

Being again equipped like a gentleman, he rode into Cambridgeshire, and met with a gentleman who informed him that he had well-nigh been robbed, and requested him to ride along with him for protection.

As a highwayman is never out of his way, he complied, and, at a convenient place, levied a contribution as protector of the gentleman by emptying his pockets of eighty guineas.

He, however, had the generosity to give him two shillings and sixpence to carry him to the next town.

One hundred robberies had the daring Ned committed when he joined the fraternity who was harboured by Mother Granville.

Such, then, was the man who volunteered to join Bill Waters in his exploit in search of the missing Clifford.

They had no sooner determined to act in concert than they prepared to put their plans into execution.

They mounted at once, and were away from the house in five minutes.

As they hastened towards the stables a tall, but not a handsome woman, ran from the house and overtook them.

"Well, Sall M'Carthy," said Bill, "what is it you want?"

"Shure," said the woman, in unmistakably Hibernian accents, "shure, it's myself as would go with ye in search of the ginthelman."

"You?"

"Yes, myself. Ah, shure, the ginthelman didn't think

much of me. He pays no attention to my ogles and sight, but I've a heart as bates for him, and I'd with you to do him a good turn if he wants it; and by the powers ye may have with ye a worse woman than Sall M'Carthy.'

"She is right," said Bill, "I've proved her a good 'un in a difficulty, many a time and oft, so let her come."

"Has she a horse?" demanded Ned.

"That I have, shure! A better one never carried a woman."

"Yes," said Bill, "and she knows how to manage him, too. Sall McCarthy can ride a horse and stop a traveller as well as any knight of the road."

"All right, then," said Ned, regarding the amazon with some delight, "let her come, if only for company."

So it was agreed that Sall should take part in the expedition, and without delay the three were dashing off at a great pace in the direction of the Willows.

Arrived at the lodge they were met by the old lodge-keeper and his wife, of whom they gained as much information as they required, for the old people were very communicative in the interest of the handsome gentleman with the beautiful white mare.

The white mare by the bye was still in the care of the lodge-keeper.

Poor Brilliant looked dejected and sorrowful without her master, but seemed to revive on the instant she heard Bill's voice: for Bill was an immense favourite with her.

"Poor mare," he said, "poor old Brilliant! Where's her master, now?"

The mare seemed to comprehend the question, and whined piteously.

"Ah," continued Bill, "we'll bring him to you, old girl—never fear, never fear."

"Now," said Ned, "let us get on to the old house and search it. There may not be a moment to lose."

They did get on, and, entering the house, searched it from top to bottom most diligently, but nowhere was to be found the slightest trace of Clifford.

In fact the house was entirely deserted!

*   *   *   *   *

It is now necessary that we take a retrospective glance at the state of affairs at the Willows.

We left Clifford, as it appeared, quite insensible, and with the treacherous Princess for his only attendant.

We saw her drug his medicine, and place it so that, on returning to consciousness, it would be the first thing he would take.

But, unfortunately for the plans of the Princess, Clifford had so far recovered his senses as to be enabled to comprehend what was passing in the chamber in which he lay.

His trance was *feigned*, and his eyes were fixed upon the woman preparing the deadly draught for his use.

It is needless to say that the poison was thrown in the fire, and that the Princess was confounded at the unexpected turn of affairs.

Clifford accused her of treachery of the deepest dye, and under the lash of his burning words she fled the apartment.

Next day the doctor came again, and found his patient very feverish and much worse than when he had left him.

Clifford was too weak to tell what happened had he been so inclined, and the old physician was at a loss to account for his miserable state.

The only thing he could do was to give a composing draught, in which laudanum was the chief ingredient.

Under its influence Clifford sank into a profound slumber, and the doctor went his way.

Meanwhile, the events already narrated had occurred.

Wild had been taken, tried, condemned, and rescued.

He had, with his companion in crime, left the inn in which they had taken shelter, and made their way once more to the Willows.

There they found poor Clifford in the precarious state we have described.

For many days he was delirious, and completely insensible.

Wild and the Princess could not agree as to what it was best to do with him.

Wild had a desire to keep him there and restore him, but the Princess was for destroying him.

Wild proved himself the best general, and had his way, and the doctor was allowed to perform his offices to the best of his ability.

Then there was held a counsel of war, as to the future movements of the pair of criminals.

Wild could not again show himself in the metropolis, and had no desire to remain in the place he so dreaded.

In the emergency Colonel Jack was summoned from London, and matters were "talked over."

There was a long and earnest talk in the little room occupied by the Princess.

Every description of plan for the future was suggested and canvassed, but none so took the taste of Wild as the suggestion of the Colonel that he should join a band of London criminals, remain concealed in the neighbourhood, and live on the prey they could get at on the road.

The *locale* was an excellent one for the purpose, and ere the meeting separated a complete plan of execution had been resolved upon.

How it worked, and of what character it was, we shall hereafter see.

But there was *an enemy in that camp* to mar its plottings and counteract its dire effects.

CHAPTER LI

THE FORTUNES OF ADA REVERTED TO — WILSNICK, WICKLES, AND WILSNICK FIND A HOME AND FORTUNE FOR HER—THE MEETING WITH LORD STORKS—GENERAL MOORE AND HIS NIECE—STORKS' REVELATION.

WILSNICK, WICKLES, AND WILSNICK, were sharp practitioners.

They generally managed to bring down two birds when they flung a stone, and the instance of the affairs of Lord Algernon proved no exception to the rule.

They disposed of his wife on the one hand, and took her friend, the homeless Ada, to snatch his fortune from him on the other.

This might have been poetical justice, but it was far from agreeable to the feelings of the party most interested.

It was the game of the three cunning lawyers to wrench the property to which Algernon was undoubtedly not entitled from his grasp, and place it in the hands of one whom they could manage with ease.

It was evident that the real heiress was not forthcoming, and the lawyers cunningly devised a scheme for finding a substitute. Chance flung in their way the orphan Ada, and they determined to use her.

It is not for us to fill these pages with a revelation of the subtle means they used to establish her as the heiress of the Algernon estates.

Suffice it to say that they did so at length, and Algernon was almost beggared!

But when he knew who the real heiress was his gloom disappeared; his sorrow vanished, and he declared himself satisfied.

"I tried to wrong her once," he said; "I am glad I did not succeed. I am still glad of this act of retributive justice."

The lawyers had not yet done with his lordship.

Their heiress was young and fascinating, and what was to prevent her marrying?

"A husband would spoil our sport," said Wickles.

"Yes," said the elephantine Wilsnick, "unless he be a husband whom we could manage !

"Algernon," suggested the parrot.

"Yes, Algernon," said the others, in a breath.

And so the matter was canvassed, and Algernon consulted.

He, of course, could find no objection.

* * * * *

A few weeks passed, and Algernon was deposed and fair Ada reigned in his stead.

But the plans of the lawyers received a gre t and unexpected check.

The moment Ada was proclaimed and recognised heiress of the Algernon property a General Moore and his daughter sought her out, and the young girl accepted the old soldier as her guardian, and went to live with him.

The General represented himself as the brother of Ada's supposed mother.

He knew Algernon slightly, but had seldom seen or conversed with him.

But as soon as the property came into the hands of his supposed niece he began to sympathise with the "poor young devil" who had got kicked out, and who must feel his reverse of fortune so much.

So he immediately forwarded him an invite to his house.

As luck would have it, Lord Storks, now indeed a widower, was by some inexplicable circumstance invited at the same moment.

Under these circumstances poor Ada felt that she had nothing to do but to reveal to Louise Moore the relationship in which she stood towards both these parties.

They arrived.

There was a meeting at dinner, and it was easy to see how miserable all were feeling.

They rose early ; the gentlemen did not join the ladies that night, and all retired early to rest.

* * * * *

Louise Moore at once sought young Algernon, and learned from him how deeply he repented of ever contemplating the outrage he had offered Ada under the roof of Storks.

Storks but barely noticed Algernon, but kept his eyes fixed on Ada, who averted her gaze from his, and avoided him.

But Storks was not to be put off.

He was now a widower, and Ada was a rich heiress, so he determined on meeting her without delay, and asking for forgiveness of the past, and propose to her out of hand.

He did so, and got snubbed for his pains.

"Ah, well," muttered his lordship, "I shall know how to avenge this. In the morning I shall give the General my version of what passed in my London house some little time ago."

Having determined on this, his lordship retired to rest, quite satisfied with himself and the state of affairs generally.

Meanwhile Louise had arranged that Algernon should meet Ada in the garden next morning, and seek her forgiveness.

To this Ada offered no objection.

Accordingly the next morning the two girls were early in the garden.

They had not walked there a great while when Algernon joined them.

Before he came up to them, the following conversation had taken place.

Said Louise—

"As I live, I do believe that Algernon deeply feels his error, and that he would have died with that feeling. And now, my dear friend, I have to ask you, not to be friends with him—not to take him into your confidence or your affection, but to forgive him, and to think of him as you did before this affair took place, and to believe it to have been, as far as he was concerned, something like

a piece of mental hallucination, for which he cannot be much blamed. Will you, for my sake, do this?"

"Yes, Louise, for your sake I will do anything ; but still it would be well that he soon left this place."

"He shall soon leave it : and before I go, I will take care that another likewise leaves it, whom you do not wish to stay."

"You allude to Lord Storks?"

"I do. I feel confident, after what has passed, that there is mischief in that man's mind, and that he will do you all the harm he can. I will take good care to thwart him ; and for that purpose I wish that during this morning you would hold yourself in readiness to act as I wish you."

"I will—I will."

"That is my own, good kind Ada. Will you, then, shake hands with Algernon to oblige me ?"

"Come, I know that Algernon will be very unhappy until you have spoken to him three little words."

"Three words, Louise ?"

"Yes, the three words, 'I forgive you.' Speak them, and he will be content."

Louise now went to a little rustic gate, and called out to Algernon to come to them.

Algernon looking rather foolish and awkward, as he might well do under the circumstances, approached. He durst hardly raise his eyes to look at Ada, who turned very pale when she saw him.

"Here is the culprit," said Louise.

Ada stepped forward, and held out her hand, as she said in a low voice—

"For the sake of her who is dear to me, I forgive you."

Algernon just touched the extended hand with the tips of his fingers, and then gently kissed it, as he replied—

"Even this is more than I deserve."

"Let the past, then, be forgotten," said Ada.

"Is that possible ?"

"Yes, it shall be so. From this moment let it never again be ever referred to by any of us. We shall all feel the happier with such a determination."

"To be sure we shall," said Louise.

Algernon looked the gratitude that he felt, but he could not say a word ; and it was quite a relief to him, as well as to the others, when a loud bell suddenly sounded from the house, and Ada said—

"That is the breakfast bell; let us all go in."

"Yes," said Louise, "for I can assure you these early paradings in the gardens and grounds without anything to eat make me feel as if I could almost consume my Lord Storks."

"I wonder where he is ?" said Ada, laughing.

In this way, talking quite pleasantly, only that Algernon wished himself anywhere now but where he was, they went to the house, and were soon in the breakfast-room.

The General was there, and one glance at his cheerful, frank-looking face was quite sufficient to convince them that as yet Lord Storks had made no sort of communication to him regarding past events, and Louise began to think that, after all, he might not be so bad as they were inclined to think him, and that, with the calm reflection of the morning, he had seen the baseness of interfering in a matter that he had nothing to do with, and that he could not say he intermeddled with but from the meanest and worst possible motives.

In this idea, though, Louise was mistaken.

The Lord Storks was by no means one of those men who are generous upon reflection.

"How are you all ?" said the General as they entered the breakfast-room. "I was late up or I should have enjoyed an early walk myself ; but I am glad to find that you have been getting appetite and health among the trees and flowers."

"We have indeed, sir," said Louise.

"Ah, my young spark, you look well indeed this morning."

"Thank you, General."

" No thanks to me.   Nature has done a great deal for you, young man, in giving you handsome looks. I am afraid as you get older you will do some havoc among the hearts of heedless girls.''

" Oh, no, sir."

"Ah, it's all very well to say ' oh, no,' but it will be ' oh, yes' in the course of time, I am sure. Well, Ada, and how are you ?"

"Quite well," said Ada, as she embraced her supposed uncle.

" Then if you are quite well, my darling, all is well.''

Ada felt as if she could have burst into tears at that moment, but she controlled the feeling, and they were upon the point of sitting down to breakfast when Lord Storks appeared.

His lordship wore a very elegant morning gown, made of tapestry embroidered with silk.

A cord and tassel of silk confined the dressing-gown round his waist, and he looked as if he had taken more than usual care with his toilette.

"Why, Storks," said the General, "how killing you look this morning.   Have you any conquest on hand ?"

"Why, a—no," said Lord Storks.

"Well, I am surprised at that, for to me you seem quite made up for storming female hearts."

" Eh ?—oh—demme!   I am afraid I am not very well."

"What a pity," said Louise.

It was the tone in which Louise said these words more than the words themselves that produced the roar of laughter with which they were greeted. Lord Storks looked very angry, and when silence was somewhat restored, he said—

"Perhaps, though—demme! I do feel a little ill, my nerves are steady enough to obey wishes."

" In what way ?" said the General.

"Oh, no particular way. Demme, nothing !"

The General was the only person who was at all in the dark respecting the meaning of Lord Storks.

The others all knew that he alluded to the possibility of being steady enough in the hand to shoot Algernon, who at the moment, but that he felt it would be very imprudent so to do, could, with great pleasure, have got up and knocked his head off; but he kept silent.

"Well, well," said the General, "we will attend to our breakfast now instead of the nerves of Lord Storks."

That something was amiss between Lord Storks and his other guests the General could not but perceive; but, like a well-bred gentleman, and a thorough man of the world as he was, he forebore to make the slightest remark upon the subject, but patiently waited until some one should think proper to let him know what it was all about.

If they did not, he would quietly make up his mind that it was no business of his, and there, to him, would have been an end of it.

What a capital thing it would be in society if everybody could act like the General, and only interfere in their own affairs, or when they are called upon specially so to do by other parties.

The breakfast, as may be imagined, with such discordant persons at it, could not pass off very sociably. As for Lord Storks, if ever he felt anything like positive amazement in his life it was at what he considered the cool conduct of Ada, who looked and spoke really as if nothing were at all wrong in her conduct.

"By Jove!" said Lord Storks to himself, " the little devil thinks that I won't tell of her, and so that she is quite safe; but she has not been civil enough for that, and tell I will, demme !"

Now, notwithstanding aggravated at the moment as Lord Storks had been to make the rather valorous speech he had made concerning the steadiness of his nerves, he had no sort of intention of fighting with Algernon, and if anything could more than another have completely fortified him in his intentions of telling all he thought

he knew to the General, the prospect of by so doing escaping the conflict he had provoked would have done so.

But the real truth was that his lordship needed no such motives to tell all that he thought he knew.

His feelings of revenge against Ada were quite sufficient to induce him to do so, and now he only waited till the breakfast was over to ask the General to give him his attention for a few minutes while he unfolded to him the story of the disgrace that had fallen upon his relative.

A few minutes after they rose from the breakfast table; and as the General went to one of the windows Lord Storks followed him, and said, in a low tone of voice—

"General, I have a private communication to make to you, if you can oblige me with an interview alone."

"Certainly, my lord. I am quite at your service."

" Thank you, General."

"Will you follow me to the library ? We shall be quite secure from any interruption there, as you are aware."

"Oh, quite.   That will do excellently well, general, Hem, demme! this is a very fine day."

"Very, my lord.''

" I a—a—admire a fine day, General, very much. By Jove, I do! 'pon soul, demme !"

With that brilliant remark, Lord Storks followed the General from the breakfast room and across the hall to the library, which was an apartment of great size and beauty, adorned as it was by some exquisite pieces of sculpture, and filled by books of the highest character.

The moment the door of the breakfast-room closed upon the General and Lord Storks Ada glanced at her friends, and the tears gushed to her eyes as she said—

" Now, if it be only for an hour, my dear friend is to be made most wretched by that base slanderer."

" Be patient, Ada—be patient," said Louise. "It shall only be for a time, and the joy that your uncle will feel when he knows, as you are aware he will soon know, that the statement of Lord Storks arose from mistake, will be great."

Ada wept.

Algernon now stepped forward, and spoke.

" Louise," he said, " you have free leave and licence from me to let the General know the truth ; and if you pleased to go after him now and confront the lord, who is, no doubt, filling his mind with lies, I will go with you."

"No—no, let us wait. If you will wait, Ada, you will do more good than by being precipitate.''

" I will wait," said Ada.

" Now, my lord," said the General, as he motioned Storks to a seat in the library, " now that we are alone, I am ready to pay every possible attention to what you may have to say to me."

Lord Storks shook his head as solemnly as if there had really been anything in it.

" Pray be seated, General."

" Thank you," said the General, with a smile, as he sat down. "Be seated yourself, and speak freely.''

" General—oh, General ?"

" Lord Storks—oh, Lord Storks !"

" Sir ?"

" Well, sir, what is the matter with you ? You put on such a dolorous face that any one would suppose that I was your physician, and that you were in the last stage of some dreadful and fatal disorder.   What have you got to say ?"

" I am very—very sorry."

" For what ?"

" That I have got to say to you, General; what I have got to say."

" Then don't say it."

" I only wish that I felt it to be consistent with my feelings and my duty not to say it; but, alas, I must—I feel that I must. You shall know all."

"All what ?"

" Oh, my dear sir, do not be impatient. It is quite

soon enough. Of course I could have told you before, but I did not wish you to spoil your breakfast; that was the reason."

"That's very kind of you, I'm sure; but, after all, perhaps you are mistaken as to the probable effect of the communication; my breakfast might have gone on just as comfortable notwithstanding."

"Oh, no—no—no! It is with regret I say no. It is really with quite a feeling of anguish that I say no. Pray excuse me for being so very sensitive, but I really cannot help it. Indeed I cannot."

"Oh, don't mention it."

'Well, General, you are an old soldier, I may truly say."

"I am, indeed, my lord, and as such, do you know, there is nothing I so much dislike as being kept in a state of suspense."

"Then, my dear sir, my friendship for you is so great that you shall know all. Hem!—You have a niece?'

"I have."

"The fair—no, not the fair, for she is rather dark, but I may truly call her the beautiful and the accomplished Ada."

"My lord, I am very much indebted to you for the highly complimentary way in which you mention my niece, and I feel sure so would she be, if she knew it.'

"Oh, General! Oh—oh—oh!"

"Why you are taken bad again," said the General, "are you? Perhaps, my dear sir, you would like a glass of wine to help you on?"

"Oh, no—no. I can well perceive, General, that you do not for one moment guess—as how, indeed, should you?—the nature of the communication that I am now about to make."

"It relates to my niece, sir."

"It does—it does."

"Then you will permit me to say that I do not see any difficulty in guessing it at all; I am led to believe that your object in coming here was to pay your addresses to my niece Ada."

"Yes, but—"

"Nay, sir, hear me out. If you had had the candour in the first instance to have spoken to me, I could have told you what, of course, I could not think of volunteering to you, namely, that I left my niece entirely to her own inclinations."

"The devil you do!"

"I do; and you will permit me to add that I don't see anything very much out of the way in so doing. It is, I am convinced, the best, as it is the only rational course for a guardian to pursue. She will please herself."

"You amaze me, General!"

"Perhaps so. And now, I suppose, with your amazement, our interview ends. If you can persuade Ada to accept you as her husband I am perfectly willing, and you will hear nothing from me to the contrary; so go to her at once, I advise you, and get her answer."

"But you understand me, my dear sir. I wouldn't have her if every hair of her head were hung with a diamond—I would'nt have her if she were the queen of Sheba or England. I don't intend to propose to her at all, I assure you, and I very much congratulate myself that I have not done so, demme!"

"Then what, in the name of all that is incomprehensible, sir, do you want to say to me?"

"Oh, General; oh, oh!"

"D—n it, my lord, don't begin that again! If you have anything to say, say it like a man, and I will hear it like one; you may depend upon that."

"Then, General—"

"Stop!"

"Yes, I will stop. As—'

"Silence! Before you say what you are going to say, let me give you one word of advice, and that is, that if it be anything which in any way attacks the honour or the feelings of my niece, it will not be the safest thing in the world for you to say it."

"Oh!"

"Yes, my lord; that is my serious advice to you."

"But do you mean to say that a fellow musn't say what he knows, and what he saw, and what is the truth? Dear me, General, you don't mean to shut your ears and your eyes to what you ought to know? Demme! you are not so mad as that?"

The General looked at Lord Storks for a few moments in silence; and then with a slightly heightened colour upon his cheeks he cried out—

"Man, if you have anything to say, say it or leave my house this moment. I will not be longer kept upon the tenter hooks by you."

"Thank you," said Lord Storks; "you are very good. I now avail myself of your gracious permission, demme! to tell you that I once slept in a chamber adjoining that occupied by your niece, and that about twelve o'clock at night, or it might be a little later, I heard some one try the handle of my bed-room door. The handle is of brass; and so you see—"

"Go on—go on, do."

"Very good. Some one tried the handle of my door, and I, thinking it might be a thief, got up and dressed myself and went out into the corridor—you comprehend? —and I saw a figure stealing——"

"What?"

"Stealing along towards another room. I think, now, that the handle of my door must have been tried by mistake, for when the figure tried another on the opposite side of the corridor it yielded, and a voice said, 'Oh, come in; is it you?' to which the other replied, 'Yes, my duck!'"

"Stuff!"

"You may say stuff as much as you like, General, but that was just what happened; and I can assure you that the stuff that the figure had on in the way of drapery was of a very limited quantity, indeed. Well, I went after it, not knowing what room it had gone into."

"What happened then?"

"I opened the same door that it had opened, and I perceived that it led to your niece's chamber, and with her was the handsome young man who is a guest in this house; and I can further assure you that I was bullied by him and by her both, and threatened very much if I dared to say anything about it; and the handsome young lord stayed with her for the rest of the night. Now, General, you can make what you like of the affair. I have done my duty as a friend, and told you all."

The General sat like a man in a trance while Lord Storks was speaking to him; and, when he had concluded, the unhappy man passed his hand several times across his brow, as though he would try to assure himself that he was awake.

"No, no," he said, "no!"

"What is no?" said Lord Storks.

"It is all a dream."

"I only wish it was, that is all; but I can assure you, General, it is very much the contrary of that same; although, at this time, it gives me great pleasure to see that you are so much of a philosopher and a man of the world as to be able to take it so easy, and you—"

"Villain!" cried the General, springing to his feet, and making a dash at the throat of Lord Storks, "villain —wretch—without remorse or pity! I will rid the world of you!"

"Murder!"

"I will make it impossible that ever again you should be able to calumniate one so fair and so good as Ada."

"Oh, mercy! I didn't—I won't—it's true. Do you want all the house to know it?"

The General let go the throat of Lord Storks, and, sinking back into a seat, he gasped out—

"Tell me that you doubt it—oh, tell me that there is a possibility your vile and criminal imagination dreamt this."

"Oh thank you, I'm sure I'm much obliged, but it isn't so nohow. It's all true, and I don't see, sir, why—"

"Why what?"

"Why a man's cravat is to be torn to pieces because a young lady follows, as you say, her own inclination—demme!"

"My Lord Storks?"

"Yes, General?"

"You are here in my house, you understand."

"Of course I do, but I shall not be for long."

"Yes, perhaps you will, for from here you do not stir, sir, till you have proved this vile calumny. If you fail in proving it you had better find yourself in the den of a lion, sir, than in the house of General Moore."

"I'm to prove it?"

"You are."

"Oh, well; I don't know how Ada will have the face to deny it if you ask her. I must say that she was pretty cool and confident about it, and the fellow himself challenged me to fight a duel about it. What do you think of that?"

"I forbid it, sir."

"Then I won't, you may depend upon it. My respect for your opinion is so—"

"Silence! Let me think."

The General paced the room to and fro for some few moments in silence, and then, stopping short before Lord Storks, he said, in a tone of deep seriousness—

"My Lord Storks, if what you have said be true, I don't, upon reflection, see that I ought to blame you in this matter; but if it be false, your life, sir, shall be the forfeit of the vile calumny. I have altered my mind about the duel."

"Oh!"

"Yes; you shall fight this fellow."

"Well, but—"

"Nay, you shall fight him, and I will see that you have every facility for so doing. You came here to propose for my daughter's hand, and let a man be what he may, a fool or a philsopher, the veriest jackass that ever lived or the profoundest genius, he pays a compliment to the woman whom he so selects to be his wife."

"You are very good, General, indeed."

"No—no, I only mean to be just, and I mean to say, sir, that this affair touches your honour as well as mine. Of course it does not touch you so nearly—it does not heap upon your head hot ashes—it does not sear your heart while you live; but it touches your honour, and therefore you shall fight. I give you my word for that."

Lord Storks looked uncommonly blue at this kindness on the part of the General, and he interfered by saying—

"Demme! I thought that it would be so much more satisfactory to settle the fellow yourself. You know, General, that—"

"No, no! If he should escape you, my dear sir—if he should leave you a corpse on the ground, weltering in your blood—I will then meet him, be assured of that. He shall not escape my vengeance."

Lord Storks groaned again, and at that moment how devoutly he wished that he had never mentioned to the General anything of the affair, but had gone quietly from the mansion at once.

"Oh, lor;" he muttered, "I am in for it now; but still there is a chance. The General and this fellow cannot meet without a collision, surely; and then I shall get out of it."

"Now, my lord," added the General, "leave me to my own reflections. God knows they are bitter enough. Leave me."

"I will—I do. And—and—"

"What now?"

"Perhaps, after all, you had better tackle the fellow first, you know; and if by any chance you should miss him, why then I will try him."

"My dear Lord Storks, I fully appreciate the tenderness that induces you to prefer my honour to your own; but I cannot allow you to make such a sacrifice; so now adieu."

"Oh, oh," thought Storks, as he left the room, "here's a pretty situation."

CHAPTER LI.

THE SCENT DISCOVERED BY THE MYSTERIOUS FRIEND—A BAND OF DESPERADOES IN A CAVERN—WILD SERVES HIS COMPANION A NEAT TRICK.

IT was all in vain.

The Old Willows was traversed from end to end; every nook—every cranny was carefully surveyed, but without success.

There were traces—many traces of Clifford's having been there, but he was gone.

Gone, and with him those who had been his companions or jailers—evidently the latter.

"Well," said Bill Waters, "this here is about the rummiest go I ever did see. If those old fogies at the door are right he must have been here, but how he could have been got away without anybody being the wiser for it beats cockfighting hollow, and no mistake about—and no—mistake—a—bout—it."

The last words were drawled out in the most impressive manner, and with a nod of the head between each syllable that would have been worthy of an Old Bailey advocate beating a fact into the head of a dubious jury.

"It's awful," said Ned, "awful to be so done."

"Done!" said Sall, with a sneer, "done is it you're afther sayin'? More power to us, but devil a bit are we done just now, boys."

"What are we to do?" said Bill, "We've follered the scent as far as we could, and now we are clean off from it, and no mistake. It's bad to be so licked."

"Ah," murmured Will, "the devil's in Jonathan Wild; there's no getting at him in a hurry. He's the boy to do the dodge in correct style, he is, and if Clifford's at his mercy, Heaven help him, for we can't."

"Ye're at it agin," said the never-to-be-daunted Sall. "Och! spalpeens not worth yer salt, will ye give up the Cap'n because it's in Wild's clutches he is?"

"Give him up? No."

"But ye're as chicken-hearted as young geese."

"Devil a bit," said Ned. "We're baffled, not beaten."

"It's not baffled that I am," said Sall. "Stay you at the door, and see that nobody comes nigh it without havin' his beautiful brains knocked out if he happens to have any, and I'll run to the lodge, and thry if I can't make something more out o' the ould people who, afther all, seem true blue, and not the sort to thry on dirthy work."

So saying, the Amazon placed Ned and Bill sentinels in the hall, and, shouldering a heavy club, she started down the lawn, and entered the avenue leading to the lodge-keeper's old hut.

She was speeding along at a great rate. When within a hundred yards of the hut, a man, completely muffled, and disguised in a great cloak shawl and slouched hat, sprang from amongst the trees and confronted her.

In a moment Sall had raised her club with the intention of bringing it down on the head of the party who had thus suddenly presented himself to her notice, but his voice withheld her hand.

"Hold!" he cried; "hold, woman!"

"Who the devil are ye?"

"A friend."

"Whose friend?"

"Yours."

"Devil a bit."

"But I would serve you."

"Och, shure I don't want anything."

"You are searching for some one."

"That's thrue."

"And you think to find him?"

"I've an idea I shall."

"You won't."

"Why won't I, *my friend?*"

"Because he is too securely entrapped."

"By whom?"

"By Wild."

"Murther! Are ye Wild?"

"Heaven save us, no."

"I don't believe ye. Blazes! but ye'll have to unmuffle, and show me yer illegant mug afore I'll take yer word."

"Listen: I am Clifford's friend."

"A while ago ye were *my* friend."

"If you are Clifford's friend, so am I; therefore we must be friends."

"Och, shure now it's the devil's own child ye are at rasonin'. It's a ra'al Oxford scholar ye were brought up, boy."

"No such luck."

"But ye said something about the gentleman?"

"I did."

"What was it?"

"I said I was his friend."

"And it was'nt stoppin' me jist to say that ye were afther?"

"Not only that."

"What else?"

"Much."

"Make a beginning."

"I will if you will only hold your abominable jaw."

"Shure, is it me ye're accusin' of talkin', when I've been quiet as a mouse, listening to ye all the while. Oh, murther!"

"Will you be quiet?"

"Before I've begun?"

"Do you wish to do Clifford a service?"

"It's myself as would go through fire and wather to serve him."

"Then hold your tongue, and listen."

"I've—"

"Silence!"

"But—"

"Will you cease?"

"Devil take the fellow if I've said a word yet—"

"Are you going to listen? My time is precious, and in a few minutes I shall be gone, and Clifford will be lost."

"Lost."

"Lost. I repeat it, and I can't repeat it too many times, or impress it too deeply on your mind. Lost—lost—mind that."

"Och, no other of us; hear that now."

"Are you ready to listen."

"I'm dumb."

"Then hear me to an end without interruption."

"I'm Clifford's friend."

"Sure, you said that before."

"Damnation!"

"I forgot."

"One more interruption, and I go."

"Don't now."

"I would stake my life to serve Clifford, and that is why I am here. I have followed you; learned your errand; watched your ill-success, and have sought this opportunity of addressing you. Clifford is concealed by Wild in a cave in the Sandstone quarry, to the left of the wood yonder. It is a dangerous place in the night time, and can only be approached at great risk. Over the mouth of the pit is a lime tree; it is skirted by a rough hedge. In the cave Wild has formed a little band of dare-devils from London. At the head of them he has placed himself, and he resides with them in that cave, for he dares not now show up in the capacity of mock footman to the woman he has chosen as his ally in guilt, and who has stood his friend with so much pertinacity."

"Well, well."

"Well, woman, at the present moment Clifford is insensible; he can neither speak nor move, but when consciousness returns he will have the option given him of swearing to relinquish his pursuit of Jonathan Wild, and become his sworn friend, for good or evil, during the remainder of his days, or to die a wretched dog's death with a stone about his neck in the pool at the bottom of the pit leading to the cave."

"Murther!"

"Murder it will be."

"And what's to be done!"

"I don't know."

"Can't ye help me!"

"No. You have friends with you."

"Yes; good friends in a stand-up fight, but no heads to plot."

"It is a pity; but you must save Clifford."

"Be dad, we will."

"How it is to be done is beyond me; I have said and done all I can for you. I dare not utter another word, or risk my life another moment by remaining with you."

"Murther! Hey, here boy a moment!"

It was in vain the Amazon called.

The mysterious man who had brought her so much information, but who had refused to utter another word or stay another instant in the service of the man he called his friend, was gone.

He darted with velocity through the trees, and was out of sight in an instant.

Sall contemplated following him.

But a moment's reflection proved to her the absurdity of that proceeding.

"There's nothing better than to go back to the house, and tell the boys what's up," she said; "but it's a devil of a thick muddle we're in this time."

She sped back to the Willows with velocity.

She found Bill and Ned posted near the door, but the air of courage and bravado she had observed in them on leaving them was now gone.

They were as pale as marble, and trembled as the few leaves that remained clinging to the parent trees.

"I've something to tell ye, boys," roared Sall, "ye can't guess what I've seen."

"And I've something to tell you, Sall, and you can't guess what I've seen," said Bill.

"What we've both seen," said Ned.

"But I've had the greatest fright."

"And so have we."

"I've met ——— "

"And so have we."

"A man muffled in a cloak, with news of Clifford?"

"No, but *a party of ghosts* comin' down those old stairs, there. Oh! my God, it was an awful sight."

"What the devil d'ye mean?"

"Briefly this," said Ned. "Not long since, as we were pacing the hall, keeping strict watch, as you bade us, we heard a dull moan sound through the hall."

"As if from above," interrupted Ned.

"Yes! as if from above," continued Bill, "and then, and then, Sall, down the stairs glided, not walked, glided two phantoms: an old man leaning on the arm of a young and beautiful woman; they reached the bottom."

"They did."

"And then the woman seemed to give a signal; and a third phantom, a being muffled and clouded up like an Italian bravo, rushed upon the old man and stabbed him to death."

"Holy Virgin!" cried Sall.

"Yes," said Bill, "that's it; and the most mysterious thing of all is, that although there's never a trace of the phantoms, the foot of the stairs is wet with with blood."

"It is."

"Whew!" said the amazon, gaining heart once more, "if ye've seed anything, it was real murther, ye gawks."

"No, no," cried the men, in a breath.

"Let me see the blood," said Sall.

She took a lantern from Bill, and walked to the bottom of the stairs.

She stooped.

Lower and lower.

She threw the full glare of the lantern on the marble flags.

Every inch was inspected with great care.

Her glance wandered over every spot in the hall and some way up the old oak stairs, but *there was no blood!*

It had disappeared!

The men looked dumbfounded.

The woman incredulous.

"It's strange," said Bill.

"Very," said Ned.

"I can't make ye out," said Sall.

"We can't make *ourselves* out," said Bill.

"If I can you may kick me," said his friend.

"It's not dreamin' ye've been?"

"No," roared both.

"Well, it's strange."

"It's an awful den."

"It is."

"Hark!"

"What's that?"

"There's some one upstairs."

"Hist!"

Instinctively they drew towards the door.

They watched the stairs.

A dull blue light seemed to fill the hall, and next moment an old woman, bent and crippled, withered and faded, stole down the stairs, followed by a great *white cat.*

In an instant she disappeared, and there was darkness again.

Without a moment's delay the three persons rushed from the haunted house, and stood under the clear blue vault of heaven once more.

The men, it is almost needless to say, had beheld the vision of the crime by which the German Princess possessed herself of the brilliants.

And with Nan they saw the crime-laden, heaven-abandoned Mother Clifford, whose presence, although a profound mystery, must be attributed to the fact of Clifford having been recently in the house of sin and crime.

The failure of young Norman to effect the vengeance she had desired had determined her on trying her infernal arts.

But her resolve was taken after Clifford had been removed to the place mentioned by the mysterious man who had accosted Sall.

*   *   *   *

In the air once more the spirits and courage of the vision-seers immediately returned.

"Whew!" cried Bill; "rum, isn't it?"

"Awful."

"It's a murther, and the blessed Virgin protect us from all sich devilments."

"It's my opinion," said Ned, "it amounts to this, and nothing else. These things have been shown us by Wild and his friend the devil just to get us out of the house where Clifford is concealed."

"And that reminds me—" said Sall.

"Of what?"

"Of the fact that you didn't hear my mysterious story."

"Tell it now."

"I will, and quickly, for a great deal may depend upon it."

"Go on, then."

"Well, ye know, I left ye jist to run down to the lodge-keeper's, and talk over matters with 'em."

"Yes."

"Well, I didn't get there."

"No?"

"No. I met a gintleman muffled to the eyes on the road, and he stopped me."

"What had he to say?"

"Jist this, that Clifford isn't in that house."

"Not in that house, Meg?"

"No."

"Then perhaps he told you where he is?"

"He did!"

"The deuce!"

"He did, sure enough."

"Then *where* is he?"

"In a cave!"

"In a cave?"

"Yis, in an illagant cave."

"Where can there be a cave about here?"

"D'ye see the wood to the left?"

"Away yonder?"

"Away yonder, sure enough."

"Yes."

"That wood skirts a quarry."

"Yes."

"T'other side of wood is rough hedge."

"Well?"

"Near the hedge is a limetree."

"Go on."

"That limetree overhangs a pit."

"Get on with the tale."

"That pit leads to a cavern."

"Yes, yes!"

"In that cavern is Jonathan Wild!"

"Hey?"

The men pricked up their ears.

"He's at the head of a band of cut-throats as lives there."

"Ho, ho, Jonathan!"

"Them cut-throats have Clifford with 'em."

"Poor Gentleman!"

"Poor Ginthelman indeed!—if you knew all."

"Then why don't you tell us all?"

"Sure and ain't I doin' it as fast as I can?"

"Go on, then."

"Well, the Ginthelman is an insensible sort of trance like."

"Well, well, Sall."

"And when he comes to hisself Jonathan Wild means to say this to him—'Either you are my brother for life, or I drown ye in the pool that lays close by awaiting your illegant and ginthelmanly body."

"Whew!"

"And that's all."

"All—who told you this?"

"Didn't I say a man muffled up to his eyes in a cloak?"

"But didn't you recognise him?"

"Shouldn't I have said so if I had?"

"Well, is he a friend?"

"He said he was."

"And will assist us?"

"Devil a bit!"

"Hey!"

"All the assistance he was inclined to give was to tell me as much as he did."

"And how are we to set to work in this matter."

"I don't know."

"How many has Wild in his band?"

"He didn't tell me that. He just said what I told ye, and flew through the trees like a spirit."

"Strange."

"Very strange."

They consulted some moments on what was next to be done, but they could only arrive at one decision, and that was to consult the lodge-keeper as to the locality of the cave, get him to guide them to the spot, and then trust to circumstances.

Acting on this determination they hastened to the lodge, and secured the services of the keeper as guide and assistant in their enterprise.

The old man was indeed astonished at what was told him by his visitors.

He had heard of robbers being in the neighbourhood.

THE SHOWMAN FINDS A MARVELLOUS DWARF.

He had heard of many and fearful depredations lately, but that the band had their quarters in the old sandstone quarries beyond the wood he had no conception of.

The men looked to their weapons. Sall flourished her club. The old lodge-keeper carried his lantern before him, and thus they proceeded to the quarry.

* * * * *

Arrived on the spot they found the place to be very like the description given by Sall's mysterious friend.

The mouth of the pit was situated in the most elevated part of the quarry.

In the limetree the friends discovered a rope, that was evidently used to facilitate the ascent and descent into and from the cave.

It was a place admirably adapted for a retreat of this description. Nothing could be better devised.

The brow of the quarry commanded a view of three roads leading to the metropolis, and two villages lying east and west. The faintest sound on these roads would echo through the quarry, and give notice of the approaching traveller. He could be immediately sighted from the mouth of the pit, and, from all accounts, when found, his doom was certain; for the men of the cave appeared to be not merely robbers, but uncompromising murderers—cold-blooded cut-throat villains, who always disposed of their victims in the most complete manner.

"Well," said Ned, "I suppose they don't always leave that rope and pulley in the tree? That ain't like Wild's tactics, anyhow?"

"It's only likely to be there at night," said Bill.

"Hist! ye devils," said Sall; "see how it shakes. Somebody's coming up."

Cautiously they withdrew.

In a few moments a head was seen rising from the pit; then a body, and then another head and body.

And from the spot where the friends stood they beheld the forms of two tall and stalwart ruffians.

"What's their game ?" whispered Ned.

"I can't make out," said Bill.

"I see," said Sall, "sure they're the sentries on the watch. Jist see how comfortably and nately they're sating themselves for the watch."

"Sall's right," said Bill, "they're sentinels, sure enough."

"We must have 'em," cried Ned; "at all risks they must be our prisoners, or we can't go on another step."

"Right."

"What d'ye propose ?"

"You and I will crawl up to the fellows," said Bill, "and try and get at their throats before they are aware of it."

"And if we don't ?"

"We shall have to fight for it."

"Be careful," said Sall, "nothin' bates caution."

"You're right."

The two men now glanced at one another, as if asking if all was right.

They nodded, and moved forward together.

Like two snakes they stole along the ground, and in a few seconds stood over their intended victims.

Ned slipped, and the movement brought the two fellows to their feet.

But on the instant Ned and Bill were upon them, and ere they well knew what was up brawny fingers were about their throats, and they felt themselves being forced to the earth.

Bill's man sank to the ground like a lump of lead.

He struggled for a moment, but it was an iron grasp that held him, and the sense was squeezed out without much trouble.

Ned's victim was a more powerful man, and Ned was a less formidable adversary.

In a brief while he freed himself, but Bill having disposed of his man, now turned his attention to him engaged by his friend.

With his left hand Bill made a grasp at the fellow's hair, which was very thick, and got a good hold of it, and at the same moment, with his right, he caught him by the throat, and with all the force he could command he compressed his neck.

The fellow felt as though he were in a vice.

"I have him !" said Bill, between his clenched teeth.

A gurgling, gasping attempt to say something was the only sound the rascal uttered, and as Bill held him tighter and tighter still in the excitement of the moment it seemed to be a settled thing that choked he must be.

"Make the least alarm, and your brains are scattered upon the earth. Be quiet, and you have a chance of your life."

The murderer of the cavern was so completely taken by surprise that for some few moments both speech and the use of his hands were denied to him.

He then made a desperate effort to free himself from the grasp that Bill had of him, but that grasp tightened only the more, and Ned said—

"If he don't be quiet, shoot him, Bill."

"I will. Hold him still a moment."

"Oh, no—no. I am still—I will be quiet. Don't kill me !"

"Put a turn or two of a rope round him, Bill."

"That will do it."

Bill pulled the rope from over the pulley, and put it to a much better use than it had been intended for by the thieves, for he firmly bound the rascal hand and foot with it.

It was a thick, well-made piece of cordage, and the prisoner was perfectly helpless when Bill finished rolling it round him. He fell to the ground with a groan.

"Now, my fine fellow," said Ned, "you had better make a clean breast of it, and tell all."

"What do you mean ? Officers, I suppose ?"

"As you please."

"Lazarus has done it—Lazarus has sold us !"

"Just as you like to think."

"I know it—I know it. Oh, I knew he would, some day. Curses on him ! He will remember me if I get a grip at him."

"Very likely. Ned, where are you ?"

"Here. I rather think the other one is not quite safe."

"Have you got any spare cord ?"

"Yes, a long piece, but I have not cut it."

"All the better. Tie it to the other fellow, and then we shall have them both in a line together."

Bill did so, and just as the half throttled thief began to show some signs of returning consciousness, Bill had wound the remainder of the cord round him, so that they were both perfectly helpless, and connected together by a couple of yards of rope.

"Bring them along," said Ned.

"Stop a minute," said Sall. "What is that strange reflected-looking light in the hedge opposite ?"

They both looked at it, but could not make out what it was. It was like a little halo of light over one spot."

"I will go and see," said Ned.

"Be careful."

"Oh, yes ; that I will be. You look to the prisoners, Bill, and if either of them gives you any trouble it is far better to put them out of the world at once ; only do it as quietly as you can."

"I will," said Bill. "A small charge of gunpowder blown down their throats would settle them, and you would hardly hear the report of the pistol on the other side of the road."

"That would do capitally."

There was no intention upon the part of either Bill or Ned to put the prisoners to this end ; but no doubt the cool way in which Bill mentioned it as a mode of quietly and effectually managing the affair had all its effect upon them.

They were as quiet as mice who suspect that a cat is close at hand.

Ned went over the way to the strange light that was in the hedge, and when he got there he could not but laugh to himself at the trifling cause that could produce so mysterious an appearance.

The little hand-lantern that the two murderers had brought with them had not been put out ; but a slide had been drawn over the glass, and then it had been laid upon the grass by the side of the hedge ; but as the slide did not fit well enough to exclude the light entirely, the faint ray or two that had looked so strange from the other side of the way had struggled out, and rested upon the grass and the weeds in the old hedgerow.

Ned brought back the lantern with him, and explained the cause of the strange light.

"It will be useful to us, Ned," whispered Bill ; "don't put it out, but don't open it, or these fellows may see that we are a very small party."

"I will be careful."

Ned thought it would be a good thing to impress the thieves with an idea that they were in great force, so he said—

"Bring them into the lane, Bill. There are enough of our party there, as you well know, to eat them, if necessary."

"Yes," said Bill ; it would be odd, indeed, if some twenty men did not succeed in the enterprise they are upon."

"Are there twenty of you ?" said one of the prisoners.

"Silence."

Bill dragged them along to the lane, and then, when they had got them some distance from the road, they all paused ; and Ned, after a brief consultation with Bill and Sall, turned to the thieves, and said—

"There is but one solitary chance you have that your lives may possibly be spared. Are you willing to take it ?"

"Oh, yes—yes. What is it, sir?"

"It is that you at once tell the whole truth respecting the gang that inhabit the cave.

"We know a great deal, and from what we do know we shall be able to judge whether you tell us honestly what we don't know."

"Mind you, we know that Lazarus is there, and we know that Gentleman Clifford is your prisoner."

"Ah!" groaned one of the fellows, "I always thought that bothering with him would be the ruin of us all. It's about him you come, I know."

"We don't give any information," said Ned. "We now wait for you, and it will be well to speak the truth."

"I will, gentleman—I will."

"Ah, do," said the other, in a very odd voice. "My throat is rather queer, and I don't think it will ever come right again; hang me if I do."

"Go on. Be quick."

"Then, gentlemen, there are only eight of us now."

"With you two?"

"No, without us. There are eight in the cave, including Wild, and there are three prisoners there now, that is, a gent as we took to-night—his horse lies dead at the bottom of the pit—Clifford, and a boy that does nothing but cry. We can't make out who he is; but he had two hundred pounds with him, and so there's a chance of getting something handsome for him."

"How do you mean?"

"Why just this way, sir: When we nab any one that seems as if they had friends who would come down handsome, we sends a letter saying that if they put a certain sum of money in such or such a place the person they have lost will be sent home. Sometimes they do it, and sometimes they don't."

"If they do it—how do you manage then?"

"Why, sir, that's about the most troublesome part of the business, you see, sir."

"As how?"

"We tells 'em to put the money we call the ransom at a particular place, and then we are afraid that it will turn out to be a sell, and that, when we go for it, the sanguinary grabs will be down upon us; but if it's all right, and *bonum fiddy*, as they calls it, why we sends the prisoner home as comfortably as nothink at all."

"A pretty set of scoundrels you are, by your own account," said Ned.

Ned now stepped aside with his friends, to consult upon the best mode of attacking the robbers in the cave.

Sall looked rather anxious, and when Ned said to her —"Why, Sall, you don't seem to think we shall succeed in this affair," she replied—

"Yes, Ned, I do indeed; of that I can have no doubt; but—but—"

"But what?"

"I am afraid we shall purchase success at by far too high a price, that is all, you see. These rascals will fight like devils; and is it worth while for one or two of us to fall?"

"Not if it can be managed in any other way, certainly; but I don't exactly see how you are to strip our adventure of all danger, Sall."

"Not of all danger."

"Stop a bit," said Dick. "We may do something by taking the rascals by detail. This fellow says that there are eight of them now in the cave."

"Nine, with a Jew."

"To be sure; but I don't think he will fight. How-ever, there is no knowing what a rat even may do when you pursue it into a corner, so it will be as well to consider them as nine. Now, we are quite a match for them, if we were to attack them; but if nine pistol shots are sent off at us, it is just possible that some one or two out of the lot may do mischief."

"It is more than possible."

"Well, it is probable, then; but I have a question to ask of this fellow, who has already been so communicative, which will guide us. Now, mind."

"Yes, sir," returned the robber.

"How long would you and your comrade have been on duty?"

"Not long, sir. We should have been relieved by another two of 'em."

"Will they come to relieve you without your going for them, or making any sort of signal that you want them?"

"No, sir."

"Well, then, what is the signal?"

"A particular sort of a whistle, sir, if you please. When they hear that they will be sure, two of them, to come, that is to say, the next two in regular turn."

"Well, you may, or you may not, set some value upon your life, and to do a great good we will do a little evil."

"Lor, sir, what do you mean?"

"Wait a moment, and I will speak to my friends."

Bill stepped back to Sall and Ned, and told them what the robber had said, and concluded by saying—

"Now, I think that this fellow may be made use of to set a trap for some of his rascally comrades. We cannot, however, expect for a moment that he will aid us while he thinks his own fate certain, and what I propose is to promise him his life and liberty on condition that he betrays the others."

"Can he be trusted, Bill?"

"I think so, for the proofs of whether he acts truly or falsely by us will be so easily made apparent."

"There is something in that."

"And what is the promise, even then," said Sall, that you advise."

"It is this. I propose to get this fellow to make the signal for two more of the gang to come up to take charge of the rope, and then that we pounce upon them instantly. That will reduce their number to six."

"Yes," said Ned, "but what the deuce are we to do with them when we have pounced upon them?"

"No killing," said Sall.

"Certainly not," said Ned.

"Wait a bit," said Bill; "if you please, both of you—I did not say anything at all about killing that I know of."

"Pardon me, Bill; I did not for a moment wish to insinuate that you did. It was the only difficulty that stared me in face, for that the rascals well and truly deserve death there is no doubt."

"None whatever; but we don't feel disposed to be their executioners, you see, Ned, so I propose that if we get hold of another two of them we take them up the lane and tie them hand and foot to the trees with a promise of instant death if they make any alarm, and then we can try for some more of them."

"But what is to be done with them in the long run?"

"See them well secured in the cave, and then write a note to the nearest country magistrate, apprising him of the fact, and leave him to take what steps he thinks proper; and, at all events, if they were all to get off again, we shall have done something, for we shall have relieved the three prisoners in the cave."

"That is everything," said Sall.

"Will the plan do, then?"

"Yes. I say yes. What say you, Ned?"

"Agreed."

Upon this, they all three went to the fellow from whose fears they had already extracted some information, and Bill stepping close up to him, spoke in a serious and impressive tone of voice—

"You are a terrible rogue!"

"I am, sir, if you please; but I never did any of the murders. It was the others did that. I never could bring my mind to them."

"So much the better. I will believe you if I can in that particular; but I have now an offer to make to you, which I think you will do well to accept."

"What is it, sir?"

"It is just that you aid us by all means in your power

to get as many of your comrades from the cave, so that we can conquer them in detail ; and if you act with good faith to us, we promise you your own life and liberty as your reward for such services."

"You mean to say you will let me go, sir ?"

"We will."

"'Pon honour, and no mistake ?"

"We pledge you our words to that effect, always provided you play fairly with us ; but be warned that if we find you are playing a double part, you will find yourself at once sacrificed ; so your life is in your own hands. If you don't like the proposition, you can remain as you are."

"And what would become of me then ? "

"The police will come and take you as soon as we can take them to this spot for that purpose."

"**I consent, sir.**"

"Very good. Now, knowing all your chances, you can manage the best way for your own life."

"But there's one thing, sir."

"What is it ?"

"I will do my best, sir ; but if the others should suspect anything is amiss, or your plans about 'em should go wrong, don't lay it to me."

"Certainly not. You do your best, and, whether our plans fail or succeed, you shall have your reward in the shape of life and liberty."

"Then I am satisfied. I have long wished to leave the gang, but I knew they would have taken my life if I had only hinted at such a thing."

"Well, well, commence operations."

"I will. Now, you will see two of 'em come crouching up to the roadside, just where one end of the rope goes, in the course of a few moments."

Ned and his friends had every reason to feel tolerably satisfied that this man would behave with candour and honesty towards them, for his own interests were so imperatively in that direction that nothing could be very well more unlikely than that he should do otherwise.

It was possible that he might have sufficient spirit and attachment to his dear friends in the cave to sacrifice himself for the purpose of giving them notice of danger, but it was far from probable ; and there was nothing at all in his conduct, as yet, to favour such a supposition.

The persons who assemble and associate together for high and noble purposes may attain to such a sublimity of virtue that they often face death in preference to disclosure ; but a thief who lives in a cave, and whose business it is to pounce out like a spider on a fly upon any unwary passenger who may be at hand, is not at all likely to have such high-flown notions of his integrity.

Hence was it that Bill placed all but a full and perfect reliance upon the honesty of purpose of the rascal who had promised to save himself by aiding in the destruction of his friends.

The lodge-keeper did not say much upon this occasion, but proffered just all the assistance he could in carrying out the designs of Bill and Ned.

"Now, then, make your signal," said Bill to the thief.

Upon this the fellow placed his fingers to his mouth in a peculiar way, and produced a long, clear whistle, without the slightest quiver in the tone of it. It lasted about a quarter of a minute.

"That will do it," he said.

"We shall see," said Bill. "Come on, Ned."

The whole party now crept very silently to the brink of the pit, where the robbers might be expected to come up, for there was one part of the little bit of double roadway where the facilities of ascent and of descent were very great compared with the others.

They all crouched down as closely as they could in the shade of a large chestnut tree, and waited with patience.

The robber repeated his whistle three times in all, and then as Bill crept to the verge of the pit he saw a light move along as if carried by some person who was looking for something far down in the depths of the excavation.

In the course of a few moments this light rose higher, and then Bill could see who carried it.

A man of large stature, with a fur cap on his head, was slowly and carefully ascending the side of the pit with the light, but he came alone.

Bill went back to his friends and reported progress.

"There is but one man," he said.

"But one ?"

"That is all I can see, but he is a big fellow, and quite size enough for two."

"Hush," said Ned, "some one speaks."

"Can't you come on, sleepy-head?" growled a voice from the pit. "Come on, will you? Do you want me to kick up a noise here when you know it's against all rule to do so?"

"I'm coming," said another voice. "Hold your row."

"Hold my row, indeed ! It's enough to make a fellow make a row when he is half way up to his duty and you merely crawling out of the cavern. Come on, do."

"I shan't unless I like. Who the devil are you ?"

"Silence, stupid."

"Go to the deuce. You are as stupid yourself as you are big, and that makes you stupid enough. Ha—ha."

The big man in the fur cap only muttered in an under tone some rather awful maledictions upon the eyes and the limbs of his friend who was following him, and then pursued his way towards the top of the pit.

"It strikes me, Ned," whispered Bill, "that it will be a good job to nab that big fellow. If I don't mistake, that's Wild."

Ned, whose eyes were intently fixed upon the point at which the robber was expected to appear, was fully of Bill's opinion when he really saw the man in the fur cap.

As the fellow came out of the pit it seemed, as Ned whispered, he would never be done coming.

"I'm afraid," said Bill, "a bullet will be about the only argument that fellow will at all understand."

"It looks like it."

"Come on," cried the fellow again. "Come on, will you ?"

He held the light extended over the brink to light up his companion, who was evidently taking his time about it.

As that companion came up the big man said, in a conciliatory tone of voice—

"I say, Mop, you didn't mean, now, that I was stupid, did you though ?"

"Yes I did, and so you are ; and if you don't mend your manners I can tell you I will make you."

"Ho !—ho ! Will you, though ? Well, well ; you know I am very much attached to you, and have been quite a father to you."

"You go to the deuce with your nonsense."

"Well, now ; but haven't I ?"

"No, stupid ; you are drunk. If I hadn't a better father than you I'd hang myself, that I would, to put a stop to the breed."

"Never mind, Mops ; never mind. I say, old fellow ; I say—"

"What now ?"

"Don't you remember when Green once came up just where you are, and toppled head over heels, and broke his neck right at the bottom of the pit, eh ?"

"Yes ; but he was drunk, and I am not."

"Oh, ah ; that does make a difference, to be sure. I didn't think of that. Can you see ?"

"Yes, yes ; all's right. Hold the light a little higher."

"Give us your hand, old boy."

"I tell you the light dazzles me. A little higher. Ah !"

"Down you goes," said the man, as, with one blow of his fist he sent his companion, who had just got to the brink of the pit, headlong down it; "down you goes, and that will stop you from calling me as stupid as I am big another time, I rather think. Ha! ha! You won't have many whole bones, old fellow, by the time you get to the pool at the bottom of the pit. There you go. Bump!—crash! There's a bound; oh, my eye! Splash! Good-bye, old Mops. Your humble servant, sir; you are done for!"

So unexpected was this proceeding on the part of the man in the fur cap that Ned and his friends for a few moments were completely taken by surprise and bewildered at it.

The idea that a man could have such a wild, vicious, and revengeful spirit as to commit such a deed, merely on account of a little wordy warfare with his fellow man was really monstrous; but there was the fact, and there was no such thing as for a moment gainsaying it.

"Hem! said the savage. "Of course they will think that he had a drop too much, and fell over. Who is to say no, that I should like to know? So he is got rid of completely."

"Ned!" whispered Bill.

"Yes, Bill."

"Have you any scruples now about shooting that fellow?"

"Upon my life no; and yet—"

"You don't like to do it?"

"I really don't."

"Very good. I will, then. Don't you see him just upon the very edge of the pit? I can hit him nicely with one of my small, single-barrel pistols, and down he will go."

Bill paused now a moment, for he expected that Sall would say something; but the fact was, she was so terrified at the diabolical way in which the man had thrown his friend and companion down the pit that she could not say a word in his defence.

"Are you going to do it, Bill?" said Ned.

"I am."

"Ha! ha!" said the man, as he waved the light to and fro; "I think I see him half in the pool and half out. I only hope his legs are out, for he put on a new pair of boots this morning, and they will just fit me; so I don't want 'em to be damp nohow."

Bang! went Bill's pistol.

There was a shriek, and the man and the lantern went over the precipice together in a moment. The shriek mingled with the report of the pistol, and awakened some strange echoes about the spot, and then all was still as the very grave.

Ned and his friends started to their feet, for the pistol report and the noise that had followed it had seemed to them so entirely subversive of all further secrecy that they almost expected the robbers of the cavern would be upon them in a few moments.

"We forgot that it would give an alarm to shoot him," said Ned. "Keep together, all of you."

"Yes, yes," said Bill; "but don't be too hasty in thinking that we have injured our chances of success in our adventure. They can't say who fired the pistol yet, you know; so I recommend that we get back."

"So do I," said Sall.

"Stop a moment or two," said the lodge-keeper. "Who knows but two or three of them may come up to see what is the matter? and if so, we can pounce upon them, you know, easily."

"Good," said Ned, "let us wait."

This advice was all very good so far as it went, and as an experiment upon the credulity or the want of caution of the thieves it did well enough; but Ned and his friends soon enough found out that if they expected a couple more of the murderers from the cave to make their appearance above the pit they were reckoning without their host, and that they might give up the idea.

That there were six still remaining after the two that had obeyed the signal of the whistle had been disposed of they had upon the word of the thief who was tied to the tree in the lane; and they had no reason to doubt his statement.

"What is to be done?" said Ned; "it is clear that they don't mean to come up."

"I am of that opinion myself, now," said the lodge-keeper, "and as it is the case, I don't see any good reason why we should not take a peep over the hedge of the pit."

"Nor I," said Ned, "let us come on."

They all made their way quite close to the hedge of the pit, from which they were not, even when hiding amid the shadow of the trunk of the large chestnut tree, above a half a dozen yards, and then they were enabled to catch a sight of the gloomy abyss, close to which they had kept watch.

That commotion and consternation reigned below they could not doubt, for there was a flashing of lights and a moving of dusky figures to and fro, and now and then a voice would sound upon the night air, but they could not catch what was said.

In the course of another five minutes all was, or seemed to be, profoundly serene in the pit and the cavern, for no light and no moving form was to be seen, let them strain their eyes ever so much.

"Well," said Ned, "now, Bill, as we have followed you more than any one else as yet in this affair, pray just say what we shall do now?"

"Come back to the lane," said Bill, "and ask our friend at the tree what his friends, or rather quondam friends, below are likely to do now; but at the same time that I advise, I also protest against being considered to be the general upon this occasion."

"Never mind who is the general, so that the advice be good. I think that we ought to consider Sall to be considered the commander-in-chief."

"Be it so."

"I accept the offer," said Sall, quietly.

"You do?"

"Yes, Ned, if you give it to me. I think that one mind had better now direct the future arrangements in connection with this adventure, and I have no objection to take the responsibility upon myself."

"Bravo! Be it so."

"Follow me to the lane, then."

They all followed Sall to the lane, and she went direct up to the thief who was tied to the tree, and said to him in a firm and decided tone—

"Did you hear a pistol-shot?"

"I did."

"Well, there was a man with a fur cap, who came up to the top of the pit a few paces before another man, whom he called Mops, and this Mops gave him some frivolous offence, upon which he flung him headlong down the pit."

"He did? Wild did that?"

"I don't know if he be Wild or not, but when the man did that one of us shot at him, and he fell after his victim."

"Served him right—served him right. But they won't come up now, they will go into the inner cavern and hide themselves, and if you want them you will have to seek for them."

CHAPTER LII.

THE MEN OF THE CAVE—THEIR HISTORIES RELATED BY
THE PRISONER—THE MYSTERY OF THE OLD SANDSTONE
QUARRY REVEALED AND EXPLODED.

"Now," said Bill, addressing his prisoner, the one who
appeared so much inclined to talk; "now, then, young
fellow, as we can't make any further progress, and don't
mean to give up the ghost, perhaps you'll put us down
to a move or two."

"What can I do?"

"In the first place you must tell us the names and the
nature of the gang in the cave, and then tell us how we
are to get into the cave—for there we are determined to
to go."

"Well, then, you'd best listen attentively to me.
There's no fear of interruption. Wild and his lieutenant
dead or wounded, the others must find the pluck to come
in just yet."

"Go on, then."

"In the cave," said the prisoner, "are eight men and the
Jew. Some of their names will be familiar to you, and
their exploits will be worth relating. Below us, then, are
Ned Burnworth, Bill Blewit, Tom Berry, Tom Dorbel,
Kit Moor, Dan Hughes, and Jack Prince. These are the
leaders; and desperate devils every one.

"The father of Burnworth was a painter, and bound
his son an apprentice to a buckle-maker.

"After the death of his father he went into the company of vagrants, and neglected his work.

"Being active in person, and enterprising in genius, he
distinguished himself in cudgel-playing and those exercises which first prepare for the highway, and then lead
to the gallows.

"There was one Frazier, who kept an inn, which was
frequented by these hopeful youths.

"His comrades were so highly pleased with Burnworth's exploits that they honoured him with the appellation of Young Frazier.

"He was proud of the compliment, and was more
generally known by that name than by that of Burnworth.

"Frazier, along with his associates, began with picking pockets, and in that way did more mischief than any
gang who had been before them.

"It happened, however, that for an action of this kind
Ned was committed to Bridewell, where he employed his
thoughts in forming a regular plan of operations, and
devising such means as would render him and his companions more secure in their lucrative employment.

"He had no sooner recovered his liberty than he sought
out his confederates, and with them walked the streets
with singular audacity, as there were warrants out against
several of them.

"In frequenting petty ale-houses one evening in the
Old Bailey he learned that one Thomas Ball, the successor to Jonathan Wild, was carousing with his servants
and attendants.

"Burnworth loaded his pistol, went into an inner
room where Ball was, and presented the pistol to him
saying—

"'Harkee, you fellow, who have served your time to
a thief-catcher, what business might you have with me
or my company? Do you think to get a hundred or two
by swearing our lives away? If you do, you are much
mistaken; but that I may be some judge of your talents
in that way, here's a glass of brandy, and swear by the
most tremendous oaths that I shall prescribe, that you
will never more attempt any mischief against me or my
company.'

"Ball had no sooner complied than the other knocked
him down, and went to inform his friends what he had
done.

"This memorable action procured him the command,
and all were willing to submit to his direction.

"In this manner union added to their strength, and
enabled them to act on a safer and more formidable plan.

"As an old justice of the peace had committed Ned to
prison, he proposed to reward him by robbing his house.

"The company were successful; but, instead of plate,
they were disappointed in finding that it was only gilt.

"He was for throwing it away, but Barton was of a
different opinion, saying, 'That they should be able to
sell it for something.'

"Burnworth replied, 'That it was good for nothing but
to discover them, therefore it should not be kept at any
rate.'

"While they were warmly disputing, several of their
companions arrived at the place of rendezvous, when it
was proposed to terminate the dispute by throwing up for
it.

"Burnworth gained the disposal of the hated property,
and instantly carried it to the river, throwing it in, saying, 'He was sorry he had not the old justice there to
share the same fate.'

"While loitering about the fields until the evening,
when they might renew either their pleasures or their
depredations, one of their companions joined them in the
greatest hurry, saying, 'Lads, beware of one thing: the
constables have been all about Chick-lane in search of
folks of our profession, and if we venture to the house
where we agreed to meet to-night, 'tis ten to one but we
are all taken.'

"Their chief admonished them to keep together, and,
as they were well armed, a small force would not venture
to attack them.

"In the evening they ventured into the town; but the
people suspecting their appearance began to assemble in
formidable numbers; on which they thought it proper
to leave the place, frequently turning about, and presenting their pistols to the crowd, and swearing that the first
man who dared to touch them should instantly be shot
dead upon the spot.

"Their pursuers being dispersed, a consultation was
held what was next to be done.

"Burnworth proposed that they should enter another
quarter of the town, and then go directly to the water
side.

"He next proposed, that in order to secure themselves
against present and future danger, there was nothing
better than to go to the house of Thomas Ball the thief-
catcher, and to kill him at once.

"They all agreed to the proposal but one, who, as soon
as the darkness of night permitted, separated from the
company.

"Having taken an oath that they would stand true,
Burnworth put himself at their head, and marched
directly for Ball's house.

"Burnworth inquired for him, and was informed by his
wife that he was in an ale-house in the neighbourhood, but
that she would go for him. He followed, and, meeting
Ball at the door, seized him by the throat, dragged him
into his own house, and began to upbraid him for attempting to betray his old acquaintance.

"Ball entreated for his life, but in vain; for Burnworth
instantly shot him dead.

"Having perpetrated this deed they were more
cautious than ever, because of the search that they were
certain would be made after them.

Three of them went over to Holland, and took shelter
until the search should be over. Hughes, who declined
engaging in that murder, was apprehended, and also one
of the name of Wilson.

"Burnworth and the remainder still continued their
depredations; so that proclamation was made, and a reward offered for any one who would apprehend them, who
were expressly named.

"Upon this proclamation, one of them, Marjoram, re_

flecting upon his danger, surrendered to a constable, upon receiving security that his own life should be spared.

"Upon the report of his surrender many of his companions changed their lodgings; but the next day, as he was conveying to the Goldsmiths' Hall, Barton planted himself in the way, presented a pistol to Marjoram, swearing, 'I'll kill you.'

"He bowed forward his head, and the ball grazed his back, but did him small injury.

"Barton, amid the surprise occasioned by this circumstance, escaped in the crowd. Marjoram made a full discovery.

"One of the gang was seized that very night, and committed to Newgate.

"Burnworth was now under the necessity of acting alone, and, a few nights after, he broke into the house of a great distiller, aud took a large quantity of plate, which, supposing that they were white metal, he threw away, and the articles being picked up by one Jones, that unfortunate man was executed as having stolen them.

"But so bold and daring did Burnworth become, that even after the proclamation was issued, he came into an ale-house, laid his pistols upon the table, and defied any person to touch him, while he called for a pint of beer, paid for it, drank it, and went off with impunity.

"There was, however, one Leonard, who, being in prison for actions similar to Burnworth's, and being informed that the latter was, at that time, lodging with his wife and sister, the desire of life, strongly implanted in every creature, suggested to Leonard the possibility of purchasing his own at the expense of that of Burnworth.

"Accordingly he sent his wife to make the proposal to government, and, matters being settled, a sufficient force was lodged in an adjoining house, which, upon a signal being given, rushed in upon him, seized him, carried him before a justice, who, upon examination, sent him to Newgate.

"He found means to communicate to his companions his suspicions that the wife of Leonard had betrayed him; so that one of them fired at her as she was entering her own door, and made other similar attempts, until the justice of the peace placed a guard at her door, when she was no more disturbed with such visitors.

"Burnworth was confined in the condemned hole; but nothing could subdue the stubbornness of his temper, and he was continually plotting his escape.

"Having procured some files and instruments for that purpose, he released himself from his irons, and broke through the wall into the women's apartment.

"The window being secured by three iron bars, he had cut one, and was keenly employed at another, when one of the women gave the alarm, and the keepers came and dragged him back to the condemned hole, and bound him down by staples to the ground, but he soon after got away.

"William Blewit was the son of a potter, and learned to be a perfumer of gloves.

"But the path of sobriety and industry was soon abandoned by him, and he became acquainted with a gang of young pick-pockets, with whom he carried on business with considerable success for several years.

"Justice, however, overtook him, and he was sentenced to transportation.

"Scarcely were the convicts on board the vessel destined to transport them when they formed the plan of their deliverance.

"Blewit informed the captain, and thus obtained his liberty.

"But being taken up because he had returned from banishment, he pleaded the service he had done, and the grant of the captain: he was, therefore, respited until the captain's return, and then set at liberty.

He met, accidentally, with Burnworth, the same evening on which they killed Ball; and the ferociousness of his temper made him readily fall in with any wicked proposal.

"He and Dickson, and Berry, having gone over to Holland, the British resident at the Hague caused search, diligently, after any persons who might be suspected of Ball's murder; and Blewit being apprehended, the others were also soon discovered.

"All three being seized, they were sent under a strong guard to Rotterdam.

"Intelligence of their being in custody was sent over to England, and an application was made to the States to allow them to be carried over to their native country, which was readily granted.

"Besides the messengers who were sent to apprehend them, six soldiers attended them on board.

"Arrived at the Tower, they were put into a boat with armed men in them, to guard them.

"They were conducted to Westminster, to be examined by a justice of the peace, the people in the meantime exulting that such notorious villains were in custody.

"Burnworth and five of his companions were conveyed in a wagon, handcuffed and in chains, to their trial, under a strong guard, the populace exulting in their fate.

"They were all found guilty, and sentenced to suffer death.

"Upon receiving sentence they requested liberty for their relations to visit them in prison, which was granted.

"Their minds were still bent upon their liberation; Burnworth's mother carried files upon her, and Blewit's mother had opium, with which the prison authorities were poisoned, and the whole gang escaped.

"About the age of nineteen Tom Dorbel ventured to appear upon the highway; but he was nearly outwitted in his first attempt.

"Meeting a Welshman, he demanded Taffy's money, or he would take his life.

"The Welshman said—

"'Hur has none of hur own, but has three score pounds of hur master's money; but Cot's blood! hur must not give hur master's money: what would hur master then say for hur doing so?'

"Tom replied—

"'You must not put me off with your cant; for money I want, and money I will have, let it be whose it will; or expect to be shot through the head.'

"The Welshman then delivered the money, saying—

"'What hur gives you is none of hur own; and that hur master may not think hur has spent hur money, hur requests that you be so kind as to shoot some holes through hur coat-lappets, that hur master may see hur was robbed.'

"So, suspending his coat upon a tree, Tom fired his pistol through it.

"Taffy exclaimed—

"'Gots splatter a-nails! this is a pretty pounce; pray give hur another pounce for her money!'

"Tom fired another shot through his coat.

"'By St. Davy, this is a better pounce than the other; pray give hur one pounce more.'

"Quoth Tom—

"'I have never another pounce left.'

"'Why, then,' replied the Welshman, 'Hur has one pounce left for hur, and if hur will not give hur money again, hur will pounce hur through hur body.'

"He quietly returned the money, and was thankful he was allowed to depart.

"But this narrow escape did not deter Dorbel, and he continued his villanies about the space of five years.

"It happened, however, that a gentleman's son was taken for robbing on the highway; and, as he was formerly pardoned, he now despaired of obtaining mercy a second time.

"Tom undertook, for the sum of five hundred pounds, to bring him off.

"The one-half was paid in hand, and the other half was to be paid when the deliverance was effected.

"When the young gentleman came upon his trial, he was found guilty; and when the judge was about to pass sentence, Tom cried out—

"'Oh! what a sad thing it is to shed innocent blood! Oh! what a sad thing it is to shed innocent blood?'

"Continuing to reiterate the expression, he was apprehended, and, the judge interrogating him what he meant by such an expression, he said—

"'May it please your lordship, it is a very hard thing for a man to die wrongfully, but one may see how hard-mouthed some people are by the witnesses swearing that this gentleman here at the bar now robbed them on the highway at such a time, when, indeed, my lord, I was the person that committed that robbery.'

"Accordingly Tom was taken into custody, and the young gentleman liberated.

"He was brought to trial at the next assizes, and being asked whether he was guilty or not, he pleaded not guilty.

"'Not guilty!' replied the judge, 'why, did not you, at last assizes, when I was here, own yourself guilty of such a robbery?'

"Quoth Tom—'I don't know how far I was guilty then; but, upon my word, I am not guilty now; therefore, if any person can accuse me of committing such a robbery, I desire they may prove the same.'

"No witnesses appearing he was acquitted.

"Tom living at such an extravagant rate in the prison had scarcely any part of the five hundred pounds remaining when he obtained his liberty; therefore, endeavouring to recruit his funds by robbing the Duke of Norfolk, near Salisbury, his horse was shot, and he taken and condemned at the next assizes.

"While under sentence, he found a lawyer who engaged, for the sum of fifty guineas, to obtain his pardon.

"He accordingly rode to London, was successful, and just arrived in time with the pardon, when Dorbel was about to be thrown off, having rode so hard that his horse immediately dropped down dead.

"Such, however, was Tom's ingratitude that he refused to pay the lawyer, alleging that any obligation given by a man under sentence of death was not valid.

"Dorbel was so much alarmed upon his narrow escape from a violent death that he resolved to abandon the collecting trade, and served in several families in the station of a footman.

"He also served six or seven years with a lady in Ormond-street, who had a brother a merchant in Bristol, who having an only daughter sixteen years of age, she prevailed upon her father to allow her to come to London to perfect her education.

"Dorbel being a person in whom her aunt thought she could place unlimited confidence he was left alone with her, when he first abused her person, then robbed her of her gold watch, diamond ring, jewels to the amount of a hundred pounds, and, cutting a hole in the back of the coach, escaped, leaving the young lady in a swoon.

"It was with difficulty she recovered to inform her relations how she had been treated.

"Her mother hastened to town to see her, and, after speaking a few words to her, the poor girl breathed her last.

"The disconsolate father soon after lost his senses.

"Dorbel was pursued in different directions, but he took refuge with Wild, and escaped justice.

"Jack Collins was a coachman to Colonel Kendal; and being sent to sell two horses, he decamped with the money.

"He was detected and sent as a soldier into Flanders, from whence he soon returned to London; and having need of a surgeon, he would give him no greater fee than a groat!

"The son of Galen spurned at the offer, but afterwards thought proper to accept it.

"Collins went after him and robbed him of his watch and all his money.

"He was chiefly employed in house-breaking for some years, then a second time enlisted in Colonel Wing's regiment; and though he attained the rank of a sergeant, he was not content with his pay, but frequently went upon the highway.

"He a second time deserted his colours, and commenced house-breaker.

"He was at last indicted for breaking into the house of John Halloway, and stealing from thence two exchequer bills of a hundred pounds each, one hundred and thirty seven pounds ten shillings in money, and one hundred and ninety-four pounds in gold.

"A woman who shared these large spoils with him and a lady were the two evidences against him.

"There was also another indictment served upon him for robbing on the highway, which was likewise proved, but Wild was then in power and got him off.

"Kit Moore was bred up as a tapster in one of the low inns in London, and soon began to break houses.

"He associated with Dan Hughes; and, though both young, they are bold and active to that degree, that they have committed fifty robberies in London and the adjacent places.

"About the age of eighteen Price was serving a gentleman in the country, who turned him off merely for his notorious falsehoods.

"In going to London he robbed a woman of eighteen shillings, was apprehended in the act, and tried before his late master, who took pity upon his situation, and saved his life.

"Informed of this, the judges at the next assizes, blamed the gentleman's conduct for allowing the man to escape who had pleaded guilty.

"The sheriff said, 'He acknowledged that such a man had been condemned at the last assizes; but, then, he knew the fellow to be such an unaccountable liar, that there was no believing one word he said; so, his pleading guilty to what was laid to his charge, was, in his opinion, an eminent sign he ought to be believed innocent of the fact, and he would not hang an innocent man for the world.'

"This reply made the judges smile, and he was dismissed with a severe reprimand, and cautioned not to come before them again.

"Upon obtaining his liberty he came to London, associated with a band of robbers, and, in a short time, was apprehended diving into another person's pocket instead of his own, and for that crime committed to Newgate.

"He was accordingly sentenced to a severe whipping, then sent on board a man-of-war; but, after he received the punishment assigned to stealing, from the sailors, he was discharged the ship.

"He hastened again to London, joined another association of thieves, and abandoned himself to all manner of wickedness.

"One evening his gang divided themselves into three companies.

"The first met an attorney, near Hampstead, whom they robbed of eight guineas.

"The unfortunate lawyer had not gone far when he was attacked by the second party, to whom he related his misfortunes, and into what cruel hands he had fallen.

"'Cruel!' said one of them, 'how durst thou use these terms? And who made you so bold as to talk to us with your hat on? Pray, sir, be pleased henceforward to learn more manners!'

"They then snatched off his hat and wig, and took a diamond ring from his finger.

"As he was plodding his way home, uncertain which road was safest, the third division came up to him near Kentish-town, bringing with them a man that they pretended to have stripped completely naked, and constrained the lawyer to clothe the naked with his own coat and waistcoat; then told him he might be thankful he got off with his life, which he employed to sow division among society.

"In a short time after this, Price and one of his companions one evening entered a garret, in which there was nothing but lumber, with the intention of robbing the house when all was silent.

THE IRISH GIRL ENTERS THE PIT.

"But, in the dark, as Price was laying his hand upon a pistol which he had laid upon the table, it went off and alarmed the people of the house.

"His comrade instantly ran to the window where they fastened a rope for their escape, and his companion attempting to slide down the rope soon broke, though he was not so much injured but he got away.

"Price, seeing his extreme danger of being caught, removed the rope to another window, and it conveyed him to a balcony.

"He was, however, scarcely there, when all the people in the house were alarmed; on which he leaped into a large basket of eggs which a man was carrying upon his head, from Newgate Market; so that the fall being broken, he was able to make his escape amid the cry of "thieves!"

"Jack now began to be so well known about town that he found it necessary to remove to the country.

"He was there most industrious in stripping the hedges of all the linen that he found upon them.

"Putting up at an inn, the landlord soon understood, from his discourse, that he was a servant that would suit him; therefore, hired him as his tapster.

"It was this miscreant's custom to murder travellers who put up at his house; but one gentleman, being warned by a maid of his danger, he provided for his safety.

"Among other things, the maid informed him that it was usual for the landlord to ring a bell, on which an assassin, pretending to be a servant, entered the chamber, and snuffed out the candle, when the other villains rushed in and murdered the stranger.

"The gentleman caused the maid to place a lantern, with a candle in it, below his stool, and he laid his arms ready, and stood upon his guard.

"Scarcely had he sat himself down, when it happened

as the girl had mentioned; but the gentleman, with the assistance of his servant, killed two of the villains, and put the rest to flight.

"He then seized the innkeeper and his wife, carried them before a magistrate, and they were indicted to stand for trial at the next assizes.

"From the maid's deposition it appeared that fourteen strangers had been murdered by them, and that their bodies were concealed in an arched vault in the garden, to which there was a passage from the cellar.

"Both were executed, and the innkeeper hung in chains.

"Jack, having once more escaped death, he returned to his pilfering trade, was committed to Newgate, and whipped for his crimes.

"But Jack was now determined to follow the example of the great ones of the earth, and to better his circumstances by marriage.

"Accordingly, he married one of the name of Betty, who gained her livelihood by running errands to the prisoners of Newgate.

"Nor was Jack, like too many, disappointed in his matrimonial connexion; for he was soon elevated to be hangman to the county of Middlesex.

"In this station he assumed great importance, and held a levee every day that he did business at Tyburn; but, though he sometimes run in debt, yet he was always very willing to work in order to pay his debt.

"But envy reached even him, and he lost his place by means of one that had *greater* ministerial interest.

"But Jack never could be destitute while he had fingers to lay hold of whatever was within his reach.

"Wild has likewise stood his friend."

"And now," continued the prisoner, "you have the stories of the men remaining in the cave; Wild, I need not tell you about, for his exploits you are doubtless well acquainted with."

"Too well," said Bill. "Too well, unfortunately."

"But the cave," said Ned, "how are we to get into that den?"

"That I will now tell you, but beware, for the danger is immense."

"Never you mind the danger," said Bill, "leave that to us."

"Well, then, the cave, or rather caves, run east and west; this is the eastern entrance. In the west we enter beneath—down in the very bowels of the quarry. At that point there is a hole closed by a single stone, which at once gives us entrance to the cave."

"And how is it that with that aisy mode of gittin' in and out of yer divil's den, ye risk yer necks by commin' up and down that ould rope?" demanded Sall.

"It is the simplest and easiest method," replied the robber; "it is a quarter of a mile to the western entrance, and the road isn't the best in the world, whereas we can, by means of the pulley, get up and down in a few seconds and with only the least bit of danger in the world."

"I see."

"This is our point of look out, and here we always establish ourselves; so you see the other entrance isn't of much service. Indeed it is understood amongst the gang that it is never to be used except in circumstances of the greatest possible need."

"Well."

"Well, gentlemen, the only way for you to release your friend is to enter by the hole in the quarry, and by surprising the band, overcome them."

"Meanwhile perhaps Clifford may be killed."

"Not if you've done for Jonathan Wild."

"How?"

"No other man in the band has any antipathy to Clifford, and he is safe with them."

"Well, there can't be a doubt that Wild is not done."

"Then you have plenty of time; with your friends in the lane you can easily overcome the little band and so effect your object."

The words "Friends in the lane" at once recalled the friends to the position in which they stood.

The plan proposed by the robber would have been simple enough had they had in reality those imaginary "friends in the lane," but under the existing circumstances they did not see their way clear.

"It's puzzled I am intirely," said Sall; "och! bother, what will I be doing now?"

"There's only one thing for us to do," said Bill, and that's to go into this cursed quarry and reconnoitre."

"Just so," said Ned, "so let us be off at once."

They stood the prisoners on their feet, and bade them point out the way, and be careful.

This they were very likely to do, seeing that each individual had a loaded pistol presented at the back of his head.

Walking in this manner, they disappeared, leaving Sall to guard the mouth of the pit.

"Och! blazes," said the Irish girl, as they disappeared, "an' this same is a nate sitiwation for a young female to to be placed in. What will I do?—what will I do?"

"Do as I bid you," said some one at her elbow.

Turning, she beheld her mysterious informant of the Willows.

"It's ould Muffled-up agin," she said, glancing at the mysterious comer.

"I have thought better of it," said the man, "and have come to give you further assistance."

"Many thanks to ye for that same, for it's the divil's own mess we're into now."

"What has happened, and where are your companions?"

"What's happened? Och, murther!"

"Murder?"

"Nothin' short of it."

"Explain."

"Ain't I a doin' of that same."

"Not that I am aware of."

"Bad scran! why don't ye keep yer *eyes* open, and then ye'd hear well—well enough."

"Should I?"

"Yes. D'ye seem to doubt it?"

"Perhaps."

"More fool ye."

"Now, are you about to commence one of your interminable dialogues, or will you give me the information I want?"

"As to thim hard words, it's not myself as understands 'em at all at all; but if it's wantin' to be told what's up, I'll do that same in a jiffy."

"A what?"

"A jiffy."

"What's that?"

"Bedad, it's myself that's puzzled to tell ye, now."

"I should say so."

"Should ye, now?"

"I certainly should."

"Well, nobody would think it to look at ye."

"Well, what has all this to do with Clifford?"

"That's what I'd like to be told."

"I've no doubt of it; but now just be brief, or I must go."

"Be brief is it? Och! and how's that same to be done with a long-winded chap like ye are?"

"Nonsense."

"That's what I say."

"Come, now, my good girl, what has been done?"

"Well, I'll begin agin at the old startin' point—murther!"

"Who is murdered?"

"Two of 'em."

"Your companions, or the robbers?"

"The robbers! Bad luck, now, d'ye think my companions would be fools enough to git murthered."

"I didn't know."

"Then ye ought to."

"Oh, did I?"

"O' course ye did."

"Well, two of the men are killed?"

"Yes."

"Which two ?"

"Wild's one of 'em."

"The devil !"

" So I say, the nasty ould devil !"

"And who is the other ?"

"Mops."

"How did it happen ?"

Sall related the story.

"If this be the case," said the mysterious man, " I think I can see my way clear to release your friend."

"Indeed, now !"

" Yes, indeed."

" How will ye do it ?"

"Listen to me."

"Och ! sure I will."

"You must bring your companions back."

"Must I ?"

"You must."

"What for ?"

" Because they're of no use where they are now, and I want to make a clear field for the escape of those in the cave."

"The robbers ?"

"Yes."

" Well, *that's* helpin' Clifford with a vengeance."

"It is."

"How so ?"

" By withdrawing the men, you can withdraw your friend ; whereas if they remain there, the possibility is that you won't be over and above successful ; *only one* can enter the cave at a time at either entrance. So you see the advantages are against you,—more particularly as those below are well armed, and seldom fail to bring down their men."

The woman looked puzzled.

"You see," continued the man, "that you must do as I bid you."

"Yes."

" Well, in return, I'll guarantee that you save Clifford."

" That's brave."

"Now give the signal for your friends to return."

"That's soon done."

Sall applied two fingers to her mouth and whistled loudly.

The whistle was immediately answered.

"They're coming."

"Very good. Then I'm going."

" Where ?"

" Down the rope."

"Good luck to ye."

"Thanks."

"And now your instructions."

" They are these. Do not let your prisoners know a word of what has passed between us."

"I won't."

"They give an alarm, bring the band upon you, and frustrate your plans."

" All right."

" In half an hour enter the cave."

" How ?"

" By the rope."

" All right."

" You understand."

"Perfectly ; but how are you going to act below ?"

" I'm going to tell them that I've planned an escape, that there are twenty soldiers here, and that here they are determined to remain until the gang is starved out."

" And by these manes ye think to make 'em cut off at the other end."

"Yes."

"Very good."

" And now I must descend ; I hear your friends, be careful."

" I will."

The man grasped the rope, and in a few moments descended into the pit.

Sall's companions soon rejoined her.

"Why did you whistle ?" asked Bill.

"Because I wanted ye."

"What for ?"

"What for ? sure, to release the Gintleman."

" And how's that to be done ?"

" By follerin' myself."

"And what will you do ?"

"Stand still for half an hour."

" Psha ! Sall, you're drunk or mad."

" Maybe."

"But how, in the devil's name, are we to save the Gentleman by standing here for half an hour ?"

"What's that to you ?"

"Bah !' said Ned ; " she's mad. Let us go back to the quarry."

"Ye'd better not."

" And why ?"

" Because I'm cap'n, and I order ye to stay here."

"It can't be done."

" It *must* be done."

" Let her have her own way," said Bill ; " she's a rum 'un, but she knows what she's about. Besides, we have made her captain, and must follow her."

" It's nothing short of madness," said Ned.

" Nonsense, ye mutinous rapscallion ! Howld yer tongue, and obey orders, or I'll break yer head with this stick."

The amazon flourished her club menacingly as she spoke, and Ned thought it best to hold his tongue.

" Now, Sall," said Bill, coaxingly, " what's the use of keeping us in all this suspense ? Why not speak out, and tell us what game you're after ?"

"I'm afther Clifford ; no more nor less."

" But this standing still for half an hour—"

" Strict orders, and must be obeyed."

" Why ?"

" What's that to ye ? Ain't it sufficient that I give the order ?"

" No, Sall ; you know how anxious we all are, and it's not sufficient to tell us to stand still, like a parcel of fools, for half an hour, when we don't know why we're doing it."

"Don't know, ye spalpeen ?" Isn't it to save the Gintleman ?

" I tell you what it is," said Ned, in a sulky voice, " I shan't play at this fool's game. If this is following a woman's leadership, save me from it ; that's all I have to say."

" You won't play at the game, won't ye ?" said Sall. " Now ye'll just play at whatever game I like to make ye, or ye'll take the consequences, and " she continued, grasping her stick, " by the powers, they'll be tremenjous !"

Ned was once more silenced.

For half an hour the amazon held her friends over the mouth of the pit, forbidding them to speak or move without her orders.

Bill, who knew the peculiarities of the woman, induced Ned to accede to her whim, as he considered it ; and thus they passed the weary minutes. At length Sall rose, and said—

" It's time."

" Time for what ?" asked Bill

" Why, to enter the cave, to be sure."

"To enter ?"

"Yes ; all the danger's over now ; or at least it ought to be. So come along."

The girl grasped the rope in her hand, and began to steadily lower herself into the pit.

"You'll follow yer captain, boys," she said, "and never mind how ye come ; for, bedad ! this sort of travelling ain't pleasant."

As soon as Sall had descended Bill took the rope and

followed her, and then Ned went down. The lodge-keeper was forced to remain in charge of the two prisoners.

The three adventurers found the cave, or caves, as singular a place as ever they beheld. At the bottom of the pit, on the one hand, was a deep pool. A natural bank divided this place from the opening into the cave.

The first care of the adventurers was to see what had become of Wild and his victim.

But they could discover no trace of them.

"Strange?" said one to the other.

But there was no further remark, for their thoughts were bent on penetrating further, in the hope of discovering the man of whom they had come in search.

Cautiously they penetrated into the cave.

The light they carried revealed a great hollow space, forming a rather comfortable chamber.

This place was furnished like a room, and had many comforts of which many rooms were destitute.

The first object the searchers encountered was an old lady, who assailed them in good broad Scotch.

It was the old Lady Bumbozeen, with whom Wild had eloped some time previous.

"A' weel," said the old lady, "and wha's here the noo?"

The light was turned full upon the old soul, and she started to her feet on the instant.

"Are ye friends or foes?"

"Friends."

"And ye're come to take me oot o' this?"

"Yes. But where is the other prisoner?"

"There's one in the inner cave."

"That's him," said Bill; "come along."

Poor old Lady Bumbozeen was left once more in solitude and darkness.

Within they found poor Clifford.

He lay stretched on a mattrass, and was just recovering consciousness.

He was pale and emaciated, and appeared to have suffered considerably.

"Och! bad cess to 'em. They've killed the poor Gintleman; they've kilt him entirely," said the Irish girl.

Bill and Ned raised poor Clifford in their arms.

"It's fresh air he wants," said Bill, "fresh air; so let us take him out of this."

The eyes of Ned had wandered about the cave, and lighted on piles of plunder, upon which he gazed in astonishment and admiration.

"By George!" he said, "they must have been sharp fellows to have been able to get all this together in so short a time."

"That's true," said Bill; "but the Gentleman."

"All right," said Ned; "we will hoist him and some of this stuff at the same time. Sall, you attend to the Gentleman, with Bill, and I'll collect a few of these trifles, they may be handy."

Sall at once supported Clifford, and with Bill's assistance, bore him into the other cave.

In a few minutes Ned followed.

He had collected a great pile of valuables, and with this and the two captives, the three friends went to the bottom of the pit.

"Now, then," said Sall; "I'll go up first. You will thin put the Gentleman on the rope, and I'll hand him up with all speed."

"The ladies first," suggested old Lady Bumbozeen.

"Divil a bit," said Sall; "and it's lucky ye may think yerself to get out at all at all."

With this she grasped the rope, and was speedily pulled up by the others.

Then Clifford was secured to the rope and dragged up. Next came the turn of the old lady, and then the two highwaymen.

"It's all right now," said Sall, glancing triumphantly at the robbers; "it's all right, ye see, boys; and it's myself as has proved the ra'al sort o' captain afther all."

But no sooner were the first outbursts of joy over than

fears possessed all, for over the face of Clifford was spreading a pallor so fearful that their alarm could not fail to be raised.

CHAPTER LIII.

RETURNS TO EVELINA—HER WANDERINGS—WINTERLEIGH ONCE MORE—THE DWARF AND THE SHOWMAN—FRIGHT OF EVELINA—THE MIDNIGHT FLIGHT OF MISTRESS AND MAID.

"WALK up, ladies and gentlemen; walk up—walk up! In the interior is to be seen one of the most wonderful exhibitions of ground and lofty tumbling, oriental magic, and French dancing ever witnessed in these parts. The great Signor Gufferini, from the Saharian desert of Hindostandee, will go through his marvellous slight-of-hand tricks. Signor Puffemlene will introduce his solo on the Pandean pipes, and your humble servant will exhibit his performing pig, who knows more than some Christians, and is studying for the professionship of *multiplication* at the great University of Oxford. In addition to these novelties we shall exhibit the world-famed Madame Gufferini, in her African war dance; also the infant Gufferini on the slack wire, the Spanish minstrels and dancers, Signoras Pakaraboo and Figarala, and the great panorama of the landing of George the First, St. Paul's by moonlight, and the Battle of Flodden. Walk up—walk up!"

It was a splendid afternoon, and the village of Winterleigh looked remarkably entrancing, as it nestled snugly among the tree-crested hills that bounded it on all sides.

Labour had ceased; and the villagers and farm servants hastened from their cottages and the fields to pass pleasantly the remaining hours of light.

It was a brilliant day for Winterleigh, for it was the occasion of its village festival and annual fair.

The village green was crowded with booths, shows, and theatrical establishments, of more or less pretensions, extent, and magnitude.

The noise was sufficient to call up reminiscences of Babel, and the confusion and mirth was of the most boisterous description.

Hundreds of rustic swains' and their lasses, bedizened in bright ribbons, were there, listening, with mouths wide open, to the harangue from the platforms, and swallowing the bait, temptingly held up to them by caterers for amusement, with the greatest avidity.

The speech, given at the opening of this chapter, was yelled at the multitude amid a fanfare of trumpets, the beating of drums, and crashing of gongs, from the stage of a rather large show, by a man dressed in a half-military, half-spangled suit—which sat on him as the proverbial purser's shirt would sit on a handspike.

He was a thin, cadaverous individual, and carried an enormous red umbrella, which he flourished about, to the danger of all others in his immediate vicinity.

This man was no other than the wandering buffoon, with whom Evelina, and her maid Rose, quitted the roof of Job Winchurst.

On the platform with him were the other members of his *troupe*, to whom the reader has been already introduced.

"Walk up, walk up! this *is* the show of the fair, so be in time, and secure the front places"—*sotto voce*—"Tattle that ere drum, and blow into them ere pipes, can't yer? They're walking up to every other show but this here one."

The first part of this speech was addressed to the British public; the remainder was hissed, in a confidential whisper, at the artiste on the drum and pipes, who, forthwith, beat the drum as if he had designed to knock its head in.

The wife of this individual—the lady whom the reader

will remember as having unfortunately descended from her high estate of tragic actress to dance in the mud—approached the manager; and, whilst "doing a short dance" for the pleasure of the aforesaid British public, managed to say—

"Why don't yer 'av them gals out (meaning Evelina and Rose)? They'd draw 'em fast enough."

"It ain't no manner of use," said the manager; "I've tried 'em. I've been down on my bended knees to 'em, but they won't see it, and obstinately refuse to appear on the outside."

"Why?"

"I don't quite know; but they seem to be known in these parts, and don't care to show their faces."

"I'd make 'em."

"*Would* you? Then all I can say is you'd better try. I've done all I can in the persuasion line, and as to force, it won't pay. I don't forget as it was them as raised us out of the mud and set us agoing in the respectable line in which we now appears. It was their voices, their dancing, and their money as made me the proprietor of this elegant establishment, and I can't and won't forget it."

"As you like."

"O' course it's as I like. I b'lieve I'm manager. I b'lieve I'm proprietor, and nobody dares go agin me here; and I don't like, and won't have, the gals put out of the way for anybody."

The lady to whom this speech was addressed began to look remarkably indignant, but her looks had no effect on the showman, who once more yelled out his programme, and had it accompanied by the pipes, the drum, and the gong.

Two or three rustics then moved forward, and mounted the platform.

"Hi! — hi!" screamed the showman, "see how they're acoming up. Now there's just room for another dozen or two in the inside, and then we shall positively commence."

The British public only want a leader, whether it's in the case of a battle to be fought, a minister's house to be torn down, a life to be saved, or a show to be patronised. Give them one who will set an example, and it is no difficult matter to get many to follow.

Our showman seemed alive to that fact.

He did not permit his three or four bumpkins to enter the show, where there was not a single individual, but handed them over to the care of Signor Gufferini, from the Saharian Desert of Hindostandee, who forthwith marshalled them to the front of the show.

He selected the most simple-looking of the lot as his victim.

"How do ye do, sir?" said the mummer, presenting his hand, and taking that of the bumpkin with mock ceremony.

"He! he!" roared Giles. "Oi'm purty wa'al."

"You hear that?" said the man, addressing the crowd, "you hear that? He's ' purty wa'al.' Now only think what a blessing that must be to his anxious parents. He's 'purty well.'"

"He, he, he!" grinned poor Giles, whilst the mob yelled at him.

"And how's your mother?" asked the buffoon.

"I ain't got no mother."

"D'ye hear that? The unhappy youth never had a mother. He was found one morning sitting on a big turnip, and with no visible clothing about him. He was then taken home and baked, and, unfortunately, was put in with the batch and pulled out with the cakes, which fully accounts for the soft place on the top of his head."

"Ho, ho, ho!" roared the crowd, at this not very elaborate or refined attempt at wit.

The public attention was now fully awakened, and a whole sea of faces was upturned to the platform.

"Can you dance?" inquired the Signor of his victim.

"Ya'as."

"He says, ' ya'as.'"

"Ho, ho, ho!"

"Do you mind showing the ladies and gentlemen *how* you can dance?"

"No; I doan't moind."

"He ' doan't moind.' Now, Madame Gufferini, be kind enough to step forward and take this noble youth for a partner, in order that the ladies and gentlemen may have a specimen of his ability. Now, Mr. Music, play up, and let us see what we shall see."

"Mr. Music" started a lively jig on the drum and fifes, and very soon poor Giles was straining away, in his hob nail boots, face to face with the Signora, and the platform shook with their joint efforts at sporting the light fantastic toe.

The multitude roared, and the proprietor of the show lost not a moment in roaring through a speaking trumpet the merits of the exhibition he had to lay before the public, and the result was that, at the end of the jig, the bumpkins swarmed up the steps, and filled the canvass tent to repletion.

When it was found that not another twopence could be forced into the place the curtain was drawn across the opening, and all went in to behold the wonders to be revealed in exchange for the twopence expended.

The programme was adhered to as closely as possible, and everybody was apparently satisfied therewith.

The pig told the fortunes of the lasses, and performed feats of mental arithmetic which certainly seemed to qualify him for the "multiplication professorship," at which, if his proprietor was to be believed, he was aiming.

At length the Spanish minstrels and dancers—the Signoras Pakaraboo and Figarala—entered to go through the items set down for them.

Poor Evelina and Rose, for it was indeed them, appeared to feel their position acutely.

The pallor of their cheeks and anxious expression of their eyes told of the emotion with which they regarded the degraded position in which fate had placed them, and also their fear of being recognised by those they faced; but their fears were unfounded. No one beheld the young mistress of Winterleigh and her maid in the painted mummers before them.

Both sang and danced neatly, and gave the greatest satisfaction, but it was evident that they escaped from the ordeal they had to encounter with the greatest pleasure.

Thrice during that summer evening had they to appear before the rural population of Winterleigh: thrice had they to risk recognition, and the unpleasantness that would naturally follow; but eventually the day ended, and the two girls could breathe freely once more.

"Thank Heaven!" said Evelina; "Thank Heaven it has ended so. I would not have been recognised for the whole world."

"And I would not have had such an event happen for the world," said Rose. "It would be the death of me."

"Not quite so bad as that?" said Evelina with a smile.

"Yes, quite," cried Rose," "I should never survive it. Oh! the horror of seeing those wretched villagers stare into your face and exclaim, 'There's Miss Evelina, late of the Hall:' my very blood curdles at the thought."

"And so does mine; but the danger is past, and to-morrow we shall be far away."

"Well, I hope the danger is past," said Rose, "but something tells me that it is not so."

"What do you mean?"

"I really don't know, Miss, but there's a presentiment in my mind that all's not right, and I only hope for all our sakes nothing will come of it."

"Rose, you alarm me."

"Then I will say no more, Miss: indeed, I am sorry I did not keep my silly fears to myself instead of alarming you with them, it was very selfish of me."

"Do not revert to the subject again, dear Rose, let us dismiss it from our mind.''

The subject was not reverted to, and at length, and ere long, Evelina and Rose, together with the other members of the company of strollers, were fast asleep.

* * * * *

The caravan which had become the residence of our heroine and her humble friend was to start at six o'clock, but long before that hour Evelina was awake.

Hastily dressing herself, she assumed her hat and cloak, and, without disturbing the others, sallied from the show.

"Dear old Winterleigh," she said as she stood on the green inhaling the morning air which came wafted along laden with the odour of a thousand flowers. "Dear old Winterleigh, how sweet and beautiful thou art!"

She gazed about her, and every now and then her eye lighted upon some object familiar to her as her own image; giving way to thought, she began to wander from the neighbourhood of the green.

The majority of the shows had disappeared in the night, and all was now silent.

The sun was just rising in the heavens, and the voices of a thousand birds as they soared from their leafy roosts and shook the dew from their wings greeted the young lady.

On walked our heroine, her head bowed on her bosom and her hands clasped before her; as one in a dream she hurried on, and now she has entered the wood of Winterleigh.

Still thinking of old times, still buried in the oblivion of thought, she allowed her feet to carry her some distance into the wood.

She paused not.

It appeared to her that old times had come again, and her day-dream brought back the happy past in which she had wandered over those woods a free, happy, and unconstrained girl.

How long she had wandered thus, how far into the wood she had penetrated, she knew not; but at length she was made conscious of her position by hearing a quick, rough breathing by her side.

She started and looked about her.

Horror !

Within a few feet of her stood the hideous dwarf who destroyed the unfortunate friend of Paul Clifford.

She shrieked, and would have fled, but that the eyes of the dwarf held her as if by fascination to the spot.

"Evelina," croaked the dwarf, "Evelina, Evelina— I know, I know!"

There was an expression in the awful face of the dwarf that maddened the poor girl.

Had she faced a savage animal thirsting for blood her terror could not have been so great as it was now, for she saw that at the hands of the being before her she could only expect worse than death—dishonour.

"Evelina," cried the dwarf, his eye blazing with an awful fire, "Evelina !—mine now—mine now !"

With the antics of an ape the wretched being capered about the terrified girl, and every moment threatened to seize her in his great naked, malformed arms.

At length he was at her side.

She felt his burning breath upon her cheek.

His great hand had grasped her.

She was strained to his bosom.

She was then conscious of falling to the earth, and being immediately snatched up again.

Next moment she opened her eyes, and found herself supported on the shoulder of the proprietor of the show.

A few yards from them was the dwarf.

His face was now expressive of the most intense malignity, and in his hand he held that fatal knife, which set free the life-blood of poor Wilfred.

Such was the position of affairs, but the showman trembled not.

He seemed rather to regard the being he had thus

unexpectedly encountered with wonder and admiration than fear.

He moreover murmured to himself—

"Well, he is a rum 'un, he is; his is a beauty, he is. He'd be a fortune, he would," and other expressions of a like character.

"Fly," cried Evelina, "fly, for God's sake? Come out of this place. Let us fly, or we shall be murdered !"

But the showman moved not.

Keeping his eyes upon the dwarf, he said to Evelina—

"Fly you, then, as fast as you can back to the show. I'll see to this fellow."

The poor girl wanted no second admonition to quit the place.

Releasing herself from the showman she fled with all the haste she could use.

As she moved away the dwarf made a step forward as if to pursue.

But the showman seemed to entertain a strong objection to this proceeding, and planted himself in his path.

Keeping his eye steadily fixed on the hideous being before him, he dived his hand into the pocket of his coat, and drew therefrom a tolerably large hammer.

It was the one he had used the previous night in taking down his show.

The dwarf seemed confounded at his temerity, and stood as still as a statue.

"Come along, ugly," said the showman, "come along, if fighting's yer game."

But the dwarf moved not.

His eye followed the retreating figure.

"Oh, you've an eye to beauty, you have, you pictur' of sin and ugliness. You're a young man of good taste, no doubt, but it won't do; you don't come any o' your tricks this fine morning if I knows it."

Of course all this was as unintelligible as double Dutch to the untutored savage he was addressing, but there was a something in the tone in which the words were uttered that kept the terrible wretch at bay.

He had never before encountered a being who had dared confront him, and speak without fear in his presence.

The proceeding astonished him.

"Come on," said the showman, flourishing his hammer, "come on. I ain't a going to stop here all day a waitin' on your pleasure. D'ye mean fighting, or don't ye ?"

The dwarf moved not.

"He ain't half a heart, no more pluck nor a cabbage," cried the showman; "but I'll give him one for his self afore I've done with him. He insulted a member of my company, and it's my dooty to take up her cause. Here's at ye." Cautiously advancing the showman got within a yard of the astonished dwarf.

The hideous being raised his knife.

The showman balanced his hammer.

With a yell the dwarf darted forward and the knife was sent at the breast of the showman.

But that individual was too quick.

He dipped under the arm of his antagonist, and ere he could turn had struck him rapid and severe blows on the back of his head.

The dwarf fell stunned, bleeding, and desperately wounded to the earth.

"Hallo," said the showman, regarding the body of his fallen foe; "hillo, that's harder than I intended; I'm afraid you're hurt."

There could be no doubt of it.

The dwarf's face became pale as death.

His eyes closed, his jaw fell, and to all appearances he was dying.

"My eye," said the showman, bending over him, "but this is a go. They'll bring it in murder, and have me scragged."

He went down on his knees and sought to restore consciousness to the dwarf.

But his efforts failed.

In despair, and much terrified at what he had done, the showman sprang to his feet with the intention of flying, when his orchestra, in the shape of the *artiste* on the pipes and big drum, came to the spot.

They stood regarding each other for an instant.

"Hillo," said the showman.

"Hillo," returned the other.

"This here's a neat go, ain't it ?"

"What ?"

"I've been and hurted somebody."

He pointed to the dwarf.

The soloist on the Pandean pipes looked at the victim.

"Well he is all a rum 'un, he is."

"He are."

"I never seed such a thing afore."

"No more did I. But how came you here ?"

"Thought to meet with a rabbit or *an* 'are here in the wood; started off; met the young gal; flying in terror, told me that you was a being murdered, pointed out the path and here I am."

"I see."

"That's all."

"Is it all ? I don't think so ! just look at that cove's head."

"A awful smash."

"Isn't it ?"

"You'll get in for it if you don't cut afore it's found out."

"But—but, hang me if I like to cut."

"Why not ?"

"'Cos he's such a beauty."

"What d'ye mean ?"

"I mean I'd like to take him with me."

"What ! If he's dead ?"

"No. If he's alive."

"He'd be a fortune."

"He would."

"Well, what's to be done ?"

The showman stooped over the prostrate dwarf.

"He's a breathing still," he said. "Vell, that's a good sign. If he wern't breathing I shouldn't have any hopes."

"Well, shall we bone him ?"

"Cut it with him ?"

"Yes."

"I wonder if he's got a mother, and if she'd miss him ?"

"No matter. What d'ye say to having him, mother or no mother ?"

"I says I'm agreeable. If he's alive we can make something out of him ; if he's dead we can carry him out of this and drop him in a convenient ditch some distance off."

"That's the game, so lend a hand."

The two men raised the insensible dwarf in their arms, and, covering him with their coats, hastened away.

* * * * * *

The caravan halted that night some twenty miles from Winterleigh.

It was near the hour of midnight, and the showman's company were nearly all fast asleep.

The night was so hot that the majority of them were sleeping in tents.

In fact, Evelina, Rose, and the little dwarf, were the only persons in the spacious caravan.

The place was partitioned off into sleeping apartments.

At the extreme end was that allotted to our heroine and her freind.

At the other end was a small closet usually occupied by the proprietor of the show.

It was the place wherein he kept his money and valuables ; a sort of treasury and repository of miscellaneous articles which were not to be scanned by the multitude.

Evelina could not sleep.

The memory of her morning's encounter in Winterleigh Wood disturbed her, and she lay tossing on her humble couch, and praying for morning and light.

Suddenly she was disturbed by a low groan, proceeding from the further end of the caravan.

At first she thought it was the child groaning in her sleep, but on hearing a repetition of the sound she started to her feet, and listened more attentively.

Again came the groan, this time much deeper and more distinct than at first.

It was the cry of a man in great pain.

Trembling with alarm, the poor girl aroused her companion.

"Rose, Rose," she cried; "pray, pray wake. I am afraid something dreadful is about to happen."

Rose started up.

"What say you ?"

"I have heard dreadful sounds from the other end of the caravan, and I shake with fear."

"Good God !"

"Listen."

Again came the sound.

There was no mistaking it.

It was the cry of some one enduring great bodily anguish.

"Where is the light ?" demanded Evelina.

"What would you do ?"

"I must see what this means."

"For Heaven's sake do not stir."

"I must. Whatever danger there is I will face. Better that than lie here. Where is the light ?"

"On the chair, but I pray you move not."

"Indeed I must."

"Then I will rise as well."

"Do so. Perhaps it were best you did."

In a few moments they were both dressed.

Meanwhile the groaning continued.

"I shake with fear," said Rose. "I cannot comprehend this."

"Silence ; let us see what these fearful sounds arise from."

Evelina grasped the lamp in her hand, and crossed the caravan.

Poor Rose followed her closely.

They paused at the door of the closet.

"It comes from within."

"Yes, it is there the sound proceeds from."

"I will open the door."

"Do not—oh, do not !"

"I must."

Evelina turned the key in the lock, and threw the door wide open.

The light filled the little place, and the women beheld a sight which thrilled them to the heart with terror.

On a pallet lay the maimed and bloody form of the dwarf.

As a ghost from the grave rose the monster, and fixed his glaring eyes on the intruders.

Spell bound the two girls remained in the same position as when the door was thrust open.

It was the voice of this monster that recalled animation, and gave activity once more to their paralysed limbs.

"Evelina," said the dwarf, "Evelina, mine—mine."

He rose on his hands, as if about to spring after the poor trembling girl ; but the effort was too great for him, and he fell back motionless and still.

The back of his head was now exposed to the young girls' view, and a thrill of horror passed through them as they contemplated that tattered and bloody skull.

One instant they gazed upon the sight.

One instant only, and then they sprang back, and closed the door after them.

The key was turned in the lock, and they had time to collect their distracted thoughts.

"He here," said Evelina, "he here. My God !"

She had related to Rose her adventure of the morning, so that the maid was at no loss to account for the presence of the hideous being who had been a source of terror to her from earliest childhood.

Rose was speechless.

"This is no place for us," continued Evelina," no place for us."

Rose clasped her arm convulsively.

The movement signified her readiness to quit the place on the instant.

"Once more homeless, once more friendless," said Evelina; "but better those alternatives than to remain another instant in a place that shelters a being so hideous."

"Yes—yes," cried the terrified Rose. "Come at once."

It did not take them long to collect their clothes, and whatever else belonged to them.

The work was soon done, hastened, as it was, by the groans of the dwarf, and another sound, which had even more terror for them.

It was evident that the monster had sprung or crawled from his couch, and was endeavouring to open the door of the closet.

The lock rattled, and the frail woodwork seemed likely to fall in at every fresh effort of the monster to effect an escape.

Under these circumstances the flight was hastened ; and, ere the hour of midnight was tolled, the poor young girls were hastening from the show.

They paused upon the brow of a gentle hill, and looked back upon the scene they had quitted.

There, in the bright moonlight, they beheld the old show that had so long been their home.

Close to it glittered two small tents, in which slumbered the talented artistes of the establishment.

It was not without regret that the fugitives beheld this scene.

Whatever the faults of the poor strollers, the poor girls could not deny that they possessed kind hearts and ready hands.

The rough kindness shown them since they had taken up their residence with the little band of vagabonds had made a deep impression upon them, and now that they were leaving them — and leaving them thus suddenly and silently—a pang of regret was experienced by them, and they stood for some time looking back with wistful glance.

"They will miss us in the morning," said Evelina, "they will miss us sadly."

"Yes," said Rose; "the poor fellows will feel our loss, for it is impossible not to comprehend that their prosperity has been due to our efforts."

"I am sorry, very sorry, to leave them, for they gave us shelter when we had none ; they shielded us from a cold and merciless world when we had not a friend to stretch out his hand to us. I can never forget their goodness."

"I trust I may never do so; but is it not time that we gave some thought to the direction in which we shall go ? We are in a strange place, and know not where to turn."

"Come," said Evelina, "come, dear Rose; we will take this road to the left, and trust in God for the direction of our footsteps."

They spoke not again, and, until daylight, pursued their journey.

Their hearts were sad, but could they have known the sorrow that was in store for them, even a deeper cloud would have rested on their brows, and a heavier weight oppressed their already grief-burthened hearts.

CHAPTER LIV.

RETURNS TO THE DUCHESS OF LAKEMONT—OF HER VISIT TO EASTERBROOK HALL—THE TWO WAITING MAIDS—AND THE FATE OF DANVERS.

EASTERBROOK HALL, the seat of Lord and Lady Easterbrook, lay in Suffolk, within a day's ride of the metropolis. It was to this point the Duchess of Lakemont hastened on resigning possession of her town mansion to the fiery old Scotchwoman, her relative.

Her Grace was quite weary of the persecutions of the old soul, and her petty tyranny became so irksome that the Duchess determined to endure it no longer.

The Easterbrooks were her intimate friends.

His lordship was an old but singularly genial man, who possessed the respect and love of all who met him.

Hortense, his wife, was young and beautiful.

They were separated from each other by a gulf of twenty years, but there was a great deal of love between them, and the union was as happy as could be desired.

There was no heir born to them, and his nephew Danvers, the friend of Lewis Norman, was generally looked upon as heir presumptive. But the estates were unentailed, and there was a chance that a child might be born to them.

There was, moreover, a probability that the old lord would leave all he was possessed of to his young and brilliant wife, and this thought by no means lightened the heart of Danvers.

He was penniless, and in debt ; but people trusted him, and encouraged him in his frightful habits until the old lord married. Then they turned round upon him, and drove him to the extremities in which we found him—a preyer upon the simple—a blackleg—a midnight bully and a cheat.

Instead of attempting to retrieve the past, and amend his ways, he became much worse now that he was without hope.

But his generous uncle did not desert him.

Indeed, he did more for him now than he had ever done before.

Hoping to keep him out of harm's way, he allowed him a liberal income, which was quite sufficient to maintain him in elegance and affluence, independent of his pay as an officer of the King's Guards.

He had even done more than this—he had paid many of his most embarrassing debts, and had invited him to Easterbrook until satisfactory arrangements could be made with his other creditors.

The Duchess found him and his man established at the Hall on her arrival.

There was nothing alluded to in connection with their last meeting, and that disagreeable episode seemed to be mutually forgotten, and they became as good friends as ever.

The Duchess was singularly grieved on her arrival at the Hall to find her friend Hortense sinking into an early grave.

It was impossible to shut her eyes to it, and had she been blind enough to have done so the Countess of Marlow and the Hon. Mrs. Gaspard, guests at the Hall, would soon have enlightened her darkness.

Their fears were beyond their control, and they expressed them in a variety of ways most unmistakable in their intensity.

The Duchess, too, became most seriously alarmed.

The state of the poor lady grew much worse day by day, and her disease completely baffled the skill of the physician.

He declared that he could discover no disorder.

Consumption had not entered the fair frame of the sufferer to devastate it with its ravages ; the heart was quite sound, and all the details of her anatomy as perfect as possible.

Nevertheless, every day the lady grew worse, and no one could account for the fact.

THE PRINCESS DISPOSES OF THE INTRUDER.

The old lord became seriously alarmed.

He fretted and fumed until he became a mere imbecile, and the Hall was as wretched a place as possible.

"There is a mystery in all this," thought the Duchess, "and as I have nothing else to do I will get at the bottom of it."

She was quite the woman who, having set herself a task, was not likely to abandon it without completing it. She set herself down to observing the actions of all those by whom the unhappy lady was surrounded, and she soon discovered that between two serving-women, named Mary and Bessy, who were constantly in attendance on the lady of the Hall, lay the secret of the illness of her friend.

These two women were as opposite in their characters and behaviour as north and south.

Mary appeared to be a sullen and morose woman.

Bessy, on the contrary, was all gentleness; ever ready at the beck and call of the invalid; always desirous of alleviating her suffering, and at any personal sacrifice to allay a pang in the heart of her mistress.

These characteristics the Duchess noted, and, giving them their due weight, she determined in her own mind that she must not suspect one who possessed them.

On the other hand, Mary was a constant source of suspicion to her Grace.

She went about her duties slowly, and with an air of calculation and seriousness well calculated to tell most seriously against her.

She was always bashful and retiring, and on encountering the Duchess alone would fly from her as from a detective officer.

It was soon apparent to the whole house that her Grace meant to unfathom the mystery of her ladyship's illness, and all silently watched her efforts.

The most demonstrative in crushing her success was Danvers, who was ever displaying a most unaccountable anxiety for the health of the woman he dreaded so much as the bar to his future greatness.

"His conduct," thought the Duchess, "would be suspicious but that he never visits his aunt, and never has any intercourse with those who do."

It was a fact; Danvers, whilst displaying the most extreme anxiety for the health of his relative, could not be induced to go into her presence.

Indeed he studiously avoided all those who did, for, as he said—

"It was too painful for him to undergo an interview, and he would save himself the distress of hearing from those who visited his aunt the tale of her sufferings."

One day it was announced that the Duchess was taken much worse, and no hopes were entertained of her surviving for more than four-and-twenty hours.

Upon this Danvers ordered his man to pack up, and gave out that he was starting immediately for the continent.

In a couple of hours he disappeared from the Hall.

*   *   *   *

Meanwhile the Duchess had made an awful discovery.

The Lady Easterbrook was being slowly poisoned.

It happened that one morning she encountered Mary approaching the bedroom of her mistress with a cup of chocolate.

She took the stuff from the hand of the girl, and dismissed her.

She thrust the spoon into the cup, and stirring its contents found a small white lozenge.

This she secreted.

Her next act was to throw away the chocolate, and procure a fresh cup.

This she did without exciting suspicion.

When the doctor next visited the patient, the cause of the awful illness was made known to him by her Grace, but she begged him to keep the secret until the author of the crime could be detected.

He consented, and the Duchess went on with her task.

She thought she had discovered the right clue, for whenever Mary brought her mistress a drink she detected in it one of the fatal lozenges.

Thus matters went on until the Duchess thought proper to give out that her ladyship was so seriously ill as to hold out no hope of improvement.

We have seen that one effect was to startle and drive away Danvers.

But this conduct excited no more suspicion than any of his previous acts.

*   *   *   *

Danvers had not left the Hall many hours when a most singular and serious accident occurred.

The whole of the landing-place outside the apartments occupied by her Grace, Lady Easterbrook, the Countess of Marlow, and Mrs. Gaspard, fell in, and sank, in a heap of dust, broken rafters, mortar and stones, into the hall beneath.

The only mode of getting down the stairs now available was the private staircase, of which, for her own reasons, the Duchess kept the key.

The accident excited but small alarm, for it had occurred when all the domestics had retired to rest.

The fall, moreover, was so silent that it was scarcely noticed by any one in the contiguous apartments except the watchful Duchess, whose quick ear detected the sound.

She at a glance saw what had happened, and immediately informed the sufferer of the mischance.

"What is to be done?" asked Lady Easterbrook.

"Nothing. Why alarm any one until the morning?"

"I do not know, but I thought it might be best—"

"No, no, let all rest for the night."

"And you really think, my dear Duchess," cried her ladyship, "that it is useless to inform my husband?"

"Useless until to-morrow," answered the Duchess. "If the household generally remain unconscious of the event, there is no use in spreading the alarm. No good could be done to-night : there are no masons at hand to commence the work of reparation; and even if there were, you could not be annoyed by the sounds of their labour while you want to sleep."

"But are the other apartments all safe?" asked Hortense.

"As safe," responded the Duchess, "as if they stood upon a solid rock."

The others echoed this assurance, and Lady Easterbrook began to regain her lost self-possession.

She, however, looked at the Duchess in a manner as if she had a request to make, but which she scarcely liked to proffer; and the Duchess quickly comprehended what was uppermost in her mind.

"My dear Hortense," she said, "I will pass the night here with you. Yes, it will be better; and this will at all events convince you of my firm conviction that there is nothing to be apprehended."

"Oh, then, pardon my foolish fears," exclaimed Lady Easterbrook; "but I accept your kind offer, Ellen, and you will not find that I shall trouble you any more with my nervous apprehensions."

All now prepared to say good night; and as they were issuing from the boudoir the Duchess whispered to them—

"It will be better for you not to mention to your maids to-night what has occurred, or the report might circulate, and an alarm would be excited in the house, which would prove most detrimental to the health of our dear friend."

The two ladies made the Duchess a sign to signify their compliance with the hint; and they took their departure to their own respective chambers.

"Whose turn is it," asked the Duchess when they were gone, "to sleep in the dressing-room to-night?"

"Mary's."

"Ah! I remember; so it is," ejaculated the Duchess. "But if you like we will dispense with her services altogether for this present occasion ——"

"Oh, no! let us have her near us," cried her ladyship; "for though I really do not anticipate the slightest danger—and, moreover, as I am not so foolish as to imagine that even if it threatened us it could be warded off by her presence—still there is that superstitious idea which in all things prompts us to have faith in numbers when assembled together."

"Well, be it so," responded the Duchess; "but do not send the girl out of the room when once she shall have entered it; for we have already agreed, you know, that the accident is not to be generally communicated until the morrow."

"You shall have your own way in all things, my dear friend," rejoined Hortense.

The Duchess now rang the bell as a summons for Mary, and this young woman almost immediately made her appearance.

As the reader has seen, she could have wished to dispense with her presence; for she thought it very likely that Bessy might in the meantime have communicated to her on the subject of her leaving the house within three days, and she did not therefore wish to have in such close vicinage a person who might have learnt how she was suspected by her. But she did not combat Lady Easterbrook's wish to have Mary's attendance, for fear of being closely questioned as to the causes of her own disinclination.

Besides, she thought to herself that however malicious, spiteful, or ill-intentioned Mary might be, she would adopt the proper precautions to prevent her from doing any harm, either to her mistress or herself. When Mary entered the boudoir she looked at her attentively, but without appearing to be thus intent on the study of her countenance. She saw that her features were calm and placid as usual—unmoved in their somewhat sullen and sinister expression; and she said to herself, "Bessy has not yet found an opportunity of touching on the point; and perhaps it is all the better under exist-ing circumstances."

"Mary," she said "come with me for a moment into the adjoining room."

She took up a taper, and the maid immediately followed her with that cold air of reserved and distant respect which she maintained towards her as well as to her noble master and mistress. She led her on as far as the bath-room; and then she said—

"An accident has occurred close by this evening, but do not be alarmed. The whole flooring of the landing-place has fallen in!"

"Indeed!"

And now Mary seemed somewhat excited above her wonted mood of frigid imperturbability.

"Yes," she continued; " but for obvious reasons I have thought it better to suffer no noise to be made upon the subject until to-morrow. Thanks to the operation of the inscrutable ways of Providence'—and here the Duchess looked her very hard in the face—"your mistress is im-proving in health; but all unnecessary excitement must be avoided."

"No doubt of it, your Grace," answered Mary, who by this time had relapsed into her cold, phlegmatic manner, and whose countenance underwent not the slightest change as the Duchess rivetted her regards so fixedly upon it.

"I am going to pass the night with Lady Easterbrook," she continued; " for she is somewhat nervous on account of this accident. But you will occupy the couch in the dressing-room all the same."

"Yes, your Grace," she responded.

They then returned into the boudoir, where Hortense almost immediately commenced the details of her night toilet by the assistance of Mary.

"I must go to my own chamber for a few minutes," said the Duchess, " and then I will return."

She proceeded to her room, and found Bessy awaiting her presence.

She had made up a good fire, as was her custom; and she was warming herself by it when the Duchess en-tered.

"Have you yet spoken to Mary," she inquired, "rela-tive to that matter which I mentioned this afternoon?"

" No, your Grace," answered Bessy; "I have not yet found an opportunity."

"Well, it is of no consequence," she said; " to morrow will do just as well."

When she had unfastened her dress, she dismissed her for the night; for she was not accustomed to engage her attentions any farther in her preparations for retiring to rest.

She thought that Bessy lingered in the chamber, and fidgetted about somewhat, as if she desired to speak to her ere she took her departure; but the Duchess said to herself—

"In the goodness of her heart she wishes to intercede for Mary. It is well-intentioned and praiseworthy on her part; but I will not afford her the opportunity."

She bade the Duchess good night, and left the room.

A few minutes afterwards the Duchess put on a morn-ing wrapper, and returned to Lady Easterbrook's boudoir. Hortense was nearly ready to seek her own couch: the Duchess sat down and conversed with her until her night-toilet was completely finished, and Mary had retired into the dressing-room.

She then proceeded to disapparel herself, and in a short time she occupied her share of Lady Easterbrook's bed.

The latter did not converse many minutes before slum-ber stole upon her eyes, and by half-past eleven o'clock she was asleep.

The Duchess lay awake, thinking of the occurrences of the day; but for no very great length of time; and at midnight she also was sinking into a profound repose.

But this was not destined to last for a considerable period

She was awakened by a sound which reached her ears It struck her that she heard a window opening at no very great distance.

She listened with suspended breath.

All was still, and she thought her imagination must have deceived her.

She was composing herself to sleep again, when she was once more startled, and she thought that it was by a similar sound.

But again, when she listened, everything was once more still, and the most solemn silence appeared to be reigning throughout the spacious habitation.

Nevertheless, as her suspicions were so strongly excited against Mary, she was determined to assure herself that there was nothing wrong.

She therefore descended with the utmost gentleness from the bed; for Lady Easterbrook was sleeping soundly by her side.

She listened at the door of the dressing-room; but all continued perfectly still.

Yet she was resolved to leave nothing to mere surmise or conjecture; she therefore opened that door of commu-nication, but in so noiseless a manner that in this respect it was the same as if she had not opened it all.

She peeped in—the light was extinguished there; but a taper was burning in the chamber which she occupied with Hortense; and by its beams she could discern that Mary was fast asleep, or at least she was lying in her couch with her eyes shut, and with the appearance of one who slumbered profoundly.

She glanced at the window; the draperies were closed almost completely over, but through the slight opening that there was in the middle she could see that the window itself was shut, and that the fastening was secure.

Closing the door as noiselessly as she had opened it, she crept back to her place by Hortense's side.

She did not immediately endeavour to compose herself to sleep again; she lay thinking and listening.

If any one had been there to put the question to her whether she now believed that she had heard a window opening, she would have been inclined to answer at once in the negative; but still there was in her soul a lurking idea—a species of vague apprehension—to the effect that it was not altogether an illusion on her part.

Not more than five minutes had elapsed after she had thus returned to bed—the most solemn silence again ap-peared to be prevailing throughout the mansion—when all in a moment that stillness was fearfully, horribly broken in upon!

First one tremendous ejaculation of mortal terror—then another! The latter following as closely upon the former as two pulsations of the heart, or two strokes of a bell that is being rung violently.

Thus they smote upon the ear.

Thus they rang horribly through the mansion, and they were accompanied by the sounds of two heavy bodies falling one after the other, just as quickly as the two cries that indicated the mortal pain of some horrible catastrophe.

The Duchess started up all shuddering and quivering: Lady Easterbrook sprang up in a similar manner by her side; then there was instantaneously the sound of Mary leaping from her bed in the next room.

"Good God!" cried Lady Easterbrook; " is it a horrible dream?" and she sank back, gasping with affright and terror, on her pillow.

" For Heaven's sake compose yourself!" the Duchess said; " but it is no dream!" and in the twinkling of an eye she sprang out of bed.

At the same instant there was a violent knocking at the door leading into the dressing-room, and which door she had locked after peeping in upon Mary.

"Open, open, for God's sake!" cried that young woman's voice. " Something terrible has occurred close by!"

The Duchess opened the door with the utmost despatch,

and, as the light streamed upon Mary's countenance, the beams showed that it was as pale as that of a corpse.

"Good God!" she murmured, clasping her hands, "what can it be? The sounds came from *there*," and she pointed in the direction of the bath-room, or rather of the private staircase which lay beyond—for the Duchess instantaneously comprehended her meaning.

Her Grace threw her morning wrapper over her shoulders, caught up a light, and rushed towards the bath-room.

Nothing unusual was there to be seen, and the window was closed; but it was with an awful shuddering throughout her entire form, and, with the horrible presentiment of being about to make some terrific discovery, she opened the opposite door of that bath-room—the door which now overhung the chasm where a landing once had been.

At the same instant a strong gust of wind blew in upon her, nearly extinguishing the light which she carried; but she instantaneously shielded it with her hand.

Mary was behind her in her night-dress; but she had not time at the moment to think of her, nor to pause to reflect how she might possibly be connected with all the horrible things that were progressing at the Hall.

And now the Duchess stood upon the threshold of that doorway which overlooked the chasm.

The window was open—the curtains were blowing with the strong current of air.

Yes, there she stood above the wreck of the fallen floor.

She plunged her eyes down into the abyss; dark objects lay there—human shapes; yes, unmistakable forms of men, but motionless as if dead.

No, they were not dead, for moans of intense agony were heard, and she ejaculated, "There is life in those wretches, and, whoever they are, they must receive prompt ministration."

The Duchess was about to step forward upon the staircase, so as to descend and see what could be done for the miserable beings lying at the bottom, when Mary caught her by the arm, exclaiming—

"For God's sake take care what you do: those steps will not bear you, all their support is gone."

The Duchess instantly recognised the truth of what Mary said.

She felt at the moment that she had actually and positively saved her life; and it struck her as singular indeed that she should owe her life to one whom she would have thought would perhaps have been only too glad to take it or to see it sacrificed.

"Go and unlock the outer door, Mary," said the Duchess, "for there is a loud knocking at it, and it is doubtless his lordship who is alarmed."

Mary at once retired, and the Duchess stooped as far over the chasm as in safety she dared, to discern, if possible, who were the men that were lying below.

But, as it was only a taper which she had in her hand, she could not throw the light in such a way, or with sufficient power, to obtain a view of the countenances of the individuals at the bottom.

They were two men, and they seemed to be very coarsely dressed, so that she could not form the slightest conjecture who they were.

It was only for a moment that she thus lingered over the abyss, and then she sped back into the bed-chamber.

Lady Easterbrook had fainted: the Countess of Marlow and Mrs. Gaspard were bending over her: they had only just thrown on some loose articles of apparel—they had been alarmed by those terrific cries which had swept like the yell of murder through the Hall.

And now the Duchess herself flung on a shawl which she caught up, and thrust her feet into slippers, and sped towards the outer door of the boudoir, at which there was renewed knocking; for Mary had locked it again after giving admission to the ladies.

It was now his lordship who entered: he was terribly alarmed—he asked a thousand questions, but she did not pause to answer one.

She left the Countess to respond, to them as best she might; for she had just hastily explained to them that a frightful catastrophe had occurred at the private staircase.

Snatching up the key of the door at the bottom of that private staircase, she rushed from the boudoir, exclaiming—

"Come with me, Mary. I insist upon it that you come!"

The young woman had also thrown on a few articles of apparel; she flung upon her a look which seemed to be full of astonishment; and then she said—

"Most decidedly, your Grace, I am prepared to go with you; and such peremptory language is not necessary."

The Duchess was just upon the point of telling her that such bold words would not serve her turn, when she thought it useless to waste a moment of precious time in bandying observations; and rushed out of the boudoir, thinking, however, to herself—

"Something has unquestionably happened which has brought matters to a crisis; and Mary will be unmasked, or, perhaps, she will fall upon her knees and confess!"

By this time the entire household was alarmed, and all the domestics were flocking from their respective apartments. In a moment she was assailed by a dozen questions.

"What is the matter, your Grace? What were those cries? Was it his lordship? Is her ladyship worse? Is she dead? Are there robbers in the house? What is it?"—and so forth.

"Come with me," the Duchess cried, "and you shall see."

"In the name of Heaven, your Grace, what is the matter?" asked Bessy, who now came rushing down the stairs, as pale as death, and only half dressed—as indeed were the generality of the servants.

"Come with me! come with me!" the Duchess ejaculated; "there is no time for explanations."

They rushed down the principal staircase, and gained the domestic offices.

The Duchess flung open one of the back doors, and they passed out into the premises in the rear of the mansion.

It was a singular spectacle.

There was the Duchess holding in her hand a taper, followed by a crowd of half-dressed domestics, some three or four of whom also carried lights; and a species of wild dismay was depicted upon all countenances.

Thus did they burst forth into the open air, and then sped straight to the private door.

Some one looking up ejaculated, "The window is open!"

"Yes," answered Mary, "it was there that they came in."

"Who came in?" demanded half a dozen voices. "What! robbers!"

At this moment the Duchess turned the key in the lock, and flung the door wide open.

The whole spectacle revealed itself completely.

The flooring that had fallen in—the broken balustrades—the staircase that jutted out, as if without support, from the wall—the mass of ruins on the ground—and two human forms stretched there motionless, in positions which made them seem as if they had been flung there by giant hands, or, what was still more natural, and was also strictly correct, as if they had fallen from the open window above.

And now a wild scream rang through the night air, and one of the half-clad female domestics sprang past the Duchess, threw herself upon one of the forms which lay prostrate there, and gave vent to all the horror of her feelings in another long loud scream of agony.

It was Bessy.

"Poor young woman!" ejaculated the Duchess; "the scene has turned her brain."

"Oh! wretch, wretch that I am!" she cried. "Kill me! slay me! take me to prison! hang me on the highest gibbet! for my crimes are immense. Will! Will! speak, speak! Are you dead? Oh, pray speak—if only for a moment."

They were literally staggered by this scene.

What! Bessy thus accusing herself? What did it mean?

"Why, this is Will Jope!" exclaimed one of the footmen, as he lifted up the individual on whose form Bessy had thrown herself, while a couple of females took charge of Bessy herself, for the wretched young woman had suddenly fallen into a state of unconsciousness.

"And who have we here?" ejaculated another of the footmen, raising the second individual. "Why, is it possible? Lieutenant Danvers."

"Danvers!" and the name was echoed by every tongue.

"Bring them forth! see if there be life in them."

"The lieutenant is a corpse, Yes; his day is over!" exclaimed a footman.

"And 'tis the same with Will!" cried the other footman.

Good heavens! was it possible that after all, the Duchess had wrongly suspected Mary of the attempt on the life of her friend, while Bessy and Will were in reality the guilty persons!

"And who is Will Jope?" demanded the Duchess; "or rather I should ask, who was he?"

"Why, didn't you know?" exclaimed the butler. "The lieutenant's servant."

There could be no longer a doubt: everything was now apparent.

"Are you sure they are both dead?" inquired the Duchess, averting her eyes from the ghastly spectacle of the two corpses.

"There's no doubt of it, your Grace," was the answer given by three or four tongues.

"Nevertheless," said her Grace, "let some one mount a horse immediately, and run and fetch the surgeon. All this is most serious, and everything must be done in a consistent and proper manner. Meanwhile, remove the bodies to some convenient place; let restoratives be at once applied—"

"The heart of the lieutenant will never beat again," said the butler, solemnly; "and I much fear that in his lifetime it was a bad heart when it did beat."

"As for his valet," said one of the footmen, "he is stone dead."

"Nevertheless," said her Grace, "let my instructions be attended to; for there's often a spark of life lingering when it seems to be extinct. Where is Bessy?"

"They have taken her indoors," answered one of the servants. "Ah, good heavens! Strange things are about to come out!"

"And it was true, you see," ejaculated one of the footmen to another, "that I did meet Will lurking about the place t'other night, when everybody thought he was in France, along with his master."

"Yes, yes; it was true enough, no doubt. And look at them—master and man—disguised as labourers. Ah, perhaps the illness of our poor mistress—"

"No doubt of it," ejaculated several voices, as suspicion all in a moment flamed up into conviction. "Ah, that wretch Bessy."

"Come with me, Mary; come with me, said the Duchess; "and let us hasten back to her ladyship!"

They re-entered the domestic offices; and, meeting one of the servants who, some few minutes back, had taken charge of Bessy, the Duchess said, "where is the wretched young woman, and how fares it with her?"

"We have taken her up to her own chamber, your Grace," was the reply; "she is still in a state of unconsciousness, and I have come down to get some vinegar."

"And when she recovers," said her Grace, "keep a strict watch upon her. She may attempt to commit suicide, or to escape—"

"We will look after her, your Grace," replied the servant.

The Duchess hastened up the stairs, followed by Mary; and on reaching the landing paused for a moment to say a kind word to the girl.

"What a shocking scene, was it not?" she remarked, throwing into her look and voice as much friendliness as possible.

"Oh, dreadful, your Grace! But I feel as if I were almost overwhelmed with consternation and dismay," continued Mary, and she looked deadly pale; "for oh, what must we think of Bessy—what must we think of dear Lady Easterbrook's illness? Oh, now a thousand little circumstances rush to my mind, fearfully proving that Bessy is the vilest of all vile creatures! But, ah, your Grace," ejaculated Mary, as a light seemed suddenly to flash upon her brain, "you have suspected it from the first! Ah, my God! and you have suspected me also."

"Mary," said the Duchess, taking her hand, and pressing it warmly, "I have suspected you—I confess it; yes, with sorrow, and almost with shame do I confess it. Forgive me! I declare to you that a number of circumstances—"

"Oh, your Grace," said Mary, the tears trickling down her cheeks, "you are so ready to speak kindly where you think that kindness ought to be shown, that you win every heart. Say no more, your Grace, unless it is to tell me that you do not suspect me now."

"Heaven forbid!" and again and again she pressed her hand with the heartiest warmth. "Now let us return to your mistress."

They entered the boudoir. Lady Easterbrook was only at that very instant opening her eyes, and the old nobleman was calling upon her in the most piteous manner to look upon him and to speak to him.

"Leave us, my lord," said her Grace, "for a few minutes; leave us, I beseech you!" for she saw that by his entreaties and whinings he was only pursuing a course that was calculated to excite Lady Easterbrook even more than other circumstances would tend to play on her nerves. "Go, my lord, I beseech you! withdraw into the boudoir! Mary will tell you the fearful discoveries that have been made."

Lord Easterbrook accordingly retired, and, by the time the door had closed behind him, his wife had completely regained her consciousness.

"Ah! then," she said, "it is not all a dream! Night! —tapers burning!—you, dear, you are here—and all half-dressed about my bed! Then something dreadful has happened! Yes, yes; I remember the landing falling in. But ah! those fearful, shocking cries! Your Grace, I beseech you to tell me what dismal tragedy has occurred beneath this roof to-night!"

Suffice it to say that the Duchess presently revealed to her the facts that her husband's nephew and the valet, disguised in the coarsest apparel, had endeavoured to enter the mansion stealthily by the window over the private staircase; that ignorant, in the darkness, of the fact that the flooring had fallen in, they had thought to let themselves down easily, one after another, upon the landing, but that they had gone headlong down to the very bottom.

Lady Easterbrook's senses seemed for a while to be so paralysed by this astounding intelligence that she made no remark, and gave no verbal expression to her thoughts.

Leaving her in the care of the Countess and Mrs. Gaspard, her Grace passed into the boudoir, where she found Lord Easterbrook still questioning Mary in reference to the circumstances which had so recently transpired, and of which she had been giving him the horrified and excited account.

"Good God! your Grace!" said the old nobleman, quivering nervously from head to foot: "to think that my own nephew—oh, the villain! it is only too clear—only too palpable! And I who used to love him, and who made a will leaving him an income that would have placed him far beyond want. But, ah! do you think—good heavens! I can scarcely find language wherein to shape the question. But do you think that he came to assassinate me, or my poor dear wife? And do you think that her illness after all—"

"My lord," said the Duchess, "it is useless now to bewilder yourself with conjectures; everything will be made apparent shortly."

At this moment a female domestic knocked at the door of the boudoir.

She came to announce that the surgeon had just arrived, and that he was examining the two bodies which had been conveyed into one of the rooms down stairs.

Almost immediately afterwards the surgeon himself made his appearance.

Lord Easterbrook at once demanded, with nervous haste—

"Well! what of that graceless nephew of mine? What of the unhappy man?"

"Whatever injury he may have done, or sought to do you or yours, my lord," answered the surgeon solemnly, "is now to be accounted for in another world. Mr. Danvers ceases to exist!"

"My lord,' said the Duchess, "I wish to say a few words to you alone immediately."

She spoke in a whisper, and then, turning to Mary, said—

"Let the medical gentleman see Bessy next. Lady Easterbrook does not now require his assistance."

*   *   *   *   *   *

The Duchess ascended to Bessy's chamber.

The surgeon and an elderly female domestic were there.

The wretched young woman seemed to be lying in an exhausted state. Her countenance was deadly pale, her cheeks looked sunken, her eyes seemed hollow. It actually appeared as if she had experienced an illness of many weeks.

As the Duchess made her appearance the surgeon and the domestic moved towards the door; and Bessy exclaimed, in a species of half-maniac tone, "Yes, go; go, I beseech you! Leave me alone with her Grace! It is to her only that I will make confession of my enormities!"

The medical man and the servant accordingly issued from the chamber; but now it seemed as if a paroxysm of mingled shame and horror seized upon the wretched young woman—for she covered her face with her hands, and burst into tears.

The Duchess sat down by the side of the couch, saying, "If your crimes have been so great, Bessy, remember that your penitence must be proportionate."

"Oh, yes; my crimes have been immense, and you know them all, your Grace," she exclaimed, wildly and passionately; "yes, you know them; because I am guilty of everything of which I felt sure that you suspected Mary. But I must confess my wickedness to you just the same as if you were ignorant of it; for it seems to me as if this is the only means by which I can demonstrate my contrition, or remove a portion of the tremendous weight which now rests upon my soul!"

"Proceed, Bessy," said her Grace; "confession has ever been held as a proof of salutary sorrow and repentance."

*   *   *   *   *   *

There was a pause, during which Bessy appeared to be collecting her ideas as well as she was able; and presently the Duchess observed that a strong shudder swept over her form, for the very bed shook beneath her.

She comprehended what was passing in her mind, and what terrible scene was conjured up to her recollection; because she turned her haggard eyes towards her, and asked, in a hollow voice, "Is it true, then, your Grace—and my fancy is not deceiving me—is it true that Will is no more?"

"It is true, Bessy," answered her Grace.

"Oh, that Heaven would now put a speedy end to my own existence!" she cried; "for I cannot bear to live! You know not the wretch that I altogether am! But, ah! Will made me his victim; and when he had seduced

me from the path of virtue—yes, when he had seduced me, for I am a fallen and degraded creature—and, oh! my God! the babe that I bear in my bosom——"

"Bessy, compose yourself," her Grace said, for she had started up in a wild paroxysm of despair, and she dreaded lest she should suddenly lay violent hands upon herself.

"I will be as calm as I can," she replied. "But, Oh! what a wicked wretch have I been! and in what horror must you hold me! Yes, it was I who administered the slow poison to that good, kind mistress who ever had a friendly word for me! It was I who continued day by day to administer the fatal lozenges,—ruthlessly beholding her pining, fading, and perishing before my eyes! Yet not altogether *ruthlessly*; for, oh! there have been bitter, bitter moments when remorse has seized upon me as if it were a vulture fastening its claws upon my heart!"

"And you tell me," her Grace said, "that it was day by day you administered the slow poison? But tell me how you did this."

"Oh! when it was my turn to attend upon her ladyship," rejoined Bessy, "it was so easy for me to slip a lozenge into the coffee or the chocolate at breakfast time—I mean into her own cup—or else into the basin of soup or beef-tea which she took for her luncheon."

"And upon those days," her Grace said, "when it was Mary's turn to wait upon her ladyship?"

"Oh! when once a person has entered upon the ways of crime," exclaimed Bessy bitterly, "the imagination becomes horribly ingenious for the carrying out of its nefarious aims! On those days, for instance, when Mary, waited upon her ladyship, I used to be upon the watch for her when she came into the kitchen to order whatsoever her ladyship preferred for luncheon; and then I would either officiously assist to prepare it, or I would take upon myself the entire task, bidding Mary go and do something else; so that this readiness on my part was set down to that character for good nature which I have always borne. Ah, your Grace! rest assured that when people make up their minds to commit crimes the ways are only too easy, and the opportunities are only too great. My God! would that it had been otherwise! I might then have hesitated—I might not be the wretch that I have become. But, oh! believe me, it was not without a severe struggle, in the first instance, that I yielded to the representations—the mingled threats and entreaties—of Will. He had seduced me; I dreaded the consequences. He promised grand things—we were to be married; we were to be enriched whenever his master should be enabled to reward us—"

"Enough, Bessy," said her Grace, "I can understand all the motives which triumphed over the weakness of your own disposition and nature. But tell me—there is one point which I can scarcely understand. How was it that Mr. Danvers sought to bring about the death of Lady Easterbrook, when it was by the death of his lordship that he might have chiefly hoped to profit?"

"Oh! his calculation, your Grace, is easily explained," answered Bessy. "It is true that if he had consigned his uncle to the grave, he would have inherited the title of Easterbrook; but of what use would the mere name have been without the family estates? Those estates are not entailed, and, therefore, Lord Easterbrook could bequeath them unto whomsoever he thought fit. Now, Mr. Danvers, knowing how dotingly attached the old nobleman is to his young wife, thought it most probable that he had made a will, bequeathing the great bulk of his property—perhaps, indeed, the whole of it—to her ladyship. Then of what use to put Lord Easterbrook out of the way under such circumstances?"

"Ah, now I begin to comprehend the deep and cunning calculations of the villain Danvers," her Grace exclaimed. "He thought that he would send her ladyship as speedily as possible to the grave, and then his uncle would once more look upon him as his sole heir, and he might in due course make certain of succeeding not only to the peerage of Easterbrook, but likewise to the estates."

"Yes, your Grace; those were the calculations of Mr. Danvers."

"Tell me," said the Duchess, after a pause, "was it suspected that Lady Easterbrook was getting better through my agency?"

"Yes—oh, yes!" answered Bessy. "Mr. Danvers said it was plain enough that you suspected what was going on, and that you were administering an antidote. Well, then, all his dreams and visions, so grand though so iniquitous, became suddenly threatened with annihilation, and he was reduced to despair. He knew not how to act. He resolved to take some little time to consider; and it was agreed that I should meet him and Will again this evening in the garden. Alas! it was at my instigation that, after a brief debate, Mr. Danvers resolved to make his entry, along with Will, through the window overlooking the private staircase, and to which it was easy to climb up by means of the grape-vine which extends its branches all over that part of the building. Oh, Heaven! now again the scene—the awful scene presents itself vividly to my view!"

She sank back as if about to faint.

The Duchess sustained the wretched young woman, and held a glass of water to her lips.

She drank some, and soon revived.

"Tell me," said the Duchess, "for you remember that your confession is to be complete—what was the manner of proceeding which the villain had sketched out for himself and his wretched follower to adopt? That it was murder I have no doubt."

"Oh, God forgive me! Yes, it was murder!"

"But how did the assassins purpose to execute their diabolical object?" inquired the Duchess.

"Mr. Danvers had provided himself with a phial of deadly poison," continued Bessy, "a single drop of which let fall betwixt the lips proves fatal. Oh, heavens! my strength seems to fail me! No, it is but a passing weakness; I will proceed. If Mary and her ladyship slept, well and good; but if otherwise, then there were two strong men ready to overpower them both."

"But was it purposed to kill Mary likewise?" asked her Grace.

"No—not unless the crime became an absolute necessity," was the reply. "And oh, your Grace, here again is it that my own conscience tortures me so terribly: for alas! I was all the time consoling myself with the idea that, whatever might ensue, suspicion never would be attached to me—that I was therefore safe—and that under all circumstances, especially with the impressions dwelling on *your* mind, it would be Mary against whom the whole weight of accusation would rest. And thus was it that I recommended the two intending murderers to enter by that window; for I thought that if they were discovered, it would be supposed they had been in collusion with Mary, as it was Mary's turn to sleep to-night in the dressing-room. Thus you see that my own thoughts were selfishly bent on calculating how in every possible contingency I must be safe!"

"Am I to understand, then, that Mr. Danvers's calculation was to accomplish his crime so secretly and cunningly that all suspicion would rest upon Mary as the authoress of the foul deed?"

"Yes—such was his main calculation: but, after all, it was a bold stroke that he was playing, leaving a great deal to the chapter of accidents."

"And if it had succeeded," said her Grace, "and if Mary had been accused of murdering her mistress—and if she had told the tale of how two persons entered by the window and perpetrated the crime—"

"Who would have believed such a tale?" asked Bessy. "Nothing would have been stolen; and Mary must have represented the men as two common-looking fellows, coarsely dressed, with masks upon their countenances—for with these were they provided. Then who would believe that two low ruffians would have stealthily entered

that chamber to poison a lady for the mere sake of committing a crime; and without the object of plunder! Ah, rest assured, that poor Mary would have been deemed guilty—and even you yourself would have suffered her to go with but little sympathy to the scaffold, for you would have been convinced of her iniquity."

"Alas! yes, it must have been so," the Duchess murmured.

"But this was not all," resumed Bessy; "there was yet another calculation. Suppose that Mary had slept soundly; suppose that Mr. Danvers had penetrated, unheard and unperceived, into her ladyship's chamber, and that she, also, was sleeping soundly, the fatal poison would have been dropped between her lips; and, then, let us suppose that the murderers succeeded in effecting a retreat as noiseless as their entry had been. Well, your Grace, what would have happened? In the morning Lady Easterbrook would have been found dead in her bed; and there was the chance that her death might have been attributed to natural causes."

"What!" exclaimed the Duchess, "Mr. Danvers calculated upon such a chance when he knew that I was at the Hall, and that my mind was filled with suspicions?"

"Ah! your Grace, he scarcely knew what to think in reference to the policy you were pursuing. There was, however, one thing which was as clear to him as the sun at noonday,—which was that you were bent on dragging the terrible facts of the case to light; and this was a constant source of fear to him."

"And well it might be," said her Grace, "but now I leave you, and trust that when we next meet—"

"We shall meet no more."

"What mean you?"

"Nothing."

The Duchess watched the girl narrowly, but her face was calm and passionless, and so she left her.

An hour passed, and then, with a little cry, the Duchess, who was sitting by the bedside of her friend, sprang to her feet.

"What is it?" demanded Lady Easterbrook, seriously alarmed at the manner of her friend.

"Good God!" cried her Grace, to think that I should have been mad enough to leave that unhappy girl alone."

"Why?"

"Why, Heaven and earth! may she not be supplied with sufficient poison to destroy her life?"

Her Grace hastened to the room in which the girl lay.

She was too late.

Bessy was dead.

By her side was a small box, in which was found a *white* lozenge."

CHAPTER LV.

WHAT BECAME OF JONATHAN WILD AFTER HIS DISAPPEARANCE FROM THE MANDSTONE CAVE—THE MAN IN THE CLOAK HAS RECOURSE TO THE SERVICES OF JACK HALL—THE CAREER OF THAT CRIMINAL—WILD ONCE MORE IN SAFETY THROUGH THE MACHINATIONS OF THE PRINCESS, WHO DISPOSES OF HIS ENEMY IN A DIABOLICAL MANNER.

FROM the events recorded in the last chapter, the reader may glean that the individual who served Sall whilst doing his best to bring out of danger those persons of whom he was beyond doubt the compatriot had contrived to carry off the band in safety.

We will leave those persons in whom we are more immediately interested for a while, in order to follow this mysterious being who was, for reasons hereafter to be revealed, playing so curious and apparently incomprehensible a part.

We hasten over his descent into the cave.

We only hint at his giving an alarm so serious that the men he had betrayed instantly followed his advice, and fled by the quarry entrance.

We cannot pause to detail the incidents of his search for the maimed body of Wild; let it suffice to say that he found that wretch lying bleeding and almost dead in a corner of the inner cave, to which spot he had been dragged by the terrified robbers.

All this took but a short time to accomplish, and ere the half hour he desired Sall to pause had elapsed they had all fled.

The mysterious man seized the form of Wild, dragged it out of the cave, closed the entrance, and staggered away under his burthen.

The task of quitting the old quarry was one of extreme difficulty, but it was at length accomplished, and the man then struck across some fields, which brought him to a point on the London road some three-quarters of a mile from the quarry.

Here he gave a long and piercing whistle, and from a dry ditch, half concealed by bushes, came lumbering out a heavy wagon, drawn by two horses, and driven by a man habited in the garb of a farmer.

The whole character of himself and his conveyance was that of a respectable countryman, conveying his produce to market for sale.

"Well?" said the driver, looking at the man who had summoned him.

The individual silently pointed to the insensible Wild.

"Told you there would be the devil's work at the cave to-night," he said, "and there has been, as you may see; but, with the exception of one man, killed by Wild, all are off in safety."

"What's the matter with Jonathan?"

"Shot by those who trapped him, and suffering from a fall into the pit."

"Dangerously hurt?"

"I think so."

"Poor devil!"

"Come, there is no time to waste in words. Now, lend a hand, Jack, and get Jonathan into the wagon."

"What's to be done with him?"

"He's to go to Cartchapel."

"To the Hall?"

"Yes, to the Hall. He must join the Princess at once."

"But will she care about having him there?"

"She must!"

"All's well, then."

They raised the prostrate form, and placed it in the bottom of the wagon.

It was then covered with straw, and the contents of the wagon skilfully piled around, so that detection was impossible.

"He's right enough there," said the driver.

"Yes, if he don't die."

"Die! Jonathan Wild die! I don't believe in the possibility of such a contingency. He'll be alive and sprightly by the time we reach Cartchapel, or my name isn't Jack Hall."

With this he set his team in motion, and hastened away.

"All right," said the man in the cloak, "I can't betray Wild; it's too dangerous a game; but, unless I'm mistaken, there's one concealed in the musty old Hall at Cartchapel who will do the business for him with expedition and care."

He stood watching the vehicle until it disappeared from view, and then struck back into the path by which he had come.

We must follow the wagon.

On the ponderous concern jogged, and Mr. Jack Hall set himself down to the enjoyment of a pipe, which he lighted and puffed at with great energy.

Jack Hall!

The reader will be familiar with the name.

It has echoed throughout England, and the acts of its possessor are generally known. But in case memory should not serve the reader, or his not having in his possession the Newgate Calendar to refer to, a few of the adventures of this outrageous thief may be reproduced and perused with interest.

This man was educated for a thief.

In a very short time he became dexterous in every species of stealing.

Housebreaking, robbing as a pad upon the highway, shop-lifting, picking pickets—all were equally at his command.

Nor could any in the trade exceed him in industry or activity.

He frequented churches, fairs, markets, public assemblies; had always some companion ready to receive the booty; so that, if he was charged with stealing, or searched, there might be nothing found to prove his guilt.

The following is an instance of the dexterity of Hall in picking pockets.

Upon a market day, a grazier in Smithfield was receiving money for some cattle, and had put a bagful into his pocket.

Jack brought it to his comrades, who were drinking in an alehouse.

Nor was this all.

To show his dexterity still further, he went in search of the same grazier, and replaced the bag in his pocket, without his knowledge.

Not long after, a farmer coming to the grazier, they went to an inn, the former having to receive some money from the latter.

He pulled out his bag, though in a very besmeared, stinking condition, exclaiming that he had put thirty pounds into it, and behold what it was now become!

The gentlemen of the fields generally love to be well provided with dung, but this honest grazier esteemed his dunghill too dearly purchased.

Jack had a strong desire to levy some contribution on a rich merchant in town; but he could not effect his purpose, though he had frequently sauntered about his shop.

Resolved, however, to gain his object, he contrived, along with one of his comrades, to be put into a bale of goods, and conveyed to the merchant's warehouse, there to lie all night, when his comrade, who was dressed as a merchant, was to come next day and settle about the price of the goods.

Accordingly this bale of iniquity, well protected on all sides with coarse cloth and fustian, was laid up in the ware-room.

Night being come, one of the apprentices, who was weary, threw himself down upon the bale, placed beside some others.

His weight so incommoded Jack, that he could scarcely breathe.

Upon this he was constrained, to prevent his being smothered to death, to make a wound in the bale with his penknife, and as great a one in the buttocks of the apprentice, who roared out that his fellow apprentice had killed him.

Running instantly to his master, the innocent lad was apprehended, until the matter was more thoroughly examined.

Meanwhile Jack made his escape out of a window, with only two pieces of velvet.

When the master saw his apprentice in such a bloody condition, he was afraid that any of the blood should have been spilt upon the bale, so that he might have been called upon to take the goods at any price; he therefore hastened to examine it, and perceived that there was a great rent in it, and that it was greatly diminished in its size.

Nay, upon further examination, he found it contained nothing valuable.

In this manner he discovered the whole matter, and the

CLIFFORD'S ARRIVAL AT MRS. GRANVILLE'S.

other apprentice was exonerated. A surgeon was also sent for to dress his wound, and it cost the master five pounds for the doctor's fee.

Jack was also an expert hand at what was termed *lob*; which was going into a shop with a companion to receive the change of a guinea, or any other piece of money, and when about one half of the change is received, then the one exclaims to the other—

" What need you to change? I have silver enough to defray our charges where we are going."

Upon this the other throws the money back into the box, but with such dexterity as to retain one of the pieces in the hollow of the hand, unperceived.

He was likewise expert at what was called " *whale-bonelay*."

This was, having a piece of whalebone daubed on the end with birdlime, and then going into a shop to purchase something, and, by asking for different articles, oblige the shopkeeper frequently to turn his back to them; then putting the whalebone into the till of the counter, they bring up whatever piece of money it happens to touch.

Then, buying some article, they pay the merchant with a pig of his own sow.

Jack having one time committed sacrilege, by robbing Radcliffe church, he hastened to London; but his money being soon spent, he was constrained, with some companions, to take a *running-smobble*.

That manœuvre is effected by one of the confederates going into a shop, pretending to be drunk, and, after some uproar, extinguishing the lights, and seizing whatever comes first to hand, while another throws handfuls of dirt and nastiness into the mouth and face of the person who cries " hold the thief!" thus preventing detection, and getting time to make off with their prize.

There was nothing that Jack would not attempt, and few things that he could not accomplish.

As he was one day dressed in the habit of a gentleman, he sat down to rest himself upon a bench in St. James's Park.

In the meantime he observed an attorney accost one of the Life Guards, and, after the usual compliments, invite him to dine with him on the following day, giving him his address, and requesting him to bring any one of his acquaintance with him.

Jack, hearing this, began to ruminate how he could make the most of this occurrence.

Accordingly he is dressed in style, and ready a little before the appointed hour of dinner, and, hovering about, discovers the Life Guardsman enter the attorney's at the time appointed.

With the greatest assurance he follows him at the heels, and in the most free and easy manner talked at dinner, the attorney supposing he was a friend of the Life Guardsman, and he, on the other hand, taking him to be a friend of the landlord.

But when Jack found a convenient moment, he stepped up to the sideboard and, taking a few silver spoons, and knives, and forks, he went off secretly, as he had come in openly.

In a little time an explanation took place, the articles were missing, and the imposition detected, but the impostor was gone.

At another time, Jack wished to act the sober man for a while, and, assuming the character of a country gentleman, took lodgings at a Quaker's house.

It was some considerable time before fortune favoured his designs.

He at last, one day, discovered the key of the Quaker's secret closet, and carefully took the impression of it in clay.

With all possible dispatch, he got the key made, and waited the wished-for moment.

At length the Quaker and his wife went to reside a few days at their country house, and leaving the care of the house to their domestics.

This was too good an opportunity to lose.

He pillaged the house of all the money and the plate he could find, as well as everything else which suited his purpose.

When the Quaker returned, he stormed and raged more like a fury than a calm and godly Quaker.

But Jack was far beyond the strife of tongues, or the reproach of the indignant Quaker.

The next adventure of our hero was in company with Stephen Bunce and Dick Low.

They, by the help of their short crows and other instruments, entered the house of a baker.

They bound the apprentice and journeyman, and threw them both into the kneading trough.

Jack stood below, and the other two went up stairs to the baker's own bed-chamber, tied both him and his wife, and threatened them with death if they did not inform them where their treasure lay.

Threats had no effect; upon which Jack, chiding their delay, ran up stairs, seized a grandchild lying in the room, and threatened to take its life, unless the old people would deal candidly.

The old man entreated them to spare the child's life, and, laying his hand upon a small iron box, below the bed, he opened it, and gave them about eighty pounds.

At another time Jack went into the shop of a robe-maker, pretending that he wished to send a gown to his brother, who was a parson in the country; adding, that he wished a good one, though he should pay the more.

"I can furnish you with all sorts and sizes," said Mr. Aspin.

He examined and turned over a great many, until he selected one which seemed to please him.

But he was still at a loss to know whether or not it would suit, pretending that it was too short; but the robemaker said he was sure that it was long enough in all conscience.

He was, at the same time, for trying it upon Jack.

"Alas! there will be no certain measure by me, because my brother is the head and shoulders taller than me."

Dick then asked the favour of Mr. Aspin to put it upon himself, and from him he would discover how it would answer, as he was a man of nearly his brother's size.

Aspin, to please his customer, consented, but, while he was putting it on, Jack seized a barrister's gown, and run off with all possible speed.

Stephen Bunce took hold of the first parcel of goods which came to his hand, and made off with it; and as the robemaker pursued hard after Jack Hall, Dick Low went up to him, and cried——

"O dear, Doctor Cross, who thought of seeing you.

"I am glad I have met with you with all my heart.

"But pray, sir, what makes you run in this distracted manner about the streets?"

"Pish," quoth Aspin, "let me go, I am no parson: you are mistaken in your man, for I am running after a rogue that has robbed me."

Then Dick Low replied, but still holding him, "I beg your pardon, sir, for my mistake, for you are as like my friend Doctor Cross as ever I saw two men in my life like one another."

During this bustle the neighbours were collected, and filled with no small admiration to see old Aspin in a canonical dress.

In this case, as usual, both invention and scandal were soon at work.

Accordingly, one more eloquent than the rest exclaimed——

"Surely he was not going to christen his own child himself that his maid Betty had to him!"

Others, with more compassion and politeness, endeavoured to calm his temper, and to advise him to go home, and lay aside his assumed dress, which exposed him to ridicule, and then to make diligent inquiry after the thief.

But when he returned home, he found that more than one thief had assailed him, and that goods, to a much greater value than the unfortunate cassock, had been extracted from his shop during his unsuccessful pursuit.

Upon this he exclaimed——

"Well might the fellow call me Doctor *Cross*, for I am *crossed* by the whole world!"

These are but a few of the many acts recorded against Jack Hall; and at the date of this tale he was in the full tide of a triumphal career of vice.

Naturally enough he became an accomplice of Wild when that gentleman fell from his high estate, and had to make friends and rely upon the aid of those who formerly stood in such terror of his very name.

He was on the night of the adventures at the cave acting under the orders of the mysterious man in whom we have so much interest, and it was his express order that Jack should lie in ambush, in order to render what assistance he could, and in order to facilitate the escape of the band of rascals in the cave.

*   *   *   *   *   *

A very capital retreat was the old Hall of Cartchapel, and the Princess exhibited great tact in selecting it.

Cartchapel was an obscure little village, and the old Hall had been for years untenanted.

It was rented for "a mere song," and there the Princess fled after rescuing Wild from the very hangman, and lived in the most secluded style.

She was attended only by members of her own gang, and to all appearances the tumble-down old house had no occupant.

It was somewhat late in the day when the wagon of Jack Hall approached Cartchapel, and skulked by an obscure and circuitous route to the stables of the old house.

He was unobserved, and Wild was placed in safety.

The Princess dismissed Hall as soon as Jonathan Wild had been placed in bed.

Her first care was to dress the wounds of the unfortunate partner of her crimes, and to endeavour to bring back life to his inanimate form.

It was long before her efforts succeeded, but a liberal application of brandy, within and without, at length brought the blood tingling through his veins, and partially restored animation.

It was long before Wild comprehended his position. but gradually the Princess detailed to him all she had heard from Jack Hall, and bitterly did the great thief-taker curse his fate.

"Curse him!" he cried, as his thoughts reverted to the safety of Clifford; "curse him! He has done me once more. It's all no use—it's all no use. I see I shall die by his hand after all."

"Psha! Fool that you have been! Why not have killed him when you had him so entirely in your power?"

"Why not?" cried Wild, starting up in his bed, and pointing angrily to the bright sky through his chamber window, "why not? Can you ask that? Why do we not bid the sunshine or the clouds gather at our will? Because we know that the ordering of such matters is beyond us! Why not fight against Fate? Because Fate is the strongest, and always wins the battle! Why not slay Clifford? Have I not tried to do so—and has not Fate defied me?"

"Fools and cowards are always ready to attribute to *Fate* the failures due to their own weakness or want of foresight. Bah! Wild; you rave. You want to talk of matters you don't understand—you want to charge the will of Heaven with an account of which it notes not! Do you think the same power that governs the elements recognises such beings as you and Clifford?—'

"And *you*."

"Yes, and myself if you will. If I but thought so I should not now be doing what I am."

Wild was about to reply when a strange sound arrested his attention.

It came from the corridor!

The Princess and Jonathan gazed at each other.

The former placed her finger upon her lip, and stole to the door.

Drawing a small stiletto from under a fold in her dress, she suddenly threw open the door of her chamber, and gazed out.

Nothing was to be *seen*, but there *was a sound* as of retreating footsteps.

"Marcus, Horace, Nat!" cried the Princess.

There was no reply.

She re-entered the chamber.

"Strange," she said.

"What is it?" asked Wild. "One of the men?"

"I ordered them not to approach this wing of the house; and, had it been either of them, they would have answered."

"Then there's some one in the place," said Wild.

"If so it is an enemy?"

"Be cautious."

"Trust me."

"I know I can do so."

The Princess glided from the room, turned the key in the door, and stole cautiously away in the direction in which she had heard footsteps retreat.

It was now dusk.

The woman, grasping her weapon, passed with a cat-like step through the grim and dusty old corridor.

She listened at each door as she passed.

No sound arrested her until she reached the end of the passage.

It was growing dark, and the shadows were falling fast.

The woman appeared to be baffled!

She paused and listened.

There was a step in a chamber on her right.

The Princess drew a deep breath, and then placed her hand on the door.

Resolution was in her face.

Her lips were compressed, and her eyes wore a fierce expression of daring and determination.

She thrust open the door, and entered a small and grimly-furnished sleeping apartment.

With his back to the window, and glancing nervously at the door, was a young and elegantly dressed man.

"So," said the Princess, confronting him, "so, Mr. Watville, the detective officer! So, sir, you have found your way to this remote hole?"

The man spoke not.

"So," continued the Princess, "we are betrayed, hunted to this den, and set at bay?"

"Yes."

"Are you alone?"

"Yes."

"What brought you here—do you want *me*?"

"No."

"Wild, then?"

"Yes."

"He is not here."

"I know better."

"How know you that?"

"That is my secret."

"Explain to me how you came here; how you knew Wild would be here."

"No."

"You won't."

"No."

"Then I can't force you."

"Just so."

"But, Mr. Watville, does it not strike you that you do rather a foolish trick in coming here alone?"

The man shook his head and smiled.

"Why should I have done a stupid trick?"

"We are not alone here."

"No; but your friends are of no service to you."

"Indeed!"

"Yes, indeed; I took care to hocus* them."

"Dead?"

"No, but dead to *you*; it's pretty much the same thing, at least, for my purpose."

The Princess looked alarmed.

The detective, for such he appeared to be, now caught sight of the weapon the Princess carried.

With great rapidity he drew a pistol, and pointed it at her head.

"No tricks," he said; just throw down that pricking machine, or I shall fire."

"Nonsense."

"There's no nonsense about it. Throw it down."

The Princess reluctantly obeyed.

"You see, I mean to have Wild in spite of you."

"But he is ill—dying!"

"I know just how he is, for I took the liberty of placing myself on the outside of his chamber door just now."

"I heard you."

"I presume so, or you would not be here now."

"But now, Watville, let us talk things over; you don't mean mischief?"

"I do."

"But I can coax—"

"No you can't; I don't mean being swindled now. The reward is a big one, and the game is in my own hands. Don't think I mean to lose it."

"But if I can make it worth your while?"

"You can't."

"Why not? I have money."

"Yes, but you can't give me the *reputation!* I'm young at the work, and have a strong ambition to gratify."

As he spoke he threw up the window, and placed himself carelessly against it.

The Princess then approached him, and commenced fondling him.

She used every art to which a woman has recource to

---

* Drugged.

make the man waver; but, although her endearments were far from distasteful to him, she failed to shake his purpose.

"Come," she cried, "come, now; let Wild get away this once. It won't be much of a loss to you in the long run."

"It won't do."

"I'll double the amount of the reward!"

"That's handsome, but still it won't do."

"And then there's my love—"

"Psha!"

"You won't have it?"

"Yes, and Wild too!"

"No, not Wild."

"Yes, I shall have Jonathan."

"Then I say you shan't."

"Shan't!"

"I am determined."

"Now, what will you do?"

"*Dispose of you!*"

The young man was seated on the ledge of the window, and was entirely off his guard.

With a bound like that of a tiger she darted upon him, and struck him on the chest.

He fell back, and was at her mercy.

"Now, Mr. Watville," she cried, "now we shall see if you will have Jonathan Wild!"

"Spare me!"

"Not I! Down with you!"

She caught him by the leg, and pitched him from the window-ledge.

There was a wild shriek, and then a dull, heavy thud.

The Princess looked out of the window, and through the gathering gloom she discovered, some forty feet below her, a dark form writhing on the ground.

It was the detective, with his back broken!

CHAPTER LVI.

EVELINA AND ROSE PURSUE THEIR JOURNEY—THE ATTACK OF THE SMUGGLERS—THE RESCUE—AND THE "GOOD WOMAN OF GLENHAVEN."

THE direction taken by Evelina and her humble friend was towards the south coast, and on the second day, as the sun was going down, the roar of the ocean fell upon their ears.

They were near the little sea port of Glenhaven.

The moon rose as they crossed some fields leading to the shore and thence to the town.

The sight of the queen of night playing upon the waters had a somewhat novel appearance to the young girls, and they paused to contemplate it for some time.

The fresh breeze and the pleasant sound of the water had a charming effect, and somewhat revived the drooping spirits of the fair wanderers.

"Oh, that we could live here," said Rose; "oh, that we could remain in this charming place."

"That may be possible," said Evelina; "there must be work to do in this place, and Heaven knows we are willing to do it."

"Yes," said Rose, "we will work hard so that we can only live in peace and retirement."

The place in which they stood was somewhat retired, and appeared to be entirely unfrequented at nightfall, so that the conversation of the girls was not interrupted.

Long did they stand gazing on the vast waste of waters, but at last the sound of a distant clock striking the hour of nine, warned them that it was time to make for the village.

They gathered their garments about them and proceeded a few paces in the direction of the lights that twinkled invitingly about a quarter of a mile from them.

Suddenly they were brought to a stand still.

Several rough-looking men came upon them from some spot near at hand, and stood in their path.

The dress of these fellows denoted their occupation was the sea, but there was an air about them that spoke plainly of lawlessness and bravado.

"Hillo," said the foremost of them; "hillo, my pretty maids, where are you trotting off at this time of night, and what's your business?"

"Business!" said another, "no good, I'll be sworn. Mischief's their business, it always is! Women never have any proper business."

The girls, trembling with fear at this unexpected appearance, made an attempt to pass on, and at first their progress was not checked, but anon they were followed.

This occurred after two of the ruffians had held the following brief conversation:—

"Well," said one, "what d'ye say, will you do it?"

"I don't know."

"There's no time to lose; what d'ye say?"

"Well, they're wanted."

"Yes; them or two others; these look likely ones. The chance is good; there's no one by; they are evidently strangers, and won't be missed—now then."

"Well, let us collar them."

The whole of the men now started off after the girls.

They heard the footsteps following them, and hurried on, their hearts sinking within them.

In a few moments the men headed them again.

"Why do you follow us?" asked Evelina, speaking to the foremost of the men.

"Because we're in love with you, my dears, and don't know how to sheer off."

"If you are men you will allow us to proceed unmolested."

"We shouldn't be men if we did."

"What mean you? If you are seeking money learn at once that we have none, so that you waste your time and risk punishment without reason."

"We ain't no robbers, my lass," said one; "that isn't our game, so don't say anything in that strain; all we want is your pretty selves."

"You terrify me."

"Ah, that's a pity, for we don't want to do that."

"No," said another; "we don't want to do that. Look here, my lasses, we want two comely lasses to take a trip with us in the Flying Betsy, as neat a little craft as either of you; clean stem and starn, and as prettily rigged as a May queen. You don't look as if the world had sarved you too well, so you see you're in luck's way. Come along without any palaver."

They advanced, as if intending to lay hands on them.

"Stand back," cried Evelina; "stand back, if you advance another step I will cry for help."

"And much good that would do you. Look here, we mean to have you gals to make a little trip along with us, so all the crying for help won't be of sarvice."

"Ruffians! there must be some help at hand, and we will not submit to your brutal outrage without a struggle."

"Struggle be d——d; here Bill, Jack, catch 'em up; put a stopper on their gab, and take 'em down to the beach; whip 'em into the boat, and have 'em aboard without delay."

The two men indicated sprang forward, and caught the two girls in their arms.

They struggled violently, and cried aloud, but the men in a few moments succeeded in overpowering them, and placing a gag in their mouths.

They then hastened with them in the direction of the beach.

Suddenly, however, cries were heard; lights were seen dancing about in all directions, and the whole neighbourhood appeared to be alarmed.

"Devil take it," said one, "they have heard the cry of the women.

"Nonsense," said another, "that can't be it; see where the lights come from, they have discovered the boat and are coming down in a shoal to snap us up."

"Drop the women," said a third. "Drop the women, and run for it."

"Devil take me if I drop them," said one of the two ruffians who held the girls; "I'll stick to them till the last!"

"Hillo!" shouted a fourth, "they're close upon us now, we shall have to fight for it."

"Fight for it! nonsense," said the one who appeared to be in command of the party; "let us cut."

The two ruffians who held the young girls acted upon this order, and threw Evelina and Rose violently to the earth!

They attempted flight; but, by this time several men bearing torches came to the spot, and brought the ruffians to a standstill.

There was a short and desperate struggle.

There were groans and cries: a few loud oaths, and then a flight and pursuit, and the girls were left with only two men stooping over them.

They were friends!

"Dang the fellows," cried one, "they had almost bolted with the lasses. What devil's game could they have been up to?"

"No matter; let us see to the poor creatures. They're faint and ill and want assistance."

The speaker raised Evelina, and gazed into her face.

"Strangers," he said, "strangers to this part. I can't make the game out; but there's no time for speculation, I must leave you here while I run to the village and get assistance."

"Yes," said the other, "I'll remain here and keep watch: you had best go to Mrs. Armer, she is the best hearted woman in the world, and will gladly give you any assistance.

* * * * *

In a short time the mission had been performed, and assistance from the village procured.

Without delay, Evelina and Rose were conveyed to the house of the lady named Armer, who received them joyfully, and at once proceeded to bring back consciousness to them, and see to their wants.

Mrs. Armer had seen trials and troubles that had chastened her, and her whole life was devoted to doing good.

Indeed, so many and important were the charitable actions she performed that she had won for herself the name of the "Good woman of Glenhaven."

We will briefly give the story of her life before returning to our heroine:—

She was the eldest of a large family of girls, who, being motherless, were brought up under her care; and her father was a clergyman.

He was poor, and could afford his daughters no education but what he gave them himself; and, to tell the truth, he tried to teach them all he knew, for he was great in Latin, Greek, and particularly mathematics. But of what use were such things to a number of portionless daughters? So she was not clever, but, to make up for it, was good tempered, unobtrusive, religious (humbly, not hypocritically so), and very loving.

We speak of Sarah Mordaunt.

He whole thoughts were centred in her home; and, as she had never thought of any different life herself, it seemed so strange when her sisters, one after the other, got married and left her.

It seemed to Sarah but yesterday when she held them on her knee, teaching them the alphabet, and promising them a pretty story when so many letters were learned. So when Effie, the youngest, got married likewise, Sarah felt quite desolate.

She had loved the pleasant routine of daily duties which she had now no longer to perform, for her father and herself required very little. Yet Sarah did not

repine, and did her duty towards her father, and tried to be happy; though the past would often rise up before her, and weaken her resolutions.

And then Mr. Mordaunt died, leaving Sarah quite alone—but not for long; as her sisters, especially Effie, all wished her to live with them.

And to the house of Effie Sarah went.

Now Effie had married an officer fond of company, so the change in Sarah's life was very great. She had lived so much alone all her life, that the present seemed like a dream—somehow, not a very pleasant one.

And Sarah thought of the quiet days spent at the old parsonage, and could not help wishing her sisters all children again, so that she might watch over them as in the dear old times.

But another greater change soon took place.

Amongst those Sarah met every day was a Lieutenant Armer—one of those young men who, disgusted with everything as it is, are always building up an ideal view of life in their own fancy. He was not *blasé*, for he had seen very little of the world. He merely (and he was sincere in his ideas, if nothing else) disliked the present ways of the world. He was anything but a recluse, with all his peculiarities; and he did not dislike quiet Sarah Mordaunt. Her simple, truthful manner amused him; he became friendly with her; then more friendly still; until, at last, he became unhappy if a day passed without their having met.

Poor Sarah! She was glad when he came, though something told her that she ought not to encourage him; but it was so nice to have all she said listened to; it put her in mind of old times again. And the strange fancy of the youth of twenty for the woman of two-and-thirty became talked about.

It was the night of a ball, and tired of the hot, crowded rooms, Sarah went out on the balcony.

She stood there some time dreaming about her former life, as she generally did when alone. Presently Frank Armer followed her, and, unseen by Sarah, quietly watched her for some minutes.

"Sarah!"

"Mr. Armer! You here? I never heard you come."

"I was afraid of disturbing you, you seemed so quiet. What were you thinking about?"

"O, many things."

"Of old times, as usual?"

"What makes you fancy I think of old times?"

"O, I can see you do; and you do not seem as if you were happy. The life you now lead does not suit you."

"I never said so."

"Of course not. You would like your sisters to think you were happy; but, Miss Mordaunt—Sarah—you are too good for this sort of existence."

"Mr. Armer!"

"Yes, much too good. The country is your sphere—some quiet village, with plenty of miserable, discontented people in it. I could fancy you, then—spending all your days in trying to make them happy. You ought to be a clergyman's wife."

"Why a clergyman's?"

Poor Sarah repented those words.

"Not necessarily a clergyman's; and you might be happy without living always in the country. But you could make one discontented person think better of the world. You know who I mean."

Of course she knew, and said so; but advised him to think no more about her. She owned she loved him; but then the difference in their ages! It would be better for him to leave her at once than have, in years to come, when she would be old and he only in the prime of life, to repent their ever having met. But Frank thought different, and—but never mind what else they said. A few months afterwards strange, eccentric Frank Armer, and quiet Sarah Mordaunt, were married.

They went into the country at first, and a quiet, pleasant time they had of it. Frank Armer found a charm in his wife's society that made him forget all his former fantastical notions. But one day Frank received a letter telling him that his regiment was ordered on foreign service.

And Sarah ?

The idea of leaving the country where her few friends lived made her feel sad, but the idea of her husband (to whom she now felt herself of so much use) going without her made her sadder still; so she resolved to accompany him. At first Frank tried to persuade her from going, telling her of the long voyage, the unhealthy climate, and the separation from her sisters ; but all he could say would not make Sarah alter her resolution. So Frank Armer, with his regiment, sailed for the West Indies, and his wife followed him.

They were far from unhappy, but Frank became used to the " customs of the country " much sooner than his wife. All was new—so strange to her—so different from what she had been accustomed to all her life ; but after a time, when her child was born, Sarah begun to like her new home almost as well as the quiet English village in which she passed the early part of her life.

The winter was over, and the approaching summer threatened to be a very hot one. Now, a very hot summer in a tropical climate is a thing somewhat dreaded by Europeans, especially when residing in a low marshy climate.

The summer came ; and ere long a fever of the most dangerous kind had spread through the camp. At first it was not much noticed ; but the mortality daily increasing, orders were given for the regiment to remove to a town some miles distant.

It was evening, and the regiment was to march the next day. It was a very sultry evening, and Sarah, complaining of a headache, lay down on the sofa. Before night came on she was suffering from the worst form of the fever, and the next morning no hopes were given of her recovery. Now the country near them had long been in an unsettled state ; and the day before Sarah was taken ill her husband had gone with a part of the regiment to quell a rising rebellion some miles off. The first news that he heard on his return was his wife's death ; and when he had reached his home, and would have taken a last farewell of her with whom he had been so happy, he found himself too late ; for her body was gone. Frank felt grieved but not surprised, for he had no doubt that she had been taken away immediately after death, and buried in the common grave ; necessity having for some time made such a proceeding the custom.

But he could do no good by remaining, so when the regiment left the town, Frank Armer, taking his infant child, accompanied it, and never again returned to the place where his short, but happy married life had been passed.

*   *   *   *   *

Twelve years passed by. It is summer, and the sun was setting at Glenhaven, a little sea-side village on the south coast of England. It had been a very hot day, and a calm, drowsy languor seemed to hang over everything and everybody. It was one of those evenings when indoor life seems so unnatural ; so the little straggling street of Glenhaven was full of people sitting in their front gardens or leaning idly against the palings. All was so calm—so still.

Close by Glenhaven village was a little house—too large for a cottage, and too unpretending for a villa—called the May Trees. It had a long garden behind it, reaching down to the sea, in which sits a pale delicate-looking lady with a little girl, golden-haired, bright-eyed, and so very pretty, by her side. But we must leave them for a minute, for along the high road comes a tired, poorly-dressed woman who seemed pleased when she reached the May Trees, and then, leaning against the palings, looked eagerly into the garden.

" I wish papa would come out," said the little girl.

" So do I, Effie dear,' answered the lady. " I do not like him to be sitting indoors writing all the evening—such a pleasant evening too."

" He is always writing now."

" A great deal too much : he will make himself ill, I'm afraid ; and, besides, I feel so lonely here without him."

" So you can't get on without me,' said a gentleman who had just entered the garden. " A pretty wife you are, who does not know what to do because her husband leaves her for a minute."

" A minute ! Oh, Frank, I have scarcely seen you all day ; whatever have you been doing ?"

" Hush ! it is a great secret at present. I am writing an essay about the foolishness and uselessness of the present ways of society, and I—"

" The old story, Frank. Are you never going to give up those eccentric ideas ?"

" Not till I have made everyone else think the same, your dear self included. But, my dear Effie, I came out on purpose to see them unloading the fishing boats. We have not been to see them for nearly a week ; so come along dear.'

Frank Armer, now a captain on half-pay, went away with his daughter, leaving his pale, pretty wife (too much of an invalid to walk far herself) sitting alone in her garden, with nothing to think of but the pleasant dreamy existence she was leading, and the kind, indulgent husband who had just left her.

She felt so happy.

And the woman, leaning over the palings, had heard all that had been said.

A strange, sorrowful expression came over her face. At first the scene she beheld seemed like a dream, but gradually the truth came upon her. It was all real. Yet it was not unkindly that she gazed upon the invalid lady sitting in her garden, and, inwardly murmuring a blessing on the little house and its inhabitants, she went to the village, and into the principal inn.

There, alone in her room, when the officious, over-kind landlady had at last left, her grief gave way, and she cried as if her heart would break.

Poor creature ! a wretched night she passed. She tried to pray, but words would not come ; and at times she felt as if her senses were leaving her. But in the morning she became calmer, and, after thinking a long time, called the landlady into the room.

" I want your advice," she said to her. " Do you think that if I was to set up here as a sick nurse, I should stand any chance of getting my living ?"

" Well, I should say so,'' answered the landlady. " I do not think we have a nurse in the village—you see it is such a healthy spot ; but people must fall ill sometimes, for all that. But do you think you are strong enough ?"

" Yes, I am quite fit for such work ; and if you could recommend me to a small, cheap cottage, I should be much obliged to you."

The landlady happened to know of one already furnished ; and, after a few days, the quiet-looking woman, who gave the name of Mrs. Elmer, took up her abode there. She was somewhat changed since the day on which she arrived at Glenhaven ; for she wore a cap, which covering nearly all her hair, came close on to her face, and used spectacles : in fact, anyone who had seen her then would not have known her to be the same person.

Her life was very retired ; but for all that she was liked by the people of Glenhaven, and found plenty of employment. Except when engaged in her duties she seldom went out, but sometimes of an evening, when it was getting dark, she would (with a thick veil on, which she always wore out of doors) haunt the May Trees, and always returned home sadder, yet somehow happier.

Now one day when it was raining, little Effie came and stood under the porch of Mrs. Elmer's cottage, and the latter recognised her at once as the little girl she had seen in the garden of the May Trees. She was a pretty little creature ; and, when Mrs. Elmer began to talk to her, seemed to take a fancy to the quiet-looking woman in the large cap at once. It is only children make friends by impulse : in after life we are suspicious of every stranger we meet, and like to know all about

them before we become communicative. But Effie
was as friendly with Mrs. Elmer as if she had
known her all her life, and made her the confidant
of all her childish joys and sorrows—how her bird died
last week, and how she had buried it in the garden. That
she was soon to go to school, though she already knew a
great deal, as her papa—who was, oh! so clever!—was
fond of teaching her. What books she had read, and
which she liked best; and Mrs. Elmer sat and listened,
and seemed as if she could have listened to little Effie for
ever.

But it was getting dark, and the rain looked as if it
would not leave off for a long time.

"How ever are you to get home, dear?" said Mrs.
Elmer. "Won't your mamma be very anxious about
you?"

"She is not my mamma. My mamma died a long
time ago."

"A long time ago! You do not recollect her,
then?"

"Oh, no! I was only a few months old at the time.
Papa says she died a very long way from here; but I
never like to talk about it; it makes him so unhappy."

"Do you recollect the time before your papa married
again?"

"I can only just remember it. We did not live here
then, but a very long way off."

What Effie had said brought strange thoughts to Mrs.
Elmer's mind, and made her love the little creature with
a love so strong that nothing in the world could break
it.

The rain at last left off, and Mrs. Elmer (for it was
now dark) took Effie home.

She would not go into the May Trees as Effie wanted,
but from that day the quiet-looking woman and the little
golden haired child often met on the beach, and after a
little time loved one another as only a child who has seen
nothing but what is good in the world, and a pure woman,
who, having lived the greatest part of her life, finds herself friendless and lonely, though wishing for some one to
be fond of—can love.

Happy hours they passed there, on the beach, listening
to the old ocean's roaring.

Mrs. Elmer would bring her work with her, and when
Effie was tired of talking would tell her some story
(generally a fairy tale, and one which Effie had often
heard before); and the quiet voice of Mrs. Elmer har-
monised so well with the music of the sea, that little Effie
almost fancied herself in fairy land itself, and never got
tired of hearing the same old stories over and over
again.

There are some hours of our existence when the place
we are in, the people we are with, the thoughts we have,
and the events around us seem to throw a certain halo of calm
happiness over our existence; and, in those hours, we
forget that the world is wicked; that we have suffered
disappointments in the past, and may expect fresh
troubles in the future. Then all seems bright, and the
past and future, reflected in the mirror of the present,
seem bright also. Sweet, dear hours! how pleasant it is
to look back to the time when we enjoyed you!

Mrs. Elmer must have thought something like this.
Effie was very happy: she had been happy all her life—
but this was a different sort of happiness.

Autumn and winter came on, and they could no longer
sit out of doors; but they were not separated; for little
Effie, on her way from school, would often go into Mrs.
Elmer's cottage, and talk to her there; but Mrs. Elmer
would never go to the May Trees.

One cold, frosty day Captain Armer was thrown from
his horse, and injured in several places. He was brought
home insensible, and inflammation soon set in. Now
they had often talked of Effie's "friend" at the May
Trees; so when the doctor said Captain Armer required
constant nursing, Mrs. Elmer was sent for. She came
(she seemed frightened, but she came), with her kind,
yet melancholy face, and her large cap, and took her

place at the invalid's bedside. He was very ill, and for
many days lay in a state of insensibility. Mrs. Elmer
never left him, and his wife and daughter were nearly all
day long in the room.

* * * *

It was a cold night; and Frank Armer, waking from a
deep sleep which had been caused by a draught the doctor
had given him, recovered his senses, and saw the quiet-
looking woman leaning over him.

"Whoever are you?" he said, after gazing at her for
some time; "you never can be real—you must be some
spirit. Oh do speak, and tell me who you are!"

"I am your nurse, sir," she answered, turning her face
away from him. "You have been very ill, and mustn't
talk now, it will excite you."

"Oh! who are you? I think—I am certain that I
have seen you before. You must be—"

"Hush! hush! if you talk so you will make yourself ill again."

There was a tenderness in her voice, and she took hold
of his hand (she couldn't help it), and looked lovingly at
his face; for there was a certain look about him which
her experience told her was the look of a man whose end
was very near. Somehow her cap came off, and her
long black hair fell down over her shoulders. Captain
Armer spoke no more, but as he looked at Mrs. Elmer,
happy thoughts seemed to be rushing back to his mind;
and with her hand in his and her face close to his own, he
died.

It was so sudden that Mrs. Elmer, had no time to call
in his wife. The latter felt the loss very severely; for
she had dearly loved him; and, as she had been accustomed to depend wholly upon him, felt, now that he
was gone, utterly helpless. How sad the May Trees
became! How dreary the time before the funeral, and the
long weary days afterwards.

Mrs. Armer, who was left very well off, still remained
at the May Trees, and persuaded Mrs Elmer, who had
been "everything" during the time of the funeral, to live
with her as housekeeper, to which arrangement the
nurse consented.

A very quiet life they lived at the May Trees. Mrs.
Armer was more of an invalid than ever, she seldom
went out, and then only to sit in the garden in the sunny
weather. Mrs. Elmer, who was singularly active, had
the whole management of the household under her care.
In the evening, when they were sitting round the fire,
and Effie had learned her lessons for the next day, the
fairy stories were told again—the same old stories that
had been told so often on the beach, and to which Effie
seemed never tired of listening.

They lived very happily at the May Trees, till one very
severe winter, two years after Captain Armer's death,
his widow was confined to her bed, lingered for a
few months, and died before the return of the warm
weather. She died very gently; and, after her funeral,
her relations and those of her late husband, held a consultation as to what was to be done with Effie. Several of
them offered her a home; but Effie, obstinate and self-
willed for once, declared she would live nowhere else but
at the May Trees, and with no one but Mrs. Elmer; so,
as she was still a child, they consented, but separation
and other dreadful things were threatened in the future.

Since the time of Mrs. Armer's death something seemed
to be weighing heavily on Mrs. Elmer's mind, and, when
separation was talked about, she was as much against it
as Effie herself, of whom she was fonder than ever.

One warm evening in May they were sitting on the
beach, listening to the waves roaring, as in the old times,
but Mrs. Elmer was less cheerful than usual, and, though
she tried to talk, her thoughts seemed to be wandering
far away from what she was saying.

"Do you often think of your mother?" she said, after
a time. "I do not mean her who died last winter, but
your own mamma, Effie."

"Sometimes I do. Papa used to say she was an angel
in Heaven, and could always see me; so when I have

been going to do anything wrong, the idea of her watching me has often prevented me from doing it. I often think of her. I often watch the stars of a night, and wonder in which one she is living."

"I will tell you something, dear—a story you have never heard before. Once upon a time a very young man married a lady much older than himself. He was very fond of her, and so was she of him; and after they had been married some fifteen months she was taken ill, and, as he thought, died But she was not dead—only in a trance; and a negro servant, fearing she would be buried alive, had her removed to a lonely hut some miles from where her husband was living. Under that servant's care the lady's health returned, but her illness had had such an effect upon her that her mind was gone, and as no one could find her husband (his regiment had been ordered home) she was placed in the hospital, where she remained nearly eight years. One morning her senses came back to her; the doctor saw her, and, her sanity being proved, she was discharged. Of course, her first inquiries were about her husband, but no one could give her any information, and as an European family were going home, she entered their service, and sailed with them to England. On the passage she by chance heard that her husband had retired from the army, and was living in a retired village, to which place she went immediately on her arrival in England."

"And did she find him?"

"She found him—she saw him; but it was too late. He had married again!"

"But did she not speak to him, and tell him who she was?"

"How could I—?"

"You, Mrs. Elmer?"

"Yes, Effie, darling; I am the lady I was telling you of; and your father was my husband. Do you not understand it, dear? For you—you—O, my darling Effie! —you are my daughter!"

Mrs. Elmer—or Sarah Armer—held her child closely in her arms, as if she was afraid of losing her; and Effie, who seemed to understand the whole story, put her arms round poor Sarah's neck, and whispered, what the latter had for years so longed to hear—

"Mamma, dear mamma."

And no one in the world felt happier than Sarah Armer. Her secret was told to Effie, but it had to be made known to the world. So Sarah wrote to her sisters (whom she had long known to be alive and well) and her late husbands relations, telling them all to come down to the May Trees on a certain day to hear an important revelation. The day came, and they all arrived; Effie—at whose house Lieutenant Armer and Sarah had first met —bringing her children with her. And then Sarah told her story. At first some of them scarcely believed it; but when they saw Sarah and her sisters kissing and crying over one another, their doubts were dispelled, and they welcomed Sarah Armer back to life unanimously.

"But why did you not let us know of your arrival in England?" asked one of her sisters.

"How could I," replied Sarah, "when the very knowledge of my existence would have made my husband unhappy; for he loved his new wife, and it was half natural, after all, that he should marry again after all those years. But he recognised me before he died; and have I not had Effie always with me? Oh! when I first found out that she was my own child, I felt satisfied with my lot, and would have been content to have remained unknown for ever."

"Dear, good Sarah," whispered her youngest sister, if anyone deserves to be happy, it is you."

Happy! and was she not so? To suddenly find herself surrounded with friends, and to be re-united to her sisters—the only links of the days gone by when she was so calmly happy in the old parsonage; and, above all, to have dear little golden-haired Effie recognised as her own daughter. Happy! of course she was.

CHAPTER LVII.

THE RETURN OF CLIFFORD TO MRS. GRANVILLE'S HOSTELRIE—THE TALE OF THE MAISON ROUGE.

IT did not take a great while to hurry Clifford to London.

His friends, Bill and Ned, soon had him in the metropolis, and insisted on taking him to his old quarters at Mrs. Granville's, there to exhibit him in triumph.

Clifford would have objected to this arrangement, but he found that remonstrance was vain, and so he submitted to be carried off to the house of his oldest, although least reputable, friend.

"Hurrah!" shouted the company in the drinking-room, as Clifford made his appearance. "Hurrah for the Gentleman! and good luck to those who have brought him back to us."

"And it's myself that's done that same," said the Amazon Sall, pushing forward and exhibiting Clifford: "shure I was cap'n, and brought him off safe; and it's a mighty queer tale I've got to tell ye about that same adventure."

"Hurrah for Sall!" they cried. "Hurrah for the brave old Sall, and let us hear her tell her story."

"Och! and it's not long I'll be about that same," said Sall; and, settling herself down, she related in her own strange fashion the story of the rescue of Clifford.

No sooner was this over than Clifford was borne off by Mrs. Granville and placed in bed.

He was carefully attended to above stairs, whilst great feasting and revelry was being held in his honour below.

Tale-telling became the order of the day—or rather of the night; and many were the thrilling tales of adventure then related.

One of them, told by an old and rather taciturn man, we will repeat, giving it in his own words:—

"I wasn't always a cracksman," he said, by way of preface; "I once was as straight-laced and right as the best of 'em; and it was in those days that the following adventure occurred to me:—

"I was once travelling over a rather desolate region in the south of France, when, as night came on I found myself a good league from the small town of Nyons.

"The country which, up to this time, I had traversed, had been uniformly flat and swampy, with but little wood about it, but now I found myself on the borders of a thick forest of pines and firs which I knew to be fully a league in length, and which I also knew I should have to traverse to reach Nyons before nightfall.

"This was by no means a pleasant prospect, for I had heard that frequent robberies and even murders had lately taken place in the forest; and although I was armed with a brace of strong pistols, I knew that in the dark it might fare ill with me, and it was therefore with feelings of great joy, that just as I had determined to make the best of a bad bargain, and was on the point of entering the forest, I thought I perceived a light glimmering faintly from behind a clump of bushes a little to the left.

"I did not hesitate, but pushed on towards the light, which proceeded, as I rightly conjectured, from an *auberge;* for, on rounding the clump of bushes, I clearly distinguished painted in large letters on a board above the entrance to the inn, *La Maison Rouge.*

"To the 'Red House' then let it be, I inwardly muttered. Doubtless I shall find a guide to lead me to Nyons, or if not, a bed for the night—to the 'Red House' then —so saying, I pushed up the slight declivity on which was situate *La Maison Rouge* (which built of red brick, fully answered to its name), and knocked loudly at the door which I found closed.

"My summons had to be repeated thrice, when, after some whispering inside, a short, stout, thick-set man made his appearance.

"The *tout ensemble* of this person (who turned out to be

CLIFFORD AWAITING THE APPROACH OF BILL WATERS.

none other than the landlord of the *Maison Rouge*) was anything but prepossessing. A large stock of coarse brown uncombed hair covered his head; and his face, which was lean and haggard, terminated in a straggling, untrimmed appendage, which I can scarcely call beard. His eyes, too, which were small and deeply set, covered with thick bushy brows, gave him a very villanous look, which was further augmented by a deep scar on his left cheek.

"'What is monsieur's business,' he said, addressing me in a gruff, surly tone, and with a strong Spanish accent; 'is monsieur *voyageur?*—if so, monsieur will be sorry to hear that we are quite full.'

"'Thanks, friend, for your gratuitous information,' I responded, answering mine host in his own tongue; 'but it is not so much a bed I seek as a guide through the

Nyons' Forest. I wish to reach Nyons this evening, if possible, where Monsieur Mordaunt, *l'avocat*, awaits me even now.'

"'Ha, senor speaks Spanish," replied the landlord in a pleased tone; 'and Monsieur Mordaunt's name is already a recommendation. Will senor not enter and take some refreshment, while I see if a guide can be procured, though I much fear this is impossible, as the Nyons' Forest is too well known as a resort for brigands and assassins. Is it not so, son Carlos?'

"This last remark was addressed—as the landlord ushered me into the parlour of the *auberge*—to a tall, gaunt young man, seated at a table with two others, and busily engaged in discussing a bottle of *vin d'Avignon*.

"'*Carrambo*, what you say is true, father,' replied the young man named Carlos; 'I would not undertake to guide the stranger; no, not for a hundred francs down on starting, and a hundred on arriving at our destination. No, Holy Virgin, I have too great a regard for my skin!'

"'You name a high price, young man,' I said, coming forward. 'After all it appears to me there is not much danger when one is well armed, and I placed my hand significantly on the butt-end of my pistols.'

"'Ah! Monsieur is English,' sneered a tall muscular-looking Frenchman, who sat opposite the landlord's son, 'and it is said the English do not know what fear is. *Allors!* Monsieur, being well armed, would, doubtless, make the journey by himself?'

"''Tis not that I'm afraid, fellow,' I answered; 'but without a guide I should risk being lost in the forest, which, at this time of night, and especially as it looks like a storm, would be far from pleasant.'

"Even as I spoke the wind came whistling with a mournful sound past the bushes which surrounded the inn, and rattled small stones and gravel against the window pane. Coupled with this a few drops of rain fell.

"'Monsieur is right,' said a short, swarthy-looking Frenchman, whose countenance was rendered peculiarly repulsive by a squint in both eyes, and the bridge of his nose being flattened to his face, 'monsieur is right. I fear we shall have a regular storm. Pity I could not make shift, and offer my bed to monsieur; but monsieur will excuse me as—'

"I cut him short. 'Thank you,' I said; 'do not incommode yourself on my account. If I am obliged to stay here I can sleep on the floor; 'twill not be the first time I have done so.' So saying I sat down at a separate table, and calling for a bottle of the best Bordeaux, I proceeded to take a survey of the apartment.

"The room in which I now found myself was on the ground floor, or *reg-de-chausée* of the inn, and was a small room, with a very low ceiling. Three tables were ranged on each side of it, and on the opposite side to myself, and round the centre table, were seated Carlos, the landlord's son, and the two Frenchmen above mentioned. The only other occupant of the room was a pale, thin, yet agile young man, seated by himself at a corner table.

"My first look assured me he was an Englishman, my second that he was an old friend.

"As I gazed hard at him, he raised his eyes, they met mine—there was no longer any doubt—we both rose simultaneously—

"'Merton, old fellow,' he said, 'how are you? This is a happy meeting!'

"'Williams, old boy,' I replied, heartily shaking hands 'what earthly chance can have brought you to this cut-throat looking place?—Whatever it was, I feel great pleasure in meeting you again. I thought you were *en route* to Paris.'

"'Hush! speak lower,' replied Williams, 'some of these fellows may understand us; or, let us talk in Gaelic when there can be no danger. I should have been in Paris, but I have been delayed, and only arrived here some ten minutes before yourself.'

"'I was going to Nyons,' I replied, 'but it came on dark just as I reached the forest, so I thought it better to turn in here; but there appears to be no guide, and no bed; so what would you advise—should I go on?'

"'No. For Heaven's sake, don't think of such a thing,' replied Williams, 'it's dangerous at this time of night, even if you are armed. I have a bed here which you can have, and if I can procure a mattress, I shall be all right on the floor; you know I'm an old soldier accustomed to rough it; and besides, there will be an advantage in our being in the same room, in case these ruffians are inclined to be troublesome.'

"'On no account will I hear of it, Williams,' I responded; 'you keep to your bed and let me sleep on the floor. Now let me hear no more about it,' I continued, as I saw Williams was inclined to remonstrate, 'I hold the matter settled, if not I shall start off *a l'instant meme* for Nyons.'

"'Well, if you will have it so, so let it be,' rejoined Williams; 'I will not dispute the point. only you had better tell the landlord so, and order a fresh bottle of Bordeaux at the same time, and let us have a chat about old times over it.'

"'Agreed!' I cried, and rising I hastened to hunt up the landlord; and, having found him, I stated my proposal to him.

"He seemed very unwilling at first to agree, and proposed that I should set out immediately, when he would himself lead me part of the way through the forest. To this, however, I objected; and it was not until I had offered to pay handsomely, and had dropped a five-franc piece into his hand, as an incentive, that he at length consented, with a bad grace, to my remaining.

"Having gained my point I rejoined Williams with a fresh bottle of Bordeaux, and we sat together, chatting of old times, when as boys we roved together through the Highlands of Scotland and discussing which of our friends were since married and which were dead

"In this way the time passed so rapidly that we were surprised to find it already half-past nine, when, a pause having ensued in our dialogue, we were aroused by a *fracas* between our French neighbours on the other side of the room.

"Looking up a strange sight met our gaze. The tallest of the two Frenchman was standing—either a good deal the worse for liquor, or pretending to be so—with one leg on his chair and the other on the table, and was shouting at the top of his voice, addressing himself fiercely to his short, stout countryman, who sat next to him—

"The quarrel raged until Maitre Canot gave vent to certain opinions that rose the ire of the others.

"The objectionable words had hardly left his mouth when the Frenchman Jacques sprang to the ground, and, drawing his poniard, made a fierce stab at him.

"Had not Maitre Canot sprung quickly to one side, those words would have been his last; as it was, in his spring he stumbled over his chair, and fell heavily to the ground. In an instant Jacques was upon him, and, raising his dagger, prepared to strike.

"Williams and I rushed forward almost at the same moment to avert the blow, and, swiftly disarming the ruffian, we assisted Maitre Canot to rise.

"'Cursed English dogs!' shouted the baffled Frenchman; 'always ready to interfere in other's quarrels. By the bones of St. Edouard, you shall smart for this!'

"'Keep a civil tongue in your head, fellow,' I replied, drawing forth one of my pistols and pointing it full at him. 'We allow no insolence here, nor will my friend and myself submit to it. Cowardly assassins like yourself never come to any good. Here, take back your weapon, and mind how you use it;' so saying, I flung his poniard on the table.

"The Frenchman seized it rapidly, re-sheathed it, and, scowling at us savagely, walked swiftly from the room without a word.

"'Those looks bode us no good,' said Williams: 'I fear we shall have a rough customer in that villain.'

"'Heaven defend us from coming into contact with him,' I rejoined; 'he looks about the most cut-throat ruffian I ever saw.'

"Here mine host of the *Maison Rouge* entered the room, carrying two large bottles of *vin d'Avignon* with him, and, having knocked the fire into a blaze, Maitre Canot, Carlos, and himself, all moved, and ensconced themselves comfortably at a table near the fire, where they soon began to smoke and enjoy their wine, cracking coarse jokes, and swearing terribly all the time.

"'Where's Jacques?' shouted mine host, as he swallowed a large draught of wine.

"'In the dumps,' responded Maitre Canot, with an oath; '*parbleu!* he nearly dealt me a blow which I doubt not would have done for me, but for the interposition of these strangers.'

"'Indeed!' replied mine host. 'Well, Jacques *is* a

hot tempered fellow, and doesn't like being interfered with. I never could understand him quite, for the years I've known him.'

" ' Nor I,' returned Maitre Canot ; ' he's a rough devil, and no mistake about it.'

" ' Our room,' said I, interrupting the dialogue.

" ' Ha ! doubtless you are tired, senors, and would wish to get to bed ? Your room is just above this, you cannot mistake it. Here is your candle, and may you sleep like dormice !' and mine host laughed jocosely.

. " ' Sleep like dormice !' I soliloquised, as Williams and I mounted the steps to our room. ' Dormice sleep as sound as death. If there is a hidden meaning in your words, good landlord, I trust I shall live to probe them.'

" ' Merton, old fellow,' said Williams, as we turned to the left at the head of the staircase and entered our room, ' I confess I don't much like the thoughts of our sleeping here, and those four ruffians downstairs.'

" ' Nor I,' I answered. ' Do you think it would be well to try and slip downstairs, and take our chance of reaching Nyons ?'

" ' No, we should be heard,' rejoined Williams ; ' better remain as we are, only we would do well to keep a good look out.'

" ' Yes, I think we should watch turn-about,' I rejoined ; ' I will keep watch till one o'clock if you take the first sleep.'

" ' No, no,' said Williams ; ' you are tired, and need rest. I will take the first watch ; but first let us see the door locked. Well, this is a nuisance,' continued Williams, after having examined the door, ' either this door has never had a lock, or, if it has, it has long since been broken off The door seems loose on its hinges, too ; however, let us make the best of it, and place something heavy against it.'

" ' A chest of drawers ?' I suggested.

" ' Aye, if there was one,' replied Williams, as he took a survey of our apartment ; ' the whole furniture of this room seems to consist of a bed and three chairs, and this small washhand-stand in the corner, which,' continued Williams, as he tried to remove it, ' appears to be a fixture. However, we must make the best of a bad concern.' So saying, Williams drew a chair, and placed it against the door. ' Now,' he said, ' if any one should try to open the door, this chair will make sufficient noise to warn us ; and, as my bed is just opposite, I shall immediately be on the alert.'

" ' Yes,' that will do for the door,' I said ; ' and now it will be as well to examine our premises,'—saying which I undid the bolt of a door situate on the same side of the room as Williams' bed, but in the opposite corner.

" This I found led into a roomy cupboard, the walls of which were unpapered. These Williams and I were examining together when we came upon what appeared to be a secret door, without any handle or means of opening. We pressed all round the wall with our hands, to try and discover some secret spring which might open the door, but in vain.

" ' Never mind,' said Williams, as we emerged from the cupboard, ' this door bolts, which is a blessing !'—saying which, he drew the bolt.

" ' I'm afraid the bolt won't be of much use ; look here,' said I, as I thrust my arm through an aperture in the door, which was on a level with the bolt, ' this seems strange, I wonder whether this is the work of accident or design. When once anyone was in the cupboard, there would not be much difficulty in unbolting the door, we must keep a sharp look-out, old fellow !'

" As I ceased speaking, Williams (who had examined the walls of our room without finding anything suspicious), stood listening by the door to the sound of voices from downstairs.

" I stole close to him, and listened also.

" ' You take the cupboard,' I distinctly heard : and, had no difficulty in determining as the speaker, Carlos, the landlord's son.

" ' No—no, pest on it—after all, they did save my life, and I won't be one of the attacking party,' replied a voice which I recognised as Maitre Canot's.

" ' Well, you take the door !'

" ' What hour ?' This time it was the Frenchman Jacques' voice.

" ' Shortly after one.' The voices now died into silence, and although we listened for some time, we could hear nothing more.

" ' They are meditating an attack, Williams,' said I. I think I had better watch too.'

" ' No—no,' said Williams, as he threw himself into his bed with his clothes on ; don't undress, but place your mattress between my bed and the cupboard and get to sleep. I will watch till past one, and if I hear anything suspicious I know how to wake you without getting up.' So saying, Williams took a roll of thin cord from his pocket, and tying one end round his wrist, he threw the other end to me, telling me to do the same.

" ' Now,' said Williams, when I had finished, ' by simply pulling the cord I shall be able to give you notice if I hear or see anything.'

" ' This plan I thought capital, and placing my watch by my bedside, I prepared to sleep.

" ' Good-night, Williams,' I said ; ' it's now eleven o'clock, be sure and wake me in two hours' time, whether you hear anything or not.'

Williams replied in the affirmative, and having placed my pistols within reach, I strove to quiet my thoughts and fall asleep.

" This, however, was not so easy, for I felt by no means certain as to what might occur, and the storm, too, blew so violently, rattling the window-panes, that I found it almost impossible to sleep ; at length, however, slumber overcame my senses, and the last thing I saw, by the faint starlight through the window, before I was fairly insensible to all around, was the tall, handsome figure of Williams stretched full length on his bed, his military sword and pistols by his side.

" How long I slept I could not undertake to say (it turned out afterwards to be shortly over two hours), but it seemed to me a long, long while, for my dreams were none of the pleasantest, when I was aroused by a gentle tug at my wrist, a second and harder tug woke me completely, and, looking round, I distinguished the form of Williams sitting up in his bed.

" ' Some one has just unbolted the cupboard door,' he whispered under his breath, ' get up gently and bolt it again, without making the least noise ; and now,' continued Williams, when I had finished, as he handed me his sword, ' cross gently to the other side of the door, and watch well, and if you notice a hand pushed through the hole in the door trying to unbolt it again, strike sharply with your sword, and I'll warrant they won't try that on again !'

" I did as Williams directed, and we both awaited breathlessly the issue.

" Presently, the door shook gently, as if some one was trying it from inside the cupboard, and then, doubtless astonished to find it bolted, a hand was thrust slowly through the aperture, and presently the whole arm of a man.

" Just as the hand reached the bolt of the door my sword descended like lightning, and half severed the thumb from it, when a loud *sacré* and the whole arm being rapidly drawn in, was the result.

" ' Jacques,' I whispered to Williams, as I recognised the tall Frenchman's voice.

" ' Aye, keep a sharp look out,' responded Williams ; ' Ha ! I hear a noise at the other door,' so saying, Williams sprang lightly from his bed.

" I listened, too, while still keeping my eye on the cupboard door, and distinctly enough I heard a grating sound, which proceeded, without doubt, from the door of our room.

" What was my surprise, on stealing a hurried glance,

to find the door moving slowly backwards as if by some unseen agency, the chair alone remaining in its place."

"Looking round I saw Williams leaning against the opposite side of the room, his face ghastly pale, whether from terror or from the pale light of the moon, which faintly lit up the room, I never knew. I tried to call him, but could not, and in another moment I saw him spring frantically forward to where the door had been, and from where it was visibly descending the stairs, and, raising his pistol, he fired; the shot perforated the door, and a frightful and most appalling shriek from a human voice, together with the crash of the door falling over the banisters, broke the stillness of the night.

"'Good God!' said Williams, 'I fear one of these ruffians has gone to his last account. Merton, look out for that fellow in the cupbard.' The warning was needful, for at the moment the cupboard-door fell outwards with a crash, and almost upon me, while three men, all masked, and with bludgeons in their hands, rushed forward with fierce cries.

"As the three ruffians were close upon me I found Williams by my side, and our three remaining pistols rang almost at the same moment, but, in the confusion of the moment, without effect.

"And now the ruffians were upon us, and, just as I had felled one to the ground with the butt-end of my pistol, Williams was hurled insensible to the ground with a blow from a bludgeon, and, as half-mad with rage and burning with revenge I rushed upon the rascal who had struck the blow, I was knocked down by a blow on the head from behind, and fell unconscious by Williams' side.

"When I partially recovered consciousness, my pockets had been rifled of nearly all their contents, and Williams and I were being dragged down stairs to the yard of the inn.

"Half-way down stairs we passed the body of Maitre Canot, perfectly dead, with a large wound in his side, from which blood had flowed in torrents, and farther on, at the foot of the staircase, we came upon the door which was shivered to atoms.

"As we passed the body of Maitre Canot, I must confess I felt a pang of regret that Williams had not shot one of the other ruffians in his stead; but there was no time for thought, for our captors dragged us into the night air, and although this only served to restore our senses, yet we were unarmed and powerless to resist, and, therefore, remained perfectly passive while they succeeded in binding firmly our arms by our sides to two firs which grew close to each other.

"Even in this horrid position I had not given up all hope, and it was, therefore, with great joy that I saw lightly tethered to a shrub not far from us, a small yet apparently strong-limbed Andalusian pony.

"'O! that I were only free,' I inwardly exclaimed, 'and upon that noble little animal with a good hundred yards start, we should never look on our captors again!'

"My soliloquy was soon broken in upon by one of our captors who, as they both drew off their masks, I recognised as the Frenchman Jacques.

"'Sacre! did I not say you should smart for it,' he exclaimed, 'and shall I not keep my oath. This will teach you to interfere in other's quarrels,' and he struck me a blow on the cheek with his clenched fist. I reddened under the insult, and would have given worlds to have been free when the ruffian would have expiated his insolence with his life, but I thought it best under the circumstances to control my feelings.

"Passing down, the ruffian struck Williams also, the blow in his case was succeeded by a livid whiteness of the face, and I thought Williams would have fainted; after a time, however, he recovered.

"'Parbleu!' and the ruffian continued his taunts. 'I can forgive you, however, when I consider that you have given Maitre Canot his *coup de grace*. But for this' and he held up his thumb, 'which of you was it that gave me this ugly wound? By the bones of St. Edouard you won't answer,' he continued as we remained silent, 'then make

your last prayers,' and the villain raised his sword to strike.

"'Hold, Jacques, you hot-headed rascal,' shouted the other ruffian, whom I recognised as the landlord; 'wait till I tell you a plan. They'll make capital targets, let's fetch our rifles and have shooting practice.'

"'Shooting practice in the dark,' shouted the other, derisively.

"No, not in the dark, we'll bring a torch with us. Come along!' and the two rascals ran off full speed to the inn.

"And now I must confess I gave up all hope, and endeavoured to compose my thoughts and prepare for death, when as chance would have it I placed my hand in my pocket. It rested on a box of lucifers which had been my constant companion in my journeys, and which I had found useful in lighting fires for my bivouac as the evenings drew in such a ray of hope as this diffused through my mind it would be impossible to describe. I felt like a criminal released from prison.

"'Thank God, we are saved, Williams,' I cried; 'cheer up, old boy, we shall cheat them yet.'—So saying, I lit a match carefully and applied it to the cord which bound me. It ignited, smouldered away, and soon snapped, and stepping out I was free. It did not take long to effect William's release, and rushing forward, I unloosened the pony tethered near us, and mounting Williams behind me, we started off at full gallop.

"And now my joy got the better of me, for as we were on the point of entering the Nyons' Forest I gave a shout of exultation, as only a Briton can shout, which woke up the echos of the forest. It did more—it alarmed our captors, who, with sundry shouts and oaths, mounted on horseback and followed us swiftly.

"And now it was a race of life and death. On—on we dashed through the forest (Williams luckily knowing the right path), while our pursuers followed close behind. When we traversed one mile, or about one third of the forest, looking behind I saw mine host of the *Maison Rouge*, place a whistle to his mouth and blow a shrill blast, which re-echoed through the wood.

"What was our alarm when presently mine host's whistle was answered by two shrill ones from different sides of the forest, and we were fired at several times. I am thankful to say, however, that the bullets missed their aim, and only served to madden our pony, which increased its pace, and soon we were clear of the forest, and on the borders of Nyons. Here our pursuers thought it wise to turn, and the sound of their horses' hoofs soon died away in the distance.

"Williams and I rode on to the residence of my friend Monsieur Mordaunt—who was greatly astonished to hear of our adventures, and delighted that we had made good our escape.

"He promised that the rascals who had thus robbed us should not escape scot free; and he kept his word—for when we had slept for an hour or two, and the morning had come, we went with our friend to call on the chief magistrate of Nyons, Monsieur Goddard, and explain the circumstances of our case.

"Monsieur Goddard promised his assistance, and shortly after we set out with a party of soldiers for the *Maison Rouge*.

"When we reached the inn everything seemed in order, and mine host was there to receive us. He turned pale when we explained our mission, but strongly denied all knowledge of us.

"This would not do, however, and he was taken into custody, as also the young man Carlos, his son. The body of Maitre Canot was not visible, and it was supposed that it had been buried during our absence. Neither could we, after a strict search, discover the Frenchman Jacques, whom we specially desired to deliver up to justice.

"We had, in fact, given up our search for him, when, passing a large chest with the lid broken, lying in the yard of the inn, I was curious enough to place my hand in the straw with which the box appeared to be filled. I felt something hard answer to my touch, and at the same instant the Frenchman Jacques sprang from the box, and made a lunge at me with his sword.

"Happily I stepped to one side, and escaped the deadly blow, and after a severe struggle, succeeded in capturing the rascal, who was placed along with the landlord and his son, when all three were conducted back to Nyons.

CHAPTER LVIII.

TALE-TELLING AT MRS. GRANVILLE'S HOSTELRIE CONTINUED—THE STORY OF THE HAUNTED HOUSE RELATED BY THE CITY SWELL.

THE mania for story telling, wherever and whenever it sets in, is sure to rage with great violence.

The meeting at Mrs. Granville's, whereat Sall's story of her adventures in search of Clifford set an example, proved no exception to the rule, and many were the tales told on that occasion.

Among the guests was a young-looking man. dressed in the most fashionable manner, and speaking in a far different style to those with whom he was associated.

He was evidently well educated and well acquainted with the world, and to him was paid a very great deal of respect.

He was addressed as the *City Swell*, a title he acquired from his peculiar occupation.

He was a swindler on a gigantic scale: started bubble schemes, traded without capital, and occasionally did some neat things in forging.

He had formerly been engaged in a city banking house, from which he had been expelled for pilfering, and was now looked upon as the most expert rascal in London.

"Now," said Sall, "shure it's the turn of the City Swell to tell us a yarn, and by jabers we're all a listening for it."

"I'll oblige you," said the man appealed to; "I'll oblige you with pleasure; do you believe in ghosts."

Sall turned pale, and looked at Bill Waters.

"Mother of us," she cried, "don't we believe in 'em—that's all!"

"Well I don't," said the Swell; "nevertheless my tale deals with ghosts to some extent; but you shall hear it from beginning to end, and I will not spoil it by telling you the *denouement* beforehand.

"Some years ago," he said, "I had occasion to pass through a small village in Berkshire.

"It was not the first time I had been there; once or twice before I had passed through on business, and had always put up at the Crown and Garter, kept by a Mrs. Baxter.

"Mrs. Baxter, the landlady of the Crown and Garter, at the time when I knew her, was a widow (the jolly host of the Crown and Garter having been defunct some years), of about forty years of age, but she seemed much younger, very bustling and active, and of a cheerful disposition, and seemed never put out under any circumstances.

"She had one child, a girl of about twenty who was a great help to her in her work, and as the Crown and Garter was the only one where travellers could be accommodated for the night, Mrs. Baxter, as most people agreed, bid fair to make her fortune.

"She was, moreover, a very courageous woman, instances of which I could relate but that I have neither the time nor the space at present.

"On my former visits I had always been in the habit of writing beforehand to Mrs. Baxter and engaging a room, and as I was one of her best customers, when I arrived I always found my room prepared, a nice fire burning, and my supper awaiting me. On the night in question, however, I did not know I should be passing through this same village till the afternoon of the same day, when I had an urgent call to meet a friend there on particular business, and, therefore, had no time to inform Mrs. Baxter of my approaching arrival.

"I arrived at the Crown and Garter at seven in the evening by the mail coach, and sure enough there was Mrs. Baxter with her smiling face ready to receive me.

"'Glad to see you again, sir,' she said in her cheerful way, 'very glad; such a long time since you were here before, but you didn't write to say you were coming or I should have——'

"I interrupted her.

"'I did not know till this afternoon that I should be passing here on urgent business, Mrs. Baxter,' I said, 'and then it would have been no use writing, for I should have arrived before the letter.'

"'More's the pity, sir; for the whole house is full at present. A party of strangers came in yesterday, and all the rooms are occupied, and there's not a spare bed in the establishment.'

"She continued;—

"'But you must be cold, sir,' and assisted me off with my great coat; 'come in and warm yourself in the parlour, there's a good fire, and I'll be off and get you a bit to eat, and then we'll talk it over about the bed.'

"Well, here was a bore. No bed for me to sleep in, all the rooms engaged! What was to be done?

"However, Mrs. Baxter had said she would talk it over, so I thought it best to warm myself, and take a survey of the room and its occupants.

"It was a small parlour, proportionate to the size of the Crown and Garter, and had nothing remarkable in it. I had often been in it before.

"There were four men in it. Two were sitting at different ends of the room, engaged in reading, and seemed to have no connection with each other.

"The other two were playing at cards on a small table in the centre of the room. One of these was a large stout man, with a stupid, senseless face, who seemed intent on his cards, and never even looked up as I entered the room.

"The other was a wiry little man, of small stature, and thin, sharp features, but a cunning, vixenish look lightened up his face every now and then, and gave him a fiendish expression.

"The other two travellers had nothing remarkable about them, and seemed quiet elderly men.

"It was at this point of my observations that Mrs. Baxter entered the room.

"'Here you are, sir,' she said; 'I've got you some refreshments; and now about a bed. I've been thinking that Kitty (that was the name of her daughter) and I could manage on the floor, and give you up our bed for the night.'

"'On no account, Mrs. Baxter,' I interposed. 'On no consideration would I wish you to put yourself to any inconvenience for my sake. No, I will not hear of such a thing,' I said decidedly.

"'Well, then, sir, I can't think how it can be arranged at all.'

"She seemed to think, then resumed—

"I have it now, sir; there's the old house opposite, that belonged formerly to Colonel Bearing, which I've got the key of, and that hasn't been inhabited for these last twenty years or more. To be sure, it's rather dilapidated looking, and the windows are mostly broken, but there's a room on the third floor in pretty good repair. I can fit you up a bed there, and have a nice fire lighted. It's what they call the Haunted House, for some people say there are ghosts, and them sort of things, that live up there. But that's all talk, for there ain't such things as ghosts now-a-days, and of course you don't believe in them no more than I don't; but perhaps you're afraid, sir?'

"The jeering tone in which Mrs. Baxter pronounced these words irritated me, and I replied in a tone of hauteur—

"'Of course I don't believe in ghosts, Mrs. Baxter; I'm thankful to say I'm not so weak-minded as some people; but the idea of sleeping all alone in a large dreary house that hasn't been inhabited for such a long time, is, to say the least of it, not at all pleasant.'

"At this moment the stout, senseless-looking man broke in——

"'If you wouldn't take it bad, sir, I would just give you a bit of advice.'

"'What is it?' I replied.

"'Why, sir, I wouldn't sleep in that 'ere house this blessed night not for twenty pounds; no, nor for twenty times twenty pounds, and that's saying a good deal.'

"'Hand your pipe, Bill Stoker, will ye?' interrupted his villanous-looking companion, with an oath; 'leave the gentleman alone, will ye. Never mind him, sir, he's maist daft. Why I'd sleep in that 'ere house for nothing, and d—d glad to do it, that's more!'

"A volley of remonstrances assailed me on all sides.

"Even Mrs. Baxter declared there was no help for it, and what could I do? I certainly didn't like the idea—but there was nothing else for it; so I yielded, and told Mrs. B. to have a fire lighted for me by ten o'clock, when I proposed going off to bed.

"During the evening, as I took out my purse, to look over my accounts, the eye of the smaller man was upon me.

"He seemed to count each piece of money.

"How fiendish he looked at me.

"Then he would turn again to his cards; now glance up furtively at my chair.

"Oh! what a villanous look was there.

"I shuddered, and instinctively I clutched my pistols in my pocket.

"Soon after Mrs. Baxter came in to say my bed was ready, and I left the room, instructing her to call me in the morning.

"The eye of the small man still followed me. Outside the room I asked Mrs. B. who he was.

"'Oh, yon mean the small man. Why he came yesterday; he's a Mr. Higgins, but where he comes from I don't know, I'm sure.'

"This was all Mrs. Baxter knew, so I betook myself to my chamber, determined to be on my guard.

"Mrs. Baxter preceded me with a light in her hand all through the long corridors and dark passages of the dreary house, through the doors of which the wind whistled with a mournful moaning sound, and every now and then a door would slam with a loud report, and give us both a start.

"At last we reached the room that was to be mine for the night.

"The window panes were nearly all broken, and large pieces of paper had been put in to keep out the cold air.

"The moon shed its cold pale light across the room, giving it a very ghastly appearance.

"Mrs. Baxter left me, saying she would call me at eight o'clock next morning.

"I heard the front door shut. She had gone, and I was alone in the dreary house.

"Alone! What a feeling it was.

"I felt the blood creep through my veins.

"I took my pistols out of my pockets, looked at them to see they were loaded, and placed them on the table near me.

"I laid my watch on the table. It wanted ten minutes to ten.

"I took a book out of my pocket, and began to read.

"It was an interesting book.

"I read on, only looking up when some shriller blast of wind than usual swept with a mournful sighing sound through the long corridors, or some door slammed to with unusual violence.

"I was at length aroused from my book by a feeling of intense cold.

"I looked around.

"The last few embers were expiring in the grate.

I tried to reanimate the fire—it was too late. It was quite out. The candle, too, was getting low, so I closed my book and prepared to undress.

"I got into bed and put out the candle after having placed my two pistols one on each side of the pillow.

"I had not locked the door, thinking it safer not to do so, for were I attacked during the night I should thus be able to escape.

"I kept my anxious eyes on the door, expecting every minute to see something enter, I knew not what.

"I had been in bed nearly half an hour, and was just falling off to sleep, when I heard a grating sound at the other end of the room.

"I looked round. The wall seemed to open, and a figure appeared.

"It was a ghastly figure, all white, as the moon shone on it.

"Slowly it glided through the room. Now it passed by my bed.

"Horror-stricken, I dared not move.

"I was ashy pale; my hair stood on end. I tried to speak, but could not; my tongue clove to the roof of my mouth.

"Slowly the figure glided through the room.

"I tried to seize a pistol: my trembling hand would not obey the impulse.

"Now the figure had passed, it seemed to vanish through the door.

"I heard a sound of doors shutting and re-opening.

"Shrieks seemed to rend the air; then a voice, as of a child in agony.

"'Help! Murder! Is there no one here?'

"Then a gurgling sound.

"Then all was still.

"I felt my heart beat.

"I would have rushed out of bed; but I could not move.

"A dead silence now seemed to reign through the house.

"The clock struck the hour of midnight, each stroke sounding like a solemn knell through the still silence.

"Scarcely had the sounds ceased, when again I heard the same strange, grating sound.

"The wall seemed to re-open in the same place.

"Good Heavens! what did I see!

"A hideous creature all covered with hair came bounding on the floor, every now and then uttering a sharp cry or snarl.

"Two large red eyes glared on me in the darkness, a large red tongue, and two sharp rows of teeth were visible in the pale light.

"I was paralysed.

"Could it be a bear, or some fiend?

"Dark thoughts came over me.

"I saw all things dark.

"A sickening terror rendered my countenance livid.

"My eyes were nearly out of their sockets.

"Nearer came the hideous thing, leaping and yelling fiercely.

"There was but one chance, that it might not see me.

"I hid my face under the bed-clothes to hide the fearful sight from mine eyes.

"Nearer it came—it bounded—now it was close by my bed.

"I could feel its hot breath.

"I was suffocating, yet I dared not look up.

"It would be my death.

"The animal seemed to raise some heavy thing in its paw; was it my pistol?

"Yes! in my hurry I had left them on the pillow.

"I heard a bang—a sharp report—then a cry, as from a frightened brute.

"I looked up; the room was filled with smoke.

"As the smoke cleared away, there was the retreating form of the beast.

"I seized my pistol and fired.

"A yell, like of some wounded animal, and the room was again filled with smoke.

"When the smoke cleared away, the room was empty, it had vanished.

"But the fright and exertion were too much for me. I lost consciousness.

"I remembered no more.

"When I recovered the grey dawn was stealing through the window.

"I got up and examined the wall of the room.

"There were no signs of any door or secret passage.

"I rose quickly, and dressed myself; but on examining my clothes I found my watch and purse missing.

"This alarmed me the more.

"Had I been robbed? and, if so, by whom?

"Suddenly a thought flashed across me.

"Heavens! Why had I not thought of it before?

"The man of the preceding evening who had looked so eagerly at my purse.

"Could he have imposed on me, disguised as the fiendish creature which had so terrified me?—and could Mrs. Baxter be the figure in white?

"Yes! I saw it all—it was a base conspiracy—a plot entered into by Mrs. Baxter.

"But I had only suspicions.

"I determined to wait for facts.

"Besides I had no time to waste. I then dressed quickly and hastened to quit the fearful place.

"But my two pistols were unloaded, and if I should meet some one on the stairs.

"I should be unarmed, but I had still a pocket knife. I opened the large blade, and holding it in my hand I hurried from the room.

"Through the long corridors, down flights of stairs, in deadly fear of meeting some one every minute but no one appeared, and now I was at the front door.

"As I passed through the doorway and into the garden traces of human feet met my eye; then, again, like animals feet.

"But I had no time to lose.

"I could not rest till I was clear of the house.

"Now the garden gate was undone, and I was in the street.

"No one was stirring, and I passed into the fields.

"A long walk of some hours refreshed me, and I returned to the inn myself again.

"As I entered the parlour I noticed the men who had been playing at cards on the preceding evening.

"The smaller one had his arm bound in a sling.

"Again my suspicions were aroused. Why his arm in a sling, if not to hide a bullet mark?"

"Mrs. Baxter was not in the room. I sat down, and took up a book.

"Presently she entered, and on seeing me, exclaimed—

"'Good morning Mr. Hartney; I hope you slept well, and where not disturbed by any ghosts, or apparitions, or them sort of things.'

"Mrs. Baxter uttered these words in a mocking tone, which irritated me.

"I was determined, then, to say nothing of what I had seen, but to pass it off.

"I therefore replied—

"'Oh, not at all, thank you. I slept as well as could be expected, and saw nothing but a bear, or some such animal, that, no doubt, had lived in the garden, and found its way into my room. But I fired at and wounded it, and next time it comes into my room I shall shoot it dead.'

"As I said these words, I noticed that the small man changed colour.

"'Ah, yes,' said Mrs. Baxter; 'Kitty and I heard a report about twelve o'clock, and it frightened us rather—didn't it, Kitty?'

"But as Kitty was not there to corroborate the fact, Mrs. Baxter was safe in her assertion.

"I had still a strong suspicion of Mrs. Baxter and the figure in white of the preceding evening being one and the same person. But here she had heard the report of my pistol when in bed in the middle of the night, so I did not know what to think.

"At this moment Mrs. Baxter seemed to perceive that the small man had his arm in a sling.

"'Dear 'a me, Mr. Higgins,' she exclaimed, 'what's happened to your arm now?'

"The man seemed to hesitate, then replied in a sullen manner that, in shaving that morning, his razor had slipped and cut his arm. Mrs. Baxter kindly asked if he would let her look at it, and perhaps she could do something for it.

"'No, hang it, no!' swore the man. 'I don't want none of your help. It's all right if you'll let it alone, d—n you.'

"Mrs. Baxter drew back terrified, and spoke no more. What was this I thought the man's unwillingness to show his wound! Was it caused by a bullet mark? It was very probable.

"As I still had a suspicion of Mrs. Baxter's playing a trick on me, I determined to pass another night in the Haunted House, more especially as I had heard no news of the friend I had to meet.

"I passed the day in writing letters, and at about ten o'clock in the evening I repaired to my room in the old building.

"I was not so frightened as the night before.

"I primed my pistols, and placed them on each side of my pillow.

"Then I undressed quickly, and got into bed, determined to keep a good look out.

"But sleep began to overwhelm me.

"The clock had already struck the hour of midnight, and the fire had nearly burnt out.

"The moon was shining in brightly, and now I was startled by the same terrible shrieks that rang through the air, coupled with doors slamming and groaning.

"I looked round alarmed.

"Again I heard the same strange grating sound.

"The wall seemed to open again in the same spot as the preceding evening, and the same tall white figure glided in.

"Now the wall had closed and still it glided on—nearer it came. Now it stretched its bony hands towards my bed, then it approached the fire and seemed to warm itself—now again it approached my bed and stood motionless before me.

"Notwithstanding my past experience I was terribly afraid.

"I looked at the figure, it was tall, and Mrs. Baxter was tall.

"I seized a pistol—my hair on end—my face livid—and cried—

"'Who art thou? Phantom, speak.'

"Still the figure stood motionless and uttered no word.

"I was determined to try the effect of Mrs. Baxter's name on it; I therefore cried—'Baxter.'

"A deep, hollow voice that seemed to come from the very heart of the figure echoed the word in a deep sepulchral tone—'Baxter.'

"'Speak,' I cried, 'If ye be a living thing speak, or I fire.'

"'I fire,' again echoed the figure.

"I was maddened with rage and terror.

"'Die,' I shouted as I raised my pistol and cocked it.

"At the noise I fancied I saw the figure start.

"A moment more and the being before me would have been extended at my feet.

"A shriek that sounded through the whole house stopped me. The figure threw itself upon me, and knocked up the barrel of my pistol, exclaiming—

"'Don't fire, sir, for Heaven's sake don't fire—it's only me;' and then the sheet that had covered her was thrown back, and there stood Mrs. Baxter—her hair dishevelled, and her face wild with terror. Yes, it was no other than Mrs. Baxter.

"I reprimanded her for her 'bit of play,' as she called it, and showed her that, had I had less strength of mind, my reason might have been affected by it.

"She seemed very penitent, hoped I would forgive her, and said she had only meant it as a joke.

"I then communicated to her the loss of my watch and purse, and my suspicions of Mr. Higgins, and asked her if she knew anything about it.

"She said, no; she had not communicated to Mr. Higgins her plan of imposing on my fears, and did not think it could have been him.

"'Perhaps there were real ghosts.'

"Here Mrs. Baxter grew alarmed, and I had to escort her out of the house.

"Next morning, as I entered the parlour, Mr. Higgins was still there. He was to depart by the mail at 12 a.m. But I was determined he should not escape me.

"I sent Mrs. Baxter off for an officer, and told her to bring him back with her, so that I might explain all the circumstances of the case to him, and then to send him into the parlour as a new arrival.

"Soon after she was to follow herself.

"Then I entered the parlour, sat down, and took up a paper, awaiting the arrival of the police officer.

"I had not long to wait.

"In a few minutes a strong, muscular-looking man entered the room, and sat down at a table near me.

"A few minutes after, Mrs. Baxter also came in on some pretence.

"Now was my opportunity. I was resolved not to lose it.

"I rose and addressed myself to Mr. Higgins, who was, no doubt, enjoying himself wonderfully.

"'I beg your pardon, sir,' I began, politely; 'but I did not observe your arm before. How did you come by it? If it is any hurt I am a medical man, and could, perhaps, do something for it.'

"The man drew back angrily.

"'I don't want none of your doctor's stuff, hang me if I do. Joe Higgins ain't come to that yet. I ain't a woman, to want a doctor for a bit of a razor scratch, hang me if I am!'

"'Ah! it is a cut with a razor,' I replied. 'When did it happen, if I may ask?'

"'What's that to you?—that's none of your business. But if you'd really like to know,' sneered the man, 'I got it yesterday morning, in shaving.'

"'Of course, then,' I replied, 'your friend, Mr. Stokes, who slept with you in the same room must have seen you do it.'

"The man seemed taken by surprise. The idea did not seem to strike him before he hesitated and stammered out 'yes.'

"I then addressed myself to the sleepy, fat man, and asked him if he had been in the room when Mr. Higgins had cut himself, and how he did it.

"He was going to answer—'No, he knew nothing about it,' when a kick, administered by Higgins from under the table, and a vehement gesture, seemed to rouse him to his senses, and he answered in the affirmative.

"Then I asked what he had cut himself with.

"I looked round quickly at Higgins to see that he made no sign.

"It was too late.

"He had passed his forefinger with the rapidity of lightning across his cheek.

"The sleepy, senseless man seemed to understand.

"'Why, in shaving, to be sure: his razor slipped,' he replied.

"'Come, this won't do, Mr. Higgins: no signs; but I know you. You imposed on me last night, disguised as a bear, to steal my watch and purse. I accuse you now of having them in your possession. Officer, do your duty!'

"The officer rose and seized him by the collar.

"He tried to resist.

"He cursed and swore, but he was soon mastered.

"His arm was stripped in spite of his efforts, and from the fleshy part a bullet was extracted which fitted exactly the bore of my pistol.

"No more evidence was needed.

"The man was evidently a coward: he was terrified, and confessed all. How he had seen Mrs. Baxter go out at night; how the idea of robbing me at occurred to him; how he had followed Mrs. Baxter through a secret passage which led to my room; how a few minutes after Mrs. Baxter had passed through the door he had followed disguised; how, in the confusion occasioned by the pistol shot he had fired, he had stolen my watch and purse; how he had hastened and got into the inn before Mrs. Baxter, and without exciting any suspicions; how I had wounded him—all came out.

"I got back my watch and purse, though he had managed to get through the greater part of the contents of the latter.

"He was tried at the next assizes, and transported.

"What became of the sleepy man I never knew.

"He evidently had not enough spirit had him to commit a daring robbery.

"And thus ended my ghost adventure, the only time I ever had anything to do with such creatures; and I think that, in most of the ghost stories told now-a-days, the ghosts generally turn out to be what mine were—nothing but real flesh and blood."

CHAPTER LIX.

THE CLOISTER OF CANTERBURY CATHEDRAL—A VISION OF DEATH—FORESHADOWINGS OF THE FUTURE.

It was midnight, and a flood of moonlight bathed the grim old town of Canterbury.

Along the High-street, and thence to the cathedral, stole the muffled figure of a man.

He appeared to be in haste, yet dared not hurry for fear of attracting attention.

He passed through the principal entrance to the precincts of the cathedral, a very beautiful structure, ornamented with angels bearing shields, small niches, armorial bearings, mitres, coronets, and the emblems of the Tudors—roses.

He glided through the east transept, where, not long ago, stood the remains of the Cemetery Gate, which, with a wall attached, was the eastern boundary of the churchyard, and the entrance from the Oaks; it presented a beautiful Norman arch, ornamented with a zigzag moulding and a fissure in the centre; but, from its dilapidated state, was considered unsafe, and the remains of the old Cemetery Gate were removed.

Passing onward he entered the convent garden, or the Oaks, called so from the rows of noble and stately oak trees that stand there. It was a cemetery, called the lesser cemetery. On the east side of this piece of ground stands the house of the Vice Dean, and at the north, the remains of the Priory. Leading from the Oaks is a passage called the Brick Walk. On the right of this walk, and north-east of the cathedral, is an ancient stone mansion, called the Maister Honours, from its being formerly the great state chamber of the Prior of the convent, and that in which he entertained his guests; it is now the residence of the eleventh prebend.

On the left of this walk is a small doorway, and over it is a much decayed figure of a man, described by Somner as holding in his hands a scroll, with the words "Ecce me Major" inscribed thereon; this inscription, scroll, and all are now quite obliterated.

Opposite the west end of the Maister Honours is a large gothic window, that appears to have been divided into four lights or upright divisions, but now quite

CLIFFORD ATTACKED BY WILD'S BAND.

blocked up, and forms part of the residence of the first prebendary—this belonged to the chapel of the infirmary ; this chapel formed part of the range of buildings built by Cuthbert, by permission of Eadbald, King of Kent, in 741. It was dedicated to John the Baptist.

Its high antiquity is proved by the existence of large circular arches, now filled up, supported by pillars, the capitals of which exhibit rude designs of animals. It is now an open court. On the right, or north side, is the garden wall of the sixth prebendary's residence, and adjoining is the prepondal house, formerly the hall of the Infirmary, and on the opposite side are the pillars first mentioned, which being filled up, form part of the first prebendary's house, and the residence of some of the minor canons; further on, on the same side of the court, are four massive Norman pillars, supporting circular arches, but not ornamented ; they formed part of the Infirmary attached to the chapel. These arches are now

walled up ; this Chapel and infirmary are supposed to have been burnt. Westward of this court is what is called the Dark Entry ; on the right is an entrance to the Cloisters, and to the left a passage into the Green Court ; at the end of this passage is the Priory Gate or Porter's Gate, being the north-west entrance to the priory ; it is supposed, from the style of the arch, to have been built by Lanfranc ; the passage is long, narrow, and dark, the outer gateway is lofty, and between the two arches is a porch ; the inner arch is small and low. The Green Court is a large open square, surrounded with buildings ; it was the court of the Priory.

On the east side of it is the Deanery, formerly the dwelling of the prior ; it is a large handsome building, with a court-yard in front.

Just within the gate of this yard, and adjoining the eastern side of the Dark Entry, are two towers with Newel staircases.

The steps are of solid stone, and derive no support but from the geometrical precision and accuracy with which they are placed one upon another.

Between these towers was situated the kitchen of the priory.

The north tower is about thirty feet high, and the entrance to the staircase is by a small Norman arch.

There is still standing, at the north west end, a gate called the Larder Gate, through which is a passage and a flight of steps leading to the ruins of the convent; adjoining these is the Chapter or Sermon House, to which the congregation repaired after prayers in the body of the Church; it is a handsome building, ninety-two feet long, thirty-seven broad, and fifty-four high, and was built by Archbishops Courtenay and Arundel, in the time of Richard II., as appears from the armorial bearings in different parts of the buildings; the ceiling is composed of squares or panels of Irish oak, twelve in the length and seven in the breadth, ornamented with escutcheons, flower work, painted, carved, and gilt; the room is divided into arches or stalls separated one from another by pillars of Sussex marble, and having above them pyramids of stone, ornamented and gilt; at the east end is a window of the breadth and height of the building; in the upper lights are Cherubim, Seraphim, Angelii, in coloured glass.

Henry II., after travelling from Normandy, to do penance at the shrine of Thomas-a-Becket, and walking barefoot through the streets for three miles, summoned the monks in this building, and submitted to be scourged.

When the fraternity of monks was abolished, this place was fitted up with a pulpit and pews as a sermon-house; this use of it being attended with inconvenience, the service was removed, and the building used as necessity required.

Between this building and the Larder Gate, extending from east to west, are the remains of the *dortors* or dormitories, where the monks of the priory dwelt; they were built by Lanfranc, over ancient vaults, as was nearly the whole of the priory.

There were two dortors, inclosing a space of one hundred and five feet north to south, and seventy-five from east to west; and the west end of one of them are the remains of a wall, in which are windows in the Norman style; the lesser dortor was towards the east, and the site is now occupied by some of the minor canons. To the right of the passage, leading from the Larder Gate to the Chapter House, stands the Baptistry; it is a circular building with a roof in the form of a cupola, underneath which is a vault raised on stone pillars, from the centre of which proceed ribs to an outer circle of pillars; the arch, which is Norman, is beautifully ornamented. On the north side of the quadrangle, is the Domus Hospitum, or Stranger's Hall, being the place in which poor pilgrims were entertained; it was one hundred and fifty feet long and forty broad, and used to be designated the hog-hall. In the north-east corner of the Green Court is the great gate of this hall, leading into a stable formerly a portion of Newington-lane.

West of the Domus Hospitum is the Almonry or Mint Yard, where the fragments of meat and drink from the large table in the convent were distributed among the poor.

After Henry VIII. had expelled the monks he converted this place into a mint for the coining of money; the chapels and premises appertaining were afterwards given by Mary to Cardinal Pole, and in 1559, they were transferred to the Dean and Chapter for the use of the school founded by Henry VIII., now known as the King's school; close to which is the Porta Prioratus, or as it is now called the Green Court Gate. It is a handsome structure having a large Norman arch, within which is a pointed arch of much later date; the style of the ornaments gives it an appearance of great antiquity, though it is in a good state of preservation. On the west side of the quadrangle is a wall enclosing a garden belonging to the surveyor of the Cathedral; on this spot near the dormitories, stood

the Frater Hall, now completely demolished. The cloister is a square building curiously arched with stone. On the west side was a communication to the cellarer's lodgings. On the north side are two very handsome curiously arched doorways, one of which seems to have opened into the vaults under the refectory; the other was the way from the pentice gate into the church. All the arches are of the same breadth, and supported by little pillars, from each capitol of which spring fifteen ribs; these are adorned at the intersections by about six hundred and eighty-three escutcheons, bearing the arms of benefactors to the church, from which we learn that the establishment has been pretty well provided for. The north wall is the remainder of a former cloister, and is ornamented with a range of stalls, every fifth of which is divided from the others by a wall; these were the seats of the monks. The east wall had several openings; one of them led to the western gallery of the dortors, and is now walled up—another to the dark entry—a third to the Chapter house, and one at the south end leading into the north wing of the western transept.

Into this dim place stepped the mysterious figure we have followed.

As soon as he had entered the cloisters he threw off his cloak, and revealed a tall weird frame, worn to a shadow, and stooping to the very earth.

The face was ghastly white, and the features cadaverous and contorted.

This awful being stretched forth his arm, and in a voice of singular power cried :

"Appear !"

A low, wailing voice answered—

"Who summonses me ?"

"It is I, the Reeve of Windsor Forest."

A moment passed, and then a shadow stood before the Reeve.

This phantom gradually assumed a more tangible form, and at length grew into the semblance of a monk of a date long passed.

"Reeve of the Forest," said this being, "why dost thou summons me ?"

"To tell thee that strange things are to happen; Wild will come to dwell in Windsor Forest, and Clifford will follow him there ; I ask thee what is to be done ?"

"Do thy best ! Wild, and, if possible, Clifford must be made to join the band of Herne the Hunter. See that it is done !"

"I will obey."

"Remember, above all things, that neither one nor the other leaves Windsor Forest without my sanction, and, above all, communicate with Mother Clifford !"

"To what purpose ?"

"Tell her that a being who is destined to ruin the plans of the presumed heir, who is to crush his and her power, and who shall destroy the charm that gives her supernatural sway, will ere long present himself at Winterleigh, and demand her hospitality, and if she refuses it she is lost."

"What then is she to do ?"

"There is but one way to save herself, and that is to crush his will and make him fly in terror from the Hall."

"And if she cannot succeed ?"

"She is lost !"

"Eternally !"

"Yes."

"And who is the being who can do all this ?"

"No matter: time will reveal that. Ask me no more questions, for I will not answer them. Am I dismissed ?"

"Yes."

A faint rustling sound, and the phantom was gone !

Then the Reeve of the forest muffled himself once more in his cloak, and hastened from the cloisters.

He glided away as hastily as he had come, but fast as he went, so fast followed a man in his footsteps.

He had been watched.

CHAPTER LX.

CLIFFORD ONCE MORE ON THE PATH OF WILD — THE
FOREST AND THE STRANGE MEETING BETWEEN CLIF-
FORD AND THE DUCHESS —WILD ONCE MORE ESCAPES
THE VENGEANCE OF HIS ENEMY.

WITH a constitution of iron, Wild was not long in shaking
off the effects of his wound and awful fall into the pit.

The Princess was skilled in surgery, and knew many
secrets of the art, that proved of infinite service to Wild
in this instance.

Fortunate for him that it was so, for, under the circumstance, the services of a surgeon could not be secured.

In one week the great thief-taker was on his legs
again, but the monotony of the old house was too much
for him, and ere long he expressed himself sick of the
inactivity.

The question was—what was to be done?

The Princess was for remaining lost to the world for
some months longer, or to go abroad.

Of this, however, Wild would not hear. He said he
loved the old country too well to quit it, and resolutely
declined remaining longer in the gloomy old hall.

"Then," said the Princess, as he delivered himself of
this determination, "you go alone; I'll risk nothing in
the matter. Here I am safe—elsewhere I may come to
grief speedily. So you have my determination."

"Then we part," said Wild.

"Very good," said the Princess; "but we can be friends
still."

"Yes, and be partners too, for all I see to the contrary,"
said Wild; "You go your path for a while, and I'll go
mine; but we share in all things."

"Agreed. Where and when do you go?"

"As to where," said Wild, "my mind is made up. I
go to the forest yonder."

He pointed to a vast wood, which lay in front of the
old hall, at a distance of some three miles, and which
formed a part of the original forest of Windsor.

"What are you going to do in the wood," asked the
Princess, with a laugh, "turn forester and hermit?"

"Not quite. I've watched that place day by day for
the last week, and I feel certain that there's good business
to be done there."

"In what way?"

"In the old way."

"Nonsense."

"I never was more serious, and time will will prove
that I am right. I know my game."

That very night Wild ventured out into the forest, and
it may be presumed that he was satisfied with the result
of his expedition, for three days afterwards he had nur-
tured the following plan.

In the forest lived a wretched old man, who was
allowed to occupy a little hut by the courtesy of the chief
ranger.

The old fellow had been a hermit for years, and was
generally looked upon in that part of the country as a
harmless old imbecile, doing no harm, and only repulsive
from the fact of his having an extreme affection for
filth.

Wild noted all this, and through the old man he determined to save himself.

This is how he did it.

He found the old man sleeping.

To open the door and stealthily enter the cottage was
the work of an instant.

He stood over the poor old hermit, who suddenly awoke
and confronted him.

"What do you want here?" asked the old man.

"Not much," said Wild, with one of his hideous
leers.

"Then get you gone. I have no wish to have you
here."

"Perhaps not. But I shall stay."

"Begone!" said the old fellow; "begone, or I shall
get angry."

Wild laughed loudly.

"Angry!" he said. "Well, you're a nice fellow to get
angry, you are. Now I'll tell you why I am here. I mean
to *kill you*."

"To kill me! What injury have I ever done you?"

"Not much; but I want you out of the way, and out
of the way you will have to go."

"Good God! I have nothing for you. I'm a poor
harmless old man. I—I—"

He could say no more. The ruffian caught him by the
throat, and gripped him in a vice of iron.

It was only a short struggle, and all was over.

Wild had done one more deed of darkness.

"Now," he muttered, as he stripped the old man of his
clothes, "now it will only be to grow my hair and beard
and get dirty, and no one will ever know that there has
been a change in the occupant of this house."

Before a week was over Wild had thoroughly made up
his new character and wandered about the forest as a
decrepid old man fast sinking into the grave.

In fourteen days a complete system of robbery was established and Wild was once more at the head of a band
in which the name of *Colonel Jack* figured.

We say his name figured, for the Colonel was only a
kind of honorary member who declined active participation in the work of the robbers.

* * * * * *

Let us pass over a period during which Clifford has
been steadily gaining health and strength.

Let us next introduce him to the reader as he sat one
day in the best room of Mother Granville's house thinking of plans for the future.

"It's no use," he muttered to himself; "it's no
manner of use. The honest members of society turn
their backs upon me, and shut their doors in my face. I
can't be the honest man I have tried to be, and the name
I own must be sullied by me! The only kindness I
have known has emanated from the Countess of Lakemont, and into her presence I dare not go, for in spite of
all I can only love Evelina; can only think of her image.
Heaven save me!"

His reflections were interrupted by the entrance of a
man who bore a letter which he presented and withdrew.

Clifford looked at it for an instant, and then broke the
seal.

It was a curious letter, without date or signature, and
ran as follows:—

"*Wild is in the forest of Windsor. I am with him
now, but to-night he will be alone. Then will be your
time. Bring one trusty friend and make up your mind
for hard work and plenty of it. Don't fail. Remember.
Three miles west of the Hall I described to you as the
residence of the Princess! Don't mistake the road or
you will be at fault, and the result will be a failure.
Disguise is necessary. Wild will be found in the garb
of an aged forester, and inhabits a little hut in the
forest; the former occupant of which he strangled, and
now personifies with a skill that defies detection.*"

Clifford was singularly puzzled on reading this strange
document.

That he knew the writer was evident, for, in a conversation that ensued between himself and Bill Waters, he
revealed his name.

But the game Wild was playing completely beat his
comprehension.

"At all events," he said to Bill, "we will go."

"Go!" said Bill, "it'll be the greatest pleasure in life
to destroy that warmint, and I'll go with ye to—to the
devil, so that I get the chance."

"Very well, then ; have the mare ready in half an hour, and get well mounted yourself. There is no time to lose if we mean to make but a day's ride of it."

Bill vanished, and, ere an hour had passed, had completed such arrangements as were necessary.

At night they were in the forest, both disguised in the most complete manner.

"You to the right and I will to the left," said Clifford to Bill. "Be careful, and meet me at this spot in half an hour."

They separated.

Clifford took a path to the left, and, ere long, came close to the cottage of the murdered forester.

He dismounted at a slight distance.

He peered through the open windows and then withdrew, satisfied that he had discovered the nest of the bird of prey.

When Clifford had made a complete survey of the premises he mounted and galloped back to the spot where he expected to meet Waters.

More than half an hour had passed, but his friend had not yet come.

Most anxiously did Clifford await the coming of Bill ; but, after the lapse of an hour, he gave him up in despair, and made up his mind to return to the cottage.

*   *   *   *   *

Meanwhile the Duchess of Lakemont and her waiting woman had come mysteriously on the scene.

They had been riding that day, and had gone far beyond the distance they at first intended, and at length missed their way.

At length they came across a man *who pretended to direct them.*

Then another and another.

And following their advice they at nightfall found themselves *in the forest,* to which they had been guided by the agents of the cunning thief-taker.

They were at once in the pathless labyrinth of trees, without discovering a trace of human beings.

The night wore away, the cold increased, and the horses could scarcely move, on account of hunger and weakness.

They heard nothing save the wind, which moaned through the primeval trees.

The darkness became greater and greater, and the unfortunate travellers had already determined to dismount from the horses, and with resignation to their fate, to spend the night in the open air, when suddenly a faint light appeared.

They urged on the horses as much as possible, and reached, at last, the miserable hut of Wild.

Hearing a noise, an old man, with a long beard and a burning chip of wood, came out.

The travellers asked him if he could give them a night's shelter ?

He replied that he could give them nothing but a litter of straw, and a shed for their horses.

The offer was accepted with great joy, and the Duchess, together with her servant, stepped into the miserable hut. It was an unfloored barn, in which were some roots of trees, that served both for chairs and tables.

In one corner lay a bundle of straw, and on the hearth a log of wood was burning, which served for warming and lighting the apartment at the same time, which caused an insupportable smoke.

Everything betrayed poverty and misery.

The travellers made themselves as comfortable as circumstances permitted, and were heartily glad at having found a protection for the night from the storm and cold.

Presently they heard a noise, as though a horseman was approaching the hut, and ere long the door was opened by Clifford, habited as an officer, who at once recognised the Duchess.

He saluted her as a stranger, and expressed his joy at finding such company in this awful desert.

She did not recognise him. He described himself as a soldier who had been on duty at Windsor Castle, and had obtained for some weeks a furlough, in order to visit his father. The conversation became lively, and they did not separate until late.

The Duchess and her maid remained in the low room, but the officer betook himself to the hay-loft above, which was separated by trap-door from the low room.

The fatigue of so long a journey soon placed the women on the litter in a sound sleep, but Clifford had much to do, and so fastened his door with a bolt, put his loaded pistols and sword beside him in order to be prepared for the worst.

Not long had he been in the loft, quietly expecting what would happen, when he heard in the room below a gentle movement.

He fancied it was like a rattling in the throat, so he peeped through a crevice in the door, and beheld a sight that made his blood run cold.

The room was dimly illumined by the moon. Two men approached the sleeping women, covered their faces with thick cloth, and deprived them of their senses in this manner.

In this terrible situation he lost not his presence of mind, but determined to sell his life as dearly as possible.

Alas ! where was Waters at this moment ?

He drew himslf upright, placed the pistols in his girdle, and stood with drawn sword, anxiously waiting for what would take place next.

He soon heard somebody gently ascending the ladder, and saw a hand through the opening remove the bolt which fastened the door.

The time for action had now come. Clifford struck so terrible a blow at the hand that it was almost separated from the arm, and the man, with a terrible scream, fell upon the ground.

His companions darted rapidly up the steps to his assistance, but Clifford received them with his pistols, and they fell back much quicker than they came.

They retreated to the door, drew their pistols and prepared for another attack, when a loud shout from without attracted their attention. They turned, and faced Bill Waters.

"Hoy, Waters,'' shouted Clifford, "upon 'em, boy, beat 'em down !"

" I'm with you, cap'en" cried Bill, throwing himself from his horse, and darting at the robbers.

Not comprehending these tactics, and finding that Clifford was again dangerous with his weapons, the fellows slammed the door in Bill's face, and ere he had time to smash in the window, *the whole troupe, including the wounded Wild, had disappeared !*

" Hillo,'' said Bill, popping his head in at the window, "hillo, cap'en, how now ?''

"All right. Get through the window and look to the women.''

" Bill did as desired.

The wet cloths were removed from the faces of the Countess and her maid, and they revived.

Clifford then made himself known to the lady, and while they were exchanging greetings Bill peered into every hole and corner of the place in search of those who had so mysteriously disappeared.

"Well,'' he said, "this here go beats all I've seen to-night, and that warn't no trifle.''

"What have you seen ?'' asked Clifford.

"Seen !—why the devil and all his imps.''

"Hush !'' said Clifford, pointing to the ladies ; "you forget.''

"Begging the ladies' pardon,'' said Bill, " but still it was the old gentleman.''

" What mean you ?''

"Simply that the old tale of Herne the Hunter ain't no fiction, but the real truth, that's all.''

"Why, Bill !'' said Clifford in amazement.

"Ha ! you may say, ' Why, Bill !' but what I says is the genuine facts. I've *seen* Herne the Hunter.''

"Seen him ?"

"Seen him and all his band in the forest; and a nice set they are, I can tell you."

"Why, what are you aiming at ?"

"Only the facts. But it's no use remaining here, for the place is no good, and we may come across some more of those fellows."

"Pray let us go," said the Countess; "I dread remaining here a moment."

"And I," said the girl; "it is a fearful place."

The Duchess then explained to Clifford how she had been staying at the house of a friend in the neighbourhood; told him of the death of Danvers, and said that she had something of importance to communicate to him in relation thereto.

They remained but a moment more, and then left the cottage.

"Better plunge into the forest," said Bill, "and get on the way "to Windsor."

"Yes," said Clifford, "to Windsor."

In a few moments they were on their way into the depths of the forest.

Suddenly the baying of dogs fell upon their ear.

"Ha!" said Bill. "they're at it again, are they ?"

"What mean you ?" asked Clifford.

"Only that you hear the hounds of Herne the Hunter."

"Pshaw!" cried Clifford; but before the ejaculation had well passed his lips, a band of weird horsemen came in sight, and, with a wild shout, fled through the forest, leaving behind them a faint stream of phosphoric light, which played about the ground for a few seconds, and then disappeared.

The group stood electrified.

"Yes," said Clifford, after a long and awful pause, "I am convinced that some supernatural agency is at work in this forest, and that Wild is at the bottom of it."

"Why you do not suppose," said Bill, "that he is in league with Herne the Hunter ?"

"He would not hesitate to become the associate of the fiend himself," said Clifford.

CHAPTER LXI.

THE LEGEND OF HERNE THE HUNTER.

OUR readers have doubtless heard of Herne the Hunter; but many of them may not be acquainted with the legend in which he plays so conspicuous a part. We will, while our friends are yet in the forest, relate the old tale, as we have found it in the old chronicles of Windsor.

"The King will hunt the stag to-day."

"Then marry, good master page, a right royal chase shall we have; for I did mark a noble hart this morning, and, if I mistake not, he will not wander far from home ere we are in full cry at his heels."

The order was given by Ralph Atheling, the favourite page of Richard II., to old Osmond, the King's chief huntsman.

The scene was the grim old castle of Windsor, and the time was a morning in the month of January, in the year 1390.

Osmond hastened to make great preparations for the royal hunt, and ere the hour of eleven had tolled from the bell tower of the castle, all within was life and activity, in anticipation of the noble sport promised that day.

Within the hour the King, attended by a noble train of knights and gentlemen, rode forth, and made their way to a particular spot in the forest, where Osmond and a troop of huntsmen awaited his coming.

The hounds bayed and the horns resounded through the woods, and the scene was gladsome and enlivening.

"By my fay," cried the King, "but this is a glorious day for the hunt, and thy promise of right royal sport will not be broken, Osmond."

"You may rely on me, my liege; I have made all due preparations to ensure your satisfaction."

The eye of the King wandered over the group of huntsmen and forest keepers.

"Thou hast a fine troop of fellows," said the King; "but we miss our favourite, young Herne—what hast thou done with him ?"

"I know not where he tarries, sire; he well knew the hour appointed."

"He is not wont to linger," said King Richard, "and much do we regret his absence, for he is the very king of foresters."

Osmond and his troop did not appear best pleased to hear the praises of their rival thus loudly sung in that royal company, and they turned away with brows darkened and eyes flashing the fire of malice and hatred.

There was a pause, and then Osmond turned to the King once more, and, blotting out all trace of the feeling that agitated him, said—

"Is it your Majesty's pleasure that we delay the chase any further ?"

"Not another instant," answered the King. "We wait for no dullard clown. Proceed to your work."

Osmond gave the signal to his men, and was proceeding with them to start the stag, when a young man, habited in the livery of the King, but bearing the arms and accoutrements of a forester, dashed through the wood on a coal black charger, and in a few seconds was up with the royal party.

Doffing his cap, he bowed reverentially to the King and courtiers.

"How now," cried the King. "Ah! By our word, it is our young favourite, Herne."

"Your Majesty's most faithful servant," said the forester.

"We have ever deemed thee so," said King Richard, "and, by Heaven! the character shall not be taken from thee until we have heard thee explain the absence that has so ruffled us. Young Herne was never wont to delay."

"And never will, your Majesty, while health and strength and the cunning of his craft be left him. My non-arrival here at the time appointed for the meet is my misfortune rather than my fault; for I have been sadly served this merry morn."

"By whom ?"

"By those who should have treated me better."

As he uttered these words he turned his gaze full upon Osmond, who avoided his head, and slunk away.

The King noted the act, and a frown spread upon his brow.

"I was sent to a distant part of the forest," continued Herne, "supposing that there the meet would be. I waited on in the vain hope that your Majesty had changed the hour, and probably should have been there now had not chance thrown in my path one better informed than myself, from whom I learned how matters really stood, and hither have I flown as fast as horse could carry me."

The young man once more threw a glance of deep meaning at Osmond as he uttered these words, and by this means accused him, as plainly as eyes could speak, of the treachery by which he had been misguided.

All this was listened to and marked attentively by the King, who said, with much severity in his tones—

"This is a matter requiring to be well looked into, and we shall not pass it by in silence. Our favourites shall not be thrust aside thus, and our displeasure shall light upon those who by such means offend us. Now, rouse the stag."

Osmond and the huntsmen, Herne among the number, rode away to perform this duty, whilst the King turned and conversed with his favourite, the Earl of Oxford.

Young Herne was an eye-sore to all his companions. As he found favour in the eyes of the King, so their hatred for him increased.

Many were the plans they concerted for his ruin, but he appeared to have a charmed life, and to be guarded by some wondrous power that thwarted their efforts and turned their poisoned shafts back upon themselves.

Anticipating a great chase, and well knowing how prominent a part Herne would be sure to play therein, the keepers and huntsmen had concerted to bar him from participation in its honours, and aided by Osmond, who trembled for his position, Herne was sent a great distance from the spot where it was intended to unharbour the deer.

How their plan succeeded is already revealed.

Ere long the loud bray of the huntsmens' horns told that the noble beast had broken away, and then the voices of the hounds conveyed to the royal party that they were in full chase :

"Delightful scene !
"When all around is gay—men, horses, dogs ;
"And in each blooming countenance appears
"Fresh-blooming health and universal joy."

"Follow," cried the King, " follow ; by our word this stag will show us noble sport."

The King was an enthusiast in the chase, and was as good a forester as ever handled horn, or broke up a stag.

As soon as he heard the first wild note of the horn he set his magnificent horse in motion, and, o'erleaping all the impediments that lay in his path, was soon leading the majority of his party.

Oxford, who rode right nobly, followed next, and then the others came in a close-packed crowd.

The stag, seemingly the noblest of his race, bounded away into open country, and so great was his pace that even the hounds lost ground at every stride, and it was feared that for once the beast was too good for the sportsmen.

Right gallantly did he bound away, taking the direction of Hungerford, and right merrily did all the field of huntsmen ride after him, but in less than half an hour he had distanced all save two, and these it seemed impossible for him to shake off.

They rode well together, giving stride and stride, as in a well-contested race.

Both were consummate horsemen, and seemed excited into wildest enthusiasm by the excitement of the hunt.

They stole a glance at each other ever and anon, as if to mark whether there was a sign of either giving up the chase.

So they sped onward until within a few miles of Hungerford, whither the borders of the forest then extended.

"He must fall from sheer fatigue," cried the King to his trusty follower. "He cannot last many minutes at this pace."

"He will turn, your Majesty," said Herne. "This will madden him, and ere long he will stand at bay."

"By our faith !" cried the King, "if that be so we shall have no easy work with him."

"See," cried Herne ; "even now he makes good my prediction."

"Steady," cried the King ; "steady. Let us act with caution, or all our pains go for naught."

"Look out, Sire. Be guarded," cried Herne.

He saw the hart turn, and with excellent judgment turned his horse on one side, out of the path of the now infuriated animal.

The King was less fortunate, and in an instant the horns of the hart was plunged deep into the body of his horse.

The fierce brute, maddened by pain and fright, roared violently, and brought his royal rider to earth.

Another moment and the terrible horns would have been doing more bloody work on the body of the King, but Herne, with the greatest resolution and coolness, threw himself from his horse, and placed his own body between the prostrate monarch and his assailant.

In a second his knife was out, but the hart evaded the fatal stroke that was aimed at him, and in return dashed upon the young huntsman with his cruel antlers, and next moment Herne lay bleeding and crushed on the earth.

Though desperately wounded the gallant man contrived to raise himself slightly, and still grasping the glittering knife he contrived to bury it in the hart's throat, and the beast fell to the earth, bleeding to death, as the King regained his feet.

"Heaven save us, man," cried the King, gazing at his deliverer with the deepest concern ; "thou art stabbed to death. What shall we do for thee ?"

"In this world," said Herne, with a sad smile, "I shall require nothing but a grave."

"Nay, nay," cried King Richard ; "it cannot be so bad as that. The care of my best leech will soon set the right again."

Herne shook his had sadly.

He felt that he was beyond the help of the most skilful of leeches.

"A hurt from a hart's horn," he said, with a melancholy smile, "bringeth to the bier."

"Out upon the proverb," cried the King ; "it cannot —shall not be justified in thy case. Thou shalt live, Herne, and here I promise thee that thou shalt have the post of head keeper of the forest, with twenty nobles a year for wages.

"If words could stay the ebbing flood of life," said Herne, "those uttered by your Majesty would surely have the desired effect, but I know I am past help, save from Heaven."

"Then if thou diest," said the King, "I do surely promise that the sum I would have given thee for wage shall year by year be laid out in masses for thy soul."

"Your Majesty has my humble thanks," said Herne, growing faint, and with the greatest difficulty keeping up his head ; "I am grateful," he continued, "such an offer is the only one likely to profit me."

Uttering these words, he put his horn to his lips, and winding the dead note with a feebleness that made it painful to hear, dropped back senseless, and, to all appearances, *dead !*

Believing that he could do no more for him, the King rose from the kneeling position he had assumed while speaking with Herne, and mounting the horse of his unfortunate servitor, rode off for succour.

No sooner had he quitted the spot than a man habited in a suit of solemn black, but wearing the arms of a woodman, appeared at the side of the unfortunate Herne.

There was a most mysterious—almost repulsive, air about this individual.

He was more than the average height of man, but lank and pale of visage.

His eyes, although sunken, were marvellously brilliant, and shaded by brows of bushy black hair that lent a fierceness to his contour, and marred the expression of an otherwise well-formed visage.

As he bent over the body of Herne, he raised his long arms aloft, and muttered—

"At last ! at last ! Ha ! ha ! the king of the craft shall be the slave of Urswick, and these wooded lands shall be the scene of unrestrained devilry."

He sprang to the dead hart, and dipping his finger in the flood that still flowed warm and fast from the wound in the throat, he again approached the inanimate form of Herne, and forcing open his lips he placed the bloody finger on his tongue.

Next moment he was gone !

Meanwhile the King rode back in the direction he had come.

After a while he blew a lusty call on his bugle, which brought to him the Earl of Oxford, who was riding hard in the direction of the King, but in another path of the forest and therefore concealed from him.

He was by the side of the monarch at the first blast.

"Well met, Oxford," cried the King; "we have had desperate work yonder."

"What has happened?" asked the Earl, alarmed at the disturbed appearance of the King, and eyeing his blood-stained garments.

"The worst that could have befallen us. Herne is killed."

"Nay, but, let us hope, sire, that it is not so bad as that."

"I fear I speak but too truly. Poor fellow, he fell in saving me."

"There may yet be hope, sire: let us try what succour is nigh."

The King and the Earl placed their bugles to their lips, called as lustily as they were able, and presently they were joined by many of the royal party, including Osmond and the other keepers.

With this help the King rode back to the fatal spot.

Osmond was secretly rejoiced at what had befallen Herne, but, in common with the other keepers, gave expression to a show of deep feeling, and appeared only too anxious to do what laid in their power.

They found Herne and the hart laying just as the king had left them, but in an instant the Earl dismounted, and stooping over the fallen man, raised his head and felt for some sign of animation.

At first there was none, but after awhile, the faintest possible beating of the heart assured the Earl that life still remained.

"He lives," he said to the king, "he lives, but it is better that he were dead, for he can only survive for awhile, and that to experience such agony as no mortal can bear."

Osmond now bent over his young rival, and being well skilled in matters such as those, the King asked his opinion.

"My lord of Oxford is right," said the old woodsman, "he cannot live, and it is a pity that he should awake to know fresh misery and pain: it were better to end all now."

As he spoke he half drew his hunting knife.

"What," cried the King, unable to restrain his fury "what, ye knave! Slay the man who has just saved our life! I'd have thee hanged if thou didst offer such thing in sober seriousness. Kill Herne, I'd as lieve be killed myself. Who can save him? What can be done? I would give a great reward to anyone who would restore him to health."

As the King uttered these words, the same mysterious man we have before noted, but now mounted on a black, wild-looking steed, galloped to the spot, and at once addressed the King:

"I accept the offer," he said, "I will cure him."

"Who art thou, fellow?"

"A forester by trade, but somewhat skilled in chirurgery and leechcraft."

"Thou art as ill-favoured a knave as any we ever gazed upon," said the King, "but, nevertheless, thou mayst possess some skill in leechcraft; although, we should be more inclined to give the credit for tact in woodcraft. Thou dost look very, very like a man who, would, without leave, make free with our venison."

"Your highness misjudges me," said the strange man, "my name is Philip Urswick, and I dwell on the Heath, near Bagshot, which you passed to day, and where I joined you."

Osmond here said that he had noted no such fellow, and his followers to a man agreed with him.

"What matters it," asked Urswick, "whether thou didst see me or not? I saw thee, and I tell thee that the man who lies there bleeding to death is worth a hundred of such scurvy knaves, for he can outdo thee all. He has been pronounced beyond help, but I again say I can cure him."

"Enough!" cried the King, "prove thy skill, and not only shall a splendid reward be thine, but we promise thee a free pardon for any offence thou mayst have committed."

"I shall not fail to remind your Majesty of your offer. I will do my best."

So saying he jumped to the ground, and, drawing his hunting knife from his girdle, *he cut off the head of the hart close to the point where the neck joins the skull,* and then laid it open from the extremity of the upper lip to the back.

"I must bind this to the head of the wounded man," he said, holding aloft the gory skull.

"Do as thou wilt," said the King.

Thereupon Urswick stripped off Herne's cap, and fixed upon his head the hart's skull, which he secured with stout leathern thongs.

"What must now be done?" asked the King.

"He must be transported to my hut at Bagshot."

"Indeed!" cried King Richard, "we would prefer that he should be taken to the castle. Thou canst take up thy quarters there as well as he, and his cure may thus be facilitated."

"Not so, my liege," said Urswick; "he *must* be taken to my cottage if I am to proceed with my task, and bring it to a satisfactory end."

"Even as thou wilt," said the King, "but be sure thou playest no pranks with our woodsman, or thy life shalt answer for it."

"I will agree to that," said Urswick. "If I do not restore him to perfect health my life shall be the penalty. I pray your highness to command these keepers to assist me in transporting the man to my hut."

"Thou dost hear, knaves," cried the King; "do his bidding with as much care as if it were our royal self thou wert handling, or thy lives are not worth an hour's purchase."

They formed a litter of the branches of trees, and on this they laid the body of Herne, with the hart's head still bound to it.

"Now," cried the King, "forward to Bagshot, and bring us word how fares our huntsman."

There was nothing for it but to obey the royal command with as much care as they were able to use. Although by no means cheerfully, they raised the litter, and followed the mysterious forester, whilst the King and his party returned to the castle by another route.

* * * * *

The keepers carried the body of Herne in silence after the mysterious forester.

Theirs was a long and somewhat tedious task, and it was some time ere the heath on which the cottage of Urswick stood was reached.

At length the task was ended, and the cottage—a very miserable one, situated in the wildest part of the heath—was entered, and the form of Herne placed upon a bed of dried fern.

He still lay prostrate and insensible.

"Ha! ha!" roared Osmond, as he glanced at the sufferer! his career has ended bravely. We shall hear no more now of his pretensions, and my post is secure."

"You, believe, then, that he is past cure?" asked Urswick.

"I am sure of it."

"We shall see anon."

The forester doffed his cap, and now turned and looked Osmond full in the face.

"Good God!" cried the latter, can it be?"

"What ails you?" asked Urswick composedly.

"My eyes deceive me," said Osmond, "or you are not Philip Urswick, but Arnold Theafe, who was hanged years ago for deer stealing."

"Ho! ho!" shouted Urswick; "is it then usual for hanged men to return to life and set up for foresters?"

"It boots not; but if thou art not Arnold Theafe thou art his twin brother."

"Psha!—but have your own will. I care not for whom you take me, and it matters but little who I am and what I have been. I have the King's pardon."

"You *will have* when you have earned it," said Osmond disdainfully.

"And even suppose that I cannot earn it?"

"I am well assured of that."

"Then thou art deceived! In a short time, within the month I named, Herne will be restored to health, and thy post of head keeper will be gone."

"How?"

"The King promised it to Herne should he regain his health and strength."

"I cannot hear aright."

"Thou hearest as I heard it, and that was from the King's own lips."

"I am dumbfounded!"

"Doubtless. I thought you would be."

"Would the deer had killed him outright."

"Aye that would have been the best thing that could have happened," cried the others.

"Ah! you all hate him bitterly," said Urswick; "I can see it in your faces. *Would you like some revenge upon him?*"

"We should."

"What will ye give me to put it in your power?"

"Save an occasional fat buck, to which, as the King said, thou can doubtless help thyself, we have but little to give," said Osmond.

The man knitted his brows, and appeared buried in thought.

After a pause he looked up and said:

"Will you all swear to grant me the first request I may make of you, provided I ask that which is in your power to give?"

"Readily!"

"Enough!"

"And Herne shall die?"

"No."

"Then we cannot grant the request."

"Thou shalt do so. I *must* keep faith with the King, and Herne shall recover, but he shall not return to the King's service. Will that suffice?"

"It is enough—too much," said Osmond, tremblingly, "for, if thou canst do all this, thou art the fiend himself."

"No matter, cried Urswick, with a mocking laugh; "No matter, fiend or no fiend, ye have made a compact with me, and I will keep ye to it. Now begone! I have work to do."

The keepers appeared only too glad to be dismissed, and, as soon as possible, they regained the open air.

"I like not that man," said Osmond to the others; "I am assured I have seen his face before, and I am almost convinced he is a being who was hung in the forest some years ago."

The others trembled.

"Nay," said one, "say not so."

"But I must say it," said the forester, "for I believe it."

They went their ways, and, on next visiting the cottage of Urswick, a surprise of the most awful nature awaited them.

They were introduced by the mysterious forester to a being whom they recognised as Herne, but whose appearance had undergone a wonderful transformation.

He now wore the skull and antlers of a stag in place of head-dress.

His costume was a rough surtout of deerskins, and from his eyes gleamed a strong and awful fire.

Two black hounds were at his feet, and a coal-black steed awaited him without.

"You see," said Urswick to the keepers, "you see I have kept my word. Herne has recovered, but he is no longer ambitious to serve the King."

"'No,' said Herne; 'henceforth I serve no master; I am lord of the forest, and *you*—you are my slaves.'"

"His slaves," echoed Urswick; "that is the condition attached to my promise. You are *his* and *mine*, soul and body for ever."

At this moment a sound as of distant thunder rent the air, and the cottage disappeared.

They were in the forest with the clear blue sky above them, and awaiting them were hounds and horses of the same colour as those of Herne.

"Mount and away," cried Herne.

"Yes, away to the cave beneath the pool," echoed Urswick.

They mounted and obeyed the command of their master, and from that time to this Herne and his phantom horsemen have haunted the forest of Windsor.

CHAPTER LXII.

MOTHER CLIFFORD, AND WHAT THE STRANGE TRAVELLER BEHELD AT WINTERLEIGH HALL.

THE young owner of Winterleigh was still absent from Winterleigh, when one evening a strange-looking traveller rode up to the Hall, and demanded the hospitality of its owner.

He was answered by Mother Clifford, who surlily told him he was welcome to a night's lodging if he was not afraid to sleep at the Hall.

"Afraid!" said the traveller; "of what should I be afraid?"

"I don't know," said the old hag; "but most people would rather not pass a night in Winterleigh Hall since I have lived in it."

The traveller looked aghast.

"What say you?" continued Mother Clifford.

"I say that I will stay," said the gentleman, and, turning to his servant, he said, "put the horses in the stable, and follow me."

The man did as desired, and in a short time was once more with his master, in the apartment to which Mother Clifford had conducted him. He also brought with him a dog, to which he appeared to be much attached.

He supped, and then drew near the fire that burned brightly in the grate of his chamber.

He then turned his attention to his dog.

He had at first run in eagerly enough, but had sneaked back to the door, and was scratching and whining to get out.

After patting him on the head, and encouraging him gently, the dog seemed to reconcile himself to the situation, and followed his master and the servant through the house, but keeping close at his heels, instead of hurrying inquisitively in advance, which was his usual and normal habit in all strange places.

They first visited the subterranean apartments, the kitchen, and other offices, and especially the cellars.

And now appeared the first strange phenomenon witnessed by the traveller in this strange abode.

He saw just before him the print of a foot suddenly form itself as it were.

He stopped, caught hold of the servant, and pointed to it.

In advance of that footprint as suddenly dropped another.

They both saw it.

The traveller advanced quickly to the place.

The footprint kept advancing before him—a small footprint—the foot of a child.

The impression was too faint thoroughly to distinguish the shape, but it seemed to them both that it was the print of a naked foot.

This phenomenon ceased when they arrived at the opposite wall, nor did it repeat itself on returning.

They remounted the stairs, and entered the rooms on the ground floor, a dining parlour, a small back-parlour, and a still smaller third room that had been probably appropriated to a footman—all still as death. They then visited the drawing-rooms, which seemed fresh and new.

EVELINA AND ROSE ON BOARD THE SMUGGLER.

In the front room the traveller seated himself in an arm chair. The valet placed on the table the candlestick, with which he lighted them.

The traveller told him to shut the door. As he turned to do so, a chair opposite to him moved from the wall quickly and noiselessly and dropped itself about a yard from his own chair immediately fronting it.

The traveller laughed, but the dog put back his head and howled.

The valet, coming back, had not observed the movement of the chair.

He employed himself now in stilling the dog.

The traveller continued to gaze on the chair, and fancied he saw on it a pale blue misty outline of a human figure, but an outline so indistinct that he could only distrust his own vision.

The dog now was quiet.

"Put back that chair opposite to me," said he to his servant; "put it back to the wall."

He obeyed.

"Was that you, sir?" said he, turning abruptly.

"I!—what?"

"Why, something struck me. I felt it sharply on the shoulder—just here."

"No," said the traveller. "But we have jugglers present, and though we may not discover their tricks, we shall catch *them* before they frighten *us*."

They did not stay long in the drawing-rooms—in fact they felt so damp and so chilly that they were glad to get to the fire up-stairs.

The bedroom the servant had selected for his master was the best on the floor—a large one, with two windows fronting the street.

The four-post bed, which took up no inconsiderable space,

was opposite to the fire, which burned clear and bright; a door in the wall to the left, between the bed and the window, communicated with the room which the servant appropriated to himself.

This last was a small room with a sofa-bed, and had no communication with the landing place—no other door but that which conducted to the bedroom he was to occupy.

On either side of his fireplace was a cupboard, without locks, flushed with the wall, and covered with the same dull-brown paper.

They examined these cupboards—only hooks to suspend female dresses—nothing else; they sounded the walls—evidently solid—the outer walls of the building.

In the landing place there was another door; it was closed firmly.

"Sir," said the servant, in surprise, "I unlocked this door with all the others when I first came; it cannot have got locked from the inside, for it is a——"

Before he had finished his sentence, the door, which neither of them then was touching, opened quietly of itself. They looked at each other a single instant.

The same thought seized both—some human agency might be detected here.

The traveller rushed in first. The servant followed.

A small blank dreary room without furniture—a few empty boxes and hampers in a corner—a small window —the shutters closed—not even a fire-place—no other door but that by which they had entered—no carpet on the floor, and the floor seemed very old, uneven, worm-eaten, mended here and there, as was shown by the whiter patches on the wood; but no living being, and no visible place in which a living being could have hidden.

As they stood gazing round, the door by which they had entered closed as quietly as it had before opened: they were imprisoned.

For the first time the traveller felt a creep of undefinable horror.

Not so the servant.

"Why, they don't think to trap us, sir: I could break that trumpery door with a kick of my foot."

"Try first if it will open to your hand," said the traveller, shaking off the vague apprehension that had seized him, "while I open the shutters and see what is without."

He unbarred the shutters—the window looked on the back yard; there was no ledge without—nothing but sheer descent.

No man getting out of that window would have found any footing till he had fallen on the stones below.

The valet meanwhile, was vainly attempting to open the door.

He now turned round to his master, and asked permission to use force.

He willingly gave him the permission required.

But though he was a remarkably strong man, his force was as idle as his milder efforts; the door did not even shake to his stoutest kick.

Breathless and panting, he desisted.

The traveller then tried the door himself, equally in vain.

As he ceased from the effort, again a creep of horror came over him; but this time it was more cold and stubborn.

He felt as if some strange and ghastly exhalation were rising up from the chinks of that rugged floor, and filling the atmosphere with a venomous influence hostile to human life.

The door now very slowly and quietly opened as of its own accord.

They precipitated themselves into the landing-place.

They both saw a large pale light—as large as the human figure, but shapeless and unsubstantial—move before them, and ascend the stairs that led from the landing into the attics.

He followed the light, and the servant followed him.

It entered, to the right of the landing, a small garret, of which the door stood open.

The traveller entered in the same instant.

The light then collapsed into a small globule exceedingly brilliant and vivid, rested a moment on a bed in the corner, quivered, and vanished.

They approached the bed and examined it—a half-tester, such as is commonly found in attics devoted to servants.

On the drawers that stood near it they perceived an old faded silk kerchief, with the needle still left in a rent half repaired.

The kerchief was covered with dust.

He had sufficient curiosity to open the drawers: there were a few odds and ends of female dress, and two letters tied round with a narrow ribbon of faded yellow.

He took the liberty to possess himself of the letters. They found nothing else in the room worth noticing— nor did the light reappear; but they distinctly heard, as they turned to go, a pattering footfall on the floor, just before them.

They went through the other attics (in all four), the footfall still preceding them.

Nothing to be seen—nothing but the footfall heard.

The traveller had the letters in his hand.

Just as he was descending the stairs he distinctly felt his wrist seized, and a faint, soft effort made to draw the letters from his clasp.

He only held them the more tightly, and the effort ceased.

They regained the bedchamber appropriated to the traveller, and he then remarked that the dog had not followed them when they had left it.

He was thrusting himself close to the fire, and trembling.

The traveller was impatient to examine the letters, and while he read them the servant opened a little box in which he had deposited the weapons his master had ordered him to bring, took them out, placed them on a table close at his bed-head, and then occupied himself in soothing the dog—who, however, seemed to heed him very little.

The letters were short. They were dated exactly thirty-five years previous to that date.

They were evidently from a lover to his mistress, or a husband to some young wife.

Not only the terms of expression, but a distinct reference to a former voyage, indicated the writer to have been a seafarer.

The spelling and handwriting were those of a man imperfectly educated; but still, the language itself was forcible.

In the expressions of endearment there was a kind of rough, wild love; but here and there were dark, unintelligible hints at some secret not of love—some secret that seemed of crime.

"We ought to love each other," was one of the sentences "for how every one else would execrate us if all was known."

Again: "Don't let any one be in the same room with you at night—you talk in your sleep."

And again; "What's done can't be undone: and I tell you there's nothing against us unless the dead should come to life."

Here there was underlined in a better handwriting (a female's), "They do."

At the end of the letter latest in date the same female hand had written these words: "Lost at sea the 4th of June, the same day as——"

He put down the letters, and begun to muse over their contents.

Fearing, however, that the train of thought into which he fell might unsteady his nerves, he fully determined to keep his mind in a fit state to cope with whatever of marvellous the advancing night might bring forth.

He roused himself, laid the letters on the table, stirred up the fire—which was still bright and cheering—and opened a book.

He read quietly enough till about half-past eleven.

He then threw himself, dressed, upon the bed, and told his servant he might retire to his own room, but must keep himself awake.

He bade him leave open the door between the two rooms.

Thus alone, he kept two candles burning on the table by his bed-head.

He placed his watch beside the weapons, and calmly resumed his reading.

Opposite to him the fire burned clear; and on the hearth rug, seemingly asleep, lay the dog.

In about twenty minutes he felt an exceedingly cold air pass by his cheek, like a sudden draught.

He fancied the door to his right, communicating with the landing-place, must have got open; but no, it was closed.

He then turned his glance to his left, and saw the flame of the candles violently swayed as by a wind.

At the same moment the watch beside the pistol softly slid from the table—softly, softly, no visible hand—it was gone.

He sprang up, seizing the revolver with the one hand, the dagger with the other: he was not willing that his weapons should share the fate of the watch.

Thus armed, he looked round the floor—no sign of the watch.

Three slow, loud, distinct knocks were now heard at the bed-head; his servant called out, "Is that you, sir?"

"No; be on your guard."

The dog now roused himself and sat on his haunches, his ears moving quickly backwards and forwards.

He kept his eyes fixed on him with a look so strange that he concentrated all his attention on himself.

Slowly he rose up, all his hair bristling, and stood perfectly rigid, and with the same wild stare.

He had no time, however, to examine the dog.

Presently the servant emerged from his room; and if ever horror was seen in the human face it was then.

He could not have recognised him had they met in the street, so altered was every lineament.

He passed by his master quickly, saying in a whisper that seemed scarcely to come from his lips, "Run! run! it is after me!"

He gained the door to the landing, pulled it open, and rushed forth.

The master followed him into the landing involuntarily, calling to him to stop; but, without heeding him, he bounded down the stairs, clinging to the ballusters, and taking several steps at a time.

He heard where he stood, the door open—heard it again clip to, and he was left alone in the house with Mother Clifford.

It was but for a moment that he remained undecided whether or not to follow his servant. Pride and curiosity alike forbade so dastardly a flight.

He re-entered his room, closing the door after him, and proceeded cautiously into the interior chamber.

He encountered nothing to justify his servant's terror. He again examined the walls, to see if there was any concealed door.

He could find no trace of one—not even a seam in the dull brown paper, with which the room was hung.

How, then, had the THING, whatever it was, which had so scared him, obtained ingress except through his own chamber?

He returned to his room, shut and locked the door that opened upon the interior one, and stood on the hearth, expectant and prepared.

He now perceived that the dog had slunk into an angle of the wall, and was pressing himself close against it as if literally striving to force his way into it.

He approached the animal and spoke to it; the poor brute was evidently beside itself with terror.

It showed all its teeth, the saliva dropping from its jaws, and would certainly have bitten his master if he had touched it.

It did not seem to recognise him.

Finding all efforts to soothe him in vain, and fearing that his bite might be as venomous in that state as in the madness of hydrophobia, he left him alone, placed his weapons on the table beside the fire, seated himself, and recommenced his book.

It was his conjecture that all that was presented, or would be presented, to his senses, must originate in some human being gifted by constitution with the power so to present them; and having some motive so to do, he felt an interest in his theory which, in its way, was rather philosophical than superstitious.

And we can certainly say that he was in as tranquil a temper for observation as any practical experimentalist could be in awaiting the effects of some rare, though perhaps perilous, chemical combination. Of course, the more he kept his mind detached from fancy, the more the temper fitted for observation would be obtained; and he therefore riveted eye and thought on the strong daylight sense in the page of his book.

He now became aware that something interposed between the page and the light—the page was overshadowed.

He looked up, and saw what we shall find very difficult, if not impossible, to describe.

It was a darkness shaping itself out of the air in very undefined outline.

We cannot say it was of a human form, and yet it had more resemblance to a human form, or rather shadow, than anything else.

As it stood, wholly apart and distinct from the air and the light around it, its dimensions seemed gigantic, the summit nearly touching the ceiling. While he gazed, a feeling of intense cold seized him. He felt convinced that it was not the cold caused by fear.

As he continued to gaze, he thought that he distinguished two eyes looking down on him from the height.

One moment he seemed to distinguish them clearly, the next they seemed gone; but still two rays of a pale-blue light frequently shot through the darkness, as from the height on which he half believed, half doubted, that he had encountered the eyes.

He strove to speak—his voice utterly failed him; he could only think to himself, "Is this fear? it is *not* fear!" He strove to rise—in vain; he felt as if weighed down by an irresistible force. Indeed, his impression was that of an immense and overwhelming power opposed to his volition;—that sense of utter inadequacy to cope with a force beyond men's, which one may feel *physically* in a storm at sea, in a conflagration, or when confronting some terrible wild beast, or rather, perhaps, the shark of the ocean—he felt *morally*.

Opposed to his will was another will, as far superior to its strength as storm, fire, and shark are superior in material force to the force of men.

And now, as this impression grew on him, now came, at last, horror—horror to a degree that no words can convey.

Still he retained pride, if not courage; and in his own mind he said, "This is horror, but it is not fear; unless I fear, I cannot be harmed; my reason rejects this thing; it is an illusion—I do not fear." With a violent effort he succeeded at last in stretching out his hand towards the weapon on the table; as he did so, on the arm and shoulder he received a strange shock, and his arm fell to his side powerless.

And now, to add to his horror, the light began slowly to wane from the candles—they were not, as it were, extinguished, but their flame seemed very gradually withdrawn: it was the same with the fire—the light was extracted from the fuel; in a few minutes the room was in utter darkness.

The dread that came over him, to be thus in the dark, with that dark thug, whose power was so intensely felt, brought a reaction of nerve. In fact, terror had reached that climax, that either his senses must have deserted him, or he must have burst through the spell.

He did burst through it.

He found voice, though the voice was a shriek.

He remembered that he broke forth with words like these—

"I do not fear, my soul does not fear."

And, at the same time, he found the strength to rise.

Still, in that profound gloom, he rushed to one of the windows, tore aside the curtain, flung open the shutters; his first thought was—LIGHT.

And when he saw the moon, high, clear, and calm, he felt a joy that almost compensated for the previous terror.

There was the moon; there was also the light from the lamps in the deserted place.

He turned to look back into the room. The moon penetrated its shadow very palely and partially—but still there was light.

The dark *thing*—whatever it might be—was gone, except that he could yet see a dim shadow, which seemed the shadow of that shade, against the opposite wall.

His eye now rested on the table; and from under the table (which was without cloth or cover—an old mahogany round table) there rose a hand, visible as far as the wrist.

It was a hand, seemingly, as much of flesh and blood as his own, but the hand of an aged person—lean, wrinkled, small too—*a woman's hand.*

That hand very softly closed on the two letters that lay on the table; hand and letters both vanished.

There then came the same three loud measured knocks he had heard at the bed-head before this extraordinary drama had commenced.

As those sounds slowly ceased, he felt the whole room vibrate sensibly; and at the far end there rose, as from the floor, sparks or globules like bubbles of light, many-coloured—green, yellow, fire-red, azure.

Up and down, to and fro, hither, thither, as tiny Will. o'-the-Wisps, the sparks moved, slow or swift, each at its own caprice.

A chair (as in the drawing room below) was now advanced from the wall without apparent agency, and placed at the opposite side of the table.

Suddenly, as from the chair, there grew a shape—a woman's shape.

It was distinct as a shape of life—ghastly as a shape of death.

The face was that of youth, with a strange, mournful beauty; the throat and shoulders were bare, the rest of the form in a loose robe of cloudy white.

It began sleeking its long yellow hair, which fell over its shoulders; its eyes were not turned towards him, but to the door; it seemed listening, watching, waiting.

The shadow of the shade in the background grew darker; and again he thought he beheld the eyes gleaming out from the summit of the shadow—eyes fixed upon that shape.

As if from the door, though it did not open, there grew out another shape, equally distinct, equally ghastly—a man's shape—a young man's.

It was in the dress of the previous century, or rather in a likeness of such dress; for both the male shape and the female, though defined, were evidently unsubstantial, impalpable—simulacra—phantasms; and there was something incongruous, grotesque, yet fearful, in the contrast between the elaborate finery, the courtly precision of that old-fashioned garb, with its ruffles and lace and buckles, and the corpse-like aspect and ghost-like stillness of the flitting wearer.

Just as the male shape approached the female, the dark shadow started from the wall, all three for a moment wrapped in darkness.

When the pale light returned, the two phantoms were as if in the grasp of the shadow that towered between them; and there was a blood stain on the breast of the female; and the phantom male was leaning on its phantom sword, and blood seemed trickling fast from the ruffles from the lace; and the darkness of the intermediate shadow swallowed them up—they were gone.

And again the bubbles of light shot, and sailed, and undulated, growing thicker and thicker and more wildly confused in their movements.

The closet door to the right of the fireplace now opened, and from the aperture there came the form of a woman, aged.

In her hand she held letters—the very letters over which he had seen the hand close, and behind her he heard a footstep.

She turned round as if to listen, and then she opened the letters and seemed to read; and over her shoulder he saw a livid face, the face as of a man long drowned—bloated, bleached, seaweed tangled in its dripping hair; and at her feet lay a form as of a corpse, and beside the corpse there cowered a child, a miserable squalid child, with famine in its cheeks and fear in its eyes.

And as he looked in the old woman's face, the wrinkles and lines vanished, and it became a face of youth, hard-eyed, stony, but still youth; and the shadow darted forth, and darkened over these phantoms as it had darkened over the last.

Nothing now was left but the shadow, and on that his eyes were intently fixed, till again eyes grew out of the shadow—malignant, serpent eyes.

And the bubbles of light again rose and fell, and in their disordered, irregular, turbulent maze, mingled with the wan moonlight.

And now from these globules themselves, as from the shell of an egg, monstrous things burst out; the air grew filled with them; larvæ so bloodless and so hideous that he could in no way describe them except the reader of the swarming life which the solar microscope brings before his eyes in a drop of water—things transparent, supple, agile, chasing each other, devouring each other—forms like nothing ever beheld by the naked eye.

As the shapes were without symmetry, so their movements were without order.

In their very vargaries there was no sport; they came round him and round, thicker and faster and swifter, swarming over his head, crawling over his right arm, which was outstretched in involuntary command against all evil beings.

Sometimes he felt himself touched, but not by them; invisible hands touched him.

Once he felt the clutch as of cold soft fingers at his throat.

He was still equally conscious that if he gave way to fear he should be in bodily peril, and he concentrated all his faculties in the single focus of resisting, stubborn will.

And he turned his sight from the shadow; above all from those strange serpent eyes—eyes that had now become distinctly visible.

For there, though in nought else around, he was aware that there was a will; and a will of intense, creative, working evil, which might crush down his own.

The pale atmosphere in the room began now to redden, as if in the air of some near conflagration.

The larvæ grew lurid as things that live in fire.

Again the room vibrated—again were heard the three measured knocks—and again all things were swallowed up in the darkness of the dark shadow, as if out of that darkness all had come—into that darkness all returned.

As the gloom receded the shadow was wholly gone.

Slowly as it had been withdrawn, the flame grew again into the candles on the table—again into the fuel in the grate.

The whole room came once more calmly, healthfully into sight.

The two doors were still closed—the door communicating with the servant's room still locked.

In the corner of the room into which he had so convulsively niched himself lay the dog.

He called to him—no movement.

He approached—the animal was dead!

His eyes protruded—his tongue out of his mouth—the froth gathered round his jaws.

He took him in his arms—he brought him to the fire.

He felt acute grief for the loss of his poor favourite—acute self-reproach.

He accused himself of his death—he imagined he had died of fright.

But what was his surprise on finding that his neck was actually broken—actually twisted out of the vertebræ.

Had this been done in the dark?—must it not have been by a hand human as his?—must there not have been a human agency all the while in that room?

Good cause to suspect it.

Another surprising circumstance—his watch was restored to the table from which it had been so mysteriously withdrawn; but it had stopped at the very moment it was so withdrawn.

Nothing more chanced for the rest of the night; nor, indeed, had he long to wait before the dawn broke.

Not till it was broad daylight did he quit the Hall.

Before he did so he revisited the little blind room in which his servant and himself had been for a time imprisoned.

He had a strong impression, for which he could not account, that from that room had originated the mechanism of the phenomena which had been experienced in his chamber; and though he entered it now in the clear day, with the sun peering through the filmy window, he still felt, as he stood on its floor, the creep of the horror which he had first there experienced the night before, and which had been so aggravated by what had passed in h's own chamber.

He could not, indeed, bear to stay more than half a minute within those walls.

He descended the stairs, and again he heard the footfall before him; and when he opened the door, he thought he could distinguish a very low laugh.

Outside the house the traveller paused, and uttered—

"Psha!"

He hesitated a moment, and then turned to re-enter the house.

As he was about to do so his servant approached him.

The poor fellow had been wandering on the terrace, and appeared glad to see his master alive and unhurt.

"I shall return," said the master; "you may follow if you will."

"I will return with you," said the servant, "at once."

"Good. I know not for what purpose, but some power is prompting me on to sift the mysteries—the terrible mysteries—of this Hall to their foundation. Will you stand by me?"

"Yes."

"Without flinching?"

"Without flinching."

They then re-opened the Hall door and entered.

They hastened to the bed room, and the traveller then set to work, taking up the skirting and then the floors.

Under the rafters, covered with rubbish, was found a trap-door, quite large enough to admit a man.

It was closely nailed down, with clamps and rivets of iron.

On removing these they descended into a room below, the existence of which had never been suspected.

In this room there had been a window and a flue, but they had been bricked over, evidently for many years.

By the help of candles they examined this place; it still retained some mouldering furniture—three chairs, an oak settle, a table—all of the fashion of centuries ago.

There was a chest of drawers against the wall, in which they found, half-rotted away, old-fashioned articles of a man's dress, such as might have been worn long ago by a gentleman of some rank—costly steel buckles and buttons, like those yet worn in court-dresses; a hand-

some court-sword—in a waistcoat which had once been rich with gold lace, but which was now blackened and foul with damp, they found five guineas, a few silver coins, an ivory ticket, probably for some place of entertainment long since passed away.

But their main discovery was in a kind of iron safe fixed to the wall, the lock of which it cost them much trouble to pick.

In this safe were three shelves and two small drawers.

Ranged on the shelves were several small bottles of crystal, hermetically stopped.

They contained colourless volatile essences, of what nature we shall say no more than that they were not poisons—phosphor and ammonia entered into some of them.

There were also some very curious glass tubes, and a small pointed rod of iron, with a large lump of rock-crystal, and another of amber—also a loadstone of great power.

In one of the drawers they found a miniature portrait, set in gold, and retaining the freshness of its colours most remarkably, considering the length of time it had probably been there.

The portrait was that of a man who might be somewhat advanced in middle life, perhaps forty-seven or forty-eight.

It was a most peculiar face—a most impressive face.

If you could fancy some mighty serpent transformed into man, preserving in the human lineaments the old serpent type, the reader would have a better idea of that countenance than long descriptions can convey: the width and flatness of frontal, the tapering elegance of contour disguising the strength of the deadly jaw, the long, large, terrible eye, glittering and green as the emerald, and withal a certain ruthless calm, as if from the consciousness of an immense power.

The strange thing was this.

The instant the traveller saw the miniature he recognised a startling likeness to one of the rarest portraits in the world, the portrait of a man of rank only below that of royalty, who in his own day had made a considerable noise.

History says little or nothing of him; but search the correspondence of his contemporaries, and you find reference to his wild daring, his bold profligacy, his restless spirit, his taste for the occult sciences.

While still in the meridian of life he died and was buried, so say the chronicles, in a foreign land.

He died in time to escape the grasp of the law, for he was accused of crimes which would have given him to the headsman.

After his death, the portraits of him, which had been numerous, for he had been a munificent encourager of art, were brought up and destroyed, it was supposed by his heirs, who might have been glad could they have razed his very name from their splendid line.

He had enjoyed a vast wealth; a large portion of this was believed to have been embezzled by a favourite astrologer or soothsayer; at all events it had unaccountably vanished at the time of his death.

One portrait alone of him was supposed to have escaped the general destruction; the traveller had seen it in the house of a collector some months before.

It had made on him a wonderful impression, as it does on all who behold it, a face never to be forgotten; and there was that face in the miniature that lay within his hand.

True, that in the miniature the man was a few years older than in the portrait he had seen, or than the original was even at the time of his death.

But a few years!—why, between the date in which flourished that direful noble and the date in which the miniature was evidently painted, there was an interval of more than two centuries.

While he was thus gazing, silent and wondering, the the servant said—

"But is it possible? I have known this man."

"How—where?" cried the traveller.

"In India. He was high in the confidence of the Rajah of ——, and well-nigh drew him into a revolt which would have lost the Rajah his dominions. The man was a Frenchman, his name De.V——, clever, bold, lawless.

"People insisted on his dismissal and banishment: it must be the same man—no two faces like his—yet this miniature seems nearly a hundred years old."

Mechanically the traveller turned round the miniature to examine the back of it, and on the back was engraved a penticle; in the middle of the pentacle a ladder, and the third step of the ladder was formed by the date 1665. Examining still more minutely, he detected a spring; this, on being pressed, opened the back of the miniature as a lid.

Within-side the lid were engraved "Mariana to thee—Be faithful in life and in death to——."

Here follows a name that we will not mention.

They found no difficulty in opening the first drawer within the iron safe—they found great difficulty in opening the second.

It was not locked, but it resisted all efforts till they inserted in the chinks the edge of a chisel.

When they had thus drawn it forth they found a very singular apparatus, in the nicest order.

Upon a small thin book, or rather tablet, was placed a saucer of crystal; this saucer was filled with a clear liquid, on that liquid floated a kind of compass, with a needle shifting rapidly round; but instead of the usual points of a compass were seven strange characters, not very unlike those used by astrologers to denote the planets.

A very peculiar, but not strong nor disagreeable odour, came from this drawer, which was lined with a wood that we afterwards discovered to be hazel.

Whatever the cause of this odour, it produced a material effect on the nerves.

They both felt it—a creeping, tingling sensation from the tips of the fingers to the roots of the hair.

Impatient to examine the tablet, the traveller removed the saucer.

As he did so the needle of the compass went round and round with exceeding swiftness, and he felt a shock that ran through his whole frame, so that he dropped the saucer on the floor.

The liquid was spilt, the saucer was broken, the compass rolled to the end of the room, and at that instant the walls shook to and fro, as if a giant had swayed and rocked them.

Meanwhile the traveller had opened the tablet.

It was bound in plain red leather, with a silver clasp; it contained but one sheet of thick vellum, and on that sheet were inscribed, within a double pentacle, words in old monkish Latin, which are literally to be translated thus:—"On all that it can reach within these walls—sentient or inanimate—living or dead; as moves the needle so work my will! Accursed be the house, and restless be the dwellers therein."

They found no more.

The servant burnt the tablet and its anathema, but as he did so Mother Clifford appeared on the scene.

CHAPTER LXIII.

THE HISTORY OF THE OLD CATHEDRAL OF CANTERBURY—THE MYSTERIOUS MONK—THE MALEDICTION—THE VAULT—THE SECRET PASSAGE, AND THE DEED OF DARKNESS.

THE Cathedral stands in nearly the south-west part of the precincts of it, adjoining to which on the north side, was the Priory of Christchurch, to which it belonged; the remains of which are converted, for the most part, into dwellings and offices for the use of the Dean and Chapter and other members of this church.

In this spot was once the palace of Ethelbert, the Saxon King of Kent, who, having become a convert to Christianity by the persuasion of St. Augustine, gave him his royal palace here, as a perpetual seat for him and his successors.

This palace, with the adjoining buildings, St. Augustine afterwards converted into a cathedral and monastery, dedicating both to the honour of Christ our Saviour, whence it afterwards obtained the name of Christ Church. From the above time for upwards of three hundred years, nothing was worthy of being recorded concerning this church, except that during this period the gifts to it were many and large; but afterwards, through the frequent ravages of the Danes, which involved this country in continued troubles, it appears to have suffered much, as well by fire as frequent neglect and dilapidation, so that when Archbishop Lanfranc came to the Archbishopric, soon after the Norman Conquest, he found it in a most ruinous state.

By his care and perseverance, he re-edified it in all parts, and that in a more novel and substantial form of structure than had been seen before in this kingdom, which made it a precedent and pattern to succeeding ones of this kind.

New monasteries and churches were built after the example of it; for before this, most of the churches and monasteries of the kingdom were made of wood, but from this time such timber fabrics grew out of use, and gave place to stone buildings raised upon arches, a custom brought from Normandy.

The stone he employed is a fine grained oolite, which he obtained from Caen, in Normandy; it is comparatively soft when quarried; and being fine and evenly grained, is well adapted for the elaborate carvings used both in the interior and exterior of Gothic structures, more especially as it hardens by exposure to the air, and tones down with a rich and mellow tint.

With this stone he rebuilt the whole church, from its foundation, with the palace and monastery, and the wall which encompassed them, and when finished, he altered the name by dedicating it to the Holy Trinity.

During the long-continued wars many repairs were effected by the use of Portland stone, a material in no way comparable to that from Caen, and not a few specimens of carpentry, painted to imitate stone, are yet to be seen that were placed up at the same period.

After Lanfranc's death, by means of Archbishop Anselm, this church was again rebuilt on a still larger and more beautiful plan.

For this purpose that part of it built by Lanfranc, from the great tower in the middle of it to the east end, was in part pulled down, and the fabric again raised up with such splendour, says Malmesbury, "that the like was not to be seen in England, in respect of the clear light of the glass windows, the beauty and comeliness of the marble pavement, and the curious painting of the roof;" after which the Prior Conrad perfected the choir, magnificently adorned it with curious pictures and other ornaments, insomuch that, from its more than ordinary beauty, it gained the name of the Glorious Choir of Conrad.

In this state, without anything material happening,

the church continued till the reign of Henry I., when it suffered some damage by fire, which was, however, repaired by Archbishop Corboyl, sufficiently for the performance of divine service, and for the Archbishop to dedicate it anew, the ceremony of which was performed with great splendour and magnificence, such as was said not to have been heard of since the dedication of the Temple of Solomon; the King, the Queen, the King of Scots, and all the prelates and nobility of both kingdoms being at it, when this church's former name was restored, being thenceforth commonly called Christ Church.

Forty-four years after this, anno. 1174, being the 20th of the reign of King Henry II., great part of this stately edifice was again destroyed by fire.

Upon this destruction of the church the prior and convent took the most speedy and effectual methods to rebuild it in such a manner as should surpass all former chairs, as well in beauty as size.

The new building accordingly exceeded in height and length, and was more beautiful in every respect than the choir of Conrad.

The roof was not only considerably advanced above what it was before, but was arched over with stone, prior to which it was composed of timber. The capitals of the pillars were now beautified with carved work, whereas they were before plain, and six more pillars were added. The former choir had but one triforium, or inner gallery, but now there are two made round it, and one in each side aisle. Before this there were no marble pillars, but such were now added in abundance.

In forwarding this great work, the monks spent eight years, when they could proceed no further for want of money; but a papal bull was issued, providing that the offerings to the then newly murdered Archbishop Becket should be appropriated to the restoration of the cathedral, and this encouraged them to set about a grander design, which was to pull down the eastern end of the church, with the small chapel of the Holy Trinity adjoining to it, and to erect, upon a stately underbroft, a more sumptuous one in the room of it equally lofty with the roof of the church, and making a part of it, which the former did not, but opened by a doorway into it.

At the east end of this chapel, another small one was afterwards erected, at the end of the building since called Becket's Crown, for the purpose of an altar, and the reception of some part of that saint's relics, further mention of which will be made.

The eastern parts of the church have the appearance of being much older than they are generally allowed to be; and indeed, if the side walls and cross wings on each side of the choir are only examined, it will appear that the whole of them were not rebuilt when the choir was, and that a great part of them was suffered to remain, though altered, added to, and adapted, as far as could be, to the new building then erected; the traces of several circular windows and other openings, which were then stopped up, removed, or altered, still appearing in the walls of both, and on the south side of the south aisle; the vaulting of the roof, as well as the triforium, which could not be adjusted to the placing of the upper windows, plainly show it.

To which may be added, that the basement of one of the westernmost large pillars of the choir on the north side is strengthened with a strong iron band round it, seeming to be one of those which had been weakened by the fire, but was judged of sufficient firmness, with this precaution, to remain for the use of the new fabric.

The outside part of the church is a corroborating proof of the preceding, as well in the method as in the ornaments of the building: on the outside of it, towards the south, from St. Michael's Chapel, eastward, there is a range of small pillars, of about six inches diameter, and about three feet high; these support little arches intersecting each other, and this chain or girdle of pillars is continued round the small tower, the eastern cross aisle, and the chapel of St. Anslem, as far as the new building

added since of the Trinity Chapel, and St. Thomas à Becket's crown, where they leave off.

At the time of the before-mentioned fire, which so fatally destroyed the upper part of the church, the undercroft, with the vaulting over it, seems to have remained entire and unhurt by it.

The vaulting of the undercroft, on which the floor of the choir end eastern part of the church are raised, is supported by pillars, whose capitals are as various and as fantastical as those of the smaller ones before mentioned, and so are their shafts, some being round, and others canted, twisted, or carved, so that hardly any two of them are alike, except such as are quite plain.

That the ornaments of the capitals were worked after the capital was placed there is good proof in this crypt; for one may be seen of four sides—the one quite plain, a second with the pattern sketched out. the third partly sculptured, and the remaining one with the pattern perfected.

That part of this undercroft now remaining as far eastward as where it begins, under the Trinity Chapel, appears to be of later date, erected at the same time as the chapel, and may well be supposed, from its appearance, to be that which was originally built by Archbishop Lanfranc, and continues as firm and entire as it was at the first building of it, though now upwards of seven hundred years old.

If this is correct it strongly corroborates Mr. Sandy's view, who is clearly of opinion that the oldest parts of this cathedral are of British and Saxon work, and done prior to the Norman invasion.

Archbishop à Beckett was murdered in it on December 29th, 1170, and his body had been privately buried towards the east end of the undercroft, soon after which miracles, as the monks tell us, began to be wrought by him; first at his tomb, then in other parts of the church, and afterwards throughout the rest of the world, so that two years afterwards, he was sainted by the Pope.

Now crowds of zealots, led on by a frenzy of false devotion, hastened to kneel at his tomb.

Kings, princes, nobles, and prelates of this and every other kingdom paid their adorations at it, watching and praying with great humility all night there, many of them in the habits of pilgrims.

The oblations of gold, silver, and jewels presented by them to the saint exceeded all credibility.

These visits were the early fruits of adoration to the newly-sainted martyr, and their examples were followed by multitudes of all sorts, who crowded with humble reverence and rich oblations to him, whilst his body lay in the undercroft.

From these liberal donations the expense of rebuilding the church seems to have been in a great measure supplied, nor did their devotions and offerings after it was completed in any way abate, but on the contrary daily increased; and the monks employed the whole of this vast income to the fabric of the church, which continued a plentiful supply to them till the Reformation, and the final suppression of the priory itself.

Besides these usual customary offerings, there was a more abundant one, which brought into the convent an incredible gain; this was a celebration of Becket's martyrdom, which was called a jubilee, being kept at the period of every fifty years from the time of his murder.

The privilege of this solemnity was purchased at a dear rate from the Court of Rome, and not without the most humble praying and solicitations.

The confluence of people of all ranks who came to them was not less than 100,000 in number, and their estimation of their liberal oblations at the saint's tomb was beyond the bounds of belief.

There had been seven of these jubilees before the Reformation; the last of them in 1520, in the time of Archbishop Warham.

In the meantime the chapel and altar at the upper part of the east end of the church, dedicated to the Holy

Trinity, were demolished, and again prepared with great splendour for the reception of this new saint, who being now placed there, not only the chapel and altar, but the whole church, from that time, became known by the name of St. Thomas the martyr.

On the 7th July, 1220, the remains of St. Thomas were transferred from his tomb to the new shrine with great solemnity and rejoicings, the Pope's Legate, the Archbishops of Canterbury and Rheims, and many bishops and abbots carrying the coffin on their shoulders, and placing it there, and the king gracing these solemnities with his royal presence.

The saint, now placed in his new repository, became the vain object of adoration to the deluded multitude, and such veneration had every one for his relics, that all endeavours were used to obtain one of them; the meanest things which had belonged to him, and even shreds of his clothes, were sought after as invaluable treasures, and each thought himself rich and happy in obtaining the smallest portion of them; in many cathedrals, monasteries, and churches, some parts of them were seen and worshipped, and the buildings themselves were dedicated to him.

At the time of Archbishop Sudbury's death, the west front of the church, with the two adjoining towers, had not been taken down, and probably the monks, from the great expense, determined to leave those parts standing, making such alterations as would render them suitable to their new building.

The great tower in the middle of the church, called Bell Harry Steeple, from a small bell of that name on the top of it (the only one remaining there, said to have been brought from France by King Henry VIII., and given by him to this church), was formerly called the Angel Steeple; it was 285 feet high, and had continued without rebuilding or want of repairs, till about the latter end of the reign of King Henry IV., when Prior Snelling began to rebuild it, and Prior Goldstone (the second of that name) his successor, finished it, assisted by Cardinal Archbishop Morton.

For the strengthening of this lofty tower, of most admirable form and symmetry, Prior Goldstone, caused two large arches, and a smaller one of stone to be fixed underneath from pillar to pillar, in the nave.

These arches and stretchers are very substantial, and are pierced in such patterns as to make them rather an ornament, although certainly designed as a security to strengthen the pillars under so great a weight; on them, as well as on the upper part of the inside tower, are the initial letters of his name, and office of Prior, his shield being three gold stones, and his motto, " Non nobis Domine," &c.

During the unhappy troubles of the great rebellion, inevitable destruction seemed to threaten the whole of this beautiful fabric, for in the year 1641 the madness of the people raged beyond all resistance; the deans and canons were turned out of their stalls; the newly erected font was pulled down and sold piecemeal; inscriptions, figures, coats of arms in brass, were torn off from the ancient grave stones, and the very graves themselves were ransacked for the sake of mere plunder; and whatever there was of decency in it was despoiled by the outrages of sacrilegious profaneness; in which forlorn state it remained till three years afterwards, when the government's committee took possession of this church and the revenue of it.

At the entrance of the Cathedral, at the west front of the buildings, the tower steeple on the south side, called Chicheley Steeple, had formerly on the outside, over the porch, at the entrance into the church, the figures cut out in stone of four armed men, representing the murderers of Archbishop Becket; the niches in which they were placed still remaining.

In this steeple there is now a fine musical peal of bells and a clock.

On the vaulting of the porch is carved a cluster of coats of arms, twenty-eight in number, in a double circle,

on the stone of the rib-work of it: among others, there are the arms of old France and England, quarterly; also those of the see of Canterbury, impaled with Chicheley and Courteney, with a label of three points.

*   *   *   *   *

The cloisters were filled with a damp and overpowering fog one night soon after the adventure of Clifford in the forest of Windsor.

There was a dismal air surrounding the wretched place, and the whole atmosphere was filled with mystery and gloom.

It was midnight.

A low piercing shriek rang through the cloisters.

Suddenly a bright phosphoric light illumined the place.

By it was seen a troop of monks, all of a by-gone time —all phantom-like and weird.

In their midst was a young girl.

Her raiment was white, and hung about her limbs closely, yet gracefully.

They grasped her tightly, and by their manner exhibited uncompromising sternness.

Then, as if out of the very stones, rose the figure of an abbess.

Her dress was black, but on her breast was a large white star.

Her face was concealed.

This figure advanced towards the young girl in white.

The girl, as she advanced, shrank back, and tried to hide herself, but the monks thrust her forward, and she had to confront the phantom abbess—for phantom the figure appeared to be.

The abbess sternly regarded the shrinking girl.

At length she spoke.

" Your time is come," she said; " the time is now come, and you must meet your fate."

" What have I done—what have I done?"

" Broken the awful oath you took; broken the vows that bound you to us and to Heaven."

" I have not—I have not!"

" Lie not—lie not! Thou hast broken the ties that bound thee. Thy doom is death!"

" Spare me—spare me!"

" I have said."

" We have said," cried the monks.

" She must die!" shrieked the abbess.

" She must die!" echoed the others.

From her kirtle the abbess drew a long and glittering blade.

The white face of the poor girl grew still more ghastly.

A moment the abbess poised the knife in the air.

Then two of the monks advanced and, forcibly tearing away her delicate hands, held them extended above her head.

Another then advanced and bared her snowy bosom.

Then the abbess stepped forward, baring her long, thin arm, and uttered a low, wailing cry.

This was continued for some moments.

With the hand unemployed she beat herself until she was lashed into a perfect fury.

Then she placed the knife against the heart of her victim.

The poor girl closed her eyes as the sharp steel touched her.

One awful moment, and then the knife was plunged into her heart.

The shriek that escaped her was heart rending.

Three times the knife was plunged into the girl's heart, and then a deep cross was cut over the region of the heart, and the victim was allowed to fall to the earth.

*   *   *   *   *

CLIFFORD AND HERNE IN WINDSOR FOREST.

CHAPTER LXIV.

RETURNS TO EVELINA AND ROSE—THE ABDUCTION FROM
THE GOOD WOMAN'S COTTAGE—ON BOARD THE FLYING
BETSY—THE FATAL REPAST.

THE good woman's cottage proved a place of rest and
retirement for the two wanderers.

They were cared for tenderly, and it appeared that
brighter times were dawning upon them, but, unhappily,
their hopes were not to be realised.

The ruffians who had checked them on their entrance
into Glenhaven had not yet done with them.

Whatever the reason, they had made up their minds
that the two girls should fall into their power, and they
set themselves to work to bring this about.

For this purpose they reconnoitred the cottage of the
good woman, and marked well the movements of its
inhabitants.

In a few days they had possessed themselves of
every particular they desired to know, and then awaited
their time.

It came at last.

One night, soon after the last link of their plan had
been joined and rivetted, three of the ruffians, muffled
and disguised, entered the cottage by a window they had
previously tampered with, and in a few moments were in
the chamber allotted to the poor girls.

There was no shriek—no scuffle.

The work was done so effectually that in less than a
minute the men had again left the house, bearing with
them the insensible forms of the young girls.

It was midnight, and the moon rode high in the heavens, throwing a lustrous light over the bright blue waters.

In a creek in the rocks of the shore lay concealed a small boat, and into this the girls were borne.

In a few seconds the men had applied themelves to the oars, and sent the boat far from the shore.

An hour's rowing brought them alongside a long, low, rakish-looking craft, that lay in the offing of Glen-haven.

The girls were carried on board, and when they recovered consciousness were informed that they were far from the land.

A glance at the bright blue waters assured them that this was the fact, and the knowledge of their position struck terror to their hearts.

The first impulse of Evelina was to throw herself over the side of the vessel, and end her sorrows in the bosom of the bright waters.

But they checked this fearful impulse, and to prevent a repetition of such an attempt, tied her side by side with Rose to a gun.

They taunted her with her position, and took a delight in annoying her.

Evelina was almost broken-hearted.

Rose sought to console her, but the effort was made in vain.

Evelina could not be comforted.

This state of things continued three days, and they found themselves far out into the Channel.

The weather now turned rough, and the girls were compelled to keep to the cabins.

Now, for the first time, they mixed with the people of this mysterious vessel.

They were numerous, and of both sexes.

Some were married couples—some were relatives—others lovers; but all appeared to be tainted more or less with crime, and to be living at variance with, and in fear of, the laws of their country.

*   *   *   *   *

They had been nearly five weeks at sea, when the captain found that they were within thirty miles of the Land's End.

Favourable winds and smooth seas had hitherto been their constant attendants.

The captain was a man of objectionable manners, and to Evelina his society—which he constantly thrust upon her—was particularly repulsive.

Although he possessed more general information than usually falls to the lot of seafaring persons, his mind was tinctured with some of their weaknesses and prejudices.

The women of the party had a great taste for natural history, and wished to obtain specimens of all the most interesting kinds of sea-birds.

They had several times requested the captain to shoot one of Mother Carey's chickens; however, he always declined doing so, but never gave any satisfactory reason for his unwillingness to oblige them in this respect.

At last one of the men, to oblige his wife, killed two of the birds, after having several times missed whole flocks of them.

The captain seemed very much startled when he saw them drop on the waves.

"Will you have the goodness to let down the boat to pick up the game?" said the woman.

"Yes," replied the captain, "if you and your husband will go off in her, and never return on board this vessel. Here is a serious business. Be assured we have not seen the end of it."

He then walked away without offering to give any orders about lowering the boat; and the seamen, who witnessed the transaction, looked as if they would not have obeyed him had he even done so.

The sky had, within a few days, begun to assume a more dazzling aspect, and long ranges of conical-shaped clouds floated along the horizon.

Land birds often hovered round the vessel, and they sometimes fancied they could discover a vegetable fragrance in the breezes that swelled their sails.

One delightful clear morning, when they were in hourly expectation of making the land, some fish appeared astern.

As the weather was very moderate, the captain proposed that they should fish; and a great many hooks were immediately baited for that purpose by the seamen.

They caught large quantities of several kinds of fish, and put the whole into the hands of the cook, with orders that part should be dressed for dinner.

When the dinner-hour arrived they all assembled in the cabin, in high spirits, and sat down to table.

It being St. George's day the captain, who was an Englishman, had ordered that everything should be provided and set forth in the most sumptuous style, and the cook had done full justice to his directions.

They made the wines, which were exquisite and abundant, circulate rapidly, and every glass increased their gaiety and good humour, while the influence of mirth rendered the women additionally amusing and animated.

From the festival, however, Evelina and Rose held aloof.

The captain remarked that, as there were two clarionet players among the crew, they ought to have a dance upon the quarter-deck at sunset.

This proposal was received with much delight, particularly by the females; and the captain had just told the servant to bid the musicians prepare themselves, when the mate entered the cabin, and said that the man at the helm had dropped down almost senseless, and that another of the crew was so ill that he could scarcely speak.

The captain, on receiving this information, grew very pale, and seemed at a loss what to reply.

At last he started from his chair and hurried up the gangway.

The mirth ceased in a moment, though none appeared to know why; but the minds of all were evidently occupied by what they had just heard, and some one remarked with a faltering voice, that seamen were very liable to be taken suddenly ill.

After a little time they sent the servant to inquire what was going forward upon deck.

He returned immediately, and informed the party that the two sailors were worse, and that a third had just been attacked in the same way.

He had scarcely said these words, when a woman gave a shriek, and cried out that her sister had fainted away. This added to the confusion and alarm; and the men trembled so much, that they were hardly able to convey the young woman to her cabin.

All conversation was now at end, and no one uttered a word till Ann Day, the wife of a seaman, returned from her sister's apartment.

While they were inquiring how the latter was, the captain entered the cabin in a state of great agitation.

"This is a dreadful business," said he. "The fact is—it is my duty to tell you—I fear we are all poisoned by the fish we have ate. One of the crew died a few minutes since, and five others are dangerously ill."

"Poisoned! my God! Do you say so? Must we all die?" exclaimed Ann Day, dropping on her knees.

"What is to be done?" cried one of the men distractedly; "are there no means of counteracting it?"

"None that I know of," returned the captain. "All remedies are vain. The poison is always fatal, except—but I begin to feel its effects—support me—can this be imagination?"

He staggered to one side, and would have fallen upon the floor, had not some one assisted him. Mrs. Day, notwithstanding his apparent insensibility, clung to his arm, crying out, in a tone of despair, "Is there no help—no pity—no one to save us?" and then fainted away on her husband's bosom, who, turning to one of his mates, said, with quivering lips, "You are a happy man; you have nothing to embitter your last moments—Oh, Providence! was I permitted to escape so many dangers, merely that I might suffer this misery?"

"Is there a little hope?" exclaimed one; "Oh, God grant it may be so. How dreadful to die in the midst of the ocean, far from friends and home, and then to be thrown into the deep!"

"There is one thing," said the captain, faintly, "I was going to tell you, that—but this sensation—I mean a remedy."

"Speak on," cried the first mate, in breathless suspense.

"It may have a chance of saving you," continued the former; "you must immediately—"

He gave a deep sigh, and dropped his head upon his shoulder, apparently unable to utter a word more.

"Oh, this is the worst of all," cried Mrs. Day, in agony; "he was on the point of telling us how to counteract the effects of the poison. Was it heavenly mercy that deprived him of the power of speech?—can it be called mercy?"

"Hush, hush! you rave," returned her husband; "we have only to be resigned now. Let us at least die together."

The men on deck had dined about an hour and a half before those of the cabin, and consequently felt the effects of the poison much earlier than they did.

Every one, except our two friends, however, now began to exhibit alarming symptoms.

Some became delirious. The mate lay upon the cabin floor in a state of torpidity; and the captain had drowned all sense and recollection by drinking a large quantity of brandy.

Mrs. Day watched her husband and her sister alternately, in a state of quiet despair.

Suddenly the steersman called out, "Taken all aback here."

A voice, which sounded like that of the mate, immediately answered, "Well, and what's that to us? Put her before the wind, and let her go where she pleases."

It was soon perceived, by the rushing of the water, that there was a great increase in the velocity of the ship's progress.

The man at the helm tied a rope round the tiller, and he had become so blind and dizzy that he could neither steer nor see the compass, and would, therefore, fix the rudder in such a manner as would keep the ship's head as near the wind as possible.

On going forward to the bows Evelina found the crew lying motionless in every direction.

They were either insensible of the dangerous situation in which the vessel was, or totally indifferent to it; and all representations on this head failed to draw forth an intelligible remark from any of them.

The ship carried a great deal of canvas, the lower studding sails being up, for they had enjoyed a gentle breeze directly astern, before the wind headed them in the way already mentioned.

About an hour after sunset almost every person on board seemed to have become worse.

Evelina and Rose alone retained their senses unimpaired.

The wind now blew very fresh, and they went through the water at the rate of ten miles an hour.

The night looked dreary and turbulent.

The sky was covered with large fleeces of broken clouds, and the stars flashed angrily through them as they were wildly hurried along by the blast.

The sea began to run high, and the masts showed by their incessant creaking, that they carried more sail than they could well sustain.

Evelina stood alone near the stern of the ship.

Nothing could be heard above or below deck, but the dashing of the surges and the moanings of the wind.

All the people on board were to her the same as dead; and she was tossed about, in the vast expanse of waters, with but one companion and fellow sufferer.

She knew not what might be her fate, or where she should be carried.

The vessel, as it careered along the raging deep, uncontrolled by human hands, seemed under the guidance of a relentless demon, to whose caprices its ill-fated crew had been mysteriously consigned by some superior power.

Evelina was filled with dread lest they should strike upon rocks, or run ashore, and often imagined that the clouds which bordered the horizon were the black cliffs of some desolate coast.

At length she distinctly saw a light at some distance.

She anticipated instant destruction.

She grew irresolute whether to remain upon deck, and face death, or to wait for it below.

She soon discovered a ship a little way ahead—she instinctively ran to the helm, and loosed the rope that tied the tiller, which at once bounded back and knocked her over.

A horrible crashing and loud cries now broke upon her ear, and she saw that they had got entangled with another vessel.

But the velocity with which they swept along rendered the extrication instantaneous; and on looking back she saw a ship, without a bowsprit, pitching irregularly among the waves, and heard the rattling of cordage and a tumult of voices.

But, after a little time, nothing was distinguishable by the eye or by the ear.

Her situation appeared doubly horrible.

When Evelina reflected that she had just been within call of human creatures, who might have saved and assisted all on board, had not an evil destiny hurried them along, and made them the means of injuring those who alone were capable of affording relief.

About midnight the fore-topmast gave way, and fell upon deck with a tremendous noise.

The ship immediately swung round, and began to labour in a terrible manner, while several waves broke over her successively.

Evelina had just resolved to descend the gangway for shelter, when a white figure rushed past her with a wild shriek, and sprang overboard.

She saw it struggling among the billows, and tossing about its arms distractedly, but had no means of affording it any assistance.

She watched it for some time, and observed its convulsive motions gradually grow more feeble; but its form soon became undistinguishable amidst the foam of the bursting waves.

The darkness prevented her from discovering who had thus committed himself to the deep, in a moment of madness, and she felt a strong repugnance at attempting to ascertain it, and rather wished that it might have been some spectre, or the offspring of her perturbed imagination, than a human being.

As the sea continued to break over the vessel she went down to the cabin, after having closely shut the gangway doors and companion.

Total darkness prevailed below.

She addressed the captain and all her fellow-passengers by name, but received no reply from any of them, though she sometimes fancied she heard moans and quick breathing, when the tumult of waters without happened to subside a little.

But she thought that it was perhaps imagination, and that they were probably all dead.

She began to catch for breath, and felt as if she had been immured in a large coffin along with a number of corpses, and was doomed to linger out life beside them.

The sea beat against the vessel with a noise like that of artillery, and the crashing of the bulwarks, driven in by its violence, gave startling proof of the danger that threatened them.

Having several times been dashed against the cabin walls by the violent pitching of the ship, Evelina groped for her bed, and lay down in it, and, notwithstanding the horrors that surrounded her, gradually dropped asleep.

When she awoke she perceived, by the sunbeams that shone through the skylight, that the morning was far advanced.

The ship rolled violently at intervals, but the noise of winds and waves had altogether ceased.

She got up hastily, and almost dreaded to look round, lest she should find her worst anticipations concerning her companions too fatally realised.

She immediately discovered the captain lying on one side of the cabin quite dead.

Opposite him was the first mate, stretched along the floor, and grasping firmly the handle of the door of his wife's apartment.

He had, in a moment of agony, wished to take farewell of the partner of his heart, but had been unable to get beyond the spot where he now lay.

He looked like a dying man, and Mrs. Day. who sat beside him, seemed to be exhausted with grief and terror.

She tried to speak several times, and at last succeeded in informing Evelina that her sister was better.

Evelina could not discover the second mate anywhere, and therefore concluded that he was the person who had leaped overboard the preceding night.

On going upon deck she found that everything wore a new aspect.

The sky was dazzling and cloudless, and not the faintest breath of wind could be felt.

The sea had a beautiful bright green colour, and was calm as a small lake, except when an occasional swell rolled from that quarter in which the wind had been the preceding night ; and the water was so clear that she saw to the bottom, and even distinguished little fishes sporting around the keel of the vessel.

Four of the seamen were dead, but the others had so far recovered as to be able to walk across the deck.

The ship was almost in a disabled state.

Part of the wreck of the foretopmast lay upon her bows, and the rigging and sails of the mainmast had suffered much injury.

The day passed gloomily.

They regarded every cloud that rose upon the horizon as the forerunner of a breeze, which they above all things feared to encounter.

Much of their time was employed in preparing for the painful but necessary duty of interring the dead.

The carpenter soon got ready a sufficient number of boards, to each of which they bound one of the corpses, and also weights enough to make it sink to the bottom.

About ten at night they began to commit the bodies to the deep.

A dead calm had prevailed the whole day, and not a cloud obscured the sky.

The sea reflected the stars so distinctly, that it seemed as if they were consigning their departed companions to a heaven as resplendent as that above them.

There was an awful solemnity, alike in the scene and in the situation.

The sea sparkled around each, as its sullen plunge announced that the waters were closing over it, and they all slowly and successively descended to the bottom, enveloped in a ghastly glimmering brightness, which enabled them to trace their progress through the motionless deep.

When these last offices were performed, they retired in silence to different parts of the ship.

About midnight the mate ordered the men to put down the anchor, which, till then, they had not been able to accomplish.

They likewise managed to furl most of the sails, and they went to bed under the consoling idea that, though a breeze did spring up, the moorings would enable them to weather it without any risk.

Evelina was roused early next morning by a confused noise upon deck.

When she got there, she found the men gazing intently over the side of the ship, and she inquired if the anchor held fast.

" Ay, ay," returned one of them, " rather faster than we want it."

On approaching the bulwarks, and looking down, she perceived, to her horror and astonishment, all the corpses lying at the bottom of the sea, as if they had just been dropped into it.

They could even distinguish their features glimmering confusedly through the superincumbent mass of ocean.

A large block happened to fall overboard, and the agitation which it occasioned in the sea produced an apparent augmentation of their number, and a horrible distortion of their limbs and countenances.

A hundred corpses seemed to start up and struggle wildly together, and then gradually to vanish among the eddying waters, as they subsided into a state of calmness.

They were now exempted from the ravages and actual presence of death, but his form haunted them without intermission.

They hardly dared to look over the ship's side, lest their eyes should encounter the ghastly features of some one who had formerly been a companion, and at whose funeral rites they had recently assisted.

The seamen began to murmur among themselves, saying that they would never be able to leave the spot where they then were, and that the vessel would rot away as fast as the dead bodies that lay beneath it.

In the evening a strong breeze sprung up, and filled them with hopes that some vessel would soon come in sight, and afford them relief.

At sunset, when the mate was giving directions about the watch, one of the seamen cried out,

" Thanked be God, there they are."

And the other ran up to him, saying,

" Where, where ?"

He pointed to a flock of Mother Carey's chickens that had just appeared astern, and began to count how many there were of them.

Evelina inquired what was the matter, and th eman replied,

" Why only that we've seen the worst, that's all. I've a notion that we fall in with a sail before twenty hours are past."

" Have you any particular reason for thinking so ?"said Evelina.

" To be sure I have," returned he ; " aren't them there birds the spirits of those brave fellows we threw overboard last night ? I knew we never would be able to quit this place till they made their appearance above water. However, I'm not quite sure how it may go with us yet," continued he, looking anxiously astern ; " they stay rather long about our ship." " Ah," said he, " they say experience teaches fools, and I have found it so ; there was a time when I did not believe that these creatures were anything but common birds, but now I know another story. Oh, I've witnessed such strange things !— Isn't it reasonable to suppose that these little creatures, having once been as such we are, should feel a sort of friendliness towards a ship's crew, and wish to give warning when bad weather or bad fortune is ahead, that every man may be prepared for the worst ?"

" Do you conceive," said another, " that any people but seamen are ever changed into the birds we have been talking of ?"

" No, for certain not," answered the man ; " and none but the sailors that are drowned, or thrown overboard after death. While in the form of Carey's chickens they undergo a sort of purgatory, and are punished for their sins. They fly about the wide ocean, far out of sight of land, and never find a place whereon they can rest the soles of their feet till it pleases the Lord to release them from their bondage, and take them to himself.'

Next morning Evelina was awakened by the joyful intelligence that a schooner was in sight, and that she had hoisted her flag in answer to their signals.

She bore down upon them with a good wind, and in about an hour hove to, and spoke them.

When they had informed them of their unhappy situation, the captain ordered the boat to be lowered, and came on board of the vessel, with three of his crew.

He was a thick, short, dark-complexioned man, and his language and accent discovered him to be a native of America.

The man in command immediately proceeded to detail minutely all that had happened to us, but the visitor paid very little attention to the narrative, and soon interrupted it by asking of what the cargo consisted.

Having been satisfied on this point, he said, " Seeing as how things stand I conclude you'll be keen for getting into some port ?"

" Yes ; that, of course, is our earnest wish," replied the man, " and we hope to be able, by your assistance, to accomplish it."

" Ay, we must all assist one another," returned the captain. " Well, I was just calculating that your plan would be to run into the first port. I'm bound for St. Thomas's, and you can't expect that I should turn about, and go right back with you, neither that I should let you have any of my seamen; for I'll not be able to make a good trade unless I get *slick* into port. Now, I have three *nigger* slaves on board of me ; curse them, they don't know much about sea matters, and are as lazy as hell; but keep flogging them, *mister*—keep flogging them, I say— by which means you will make them serve your ends. Well, as I was saying, I will let you have them blacks to help you if you'll buy them of me at a fair price, and pay it down in hard cash."

"This proposal,' said the man, " sounds strange enough to a British seaman. And how much do you ask for your slaves ?'

" I can't let them go under three hundred dollars each," replied the captain; " I guess they would fetch more in St. Thomas's, for they're prime, I swear."

" Why, there isn't that sum of money on board this vessel that I know of," answered the man; " and though I could pay it myself, I'm sure the owners never would agree to indemnify me. I thought you would have afforded us every assistance without asking anything in return—a British sailor would have done so, at least."

" Well, I vow you are a strange man," said the captain. " Isn't it fair that I should get something for my *niggers*, and for the chance I'll run of spoiling my trade at St. Thomas's, by making myself short of men ? But we shan't split about a small matter, and I'll lessen the price by twenty dollars ahead."

" It's out of the question, sir," cried the man, " I have no money."

" Oh! there's no harm done," returned the captain; we can't trade, that's all. Get ready the boat, boys—I guess your men will soon get smart again ; and then, if the weather holds moderate, you'll reach port with the greatest of ease."

" You surely do not mean to leave us in this barbarous way ?" cried Evelina.

" Well, ma'am, I've got owners," replied he, " and my business is to make a good voyage for them. Markets are pretty changeable just now, and it won't do to spend time talking about humanity—money's the word with me."

Having said this he leaped into the boat, and ordered his men to row towards his own vessel.

As soon as they got on board they squared their topsail, and bore away, and were soon out of sight.

They looked at one another for a little time with an expression of quiet despair ; and then the seamen began to pour forth a torrent of invectives and abuse against the heartless and avaricious shipmaster, who had inhumanly deserted them.

When the captain first came on board all were filled with rapture, thinking that they would certainly be delivered from the perils and difficulties that environed them, but, as the conversation proceeded, their hopes gradually diminished, and the conclusion of it made Mrs. Day give way to a flood of tears, in which Evelina found her indulging when she went below.

The third mate now endeavoured to encourage the seamen to exertion.

They cleared away the wreck of the fore-topmast, which had hitherto encumbered the deck, and put up a sort of jurymast in its stead, on which they rigged two sails.

When these things were accomplished they got up their moorings, and laid their course for the Land's End.

The mate had fortunately been upon the course before, and was aware of the difficulties he would have to encounter in navigating them.

The weather continued moderate ; and, after two days of agitating suspense, they made the land.

CHAPTER LXV.

CLIFFORD MEETS HERNE THE HUNTER ONCE MORE— THE DEMON OF THE FOREST TELLS HIM A TALE OF HORROR, AND TEMPTS HIM TO THE CASTLE—THE TALE OF THE BETRAYED—A MEETING.

CLIFFORD took the earliest opportunity of sending the Duchess and her maid from the forest.

He placed them under the care of Bill Waters, and bade him see them safe to London, and then return.

" I dare not go and leave you here alone," said Bill.

" And I would not be selfish enough to take him from your side," added the Duchess.

" Psha," said Clifford, " I have no fears, so prythee let me have my way."

It took a long time to induce the Duchess to consent to this course, but at length she yielded to Clifford's importunities, and, under the care of Bill Waters, was soon on the road to London.

The only thing that induced Waters to leave Clifford for an instant was the hope he had of getting together a sufficient number of men to assist him in the extermination of Wild, and fathoming the mystery of Windsor Forest.

*   *   *   *   *

It was night, and Clifford was keeping watch in the forest.

Suddenly a sound with which he was now tolerably acquainted, fell upon his ear, and turning his head he beheld Herne the Hunter close by his side.

Clifford started, but, regaining his composure, he boldly confronted the demon.

" So," cried Herne, " you bear yourself bravely."

" Why should I not ?"

" Why, indeed ! But most people shudder at the sight of me."

Clifford shrugged his shoulders.

" I like your indifference," continued Herne, " and I like you on other grounds, and would serve you."

" I don't desire your service," said Clifford.

" Be not too sure of that."

"I repeat, I desire not your services."

"You may."

"Never."

"I repeat, you may."

"I repeat, never."

"The point is not worth arguing, but we shall see."

"We shall."

"And now to the real business that brings me here. I have been seeking you through the forest."

"For what purpose?"

"Because I know you are chivalrous and brave, and because I can entrust a mission to you which I cannot myself perform."

"I will execute none of your missions."

"Indeed! Then I have been deceived in you. I thought Clifford would serve a woman, even at the bidding of the devil himself."

"I *would!*"

"So I believed, or I should not have troubled about you. Listen. In the castle yonder lies a young girl, brought thither by the kingly lord of these domains. In the forest my power is paramount; in the castle I am useless. Therefore, I ask you to enter the place and snatch from bondage and from a life of terrible shame, the girl you shall find a prisoner in the upper chamber of the curfew tower."

"The curfew tower!"

"Yes ; you can see it even from here. Enter as you will, but be sure to enter and perform the mission I have entrusted to you."

"But why should I be selected for this task?"

"No matter. You would be avenged upon Jonathan Wild ! The only means you will ever again have of executing your purpose will be by my aid, and that aid you will not have without obeying my commands. Go to the tower, release the woman and bring her to the forest. Then I will show you how to avenge yourself on Jonathan Wild."

The demon mounted and vanished as he spoke.

Clifford hesitated.

He liked not this task, and yet to refuse to execute it was to evince a fear which he was far from feeling.

He lingered on the proposition of Herne for some time and at last determined on attempting to execute the task set down for him.

"At least," said Clifford, "there can be no more harm in visiting yonder old tower than in remaining here. I will go, and Heaven direct me."

*   *   *   *

He hastened away as he spoke, and a short ride brough him to the curfew tower.

Escaping the sentinel, he effected an entrance into the old tower, and ascending through two large rooms or lofts, at length found himself in the topmost storey of the building.

Sitting disconsolately on a rough bench was a young and beautiful girl.

Clifford approached and touched her on the shoulder. She started to her feet.

"Who and what are you ?" she cried.

"I am a friend," answered Clifford, "and I am here to save you."

"To save me ?"

"Yes ; to save you."

"Alas! are you sure you have it in your power?"

"I believe so."

"I doubt it."

"No matter. Let me try. I will do so if I can."

"But why do you take this interest in one so fallen and base?"

Clifford paused.

"I see you know nothing of my story," said the girl, "begone, and leave me to my fate."

"Never," said Clifford, "never ! I care not what your

life may have been ; I only know that you are unfortunate, and that I can save you from an unhappy position. Come with me."

"Not until I have told you all."

"All what ?"

"The history of my wrongs. When you have heard my tale, I will leave you to reflect whether it will be worth your while to attempt my deliverance from this place."

Clifford listened, and the young girl spoke as follows :—

"I am called Adèle.

"My parents I never knew.

"Both died, I believe, when I was very young, and I was brought up under the care of my father's sister and her husband.

"My parents were wealthy, and occupied a high position. My uncle inherited their wealth, and out of that kept me on his bounty.

"A certain position was accorded me, but not that which was mine by right.

My uncle had sons, to one of whom it was his wish I should be united.

"The one he had selected for me was his youngest Charles, and at a very early age I was to be led to the altar, to be sacrificed to one for whom, if I entertained any feeling, it was one of the most disdainful contempt.

"Young as I was, I had a naturally strong mind, and I refused to be bartered away in such a manner.

"Besides, I had learned to love a young sculptor, Marcus by name, to whom I had resolved, if to any, my hand should be given.

"My uncle made but little comment when I informed him of my resolve.

"His son was present, and I could see by the cunning look that passed between them that they were prepared for my refusal, and determined to effect by other means what they could not fairly attain.

"That look put me on my guard, but for some time nothing occurred to justify my suspicions.

"But one night—

"Shall I ever forget it ?

"I was awoke suddenly by a noise in my room.

"My horror may be conceived when I saw, by the light of the struggling moon, the features of Charles and his villanous parent.

"Seeing that I was awake, the treacherous Charles came to my bedside, and told me, in a tone of cold-blooded atrocity, that he had come to subject me to that treatment which should overcome my scruples respecting the marriage, and make me more anxious than otherwise.

"My black-hearted uncle had projected this scheme, and had come to witness its consummation, and to aid, lest my strength should be too great for his cowardly son."

Clifford shuddered, and the hapless reciter of so sad a history resumed :—

"The elder miscreant then, with a fiendish grimace, seized me by the shoulders, and held me, that his son might effect his diabolical purpose.

"I was endowed with a sudden power.

"My shrieks ran through the house.

"I struggled fearfully with my atrocious assailants.

"But of what avail is even the maddened strength of a woman against that of two determined men ?

"My struggles grew weaker, and I felt that, sooner or later, I must yield to the terrible outrage.

"But my screams increased in fury, and just as my power of resistance totally departed, and the trembling Charles (who was appalled by my screams) had seized me in his loathsome embrace, a loud knocking at the street door alarmed them, and became so continuous and imperative, that my uncle, becoming fearful as to who it might be, descended to ascertain, leaving his cowardly son with me.

"Knowing that I only had him to contend against, and deeming that perhaps some one, attracted by my screams, had come to my assistance, I shrieked more violently, and, gaining fresh strength, fought with the terrified Charles, whom my wildness had rendered as timid as a child.

" I had just succeeded in beating him off, when steps were heard outside, and my uncle entered, followed by a tall man in a cloak.

" I instantly besought his aid, imploring him to save me from his violence ; but stopped suddenly in my appeal when I caught sight of his face.

" I remembered him too well to hope for assistance : it was the face of one who, more than once, had beset me with the importunities of his suit, and had even, in the excess of his passion, when I had repulsed him with scorn, offered to make me his wife by a Catholic marriage.

" In the circles to which, by right of my parent's rank, I had access, I had more than once been compelled to listen to his insulting proffer.

" I felt, indeed, helpless when I found who it was that my screams had summoned.

"Those terrible wretches, my uncle and cousin, immediately, and to my horror, informed him that I was mad, and that their greatest endeavours had only succeeded in preventing me from doing murder ; to my surprise he gave no credence to the assertion, but, approaching me, took my hand, and placed his own on my hot and panting brow.

" ' She is not mad,' he said sternly, ' though you have well nigh driven her so ; let her receive no further harm at your hands, or I myself will see her wrongs amply atoned for.'

" He then addressed himself to me, adding, in a tone of strange tenderness—

" ' Lady, you have sustained great indignities at the hands of those who should most have protected you ; after what has already occurred between us I will not insult you by offering you that protection which you have rightly, though to my sorrow, declined ; yet, if you would see yourself justified, and these outrages avenged, seek me at my palace, and I will see that in everything justice is accorded you.'

" I was amazed at his words.

" His tones were so mild and his looks seemed to bespeak such pity, that I felt disposed to confide in him ; and when he respectfully and tenderly raised my hand to his lips, and angrily bade my brutal relations send fit attendance to me, and to beware how they offered me further indignity, my heart was strangely drawn towards him, and I felt a gratitude I could not express.

" He left ; my uncle, awed by his manner, retired with his son ; and my aunt, who, if cognisant of their purpose, affected total ignorance, came with my maid to my assistance.

" I concealed from my lover the outrage to which I had been subjected, knowing too well the results his hot temper would infallibly lead to ; and, believing that I should have no further molestation, did not avail myself of the offer of the nobleman (for he was of high rank) who had opportunely aided me.

" But by accident I again encountered him, when, from what he informed me, I discovered that what I had always suspected was true—the estates of which my evil relatives were enjoying the benefits were lawfully mine, and they had defrauded me of their possession.

" He told me this, and affecting such interest as a father might take in a daughter, offered to aid me in their recovery.

" I was not insensible of the insults I had received from my relatives, and I eagerly grasped at the opportunity of retaliating upon them and reducing them to beggary.

" It was a fatal resolve.

" Brought more frequently into the society of my defender, treated by him with uniform kindness and re-
pe ct, the feelings which I had first entertained towards him wore off, and I learned to look upon him with grateful regard.

"I will not tell you how he made the most of the change of my sentiments towards him—how he painted in glowing colours the position I was fitted and entitled to occupy—how he hinted at rank, a coronet, and all the elegances which instil ambition, and make life proudly desirable.

" It is enough.

" I was young, reputed beautiful, and proud

" Honeyed flattery effected what dazzling offers, which only showed me as a being to be raised by depravity to superior rank, had failed to accomplish.

" Step by step I was weaned from my love for Marcus —step by step I became deeper in the entangling meshes —till at length one fatal night saw me, the dazzling bauble of rank yet before my eyes, his winning flattery singing in my ears, enter here within his castle, his too blind dupe—his willing paramour.

" Don't wrong me.

" Foolish, vain as I was, I deemed not that I was consenting to a life of infamy.

" When, in the seclusion of my chamber, he fell upon his knees, and, grasping my hand, shed his burning tears upon it, while he poured out the adoration of his impassioned soul, and conjuring me, in love's pleading and most fervent tones, to trust myself with him for one night —one night of intoxicating happiness, as he expressed it, and which his eager soul could no longer bear delayed— swore, by the remembrance of his noble race, that the morning should see me, in pride and magnificence, allied to him at the altar. I could not withstand.

" I was not ice, nor marble.

" I was but a woman—nay, a youthful girl—grateful to one who had done so much to serve me, and whose love was freely poured out before me.

" I was delirious with excitement.

" I could not think.

" I only murmured a faint acquiescence.

" His arms were round me, his hot lips pressed to mine, and in the fulness of this draught of love my soul was melted to yielding tenderness.

" A carriage was at the door.

" In this we hastily entered.

" We left the house that my cruel relatives might not discover that he had remained all night in my chamber.

" Oh, mad that I was !

" I had consented to grant his passion that indulgence.

" My maid accompanied us, and I knew not that it was to this castle I was being conducted till I found myself within its solid walls.

" Oh, God ! that man should so deceive—that when the tongue drops honey the soul should flow with gall !

" When he held me in his arms that night, his ravishing accents—his grateful protestations—reconciled me to the rashness of my act.

" The morning come, I dared not look in his face, but took my hot head from his burning bosom, and faintly mentioned marriage.

" They who have seen the darkening storm sweep over the beauty of a gorgeous sunset may conceive the change that came over his features.

" It was the change from the Archangel to Satan.

" I was appalled.

" And when his hideous laughter fell on my ears, and he scoffingly told me where I was and what I was, oh, heaven ! it sent every drop of my fevered blood like icicles through my frozen veins.

" I did not speak.

" I did not reproach him.

" I was stricken dumb ; and, as his mocking taunt jarred on my ears, and he told me how he had planned my ruin, and how those I had deemed I was triumphing over had aided him in his villany, I could only gaze upon him in speechless terror until, in the rigidity and pallor of my features, he thought he traced death."

The narrator paused, the colour had fled her cheek, her lips were hueless, and quivering, and in her eyes the big tears gathered, like two fine diamonds.

A moment she was painfully agitated, and then, dashing the tears from her eyebrows, she resumed—

"Thus, by his villany and my credulity had he triumphed: and I, too humiliated to think of returning where I might be seen and recognised, made no use of the chance of escape he afforded me, for he had accomplished his purpose, and I might wander or die.

"I remained till imprisonment became irksome, and I longed to go, that I might roam in wretchedness over the globe; but he, with the devilry of his nature, laughed at my desire for freedom, and kept me here.

"So the days passed.

"Days and weeks of shame and bitterness.

"One day when, as usual, I sought my chamber, in order that I might weep and pray, I perceived upon my table a man's glove.

"As I laid my hand upon it, surprised at it being there, I heard a light step behind me.

"I turned and shrieked.

"I stood face to face with him I had so cruelly wronged, Marcus.

"There was more of sadness than reproach in his look, and when I cast myself at his feet, and besought him, degraded thing as I was, to spurn me and despise me, he raised me gently from the ground, and suffered my guilty head to lie upon his bosom.

"Often in innocence had my head lain there; often in guileless love had I looked in those earnest eyes, and gazed on that fervent countenance; and now, what was I?—a wretched minion, a thing of guilt, unfit even to breathe the same air with him.

"Yet, with his nobleness of soul, he kissed away the tears that trickled down my cheeks, he held me to his heart, and in tones whose rich familiar softness awoke the brilliant memories of the past, said—

"'Adèle, I know by what foul arts that devil incarnate has triumphed: I know, too, the misery of your weary existence; you have sinned, but not willingly. By that love which once you bore me, let me lead you from this house of infamy; come with me to my home—more humble it is that this gilded pandemonium, but there, at least, guilt does not raise its polluting head: contentment will be there, and love, if you will come, the past shall be forgot, and as my lawful, honoured wife, you shall yet gain that happiness this miscreant has dashed from your lips, though not for ever.'

"Oh! how noble he looked; I could have worshipped him.

"I grovelled in the dust.

"I lavished kisses on his feet.

"I pressed my lips where his feet had trod.

"I thanked him.

"But to leave with him!

"To go to his honest heart!

"A thing of infamy!

"A rich man's cast-away!

"The offspring of illicit guilt maturing to its birth!

"I could not—I would not.

"I refused.

"He pleaded—oh! how fervently.

"He strove to drag me away.

"I resisted.

"Shrieked, for I would not dishonour him.

"My cries brought others to my apartment.

"He came with them.

"Black passion was on his brow.

"Red anger in his eye.

"He called on his men to seize Marcus, and drag him to a dungeon: but ere the words had well left his lips, the youth sprang upon him and dragged him to the floor.

"A dagger flashed in air, and that moment had ended the miscreant's life, but that beneath his robe was a panoply of mail, which turned aside the point, and saved his foul heart from the avenging blow.

"They seized him then, and with his last glance of tenderness beaming upon me, he was dragged away, spite of my shrieks and entreaties, wrung from my heart in its bitterness.

"Time passed on.

"Still I was a captive.

"I saw my lover no more.

"But once, when in my desolation, the void in my heart was as wormwood, he came, and with the smile of the Evil One on his lips, bade me follow.

"Dreading some terrible confirmation of my harrowing fears, I dragged by trembling limbs along.

"He led me down deep beneath the castle's base, to a small dark hole like a hideous coffin.

"He bade me enter, and look upon its inmate.

"When my eyes had become accustomed to the gloom, I put forth my hand and touched the only object I could perceive.

"*It was a skeleton.*

"My conductor brought forth a lamp, and mockingly asked me if I could recognise the features.

"Features! in that eyeless skull, with the grinning, horrid teeth!

"I shuddered and shivered till I fell beside it.

"I had not seen all.

"On the bony finger of one fleshless hand I saw a ring.

"Oh, heavens! how well I remembered it; in our early days of love I had given it to Marcus.

"My shrieks of horror moved not the cold fiend who stood over me.

"He smiled at my despair.

"And I heard his cold, awful laugh as I sank fainting beside all that remained of the noble-souled Marcus."

"Adèle ceased: her tones were faltering and faint: emotion seemed choking her, and when Clifford, in tender sympathy, wound his arms round her, she uttered a half shriek, and seemed to die in frozen anguish.

"In his interest for that sad recital Clifford had forgotten his errand.

For some time both sat in silence.

Then Clifford spoke.

"Alas! you have indeed experienced misery; cruel, indeed, must be the heart, and evil the nature of this terrible being. You have spoken of a maid who accompanied you. Was she, too, an accomplice in this deed?'

"She loved me too well. Of her fate nothing have I ever discovered, and it is, like other deeds that were they known would shake the earth, plunged in mystery."

Further would Clifford have questioned, but at that instant footsteps were heard outside, and Adèle, rising, said coldly—

"It is *he.*"

Clifford's calmness returned as he heard this mysterious man approaching.

The door was pushed open, and the profligate abductor entered.

CHAPTER LXVI.

EVELINA AND ROSE FREE THEMSELVES FROM THE SOCIETY OF THE CREW OF THE FLYING BETSY—THEY FIND AN ASYLUM IN THE VICARAGE OF ST. LEONARDS.

THE crew of the Flying Betsy were so far pre-occupied by their own distresses to note the doings of others, and so Evelina and Rose managed to get on shore unobserved.

They at once made for the country, not daring to re-

main in Falmouth a single moment for fear of being again thrust into the power of the men from whom Providence had torn them.

They walked for some miles, and at length paused before a little retired vicarage in a parish which we will call St. Leonards.

The vicar, a sad and broken-down gentleman, noted their approach and invited them to enter his humble dwelling.

They found him alone in his sweet cottage, and there was a something in his demeanour that assured them solitude was to him indeed a blessing.

His had been a life of toil and sorrow, and as he is to hereafter figure in our pages we may may as well relate the story of his life.

It was on a Sabbath evening, towards the latter end of the month of July, that the Rev. Mr. Lloyd, of St. Leonards

set forth to visit his daughter Hester, who resided in one of those romantically situated cottages which form so interesting a feature in the scenery of Cornwall.

The distance he had to go was scarcely a mile; but the walk was toilsome, for his path lay among the hills, through which it was rudely cut, and the loose fragments of rock on which he trode gave away at every step.

His thoughts, however, were too much occupied with the sad object of his visit to permit of his heeding the rugged road or even the sublime beauties of nature which were spread around him.

Hester was his eldest daughter, and the eldest also of nine brothers and sisters—a large family to feed, clothe, and educate, upon the scanty stipend of his curacy, though eked out by a small patrimonial property, and a fortune of two hundred pounds, which he had with his wife.

When all was put together, and the profits of a small school added, as well as those which he received from the sale of a quarto volume, Parson Lloyd was a somewhat poorer man than his neighbour, Farmer Morgan, who always boasted that he could spend a hundred and twenty pounds a-year, and pay every body his own.

But Farmer Morgan, at last, did not pay everybody his own ; for he went into the *Gazette*, and ther were only three shillings in the pound for his creditors, while Parson Lloyd contrived to make both ends meet ; perhaps, because he took care never to have a creditor, always deferring the purchase of anything he wanted till he could spare the money to pay for it.

" He who makes his necessities wait upon his means," he would often say, " will never find them troublesome ; but reverse the order, and let your means be the drudges of your necessities, and, run as fast as they may, they will never overtake them."

Hester Lloyd had married Farmer Morgan's second son, David ; and it was always said, by those who pretended to know the secret, that she did so, more from a desire to diminish the heavy burden of her father's family than from any violent affection she had for the young man.

To say the truth, they were a mismatched pair.

David was a coarse rustic, of violent passions, a moody temper, and suspected of dissolute habits.

Hester, on the contrary, was mild and gentle in disposition. affectionate, and trained up in the strict observance of those simple, unobtrusive virtues which became the comparative humility of her station, and the character of her parental roof.

When, therefore, she married David Morgan, some shook their heads, and pitied the poor girl for the sacrifice she made ; while others turned up their eyes, and wondered how even love could be so blind.

The union had neither the approbation nor the disapprobation, properly so called, of Hester's father.

She was of an age to choose discreetly (having passed her three-and-twentieth year), when, as was certainly her case, the heart did not take the lead in choosing ; and he left her, therefore, to decide for herself, after temperately discussing with her, upon several occasions, whatever might fairly be urged in favour, or to the prejudice, of the young man.

Hester, herself, took a twelvemonth to consider of her decision ; and, finally, yielded her consent to the pertinacious, rather than the ardent, solicitations of David Morgan.

It has been said by an ancient cynic, that marriage has only two happy days, the *first* and the *last ;* but Hester was doomed to find even this stinted portion of matrimonial felicity too liberal an allowance.

On their return from church, an unfortunate difference arose between her husband and her father upon some trifling subject of rural economy—the breeding of pigs, or the cultivation of barley, or some matter not a whit more important.

David was loud, overbearing, and, at last, insolently rude.

Nay, he so far forgot himself, at one moment, that his hand was raised to seize Mr. Lloyd by the collar.

" Forbear, young man !" said the reverend pastor, mildly ; " and learn to have more command over your passions, or they will one day hurry you into conduct which all the rest of your days may not be sufficient to atone for."

David felt the rebuke.

He felt ashamed.

He saw the cheek of Hester turn pale, and he felt sorrow for what he had done.

But his father-in-law also felt the indignity that had been offered to him, and he slowly walked away towards his own house.

Hester looked after him.

She said nothing.

She only thought, as she leaned upon her husband's arm, and proceeded silently towards *his* father's house, —what a change one little half hour had wrought in her condition !

Her now obedient steps went one way ; her heart, at that moment, another.

The former taught her she was a wife ; the latter, that she must cease to be a daughter.

It was a sharp lesson to come so early.

She said nothing.

But though her tongue spoke not, the uneasy reflections of David clothed it with words of bitterness ; and he strove, as much as his nature would let him, during the rest of the day, to dispel the gloom with which his violence of temper had clouded the beginning.

Hester was neither angry nor sullen, but she was sad ; and she could not conceal that her sadness was greatest when, as she sat down to dinner, the marriage feast lacked one guest, whose absence was to her, if not the absence of all, at least, the absence of all comfort.

Mr. Lloyd was a sincere Christian.

Without any parade of sanctity he diligently endeavoured, in all his dealings with his fellow-creatures, to fulfil the commands of Him whose minister he was.

He could not, therefore, let the sun go down upon his wrath ; but, like a primitive disciple of his Master, he sought the dwelling of his enemy, with the word of peace and the hand of fellowship.

So pure a judge had he been in his own cause that he considered he had done wrong, very wrong, in suffering himself to be kept away from the wedding table of his daughter by his resentment for a hasty speech uttered by her husband.

" I will go," said he, " and heal this wound before I sleep."

And he did go ; and it was a blessed sight for Hester to behold, as she saw her father enter, with a benignant smile upon his countenance. walk up to her husband, and taking him by the hand, exclaim—

" Son, we have never been enemies ; let us then continue to be friends !"

David was overpowered by this unexpected display of meek goodness, and his voice really faltered as he replied, grasping Mr. Lloyd's hand with honest warmth—

" God forbid we should not."

Hester kissed her father, and wept , but they were tears of much gladness. It was a peaceful evening after this.

Mr. Lloyd showed, by his cheerful conversation and kindly manner, that the spirit of anger had entirely departed from him, and, with it, all recollection of the offence.

David did not shake off quite so soon his remembrance of the morning ; for he was vanquished in spite of himself ; and he felt—as a man generally does who commits a wrong, and finds coals of fire heaped upon his head by the generous conduct of the person whom he has wronged —humbled and ashamed in his presence.

Hester was supremely happy ; for she beheld her father and her husband, side by side, under her own roof.

Months rolled on, and the neighbours began to think David Morgan quite an altered man since his marriage.

He was civil and obliging, went regularly to church every Sunday, rose early to his work, attended to his farm, returned home sober and before dark on market-days, got into no quarrels, smoked his pipe in the evening on a bench before his own door, and drank a pint or two of his own home-brewed ale.

In short, he exhibited all the outward qualities of a steady, thriving, and industrious farmer ; and it was prophesied, if he went on so, that he would soon become a better man than his father by the difference of many an acre added to those which he already rented.

Hester observed this auspicious change, and might almost be called a happy wife.

She was not entirely so; for there were out-breakings of temper at home, lightning-flashes of the mind, and distant thunder-murmurings of the heart, which the eyes and ears of friends and neighbours nor saw nor heard.

The sky was clear above—the sun shone brightly—but the elements of storm and tempest perpetually loured along the horizon, which the first gust of wind would drive into angry collision.

To Hester's watchful eye alone, and to her anxious spirit, were these signs revealed.

She could not conceal from herself the trials and the dangers they hourly menaced; but she could conceal them from all the rest of the world—and she did.

Not even to her father did she speak of them.

They were the griefs of her own foreboding heart, and they were buried there.

If they should ever be disinterred thence—if they should ever be realised, and write themselves in such characters upon her face as she could not hide—if her countenance complained for her—she must submit; but till then, she was resolved hope should chasten fear, and the faith she plighted at the altar forbade her lips to become the accusers of her husband.

It was about two years after her marriage that the bankruptcy of old Morgan happened.

For some months previously Hester suspected matters were going wrong; not from anything which her husband communicated to her, for he had grown reserved, sullen, and morose, but from the manner of the old man himself, from their frequent conferences in secret, and from his total neglect of his farming stock.

David, too, instead of minding his own affairs, and looking after his own crops, or attending the markets, as he was accustomed to do, sold hand over head upon the ground; took the first price that was offered; replaced nothing which he sold, but kept the money, and talked of setting up, by and by, as an innkeeper at Bodmin.

Meanwhile debts were contracted, and none were paid; creditors became clamorous, and David grew more and more reckless of their clamours.

At first he could not pay; at last he would not, and they might do as they liked.

If Hester ventured to remonstrate she was churlishly told to mind her own business, and look after the house, though there was less and less in it to look after; for whatever could be spared, and often what could not, was converted into money.

Old Morgan pursued much the same course; and it seemed as if father and son were striving with each other who should make most speed in the race of destruction.

Thus matters went on from bad to worse, and from worse to worst, for nearly three months; and then old Morgan was made a bankrupt.

Every one predicted that David would soon follow; but everyone lamented it at the same time, on account of poor Hester, who was universally respected.

Indeed, it was mainly owing to this feeling of respect for her that her husband's creditors had not either enforced their claims or thrown him into a prison.

They did not scruple to tell her so; and though she felt grateful for their kindness, she knew it was a forbearance that hung by a very slender thread, and each day she expected to see him dragged to jail.

If that did happen, what was to become of her, far advanced in pregnancy with her second child, and not a roof to shelter her except her father's?

She was sitting one evening, sadly ruminating upon all these things, and expecting David's return, who had gone out early in the morning, she knew not whither, when Jacob Griffiths, a maternal uncle of her husband, a respectable but poor old man, dropped in.

He sat down, and she drew him a mug of ale, which, however he scarcely touched.

She talked to him, first upon one subject, and then upon another; but he hardly answered her, and altogether his behaviour was so strange, that she looked at him as if she thought he had already had a little too much—a failing which she knew sometimes overtook "uncle Jacob."

She was soon convinced, however, that the old man was not now in his cups, whatever else might be the matter with him, for he was leaning forward on his staff, which he held with both his hands, and the tears were trickling down the furrows of his sun-burnt face.

"In the name of heaven, Jacob, what ails you?" said Hester, laying down her work, and going towards him.

"I am thinking," said Jacob, with a heavy groan, that burst from him as he spoke,—"I am thinking, Mrs. Morgan, how my poor sister Jane would have taken it to heart if she were alive now, which, thank God, she is not! But the Lord help us! what we may come to in this world!"

Hester's knees tottered—her colour fled—and she seated herself gently by his side, and she exclaimed in a tremulous voice, "What is the matter, Jacob, that you talk thus?"

The old man shook his head, while he answered, "Matter enough, I fear; but who would have thought it?"

"For God's," sake replied Hester, "tell me what it is you mean. Has anything happened to David?"

"Ay," said Jacob, "and his father too. I was coming into Monmouth to day at noon, and had just crossed, over the Munny bridge, when I saw a sight of people afore me; I walked up to them to find out, if I could, what was going on—and you might have knocked me down with a feather the next moment—for what should I see but David and his father, old George Morgan, handcuffed together like two thieves, and being led to prison!

"They did not see me, and I was glad on't, for I couldn't have spoke a word to them, my tongue stuck so to the roof of my mouth, like.

"I shall never forget how I shook."

"Are you sure you were not mistaken?" inquired Hester, in a tone of voice so thick and inarticulate that Jacob suddenly raised his head from the staff on which he had continued to support it.

"Am I sure this is my right hand?" answered Jacob. "But, Lord preserve you! what ails you, Mrs. Morgan? You look as white as your apron; you are not faintish, sure? Here, take a sup at this ale—'twill warm you, like, and do you good."

Hester was indeed pale enough, and she trembled so violently that Jacob might well suppose she needed something to warm her; but she kept from fainting, and after a few minutes she was able to ask him whether he knew what they had done that they were taken to prison?

"I could not get at the rights of the matter," said Jacob, "but, from what I understood, I should guess it was something about old Morgan's bankrupt job; though I don't see, for my part, how that could concern David."

"Nor I either," replied Hester, wiping her eyes, and sighing as if her heart would break. "But, whatever it is, I have had the dread of it upon my spirits for these many months. I felt certain that some misfortune or other was hanging over me; and it has come at last.

"My husband's conduct was so changed—he had grown so careless about everything, had so entirely neglected his affairs and his home—that I was sure, unless some change for the better took place, nothing but ruin could come of it in the end.

"Oh dear!

"God knows, my situation is bad enough just now, at any rate."

And Hester's tears flowed afresh, as the thought of what her situation was presented itself to her mind.

"Don't take on this way, Mrs. Morgan," said Jacob, "After all, things may not be so bad as they appear ; and, be they never so bad, fretting, you know, won't mend them. It is a sad business, to be sure ; but we must hope for the best. Besides, many an innocent man has been wrongfully suspected, and taken to prison, before now ; and who knows but this may be David's case, ay, and old Morgan's, too ? So keep up your spirits, Mrs. Morgan, and don't grieve. Here, take a drop of ale."

Hester had much cause to grieve.

She had said truly that the conduct of her husband for a long time past had been such as to prepare her for trouble of some kind or other ; and her grief, therefore, on the present occasion was less acute than if she had fallen suddenly from the sunny height of domestic happiness by an unforeseen and unexpected blow.

But who ever found himself sufficiently prepared for misfortune ?

Who, *till* it came, ever ceased to hope that it might *not* come ?

And who, *when* it comes, can say, "I have watched for you so long with a troubled heart, that now you find me without a tear to shed, or a sigh to breathe ?"

Alas ! the stern reality has a pang of its own, unlike that we feel in the most vivid anticipation.

Does the child you love, the mistress you adore, the parents you venerate, lie on the bed of death ?

What though you have whispered this fatal secret to yourself, again, and again, and again ?

What though your spirit have mourned over the dying object, in all the anguish of inevitable bereavement ?

Ah me ! wait till the eye *is* closed, and the tongue *is* mute—for ever ; tarry till the soul *is* departed—till the thing you dreamed is the thing you feel—and then you will know the difference between the fear of losing, ay, and even between what constitutes mere man's certainty of losing, and the miserable certainty that you HAVE lost.

Hester felt this difference.

She had insensibly trained her mind to meet an undefined calamity ; but now, when it came upon her in a specific shape and character, she almost sank beneath the shock.

It was too true what Jacob Griffiths had told her.

David and his father were both in Monmouth jail ; and they were there upon a charge of having contrived, and brought about, a fraudulent bankruptcy in the case of old Morgan, under such circumstances as made it doubtful, at one time, whether their lives would not be forfeited.

Matters, however, were not pushed to that extremity.

They were tried, found guilty, and received sentence of transportation—the father for life, and David for fourteen years.

Hester was far advanced in pregnancy when her husband was thrown into prison ; and the very day on which the judges entered Monmouth she became the unhappy mother of a son, whose father, scarcely more than eight-and-forty hours afterwards, was branded as a felon by the verdict of a just and impartial jury.

She had visited him several times in jail before his trial, and administered to him all the comfort and consolation which it was in her power to bestow, or in his nature to receive ; for it distressed her much to find that he manifested great hardness of heart, and that he was alike insensible to her sufferings and his own disgrace.

But she had not seen him since his trial.

She had not, indeed, been able to get so far, for her recovery, after her lying in, was slow ; and she was extremely delicate and feeble when, at the expiration of about six weeks, she learned, by a harsh letter from her brutal husband, that if she " wanted to see him again," she must go to Bodmin before a day named, as he was on that day to be conveyed, with other convicts, to the seaport, whence they were to embark for New South Wales.

She did wish to see him again ; and it was on the following morning of that very Sabbath evening, in the month of July, when her father set forth to visit her, as already mentioned, that she intended to do so.

Mr. Lloyd was desirous of seeing his daughter, not only to prepare her, by his conversation, for the melancholy task of taking, in all probability, a last farewell of one who, criminal and churlish as he was, was still her husband,—but also to arrange with her the time and manner of proceeding to Bodmin the next morning, whither he intended accompanying her himself.

He found her weeping over her last-born, which lay asleep in her lap.

He did not chide her tears, for they were the natural channels of her grief ; but in his twofold character of her spiritual and paternal monitor, he applied himself to assuage the sorrow which was their fruitful source.

And he had the consolation to observe, ere he departed, that Hester was so far tranquil and resigned, as to discourse calmly upon her approaching interview with David.

In this frame of mind he left her, and in this frame of mind he found her on the following morning, when, at the early hour of five, she met him, as had been agreed upon.

She had her infant in her arms, and was accompanied by a neighbour's daughter, a hale buxom wench about fifteen, who kindly offered to go with her, and help to carry the child, a labour for which the still impaired health and delicate frame of Hester were hardly sufficient.

They set forth, Hester leaning for support upon her father, having, at his suggestion, transferred her sleeping baby to the care of her young companion.

When they arrived in Bodmin, she expressed an eager desire to go at once to the prison, anxious to have the full benefit of her composed and re-animated feelings in the interview with her husband.

It was well she yielded to this desire ; for had there been the further delay of but half a n hour the object of her journey would have been frustrated.

Contrary to what was first intimated to the prisoners, the day fixed for their departure was hastened, in consequence of the transport appointed to receive them having received peremptory orders to sail immediately.

Due notice of this change was given to them all, that they who had friends, and wished to see them, might do so.

But David Morgan did not trouble himself about the matter ; and when Hester, with her child in her arms, presented herself at the prison gates, the vehicle in which the convicts were to proceed to the port of embarkation was already there.

She told her business in a faltering voice, and was conducted by the turnkey to an inner yard, where were assembled about a dozen men, whose scowling looks and ferocious countenances terrified her.

They were mustered preparatory to removal.

Among them stood David and old Morgan, handcuffed together, as were the others.

Hester did not perceive them at first ; but as they slowly approached her, she recognised her husband, and burst into tears.

She was shocked at his altered appearance, for he was now in the dress of a convict, with his hair cut close to his head.

She was still more shocked at beholding the iron manacles which bound him to his father.

She could not speak.

Old Morgan was silent.

David, in a hard, unfeeling tone, while not a feature of his face relaxed from its rigid hardness, merely said, " You are come at last ; I thought you might have found your way here a little sooner."

Hester could only reply by pointing to her baby, with a look of beseeching anguish, which seemed to say,

" Do not upbraid me : you forget I have given birth to this innocent."

The mute appeal appeared to touch him, for he took her hand, and gazing for a moment upon its thin white fingers, and the blue veins that were not used to be so visible, till sickness had made them so, he kissed it.

Hester drew nearer—leaned against her husband's bosom—and raising the infant towards his lips, whose sparkling little eyes unclosed themselves, as if to look upon its father, she exclaimed, in a scarcely articulate voice—

" Kiss it, too, David—kiss our son, and bless him."

The felon father bowed his head and kissed his innocent child, while, with his unfettered arm, he clasped closer to his breast its weeping mother.

Nature asserted her prerogative for an instant ; the husband and the father prevailed over the hardened criminal, and the heart of David owned that he was both.

But the next instant he was neither.

As if he thought it became him to play the churl, even at such a moment, or that he should lose character with his new companions, who were standing round, witnesses of this scene, he put Hester coldly from him, and muttered, as he turned away—

" There—we have had enough of this nonsense."

Before Hester could reply, or remove her handkerchief from her eyes, one of the officers of the prison entered the yard, and ordered the convicts to follow him.

David and old Morgan hurried out the first ; and in less than a minute there were left only Hester, her father, and the girl who had accompanied them.

Mr. Lloyd waited till he heard the rattling of the lumbering machine as it drove off, and he then led Hester out.

He had been a silent and a sad spectator of the interview, and he felt that it would be only an unnecessary pang, added to those she had already endured, if he permitted her to witness the actual departure of her husband.

Her emotions, when he told her that he was gone, satisfied him he had judged rightly, and acted wisely.

They were not those deep and maddening emotions which lacerate the heart when a beloved object is torn from it for ever.

It was impossible they should be.

But Hester had stood at the altar with David.

She was a wife.

He was her husband.

She was a mother.

He was the father of her children.

Ill usage may destroy all the finer sympathies which hallow those relations in a woman's gentle and affectionate nature ; but it is death alone, or its equivalent, eternal separation in this world, that can make her feel she has no longer a husband, and her children no longer a father.

And when that feeling does come, it will wring the bosom with a sorrow unlike any other.

Hester returned to her father's house that day, and remained there thenceforward with her two children.

The cottage which she had occupied since her marriage was given up, and the produce of the little furniture it contained, when sold, her husband's creditors allowed her to keep, out of respect for herself, and pity for her misfortunes.

It was an additional burden which Mr. Lloyd was ill able to bear ; but his trust was in Him whose command it is that we should succour the distressed, protect the fatherless, and do all manner of good.

In the bosom of her family, in the discharge of her maternal duties, in the occupation afforded her by superintending the education of the daughters of some of her neighbours, which enabled her to meet many of her own personal expenses without drawing upon her father's

slender means, and in her peaceful retreat, her mind gradually recovered much of its former tranquillity.

A more pleasing retreat could not easily be found.

In this place did Edmund, the son of David Morgan, pass his youth.

It was his supreme delight, while yet a boy, to wander the livelong day amid the wild and craggy steeps, the tangled thickets, the solitary glens, and the variously wooded slopes of that magnificent amphitheatre, laid out by the hand of nature.

Edmund Morgan was in his thirteenth year.

He was no common boy ; and his grandfather, who had watched the dawnings of his character, moral and intellectual, prided himself upon his cultivation of both.

Enthusiasm was its basis.

In whatever he engaged it was with the whole energy of his nature.

It may be supposed, therefore, that he quickly mastered those branches of knowledge which were within the compass of Mr. Lloyd to teach, and who was also anxious that he should have the advantage of a more comprehensive education.

But how was his benevolent desire to be accomplished ?

He was too poor to pay for it ; and he was too friendless to obtain it from patronage.

Accident, at length—if such events in the life of man may rightly be called accidents—shaped his destiny.

Some trifling circumstance, so unheeded at the time that no distinct recollection of it survived the occurrence, brought him into contact with an eccentric old gentleman of the neighbourhood, who had signalised himself on more than one occasion by the apparent caprice with which he bestowed his bounty.

The last act of the kind which had been talked of was his stocking a small farm for an industrious young man, and giving him besides a hundred pounds to begin with, to whom he had never spoken till he called upon him to announce his intention.

But he had observed him frequently, in his walks, labouring early and late in a little garden which was attached to his cottage ; and had learned, upon inquiry, that he kept an aged mother, and a sister, who was a cripple, out of the workhouse by his scanty earnings.

It was Edmund's good fortune to attract the notice of Squire Jones in the way described ; and it was not long after that he paid a visit to Mr. Lloyd, for the express purpose of asking a few questions about him.

The good old man spoke with pride and affection of his pupil and grandson, but with despondency of his future prospects.

" I have reared him as my own," said he, " from his cradle, and I should close my eyes in peace if I could know, or reasonably hope, so goodly a branch would not be left to float like a worthless weed upon the stream of time."

" He shall be planted," replied Squire Jones.

" Send for the boy. But never mind, just now. You know in what soil he will be most likely to thrive. I shall call again to-morrow. By that time make your choice, and leave the rest to me." ·

The morrow came, the choice was made, and Edmund was to study for the church at Oxford (the great ambition of his youthful mind), upon an ample allowance secured to him by Squire Jones, in such a way as nothing but his own misconduct could forfeit.

If Edmund was the pride of his grandfather, he was no less the idol of his mother, who would sometimes think that Heaven had bestowed such a treasure upon her in compensation for what it had taken away.

Perhaps her love for Edmund was somewhat heightened by the circumstance that she had lost her first child when it was only four years old, and he had become, therefore, her only one ; but, in truth, his own affectionate disposition, his ingenuousness of character, and his intellectual endowments, were of themselves sufficient passports to all the love of a fond mother's heart.

And Hester was a fond mother, though not a weak one.

She looked forward with dejected feelings to the now approaching moment of her first separation from her dear boy; but she was too gratefully conscious of the benefit he was to derive from that separation to repine at it.

There had always been one subject which, whenever it occupied the thoughts of Hester, was most painful and distressing to her.

It was the mystery of Edmund's birth.

She could not tell him his father was a convict, and she had no reason to believe that any one else had done so.

She could not even tell him that he lived.

From the moment of his leaving Bodmin prison, down to that of which we are now speaking, no tidings of him had reached her.

Neither he nor old Morgan had written a single line to any relative or friend they had left behind.

All she ever learned concerning him was that he had arrived safely at New South Wales.

Edmund, when a child, would often talk of his father, merely because the word was constantly upon the lips of his playmates, and because he saw they had fathers.

But as he grew older, and began to reflect, a thousand little circumstances presented themselves to his mind, which convinced him there was some mystery, though he knew not what, that hung over his infancy.

Once, and once only, he asked his mother—

"Who is my father? and where is he?"

But the silent agitation of Hester, for she could not answer him, sealed his lips upon that subject ever afterwards.

Edmund was in his sixteenth year when he went to the University, and he remained there, with the usual visits at home during the vacations, till he was one-and-twenty.

The progress he made in his studies, and the character he bore for strict propriety of conduct, well justified the munificent liberality of his patron.

But he was denied one gratification, that of gladdening his grandfather's pride in him by the display of his scholastic attainments.

The good old man, full of years and ripe in virtue, had breathed his last, from the gradual decay of nature rather than from the inroads of disease, not long after he had seen the wish nearest his heart realised.

Edmund was with him when he died, and he followed him to the grave with feelings which emphatically told him how he could have loved and how mourned—a father!

By the interest of his benefactor (who, the more he saw, and the more he knew of Edmund, found what had originally borne the stamp of a benevolent whim merely, gradually assuming the better quality of a permanent desire to befriend him), the Rectory of St. Leonard's was reserved for his benefit, when he should be duly qualified, by ordination, to assume its pastoral functions.

Meanwhile the place of Mr. Lloyd was supplied by a neighbouring clergyman, to whom the fatigues of double duty were sweetened by something beyond the allotted stipend out of the purse of Squire Jones.

The Rev. Edmund Morgan was in his three-and-twentieth year, when, as the rector of St. Leonard's, he took possession of the little parsonage house in which his youth had been passed, and which was endeared to him by the recollection of almost every incident in his yet spring-tide of life that could shed a charm upon the retrospect.

He brought to his sacred office a larger stock of theological erudition, and a mind naturally of a higher order, than had belonged to his grandfather; but in the purity of his life, in the holiness of his zeal, and in his exemplary discharge of the numerous duties that belong to a faithful minister of the gospel, he had an example ever present to his memory, which it was his constant prayer he might be able to follow.

One only circumstance troubled the calm and peaceful flow of the serene current of his life.

A heavy grief—some untold sorrow—lay like a canker at his mother's heart; its ravages were undermining her health, and contracting, with fearful rapidity, the already too little space which stretched between her and the grave.

Her wan features, her secret tears, whose traces were frequently visible in her swollen eyes when she appeared at the breakfast table, and those unbidden sighs that would burst from her at times, as if her heart were full to breaking, caused Edmund many a sleepless night, and many a waking hour of melancholy thoughts.

There had ever been so much of unreserved communication between himself and his mother upon all things save this one, that he felt he had here no right to intrude upon the sanctuary of her grief, because he concluded she must have sufficient reasons for drawing around it so impenetrable a veil.

When, however, he perceived what inroads it was making upon a life so dear to him, he could no longer be restrained by these delicate considerations.

A higher duty than even the respect inspired by filial obligations—the sacred duty of his calling, which enjoined him to breathe the word of comfort over the wounded and mourning spirit, made him resolve to seek an opportunity of tenderly imploring from his mother a disclosure of the affliction that preyed thus fatally upon her peace of mind.

But ere he found an opportunity, events forced themselves a passage to his ear.

His mother entered his room one morning in extreme agitation.

"You have heard," she said, with a faltering voice, "of the dreadful business that took place last week; the murder, for so it is considered, of one of the Duke of Cornwall's gamekeepers, in a scuffle between him and the poacher, Isaac Price."

"I have," replied Edmund, "and the wretched man will surely be hung if he is taken."

"He is taken," answered Mrs. Morgan, "and lodged in Bodmin jail."

"It is the law of God and man," said Edmund, "that whoso sheddeth the blood of another, his own blood shall be the atonement. This Isaac Price, moreover, is spoken of as a culprit inured to many crimes—one who has walked in the paths of vice all his life. But why is this excessive agitation, my dear mother? What is it that troubles you so grievously, and that has so long troubled you?"

"You shall know, Edmund, for it is better you should hear it from my lips than from those of others, and concealment is now no longer possible. Isaac Price is YOUR father!"

"My father!" exclaimed Edmund; and he spoke not another word.

His mother wept bitterly.

For several minutes they sat in silence; the thoughts of Mrs. Morgan travelling through a miserable past, and those of her son absorbed in the conflict of present amazement and future suffering.

He had found a father, but the first impulse of his feelings was to blush at the discovery.

He had learned the secret of his birth, and the knowledge of it tinged his cheek with shame.

He waited till his mother became more calm, and then prepared to listen to a tale which he knew must deeply afflict him.

She, with as much composure as she could command, related all the circumstances attending her marriage with David Morgan, and of the crime for which he was transported.

But in what she further disclosed, Edmund at once discovered the cause of that ceaseless sorrow which had so long harassed her.

The term of his sentence having expired, and his father being dead, David obtained a passage back to England; and it was in the summer of the year following that in which Edmund went to Oxford, that he reappeared in his native place.

He did not make himself known; and, indeed, his appearance was so altered in the seventeen years he had been absent, that no one could have recognised him at first sight.

But he prowled about the neighbourhood; and one evening, when Hester was walking out alone, he suddenly presented himself before her.

She was alarmed, thinking he was some man who intended to insult, or perhaps rob her.

He called her by name; his voice awakened the recollection of him in her memory, and gazing at him for a moment, she knew it was her husband.

He made a few inquiries about herself, her father, and her children; but told her he never meant to trouble her by claiming her as his wife. "I am poor enough," said he, "and I suppose you are not over rich; but when I want a guinea, I shall not be particular in looking to you for it; and I expect you will not begrudge to get rid of me upon such easy terms. If you have any money in your pocket now, it is more than I have in mine, and a few shillings will be acceptable to me." Hester gave him what she had; but before she could utter a word in reply he had turned upon his heel and entered a coppice by the road-side, observing, as he went away, "Remember, if you wish to be free from David Morgan, you will not deny Isaac Price, whenever he sends or watches for you."

From that time he had continued to persecute her; sometimes with threatening messages, and sometimes by dogging her steps, so that she almost dreaded to leave the parsonage house.

How he contrived to live she could only surmise from what she heard about him, every now and then, as Isaac Price, till at length the affray between him and one of the Duke of Cornwall's gamekeepers led to the awful catastrophe which caused him to be apprehended as a murderer.

Then, too, it began to be whispered in St. Leonards that Isaac Price the poacher was no other than David Morgan, who had been transported upwards of twenty-one years ago, and who was the father of that excellent young man, the Rev. Edmund Morgan.

Edmund listened to this recital with deep attention; and, when it was concluded, he exclaimed, after a short pause—

"Mother, I will see my father. I can do nothing for him in this world, which he must so soon leave: but he is not prepared for the next! and his eternal soul must not perish. I will visit him in prison; talk with him; and, if Almighty God bless my purpose, I may become an instrument, in His hands, for bringing him to the true repentence of a contrite sinner."

There was consolation to Hester's heart in these words of her son; and her sorrow was not without gladness, when she thought of the good work which filial piety might accomplish.

The very next day Edmund went to Bodmin, and procured an interview with Isaac Price.

He did not disclose himself, but assumed the character of a friend of Mrs. Morgan merely, sent by her to know if there were any service which she could render him in his present situation.

It may be imagined with what feelings he beheld, for the first time, him who was his father in the degraded condition of a felon and a murderer.

His appearance was that of a man between fifty and sixty, with a powerful make of body, and a countenance which indicated a rough and daring spirit rather than the prevalence of ferocious passions.

His eye was dull and heavy, and sunk deep into his head; and on his right cheek there were the traces of a severe wound, which, it was supposed, he had received in his desperate struggle with the gamekeeper.

The top of his head was entirely bald; and, when his hat was off, the bold projection of his forehead gave a vigorous determined character to the general expression of his face.

He scarcely looked at Edmund while speaking to him; but once or twice their eyes met, and—it might be fancy —but his manner seemed disturbed, as if some dimly remembered resemblance of features once familiar to him were suddenly awakened; for Edmund was exceedingly like his mother.

To the pretended message, of which Edmund represented himself as the bearer, his answer was, that he knew of no service which Mrs. Morgan, or anybody else, could render him, unless she could save his neck from the halter; and if she would supply him with money to pay the lawyers well, perhaps he might get off.

Edmund, who felt deeply shocked at this reprobate speech, and at the reckless insensibility it evinced of the awful situation in which his father stood, said he would undertake to promise for Mrs. Morgan, that whatever money might be required to obtain for him the utmost benefit of legal assistance should be ready.

He then endeavoured, indirectly, to lead him into a conversation upon the nature of the crime with which he was charged, and the certain consequences of his conviction; but he maintained a sullen silence; and, at last, manifested no equivocal symptoms of a determination to put an end to the interview.

Edmund, therefore, took his leave.

It wanted full two months of the time when the assizes would commence, and during the whole of that period Edmund sought frequent opportunities (sometimes twice or thrice in the course of a week) of visiting his father as the messenger of Mrs. Morgan; but at none of these visits did he give him to understand he was indebted for this solicitude, on her part, to that which was the real cause.

Edmund at length beheld the ripening harvest which was to reward his hallowed labours.

Inspired with a holy ardour, beyond what even his sacred zeal in the cause of heaven could excite in ordinary circumstances, and his fervent piety exalted by the consciousness that it was a father's salvation he was seeking, every impulse of his heart and mind, every energy which religion could animate, was employed to regenerate the sinful nature, and touch the hardened bosom of the criminal.

Much, he considered, was accomplished, when he had brought him into such a state of feeling that he would listen patiently and attentively to his mild yet earnest exhortations, though they elicited no corresponding demonstrations of repentant sorrow.

But most was he rejoiced, and most assured did he then feel of ultimate success when, as he was one evening about to depart, after having enforced, with more than his usual eloquence, the great doctrine of a sincere repentance, his father took him by the hand, and in a voice of supplication almost rather than of inquiry, said—

"When shall I see you again, sir?"

He had never before asked a similar question: he had never before manifested the slightest desire for his return; and his doing so now was a grateful evidence to Edmund that his awakened heart began to hunger for the words of eternal life—for the consolation of believing, with a devout and lively faith, that "if we confess our sins, God is faithful and righteous to forgive us our sins, and to make us clean from all wickedness."

Nor was this a delusive promise.

The seed of righteousness had been sown; the tree had taken root; and the diligent labourer in the vineyard saw its green branches shoot forth, bearing goodly and pleasant fruit.

The day of trial came, and David was arraigned as a

criminal before man; but stood before his judges as one who, having made his peace with God, was prepared to atone for the life he had taken by the just forfeiture of his own.

He was convicted, and sentence of death passed upon him.

He heard it with an air of composure and resignation, which even they who knew not the conversion that had been wrought within him still recognised as the workings of a contrite heart, and not as the insensibility of an obdurate and callous one.

He returned to his cell, and greeted Edmund, whom he found waiting for him with a serene smile, that seemed to say, "The last mortal pang will soon be past, and you have taught my soul how to pray for mercy, and hope for happiness hereafter."

The short interval that remained to him before he ascended the scaffold was so employed, and his demeanour such that Edmund's heart yearned to receive a blessing from lips which were now washed pure from guilt.

He could not endure the thought that his father should quit the world in ignorance that the son, whom he knew not, had been a shining light to show him the path of salvation.

And yet he feared lest the disclosure might discompose his thoughts, and bring them back again to earth.

He was thus unresolved, and the fatal morning approached.

Edmund passed the whole of the preceding night with his father, in those solemn exercises of devotion which are the fitting preparations of an immortal soul for heaven.

The dim light of a lamp fell upon his features as he bent over a Bible which lay open before him, and from which he was reading such passages as were most appropriate to the situation of his father.

David fixed his eyes upon him with sudden emotion, and exclaimed—

"It is very striking!"

Edmund looked up.

"I was thinking that moment," he continued, "of one whom it would have delighted me to see ere I die, though I have never mentioned her to you, sir, as my wife.

"But you are her friend, and I hope you have found cause to speak of me to her in such a way that I may feel assured of her forgiveness for all the misery I have occasioned her."

"My mother," exclaimed Edmund, with an emphatic solemnity of voice, "is on her knees this night to pray for you, and to join her intercessions with those of your son."

David's breathing was quick, and his whole frame violently agitated, but he could not utter a word.

"Father!" cried Edmund, and knelt before him.

David took his son's hands and pressed them convulsively to his bosom; but still he could not speak, though he wept as a child.

In a few minutes the struggle was over, and he was able calmly to learn how mysteriously the will of God had brought about his conversion by the holiness of his own issue.

The morning dawned, and only a few hours now remained before he would have to suffer the brief agony of a death which no longer appalled him by its terrors.

He earnestly entreated Edmund to accompany him to the scaffold, that he might see with how much Christian fortitude he could meet his doom.

It was a dreadful task, but he shrank not from it.

He walked by his father's side.

As they passed through one of the yards leading to the place of execution, David stopped and spoke to his son.

"It was on this very spot," said he, "that I first looked upon you, then an infant in the arms of your mother; and she held you to me, and bade me kiss you, and I did so. It was my first kiss. Receive here, my son, my last; and if I am worthy to beg a blessing from

heaven upon you, may your life be spared till a child of your own shall smooth your path to the grave as you have smoothed mine."

So saying, he bent forward, pressed his lips gently on the forehead of Edmund, then walked on with a firm step; and, in a few moments, David Morgan had satisfied alike the laws of God and man, by rendering life for life.

CHAPTER LXVII.

THE ESCAPE FROM THE CURFEW TOWER—THE PURSUIT—THE PERIL—THE TWO BLACK HOUNDS—AWFUL APPEARANCE OF HERNE—THE IMPRECATION—THE KING'S MINIONS—THE FOREST— DISAPPEARANCE OF THE RESCUED GIRL—CONSTERNATION OF CLIFFORD, AND THE VISION.

THE man who appeared before Clifford and the poor prisoner was tall and powerful in frame.

He was dressed in a peculiar suit of black, and appeared of a melancholy and morose turn.

His aspect was calm and dignified, but calculated to repulse the observer rather than impress him with admiration.

He regarded Clifford and the girl for some moments in profound silence.

Clifford stirred not, but kept his eyes fixed on the pale face of the comer.

"So," said the being, whom the girl recognised as her seducer, "so you have a friend with you, it appears."

"A friend," said Clifford, "who at least will protect her against thee."

"Slave!"

"That I am not."

"Minion, dare you address me?"

"You or your betters," said Clifford. "What care I for you?"

"Do you know who I am?"

"No; and what is of more importance, I do not care."

"You bear it bravely."

"I am used to do so."

"Ah, we shall see if we cannot make you change your habit."

The man smiled malignantly as he spoke.

Clifford, nothing daunted, grasped the girl's arm, and spoke as follows:—

"Tell me, man, do you keep this wretched girl here against her will?"

"What is that to thee?"

"No matter: answer my question."

"What if I say yes?"

"Then I reply that you are a vagabond, and unworthy the name of a man."

The strange being glared at Clifford in anger of the most intense description.

For some moments he could not sufficiently govern himself to speak.

At length he clutched the handle of his sword, and tearing it from his sheath, and making a rush at Clifford, attempted to drag the girl from his grasp, uttering, at the same time, a volley of imprecations of the most awful nature.

Clifford was fully on his guard, and catching the weapon of his adversary under his arm, he, by a skillful turn of the wrist, wrenched it from his grasp.

"See," said Clifford, snapping the sword in two pieces, "see how I serve you. If you are not gone on the instant my weapon shall find a way to your heart."

The man started back.

"What, ho!" he cried; "below, there, below! Quick—to the rescue!"

HERNE SEIZES THE RESCUED MAIDEN FROM CLIFFORD.

There was a rapid trampling of feet
Clifford was puzzled how to act.
He glanced rapidly about him.
There was no mode of escape.
The steps!
A glance was sufficient to show him that they were occupied by the minions of this mysterious man.
"Devil take it!" cried Clifford, drawing his sword, "I see I must cut my way through them."
"Useless," said a deep voice, coming from some unseen person, "useless. Ha! ha! Gentleman Clifford, you are entrapped now, cunning as you are."
Clifford saw no one, but he comprehended that the voice was that of Herne the Hunter.

    *   *   *   *   *

Clifford found his brain reel.
His senses appeared to leave him.
A dim idea of some awful crash, followed by a loud shriek, rang through his brain, and then there came a rushing sound, as of water, and then all was still and dark.
Clifford's next experience was that a cold air fanned his cheek, and that he was lying on green sward.
Gradually his senses returned, and on rising to his feet and opening his eyes, he found that he was in the forest, and that the moonlight was shining down upon him.
He gazed about him.
At his feet lay the girl he had rescued from the Curfew Tower.
She was bereft of her senses.

He stooped and raised her from the earth.

Cold, cold and motionless!

"What shall I do with her?—what will become of her?" cried Clifford, in an agony of doubt and fear.

He was answered by a voice with which he was now fully acquainted.

Glancing upward he beheld the ghostly form of Herne the Hunter.

At his heels were the two black hounds.

They came close to the poor girl, and their burning breath was upon her.

"Call them off!—call them off!" cried Clifford.

Herne smiled.

"Ho, ho," he cried, "dost thou fear?"

"Not I."

"And yet you well might; they are not pleasant neighbours."

"Call them off."

"Spit! Azale! down!" cried the demon huntsman, and the two hounds cowered at his feet.

"Hark!" continued the huntsman; "do you hear those sounds?"

Clifford listened.

There were voices in the forest.

"They are the minions of the King," cried Herne; "they seek *you!*"

"What is to be done?"

"*You* may do the best you can."

"But the poor girl?"

"Trust her to me."

"By Heaven I will not!"

"By Hell you cannot prevent it!"

"We shall see."

Herne advanced, and Clifford put himself in an attitude of defence.

Herne smiled.

He waved his hand, and Clifford was paralysed.

Another moment, and Clifford beheld his rescued maiden in the power of Herne.

Another moment, and the demon huntsman disappeared with the woman.

At the same time the sound of voices fell more distinctly upon his ear.

CHAPTER LXVIII.

THE STORY OF WINDSOR CASTLE AND THE FOREST.

It is now time that we gave the reader some idea of the place in which this epoch of our tale takes place.

All those who have read Harrison Ainsworth's romance of "Windsor Castle" will be thoroughly acquainted with the quaint old pile embosomed in the forest of Windsor, and all those who have not read the work should hide their heads for very shame.

We know of no better guide to Windsor, and we take advantage of it to place the scene more vividly before our readers:—

Amid the gloom hovering over the early history of Windsor Castle appear the mighty phantoms of the renowned King Arthur and his knights, for whom, it is said, Merlin reared a magic fortress upon its heights, in a great hall whereof, decorated with trophies of war and of the chase, was placed the famous Round Table.

But if the antique tale is now worn out, and no longer part of our faith, it is pleasant at least to record it, and, surrendering ourselves for awhile to the sway of fancy, to conjure up the old enchanted castle on the hill, to people its courts with warlike and lovely forms, its forests with fays and giants, and its stream with beauteous and benignant sprites.

Windsor, or Wyndleshore, so called from the winding banks of the river flowing past it, was the abode of the ancient Saxon monarchs; and a legend is related by William of Malmesbury, of a woodman named Wulwin, who being stricken with blindness, and having visited eighty-seven churches and vainly implored their tutelary saints for relief, was at last restored to sight by the touch of Edward the Confessor, who farther enhanced the boon by making him keeper of his palace at Windsor.

But though this story may be doubted, it is certain that the pious king above mentioned granted Windsor to the abbot and monks of St. Peter at Westminster, "for the hope of eternal reward, the remission of his sins, the sins of his father, mother, and all his ancestors, and to the praise of Almighty God, as a perpetual endowment and inheritance."

But the royal donation did not long remain in the hands of the priesthood.

Struck by the extreme beauty of the spot, "for that it seemed exceeding profitable and commodious, because situate so near the Thames, the wood fit for game, and many other particulars lying there meet and necessary for kings—yea, a place very convenient for his reception," William the Conqueror prevailed upon Abbot Edwin to accept in exchange for it Wakendune and Feringes, in Essex, together with three other tenements in Colchester; and having obtained possession of the coveted hill, he forthwith began to erect a castle upon it, occupying a space of about half a hide of land.

Around it he formed large parks, to enable him to pursue his favourite pastime of hunting; and he enacted and enforced severe laws for the preservation of the game.

As devoted to the chase as his father, William Rufus frequently hunted in the forests of Windsor, and solemnised some of the festivals of the church in the castle.

In the succeeding reign—namely, that of Henry the First—the castle was entirely rebuilt and greatly enlarged, assuming somewhat of the character of a palatial residence, having before been little more than a strong hunting-seat.

The structure then erected, in all probability, occupied the same site as the upper and lower wards of the present pile, but nothing remains of it except, perhaps, the keep, and of that little beyond its form and position.

In 1109 Henry celebrated the Feast of Pentecost with great state and magnificence within the castle.

In 1122 he there espoused his second wife, Adelicia, daughter of Godfrey, Duke of Louvaine; and failing in obtaining issue by her, assembled the barons at Windsor, and caused them, together with David, King of Scotland, his sister Adela, and her son Stephen, afterwards King of England, to do homage to his daughter Maud, widow of the Emperor Henry the Fifth.

Proof that Windsor Castle was regarded as the second fortress in the realm is afforded by the treaty of peace between the usurper Stephen and the Empress Maude, in which it is coupled with the Tower of London, under the designation of *Mota de Windsor.*

At the signing of the treaty it was committed to the custody of Richard de Lucy, who was continued in the office of keeper by Henry the Second.

In the reign of this monarch many repairs were made in the castle, to which a vineyard was attached—the cultivation of the grape being at this time extensively practised throughout England.

Strange as the circumstance may now appear, Stow mentions that vines grew in abundance in the Home Park in the reign of Richard the Second, the wine made from them being consumed at the King's table, and even sold.

It is related by Fabian, that Henry, stung by the disobedience and ingratitude of his sons, caused an allegorical picture to be painted, representing an old eagle assailed by four young ones, which he placed in one of the chambers of the castle.

When asked the meaning of the device, he replied—"I am the old eagle, and the four eaglets are my sons, who cease not to pursue my death. The youngest bird, who is tearing out its parent's eyes, is my son John—my youngest and best-loved son—and who yet is the most eager for my destruction."

On his departure for the holy wars, Richard Cœur de Lion entrusted the government of the castle to Hugh de Pudsey, Bishop of Durham and Earl of Northumberland.

But a fierce dispute arising between the warrior prelate and his ambitious colleague, William Longchamp, Bishop of Ely, he was seized and imprisoned by the latter, and compelled to surrender the castle.

After an extraordinary display of ostentation, Longchamp was ousted in his turn.

On the arrival of the news of Richard's capture and imprisonment in Austria, the castle was seized by Prince John.

But it was soon afterwards taken possession of in the King's behalf by the barons, and consigned to the custody of Eleanor, the Queen Dowager.

In John's reign the castle became the scene of a foul and terrible event.

William de Braose, a powerful baron, having offended the King, his wife, Maud, was ordered to deliver up her son as a hostage for her husband.

But, instead of complying with the injunction, she rashly returned for answer—

"That she would not entrust her child to the person who could slay his own nephew."

Upon which the ruthless King seized her and her son, and, enclosing them in a recess in the wall of the castle, built them up within it.

Sorely pressed by the barons in 1215, John sought refuge within the castle, and in the same year signed the two charters—Magna Charta, and Charta de Foresta—at Runnymede, a plain between Windsor and Staines.

A curious account of his frantic demeanour after divesting himself of so much power, and extending so greatly the liberties of the subject, is given by Holinshed.

"Having acted so far contrary to his mind, the king was right sorrowful in heart, cursed his mother that bare him, and the hour in which he was born, wishing that he had received death by violence of sword or knife, instead of natural nourishment.

"He whetted his teeth, and did bite now on one staff, now on another, as he walked, and oft brake the same in pieces when he had done, and with such disordered behaviour and furious gestures he uttered his grief, that the noblemen very well perceived the inclination of his inward affection concerning these things before the breaking-up of the council, and therefore sore lamented the state of the realm, guessing what would follow of his impatience and displeasant taking of the matter."

The faithless king made an attempt to regain his lost power, and, war breaking out afresh in the following year, a numerous army, under the command of William de Nivernois, besieged the castle, which was stoutly defended by Inglehard de Achie and sixty knights.

The barons, however, learning that John was marching through Norfolk and Suffolk, and ravaging the country, hastily raised the siege, and advanced to meet him.

But he avoided them, marched to Stamford and Lincoln, and from thence towards Wales.

On his return from this expedition he was seized with the distemper of which he died.

Henry the Third was an ardent encourager of architecture, and his reign marks the second great epoch in the annals of the castle.

In 1223 eight hundred marks were paid to Engelhard de Cygony, constable of the castle, John le Draper, and William, the clerk of Windsor, masters of the works, and others, for repairs and works within the castle—the latter, it is conjectured, referring to the erection of a new great hall within the lower ward, there being already a hall of small dimensions in the upper court.

The windows of the new building were filled with painted glass, and at the upper end, upon a raised dais, was a gilt throne sustaining a statue of the king in his robes.

Within this vast and richly decorated chamber, in 1240, on the day of the Nativity, an infinite number of poor persons were collected and fed by the king's command.

During the greater part of Henry's long and eventful reign the works within the castle proceeded with unabated activity.

Carpenters were maintained on the royal establishment; the ditch between the hall and the lower ward was repaired; a new kitchen was built; the bridges were repaired with timber procured from the neighbouring forest; certain breaches in the wall facing the garden were stopped; the fortifications were surveyed, and the battlements repaired.

At the same time the queen's chamber was painted and wainscoted, and iron bars were placed before the windows of Prince Edward's chamber.

In 1240 Henry commenced building an apartment for his own use near the wall of the castle, sixty feet long and twenty-eight high; another apartment for the queen contiguous to it; and a chapel seventy feet long and twenty-eight feet wide, along the same wall, but with a grassy space between it and the royal apartments.

The chapel, as appears from an order to Walter de Grey, Archbishop of York, had a galilee and a cloister, a lofty wooden roof covered with lead, and a stone turret in front holding three or four bells.

Withinside, it was made to appear like stone-work with good ceiling and painting, and it contained four gilded images.

This structure is supposed to have been in existence, under the designation of the Old College Church, in the latter part of the reign of Henry the Seventh, by whom it was pulled down to make way for the tomb-house.

Traces of its architecture have been discovered by diligent antiquarian research in the south ambulatory of the Dean's Cloister, and in the door behind the altar in Saint George's Chapel, the latter of which is conceived to have formed the principal entrance to the older structure, and has been described as exhibiting "one of the most beautiful specimens which time and innovation have respected of the elaborate ornamental work of the period."

In 1241 Henry commenced operations upon the outworks of the castle, and the three towers on the western side of the lower ward—now known as the Curfew, the Garter, and the Salisbury Tower—were erected by him.

He also continued the walls along the south side of the lower ward, traces of the architecture of the period being discoverable in the inner walls of the houses of the alms-knights as far as the tower now bearing his name. From thence it is concluded that the ramparts ran along the east side of the upper ward to a tower occupying the site of the Wykeham or Winchester Tower.

The three towers at the west end of the lower ward, though much dilapidated, present unquestionable features of the architecture of the thirteenth century.

The lower story of the Curfew Tower, which has been but little altered, consists of a large vaulted chamber twenty-two feet wide, with walls of nearly thirteen feet in thickness, and having arched recesses terminated by loopholes.

The walls are covered with the inscriptions of prisoners who have been confined within it.

The Garter Tower, though in a most ruinous condition, exhibits high architectural beauty in its moulded arches and corbelled passages. The Salisbury Tower retains only externally, and on the side towards the town, its original aspect.

The remains of a fourth tower are discernible in the Governor of the Alms-Knights' Tower; and Henry the Third's Tower, as before observed, completes what remains of the original chain of fortifications.

On the 24th November, 1244, Henry issued a writ enjoining "the clerks of the works at Windsor to work day and night to wainscot the high chamber upon the wall of the castle near our chapel in the upper bailey, so that it may be ready and properly wainscoted on Friday next (the 24th occurring on a Tuesday, only two days were allowed for the task), when we come there with boards radiated and coloured, so that nothing be found reprehensible in that wainscot; and also to make at each gable of the said chamber one glass window, on the outside of the inner window of each gable, so that when the inner window shall be closed the glass windows may be seen outside."

The following year the works were suspended, but they were afterwards resumed and continued, with few interruptions.

The keep was new constructed; a stone bench was fixed in the wall, near the grass-plot by the king's chamber; a bridge was thrown across the ditch to the king's garden, which lay outside the walls; a barbican was erected, to which a portcullis was subsequently attached; the bridges were defended by strong iron chains; the old chambers in the upper ward were renovated; a conduit and lavatory were added, and a fountain was constructed in the garden.

In this reign, in all probability, the Norman tower, which now forms a gateway between the middle and the upper ward, was erected.

This tower, at present allotted to the housekeeper of the castle, Lady Mary Fox, was used as a prison lodging during the civil wars of Charles the First's time; and many noble and gallant captives have left mementoes of their loyalty and ill-fate upon its walls.

In 1260 Henry received a visit at Windsor from his daughter Margaret, and her husband, Alexander the Third, King of Scotland.

The queen gave birth to a daughter during her stay at the castle.

In 1264, during the contest between Henry and the barons, the valiant Prince Edward, his son, returning from a successful expedition into Wales, surprised the citizens of London, and carrying off their military chest, in which was much treasure, retired to Windsor Castle, and strongly garrisoned it.

The queen Eleanor, his mother, would fain have joined him there, but she was driven back by the citizens at London Bridge, and compelled to take sanctuary in the palace of the Bishop of London, at Saint Paul's.

Compelled, at length, to surrender the castle to the barons, and to depart from it with his consort, Eleanor of Castile, the brave prince soon afterwards recovered it, but was again forced to deliver it up to Simon de Montford, Earl of Leicester, who appointed Geoffrey de Langele governor.

But though frequently wrested from him at this period, Windsor Castle was never long out of Henry's possession; and, in 1265, the chief citizens of London were imprisoned till they had paid the heavy fine imposed upon them for their adherence to Simon de Montford, who had been just before slain at the battle of Evesham.

During this reign a terrific storm of wind and thunder occurred, which tore up several great trees in the park, shook the castle, and blew down a part of the building in which the queen and her family were lodged, but happily without doing them injury.

Four of the children of Edward the First, who was blessed with numerous offspring, were born at Windsor; and as he frequently resided at the castle, the town began to increase in importance and consideration.

By a charter, granted in 1276, it was created a free borough, and various privileges were conferred on its inhabitants.

Stow tells us that, in 1295, "on the last day of February, there suddenly arose such a fire in the castle of Windsor that many offices were therewith consumed, and many goodly images, made to beautify the buildings, defaced and deformed."

Edward the Second, and his beautiful but perfidious queen, Isabella of France, made Windsor Castle their frequent abode; and here, on the 13th day of November, 1312, at forty minutes past five in the morning, was born

a prince, over whose nativity the wizard, Merlin, must have presided.

Baptised within the old chapel by the name of Edward, this prince became afterwards the third monarch of the name, and the greatest, and was also styled, from the place of his birth, Edward of Windsor.

CHARTER LXIX.

SHOWING HOW THE ORDER OF THE GARTER WAS INSTITUTED.

STRONGLY attached to the place of his birth, Edward the Third, by his letters patent, dated from Westminster, in the twenty-second year of his reign, now founded the ancient chapel, established by Henry the First, and dedicated it to the Virgin, Saint George of Cappadocia, and Saint Edward the Confessor; ordaining that to the eight canons appointed by his predecessor, there should be added one custos, fifteen more canons, and twenty-four alms-knights; the whole to be maintained out of the revenues with which the chapel was to be endowed.

The institution was confirmed by Pope Clement the Sixth, by a bull issued at Avignon, the 13th November, 1351.

In 1349, before the foundation of the college had been confirmed, as above related, Edward instituted the order of the Garter.

The origin of this illustrious order has been much disputed.

By some writers it has been ascribed to Richard Cœur de Lion, who is said to have girded a leathern band round the legs of his bravest knights in Palestine.

By others it has been asserted that it arose from the word "garter" having been used as a watchword by Edward at the battle of Cressy.

Others, again, have stoutly maintained that its ring-like form bore mysterious reference to the Round Table.

But the popular legend, to which, despite the doubts thrown upon it, credence still attaches, declares its origin to be as follows:—

Joan, Countess of Salisbury, a beautiful dame, of whom Edward was enamoured, while dancing at a high festival, accidentally slipped her garter, of blue embroidered velvet.

It was picked up by her royal partner, who, noticing the significant looks of his courtiers on the occasion, used the words to them, which afterwards became the motto of the order, " *Honi soit qui mal y pense ;*" adding, that " in a short time they should see that garter advanced to so high honour and estimation, as to account themselves happy to wear it."

But whatever may have originated the order, it unquestionably owes its establishment to motives of policy.

Wise as valiant, and bent upon prosecuting his claim to the crown of France, Edward, as a means of accomplishing his object, resolved to collect beneath his standard the best knights in Europe, and to lend a colour to the design, he gave forth that he intended a restoration of King Arthur's Round Table, and accordingly commenced constructing within the castle a large circular building of two hundred feet in diameter, in which he placed a round table.

On the completion of the work, he issued proclamations throughout England, Scotland, France, Burgundy, Flanders, Brabant, and the Empire, inviting all knights, desirous of approving their valour, to a solemn feast and jousts to be holden within the castle of Windsor, on St. George's Day, 1345.

The scheme was completely successful.

The flower of the chivalry of Europe—excepting that of Philip the Sixth of France, who, seeing through the design, interdicted the attendance of his knights—were present at the tournament, which was graced by Edward and his chief nobles, together with his queen and three hundred of her fairest dames, " adorned with all imaginable gallantry."

At this chivalrous convocation the institution of the order of the Garter was arranged ; but before its final establishment Edward assembled his principal barons and knights, to determine upon the regulations, when it was decided that the number should be limited to twenty-six.

The first installation took place on the anniversary of St. George, the patron of the order, 1349, when the king, accompanied by the [twenty-five]knights-companions, attired in gowns of russet, with mantles of fine blue wollen cloth, powdered with garters, and bearing the other insignia of the order, marched, bareheaded in solemn procession, to the chapel of St. George, then recently rebuilt, where mass was performed by William Edington, Bishop of Winchester, after which they partook of a magnificent banquet.

The festivities were continued for several days.

At the jousts held on this occasion, David, King of Scotland, the Lord Charles of Blois, and Ralph, Earl of Eu and Guisnes, and constable of France, to whom the chief prize of the day was adjudged, with others, then prisoners, attended.

The harness of the King of Scotland, embroidered with a pale of red velvet, and beneath it a red rose, was provided at Edward's own charge.

This suit of armour was, until a few years back, preserved in the Round Tower, where the royal prisoner was confined.

Edward's device was a white swan, gorged or, with the " daring and inviting " motto—

Hay hay the wythe swan
By God's soul I am thy man.

The insignia of the order in the days of its founder were the garter, mantle, surcoat, and hood ; the George and collar being added by Henry the Eighth.

The mantle, as before intimated, was originally of fine blue woollen cloth, but velvet, lined with taffeta, was substituted by Henry the Sixth, the left shoulder being adorned with the arms of St. George, embroidered within a garter.

Little is known of the materials of which the early garter was composed ; but it is supposed to have been adorned with gold, and fastened with a buckle of the same metal.

The modern garter is of blue velvet, bordered with gold wire, and embroidered with the motto—"*Honi soit qui mal y pense.*"

It is worn on the left leg, a little below the knee.

The most magnificent garter that ever graced a sovereign was that presented to Charles the First by Gustavus Adolphus, King of Sweden, each letter in the motto of which was composed of diamonds.

The collar is formed of pieces of gold fashioned like garters, with a blue enamelled ground.

The letters of the motto are in gold, with a rose enamelled red in the centre of each garter.

From the collar hangs the George, an ornament enriched with precious stones, and displaying the figure of the Saint encountering the dragon.

The officers of the order are, the prelate, represented by the Bishop of Winchester ; the chancellor, by the Bishop of Oxford ; the registrar, dean, garter king-at-arms, and the usher of the black rod.

Among the foreign potentates who have been invested with the order are, eight emperors of Germany; two of Russia ; five kings of France ; three of Spain ; one of Arragon ; seven of Portugal ; one of Poland ; two of Sweden ; six of Denmark ; two of Naples ; one of Sicily and Jerusalem ; one of Bohemia ; two of Scotland; seven princes of Orange ; and many of the most illustrious personages of different ages in Europe.

Truly hath the learned Selden written, " that the order of the Garter hath not only precedency of antiquity before the eldest rank of honour of that kind anywhere established, but it exceeds in majesty, honour, and fame all chivalrous orders in the world."

" Well, also, hath glorious Dryden, in the "Flower and the Leaf," sung the praises of the illustrious institution :—

" Behold an order yet of newer date,
Doubling their number, equal in their state :
Our England's ornament, the crown's defence,
In battle brave, protectors of their prince ;
Unchanged by fortune, to their sovereign true,
For which their manly legs are bound with blue,
These of the Garter call'd, of faith unstain'd,
In fighting fields the laurel have obtain'd,
And well repaid the laurels which they gain'd."

In 1357, John, King of France, defeated at the battle of Poitiers by Edward the Black Prince, was brought captive to Windsor; and on the festival of Saint George in the following year, 1358, Edward outshone all his former splendid doings by a tournament which he gave in honour of his royal prisoner.

Proclamation having been made as before, and letters of safe-conduct issued, the nobles and knighthood of Almayne, Gascoigne, Scotland, and other countries, flocked to attend it.

The Queen of Scotland, Edward's sister, was present at the jousts ; and it is said that John, commenting upon the splendour of the spectacle, shrewdly observed " that he never saw or knew such royal shows and feasting without some after rec koning."

The same monarch replied to his kingly captor, who sought to rouse him from dejection, on another occasion—

" Quomodo cantabimus canticum in terra alienâ !"

That his works might not be retarded for want of hands, Edward, in the twenty-fourth year of his reign, appointed John de Sponlee master of the stonehewers, with a power not only " to take and keep, as well within the liberties as without, as many masons and other artificers as were necessary, and to convey them to Windsor, but to arrest and imprison such as should disobey or refuse ; with a command to all sheriffs, mayors, bailiffs, &c., to assist him."

These powers were fully acted upon at a later period, when some of the workmen, having left their employment, were thrown into Newgate! while the place of others, who had been carried off by a pestilence then raging in the castle, was supplied by impressment.

In 1356, William of Wykeham was constituted superintendent of the works, with the same powers as John de Sponlee, and his appointment marks an important era in the annals of the castle.

Originally secretary to Edward the Third, this remarkable man became Bishop of Winchester and prelate of the Garter.

When he solicited the bishopric, it is said that Edward told him he was neither a priest nor a scholar ; to which he replied that he would soon be the one, and in regard to the other, he would make more scholars than all the Bishops of England ever did.

He made good his word by founding the collegiate school at Winchester, and erecting New College at Oxford.

When the Winchester Tower was finished, he caused the words Hoc fecit Wykeham to be carved upon it ; and the king, offended at his presumption, Wykeham turned away his displeasure by declaring that the inscription meant that the castle had made *him*, and not that *he* had made the castle.

It is a curious coincidence that this tower, after a lapse of four centuries and a half, should become the residence of an architect possessing the genius of Wykeham, and who, like him, had rebuilt the kingly edifice—Sir Jeffry Wyatville.

William of Wykeham retired from office, loaded with

cayed, were carefully and consistently restored by Mr. Blore, and the ancient stained glass replaced.

Not only does Saint George's Chapel form a house of prayer and a temple of chivalry, but it is also the burial-place of kings.

At the east end of the north aisle of the choir is a plain flag, bearing the words—

"King Edward IIII. and his Queen Elizabeth Widville."

The coat of mail and surcoat, decorated with rubies and precious stones, together with other rich trophies once ornamenting this tomb, were carried off by the Parliamentary plunderers.

Edward's queen, Elizabeth Woodville, it was thought slept beside him; but when the royal tomb was opened in 1789, and the two coffins within it examined, the smaller one was found empty.

The queen's body was subsequently discovered in a stone coffin by the workmen employed in excavating the vault for George the Third.

Edward's coffin was seven feet long, and contained a perfect skeleton.

On the opposite aisle, near the choir door, as already mentioned, rests the ill-fated Henry the Sixth, beneath an arch sumptuously embellished by Henry the Eighth, on the keystone of which may still be seen his arms, supported by two antelopes connected by a golden chain.

Henry's body was removed from Chertsey, where it was first interred, and reburied in 1484, with much solemnity, in this spot.

Such was the opinion entertained of his sanctity that miracles were supposed to be wrought upon his tomb, and Henry the Seventh applied to have him canonised, but the demands of the pope were too exorbitant.

The proximity of Henry and Edward in death suggested the following lines to Pope:—

"Here, o'er the martyr-king the marble weeps,
And fast beside him, once fear'd Edward sleeps:
The grave unites, where e'en the grave finds rest,
And mingled lie the oppressor and the opprest."

In the royal vault in the choir repose Henry the Eighth and his third queen, Jane Seymour, together with the martyred Charles the First.

Space only permits the hasty enumeration of the different beautiful chapels and chantries adorning this splendid fane.

These are Lincoln Chapel, near which Richard Beauchamp, Bishop of Salisbury, is buried; Oxenbridge Chapel; Aldworth Chapel; Bray Chapel, where rests the body of Sir Reginald de Bray, the architect of the pile; Beaufort Chapel, containing sumptuous monuments of the noble family of that name; Rutland Chapel; Hastings Chapel; and Urswick Chapel, in which is now placed the cenotaph of the Princess Charlotte, sculptured by Matthew Wyatt.

In a vault near the sovereign's stall lie the remains of the Duke of Gloucester, who died in 1805, and of his duchess, who died two years after him.

And near the entrance of the south door is a slab of grey marble, beneath which lies one who in his day filled the highest offices of the realm, and was the brother of a king and the husband of a queen.

It is inscribed with the great name of CHARLES BRANDON.

At the east end of the north aisle is the chapter-house, in which is a portrait and the sword of state of Edward the Third.

Adjoining the chapel, on the east, stands the royal tomb-house.

Commenced by Henry the Seventh as a mausoleum, but abandoned for the chapel in Westminster Abbey, this structure was granted by Henry the Eighth to Wolsey, who, intending it as a place of burial for himself, erected within it a sumptuous monument of black and white marble, with eight large brazen columns placed around it, and four others in the form of candlesticks.

At the time of the cardinal's disgrace, when the building reverted to the crown, the monument was far advanced towards completion, the vast sum of 4,280 ducats having been paid to Benedetto, a Florentine sculptor, for work, and nearly four hundred pounds for gilding part of it.

This tomb was stripped of its ornaments, and destroyed, by the Parliamentary rebels in 1646; but the black marble sarcophagus forming part of it, and intended as a receptacle for Wolsey's own remains, escaped destruction, and now covers the grave of Nelson in a crypt of St. Paul's Cathedral.

Henry the Eighth was not interred in this mausoleum, but in Saint George's Chapel, as has just been mentioned, and as he himself directed, "mid-way between the state and the high altar."

Full instructions were left by him for the erection of a monument, which, if it had been completed, would have been truly magnificent.

The pavement was to be of oriental stones, with two great steps upon it of the same material.

The two pillars of the church, between which the tomb was to be set, were to be covered with bas-reliefs, representing the chief events of the Old Testament, angels with gilt garlands, fourteen images of the prophets, the apostles, the evangelists, and the four doctors of the church, and at the foot of every image a little child, with a basket full of red and white roses, enamelled and gilt.

Between these pillars, on a basement of white marble, the epitaphs of the king and queen were to be written in letters of gold.

On the same basement were to be two tombs of black touchstone, supporting the images of the king and queen, not as dead, but sleeping, "to show," so runs the order, "that famous princes, leaving behind them great fame, do never die."

On the right hand, at either corner of the tomb, was to be an angel, holding the king's arms, with a great candlestick, and at the opposite corners two other angels, bearing the queen's arms and candlesticks.

Between the two black tombs was to rise a high basement, like a sepulchre, surmounted by a statue of the king on horseback, in armour, both figures to be "of the whole stature of a goodly man and a large horse."

Over this statue was to be a canopy, like a triumphal arch, of white marble, garnished with oriental stones of divers colours, with the story of Saint John the Baptist wrought in gilt brass upon it, with a crowning group of the Father holding the soul of the king in his right hand, and the soul of the queen in his left, and blessing them.

The height of the monument was to be twenty-eight feet.

The number of statues was to be one hundred and thirty-four, with forty-four bas-reliefs.

It would be matter of infinite regret that this great design was never executed, if its destruction by the parliamentary plunderers would not, in that case, have been, also, matter of certainty.

Charles the First intended to fit up this structure as a royal mausoleum, but was diverted from the plan by the outbreak of the civil war.

It was afterwards used as a chapel by James the Second, and mass was publicly performed in it.

The ceiling was painted by Verrio, and the walls highly ornamented; but the decorations were greatly injured by the fury of an anti-catholic mob, who assailed the building, and destroyed its windows, on the occasion of a banquet given to the Pope's nuncio by the king.

In this state it continued till the commencement of the present century, when the exterior was repaired by George the Third, and a vault, seventy feet in length, twenty-eight in width, and fourteen in depth, constructed within it, for the reception of the royal family.

Catacombs formed of massive octangular pillars, and supporting ranges of shelves, line the walls on either side.

At the eastern extremity, there are five niches, and in the middle twelve low tombs.

A subterranean passage leads from the vault beneath

the choir of St. George's altar to the sepulchre. Within it are deposited the bodies of George the Third and Queen Charlotte, the Princesses Amelia and Charlotte, the Dukes of Kent and of York, and the two last sovereigns, George the Fourth and William the Fourth.

But to return to the reign of Edward the Fourth, from which the desire to bring down the history of Saint George's Chapel to the present time has led to the foregoing digression.

About the same time that the chapel was built habitations for the dean and canons were erected on the northeast of the fane, while another range of dwellings for the minor canons was built at its west end, disposed in the form of a fetter lock, one of the badges of Edward the Fourth, and since called the Horse-shoe Cloisters.

The ambulatory of these cloisters once displayed a fine specimen of the timber architecture of Henry the Seventh's

time, when they were repaired; but little of their original character can now be discerned.

In 1482, Edward, desiring of advancing his popularity with the citizens of London, invited the lord mayor and aldermen to Windsor, where he feasted them royally, and treated them to the pleasures of the chase, sending them back to their spouses loaded with game.

In 1484 Richard the Third kept the feast of St. George at Windsor, and the building of the chapel was continued during his reign.

The picturesque portion of the castle on the north side of the upper ward, near the Norman gateway, and which is one of the noblest Gothic features of the proud pile, was built by Henry the Seventh, whose name it still bears.

The side of this building, looking towards the terrace, was originally decorated with two rich windows, but one of them has disappeared, and the other has suffered much damage.

In 1500 the deanery was rebuilt by Dean Urswick.

At the lower end of the court, adjoining the canons' houses behind the Horse shoe Cloisters, stands the Collegiate Library, the date of which is uncertain, though it may, perhaps, be referred to this period.

The establishment was enriched in later times by a valuable library, bequeathed to it by the Earl of Ranelagh.

In 1506, Windsor was the scene of great festivity, in consequence of the unexpected arrival of Philip, king of Castile, and his queen, who had been driven, by stress of weather, into Weymouth.

The royal visitors remained for several weeks at the castle, during which it continued a scene of revelry, intermixed with the sports of the chase.

At the same time, Philip was invested with the order of the Garter, and installed in the chapel of Saint George.

The great gateway to the lower ward was built in the commencement of the reign of Henry the Eighth.

It is decorated with his arms and devices—the rose, portcullis, and fleur-de-lis, and with the bearings of Catharine of Arragon.

In 1522, Charles the Fifth visited Windsor, and was installed Knight of the Garter.

During a period of dissension in the Council Edward the Sixth was removed for safety to Windsor, by the lord protector, Somerset ; and here, at a later period, the youthful monarch received a letter from the council, urging the dismissal of Somerset, with which, by the advice of the Archbishop of Canterbury, he complied.

In this reign an undertaking to convey water to the castle from Blackmore Park, near Wingfield, a distance of five miles, was commenced, though it was not till 1555, in the time of Mary, that the plan was accomplished, when a pipe was brought into the upper ward, "and there the water plenteously did rise thirteen feet high."

In the middle of the court was erected a magnificent fountain, consisting of a canopy raised upon columns, gorgeously decorated with heraldic ornaments, and surmounted by a great vane, with the arms of Philip and Mary impaled upon it and supported by a lion and an eagle, gilt and painted.

The water was discharged by a great dragon, one of the supporters of the Tudor arms, into the cistern beneath, whence it was conveyed by pipes to every part of the castle.

Mary held her court at Windsor soon after her union with Philip of Spain.

About this period the old habitations of the almsknights on the south side of the lower quadrangle were taken down, and others erected in their stead.

Fewer additions were made to Windsor Castle by Elizabeth than might have been expected from her predilection for it as a place of residence.

She extended and widened the north terrace, where, when lodging within the castle, she daily took exercise, whatever might be the weather.

The terrace at this time, as it is described by Paul Hentzner, and as it appears in Norden's view, was a sort of balcony projecting beyond the scarp of the hill, and supported by great cantilevers of wood.

In 1576 the gallery still bearing her name, and lying between Henry the Seventh's buildings and the Norman Tower, was erected by Elizabeth.

This portion of the castle had the good fortune to escape the alterations and modifications made in almost every other part of the upper ward after the restoration of Charles the Second.

It now forms the library.

A large garden was laid out by the same queen, and a small gateway on Castle Hill built by her—which afterwards became one of the greatest obstructions to the approach, and it was taken down by George the Fourth.

Elizabeth often hunted in the parks, and exhibited her skill in archery, which was by no means inconsiderable, at the butts.

Her fondness for dramatic performances likewise induced her to erect a stage within the castle, on which plays and interludes were performed.

And to her admiration of the character of Falstaff, and her love of the locality, the world is indebted for the "Merry Wives of Windsor."

James the First favoured Windsor as much as his precedessors ; caroused within its halls, and chased the deer in its parks.

Christian the Fourth of Denmark was sumptuously entertained by him at Windsor.

In this reign a curious dispute occurred between the king and the dean and chapter respecting the repair of a breach in the wall, which was not brought to issue for three years, when, after much argument, it was decided in favour of the clergy.

Little was done at Windsor by Charles the First until the tenth year of his reign, when a banquetting-house erected by Elizabeth was taken down, and the magnificent fountain constructed by Queen Mary demolished.

Two years afterwards "a pyramid or lantern," with a clock, bell, and dial, was ordered to be set up in front of the castle, and a balcony was erected before the room where Henry the Sixth was born.

In the early part of the year 1642, Charles retired to Windsor, to shield himself from the insults of the populace, and was followed by a committee of the House of Commons, who prevailed upon him to desist from the prosecution of the impeached members.

On the 23rd of October, in the same year, Captain Fogg, at the head of a parliamentarian force, demanded the keys of the college treasury, and not being able to obtain them, forced open the doors, and carried off the whole of the plate.

The plunder of the college was completed by Vane, the parliamentary governor of the castle, who seized upon the whole of the furniture and decorations of the choir, rifled the tomb of Edward the Fourth, stripped off all the costly ornaments from Wolsey's tomb, defaced the emblazonings over Henry the Sixth's grave, broke the rich painted glass of the windows, and wantonly destroyed the exquisite woodwork of the choir.

Towards the close of the year 1648 the ill-fated Charles was brought a prisoner to Windsor, where he remained while preparations were made for the execrable tragedy soon afterwards enacted.

After the slaughter of the martyr-monarch, the castle became the prison of the Earl of Norwich, Lord Capel, and the Duke of Hamilton, and other royalists and cavaliers.

Cromwell frequently resided within the castle, and often took a moody and distrustful walk upon the terrace.

It was during the Protectorate, in 1677, that the ugly buildings, appropriated to the naval knights, standing between the Garter Tower and the Chancellor's Tower, were erected by Sir Francis Crane.

CHAPTER LXXI.

CONCERNING THE PARKS AND THE FOREST.

On the Restoration the castle resumed its splendour, and presented a striking contrast to the previous gloomy period.

The terrace, with its festive groups, resembled a picture by Watteau.

The courts resounded with laughter ; and the velvet sod of the Home Park was as often pressed by the foot of frolic beauty as by that of the tripping deer.

Seventeen state apartments were built by Sir Christopher

Wren, under the direction of Sir John Denham ; the ceilings were painted by Verio, and the walls decorated with exquisite carvings by Grinling Gibbons.

A grand staircase was added at the same time.

Most of the chambers were hung with tapestry, and all adorned with pictures and costly furniture.

The addition made to the castle by Charles was the part of the north front, then called the " Star Building," from the star of the order of the Garter worked in colours in front of it, but now denominated the " Stuart Building," extending eastward along the terrace from Henry the Seventh's building one hundred and seventy feet.

In 1676 the ditch was filled up, and the terrace carried along the south and east fronts of the castle.

Meanwhile the original character of the castle was completely destroyed and Italianised.

The beautiful and picturesque irregularities of the walls were removed ; the towers shaved off, the windows transformed into common-place circular- headed apertures.

And so the castle remained for more than a century.

Edward the Third's Tower, indifferently called the Earl Marshal's Tower and the Devil Tower, and used as a place of confinement for state prisoners, was now allotted to the maids o' honour.

It was intended by Charles to erect a monument in honour of his martyred father on the site of the tomb-house, which he proposed to remove, and £70,000 were voted by Parliament for this purpose.

The design, however, was abandoned under the plea that the body could not be found, though it was perfectly well known where it lay.

The real motive probably was that Charles had already spent the money.

In 1680, an equestrian statue of Charles the Second, executed by Strada, at the expense of Tobias Rustat, formerly housekeeper at Hampton Court, was placed in the centre of the upper ward.

It now stands at the lower end of the same court.

The sculptures on the pedestal were designed by Grinling Gibbons ; and Horace Walpole pleasantly declared that the statue had no other merit than to attract attention to them.

In old times a road, forming a narrow irregular avenue, ran through the woods from the foot of the castle to Snow Hill.

But this road having been neglected, during a long series of years, the branches of the trees and underwood had so much encroached upon it as to render it wholly impassable.

A grand avenue, 240 feet wide, was planned by Charles in its place ; and the magnificent approach called the Long Walk laid out and planted.

The only material incident connected with the castle during the reign of James the Second has been already related.

Windsor was not so much favoured as Hampton Court by William the Third, though he contemplated alterations within it during the latter part of his life, which it may be matter of rejoicing were never accomplished.

Queen Anne's operations were chiefly directed towards the parks, in improving which nearly £40,000 were expended.

In 1707 the extensive avenue running almost parallel with the Long Walk, and called the " Queen's Walk," was planted by her ; and three years afterwards a carriage road was formed through the Long Walk.

A garden was also planned on the north side of the castle.

In this reign Sir James Thornhill commenced painting Charles the Second's staircase with designs from Ovid's Metamorphoses, but did not complete his task till after the accession of George the First.

This staircase was removed in 1800, to make way for the present Gothic entrance erected by the elder Wyatt.

The first two monarchs of the House of Hanover rarely used Windsor as a residence, preferring Hampton Court and Kensington ; and even George the Third did not actually live in the Castle, but in the Queen's Lodge—a large detached building, with no pretension to architectural beauty, which he himself erected opposite the south terrace, at a cost of nearly £44,000.

With most praiseworthy zeal, and almost entirely at his own expense, this monarch undertook the restoration of Saint George's Chapel.

The work was commenced in 1787, occupied three years, and was executed by Mr. Emlyn, a local architect.

The whole building was re-paved, a new altar-screen and organ added, and the carving restored.

In 1796, Mr. James Wyatt was appointed surveyor-general of the royal buildings, and effected many internal arrangements.

Externally, he restored Wren's round-headed windows to their original form, and at the same time gothicised a large portion of the north and south sides of the upper ward.

Before proceeding further a word must be said about the parks.

The Home Park, which lies on the east and north sides of the castle, is about four miles in circumference, and was enlarged and enclosed with a brick wall by William the Third.

On the east, and nearly on the site of the present sunk garden, a bowling-green was laid out by Charles the Second.

Below, on the north, were Queen Anne's gardens, since whose time the declivity of the hill has been planted with forest trees.

At the east angle of the north terrace are the beautiful slopes, with a path skirting the north side of the Home Park, and leading through charming plantations in the direction of the royal farm and dairy, the ranger's lodge, and the kennel for the queen's harriers.

This park contains many noble trees ; and the grove of elms in the south-east, near the spot where the scathed oak assigned to Herne stands, is traditionally asserted to have been a favourite walk of Queen Elizabeth.

It still retains her name.

The Great Park is approached by the magnificent avenue called the Long Walk, laid out, as has been stated, by Charles the Second, and extending to the foot of Snow Hill, the summit of which is crowned by the colossal equestrian statue of George the Third, by Westmacott.

Not far from this point stands Cumberland Lodge, which derives its name from William, Duke of Cumberland, to whom it was granted in 1744.

According to Norden's survey, in 1607, this park contained 3,050 acres ; but when surveyed by George the Third, it was found to consist of 3,800 acres ; of which 200 were covered with water.

At this time the park was overgrown with fern and rushes, and abounded in bogs and swamps, which in many places were dangerous and almost impassable.

It contained about three thousand head of deer in bad condition.

The park has since been thoroughly drained, smoothed, and new planted in parts ; and two farms have been introduced upon it, under the direction of Mr. Kent, at which the Flemish and Norfolk modes of husbandry have been successfully practised.

Boasting every variety of forest scenery, and commanding from its knolls and acclivities magnificent views of the castle, the Great Park is traversed in all directions, by green drives threading its long vistas, or crossing its open glades, laid out by George the Fourth.

Amid the groves at the back of Spring Hill, in a charmingly-sequestered situation, stands a small private chapel, built in the Gothic style, and which was used as a place of devotion by George the Fourth during the progress of the improvements at the castle, and is sometimes attended by the present queen.

Not the least of the attractions of the park is Virginia Water, with its bright and beautiful expanse, its cincture of green banks, soft and smooth as velvet, its screen of noble woods, its Chinese fishing temple, its frigates, its ruins, its cascade, cave, and Druidical temple, its obelisk and bridges, with numberless beauties besides, which it would be superfluous to describe here.

This artificial mere covers pretty nearly the same surface of ground as that occupied by the great lake of olden times.

Windsor Forest once comprehended a circumference of a hundred and twenty miles, and comprised part of Buckinghamshire, a considerable portion of Surrey, and the whole south-east side of Berkshire, as far as Hungerford.

On the Surrey side it included Cobham and Chertsey, and extended along the side of the Wey, which marked its limits as far as Guildford.

In the reign of James the First, when it was surveyed by Norden, its circuit was estimated at seventy-seven miles and a half, exclusive of the liberties extending into Buckinghamshire.

There were fifteen walks within it, each under the charge of a head keeper, and the whole contained upwards of three thousand head of deer.

It is now almost wholly enclosed.

CHAPTER LXXII.

THE LAST GREAT EPOCH IN THE HISTORY OF THE CASTLE.

A PRINCE of consummate taste and fine conceptions, George the Fourth, meditated, and what is better, accomplished, the restoration of the castle to more than its original grandeur.

He was singularly fortunate in his architect.

Sir Jeffry Wyatville was to him what William of Wykeham had been to Edward the Third.

All the incongruities of successive reigns were removed; all, or nearly all, the injuries inflicted by time repaired; and when the work, so well commenced, was finished, the structure took its place as the noblest and most majestic palatial residence in existence.

To enter into a full detail of Wyatville's achievements is beyond the scope of the present work; but a brief survey may be taken of them.

Never was lofty design more fully realised.

View the castle on the north, with its grand terrace of nearly a thousand feet in length, and high embattled walls; its superb facade, comprehending the stately Brunswick Tower; the Cornwall Tower, with its gorgeous window; George the Fourth's Tower, including the great oriel window of the state drawing-room; the restored Stuart buildings, and those of Henry the Seventh and of Elizabeth; the renovated Norman Tower; the Powder Tower, with the line of walls as far as the Winchester Tower;—view this, and then turn to the east, and behold another front of marvellous beauty, extending more than four hundred feet from north to south, and displaying the Prince of Wales's Tower, the Chester, Clarence, and Victoria Towers—all of which have been raised above their former level, and enriched by great projecting windows; behold, also, the beautiful sunken garden, with its fountain and orangery, its flights of steps, and charming pentagonal terrace;—proceed to the south front, of which the Victoria Tower, with its machicolated battlements and oriel window, forms so superb a feature at the eastern corner, the magnificent gateway receiving its name from George the Fourth, flanked by the York and Lancaster Towers, and opening in a continued line from

the Long Walk;—look at St. George's gate, Edward the Third's renovated tower, and the octagon tower beyond it;—look at all these, and if they fail to excite a due appreciation of the genius that conceived them, gaze at the triumph of the whole, and which lords over all the rest, —the Round Tower—gaze at it, and not here alone, but from the heights of the Great Park, from the great vistas of the Home Park, from the bower of Eton, the meads of Clewer and Datchet, from the Brocas, the gardens of the naval knights—from a hundred points;—view it at sunrise when the royal standard is hoisted, or at sunset when it is lowered, near or at a distance, and it will be admitted to be the work of a prodigious architect.

But Wyatville's alterations have not yet been fully considered. Pass through St. George's gateway, and enter the grand quadrangle to which it leads. Let your eye wander round it, beginning with the inner sides of Edward the Third's Tower and George the Fourth's gateway, and proceeding to the beautiful private entrance to the sovereign's apartments, the grand range of windows of the eastern corridor, the proud towers of the gateway to the household, the tall pointed windows of St. George's Hall, the state entrance tower, with its noble windows, until it finally rests upon the Stuart-buildings and King John's Tower at the angle of the pile.

Internally the alterations made by the architect have been of corresponding splendour and importance.

Around the south and east sides of the court at which you are gazing a spacious corridor has been constructed, five hundred and fifty feet in length, and connected with the different suites of apartments on these sides of the quadrangle.

Extensive alterations have been made in the domestic offices.

The state apartments have been repaired and rearranged.

Saint George's Hall has been enlarged by the addition of the private chapel (the only questionable change), and restored to the Gothic style; and the Waterloo chamber, built to contain George the Fourth's munificent gift to the nation of the splendid collection of portraits now occupying it.

" The first and most remarkable characteristic of the operations of Sir Jeffry Wyatville on the exterior," observes Mr. Poynter, " is the judgment with which he has preserved the castle of Edward the Third. Some additions have been made to it, and with striking effect, as the Brunswick Tower, and the western tower of George the Fourth's gateway, which so nobly terminates the approach from the Great Park. The more modern buildings on the north side have also been assimilated to the rest; but the architect has yielded to no temptation to substitute his own design for that of William of Wykeham, and no small difficulties have been combatted and overcome for the sake of preserving the outline of the edifice, and maintaining the towers in their original position."

The Winchester Tower, originally inhabited by William of Wykeham, was bestowed upon Sir Jeffry Wyatville as a residence by George the Fourth; and on the resignation of the distinguished architect, was continued to him for life by the present queen.

The works within the castle were continued during the reign of William the Fourth, and at its close the actual cost of the buildings had reached the sum of £771,000, and it has been asserted that the general expenditure up to the present time has exceeded a million and a half of money.

The view from the summit of the Round Tower is beyond description magnificent, and commands twelve counties—namely, Middlesex, Essex, Hertford, Berks, Bucks, Oxford, Wilts, Hants, Surrey, Sussex, Kent, and Bedford; while, on a clear day, the dome of Saint Paul's may be distinguished from it.

This tower was raised thirty-three feet by Sir Jeffry Wyatville, crowned with a machicolated battlement, and surmounted with a flag-tower.

The circumference of the castle is 4,180 feet; the length from east to west, 1,480 feet; and the area, exclusive of the terraces, about twelve acres.

For the present the works are suspended.

But it is to be hoped that the design of Sir Jeffry Wyatville will be fully carried out in the lower ward, by the removal of such houses on the north as would lay Saint George's Chapel open to view from this side; by the demolition of the old incongruous buildings lying westward of the bastion near the hundred steps; by the opening out of the pointed roof of the library; the repair and reconstruction in their original style of the Curfew, the Garter, and the Salisbury Towers; and the erection of a lower terrace, extending outside the castle, from the bastion above mentioned to the point of termination of the improvements, and accessible from the town; the construction of which terrace would necessitate the removal of the disfiguring and encroaching houses on the east side of Thames-street.

This accomplished, Crane's ugly buildings removed, and the three western towers laid open to the court, the Horseshoe Cloisters consistently repaired, Windsor Castle would indeed be complete.

And fervently do we hope that this desirable event may be identified with the reign of Victoria.

CHAPTER LXXIII.

MOTHER CLIFFORD FINDS THE MYSTERIOUS TRAVELLER —THE STORY OF HIS LIFE.

WE left the traveller confronting the weird woman of the old Hall.

"So," cried the hag; "so you would seek to unravel the mystery of my power, and destroy the charm by which I hold sway over the minds and bodies of men. You have been too bold. Take your reward."

Uttering these words, the old hag lifted her hand, and the traveller fell senseless at her feet.

The great white cat, which ever followed the old hag as some familiar spirit, now approached the prostrate man; and his servant, terrified beyond expression, fled from the spot.

"So," cried the hag; "so he is in my power now."

Here we must leave them for awhile.

The mysterious appearance of the traveller, and his subsequent act, demand some explanation, and in as few words as possible we put the story of his life before the reader.

*   *   *   *

It was fair day at Croydon, but the sun was disappearing beyond the hills, and the festivities were over.

Along the road from London a man and woman were hurrying, and scarcely stopping to take refreshment.

By their side trotted a little girl, of some five or six years of age, who seemed to accord even less attention than they did to the adverse climate and the ruggedness of the highway.

The woman, as far as you could judge of her in her drenched and ragged state, was about five-and-twenty; her face was pale, wan, and careworn, though her form was somewhat robust, as well as gracefully moulded, and her white hands indicated that work had never claimed her as its victim.

The man who accompanied her was somewhat older than herself, and of a different type of mind as well as of person.

He was tall, and strongly built, with long dark hair hanging over his shoulders, small, keen eyes, and a mouth indicative less of firmness than of obstinacy.

He was either labouring under the influence of intense sorrow or fierce anger at the moment we introduce him to our readers; for his brow was contracted, his lips set, and he had uttered no sound for hours.

"We shall never reach the town!" he cried, at length, petulantly. "I knew it would be thus! I knew you desired me to be overtaken, that you might be rid of me for ever!"

These words, implying more than the simple syllables expressed, appeared to rend the woman's heart. She gazed up into his face imploringly for a moment, and then, as if suddenly abandoning her resolution to plead with him, she said, "Do not despair, dear Alfred, we shall soon be there. See the houses yonder! The town cannot be far distant."

They were still in the open country, but the cottages were becoming more frequent and more closely built.

Then they passed the last farm, with its cows and horses standing dreamily beneath the trees to shelter themselves from the rain, and the pigs wallowing in the dirt, and giving vent to their delight in monotonous gruntings.

Then came a large church, then an inn, and then again there was a pause, as if the builders had doubted where the town should really commence.

Between this inn and the High-street at Maylsworth lay about half a mile of road, skirted on one side by meadow land, and on the other a thickly wooded heath— for it could not properly be termed a wood.

The trees came down to the very edge of the pathway, and through this, on bright sunny days, was a nearer and pleasanter road to the town.

Here, on a rude seat by the roadside, where a temporary shelter could be obtained from the rain, the man sat down sullenly, and the woman joined him, while the child, caring little for the weather, and knowing less of what engrossed their thoughts, wandered among the trees near at hand.

"Why do you stop here, Alfred?" asked the woman, in a tremulous voice. "If you were too tired to go on, why did you not rest at the inn we have just passed?"

The man muttered an oath.

"I'm going to let you have your own way," he said, morosely. "I'll stop here till they overtake us, and then you'll be relieved of me altogether."

The woman laid her hand gently upon his arm.

"Tell me, Alfred," she murmured, "tell me what ails you to-day? Why do you speak thus cruelly to me, when I have walked fifty miles with you through rain and storm, with scarcely a rest between our journeys, to aid you in escaping the consequences of your own folly? Tell me what I have done to deserve your anger."

The man glanced round, and seeing the child was not near him, but was stooping down to gather some wild flowers which were nestling from the rain beneath a tree, he leaned forward, and said, in soft tones, "Did I not wish to reach Croydon during the fair day? Was it not a necessity—was it not life itself—for me to do this simple thing? What has prevented me?"

"Yes—what indeed?"

The man eyed her fiercely once more.

"You have prevented me!" he cried, "you!—because you have fixed your heart upon that child, and you have sacrificed me. Have you not dragged her with you through this long, weary journey? Have you not toiled and fretted through this desperate wandering, when you might have gone on rapidly, and with hope in your breast, if she had been left behind? Now I dread every step, and start at every shadow; and I would sooner have done with it at once. Let them take me, if you will,— but with that child I go no further."

The man's voice was hard and determined.

She knew it was useless to combat his will when he spoke thus; yet she ventured to say—

"And what can we do with her? Can we leave her in the road to die?"

"Die! Just heavens! your words would make an angel desperate. Are we taking her to luxury, or are we taking her from it? Are we able to promise her anything in the future beyond a slow but certain starvation, and a death in a cold barn? Is she better with us than playing there, where she will be found by the good Samaritan who has, through all my life, avoided me."

There was a bitter mockery in the man's voice which made the woman tremble.

"Any one would think that the girl was your own," he cried, "to see the tears in your eyes, and the trembling in your form. Either leave the child here, or prepare to see me to-night in the hands of those I hate, and who are pursuing me to my ruin. Come," he added, in a gentle tone, "come."

The woman glanced at him in terror for a moment, and then muttered to herself—

"They cannot be far off now. They must be within a few miles of us," she said. "He is right; the child must be left."

She rose and approached the little girl, who glanced at her with a smile.

"Alice, darling," she says; "wait here a few moments while I and Alfred go to the town and fetch something to eat. We shall not be long."

The little girl loooked wistfully at her.

"Why must I not come too?" she asked.

"Because it rains, and it is some distance to Maylsworth. You can rest here."

"Don't go away and leave me," said the little girl, plaintively.

"Leave you, dear one!" whispered the woman, as she kissed her, eagerly; "no, no! We will soon be back—soon be back."

And she hurried away after Alfred, who had already started.

Meanwhile Alice sat down on the bench with her wild flowers, wondering why Mary had kissed her at parting, and why, too, she had wept so bitterly.

Their forms had scarcely disappeared in the twilight, when a man stepped from out the trees close by the bench, and after looking up and down the road, approached the child.

He was a tall, finely-built man, dressed in the picturesque and somewhat grotesque garb of the gipsies.

His appearance, however, seemed to belie his costume; his hands and his face, too were but little bronzed, and his hair, long, curly, and abundant, was of a golden auburn tint.

He sat down by the child on the bench, and smiled gently upon her.

This great rudely-attired man would certainly have alarmed her had he not spoken; but when he spoke, his voice, rich, low, and melodious, at once won her heart.

"And so they've gone away and left you, little Alice!" he said, familiarly, as if he had known her all her life.

"They're coming back presently," answered the child, glancing up at him half inquiringly, half deprecatingly.

"No, no, my little one they are not," he said kindly; "they've left you here by yourself, and they are not coming back. Never mind, my child, there are others in the world who will love you; and some, perhaps, whose hearts are breaking for you now."

The little girl did not understand one-half he said; but she understood well enough that she had been deserted.

Somehow or another she did not feel inclined to cry.

Her little heart throbbed and ached as it were with terror, and looking up into the kindly blue eyes of the strange gipsy, she placed her hand in his.

"Let us go after them," she said.

"No, no," he cried, "that will be of no use. I heard all they said; they do not want you, and would be unkind to you were you to follow them. Come with me; perhaps some day I may find your friends."

The girl smiled.

"That is what Alfred always said," she cried, as she walked away through the wood with her new protector.

In the deepening shadows of the gathering night, more dense and gloomy than elsewhere, in that wood-encircled glen, the gipsies had pitched their tents; and as Alice and her friend approached they could see twinkling through the trees the bright fires, and hear the voices of men and women borne on the evening breeze. The man who accompanied this little child, and had assumed the grave relationship of guardian after but a few moments' reflection, seemed to be some one of consequence among the tribe; for the songs ceased, and the talking became less loud, as he entered the throng and sat down.

"Whom have we here?" cried an old crone, who was busily engaged preparing some kind of savory stew in an iron cauldron, suspended by a few sticks over a blazing fire.

The gipsy eyed her somewhat sternly.

"I do not know, therefore I can answer no questions, mother," he replied. "She is cold, wet, and hungry; let her have some supper."

Beneath the shelter of some canvas rudely cast from branch to branch, twelve gipsies, men and women, crouched, a motley, wild group, which at first surprised and terrified the new comer, but which, after a time, became familiar to her, as anything would become familiar to a child who had just eaten a hearty meal after a long and painful fast.

About half-past eight o'clock Alice lay quietly sleeping within one of the tents, and the young gipsy, without a word to any one, rose from his seat by the fire, and made his way towards the town.

CHAPTER LXXIV.

THE STORY OF THE TRAVELLER'S LIFE CONTINUED.

ABOUT six o'clock that evening two persons were seated in a drawing-room at the Lion Hotel, Ayledown—a town which lay about ten miles from Maylsworth, on the London road

The one was a gentleman of some forty-five years—a fine, noble-looking man, with a benevolent and aristocratic cast of features, and hair slightly tinged with grey.

The lady, who sat opposite to him, and who was playing with a tiny dog, was perhaps three and-twenty.

She was very beautiful, with a slight figure, an oval, pale face, and golden hair, which clustered round it in rich waves.

Her eyes were large and bright, her nose small and finely chiselled, her mouth petite and rosy.

Her hands, small and plump, lay luxuriously upon her lap, calmly and cosily, as if no agitation was within that fair and graceful form.

On the table were two decanters of wine, and the remains of a dessert; but neither of the personages of whom we have spoken seemed to pay any attention to it.

"When you have quite rested, my dear," said the elderly gentleman, kindly, "we will go on. I become alarmed at this long and useless chase."

He was looking at the fire as he spoke, and could not see the smile which passed over his wife's features as she listened.

The smile, whatever was its cause, passed away in a moment; and with a look of deep concern, she flung the dog from her lap, and knelt by his side.

"My dear, kind husband," she said, looking up into his face, "I grieve to see you thus agitated. We will go on at once if you wish it; though, as they are wandering on foot, and we are travelling with our carriage, we should catch them even if we remained here till morning."

Her husband smoothed her golden tresses and kissed her brow.

"Wandering, wandering on foot," he said ; that is the very thought which terrifies me. Even if no harm comes to the child, they may follow out-of-the-way paths and bye-lanes, where we may lose every clue to their whereabouts."

The young wife rose in haste, either to display her eagerness to please him, or to hide some transient emotion.

"Ring, my dear," she said, carressing him. "Ring, and tell them to get the carriage ready, and I will be with you in a moment."

She then passed out of the room, and into her bedchamber, where a young girl, dressed with the plain neatness peculiar to lady's-maids, stood gazing out of the window.

She started as her mistress entered, and looked around.

Her rosy face and black hair contrasted strangely with the bright golden hair and somewhat pallid complexion of Lady Moore.

"Have you any message for me?" cried the latter, in a hushed, eager tone.

The girl gave her slip of paper. Lady Moore read it anxiously, and the colour came and went upon her face as she did so.

Suddenly she glanced up at the servant.

"You have read this?" she said, quickly.

"I have, madam," replied the lady's maid, whose face was averted.

"You know all my secrets, Annette," said Lady Moore, while a strange light illuminated her eyes, and her bosom heaved convulsively. "Take care you guard this one well."

Annette did not answer, but busied herself with preparing her mistress for the journey.

The lady was still pondering over the slip of paper, when Sir Charles Moore knocked and entered.

He smiled on seeing the paper, which his wife crushed in her hand.

"Has some friend found us out, even here?" he asked.

She smiled sweetly.

"No," she said ; "its only a fragment of an old letter which recalls foolish days. I am quite ready"

Sir Charles gave her his arm, and they descended the stairs.

"I am very sorry we had to stop so long," he murmured, as their carriage was once more on its way.

"It *is* a pity," said Lady Moore, languidly ; "but I really could not have borne further fatigue without some rest. Even now I feel very ill."

"Poor Maud," replied Sir Charles, carressing her fondly "it was a pity that you came with me,"

After this there was a silence.

Lady Moore appeared to relapse into a slumber, while Sir Charles sat up, glancing to the right and the left, and in the dim uncertain light scrutinising the face of every traveller.

And so they passed along the road which the child's weary feet had trodden an hour before, whirled by the gipsies' encampment, where she sat quietly eating her evening meal with her new friends, and dashed into the High-street at Croydon.

At the first inn they pulled up, and Sir Charles Moore alighted.

Lady Maud sat in her carriage, and listened eagerly. The os'ler came out.

"Put up the horses, sir?"

"No, no," cried the baronet, placing a crown in the man's hand ; "I wish you to answer me some questions. I am seeking a person whom I believe to have passed along this road."

"Yes, sir."

He is a tall well-built fellow, dressed in an uncouth style, and has with him a woman and a child."

"Yes, sir."

"Have you seen them?"

"Yes, sir ; I've seen the man and the woman—at least, so I think, by your description, sir."

"But the child—the child—what of her?" asked the baronet eagerly.

"I didn't see a child, sir ; leastwise, it was dark, and it might be a little one that I couldn't see. They sat out here and had some beer and a biscuit between 'em, and then they walked off like mad, and were gone in a moment."

"And you saw no child?"

"No sir."

Lady Moore leaned out of the carriage window.

"We are losing time, Sir Charles," she said ; "these people are clearly not those we seek."

"I fear not," murmured the baronet, in a voice which proved how loth he was to lose this faint clue to hope. "And you are quite sure they carried no child away with them?"

"Quite sure, sir."

"This is conclusive, Charles," said Lady Maud, somewhat coldly. "This child is five years old, and must have been seen had she been here."

Her hands were working nervously as she spoke ; her face, her very lips, were pale with emotion.

"What are we to do?" inquired the baronet, disconsolately.

"I think we had better return, and trust to others, my dear husband," said Lady Moore, gently. "Your health will suffer for all this anxiety and trouble, indeed it will."

"I do not like so easily to abandon the search," said the baronet, as if to himself.

"Leastwise, they cannot have gone far," cried the ostler. "They ain't been gone long, not more than half an hour. They took the main road."

"Drive on!" said Sir Charles to the coachman, as he re-entered the carriage. Drive on as quickly as you can."

Lady Moore sank back in her seat, and pretended to sleep.

If her desire was that her husband should be unsuccessful in his pursuit, and if her anxiety was produced by the faint glimmer of hope now offered to him, she might, by a little thought, have spared herself much perplexity and agitation.

The night was dark and gloomy, and though the rain had now ceased to descend, heavy clouds still obscured the heavens.

The town itself was dismal enough, and out in the country it was as black as pitch.

Alfred and Mary, notwithstanding, had forsaken the high road about a mile from Croydon, and were at that very moment making their way, through dirt and darkness, across country.

A good piece of mystery is a blessing in any society, more especially in a country town ; and, as soon as the carriage had rolled out of the court-yard, the baronet and his lady were introduced by the ostler into the conversation of the public room, and various were the opinions exchanged on the subject.

In the room, on that evening, were represented the remnants of the festive gathering of the last few days.

A few dogs, decorated with coats and bells, lay lazily in a corner ; a boy and a girl, crouched asleep, were there, dressed in spangled attire, and hugging in their sleep a pair of stilts ; a miniature stage nearly blocked up one window, and several rough-looking men were disposed in various groups.

About half-an-hour after the departure of Sir Charles and Lady Moore, the door was flung open, and the gipsy who had befriended little Alice entered.

"Ah, the White Gipsy," cried Paunch, a Punch and Judy man. "Why, Ashworth, my boy, I thought you had given us all the slip, and was going to reach Freetop before us."

"No," he answered. "We start to-morrow. I see we shall not be quite alone, either, since all of you here have remained behind for the wet weather. We number one more, for we've picked up a little one to-night."

The men looked from one to another, and Job, the ostler, smiled wisely.

"What do you mean?" said the gipsy, somewhat testily. "Do you knew anything about it?"

"Well," said Job, who by general consent seemed to be chosen as spokesman, "there's been a gentleman and lady here to-night after a child ; maybe it's the same."

"Did they give no name?" asked Ashworth, who now seemed to draw back and reserve the confidence he had intended to make.

"Well, I think I heard the coachman say Moore," replied the ostler; "I know the lady said Sir Charles."

The gipsy's face grew deadly pale as the man spoke; and, then, as if swayed by some sudden impulse, he sprang up and left the room.

"Better as it is," he muttered, as he strode down the dark road towards the gipsies' tents. "Anywhere—anywhere better than in their hands."

CHAPTER LXXV.

THE STORY OF THE TRAVELLER CONTINUED.

AT the period of our story, London was little like the London of to-day.

It was the centre of innumerable little hamlets or suburbs, now joined to it by stately streets, but then only to be reached by gloomy highways, or gloomier bridle-paths, where crime lurked in every shadow, and where the highwayman loitered carelessly under the protecting shade of dense and lofty trees.

The streets themselves,—lit by dim and melancholy-looking oil lamps—were gloomy, too; and here and there, where the wind or an interested person had extinguished the lights, they were buried in impenetrable obscurity.

In these places hid the thief escaping from justice—the gambler who had left his fortunate companion on the ground with a stab in his back—the man whom society had rendered an outlaw, and who preyed upon his fellows.

For hours the silence of these dark corners was unbroken, save by the dreary voice of the watchman, or the bawling of some sedan chair bearers, as they rushed along, preceded by lackeys, with flaming flambeaux.

Along these still and gloomy streets a man was wandering on the night before the arrival of Sir Charles Moore, at Croyden.

A man, tall, and spare, and sallow—one upon whom misfortune had placed the stamp of the most wretched of her children—a man who, when he passed you, shrunk from you, and darted away into darkness.

You could see his stealthy backward glance as he passed, and feel involuntarily how he avoided you, as if contact with you were a terror to his mind.

At twilight he had emerged into the streets.

Whence he came no one knew, for none had seen him issue forth.

All the watchman knew was that a noiseless, creeping figure had suddenly passed him, and startled him from a reverie.

He was evidently alone in the city ; and it was evident, too, that his heart sank at the thought.

You may be alone out in the dark country, when the only sound you hear is the pattering of the unwelcome rain, and the only shelter is the hayrick or the deserted barn.

This is cheerless and wretched enough, but how far more lonely is loneliness in the heart of a great city—how much more dismal is it to feel that thousands of human beings are living and breathing around you—that they are sleeping the sleep in which all are equal, and that among the gaiety and quiet, the dissipation and the home happiness, the bustling and slumbering citizens, you are the chosen one of despair !

These are the dread feelings which drive men to evil deeds—these are the miseries over which the dark rivers of great cities close each night.

When the evening had passed away, he left the streets of the city, and plunged into the dreary road which then lay between London and Hampstead.

There were but few stars in the sky, and the country looked dismal, wet, and uninviting.

It would have been full of terrors, too, for most people. But Magsworth feared nothing.

Who is so bold as he who has nothing to lose ?

He held in his hand a stout stick, which he clutched as if it were the arm of a companion.

And when he had passed the last house he never paused a moment to see if there were any lights before him, but plunged boldly onward.

If, however, he feared detection, he would have glanced behind him.

Scarcely had he left the long stream of flickering light which issued from the Rising Sun Tavern, when two men, clad in rough jackets, who had been following him a long way off, quickened their pace, and passed after him into the gloom of the high road.

He walked along so eagerly and so rapidly that it was evident he had a great object a-head of him.

But a man who is thrown much upon the cold mercy of the world is suspicious of every sound, and is never quite lost to outward things.

So, although his eyes were fixed before him, his ear quickly detected the sound of footsteps behind him.

He trembled violently.

Was his hand against every one, and was every one's hand against him, that he thus feared his fellow men ?

However this may be he took a very sudden resolution.

Without wasting a moment in reflection, he slid down from the pathway into a deep ditch, where a stream of gently running water gurgled over the pebles amid the slimy seeds, and hid himself away in the shadow.

Presently the two men approached.

The silence which pervaded the country evidently puzzled them, and they were talking earnestly as they passed him.

"He must have turned aside near this spot," said one of them. "I'll swear that up to this point he kept along the road."

They stopped still a few yards a-head of him and consulted.

"Well," said the second traveller. "we need not wait. We know his destination ; and all we have to do is to keep on and reach the place before him, or, at any rate, as soon as he does."

"Yes ; but much good might be done if we could prevent his going there, or, at least, see him before he does go."

He paused a moment to think.

"Well, well," he said, "it is of no use to remain here. Let us go forward."

And so, after this short interruption, they went on very rapidly, until they almost increased their pace to a run.

The traveller rose from his strange hiding-place, and laughed bitterly to himself.

"What good do they propose by hunting me thus ?" he muttered, as he left the high road and passed along a narrow path across a dank and oozy field. "If the child be still alive, she shall come with me if the whole world is there to prevent me."

Meanwhile, the two men, who, for some strange reason

THE WHITE MARE IN THE FOREST.

were dogging his footsteps, continued their progress until they reached a little cottage which stood by itself a short distance from the high road.

A light trembled in the window.

A shadow now and then fell upon the blind above.

That was all, in that still dark spot, which proved that human beings were there.

In the front room of that cottage—there were but two rooms—sat a woman who had scarcely yet quitted the period when one can lay claim to youth.

Her hair was neatly braided beneath a widow's cap—her hands were folded on her lap—her eyes were fixed upon the flames in the reviving fire.

At her feet lay a large black dog, asleep, with his nose flattened out along his massive paws.

The furniture of the place was scanty, but what there was was good.

It seemed to tell a story of days when it had only been a portion of the stock of a well-filled house.

On the black shelves that stood in one corner were many volumes of all imaginable sizes and characters but on this evening evidently the widow's books were in the flames, and in them she was reading the past, or striving to understand the future.

Suddenly the dog started, and uttered a low, plaintive growl.

The widow gazed at him with alarm in her face, but she had not much time left for surmise.

Before she could collect her thoughts a loud knock called her to the door.

She drew back, and then closed the door again somewhat tremulously, as there entered one of the pursuers of Magworth.

He was a tall, well-built man, of some forty years of age—a man with whom nature had dealt kindly, and who rewarded her for it by his evident enjoyment of life.

He was dressed in a rough coat, and wore his hat with a dash of jauntiness on one side of his head, but his attire was altogether of a character which was evidently a disguise.

"Good evening, Mistress Bellingham," he said. "Have you seen anything this night of Magsworth?"

The woman clasped her hands in mute terror.

"Tell me the truth," he added, sternly. "I am seeking him for his own good."

"I *will* tell the truth," she cried. "I have *not* seen him; and, what is more, I hope and trust he will not come here. His coming is always the sequel of sorrow to himself or to others."

"He is a rash and foolish man," muttered the gentleman, who was evidently convinced by the widow's earnest manner; "but he ought by this time to be aware that from Sir Vere de Vere he need fear no evil. He is coming here to-night, I am certain, so I will await him here."

The widow gazed at him in fear.

"Oh, Sir Vere, let him not find you here," she supplicated. "You know his fierce and ungovernable temper."

"Tush, woman!" cried Sir Vere, interrupting her impatiently. "What do you fear? Tell me, where is the child?"

"It is gone," said Mrs. Bellingham.

The baronet's cheek blanched.

"Gone!" he cried in a hoarse voice; "what mean you—is it dead?"

"Dead! No, no, not dead — not so terrible a misfortune as that. But I have lost it. Mary has taken it away with her—where no one knows; and Sir Charles and Lady Moore are even now in search of it."

Sir Vere de Vere remained for a few moments in thought. Then he rose slowly.

"Mrs. Bellingham," he said, sternly, "I will leave you; my servant has gone up to the hall; I will follow him thither. Upon your own head be the result of this crime, for so your neglect may justly be termed. To you, then, I abandon the task of telling this terrible news. Hark!"

He stood still, with his arm uplifted.

There was a sound as of footsteps approaching the house, but no one raised the latch of the door, though both felt *he* was there.

There was a shadow at the window—a glare of bloodshot eyes at the bright fire—the stain of breath upon the glass, and he was gone.

Sir Vere, yielding to his first impulse, rushed to the door.

A dim, hurrying figure passed between him and the horizon.

"Come back, come back."

He would have followed, but the widow clung to him with the eagerness of terror.

"Oh! molest him not," she cried, in a voice of earnest entreaty; "molest him not. Remember his child is gone, and I have to answer to him for her. Think of his fearful anger, Sir Vere, and, for the love of heaven, leave him to himself."

The baronet thought a moment, and then slowly and in silence took his way towards Moore House, which stood about a mile beyond.

When he had advanced some few hundred yards he stopped and glanced back.

The light in the cottage had been extinguished.

Fearing that some evil deed had been perpetrated since his departure by the man whose anger the widow seemed so greatly to dread, he at first thought of going back, but then with a shudder he turned away, and hurried onwards towards Moore House.

CHAPTER LXXVI.

THE TRAVELLERS—THE CHILD.

THERE had been a feud for many years in the family of the Moores. Sir Charles Moore, the elder brother, had ever been the favourite both of his father and mother, and Magworth Moore, the younger, had suffered the inevitable consequence.

He had been brought up in the atmosphere of indifference, and had learned to hate him who should have been his companion and friend.

When Charles became baronet by the death of his father—the mother had been dead some years before— Charles left Moore Castle and proceeded to London.

A moderate competence had been secured to him by his father, and on this he lived for some time, scorning to work honestly, because, as he imagined, it was ungentlemanly.

After a time, however he married, and had one child.

His marriage altogether changed the aspect of affairs.

His wife, a young and beautiful woman, was always ailing; and his money, forestalled by loans and mortgages, soon evaporated.

Then he applied to his friends, who refused him help, and referred him to his brother.

His brother, however, was the last person in the world to whom he would have gone in such an emergency, and she died and was buried in poverty.

The child, little Alice Moore, was placed by her father under the care of Mrs. Bellingham, at the cottage near Moore House.

Why he chose this spot it is difficult to say, but it might have been with a dim, undefined hope that if fortune proved fickle to himself, Alice, at least, might be near the home of a friend.

The child was placed at the cottage under the name of Alice Wentworth, and he himself, from the moment of his poverty, assumed that of Paisley Wentworth.

He disappeared.

Meanwhile Sir Charles Moore's wife died, leaving no issue.

Then, after a time of mourning, he married again, a Mrs. Maud Le Mot, the young widow of a French captain, who brought to him a pretty face, a handsome person, a little child, and no fortune.

She was an English woman, had married out of spite, and had taught her boy, a fine fellow of five, to hate his father, and ridicule his memory.

Sir Charles Moore soon discovered the propinquity of of his niece, and after a variety of coaxings and persuadings, he induced Mrs. Bellingham to allow the child to visit Moore House.

Little Alice, as she was called, was a winning child, and it was not long ere the baronet became devotedly attached to her.

His second marriage was, at the period our story opens, as unfortunate as the first.

No children blessed the union, and although Henri, his step-child, engrossed a considerable amount of his attention, his heart yearned towards Alice, who was, strictly speaking, his heiress.

And so some said she would be.

Others, on the contrary, spoke of another child, a boy, who, if he were living, would be nearly of age.

But of him nothing was known, neither of his birth, nor of his mother, nor of his subsequent life.

His name was a memory, that was all.

It was a week before the scene at Mrs. Bellingham's cottage that an event had occurred which plunged, not only Moore House, but the whole neighbourhood into consternation.

In the service of Sir Charles was a young woman named Mary Leyton, who had been imported into the establishment by Lady Maud, and who occupied an anomalous position, something between that of a lady's-maid and that of a companion.

Mary was but twenty years of age, and very pretty; but she looked older, and had an expression in her face which was anything but pleasing.

For some time she had been engaged to be married to Charles Ledbitter, the gardener at Moore House—a rough, ill-looking fellow, who appeared anything but a fit mate for her, but who, it is said, had saved a little money, and who seemed also to have a strange influence over her.

Lady Maud favoured this union, principally, it was believed, because she had some idea of getting rid of both of them, for some hidden reason.

A week before the opening of our story, as we have said, Lady Maude Moore called her maid Mary into her room.

"Mary," she said, "I have always placed great confidence in you."

Mary smirked.

"Yes, my lady," she answered, "in me and Florette, your other maid."

Lady Maud detected the slightest possible shade of annoyance in the reply.

She hastened to remove it.

"Yes," she said, "I have trusted Florette, too, because when I lose you it will be necessary to have some one to replace you. You know it is not easy to find one who can be trusted as you can."

"You are very good, my lady, I am sure," said Mary, curtseying.

"No; I am only telling the truth. But come, let me tell you why I have sent for you to-night. I wish you to get married."

Mary started.

"Get married!" she cried, in wonder.

"Yes; you have always told me you would like to marry Charles Ledbitter; now I will give you the means. But it must be on one condition that I help you, and one only."

"What is that, my lady?"

"That you leave the country. Nay, do not speak, do not offer any objections; there must be none. You must leave the country, and with you you must take Alice Wentworth—this child whom they pretend to be my husband's brother's daughter. It must be done at once, for Paisley Wentworth is expected home day by day, and if we delay it will be too late."

Mary thought a moment.

"Good, my lady!" she said. Shall I tell Charles?"

"No; let me do so myself. Send him to me."

Mary trembled, and her face changed colour rapidly.

She seemed under the influence of some unaccountable fear.

"What ails you?" asked Lady Moore.

Mary smiled faintly.

"I feel excited by this sudden announcement of yours, that is all," she said; "but had I not better tell Charles myself? If he be seen coming hither it may excite suspicion after I have gone."

Lady Moore thought a moment.

"True—you are right; so tell him at once. Say he must marry you the day after to-morrow. Give him these ten sovereigns, and explain that if he consents to my arrangement he shall have two thousand. But remember one thing. Not a penny more shall he have until he reaches Liverpool. There a man shall be in waiting to see him on board a vessel; once on board, the money shall be given him; but the journey from London to Liverpool must be performed on foot, that no one may suspect my connivance, if you are discovered, and that, moreover, you may not be traced. Go and tell him my plan, and when I have heard what he says I will give you minuter details."

Ten minutes after, Mary, attired in a neat bonnet and shawl—dressed, in fact, as little conspicuously as possible—took her way towards Hampstead.

The cottage where Charles Ledbitter resided was situated at one end of the grounds of Moore House, where it formed a kind of back lodge.

It was not, however, towards this lodge that Mary took her way.

After crossing the gardens, as much as possible in the shady portions, she glanced round after she reached the front lodge, to see if she was not followed, and then plunged down along the dark road.

Presently, amid the dense obscurity, burst forth a bright light, and she saw the sign of the 'Traveller's Rest" swinging to and fro in the wind.

She approached noiselessly, and peeped into the public room.

The light was dim and muffled in that room, for the smoke was dense, and the lamp fed with oil, which was far from the best; but near the window she could distinguish the form and face of one who was strikingly distinguished from the other occupants of the room.

He was young, tall, well-built, with a face which was intelligent and manly, without being handsome; but which was not so fortunate in expression as in feature.

His hair fell in long, light waves over his shoulders, and he wore his dress with an air of devil-may-care confidence, which, in him, was scarcely displeasing.

A smile passed over the girl's features as her eyes rested on him.

She then tapped the window three times.

The summons was at once understood.

The young man leaped up.

"I must go, my friends," he cried, gaily, as he caught up his hat. "Adieu, until our next merry meeting!"

In another moment he was at Mary's side.

"Why, Mary, my charmer," he cried, "you are, indeed, early! But what is the matter? You seem pale, and ill, and excited."

"I am, Alfred," said Mary. "I have much to tell. Listen, and I will explain all."

The young man listened—not very patiently, be it said—to her recital.

He laughed when she had finished her story.

"What has all this to do with me, my dear one?" he cried; "my name is not Charles Ledbitter?"

"No, no, Mark; you do not understand me," said Mary. "Lady Moore does not mean to see Charles, lest he should excite suspicion. Charles, therefore, will know nothing of all this. You must marry me, and have the two thousand pounds."

Alfred started.

"By Jove, Mary," he cried, "you are an angel. I have been at my unfortunate tricks again. I stopped a gentleman a week since in Lambeth Fields, and the rascally moon broke out full in my face, and he recognised me—not, however, till his purse was safe in my pocket. The Bow-street runners are after me; and I'll swear that every sound in yonder inn frightened me from my senses."

"You need be frightened no longer, then," said Mary.

"No, dear one; you have come in the nick of time. But, tell me, how is the matter to be arranged?"

"You must go to London, obtain a license in the name of Charles Ledbitter, marry me at once, and we will go. Here are the ten pounds my lady gave me to-night. When I tell her I have arranged matters, she will explain all the details, she says."

"Good, my little philosopher," cried Alfred, as he pocketed the ten sovereigns with gusto; "but there is one point you have overlooked."

What is that.

"Charles will be at Moore House, and will betray us by his very presence."

Mary thought a moment.

"I will concoct a letter," she said, "which will take him out of the neighbourhood for three days. By that time we shall be far on our journey."

"Well, well; time will prove. When am I to see you again?"

" To-morrow night."

" Good.   By that time I will have the license."

On the following night Mary met her lover, and having explained their future plans, and arranged the meeting for the morrow, left him, and betook herself towards home.

The night was dark and gloomy.

Heavy clouds swept across the sky, and the face of the country round, gloomy at all times, was now ten fold as black as usual.

Hampstead, as I have said elsewhere, was then a small and isolated village.

Broad roads and dark bridle-paths swept away from it everywhere, and the din of the mighty city beyond was drowned amid the voice of the trees.

At the corner of Lenford-lane—a narrow turning which, at that time, led from the main road towards Highgate Hill—he started as a tall figure suddenly stood beside him.

He drew back.

" You startled me, my friend," cried Alfred.   " Let me pass; I am in a hurry."

The other chuckled derisively.

" Not so fast, my friend," returned he; " I've got something to say to you."

" Indeed ! You might, then, have chosen a better place than this," replied Alfred; " some spot where we could see one another's faces."

" It's not necessary.   In such a place we might be overheard.   If you can't see my face, and don't know me, I'll tell you who I am and who you are.   I am Charles Ledbitter, and your name is Alfred Durant."

" Well, and what then ?"

" You have just left Mary."

" I have."

" What would you with her ?"

Alfred laughed loudly.

" What is that to you, Master Ledbitter ?"

" Everything.   She be going to marry me."

" Indeed ! Well, every woman to her taste.   I don't see what one need say more just now; so let me pass, as I am in a hurry."

" Now, understand me, Alfred Durant," cried Charles Ledbitter, sternly, " I didn't come here to jest; I came here to tell you, once for all, that I won't be made a fool of.   You've no right to be with Mary.   She's my sweetheart, and is going to be my wife; so look to it I don't meet you with her again.   I have seen you loafing about here for some time; and I'll tell you what, if I catch you at it again I'll set the Bow-street runners on to you. I know they're main anxious to catch hold of you."

The blood of the highwayman—for such truly was Alfred Durant—rose at these words.

" Stand aside," he cried hoarsely, " and molest me not, or, by Heavens, it will be the worse for you."

" Oh ! I've a little more to say, and you shall hear me out," said Charles.   " Ah ! would you come to blows so soon ?"

Alfred raised his heavy stick and rushed upon him.

Charles Ledbitter was active, but no match for his experienced opponent, and the combat was of but short duration.

In less than ten minutes Charles was lying, stunned and bleeding, on the earth.

Alfred knelt down, and by the pale light of the moon glanced at the man's face.

" He isn't dead—more's the pity," he muttered.   " If he were dead, and out of the way, why the cheat would never be discovered."

The cold sweat stood on his brow, and he glanced uneasily round him.

Then he drew from his breast a long, thin knife, and plunged it again and again into the chest of his senseless opponent.

A long-drawn sigh, a gush of blood, and all was over.

The cheat was safe from discovery.

But there was something more, though Alfred knew it not.

The Moores secret was safe.

On the next day Alfred and his wife left London, and Alice Wentworth went with them.

How they guarded their charge we already know.

CHAPTER LXXVII.

THE TRAVELLER'S TALE CONTINUED.

GREAT was the consternation of Sir Charles Moore when he discovered that the child he loved was gone.

The news came upon him like a thunderbolt.

Mrs. Bellingham came sobbing and in fear to Moore House to tell her story, and was listened to, first in wild astonishment by the baronet, and then in deep sorrow.

" I will immediately proceed in search of her, my good woman," he said, as he dismissed her and hurried to the room where sat Lady Moore.

The lady had heard of her coming, and was prepared for her husband's burst of grief and indignation.

She listened with apparently deep concern to her husband's story, and then throwing herself down, in her childish way, before him, she leaned on his knees, looking up at him with her blue, bright eyes, from beneath the wild waves of her golden hair.

" Sir Charles," she said, in a low, murmuring voice of sympathy, " what a sad disappointment for you."

The baronet started.

" Disappointment, madam," he cried; " I tell you it's no disappointment—I will not have it so.   This child is gone, but I will go after—I will find her—I will—"

The young wife's eyes filled with tears as he spoke.

He took her fair head between his hands, and caressed it fondly.

" Forgive me," he said, for my roughness.   I am very rude and passionate with you sometimes, my darling. But I am really very, very much grieved, and so excited that I scarcely know what I say or do."

" What purpose had these people in carrying away the child ?" asked Lady Maud quite innocently.

" I know not; Mrs. Bellingham could not tell me," returned Sir Charles.   " But I will soon ascertain it, for I will pursue them at once, and they shall answer for their conduct before a court of justice."

But the search was in vain, and in four days Sir Charles and his wife returned to Moore House.

" Now, my boy," murmured Lady Moore, as, upon her return, she patted the head of her fair boy; " now, my boy, we are safe, and you will be the heir to all."

Meanwhile, as we have said, Magworth came, on that black and threatening night, to the cottage of Mrs. Bellingham, but had rushed away in wild despair when Sir Vere de Vere appeared in the doorway.

The widow expected not his return, and so, bolting her door, she extinguished the lamp in the front room and retired to her bedchamber.

She had not been there many minutes, however, before a violent knocking again aroused her.

She went tottering to the door, opened it cautiously, and started back as Magworth entered, pale and haggard, with features distorted by passion.

" Where is my child ?" he cried fiercely.

" She is gone," said Mrs. Bellingham, falling on her knees before him, and clasping her hands in earnest supplication.   Pray—pray do not blame me, for I am guiltless."

The man slammed to the door, through which the night wind was blowing coldly, and raising the woman somewhat roughly, cried, " I want none of your crying and fooling.   Tell me, where is my child ?"

" I know not.   She is gone ; whither, no one can tell."

Magworth started up.

'It is to that man, Sir Vere!" he exclaimed, " you have given her up to him. Curses on him ! He shall rue this day."

" No, no, Mr. Moore," cried Mrs. Bellingham, calling him by his real name; "no—no; it is not he whom you have to blame—he has ever been a friend to you and yours. If you will let me, I will tell you the story, and you will then see who are your enemies."

Magsworth answered not, and the widow, taking his silence for consent, began her narrative.

" Sir Vere," she added, "has, I can assure you, been ever your best friend. He has spoken of you to Sir Charles in terms of much regret and sorrow, and was as grieved as any man could be when he heard of your loss."

Magsworth mused awhile.

"And so," he said, at length, " my brother professes to be fond of my little Alice ?"

" Yes ; he loved her as if she had been his own."

" And Lady Maud ?"

" I know not. Alice did not care much for her, I fancy. There was a kind of rivalry between her and Henri, the child of my lady by her former husband."

A strange gleam passed over the face of Magsworth as the widow.

" Good !" he said to himself—good ! I see through this most worthy plan now. Lady Moore is anxious that her son Henri shall inherit the estate ; so my poor child was in her way, and she has rid herself of it. These two people had no interest in her abduction, save the gain attaching to it through the malice of another person. I see my way clear before me, Mrs. Bellingham," he added aloud, in a voice of subdued emotion quite unusual to him, "I relieve you of all blame. I thank you for all the kindness you have shown me through my child, whom I could have taken so little care of in my rough and wandering life. Adieu, madam ; and, believe me, I shall never forget you."

" But the child—the child !" said the widow. " What of her ?"

Magsworth smiled.

" I believe in a providence," he answered, solemnly ; " I shall find her in good time. Meanwhile, I will punish her enemies."

He then rose, opened the door, and passed out into the night.

Three nights after the servant announced to Lady Moore that a man desired to speak with her.

"I can receive no one," she said, " who does not give his name. Did he mention none ?"

" Yes, my lady. It was something like Gaston Magsworth, but I am not sure. He had no card."

Lady Moore trembled slightly.

She had often heard her husband pronounce the name of Magworth ; knew that he was the younger brother of the Moore family, and feared he might come to demand what she had done with his child.

" But no," she murmured, as she dismissed the servant, and told him to admit the stranger, " no ; these are idle, foolish fears. He cannot suspect me."

In another moment Magsworth entered.

Lady Moore gazed at him in utter bewilderment for some moments.

" Can this pallid, ragged, desperate man be my husband's brother ?" she thought.

Truly, they were a contrast.

He tall, gaunt, in tattered dress, and with a figure fragile with misery.

She lovely, fairy-like, gentle-eyed, with a halo of golden curls around her marble brow, and the glow of health upon her cheeks.

They were both deceivers in their way.

In his dejected, wretched gait and manner one could scarcely discern one ray of the great hope that was in him.

In her bright eyes, her sylph-like beauty, her gentle voice, her whole air and carriage, you could never have beheld a part of that deadly, serpent-like hate which coiled around her heart.

Magsworth sat down upon a chair opposite to her, and gazed at her.

" A pretty toy my brother has bought himself," he muttered. " The son of such a woman shall never be a bar to a child of mine."

Lady Moore was impatient of his gaze.

" Pray, Mr. Magsworth," she said, " may I be favoured with your reason for this sudden reappearance under the paternal roof ?"

" Yes, madam," said Magsworth ; " I will explain it readily. I have lost my child ; I want money to enable me to search for her ; and I have come for this money to the woman who has wrought me this foul wrong."

Lady Moore started.

" I do not understand you, sir," she answered. " Who has deprived you of this child ?"

Magsworth's brow darkened with a cloud of terrible hate.

" You, madam ; you are the woman who has done this evil deed. I know it, there is no need to deny it ; but I can tell you this. Your son Henri shall never inherit the wealth that is my daughter's. Either I find her, or I take a deadly revenge !"

Lady Moore rose and approached the bell. The colour had left her pretty cheeks, and she had bitten her lips until the blood had stained them.

" I cannot suffer myself to be insulted in my own house," cried she ; " I will see that my servants turn you hence."

He rose also, and caught her wrist.

" Sit down, madam ; I am in my brother's house, and if it be necessary will let him share in our conference. I will let him know all this precious scheme, let him see how you are plotting to obtain for your son the estate of the Moores, after the death of this Sir Charles, whom you affect to love. Come, madam, understand me. What I will not ask at the hands of my brother I demand of you, because you, and you only, are the destroyer of my happiness."

" What is it you want, asked Lady Moore quietly.

" Five hundred pounds. No doubt you gave more to rid yourself of this obstacle."

Lady Moore tapped the fender with her tiny foot, and glanced confidingly into the fire.

" And supposing that I *had* paid these people to take away the child ?" she said, with a smile which made her rosy lips seem ghastly ; " do you not suppose that by this time they would be so far away as to be beyond your reach ?"

" I will search the world, madam," returned Magsworth. " I am not a man to be defeated ; and mark me well, if I find that any foul means have been adopted, there is a little boy in this house who shall be offered up as a sacrifice to my child."

Lady Moore shuddered.

" Your child's life is safe," she said ; " I am no murderess."

" You confess, then ?" cried Magsworth ; " you confess, then, you have done me this cruel wrong ?"

The ready tears—the ever-ready tears—burst into the large blue eyes, the plastic mouth worked, and the fair bosom heaved with simulated emotion.

" I *do* confess, Mr. Magsworth," she said in a low, hushed voice, which could be heard by none but he. " I *do* confess that in a moment of madness I *did* send your child away. But I *have* repented—indeed, indeed I have. Come to me to-morrow night, and you shall have all you require—even the latest clue I have to her present home. I will do this ; but I ask of you one thing in return — secrecy."

" I *will* be secret," returned Magsworth, " as long as I find you are not deceiving me. Once let me discover a proof of your deceit, and my vengeance will fall heavily —unerringly upon you."

He rose, and moved towards the door.

"Adieu, madam," he said.   "To-morrow at this hour expect me."

He then passed out, and his footsteps died away in the distance."

"Poor fool!" murmured Lady Moore, as she complacently lolled back in her easy chair.   "Poor fool! he thinks to beat me with my own weapons.   He little knows with whom he has to deal."

CHAPTER LXXVII.

THE TRAVELLER'S TALE CONTINUED.

LADY MAUD MOORE was lying on the following morning in bed, when her servant (Florette) brought her a note.

Lady Moore looked the picture of beautiful innocence.

Her night-dress was just sufficiently open to reveal her plump and alabaster shoulders, over which, and down her bosom coiled the rich golden waves of her glossy hair.

One rounded arm was thrown above her head, and her large dreamy blue eyes were cast upon vacancy.

Probably she was dreaming of some dire scheme of treachery.

Her sunny, innocent face might have suggested a dream of heaven.

She opened the note languidly.

Had she glanced at the direction, she would have started up and turned pale, for she would have recognised the handwriting.

When she opened it, and read the few first lines, the expression of her face altered instantaneously; a deadly pallor overspread her face, her neck, her bosom, and she became white as a statue.

The letter ran thus:—

"Liverpool.

"MY DEAR MADAM,—The ship sails in half-an-hour, and even these few lines I write in secret.

"You know already that I have deceived you, but you do not know how I have repented it.

"Alfred insisted upon my leaving the child behind on the journey.

"She is now, as far as I can tell, in the neighbourhood of Croydon.

"I can write no more, as I am watched.

"MARY DURANT.

Lady Moore crushed the letter in her hand, and held it over the flame of a taper.

"Baffled—baffled!" she murmured, as she stepped from the bed.   "What shall I do now?"

Sir Charles met her at breakfast, and was welcomed with the usual smiles and caresses.

"I am obliged to leave you to-day, my darling," said Sir Charles, "and I fear I shall not be able to return home until to-morrow.   I have received a letter which necessitates my being in London all day; and with your leave, Maud, I will remain at night, as the road is so lonely and so unpleasant."

Lady Maud assumed an air of concern.

"I shall be sorry for you to leave me," she said, "even for a day; but yet I would rather it were so than trust you to those dark high roads at night."

So Sir Charles Moore quitted the house at one in the afternoon, and Lady Maud was left alone with her thoughts.

For hours she sat alone.

She would admit no one, not even her son.

Late in the evening she called her maid, Florette, and, after an hour's conference, they went up to the lady's bed-chamber.

Then a curious scene was enacted.

Lady Maud deliberaeely broke open her jewel casket, and laid it open on the table.

The same thing was performed, in turn, to her dressing case and her trunks.

Then, leaving the window wide open, they quitted the room.

What did this mean?

At nine o'clock Magsworth approached the house.

It looked dark, shadowy, uninviting.

Something warned him not to go.

Yet he went.

"What have I to fear," thought he, "in this house in which I spent my earliest infancy?   Why should I dread this woman — poor painted toy — poor puppet of an hour?"

He sat down on the stone steps outside, and thought.

Years were coming over him, and clouds had ever obscured the brightness which might be before him.

His path had ever been over thorny ground, and the seeds of joy he had sown had grown up in crops of bitterness and misery.

Yet might not this be, after all, his own error—his own fatal error?

Might he not, all along, have been sailing against the wind, merely because he refused to see that from other quarters cheerful breezes would have filled his canvas?

Magsworth wept.

Well he might!

Sitting there upon that moss-grown step, where his mother's eye had often watched him bounding along the road upon his pony—sitting in the shadow of the great house which might still have been his home—sitting, too, in the shadow of a great sorrow which might never have been.

Strange, bewildering thoughts, dreads, misgivin s, griefs, set in upon his heart, and took possession of it; and when he arose and approached the gate, with his brow damp with the dew of fear or sorrow, he was not himself.

It was not strange, then, that he started, and uttered an exclamation, when he saw, standing by the little gate through which he was about to enter, a young woman and a man on horseback—a mounted patrol.

The woman eyed him narrowly.

The constable did not; his attention was too much directed towards the face and figure of the pretty girl before him.

Magsworth passed through the gate with assumed indifference, and walked rapidly up the path towards the house.

Lady Maud was awaiting him in the grounds, and pretended the utmost surprise on seeing him.

"I did not expect you so early," she said.   "I feel lonely, for Sir Charles is absent for the night; and I took a walk here to divert my thoughts."

Magsworth sighed.

Sir Charles was absent!

At that moment the weary, weary wanderer—tired with waiting for the end which would not come—would gladly have forgotten old enmities and crushed old hatreds.

But it was not to be.

"Perhaps it is all for the best," said Lady Moore. "You can now come up with me, and no one will know you have been."

Magsworth followed her unsuspectingly.

They met no one.

Entering her room unperceived, she closed the door, saying, "I have done my best to obtain the money you sought, but I have not succeeded."

Magsworth trembled.

"Another disappointment—another delay!" he cried. "Had you tried, madam, you could have succeeded. This is but a *ruse* to deceive me."

Lady Moore looked hurt.

"Mr. Magsworth," she said, "I forgive you on account of your great sorrow; but you are wronging me sadly.

I was about to tell you that as I could not obtain the money I have brought you some jewels which you can dispose of. Here are twenty pounds and two diamond crosses. You will find them fully worth the money you desire."

Magsworth took them unsuspectingly and placed them in his pocket.

"Many thanks, my lady," he said; "this at least will be some reparation for your crime—for crime it truly is. I will say adieu now madam, for time is precious."

He took his hat and approached the door.

"Can you find your way out?" asked Lady Maud, somewhat eagerly.

Magsworth smiled.

"Every nook and corner of this old house is known to me as well as it can possibly be to others," he said. "Farewell, Lady Moore. May Heaven forgive you for the great wrong you have done me."

Then he passed from the room.

Lady Moore threw open the window and listened.

Presently she heard the creak of a man's boot in the gravelled path.

Then she uttered a loud cry, and rang her bell violently.

Magsworth glanced up at the terrace casement where he heard the cry, and saw Lady Moore's form recede rapidly.

Then he heard the bell ringing loudly, and a vague sense of uneasiness crept over him.

How Lady Moore proposed to betray him he could not tell, but it was certain to his mind that some treachery was intended; and acting upon a sudden impulse, which was afterwards brought to bear against him, he ran hastily across the grounds.

The space separating him from the gate leading to the highway was not very considerable, and as he ran, he could see the figures of Florette and the horse patrol still between the overarching trees.

Trusting, therefore, to chance, and bewildered by the darkness, the rush of feet behind him, and a sense of unknown danger, he turned suddenly aside, and darted through the hedge.

As he burst out on the other side, he saw that he had entered a little narrow lane, which led down towards Mrs. Bellingham's cottage, and without reflecting he dashed onwards.

As he did so, he could hear the gallop of a horse, and knew that the patrol was on the scent.

As he neared the cottage he paused for a moment.

"What is this danger from which I am escaping?" thought he. "What have I done that I should fly?"

But there was no time left him for lengthened reflection.

Behind was again the sound of hurrying feet, and he once more plunged onwards.

To scale the low wall of the cottage, to rush into the back yard, and knock loudly was the work of a moment.

The widow hastened to the entrance in much alarm.

"Hide me somewhere—hide me!" cried he. I am pursued, and if discovered I am a lost man."

"Run through the cottage and over the road. Hide there in the shrubberies. You will be safer there than here."

He hesitated not, but, following the widow, rushed into the front room and out into the night.

Quick as was the action—quick almost as was the thought which prompted it, the steward of Moore House was upon him.

This man—a servant who had for many long years served the Moores—had been the most active in the chase.

He was upon the fugitive—the skirts of his streaming garments were already in his hand, when the widow flung herself before him—clung to him—detained him.

"That way—that way!" she cried; "he went that way."

"That way!" exclaimed he. "No, no! see, there he goes. I can see his figure crossing yonder light. Great Heavens! whose form is that? It is—"

"Hush!" said the widow; "speak not his name. He carries others' lives besides his own. Let him go—let him be free!"

The steward stood as one paralysed.

As far as he was concerned Magsworth was safe.

But safety was not to be his.

Hardly had Mrs. Bellingham finished speaking, when there was the rush of a horse—a dark figure sprang from its back, and just as he was about to dart into the shrubbery, Magsworth was seized.

"In the King's name I arrest you!" cried the horse patrol, panting with his fierce ride, "for robbery!"

"Robbery! Where?"

"At Moore House. Come, let us have no altercation. I have fire-arms with me, and shall use them if I find them needful."

"Keep your threats for the vulgar pickpockets whose overseer you are!" cried Magsworth, haughtily. "Let us go at once. The night is cold, and the air of a guard house would be preferable to that of the highway."

By this time the steward came up.

"Why, Mr. Magsworth," he said, "how is this? It is some mistake, I presume."

Magsworth smiled bitterly.

"I can scarcely say what it is," he answered; "because, as yet, I do not know what was the reason of my pursuit."

"There has been a robbery at Moore House," returned the steward; "some jewellery and money has been carried off, and as you were seen running across the grounds, we naturally followed you."

Magsworth turned deadly pale.

He saw clearly through the plot of this diabolical woman.

But what could he say?

What could he do?

"Shall we return to the house?" said the horse patrol. "Perhaps there is some mistake which my lady may clear up."

"Yes—yes," replied the steward, eagerly; "that will be the best thing to do. This is Mr. Magsworth Moore, Sir Charles's brother. There must be some absurd blunder."

The two then returned to Moore House.

Lady Moore was sitting in the drawing-room, very pale and agitated, when they entered.

"You have caught the man, then," she said, rising and gazing at Magsworth firmly, while she grasped the back of the chair.

"Why, yes—at least, no, my lady," returned the steward. "This is not a thief; this is Mr. Moore, the brother of the baronet, my lady."

Lady Maud eyed the steward coldly.

"I know nothing of Sir Charles's brother," she said, quietly. "That is the man whom I saw leaping from my window on the terrace, and dropping into the grounds—I swear it."

Magsworth trembled.

"Great Heavens, madam!" he cried. "Is it possible you will swear away my life?"

"If I am wrong, let it be proved. Search him, and see if my jewels are not in his possession."

Magsworth waved the constable back.

"I have," he said, some jewels and some money which her ladyship herself gave me. These cannot possibly be the things she pretends to have been stolen?"

As he spoke, he drew them forth, and laid them on the table.

"The man's impudence disgusts me," said Lady Moore. "These are the very things I have missed. Take him away. I can do nothing until my husband returns."

"Wretched woman!" cried Magsworth Moore, drawing himself up proudly. "Heaven will yet judge between you and me. I fear nothing, for I am innocent ; and if I die, Providence will watch over my child. My death would be a triumph for me—a terror, and a lasting haunting phantom for you !"

He then turned and left the room, guarded by the patrol.

"It is done," murmured Lady Moore, gasping, as she sank down in her chair ; "it is done ! He will die ; she will be lost for ever ; and my son is safe."

CHAPTER LXXIII.

THE TRAVELLER'S TALE CONTINUED.

SIR CHARLES MOORE arrived at Moore House on the day following the arrest of his unfortunate brother.

He could see immediately he entered that something unusual had occurred.

There was a gloom over everything, a stillness in the very grounds, a sadness on the faces of the servants, and hesitation and awkwardness in their manner.

He found Lady Moore already up, although it was early in the morning.

She was seated before an untasted breakfast.

Her face was pale ; her attitude that of one who grieves deeply.

She acted her part well.

On perceiving her husband, she rose, flung herself into his arms, and burst into a passion of tears.

"What ails you, my darling ?" asked Sir Charles kindly.

Well he might ask !

Her fresh rosy colour was gone ; her face, her neck, her bosom, under its gauzy covering, were white as alabaster, and contrasted strangely with the wayward golden tresses.

For some moments she did not answer.

"Tell me, dear one," again said Sir Charles—"tell me what is the matter."

Then leading him to a seat, and assuming her usual attitude of childish innocence, kneeling before him, and looking up into his face, she poured forth her version of the tale of her guilt.

Sir Charles listened in silence.

The colour slowly faded from his cheek, and his lips became white.

At length he said—

"Maud, you have done a grievous wrong."

She trembled.

Had she gone too far ?

The tears again welled up, and obscured her bright eyes.

"A wrong to you, Sir Charles ? Heaven forbid it !" she murmured.

"Why did you accuse this man ?"

"I knew him not. Had I ever seen him before—had you ever introduced me to him ?"

"No, no ; you are right. But when you found who he was—when Andrew told you his name—why then did you not obtain his release ?"

Lady Moore replied not ; she was, in truth, at a loss for words.

At length she said, rising up tragically, and sitting down again in her chair, as if crushed by his censure, slight and simply implied as it was—

"Sir Charles, I regret my offence. The man who came into my room as a thief could scarcely hope to be recognised as your brother."

"No ; but Andrews had told you that he was."

"I did not believe him."

"Why ?"

"Because I could not think that one of the same flesh and blood as my husband could be guilty of such a paltry crime."

Sir Charles thought a moment.

"Did he assign no reason for this robbery ?"

"None."

"Did he ask after his child ?"

"No."

The baronet rose, and paced the room.

"You must be mistaken, Maud," he cried ; "you must be mistaken. My brother would never commit a theft. Come, tell me you are not certain of his identity. Tell me it was too dark to see him plainly."

"I cannot, Sir Charles Moore. I have already told the servants that I could swear to him."

The baronet was very pale, and his lips trembled with emotion

"Maud," he said, "this trial will entail endless disgrace upon our family. It must not take place. You must save him."

The blue eyes were upturned in surprise.

"How—how can I save him ?" she asked, in pretty bewilderment.

"You must unsay your words," cried Sir Charles Moore ; "you must declare that you are wrong ; you must tell the Court that the night was dark ; and you decline to swear to his identity."

"Oh, what folly is this ?" Lady Moore muttered. "Sir Charles," she said, firmly, "which is the greater disgrace ?—the fact of your wife committing a perjury, or that of a man committing a robbery who has no proof of his identity—who does not even assume your name, and whom you can accordingly refuse to acknowledge ?"

Sir Charles eyed her in alarm.

Was this his gentle wife ?

"Maud," he said ; "I am asking you to save my honour, and do you refuse ?"

Then there was a rush of tears again, and she sank at his feet, looking like a little white tremulous cloud in her white muslin dress.

"Oh, my husband !" she sobbed, "do not—do not ask me to tell a lie !"

Sir Charles raised her up.

"Maud," he said, kindly—for he was deceived by her emotion—"I could have wished it otherwise ; I could have wished that you could have thought it consistent with your conscience to save our house from a dread disgrace. You have not thought it so, therefore it remains for me to save him if I can."

She twined her soft white arms round his neck.

"Oh, I shall be glad to hear that you have saved him, dear husband," she cried ; "yet do not indulge in false hopes. I fear very much it will be impossible."

Sir Charles said no more, partook of a hasty meal, and left the house.

He went alone, on horseback.

Sir Vere de Vere was in the house, ready to console with him and aid him ; but he refused to see him.

Every one seemed like his enemy.

Who can tell what thoughts careered through his brain—what feelings overwhelmed his heart — during that silent ride ?

Sir Charles loved his brother, wild and ill-regulated as Magsworth was.

As we have before said, his was not the hand which was held back—his was not the heart which refused to open—his were not the fierce feelings of hate and false pride.

So, fallen and wretched as was Magsworth, Sir Charles was going to see him.

Going to comfort him, to save him—if save him he could ; and if not, to crave his forgiveness.

For what ?

For the mere fact that he was remotely connected with the cause of his arrest.

The constable at the lock-up knew Sir Charles at once.

"Do you wish to see the prisoner, Sir Charles ?" he asked, respectfully.

"I do."

"Shall I tell him you are here, sir ?"

"No, no; let me enter the room unannounced. If he knew that I was here, he would refuse to see me."

The man grinned to himself as he led the way.

"Refuse!" he muttered; "I don't think it very likely he'd refuse, because he couldn't help himself."

Magsworth was seated at a table in the bare, cold room of the lock-up, and was so wrapped in his own thoughts that he did not hear the door open.

He was recalled to himself by Sir Charles' voice.

"Magsworth," he said in a voice of much emotion; "I am here—your brother—to console you."

What years had passed since they had met.

Magsworth turned savagely.

Then, as he glanced at his brother, a withering smile wreathed itself over his lips.

"You have come here to triumph over my fall," he said. "Triumph and welcome! It would better have become a Moore, notwithstanding, to have abstained from insult."

Sir Charles shook his head sadly; then, removing his hat, he advanced respectfully towards his brother.

"Magsworth," he said, "I beg of you, at such a moment as this, to cast aside your mad prejudices."

"Prejudices!" exclaimed Magsworth; "I have no prejudices, but a deep sense of wrong."

"Wrong! from whom?"

"From all. Have I not for years been an outcast and a wanderer on the earth? Whom, then, am I called upon to love?"

"If you have been a wanderer and an outcast, Magsworth," said the Baronet, "it is from no fault of mine. Believe me, my dear brother, I came here to save you."

Magsworth laughed bitterly.

"Save me! It is impossible. Your wife, whom you love so much, has betrayed me, and will swear my life away."

Sir Charles gazed at him in alarm.

" Tell me—tell me," he said, " what is it you mean ?"

" Tell you ! Why should I ? Why should I tell an infatuated old maid that her pet lap-dog bites ? Why tell an old man his young wife is a traitor ?"

His brother clutched his arm as in a vice.

" Magsworth," he said solemnly, " I come here to save you—if it be in mortal power to save you. Cast your eyes back upon the past, and ask yourself upon what occasion I have ever injured, or even thwarted you ? Believe me, then, when I say I will move heaven and earth to save you. I came here to save you—to save, too, the honour of the family—and am ready to submit to any sacrifice for the purpose."

The earnestness with which these words were spoken would have convinced one less inclined to belief than Magsworth.

He sat moodily for some moments, then he suddenly extended his hand to his brother.

" We will shake hands, Sir Charles," he said. " It is better we should, since after I have told you my story you will be less inclined to be friendly."

Sir Charles pressed his brother's hand warmly.

" Be not afraid," he said; " tell your story fearlessly."

So Magsworth told his story. Sir Charles listened in amazement and alarm, but kept silent until Magsworth had concluded.

" Wentworth," he said at length, this is a strange story you have told me, and I know not what to say to it."

The old smile wreathed itself over Magsworth's lips.

" As I thought," he murmured. " You refuse to believe me."

" Not so—not so, indeed !" cried the Baronet. " But I have ever found my wife so good—so innocent. It would be a terrible thing for me to think that you were not mistaken."

Magsworth, rose and paced the room hurriedly. At length he stopped near his brother and took his hand.

" Charles," he said, " I can well understand your feelings. Were my wife living, I would not believe any one who spoke ill of her. So let it pass. Believe me guilty if you please, and say no more of it. The only thing I ask you is that you will let me die as Magsworth and endeavour to find my child. I forgive you, Charles, for your suspicions. I would forgive you for more were you to make me this promise."

Sir Charles was much moved.

" Magsworth," he said, " I should be sorry to disbelieve either. I am positively certain in my own mind that you are incapable of the crime ascribed to you. I am equally certain that my wife is incapable of telling a deliberate lie. Therefore what am I to do ? What can I think but that there has been some terrible mistake ?"

" Be it so, then. Give me the promise I ask, and let me die unknown."

The tears stood in Sir Charles's eyes, and he flung himself on his brother's neck.

" I will promise," he cried wildly—" I will promise to search the world for your child, but I will not let you die. Come, change dresses with me. I will remain here ; you can escape, and justice will not pursue me for saving my own brother from punishment for an offence of which I believe him to be innocent."

Magsworth hesitated for a moment, but it was but for a moment.

" Heaven bless you, my brother !" he said, with deep emotion. " Heaven bless you! But I will accept no such sacrifice. No, no, I will go through with it now. The greater the injustice which is done me, the greater will be the retribution which will, one day, fall on the one who has injured me."

Sir Charles was silent. Magsworth proceeded.

" What have I to live for, Sir Charles ? What has my life been but one great and terrible mistake ? What charm has this world for me—this world in which I am

an outcast ? There was only one charm—my little child —my sweet daughter, my Alice. Where is she now ? Gone for ever. Gone for ever, then, is all that made life dear. What had I done for her ? Leaving her fatherless, as it were, in the hands of strangers, but near the home of her natural friends, I went through the world, striving to win for her a fortune. I failed miserably, as I have ever done, and I came back, thinking I would carry her away with me to a foreign land."

" And all this time you would not apply to me," murmured Sir Charles.

" I could not bring my mind to such a humiliation."

CHAPTER LXXX.

CLIFFORD AND HIS FRIENDS—THE RESOLVE TO RESCUE THE FAIR PRISONER FROM THE DEMON HUNTER.

CLIFFORD, after Herne had carried off the girl rescued from the Curfew Tower, ranged the forest for a week, but without a gleam of hope—without success of the faintest character.

Many times he caught glimpses of the demon, as he flew at midnight through the forest, and still more frequently did he hear the deep baying of his black hounds.

Once, and once only, he caught sight of Wild.

It was but for a second.

The robber was mounted on one of Herne's coal-black steeds.

He gave Clifford a look of defiance, laughed derisively, and disappeared.

But the perseverance of Clifford did not go entirely unrewarded.

He had discovered the retreat of the demon hunter and his band.

It was a sandstone cave, entered near the margin of the lake.

It was of considerable width, and hewn out of a bed of the soft stone.

The roof was supported by the trunks of three large trees, and was about ten feet high.

Several narrow passages apparently led to other caves, and at the further end was a gleam like the reflection of torch-light upon water.

On the right was a pile of huge stones, somewhat resembling a Druidical altar, on the top of which, as on a throne, sat the demon hunter, surrounded by his satellites.

Such was the retreat of Herne.

And such was the description of it given by Clifford to Bill Waters and Long Ned, his companions, who had returned to the forest to assist Clifford.

The three met at the deserted hut of the old recluse murdered by Wild when he first determined to enter the forest.

Their conference was a long and serious one.

Bringing it to a close, they separated, each taking different ways.

As they left the hut, two figures dropped from a sort of loft in the roof.

" Ho, ho, ho !" laughed the foremost, whose antlered helm and wild garb proclaimed him to be Herne, " they little dreamed who were the hearers of their conference. So they think to take me, Wild ? Ha !"

" They know not whom they have to deal with," rejoined the latter.

" They *should* do so by this time," said Herne; " but I will tell thee why Clifford has undertaken this enterprise. It is not to capture me, though that may be one object that moves him. But he wishes to see the girl. The momentary glimpse he caught of her bright eyes was sufficient to inflame him."

"Ah!" exclaimed Wild; "think you so?"

"I am assured of it," replied Herne. "He knows the secret of the cave, and will find her there."

"But he will never return to tell what he has seen," said Wild, moodily.

"I know not that," replied Herne. "I have my own views respecting him. I want to renew my band."

"He will never join you," rejoined Wild.

"What if I offer him the girl as a bait?" said Herne.

"You will not do so, dread master?" rejoined Wild, trembling, and turning pale "She belongs to me."

"To thee, fool!" cried Herne, with a derisive laugh. "Thinkest thou I would resign such a treasure to thee? No, no. But rest easy, I will not give her to Clifford."

"You mean her for yourself, then?" said Wild.

"Darest thou to question me," cried Herne, striking him with the hand armed with the iron gyves. "This to teach thee respect!"

"And this to prove whether thou art mortal or not," rejoined Wild, plucking his knife from his belt, and striking it, with all his force, against the other's breast.

But, though surely and forcibly dealt, the blow glanced off as if the demon were cased in steel.

The intended assassin fell back in amazement, while an unearthly laugh rang in his ears.

Never had Wild seen Herne wear so formidable a look as he at that moment assumed.

His giant frame dilated.

His eyes flashed fire.

The expression of his countenance was so fearful that Wild shielded his eyes with his hands.

"Ah, miserable dog!" thundered Herne; "dost thou think I am to be hurt by mortal hands, or mortal weapons? But, since thou hast provoked it, take thy fate!"

Uttering these words he seized Wild by the throat, clutching him with a terrific grip.

In a few seconds the miserable wretch would have paid the penalty of his rashness, if a person had not at the moment appeared at the doorway.

Flinging his prey hastily backwards, Herne turned at the interruption, and perceived one of his band, who looked appalled at what he beheld.

"Ah, is it thou, Tristram," cried Herne. "Thou art just in time to witness the punishment of this rebellious hound."

"Spare him, dread master—oh, spare him," cried Tristram, imploringly.

"Well," said Herne, gazing at the half-strangled caitiff, "he may live; he will not offend again. But why hast thou ventured from thy hiding-place, Tristram?"

"I came to inform you that I have just observed a person row across the lake in the skiff," replied the old man. "He appears to be taking the direction of the secret entrance to the cave."

"It is Clifford," replied Herne; "I am aware of his proceedings. Stay with Wild till he is able to move, and then proceed with him to the cave. But, mark me, no violence must be done to Clifford if you find him there. Any neglect of my orders in this respect will be followed by severe punishment. I shall be at the cave ere long; but, meanwhile, I have other business to transact."

And, quitting the hut, he plunged into the wood.

Meanwhile Clifford, having crossed the lake, landed, and fastened the skiff to a tree, struck into the wood, and presently reached the open space in which lay the secret entrance to the cave.

He was not long in finding the stone, though it was so artfully concealed by the brushwood that it would have escaped any uninstructed eye, and, removing it, the narrow entrance to the cave was revealed.

Committing himself to the protection of Heaven, Clifford entered, and, having taken the precaution of drawing the stone after him, which was easily accomplished by a handle fixed to the inner side of it, he commenced the descent.

At first he had to creep along, but the passage gradually got higher, until at length, on reaching the level ground, he was able to stand upright.

There was no light to guide him, but, by feeling against the sides of the passage, he found that he was in the long gallery he had formerly threaded.

Uncertain which way to turn, he determined to trust to chance for taking the right direction, and, drawing his sword, proceeded slowly to the right.

For some time he encountered no obstacle, neither could he detect the slightest sound, but he perceived that the atmosphere grew damp, and that the sides of the passage were covered with moisture.

Thus warned, he proceeded with greater caution, and presently found, after emerging into a more open space, and striking off on the left, that he had arrived at the edge of the pool of water which he knew lay at the end of the large cavern.

While considering how he should next proceed, a faint gleam of light became visible at the upper end of the vault.

Changing his position, for the pillars prevented him from seeing the source of the glimmer, he discovered that it issued from a lamp borne by a female hand, who, he had no doubt, was the girl he had rescued.

On making this discovery he sprang forwards, and called to her, but instantly repented his rashness, for as he uttered the cry the light was extinguished.

Clifford was now completely at a loss how to proceed.

He was satisfied that the girl was in the vault; but in what way to guide himself to her retreat, he could not tell; and it was evident she herself would not assist him.

Persuaded, however, if he could but make himself known, he should no longer be shunned, he entered one of the lateral passages, and ever and anon as he proceeded he called her in a low, soft tone.

The stratagem was successful.

Presently he heard a light footstep approaching him, and a gentle voice inquired—

"Who calls me?"

"A friend," replied Clifford.

"Your name?" she demanded.

"You will not know me if I declare myself", he replied; "but I am called Clifford."

"The name is well known to me," she replied in trembling tones; "and I have seen you before. But why have you come here? Do you know where you are?"

"I know that I am in the cave of Herne the Hunter," replied Clifford; "and one of my motives for seeking it was to set you free. But there is nothing to prevent your flight now."

"Alas! there is," she replied. "I am chained here by bonds I cannot break. Herne has declared that any attempt at escape on my part shall be followed by the death of my grandsire, whom he has here in his power. And he does not threaten idly, as no doubt you know. Besides, the most terrible vengeance would fall on my own head. No—I cannot—dare not fly. But let us not talk in the dark. Come with me to procure a light. Give me your hand, and I will lead you to my cell."

Taking the small, trembling hand offered him, Clifford followed his conductress down the passage.

A few steps brought them to a door, which she pushed aside, and disclosed a small chamber, hewn out of the rock, in a recess of which a lamp was burning.

Lighting the other lamp which she had recently extinguished, she placed it on a rude table.

"Oh, that I could behold the sun again, and breathe the fresh, pure air!" cried the girl.

"Come with me, and you shall do so," rejoined Clifford.

"I have told you I cannot fly," she answered. "I cannot sacrifice my grandsire."

"But if he is leagued with this demon he deserves the worst fate that can befall him," said Clifford. "You should think only of your own safety. What can be the motive of your detention?"

"I tremble to think of it," she replied, "but I fear that Herne has conceived a passion for me."

"Then, indeed, you must fly," cried Clifford; "such unhallowed love will lead to perdition of soul and body."

"Oh, that there was any hope for me!" she ejaculated.

"There is hope," replied Clifford. "I will protect you."

"Ha!" the girl exclaimed suddenly, "footsteps are approaching; it is Wild. Hide yourself within that recess."

Though doubting the prudence of the course, Clifford yielded to her terrified and imploring looks, and concealed himself in the manner she had indicated.

He was scarcely ensconced in the recess, when the door opened, and Wild stepped in, followed by her grandfather.

Wild gazed suspiciously round the little chamber, and then glanced significantly at old Tristram, but he made no remark.

"What brings you here?" demanded the girl tremblingly.

"You are wanted in the cave," said Wild.

"I will follow you anon," she replied.

"You must come at once," rejoined Wild, authoritatively. "Herne will become impatient."

Upon this the girl rose, and without daring to cast a look towards the spot where Clifford was concealed, quitted the cell with them.

No sooner were they all out, than Wild hastily shutting the door, turned the key in the lock, and taking it out, exclaimed—

"So we have secured you, Master Clifford. No fear of your revealing the secret of the cave now, or flying with our prisoner—ha! ha!"

CHAPTER LXXXI.

HERNE AND HIS PRISONER.

UTTERLY disregarding her cries and entreaties, Wild dragged the girl into the great cavern, and forced her to take a seat on a bench near the spot where a heap of ashes showed that the fire was ordinarily lighted.

All this while her grandfather had averted his face from her, as if fearing to meet her regards, and he now busied himself in striking a light and setting fire to a pile of faggots and small logs of wood.

"I thought you told me Herne was here," said the girl, in a tone of bitter reproach, to Wild, who seated himself beside her on the bench.

"He will be here ere long," he replied sullenly.

"Oh, do not detain Clifford!" cried the girl piteously; "do not deliver him to your dread master! Do what you will with me, but let him go."

"I will tell you what I will do," replied Wild, in a low tone; "I will set Clifford at liberty, and run all risks of Herne's displeasure, if you will promise to be mine."

The girl replied by a look of unutterable disgust.

"Then he will await Herne's coming where he is," rejoined Wild.

Saying which he arose, and pushing a table near to the bench, took the remains of a huge venison pasty and a loaf from a hutch standing on one side of the cavern.

By this time, old Tristram, having succeeded in lighting the fire, placed himself at the further end of the table, and fell to work upon the viands with Wild.

The girl was pressed to partake of the repast, but she declined the offer.

A large stone bottle was next produced and emptied of its contents by the pair, who seemed well-contented with their regale.

Meanwhile the girl was revolving the possibility of flight, and had more than once determined to make an attempt, but fear restrained her.

Her grandsire, as has been stated, sedulously avoided her gaze, and turned a deaf ear to her complaints and entreaties.

But once, when Wild's back was turned, she caught him gazing at her with peculiar significance, and then comprehended the meaning of his strange conduct.

He evidently only waited an opportunity to assist her.

Satisfied of this she became more tranquil, and about an hour having elapsed, during which nothing was said by the party, the low winding of a horn was heard, and Wild started to his feet, exclaiming—

"It is Herne!"

The next moment the demon huntsman rode from one of the lateral passages into the cave.

He was mounted on a wild-looking black horse, with flowing mane and tail, eyes glowing like carbuncles, and in all respects resembling the sable steed he had lost in the forest.

Springing to the ground he exchanged a few words with Wild in a low tone, and delivering his steed to him with orders to take it to the stable, signed to Tristram to go with him, and approached the girl.

"So you have seen Clifford, I find," he said, in a stern tone.

The girl made no answer, and did not even raise her eyes towards him.

"And he has urged you to fly with him—ha?" pursued Herne.

The girl still did not dare to look up, but a deep blush overspread her cheek.

"He was mad to venture hither," continued Herne; "but having done so, he must take the consequences."

"You will not destroy him?" cried the girl, imploringly.

"He will perish by a hand as terrible as mine," laughed Herne—"by that of famine. He will never quit the dungeon alive, unless—"

"Unless what?" gasped the girl.

"Unless he is leagued with me," replied Herne. "And now let him pass, for I would speak of myself. I have already told you that I love you, and am resolved to make you mine. You shudder; but wherefore? It is a glorious destiny to be the bride of the wild hunter—the fiend who rules the forest, and who, in his broad domain, is more powerful than the king. The old forester, Robin Hood, had his maid Marian; and what was he compared with me? He had neither my skill nor my power. Be mine, and you shall accompany me on my midnight rides; shall watch the fleet stag dart over the moonlight glade, or down the lengthened vista. You shall feel all the unutterable excitement of the chase. You shall thread with me the tangled grove; swim the river and the lake, and enjoy a thousand pleasures hitherto unknown to you. Be mine, and I will make you mistress of all my secrets, and compel the band, whom I will gather round me, to pay you homage. Be mine, and you shall have power of life and death over them, as if you were absolute queen. And from me, whom all fear, and all obey, you shall have love and worship."

And he would have taken her hand, but she recoiled from him with horror.

"Though I now inspire you with terror and aversion," pursued Herne, "the time will come when you will love me as passionately as I was beloved by one of whom you are the image."

"And she is dead?" asked the girl, with curiosity.

"Dead!" exclaimed Herne. "Thrice fifty years have flown since she dwelt upon earth. The acorn which was then shed in the forest has grown into a lusty oak, while trees, at that time in their pride, have fallen and decayed away. Dead !—yes, she has passed from all memory save mine, where she will ever dwell. Generations of men have gone down to the grave since her time—a succession of kings have lodged within the castle—but I am still a denizen of the forest. For crimes I then committed I am doomed to wander within it; and I shall haunt it, unless released, till the crack of doom."

"Liberate me !" cried the girl; "liberate your other prisoner, and we will pray for your release."

"No more of this !" cried Herne, fiercely. "If you would not call down instant and terrible punishment on your head—punishment that I cannot avert, and must inflict—you will mention nothing sacred in my hearing, and never allude to prayer. I am beyond the reach of salvation."

"Oh, say not so !" cried the girl, in a tone of commiseration.

"I will tell you how my doom was accomplished," rejoined Herne, wildly. "To gain her of whom I have just spoken, and who was already vowed to Heaven, I invoked the powers of darkness. I proffered my soul to the Evil One if he would secure her to me; and the condition demanded by him was that I should become what I am—the fiend of the forest, with power to terrify and to tempt, and with other more fearful and fatal powers besides."

"Oh !" exclaimed the girl.

"I grasped at the offer," pursued Herne. "She I loved became mine. But she was speedily snatched from me by death, and since then I have known no human passion except hatred and revenge. I have dwelt in this forest, sometimes alone, sometimes at the head of a numerous band—but always exerting a baneful influence over mankind. At last, I saw the image of her I loved again appear before me, and the old passion was revived within my breast. Chance has thrown you in my way, and mine you shall be."

"I will die rather," she replied, with a shudder.

"You cannot escape me," rejoined Herne, with a triumphant laugh; "you cannot avoid your fate. But I want not to deal harshly with you. I love you, and would win you rather by persuasion than by force. Consent to be mine, then, and I give Clifford his life and liberty."

"I cannot—I cannot !" she replied.

"Not only do I offer you Clifford's life as the price of your compliance," persevered Herne, "but you shall have whatever else you may seek — jewels, ornaments, costly attire, treasure—for of such I possess a goodly store."

"And of what use would they be to me here ?" said the girl.

"I will not always confine you to this cave," replied Herne. "You shall go where you please, and live as you please, but you must come to me whenever I summon you."

"And what of my grandsire ?" she demanded.

"Tristram is no relative of yours," replied Herne.

And then he continued—"You now know my resolve. To-morrow night at mid-night our nuptials shall take place."

"Nuptials !" echoed the girl.

"Ay, at that altar," he cried, pointing to the Druid pile of stones—"there you shall vow yourself to me and I to you, before terrible witnesses. I shall have no fear that you will break your oath. Reflect upon what I have said."

With this, he placed the bugle to his lips, blew a low call upon it, and Wild and Tristram immediately answering the summons, he whispered some instructions to the former and disappeared down one of the side passages.

Wild's deportment was now more sullen than before.

In vain did the girl inquire from him what Herne was about to do with Clifford.

He returned no answer, and at last, wearied by her importunity, desired her to hold her peace. Just then Tristram quitted the cavern for a moment, when he instantly changed his manner, and said to her quickly—

"I overhead what passed between you and Herne. Consent to be mine, and I will deliver you from him."

"That were to exchange one evil for another," she replied. If you would serve me, deliver Clifford."

"I will only deliver him on the terms I have mentioned," replied Wild.

At this moment Tristram returned, and the conversation ceased.

Fresh logs were then thrown on the fire by Wild, and, at his request, Tristram proceeded to a hole in the rock, which served as a sort of larder, and brought from it some pieces of venison, which were broiled upon the embers.

At the close of the repast, of which she sparingly partook, the girl was conducted by Wild into a small chamber opening out of the great cavern, which was furnished like the cell she had lately occupied, with a small straw pallet.

Leaving her a lamp, Wild locked the door, and placed the key in his girdle.

CHAPTER LXXXII.

CLIFFORD HAS AN INTERVIEW WITH HERNE.

MADE aware by the clangour of the lock, and Wild's exulting laughter, of the snare in which he had been caught, Clifford instantly sprang from his hiding place, and rushed to the door; but being framed of the stoutest oak, and strengthened with plates of iron, it defied all his efforts, nerved as they were by rage and despair, to burst it open.

The girl's shrieks, as she was dragged away, reached his ears, and increased his anguish; and he called out loudly to her companions to return, but his vociferations were only treated with derision.

Finding it useless to struggle further, Clifford threw himself upon the bench, and endeavoured to discover some means of deliverance from his present hazardous position.

He glanced the cell round to see whether there was any other outlet than the doorway, but he could discern none, except a narrow grated loophole opening upon the passage, and contrived, doubtless for the admission of air to the chamber.

No dungeon could be more secure.

Raising the lamp, he examined every crevice, but all seemed solid stone.

The recess in which he had taken shelter proved to be a mere hollow in the wall.

In one corner lay a small straw pallet, which, no doubt, had formed the couch of the girl; and this, together with the stone bench and rude table of the same material, constituted the sole furniture of the place.

Having taken this careful survey of the cell, Clifford again sat down upon the bench with the conviction that escape was out of the question; and he therefore endeavoured to prepare himself for the worst, for it was more than probable he would be allowed to perish of starvation.

To a fiery nature like his, the dreadful uncertainty in which he was placed was more difficult of endurance than bodily torture.

And he was destined to endure it long.

Many hours flew by, during which nothing occurred to relieve the terrible monotony of his situation.

At length, in spite of his anxiety, slumber stole upon him unawares; but it was filled with frightful visions.

How long he slept he knew not, but when he awoke, he found that the cell must have been visited in the interval, for there was a manchet of bread, part of a cold neck of venison, and a flask of wine on the table.

It was evident, therefore, that his captors did not mean to starve him, and yielding to the promptings of appetite he attacked the provisions, determined to keep strict watch when his goaler should next visit him.

The repast finished, he again examined the cell, but with no better success than before ; and he felt almost certain, from the position in which the bench was placed, that the visitor had not found entrance through the door.

After another long and dreary interval, finding that sleep was stealing upon him fast, he placed the bench near the door, and leaned his back against the latter, certain that in this position he should be awakened if any one attempted to gain admittance in that way.

His slumber was again disturbed by fearful dreams ; and he was at length aroused by a touch upon the shoulder, while a deep voice shouted his own name in his ears.

Starting to his feet, and scarcely able to separate the reality from the hideous phantasms that had troubled him, he found that the door was still fastened, and the bench unremoved, while before him stood Herne the Hunter.

"Welcome to my cave, Gentleman Clifford !" cried the demon, with a mocking laugh ; " I told you you would not escape *me*. And so it has come to pass. You are now wholly in my power, body and soul—ha ! ha !"

" I defy you, false fiend," replied Clifford.

"You alarm yourself without reason, good Clifford," replied Herne, in a slightly sneering tone. " I am not the malignant being you suppose me ; neither am I bent upon fighting the battles of the enemy of mankind against Heaven. I may be leagued with the powers of darkness, but I have no wish to aid them ; and I therefore leave you to take care of your soul in your own way. What I desire from you is your service while living. Now listen to the conditions I have to propose. You must bind yourself by a terrible oath, the slightest infraction of which shall involve the perdition of the soul you are so solicitous to preserve, not to disclose aught you may see, or that may be imparted to you here. You must also swear implicit obedience to me in all things—to execute any secret commissions, of whatever nature, I may give you—to bring associates to my band—and to join me in any enterprise I may propose. This oath taken, you are free. Refuse it, and I leave you to perish.'

" I do refuse it," replied Clifford, boldly. " I would die a thousand deaths rather than so bind myself. Neither do I fear being left to perish here. You shall not quit this cell without me."

"You are a stout robber, Clifford," rejoined the demon, with a scornful laugh ; " but you are scarcely a match for Herne the Hunter, as you will find, if you are rash enough to make the experiment. Beware !" he exclaimed, in a voice of thunder, observing Clifford lay his hand upon his sword, " I am invulnerable, and you will, therefore, vainly strike at me. Do not compel me to use the dread means, which I could instantly employ, to subject you to my will. I mean you well, and would rather serve than injure you. But I will not let you go, unless you league yourself with me. Swear, therefore, obedience to me, and depart hence to your friends, and tell them you have failed to find me."

"You know, then, of our meeting ?" exclaimed Clifford.

"Perfectly well," laughed Herne. "It is now eventide, and at midnight the meeting will take place in the forester's hut. If *you* attend it not, *I* will. They will be my prisoners as well as you. To preserve yourself and save them you must join me."

"Before I return an answer," said Clifford, "I must know what has become of the girl."

"The girl is nought to you, Clifford," rejoined Herne, coldly.

"She is so much to me that I will run a risk for her which I would not run for myself," replied Clifford. "If I promise obedience to you, will you liberate her—will you let her depart with me ?"

"No," replied Herne, peremptorily. "Banish all thoughts of her from your breast. You will never behold her again. I will give you time for reflection on my proposal. An hour before midnight I shall return, and if I find you in the same mind, I abandon you to your fate."

And with these words, he stepped back towards the lower end of the cell.

Clifford instantly sprang after him, but before he could reach him a flash of fire caused him to recoil, and to his horror and amazement, he beheld the rock open, and yield a passage to the retreating figure.

When the sulphurous smoke, with which the little cell was filled, had, in some degree, cleared off, Clifford examined the sides of the rock, but could not find the slightest trace of a secret outlet, and, therefore, concluded that the disappearance of the demon had been effected by magic.

CHAPTER LXXXIII.

THE ESCAPE.

THE next day the girl was set at liberty by her jailer, and the hours flew by without the opportunity of escape, for which she sighed, occurring to her.

As night drew on she became more anxious, and at last expressed a wish to retire to her cell.

When about to fasten the door, Wild found that the lock had got strained, and the bolts would not move, and he was, therefore, obliged to content himself with placing a bench against it, on which he took a seat.

About an hour after the girl's retirement, old Tristram offered to relieve guard with Wild, but this the other positively declined, and leaning against the door, disposed himself to slumber.

Tristram then threw himself on the floor, and in a short time all seemed buried in repose.

By and by, however, when Wild's heavy breathing gave token of the soundness of his sleep, Tristram raised himself upon his elbow, and gazed round.

The lamp placed upon the table imperfectly illumined the cavern, for the fire which had been lighted to cook the evening meal, had gone out completely.

Getting up cautiously, and drawing his hunting-knife, the old man crept towards Wild, apparently with the intent of stabbing him, but he suddenly changed his resolution, and dropped his arm.

At that moment, as if perternaturally warned, Wild opened his eyes, and seeing the old forester standing by, sprang upon him, and seized him by the throat.

"Ah ! traitor !" he exclaimed, " what are you about to do ?"

"I am no traitor," replied the old man. "I heard a noise in the passage leading to Clifford's cell, and was about to rouse you, when you awakened on your own accord, probably disturbed by the noise."

"It may be," replied Wild, satisfied with the excuse, and relinquishing his grasp ; " I fancied I heard something in my dreams. But come with me to Clifford's cell. I will not leave you here."

And snatching up the lamp he hurried with Tristram into the passage.

They were scarcely gone, than the door of the cell was opened by the girl, who had overheard what had passed ; and so hurriedly did she issue forth that she overturned the bench, which fell to the ground with a considerable clatter.

She had only just time to replace it, and to conceal herself in an adjoining passage, when Wild rushed back into the cavern.

"It was a false alarm," he cried. "I saw Clifford, in his cell through the loophole, and I have brought the key away with me. But I am sure I heard a noise here."

"It must have been mere fancy," said Tristram. "All is as we left it."

"It seems so," said Wild doubtfully. "But I will make sure."

While he placed his ear to the door the girl gave a signal to Tristram that she was safe.

Persuaded that he heard some sound in the chamber, Wild nodded to Tristram that all was right, and resumed his seat.

In less than ten minutes he was again asleep.

The girl then emerged from her concealment, and cautiously approached Tristram, who feigned, also, to slumber.

As she approached him he rose noiselessly to his feet.

"The plan has succeeded," he said in a low tone. "It was I who spoiled the lock. But come with me. I will lead you out of the cavern."

"Not without Clifford," she replied; "I will not leave him here."

"You will only expose yourself to risk, and fail to deliver him," rejoined Tristram. "Wild has the key of his cell.—Nay, if you are determined upon it, I will not hinder you. But you must find your own way out, for I shall not assist Clifford."

Motioning him to silence, the girl crept slowly, and on the points of her feet, towards Wild.

The key was in his girdle.

Leaning over him, she suddenly and dexterously plucked it forth.

At the very moment she possessed herself of it Wild stirred, and she dived down and concealed herself beneath the table.

Wild, who had only been slightly disturbed, looked up, and seeing Tristram in his former position, which he had resumed when the girl commenced her task, again disposed himself to slumber.

Waiting till she was assured of the soundness of his repose, the girl crept from under the table, signed to Tristram to remain where he was, and glided with swift and noiseless footsteps down the passage leading to the cell.

In a moment she was at the door, the key was in the lock, and she stood before Clifford.

A few words sufficed to explain to the astonished man how she came there, and comprehending that not a moment was to be lost, he followed her forth.

In the passage they held a brief consultation together, in a low tone, as to the best means of escape, for they deemed it useless to apply to Tristram.

The outlet with which Clifford was acquainted lay on the other side of the cavern; nor did he know how to discover the particular passage leading to it.

As to the girl she could offer no information, but she knew that the stable lay in an adjoining passage.

Recollecting, from former experience, how well the steeds were trained, Clifford eagerly caught at the suggestion, and the girl led him further down the passage, and, striking off through an opening on the left, brought him, after a few turns, to a large chamber, in which two or three black horses were kept.

Loosening one of them, Clifford placed a bridle on his neck, sprang upon his back, and took up the girl beside him.

He then struck his heels against the sides of the animal, who needed no further incitement to dash along the passage, and in a few seconds brought them into the cavern.

The trampling of the horse wakened Wild, who started to his feet, and ran after them, shouting furiously.

But he was too late.

Goaded by Clifford's dagger, the steed dashed furiously on, and, plunging with its double burthen into the pool at the bottom of the cavern, disappeared.

CHAPTER LXXXIV.

WILD'S RAGE - A SCHEME FOR THE DESTRUCTION OF THE DEMON.

TRANSPORTED with rage at the escape of the fugitives, Wild turned to old Tristram, and drawing his knife threatened to make an end of him.

But the old man, who was armed with a sword, stood upon his defence, and they remained brandishing their weapons at each other for some minutes, but without striking a blow.

"Well, I leave you to Herne's vengeance, said Wild, returning his knife to his belt. "You will pay dearly for allowing them to escape."

"I will take my chance," replied Tristram, moodily— "my mind is made up to the worst. I will no longer serve this fiend."

"What, dare you break your oath?" cried Wild. "Remember the terrible consequences."

"I care not for them," replied Tristram. "Harkee, Wild, I know you will not betray me, for you hate him as much as I do, and have as great a desire for revenge. I will rid the forest of this fell being."

"Would you could make good your words, old man!" cried Wild. "I would give my life for vengeance upon him."

"I take the offer," said Tristram, "you *shall* have vengeance."

"But how?" cried the other. "I have proved that he is invulnerable—and the prints of his hands are written in black characters upon my throat. If we could capture him, and deliver him to the king, we might purchase our own pardon."

"No, that can never be," said Tristram. "My plan is to destroy him."

"Well, let me hear it, said Wild.

"Come with me, then," rejoined Tristram.

And taking up the lamp, he led the way down a narrow lateral passage.

When about half way down it, he stopped before a low door, cased with iron, which he opened, and showed that the recess was filled with large canvas bags.

"Why, this is the powder magazine," said Wild. "I can now guess how you mean to destroy Herne. I like the scheme well enough; but it cannot be executed without certain destruction to ourselves."

"I will take all risk upon myself," said Tristram, "I only require your aid in the preparations. What I propose to do is this. There is powder enough in the magazine, not only to blow up the cave, but to set fire to all the wood surrounding it. It must be scattered among the dry brushwood in a great circle round the cave, and connected by a train with this magazine. When Herne comes back I will fire the train."

"There is much hazard in the scheme, and I fear it will fail," replied Wild, after a pause, "nevertheless, I will assist you."

"Then, let us go to work at once," said Tristram. "for we have no time to lose. Herne will be here before midnight, and I should like to have all ready for him."

Accordingly they each shouldered a couple of the bags, and, returning to the cavern, threaded a narrow passage, and emerged from the secret entrance in the grove.

While Wild descended for a fresh supply of powder Tristram commenced operations.

Though autumn was now far advanced, there had been remarkably fine weather of late; the ground was thickly strewn with yellow leaves; the fern was brown and dry; and the brushwood crackled and broke as a passage was forced through it.

The very trees were parched by the long-continued drought.

Thus favoured in his design, Tristram scattered the contents of one of the bags in a thick line among the fern and brushwood, depositing here and there, among the roots of a tree, several pounds of powder, and covering the heaps over with dried sticks and leaves.

While he was thus employed, Wild appeared with two more bags of powder, and descended again for a fresh supply.

When he returned, laden as before, the old forester had already described a large portion of the circle he intended to take.

Judging that there was now powder sufficient, Tristram explained to his companion how to proceed; and the other commenced laying a train on the left of the secret entrance, carefully observing the instructions given him.

In less than an hour they met together at a particular tree, and the formidable circle was complete.

"So far, well!" said Tristram, emptying the contents of his bag beneath the tree, and covering it with leaves and sticks, as before; "and now to connect this with the cavern."

With this, he opened another bag, and drew a wide train towards the centre of the space.

At length he paused at the foot of a large hollow tree.

"I have ascertained," he said, "that this tree stands immediately over the magazine; and by following this rabbit's burrow, I have contrived to make a small entrance into it. A hollow reed introduced through the hole, and filled with powder, will be sure to reach the store below."

"An excellent idea!" replied Wild. "I will fetch one instantly."

And starting off to the side of the lake, he presently returned with several long reeds, one of which was selected by Tristram, and thrust into the burrow.

It proved of the precise length required; and as soon as it touched the bottom it was carefully filled with powder from a horn.

Having connected this tube with the side train, and scattered powder for several yards around, so as to secure its instantaneous ignition, Tristram pronounced that the train was complete.

"We have now laid a trap from which Herne will scarcely escape," he observed, with a moody laugh, to Wild.

They then prepared to return to the cave; but had not proceeded many yards when Herne, mounted on his sable steed, burst through the trees.

"Ah! what makes you here?" he cried, instantly checking his career. "I bade you keep strict watch over the girl. Where is she?"

"She has escaped with Clifford, replied Wild; "and we have been in search of them—"

"Escaped!" exclaimed Herne, springing from his steed, and rushing up to him; "dogs! you have played me false. But your lives shall pay the penalty of your perfidy."

"We had no hand in it whatever," replied Wild, doggedly. "She contrived to get out of a chamber in which I placed her, and to liberate Clifford. They then procured a steed from the stable, and plunged through the pool into the lake."

"Hell's malison upon them and upon you both!" cried Herne; "but you shall pay dearly for your heedlessness, if, indeed, it has not been something worse. How long have they been gone?"

"It may be two hours, replied Wild."

"Go to the cave," cried Herne, "and await my return there; and if I recover not the prize, woe betide you both!"

And with these words he vaulted upon his steed, and disappeared.

"And woe betide you too, false fiend!" cried Wild. "When you come back you shall meet with a welcome you little expect. Would we had fired the train, Tristram, even though we had perished with him!"

"It will be time enough to fire it on his return," replied the old forester; "it is but postponing our vengeance for a short time. And now to fix our positions. I will take my station in yon brake."

"And I in that hollow tree," said Wild. "Whoever first beholds him shall fire the train."

"Agreed! replied Tristram. "Let us now descend to the cave, and see that all is right in the magazine, and then we will return and hold ourselves in readiness for action."

CHAPTER LXXXV.

THE CRISIS.

HOURS passed.

At length the two watches heard the tramp of hoofs.

It was Herne, and followed by Clifford and his friends.

"It is Herne! it is Herne!"

All were in pursuit, urging the horse to the utmost speed, Clifford foremost.

Herne's triumphant and demoniacal laugh was heard as he scoured with the swiftness of the wind down the long glade.

But the fiercest determination animated his pursuers, who being all admirably mounted, managed to keep him fully in view.

Away, away, he speeded in the direction of the lake; and after him they thundered, straining every sinew in the desperate chase.

It was a wild and extraordinary sight, and partook of the fantastical character of a dream.

At length Herne reached the acclivity, at the foot of which lay the waters of the lake glimmering in the starlight, and by the time he had descended to its foot, his pursuers had gained its brow.

The exertions made by Clifford had brought him a little in advance of the others.

Furiously goading his horse, he dashed down the hill side, at a terrific pace.

All at once, as he kept his eye on the flying figure of the demon, he was startled by a sudden burst of flame in the valley.

A wide circle of light was rapidly described, a rumbling sound was heard like that preceding an earthquake, and a tremendous explosion followed, hurling trees and fragments of rock into the air.

Astounded at the extraordinary occurrence, and not knowing what might ensue, the pursuers reined in their steeds.

But the terror of the scene was not yet over.

The whole of the brushwood had caught fire and blazed up with the fury and swiftness of lighted flax.

The flames caught the parched branches of the trees, and in a few seconds the whole grove was on fire.

The sight was awfully grand, for the wind, which was blowing strongly, swept the flames forward, so that they devoured all before them.

When the first flash was seen, the demon had checked his steed, and backed him, so that he escaped without injury, and he stood at the edge of the flaming circle watching the progress of the devastating element, but at last, finding that his pursuers had taken heart, and were approaching him, he bestirred himself, and rode round the blazing zone.

Having by this time recovered from their surprise, Bill and Long Ned dashed after him, and got so near that they made sure of his capture.

But at the very moment they expected to reach him, he turned his horse's head, and forced him to leap over the blazing boundary.

In vain the pursuers attempted to follow.

Their horses refused to encounter the flames; while Clifford's steed, urged on by its frantic master, reared bolt upright, and dislodged him.

But the demon held on his way, apparently unscathed, in the midst of the flames, casting a look of grim defiance at his pursuers.

As he passed a tree, from which volumes of fire were bursting, the most appalling shrieks reached his ear, and he beheld Wild emerging from a hole in the trunk.

But without bestowing more than a glance upon his unfortunate follower, he dashed forward, and becoming involved in the wreaths of flame and smoke, was lost to sight.

Attracted by Wilds' cries, the pursuers perceived him crawl out of the hole, and clamber into the upper part of the tree, where he roared to them most piteously for aid.

Attributing its outbreak to supernatural agency, the party gazed on in wonder at the fire, and rode round it, as closely as their steeds would allow them.

But though they tarried till the flames had abated, and little was left of the noble grove but a collection of charred and smoking stumps, nothing was seen of the fiend or of the hapless girl he had carried off.

It served to confirm the notion of the supernatural origin of the fire, in that it was confined within the mystic circle, and did not extend further into the woods.

Waters dashed forward as the flames abated, and dragged Wild from his hole.

"Ah!" he cried, "at length—at length! Now Jonathan Wild your days are numbered."

They tied him hand and foot, and he was powerless.

* * * o * *

"Alas!" cried Clifford. after a pause, "Alas for the poor girl. What is to become of her?"

"Why, ride through the flames after her," cried Long Ned.

Clifford spurred the horse he rode, but to no avail. The animal would not move.

"Oh, that Brilliant were here!" cried the highwayman, in a frenzy of fears and doubts.

As if some good angel had heard the wish and granted it, at that moment the white mare dashed into sight.

"Halt, mare; halt!" cried Clifford.

But, heeding him not, the mare then dashed forward into the blazing forest.

* * * * * *

Half an hour elapsed.

It appeared to the watchers an age.

Then their eyes were blessed with another sight of the white mare.

To the stirrup iron clung the girl, Clifford had rescued from the Curfew Tower.

At the heels of the mare were Herne's beadles—hounds; but on seeing the band before them they disappeared, as if by magic.

CHAPER LXXXVI.

CLIFFORD ONCE MORE IN THE POWER OF HERNE.

WILD was made safe, and ere long the young girl of the Curfew Tower was brought to consciousness

In the charge of Bill Waters Clifford placed Wild. To Long Ned he handed the girl.

To both he gave instructions to proceed without delay to London, promising to return as soon as he satisfied himself concerning the mysteries of the forest of Windsor.

They left him.

Suddenly all grew dark.

Clifford staggered.

He was helpless.

"Ho! ho!" roared a voice in his ear, " you would remain, would you? It was well. You shall know all you desire of the mysteries of the forest."

It was the voice of Herne.

Clifford found himself lifted from his feet, and in a few moments he was being hurried at a frightful pace through the forest.

When they halted Clifford once more found himself in the sandstone cave.

It was untouched.

The powder had not affected it.

Half-stifled by the noxious vapour he had inhaled, and blinded by the tightness of the bandage, it was some time before Clifford fully recovered his powers of sight and utterance.

"Why am I brought hither, false fiend?" he demanded, at length.

"To join my band," replied the demon, harshly and imperiously.

"Never!" rejoined Clifford. "I will have nought to do with you except as regards our compact."

"I mean you fairly, and will not delude you with false expectations. I know what you seek, and it cannot be accomplished on the instant. Ere three days Evelina shall be yours."

"Give me some proof that you are not deceiving me, spirit," said Clifford.

"Come, then!" replied Herne.

So saying, he sprang from the stone, and, taking Clifford's hand, led him towards the lower end of the cave, which gradually declined till it reached the edge of a small, but apparently deep pool of water, the level of which rose above the rock that formed its boundary.

"Remove the torch!" thundered the demon to those behind. "Now summon your love, Clifford," he added, as his orders were obeyed, and the light was taken into one of the side passages, so that its gleam no longer fell upon the water.

"Appear, Evelina!" cried Clifford.

Upon this, a shadowy resemblance of her he had invoked flitted over the surface of the water, with hands outstretched towards him.

So moved was Clifford by the vision, that he would have flung himself into the pool to grasp it, if he had not been forcibly detained by the demon.

During the struggle, the figure vanished, and all was buried in darkness.

"I have said she shall be yours," cried Herne; "but time is required for the accomplishment of my purpose. I have only power over her when evil is predominant in her heart. But such moments are not unfrequent," he added, with a bitter laugh. "And now to the chase. I promise you it will be a wilder and more exciting ride than you ever enjoyed in the king's company. To the chase!—to the chase, I say!"

Sounding a call upon his horn, the light instantly reappeared.

All was stir and confusion amid the impish troop—and presently afterwards a number of coal-black horses, and hounds of the same hue, leashed in couples, were brought out of one of the side passages.

Among the latter were two large sable hounds of Saint Hubert's breed, whom Herne summoned to his side by the names of Saturn and Dragon.

A slight noise, as of a blow dealt against a tree, was now heard overhead, and Herne, imposing silence on the group by a hasty gesture, assumed an attitude of fixed attention.

The stroke was repeated a second time.

"It is one of our brothers," cried the demon.

Catching hold of a chain hanging from the roof, which Clifford had not hitherto noticed, he swung himself into a crevice above, and disappeared from view.

During the absence of their leader the troop remain motionless and silent.

A few minutes afterwards Herne re-appeared at th upper end of the cave.

He was accompanied by a demon, between whom and Clifford a slight glance of recognition passed.

The order being given by th demon to mount, Clifford, after an instant's hesitation, seized the flowing mane of a horse nearest him—for it was furnished neither with saddle nor bridle—and vaulted upon its back.

At the same moment Herne uttered a wild cry, and plunging within the pool, sunk within it. Clifford's steed followed, and swam swiftly forward beneath the water.

When Clifford rose to the surface, he found himself in the open lake, which was gleaming in the moonlight.

Before him he beheld Herne clambering the bank, accompanied by his two favourite hounds, while a large white owl wheeled round his head, hooting loudly.

Behind came the grisly cavalcade, with their hounds, swimming from beneath a bank covered by thick, overhanging trees, which completely screened the secret entrance to the cave.

Having no control over his steed, Clifford was obliged to surrender himself to its guidance, and was soon placed by the side of the demon hunter.

"Pledge me, Clifford," said Herne, unslinging a gourd-shaped flask from his girdle, and offering it to him, "'Tis a rare wine, and will prevent you from suffering from your bath, as well as give you spirits for the chase."

Chilled to the bone by the immersion he had undergone, Clifford did not refuse the offer, but placing the flask to his lips, took a deep draught from it.

The demon uttered a low, bitter laugh, as he received back the flask, and he slung it to his girdle without tasting it.

The effect of the potion upon Clifford was extraordinary.

The whole scene seemed to dance around him; the impish figures in the lake, or upon its bank, assumed forms yet more fantastic; the horses looked like monsters of the deep; the hounds like wolves and ferocious beasts; the branches of the trees writhed and shot forward like hissing serpents; and though this effect speedily passed off, it left behind it a wild and maddening feeling of excitement.

"A noble hart is lying in yon glen," said the attendant demon, advancing towards his leader; "I tracked his slot thither this evening."

"Haste, and unharbour him," replied Herne, "and as soon as you rouse him give the halloa."

The fellow obeyed; and, shortly afterwards, a cry was heard from the glen.

"List halloa! list halloa!" cried Herne, "that's he! that's he! hyke, Saturn! hyke, Dragon!—Away!—away, my merry men all."

Accompanied by Clifford, and followed by the whole cavalcade, Herne dashed into the glen, where the demon keeper awaited him.

Threading the hollow, the troop descried the hart, flying swiftly along a sweeping glade, at some two hundred yards distance.

The glade was passed—a woody knoll skirted—a valley traversed—and the hart plunged into a thick grove clothing the side of Hawk's Hill.

But it offered him no secure retreat.

Dragon and Saturn were close upon him, and behind them came Herne, crashing through the branches of the trees, and heedless of all impediments.

By and by the thicket became more open, and they entered Cranbourne Chase.

But the hart soon quitted it to return to the Great Park, and darted down a declivity skirted by a line of noble oaks.

Here he was so hotly pressed by his fierce opponents, whose fangs he could almost feel within his haunches, that he suddenly stopped, and stood at bay, receiving the foremost of his assailants, Saturn, on the points of his horns.

But his defence, though gallant, was unavailing.

In another instant Herne came up, and dismounting, called off Dragon, who was about to take the place of his wounded companion.

Drawing a knife from his girdle, the hunter threw himself on the ground, and advancing on all fours, towards the hart, could scarcely be distinguished himself from some denizen of the forest.

As he approached, the hart snorted and bellowed fiercely, and dashed its horns against him; but the blow was received by the hunter upon his own antlered helm, and at the same moment, his knife was thrust to the hilt into the stag's throat, and it fell to the ground.

Springing to his feet, Herne whooped joyfully, placed his bugle to his lips, and blew the dead mot.

He then shouted to the keeper to call away and couple the hounds, and striking off the deer's right fore foot with his knife, presented it to Clifford.

Several large leafy branches being gathered and laid upon the ground, the hart was placed upon them, and Herne commenced breaking him up, as the process of dismembering the deer is termed in the language of woodcraft.

His first step was to cut off the animal's head, which he performed by a single blow with his heavy trenchant knife.

"Give the hounds the flesh," he said, delivering the trophy to his attendant; "but keep the antlers, for it is a great deer of head."

Placing the head on a hunting-pole, the keeper withdrew to an open space among the trees, and halloing to the others, they immediately cast off the hounds, who rushed towards him, leaping and baying at the stag's head, which he alternately raised and lowered, until they were sufficiently excited, when he threw it on the ground before them.

While this was going forward, the rest of the band were occupied in various ways—some striking a light with flint and steel—some gathering together sticks and dried leaves to form a fire—others producing various strange-shaped cooking utensils—while others were assisting their leader in his butcherly task, which he executed with infinite skill and expedition.

As soon as the fire was kindled, Herne distributed certain portions of the venison among his followers, which were instantly thrown upon the embers to broil; while a few choice morsels were stewed in a pan with wine, and subsequently offered to the leader and Clifford.

This hasty repast concluded, the demon ordered the fire to be extinguished, and the quarters of the deer to be carried to the cave.

He then mounted his steed, and attended by Clifford and the rest of his troop, except those engaged in executing his orders, galloped towards Snow Hill, where he speedily succeeded in unharbouring another noble hart.

Away then went the whole party—stag, hounds, huntsmen, sweeping, like a dark cloud, down the hill, and crossing the wide moonlit glade, studded with noble trees, on the west of the great avenue.

For awhile, the hart held a course parallel with the avenue; he then dashed across it, threaded the intricate woods on the opposite side, tracked a long glen, and leaping the pales, entered the Home Park.

It almost seemed as if he designed to seek shelter within the castle, for he made straight towards it, and was only diverted by Herne himself, who, shooting past him with incredible swiftness, turned him towards the lower part of the park.

Here the chase continued with unabated ardour, until, reaching the banks of the Thames, the hart plunged into it, and suffered himself to be carried noiselessly down the current.

But Herne followed him along the banks, and when sufficiently near, dashed into the stream, and drove him again ashore.

Once more they flew across the Home Park—once more they leaped its pales—once more they entered the

Great Park—but this time the stag took the direction of Englefield Green.

He was not, however, allowed to break forth into the open country; but driven again into the thick woods, he held on with wondrous speed, till the lake appeared in view.

In another instant he was swimming across it.

Before the eddies occasioned by the affrighted animal's plunge had described a wide ring, Herne had quitted his steed, and was cleaving with rapid strokes, the waters of the lake.

Finding escape impossible, the hart turned to meet him, and sought to strike him with his horns, but, as in the case of his ill-fated brother of the wood, the blow was warded by the antlered helm of the swimmer.

The next moment the clear water was dyed with blood, and Herne, catching the gasping animal by the head, guided his body to shore.

Again the process of breaking up the stag was gone through; and when Herne had concluded his task, he once more offered his gourd to Clifford.

Reckless of the consequences the highwayman placed the flask to his lips, and draining it to the last drop, fell from his horse insensible.

When perfect consciousness returned to him, Clifford found himself lying upon a pallet in what he at first took to be the cell of an anchorite; but as the recollection of recent events arose more distinctly before him, he guessed it to be a chamber connected with the sandstone cave.

A small lamp, placed in a recess, lighted the cell; and upon a footstool by his bed stood a jug of water, and a cup containing some drink, in which herbs had evidently been infused.

Well nigh emptying the jug, for he felt parched with thirst, Clifford attired himself, took up the lamp, and walked into the main cavern.

No one was there, nor could he obtain any answer to his calls.

Evidences, however, were not wanting to prove that a feast had recently been held there.

On one side were the scarcely-extinguished embers of a large wood fire; and in the midst of the chamber was a rude table, covered with drinking horns and wooden platters, as well as with the remains of three or four haunches of venison.

While contemplating this scene Clifford heard footsteps in one of the lateral passages, and presently afterwards the keeper made his appearance.

"So you are come round at last, Clifford," observed the keeper, in a slightly sarcastic tone.

"What has ailed me?" asked Clifford, in surprise.

"You have had a fever for three days, and have been raving like a madman."

"Three days!" muttered Clifford. "The false, juggling fiend promised her to me on the third day!"

"Fear not;—Herne will be as good as his word," said the keeper; but will you go forth with me. I am about to visit my net. It is a fine day, and a row on the lake will do you good."

Clifford acquiesced, and followed the keeper, who returned along the passage.

It grew narrower at the sides, and lower in the roof, as they advanced, until at last they were compelled to move forward on their hands and knees.

For some space, the passage, or rather hole (for it was nothing more), ran on a level.

A steep and tortuous ascent then commenced, which brought them to an outlet concealed by a large stone.

Pushing it aside, the keeper crept forth, and immediately afterwards Clifford emerged into a grove, through which, on one side, the gleaming waters of the lake were discernible.

The keeper's first business was to replace the stone, which was so screened by brambles and bushes that it could not, unless careful search were made, be detected.

Making his way through the trees to the side of the lake, the keeper marched along the greensward, in the direction of the old cottage.

Clifford mechanically followed him.

It was high noon, and the day was one of resplendent loveliness.

The lake sparkled in the sunshine, and as they shot past its tiny bays and woody headlands, new beauties were every moment revealed to them.

But while the scene softened Clifford's feelings it filled him with intolerable remorse, and so poignant did his emotions become, that he pressed his hands upon his eyes to shut out the lovely prospect.

When he looked up again the scene was changed.

The skiff had entered a narrow creek, arched over by huge trees, and looking as dark and gloomy as the rest of the lake was fair and smiling.

It was closed in by a high overhanging bank, crested by two tall trees, whose tangled roots protruded through it, like monstrous reptiles, while their branches cast a heavy shade over the deep, sluggish water.

"Why have you come here?" demanded Clifford, looking uneasily round the forbidding spot.

"You will discover anon, replied the keeper, moodily.

"Go back into the sunshine, and take me to some pleasant bank,—I will not land here," said Clifford, sternly.

"Needs must when—I need not remind you of the proverb," rejoined the man, with a sneer.

"Give me the oars," cried Clifford, fiercely; "and I will put myself ashore."

"Keep quiet," said the man, "you must, perforce, abide our master's coming."

Clifford gazed at the keeper for a moment, as if with the intention of throwing him overboard; but, abandoning the idea, he rose up in the boat, and caught at what he took to be a root of the tree above.

To his surprise and alarm, it closed upon him with an iron grasp, and he felt himself dragged upwards, while the skiff, impelled by a sudden stroke, shot from beneath him.

All Clifford's efforts to disengage himself were vain, and a wild, demoniacal laugh, echoed by a chorus of voices, proclaimed him in the power of Herne, the hunter.

The next moment he was set on the top of the bank, while the demon greeted him with a mocking laugh.

"So, you thought to escape me, Clifford!" he cried, in a taunting tone; "but any such attempt will prove fruitless. The murderer may repent the blow when dealt; the thief may desire to restore the gold he has purloined; the barterer of his soul may rue his bargain; but they are Satan's, nevertheless. You are mine, and nothing can redeem you!"

"Woe is me, that it should be so!" groaned Clifford.

"Lamentation is useless and unworthy of you," rejoined Herne, scornfully. "Your wish will be speedily accomplished. This very night your love will be placed in your power."

"Ha!" exclaimed Clifford, the flame of love again rising within his breast.

"She is now in the power of the king. He has sought to make her his mistress; until now he has failed. Be true to me, and he shall still fail. You can make your own terms with him for the lady," pursued Herne. "His life will be at your disposal."

"Do you promise this?" cried Clifford.

"Ay," replied Herne. "Put yourself under the conduct of the keeper, and all shall happen as you desire. We shall meet again at night. I have other business on hand now. Meschines," he added, to one of his attendants, "go with Clifford to the skiff."

The personage who received the command, and who was wildly and fantastically habited, beckoned Clifford to follow him, and, after many twistings and turnings, brought them to the edge of the lake, where the skiff was lying, with the keeper reclining at full length upon its benches.

He arose, however, quickly, on the appearance of Meschines, and asked him for some provisions, which the latter promised to bring; and while Clifford got into the skiff, he disappeared, but returned, a few minutes afterwards, with a basket, which he gave to the keeper.

Crossing the lake, the keeper then shaped his course towards a verdant bank, enamelled with wild flowers, where he landed.

The basket being opened was found to contain a flask of wine and the better part of a venison pasty, of which Clifford, whose appetite was keen enough after his long fasting, ate heartily.

He then stretched himself on the velvet sod and dropped into a tranquil slumber, which lasted to a late hour in the evening.

He was roused from it by a hand laid on his shoulder, while a deep voice thundered in his ear—"Up, up, Clifford, and follow me, and I will place the king in your hands!"

CHAPTER LXXXVII.

THE TRAVELLER'S TALE CONTINUED.

MAGSWORTH was in the solitary prison-room at Croydon.

The day of trial arrived.

Sir Charles Moore had refused to prosecute, saying that he felt convinced that some error had been the cause of Magsworth's arrest.

But the law itself took the matter up.

Judges, in those days, were as bloodthirsty in their way as Judge Jeffreys.

Men who ordered their fellow creatures to be strung up eight at a time for trifling offences, naturally became callous, and were in want of excitement if there was no one to hang.

So, as the baronet declined to prosecute the burglar, the law did—having for its principal witness Lady Moore.

Many were the bitter scenes between Sir Charles and his young wife.

Fresh from his melancholy scene with Magsworth, he had entered her room; and, for the first time in his married life, repelled the advances of Lady Maud.

She sank down into her chair aghast, and in deadly fear.

Fear, lest he had discovered her secrets—for two deadly secrets now were hers.

"I much fear you are angry with me, Sir Charles," she said in a tremulous voice, "though why I know not."

Sir Charles sighed.

"Alas, Maud," he replied, "my brother has made grave charges against you. If they were true they would tend to destroy all my hopes in life."

"Why so, Charles?"

And the blue eyes were upturned innocently—sorrowfully.

"Because they would make me lose my faith in you. But setting this aside, I must again urge my wishes on you. A great curse is threatening our house; it is in your power to avert it, and you have refused."

"It is not in my power, Sir Charles," returned Lady Moore, quietly; "otherwise, you know I would do it."

"There is one thing I shall do to save him," said the baronet. I shall refuse to prosecute. You cannot."

The ready tears welled up to Lady Maud's eyes.

"You think I am vindictive—I see you do!" she cried. "Believe me, dear Charles, if you can stay this prosecution by refusing to appear in it, I shall bless the hour which preserves me from uttering fatal truths."

She could say this fervently.

She had consulted a good solicitor, and he had advised her that, if all else failed, the law would be her catspaw.

Sir Charles loved his wife dearly—passionately—shall we say doatingly?—and he was quite willing to believe that this show of feeling was real.

Yet, in that sunlight there was a cloud.

The extreme abhorrence she professed for falsehood—the intense anxiety with which she disclaimed the possibility of error—had something suspicious in it.

Yet he, who could not believe in the depth of her malignity, could not see the motive of her movements, if that motive were antagonistic to the interest of his brother.

He determined to put her to the test.

"There is one way," he said, smiling, "one way in which I feel sure we can save my brother, without compromising your conscience."

Lady Moore's heart grew faint, but she responded cordially.

"And what is that?" she cried eagerly.

"If it is beyond your power to appear at the court—what then?"

"I do not understand you."

"Suppose you were ill in bed?"

"I might as well speak a lie as act one," returned Lady Moore.

"Supposing, then, I were to lock you in your room? You cannot object to this, Maud, because it is not your wish that my brother should die. I will lock you in your room on that day, and the trial must take place without you."

Lady Moore shook with anger.

She was a woman, and did not see the flimsiness of Sir Charles' day-dreams.

Very well, Sir Charles," she said. "If this will satisfy you, let it be so."

"Sir Charles glanced at her sharply, but answered not.

She rose and left the room to hide the workings of her anger in her features.

"I verily believe," said Sir Charles, murmuringly, musingly, as he gazed at her departing form,—"I verily believe she desires my brother to die!"

So the day of trial came.

Magsworth, still studying his family dignity, refused to appear as a Moore.

So the Court knew him only as Magsworth.

The judge was Judge Nicholet—a fierce, uncompromising man, who had sent unnumbered victims of a savage law to their last account.

The counsel for the prosecution was Horatio Vallance, the Attorney General—a tall man with grey hair, and a mild, benevolent face.

He was as savage and uncompromising as the judge.

But people did not see through him.

His mildness of appearance was such, that when he broke forth into eloquent barbarity it was imagined at once that the extreme villany of the prisoner had roused him from his quiet and benevolent nature, and that his outburst was the result of virtuous indignation.

Whenever, therefore, he appealed to the jury with tears in his eyes, and called upon them with deep emotion to deliver a verdict of guilty, the audience transferred to him the pity they should have bestowed upon his victim.

Against him the counsel whom Magsworth had employed was a mere plaything—a puppet to be set up and knocked down.

But Magsworth was his own best defender.

When the counsel for the prosecution had finished his peroration he demanded leave to speak.

His words were impassioned, burning, eloquent.

He detailed in glowing terms the miserable life he had led, the privations he had suffered, and the love he bore his child.

Then he told them how this child had been dragged from him, how she had disappeared, and how he suspected Lady Moore of bringing about this disappearance.

Yet through all his speech he kept up his character.

Never once did he allow it to be seen that his was more than a distant connection with the Moore family.

When he accused Lady Moore of having blamed him falsely a murmur of indignation ran through the audience.

The counsel for the prosecution had taken them by storm.

He had dwelt long upon the fact that Lady Moore would not appear against him, even though foully wronged.

But just as he spoke there was a commotion without the court, and Lady Moore was led in.

Sir Charles, who had, as the saying is, " been accommodated with a seat on the bench," turned deadly pale as he saw her enter.

" He is lost now !" he murmured.

Late in the day as it was, her evidence was received, and the judge summed up.

As might have been expected, he did so dead against the prisoner.

Just before the jury retired, Sir Charles Moore asked to be allowed to speak.

He was very pale, and almost fell as he rose up.

" I wish," he said, " to make a statement which I thought unnecessary before. I imagined that the charge was so light that the prisoner would at once be acquitted. As, however, it seems likely to be a more serious matter, I will declare that which, for the sake of the family, both I and your prisoner resolved to keep secret. Magsworth is Magsworth Moore, my younger brother, and I believe him incapable of such an action as that he is charged with."

A murmur ran through the court.

Yet, strange to say, it was not a murmur of sympathy with the prisoner, but with his brother.

" The jury will form their own opinion of what Sir Charles Moore has stated. I have nothing to add to the remarks I have already made," said the judge.

So the jury retired, and the usual excitement pervaded the assembly.

The usual remarks were made, the usual queries ventured.

Bets, even, were laid as to the verdict.

At length the twelve came in.

Twelve as dogged, stolid, impassable-looking beings as might well be met in a month's journey.

Few people doubted the verdict.

The ordinary question was asked—the ordinary answer given.

Then the verdict came—

" Guilty with a strong recommendation to mercy, on account of his perturbed state of mind, and the anguish he felt at the loss of his child."

A gleam of pleasure was in the eyes of Lady Moore.

This she could not repress, though she did repress the smile of triumph which would otherwise have wreathed itself over her lips.

And so—dear lady—when she covered her face with her handkerchief, and bowed her head, as the judge pronounced sentence, men pitied her, and women wept.

" Poor thing ! It was sad that she should be dragged into a court of justice—she, the beautiful, the innocent, the fascinating Lady Moore!

And so the judge gave sentence, saying that the merciful words of the jury should be spoken of in the proper quarter, but giving no hope to the prisoner that the extreme penalty of the law would not be enforced.

Sir Charles Moore, bowed down with grief, feared to glance at his brother.

He need not have feared.

Magsworth stood with his crest erect—his arms folded proudly over his breast—his eyes fixed upon the judge, who scarcely dared meet his gaze.

When Judge Nicholet had finished Magsworth spoke.

" The worst is over now," he said ; " but before I leave this court let me tell you that I fear not the law's revenge. Death to me has few terrors. What I dreaded in this trial was the fact of being disgraced, because my disgrace will be transmitted to my child. Had not my brother spoken, I would have allowed myself to have been murdered under the name of Magsworth, that my daughter might not, in after years, have been identified with me. For the recommendation of the jury I thank them—I desire it not. Let me die, since death to me is preferable to a life of dishonour."

And so it ended.

Sir Charles and Lady Moore drove away in their carriage, and the crowd dispersed to chat, and jeer, and pay its bets, while Magsworth was left to die.

" And so," said the baronet, to his beautiful wife, as she sat by his side, in simulated sorrow, " so, against my express wish—in spite of all my precautions—you bore witness against my brother !"

" Indeed, indeed I was forced to the court," she cried, passionately. " The officers found their way to my chamber, and compelled me to attend."

Sir Charles said no more.

In his inmost heart he disbelieved her statement, but yet he feared to confess this disbelief to himself.

What would his future be if he *did* disbelieve her thoroughly ?

What would life be to him — a lone man without children—if she were proved false ?

What could he hope for if she—the sunny, beautiful woman whom he had loved the more because of her contrast to himself—were found indisputably his enemy ?

He said no more, then, of the cause of his brother's sentence.

This only he murmured :—" Condemned as he is, I will save him, if my own life is lost in the attempt."

The voice in which these words were uttered proved their intense sincerity, and Lady Moore changed colour.

The baronet observed this, and took a note of it.

CHAPTER LXXXVIII.

THE TRAVELLER'S TALE CONTINUED.

THE day fixed for the execution of Magsworth Moore was the eighth day after the trial, and the baronet, therefore, had little time before him.

He lost not a moment.

He had considerable influence with the Government, and had powerful friends, too, in other quarters.

Day after day saw his carriage at the office of the Home Secretary ; and day after day his carriage bore him thence to prison.

" Charles," said Magsworth, at the last interview but one, " do not pursue this useless scheme."

" Useless ! It shall not be useless !"

" Indeed it will be, my dear brother : believe me, they will not save me."

" They shall—they must !"

Magsworth smiled.

" And if they do, what then ? What is life in a penal settlement ? What is life to which there is no end but a felon's grave ? How could I exist at all when I should dream by night and think by day of nothing but one thing —that my daughter is a wanderer and an outcast, and has no one to protect her, to be kind to her, to talk to her of me."

He broke down as he spoke thus, and the tears welled from his eyes.

" Listen to me, Magsworth," said the baronet, lowering his voice. " If you die, you die a felon's death ; and you have the felon's grave, too, which you so much dread ! Your child will be irretrievably lost or irretrievably disgraced."

" I know it—I know it !"

" Remember if I save you—if I succeed, as I now sincerely hope I may in moving the stony heart of the Home Secretary—you have life. That is one thing."

Magsworth smiled bitterly.

"A convict's life," he said.

"No; the life of a man whose monomania is but to escape! You will exist but to escape—to return to this country—to retrieve your character—to find your child—to take this deadly, dreary weight from off my heart."

Magsworth turned pale, and grasped his brother's arm.

"You are giving me hope but to make me more wretched still!" he said. "How could I escape!—how could I leave the penal settlements if I did escape?"

Sir Charles still spoke in a whisper—an eager, hurried whisper, though, which proved his plan was well matured.

"I have it all," he said. "Every mail I will forward a certain sum to the principal bank of the nearest city to the credit of Henry Dumont. This sum will accumulate by the time you have matured your plan of escape, and before you go I will give you a letter to a merchant in the city, to whom I will address for you all my letters of advice. Thus, when you have fled the prison, there will be no delay in obtaining your money."

The words of Sir Charles roused a new current of feeling in the breast of Magsworth.

He rose, paced his cell—agitated and pale—for some moments.

Then he stopped, pressed his brother's hand, and looked wistfully in his face.

"Yes," he said, "I would live—I would live. Save me, Charles, that I may save my child."

A look of extreme joy passed over the baronet's features.

"At last I have persuaded you," he said.

Magsworth smiled sadly.

"Yes," he answered, "you have persuaded me to live, when, doubtless, they will not permit me to live."

On the following day the cell door opened as usual, and the baronet, flushed and eager, rushed in.

"It is done!" he cried. "You are saved!"

Magsworth trembled violently.

"Have they pardoned me?" he said, in a voice of fear.

"No, my brother," said Sir Charles, sorrowfully, "you are saved from death; but the sentence, even now, is fifteen years' transportation."

"A living death," muttered Magsworth.

"Not so, even if death were impossible," returned the baronet. "You are not an old man, and can return at the expiration of your sentence. But you can and shall escape."

A week after a convict ship left the shores of England. A heavy freight it was.

Heavy in numbers—heavy in crime.

Those were ill-looking faces which surrounded Magsworth, and an ill looking ruffian, indeed, was it that was chained to him on that fearful voyage.

Magsworth obtained the appellation of the "Silent Prisoner," on the journey.

He spoke to no one.

The thieves and murderers, and low felons, by whom he was surrounded, hated him for it, and swore desperate oaths that they would punish him for his implied insults to them.

"I'll make you think of this, my fine covey," growled the convict to whom he was chained. "Wait till we gets 'home,' and then see how much your gentleman's airs will aid you. It don't do no good, I can tell you, to make enemies among your comrades there."

These words convinced Magsworth that he had made a mistake.

Low and depraved as were his companions, they were his companions, and would continue to be so.

And more than this, at any attempt at escape, he *must* fail, unless he had the co-operation, or at least the friendly feelings of the convicts on his side.

So, one evening, when they were collected together in the hold, without any keepers (they were chained, and the hatchways were down, so they could do no harm), he spoke.

"Comrades," he said, "I've something to say."

A murmur, partly of derision, partly of curiosity, ran through the assembly.

"The Silent Man's going to speak," growled his comrade. "The gentleman's condescension is summut quite unnateral."

Magsworth looked round proudly in spite of his chains.

"Gentleman!" he cried. "Ah! that is your great mistake. I *am* a gentleman—the only one here, I fancy. What then? I will be your leader—I will use my knowledge to find a means of escape, and when we *have* escaped, we will be a warning and a curse to those who have now kept us in chains. If I have been silent on the voyage, it is because I wish to keep up my character. I wish them to trust me, that they may not be on their guard against me, and that I may thus more easily fling off my bondage."

He paused.

He had been listened to in silence—a loud roar of applause greeted the conclusion of his speech.

"Go on—go on!" cried many voices.

Magsworth smiled.

"I have said all I have to say," he answered. "The Silent Man has spoken. When he reaches 'home' he will speak again."

It was not so much the words, but the manner in which they were spoken, which brought forth the second round of applause.

From that moment Magsworth Moore was the most popular man on board the ship; and when he landed he had inspired the men with such confidence, that one and all looked forward to escape as a certainty.

But there were rude stone walls round their "home," as they termed it in their slang vocabulary, and high spikes upon them, and deep ditches and marshes beyond.

The Silent Man, as he was called, soon became as popular with the governor and the chaplain as he had among the convicts.

His elegant manners, and his education, aided by his fervent asseverations of innocence, obtained from them an earnest good will, and at the end of two years he was comparatively free from restraint.

Yet they feared him.

They knew his story.

They knew his wild, daring spirit.

They knew, too, the earnest hope which bound him to life.

This knowledge it was that made them fear him, and feel sure that he would attempt escape.

It was one evening when the governor gave a ball that a cry was raised that prisoners were escaping.

The guests hurried to the windows, and looked out.

Shouting, and then the report of musketry was heard.

Then the light of torches held by hurrying men were seen, and the flash again of pistols.

Presently the Governor, who had run out on the first alarm, re-entered the ball-room.

"What is the matter?" asked one of the guests.

"Magsworth Moore, with some other convicts," he said, "has been attempting an escape, and he is shot. They are bringing his body into the prison."

————

CHAPTER LXXXIX.

THE TRAVELLER'S TALE CONTINUED.

ABOUT thirteen years after the events narrated in our last chapter, a man, ill-clad, and bent either with old age, or hunger, or cold, was hastening along one of the narrow thoroughfares which intersect the neighbourhood of Bloomsbury.

London was white with snow.

Snow everywhere—in the air, on the ground, on the broad steps, on the lamp-posts, beating in your face, blinding you, bewildering you — mingling street and pavement in one confused mass.

But the man has a track through the snow.

His clothes are threadbare, and cling to him with a poverty-stricken embrace.

He has walked a long journey, too; for his shoes are worn in holes.

Yet he slackens not his pace.

The cold without is driven away by the raging fever within.

He is ill-looking, unshorn, hard-featured, dark-skinned; and policemen eye him askance.

He slinks from them.

Who is he?

Is he a housebreaker, or one who wishes to be one?

Is he not, perhaps, and far more probably, some half-starved wretch whose poverty is a crime?

He is neither.

Onward he rushes, while the majesty of the law terrified by his proximity to well-stored plate-rooms, stalks at his heels.

He is a tall, broad fellow, though the cold has bent him ; and he could crush, at one blow, that white-faced, narrow-waisted policeman.

But that white-faced, narrow-waisted policeman is the law for the nonce, and so our traveller eyes him fearfully, and slinks away into a maze of courts.

You would hardly have conceived it possible that such a man—looking so and dressing so—could have had a fixed object at any one moment.

Yet it was so.

He moved on steadily until he reached the entrance of a court, which, even in the snow storm, looked black within, for the lamp swung at its entrance only illuminated the arch which served as a portal.

Arrived here he glanced hastily, nervously, up and down the street.

No one was in sight.

He had eluded the majesty of the law—the policeman was baffled.

" If he keeps me long here," he mutterered, as he shivered beneath the dim and dingy lamp—" if he keeps me here long, he'll find a dead man, for, by heaven, the life's nearly frozen out of me."

A step approached.

The tattered stranger slunk beneath the dark archway, and listened.

Softly—softly—stealthily—steadily it came along the snow and stopped by the lamp.

The new-comer was a man of perhaps some twenty-one years of age, tall, well built, fashionably, if not elegantly dressed, with an air of society, if not of *haut ton*, about him.

" The ragged ruffian has deceived me," he cried impatiently ; " and in this deuced cold night too."

" The ragged ruffian was here before you, and is at your service," said the other, advancing. " The night, as you say is very cold, and I should like to retire to warmer lodgings."

" Ah Morley, you are here!" cried the young man. " Well, I'm glad of that. I've been deucedly out of luck to-night, and to-morrow must decide my fate."

The face of the man whom he addressed as Morley was hidden in the shadow, or he would have seen the curl of disdain that wreathed his lip at these words.

" You should be glad to have a fate yet to be decided, Mr. Henri le Morneaut," returned Morley. " Mine was decided long ago. However, hard by here is the ' Four Spies.' There we can talk without fear of listeners."

" An ominous name."

" *Lucus a non lucendo*, my worthy friend," returned the ragamuffin, with gay familiarity, and led the way.

" The Four Spies" looked like a beershop of the lowest order, but it retailed spirits of unexceptional strength. Morley evidently knew it.

He ordered a bottle of brandy—the best, you may be sure, as he had no money to pay for it with—and sat down in a remote corner of the parlour, where a dim lamp flickered above a dingy table.

After the first draught of the invigorating fluid, his manner changed.

He pushed his hat off his brow, tucked down the collar of his threadbare coat, leaned back on his seat, and placing his thin hands in his breeches pockets, ejaculated—

" This is a strange world !"

The man, as he said this, was in the full glare of the lamp, and Henri le Morneaut could see his features.

He was apparently about seven-and-forty.

His locks were grey, his face was thin, and you might readily have taken him for ten years older, had it not been for his eyes, which were lit up with the brilliancy of youth.

It was a strange, strong, weather-beaten face.

The face of a man who had knit his brows when he had started in life, and who had never been called upon to change his frown into a smile.

" That man is an honest man," thought Henri le Morneaut ; " if so, he is of no use me !"

" Well, now my friend," he said aloud, " let us at once to business."

" Yes," returned Morley, as he stretched his legs out at the fire, with the thorough enjoyment of a man who had not seen such a sight for many a night—" yes, let's to business. We meet under strange circumstances, and and I've thought over it many a time to-day. When I was sitting on that step in the dark, and heard you talking to yourself, I'd no idea that our roads laid in such similar directions. But, however, they do, and we must make the best of our way together.

Henri le Morneaut glanced at his companion angrily.

" Our ways will soon diverge, my friend," he cried testily.

The man turned round upon him with a look of expressive amusement, not unmingled with contempt.

" We don't understand one another yet," he said ; " it is time we should."

Le Morneaut did not answer.

He proceeded therefore :—

" You stood on the step of the large house in Montague-square, and said to yourself—' I am sick of these silly fellows ; if I knew but one brave man, I could be rich and powerful.' Then I leaped up, and caught your arm, saying, ' Here is your brave man—be rich and powerful.' Are not these my words?"

" They are."

" Did I say ' Here is your villain?' No, Henri le Morneaut, I never told you I was a rogue—I said I was an outcast."

" Which generally means the same thing," sneered the other."

Morley took no notice of the interruption.

" If we are to work together, we must work as equals," he continued. ' I am a man battered and beaten through life, but I am your equal, and in all we do must be recognised as such. To-morrow my dress shall be altered—you shall walk London with me, and not be ashamed. But come, tell me all your wants."

The young man leaned across the table, and dropped his voice to a whisper.

"I have told you," he said, "that my father, or, rather, my stepfather, Sir Charles Moore, is very old."

"Yes."

"He is now nearly bed-ridden—at least, he can only move about on crutches, and very rarely leaves his chamber."

Morley made no observation, but the muscles of his face moved convulsively.

"Well, the old man still nourishes in his heart a hope which implies my ruin. Many years ago a brother of his was transported for a robbery committed upon my mother. This brother had a daughter who was carried away by an old servant of my mother's, and Sir Charles has made some foolish vow to find this child, and reinstate her in her position. No doubt the girl is dead."

"You have no proof."

Henri laughed.

"Why, you appear as excited as I am," he said.

"Of course; if this child were dead your position would be far more safe," returned Morley, wiping the sweat from his brow.

"Just so; however, he does not believe the child is dead, and, until he has satisfactory proofs that she is no more, he refuses to alter the will he has made in her favour."

Morley's eyes gleamed.

"I begin to see daylight," he muttered, "but come—tell me what is the last trace you have found?"

The young man drew from his bosom a pocket book, and from this a paper yellow with age, and dirty and crumpled with much folding and unfolding.

"Look at this," he said, passing it over to Morley.

The man took it, asking "What is it?"

"It is a copy of the ship's register kept at the owner's in Liverpool."

It ran thus:—

"Mr. and Mrs. Durant and child. Passengers to Australia. Sailed June 10th."

"That is a lie," cried Morley, hoarsely. "They never took the child."

Henri le Morneaut started back in fear and astonishment.

"What do you know of it?" he cried.

The man laughed bitterly.

"I know everything," he said, "and will tell you a little of it."

"Tell me all or none."

He proceeded without noticing the last words:—

"I am a returned convict. My name is Morley Bridgenorth. Nay, do not start—there is no harm in me, for I was convicted on false evidence. In the penal settlement I became acquainted with Magsworth Moore—Sir Charles's brother—and also with Alfred Durant."

"He was no convict."

"No; not when he left England. But he had not long been in Australia when he resumed his thieving habits, and, being tried and condemned, came to prison with us. From him and Magsworth Moore I learned the whole story of which you have told me a part. Alfred never took the child, but left it behind him, outside the town of Croydon."

"And where is she now?"

"That remains to be seen."

"And her father—what of him?"

"He is dead," said Morley.

A gleam of joy shot from Henri de Morneaut's eyes as the returned convict uttered these words.

"Dead!" he cried. "How did he die?"

"Magsworth was a monomaniac," said Morley; "his mania was escape. He was sentenced—as, of course, you know—to fifteen years' penal servitude. In two years he matured his plans of escape, and reached the outside of the prison, with several of his companions. Here, however, they were surrounded, and he was brought back for dead, having been wounded by a shot from one of the muskets of the soldiers."

"He died, then, from his wound?"

"Not so; he lived many years after this accident. About eight months ago, he, and I, and Alfred Durant hit upon a scheme which we considered a certainty, and we put it immediately in practice. We passed the walls —we reached the swamp in safety. The moon was very bright, however, and lit up patches of water and the dew-bespangled grass, and we were again pursued. Two of us escaped; the other, whose face was completely shot away by the bursting of a gun, was carried back to be buried in a felon's grave."

"This man was—"

"Magsworth Moore."

"And where is Alfred Durant?"

"He is in London with me. We live in the same house."

Henri turned deadly pale.

"That man's being here may ruin all my plans," he muttered to himself. "Is he to be bought?" he asked aloud.

"Oh, yes; I daresay."

"Can I see him?"

"Not at present, I think. But tell me what it is you want, and I can do just as well.

"Well," said Henri, "if there were satisfactory proofs of the girl's death, old Moore would make his will in my favour. Now, as the ship's register says 'Mr. and Mrs. Durant and child,' he has but to say that he took the child away, and produce a certificate of her death."

"A forged one, you mean," returned Morley, eyeing him closely.

"That has nothing to do with me, said Henri, petulently. "I suggest no means whatever. All I ask is that Alfred Durant shall produce a certificate of the death of Alice Moore. When he does that I will give him my note of hand for five thousand pounds."

Morley exhibited no emotion at the mention of this large sum.

"A fine offer," he said; "but one, my young friend, which requires consideration. We will speak of that anon. What are your present requirements?"

"Money."

Morley laughed, and pointed to his dress.

"I seem the right one to apply to for money," he said.

Henri stamped his foot impatiently on the floor.

"Bah!" he cried; I thought you understood me; I thought you were a brave man."

"I am a brave man," returned the other; "a brave, bold man; and I have done many things in my time which would make you (young, strong, and active as you may be), shudder at the very thought, though I never shuddered at the deed. But I can tell you this; I am not a thief, and therefore have no money."

Henri was rapidly losing his temper.

He could not understand the man to whom he was talking; he could not comprehend why he had formed his acquaintance, or what good could accrue to him from it.

"It seems to me," he said, "that we are losing valuable time. I don't see what you are going to do for me."

"You asked me for money," returned Morley. "I cannot lend you any, because I have none; "but I can procure it for you, if you have any security to offer."

"I have," said Henri. "I have jewellery belonging to my mother, which she has lent me. This will bring in two thousand pounds."

Morley smiled.

"I am not a pawnbroker," he answered. "What else is there?"

"I have a signature of Sir Charles' for four thousand pounds."

"Let me see it."

The young man drew out his pocket-book again, and, with a trembling hand, passed over the bill to his companion.

The returned convict glanced at the signature carefully.

Then he raised his eyes slowly, till they met those of the young man.

"How did you obtain this?" he asked.

"My mother obtained it from Sir Charles, for her private use," returned Henri.

"Are you quite sure that Sir Charles himself signed this check?"

Henri turned pale.

"Of course. Do you think it's a forgery?"

"No, no; I think nothing. I asked a simple question. You have answered it. When do you want the money?"

"To-morrow."

"Good! you shall have it."

"And when and where shall I meet you?"

"If you will come to No. 10, Harley-terrace, Bloomsbury, at seven to-morrow evening, you shall receive the cash. Meanwhile, you will of course trust me with this bill."

Henri eyed him with surprise.

"How am I to trust you," he cried, "when I know nothing of you?"

Morley handed it back to him.

"Take it," he said; "if you do not care to trust me, there is an end to the matter."

There was a quiet dignity in his manner which completely reassured Henri.

He handed him the note again.

"Take it," he said. "I will trust you, though why I should I know not."

He then rose, rang the bell, paid the score, and saying, "To-morrow at seven," left the room.

Morley Bridgenorth drew his chair to the fire brewed another glass of grog, and rubbed his hands.

"This is the first link in a chain," he murmured, "which Henri le Morneaut will find it difficult to break."

CHAPTER XC.

CLIFFORD MEETS THE KING—HIS BLIND FURY.

HERNE guided Clifford through the forest, and soon brought him to a spot where a herd of deer quietly reposed.

"Hither will he come," said the demon huntsman.

"For what purpose?"

"To hunt the stag."

"And she?"

"Will be with him."

"Is she then fallen so low?"

"She has been sorely tried. She was found by one of the king's minions in the depths of Cornwall. Thither she had been carried by smugglers who intended to carry her to the coast of France. A fearful calamity prevented them, and the girl found a home with the rector of a small parish church, who took a great fancy to her. In the house of this man she was found by the king's servants. Struck by her beauty, he determined to bring her to his master, and by persuasion succeeded in effecting his object. Promises of a brilliant career induced the girl to come to Windsor, and here she is, in the power of the king."

"But she is yet————"

Clifford paused.

"But she is yet uncontaminated, you would ask. Yes; but will not long remain so. The king burns with passion for her. To-night——"

"Never!"

"Hey-dey."

"Never, I say. I will strike him dead first."

"'Tis well, and the opportunity will soon occur—Hark!"

They listened.

There was a sound of horns and merry laughter, mingling with the clash of horse's gear in the distance.

Gradually it drew nearer.

Nearer and nearer.

And now it was possible to distinguish the sound of voices.

"Hide," said Herne, dragging Clifford into the hollow of a large tree. "Hide, and await your opportunity."

Next moment a brilliant cavalcade burst into the open space where Clifford and Herne had stood.

Clifford, from his hiding place, at once recognised Evelina.

She rode a chesnut palfrey, and was attired in the most sumptuous manner.

Clifford's heart sank within him.

He gazed into her face expecting, doubtless, to see it flushed with pride and joy, but, to his surprise, it was pale, thin, and filled with grief.

Near her rode the king.

Ever and anon the old German turned from his antique painted courtesans, and gazed upon Evelina.

Of course the others were scandalised by such a proceeding.

They were unusually moral in every particular in in which they were not personally concerned.

Clifford beheld the burning glances of the king with indignation.

He watched with growing impatience.

At length an immense hart was started and the cavalcade set off in pursuit.

The horse Evelina rode stood still, and refused to move.

She was left alone.

Gradually the others drew away.

Suddenly, however, the king missed her.

Glancing round he caught sight of her, and, turning his horse, rode back.

In a moment he was by her side.

"Come," he said, "come, fair young mistress; let us not be deprived of your society."

"I beseech your majesty to leave me. I desire not to join the hunt; I would rather return."

"Nay, sweet chuck, nay; we cannot sanction that."

He drew nearer, and attempted to place his arm about her waist.

"Your Majesty had best leave me. I will cry for help."

"Help, fair one; what help do you require? Is a king so objectionable a sweetheart?"

"For Heaven's sake begone, sire, or I will shriek."

"Nay, that were a useless exertion. Who would hear thee? Now, I must have one kiss. You have lost me all my sport, and I should have some little recompense."

He had both arms about her when Clifford, urged by Herne, sprang from his hiding place, and, seizing the king by the throat, tore him from his horse.

His sword was drawn in an instant, and the fate of the king was about to be sealed, when a horseman dashed to the spot, and, seizing Clifford's weapon, drew it from his grasp.

Clifford turned on the new comer, and beheld Colonel Jack.

The colonel's steed was followed by the white mare Brilliant.

"Mount and away," said the colonel, "not a moment must be lost. Get to London, and thence to the —— devil as long as you get out of England."

Clifford lost not a moment.

Seizing the bridle of the white mare, he leaped lightly into the saddle.

To snatch Evelina from her horse was the work of a moment, and ere the king had recovered his feet Clifford and Evelina were flying through the forest.

"This is not the proper position for your Majesty," said the Colonel, as he assisted the King to remount. "Rejoin the hunting party at once. You were mad to quit them."

The King, thoroughly confused, obeyed with the readiness of a child.

Next moment he was gone.

Then Herne, fearful in his rage, stalked from his tree, and confronted the Colonel.

"So," he cried, "so you have baulked me."

The Colonel, not in the least alarmed, answered—

"Yes; it is I."

"Do you know the consequences?"

"I know what they *would be*, if you had the power to work them."

"And think you I have not the power?"

"I am assured of it."

"This to convince you."

He drew from his kirtle a long hunting knife, and made a spring at Colonel Jack.

The Colonel stepped back, and placing his hand in his bosom, drew forth a small cross, thickly studded with gems.

This he held before him.

With a wild yell Herne fell back.

"Confusion!" he cried; "I knew you possessed some charm. Had it not been so, I would have struck thee dead the moment I saw thee."

"I know thou wouldst. But no more of this; I charge thee begone."

There was another yell from Herne as the Colonel flashed his charm before his eyes.

Next moment there was a flash of fire, and the fiend vanished.

"So," said the Colonel, "Clifford is saved. I've had enough to do to look after him, and keep him out of mischief; but now he is saved, and my task is over."

CHAPTER XCI.

THE TRAVELLER'S STORY CONTINUED—THE SEARCH AND THE RESULT.

As the reader may have imagined, the man who held the conversation with the son of Lady Moore was no other than the persecuted Magsworth.

With the money he had obtained from the wretched son of a still more wretched mother, he provided himself with ample clothing.

He also purchased a horse, and hired a servant.

Thus provided, the returned convict set out in search of his daughter.

We need not trace his career until we find him at Canterbury.

Here, following the dictates of a power which swayed him in all things, he walked on right into the old cathedral.

He wandered about until he reached the cloisters, and there he was suddenly confronted by a tall and mysterious monk.

Magsworth started.

The monk beckoned him not to stir.

"I know you," said the phantom, for such it appeared to be; "I know you, and would serve you."

"Serve me?"

"Yes. You seek a child."

"I do."

"You know not where to find her."

"True."

"What danger would you face to find her?"

"What danger would I not face?"

"Ah! I can believe thee brave when man is your antagonist, but to deal with fiends—"

"I would struggle with the devil to regain possession of my child."

"'Tis well. I see you are in earnest. I will tell you where to find your child."

"Oh! where—where?"

"Know you the old village of Winterleigh?"

"Winterleigh in Buckinghamshire?"

"Yes."

"I do.'

"To that place was your child taken by a man who found her on the road side after she had been deserted by those who stole her."

"Say you so?'

"Listen. Knowing the disposition of the Knight of Winterleigh, the preserver of your child took her to his Hall, and placing her on the very threshold of his door, left her."

"Yes, yes."

"She was taken into the house by a woman servant, and carried to the knight. He ordered her to be taken care of, gave her a name, and reared her as his own. She was the only being for whom he had any love."

"God bless him!"

"He has need of your prayers, for he was a bad man."

"He is dead, then?"

"Yes."

"And the girl?"

"She has been subjected to many changes of fortune."

"Indeed!"

"Yes, indeed."

And hereupon the monk related to Magsworth all that had befallen Evelina, from the moment of her meeting Clifford, and with which the reader is already acquainted.

"And now what is to be done," asked the father, when he had heard the monk to an end.

"Listen to me. At this moment the girl is in the hands of her enemies. You must fly to Winterleigh, and await her coming, for come she will, and accompanied by her lover."

"That is simple enough."

"Not quite so. You must take up your place in the house, and defeat Mother Clifford, the witch who sways the place. It is the destiny of the young people that they return to the Hall. Should they find the witch of Winterleigh there they are lost; should you have conquered her, all will be well."

"Trust me."

"I do; but you have a sore trial, not a trial of strength, but of mind, over unnatural things. You must probe the mysteries of the Hall to the very quick, and if you falter all is lost. Farewell!" The monk vanished.

Magsworth hesitated not a moment.

As fast as horse could carry him he rode to Winterleigh.

With his arrival there, and what followed, the reader is already acquainted.

*   *   *   *   *   *

We left the traveller, whom, of course, we shall now continue to call Magsworth Moore, prostrated at the feet of Mother Clifford.

The old crone muttered some awful words over her intended victim, and the great white cat screamed as she flew about him.

Magsworth had no power to move hand or foot.

"Now," cried the crone, "now, man, I triumph. I will see whether I cannot shake your iron will."

Magsworth comprehended her.

He nerved himself for the worst, and awaited what was to follow.

Mother Clifford lashed herself into an unearthly fury, and then, casting the contents of a glass phial on the floor, filled the room with a cloud of vapour.

Then she murmured her terrible incantations, and the very air became filled with shapes which made Magsworth's brain reel to contemplate.

He knew they were brought against him.

He knew they were to battle with him for supremacy, and he muttered to himself—

"I place my cause in the hands of God. I will be firm."

The spirits seemed to enter into his brain.

He felt them pressing upon that organ until an awful madness seemed to creep upon him.

He felt that he was becoming afraid.

He used one gigantic effort, and cried—

"Fear not, my trust is in God. This is an awful trial but I fear nothing. I defy the works of the devil."

Fresh tortures were brought to bear upon him.

Too terrible to think of.

Not one point was left untried.

Not one weak spot in his mental armour but what was tested, but still no success.

The mind was yet perfect.

The brain did not reel.

Gradually he found strength returning to him.

At length he stood upon his feet once more, and spreading forth his arms, he cried—

" Fiends, I conquer ! Your machinations affect me not. I can defy ye."

He saw Mother Clifford.

She was crouching in a corner.

He fixed his eyes upon her, and she, as if drawn by some irresistible power, crawled to his feet.

" The curse of God light upon you," he cried, " the curse of the just on the tool of the fiend."

He saw her crouch and grovel ; he heard her moan and shriek.

Gradually she diminished in size as he looked upon her, and at last *she disappeared.*

His *will* had conquered her *might.*

CHAPTER XCII.

THE END OF JONATHAN WILD.

THE captors of Wild hurried him to Windsor.

They lodged him in the gaol, and the news of his capture soon spread over the town.

It was not long in reaching the ears of the king.

The monarch appeared highly delighted at the capture of this much-talked-of thief, and gave orders for his immediate execution in the town of Windsor.

" For," said he, " trust him in London, and he will escape, though guarded by an army."

It was thus settled that Jonathan Wild was to die untried, and forthwith the gallows sprang up over the prison gate.

Meanwhile Wild behaved with his usual coolness.

" Herne will save me," was the thought uppermost in his mind. " He swears never to desert a friend and follower, so he will snatch me from them, even with the rope about my neck."

Vain hope.

The day and night passed over, and the morn of execution came.

The little town was all astir, and at daylight an immense concourse of people had assembled in front of the prison, to see Jonathan Wild die.

At eight o'clock he was led forth.

The mob saluted him with loud howls and groans.

To this greeting Wild bowed, as if he had been the recipient of a great compliment.

He returned the gaze of the populace with a defiant air, and with a sneer on his lip.

This raised the indignation of the mob to the highest point, and its members called aloud for the instant despatch of the great criminal.

Fearing a riot, the officials hastened the ceremony as fast as possible.

Wild was under the beam, when a loud cry of delight from him startled all who heard it.

The thieftaker fixed his eyes upon some object unseen by all but himself, and stretched forth his arms.

" Save me !" he shrieked ; " save me !"

The officials thought that this wild appeal was addressed to Heaven ; but on the edge of the scaffold stood a being in whom Wild's hopes were centred.

It was Herne the Hunter, unseen by all but Wild.

" Save me !" he repeated ; " save me ! I have served you faithfully ; now save me."

The phantom regarded him sternly.

" Ask not me to save thee," he said ; " seek not mercy at my hands, for you will find it not."

These words fell upon Wild's ear, but they reached that of no other person ; and those on the scaffold stared aghast at what was proceeding.

They began to deem Wild mad.

" Am I to die ?" shrieked the unhappy wretch ; " will you leave me to perish like a dog ?"

" Like a dog," repeated Herne.

" No, no ! I cannot believe it. You will snatch me from this !"

" Never."

" Yes, yes ! I will be your slave ; I will bless you, worship you ; only snatch me from this place."

" Too late !"

" No, no—not too late ! Say not so, for the love of God, say not so ! Not too late !"

" Too late," repeated the fiend.

" Oh !" groaned Wild, " this is terrible !"

" It is your just reward. You prepared a trap for me. You sought to blow me into eternity ; but I frustrated your plans. I cheated you ! Fool that you were, to think that such as you could harm Herne the Hunter."

" Forgive me ; I was mad ; I knew not what I did. Oh, forgive me !"

" No."

Herne began to descend the steps of the scaffold.

" Oh !" yelled Wild, who felt hope leaving him fast ; " oh, save me, save me !"

" Too late."

" Not too late ! My life, my soul—"

" Are mine already. Ha ! ha ! Die, wretch ! it is your doom."

Herne disappeared.

Jonathan Wild staggered back, and fell into the arms of the executioner.

Quick as thought the rope was fixed about his throat.

With lightning-like rapidity the hangman drew the bolt, and Jonathan Wild was *launched into eternity.*

The body was to hang an hour.

Long before that time the mob dispersed, and most of the officials of the gaol had gone.

Some few, however, remained, and these declared that, after hanging about half an-hour, the body of Wild fell upon the scaffold and disappeared.

They knew not that Herne the Hunter had been there and carried it off !

Such was the case.

That night *two* phantoms made night hideous in the forest, Jonathan Wild and Herne the Hunter.

CHAPTER XCIII. AND LAST.

HOW CLIFFORD TOOK EVELINA TO WINTERLEIGH, AND WHAT BEFEL THEM IN THAT PLACE.

URGED by an irresistible impulse, Clifford, instead of riding to London, made his way to Winterleigh.

He felt that that was the place, above all others, for him to reach, and thither he flew.

The road was dark and drear, and Evelina was weak and faint.

He had as much as he could do to support her in the saddle.

On they flew, over the bleak and desolate heath where the criminals hung in chains.

On, over meadow land, through brooks, and by unfrequented roads.

Still on, and night had passed, and day far advanced when the horseman drew rein at the entrance to Winterleigh Hall.

Evelina had long since recovered from her trance-like stupor. She glanced upon—into—Clifford's face.

The poor fellow turned away his head.

He felt ashamed to look into those eyes again.

It will be remembered how they parted.

" Turn not from me," said Evelina ; " turn not from me, Clifford."

"I dare not look upon you lady," replied Clifford; "remember who and what I am."

"I cannot—will not," said Evelina; "I only know that I love you. Oh, Clifford, Clifford; I am yours though you were the worst of men. I have fought against the feeling; I thought it right to battle it down, but I cannot—I cannot. I love you. You are mine, and I am thine. You will not turn from me now?"

"God forbid," cried Clifford, clasping her more closely to his bosom, "God forbid, sweetest. You have made a man of me. Ah, you shall yet be proud of me!"

In silence the remainder of the journey was performed.

"Why have you brought me here?" asked Evelina, as they stopped at the door of the old hall.

"Because this house is mine," said Clifford, "mine, and I will have it. I come to claim it, and I feel that Heaven will sustain my right."

The door of the great Hall opened, and a man in solemn black appeared.

He advanced to the head of the horse, whilst Clifford and his fair companion dismounted.

"Welcome," he said, "welcome to Winterleigh."

"Thanks," said Clifford, "but—"

"You know me not," said the stranger, "I will introduce myself. I am Magsworth Moore, and that lady is my daughter."

"Your daughter," said Clifford.

"Yes," continued Magsworth, "my long-lost child;" and then, turning to Evelina, he continued, "does not your heart endorse my words? Are you not my daughter?"

"Yes, yes," cried Evelina, a flood of joy bursting upon her; "my heart does speak, and it tells me you are my father."

In a moment they were in each other's arms.

"No time for explanations now," continued Magsworth, "lead us in."

Evelina and Clifford paused.

"Fear not," said Magsworth, "I have prepared the house for your coming. You will find it free from those evil influences which formerly characterised it."

They entered.

Ere long the tale of each was told, and they sat together in the sweet twilight, a happy trio.

* * * * *

Meanwhile there had been fresh arrivals at Winterleigh.

Her old acquaintances, the show people, had arrived in the village, and with them the dwarf.

His masters had thoroughly conquered him.

They had, as they expressed it, "made a regular christian of him."

He now spoke well and reasonably.

He was subdued in manner, and became gentle in his demeanour.

Such a change was indeed marvellous.

As Clifford was seated with Magsworth and his daughter, the two showmen and the dwarf were making their way into Winterleigh woods.

The dwarf led the way, and he conducted his master straight to the ruined cottage of Mother Clifford.

"Well," said one, "there don't appear to be much here, that's certain; what the deuce did yer bring us here for, eh, handsome?"

"See, there, there," said the dwarf, stamping on the stone underneath which Mother Clifford had buried the will.

"Well, I don't see anything," said the showman.

"Nor I," said the other.

The dwarf stooped, and applying his whole strength to the stone, tore it from its resting-place.

The eyes of the showmen fell upon the parchment.

"What's this," said the foremost, picking up the document, and reading it. "Hillo, this appears to be a valuable piece of paper to somebody. I think it had better go up to the Hall."

"You go up with it," said the other showman; "tell 'em as how Handsome says it was buried there by the old witch, and ask 'em for summut strong, for picking it up."

"All right," said the other. And so they separated.

In a few minutes the showman was at the Hall.

As a matter of course he was at once introduced to Clifford and his friends.

The delight of the three on perusing the will can be better imagined than described.

Here, then, at last, was the realisation of Clifford's dream.

Here was the confession of his uncle's guilt, and his atonement.

It is needless to trace this story beyond this point.

It is needless to tell, how when the false heir returned to the Hall, he found himself pitched out, and dragged through the very river into which he so cruelly plunged poor Rose.

It is needless to tell how happiness was heaped upon Clifford each moment, and what joy he felt at finding himself the honoured heir of Winterleigh.

As to the Moore property, he positively forbade Evelina to think of it.

"I have plenty for all," he said, "and therefore touch not that which will only lead one or other party into further misery."

The showman was magnificently rewarded, not alone for his discovery of the will, but for his goodness to Evelina when she was an outcast.

Two days after all these matters came to pass at Winterleigh, who should alight at the Hall but Colonel Jack, and with him the Duchess, now his bride.

She had conquered her passion for Clifford, and had consented to be the wife of his nearest and best friend, for, as the reader may have already divined, Colonel Jack was the unseen agent, who was ever frustrating the plans of Jonathan Wild and his accomplice the Princess.

* * * * *

A month passed, and Sir Clifford Winterleigh led to the altar the daughter of Sir Magsworth Moore.

Sir Charles had died, and the title descended to him.

The property passed into the hands of Evelina at last, although Clifford would fain have not had it so.

Lady Moore and her son fled the country.

The German Princess was, thanks to Colonel Jack, hung at Newgate, and her accomplices shared a similar fate.

Mrs. Granville, the early friend of Clifford, was not forgotten by him in his prosperity.

He forced her to abandon her calling, and retire to a neat little farm on the Winterleigh estate.

Bill Waters and Long Ned gave up the road, and were content to settle down respectably as Sir Clifford Winterleigh's gamekeepers.

Sall, the Irish girl, married Long Ned, and resided with him in a neat little cottage built for them in the wood.

Lewis, the bold, bad man, who had so long defrauded Clifford, broke his neck riding across the country, after being ejected from the Hall.

The dwarf died of convulsions the very night of his finding the will.

But three more characters remain to be mentioned.

Job Winchurst, and his friend Bob, jogged along as usual for a time, but one day a change came over the whole spirit of the landlord's dream.

Little Rose, the companion and friend of Evelina Moore, consented to become the hostess of the Harvest Home, and the rejoicing thereat was great, and the consumption of pine apple rum was enormous.

Bob married the servant who had such an affection for sleep, and when Job retired, and took up his quarters at one of Sir Clifford Winterleigh's best farms, Bob reigned supreme.

And be sure that, to his last day, he found a true friend in GENTLEMAN CLIFFORD.

www.ingramcontent.com/pod-product-compliance
Lightning Source LLC
Chambersburg PA
CBHW081146020726
47504CB00009B/2023